MOUNT MISERY

BY SAMUEL SHEM:

Novels

The House of God
Fine

Plays

Bill W. and Dr. Bob (with Janet Surrey)
Napoleon's Dinner
Room for One Woman

SAMUEL SHEM

MOUNT MISERY

FAWCETT COLUMBINE
NEW YORK

A Fawcett Columbine Book
Published by Ballantine Books

http://www.randomhouse.com

LIBRARY OF CONGRESS CATALOGING-IN-PUBLICATION DATA
Shem, Samuel.
Mount Misery / Samuel Shem.
p. cm.
ISBN 0-449-91118-7
I. Title.
PS3569.H39374M68 1997
813'.54—dc21 96-45629

Manufactured in the United States of America

First Edition: March 1997

10 9 8 7 6 5 4 3 2 1

For Janet and Katie and Rose

Thanks to Judith Abbott, Joy Harris, Les Havens,
Ben Heineman, and Chris Robb.

"It was how the sun came shining into his room:
To be without a description of to be,
For a moment on rising, at the edge of the bed, to be,
To have the ant of the self changed to an ox
With its organic boomings, to be changed
From a doctor into an ox, before standing up,
To know that the change and that the ox-like struggle
Come from the strength that is the strength of the sun,
Whether it comes directly or from the sun.
It was how he was free. It was how his freedom came."

—WALLACE STEVENS
The Latest Freed Man

EMERSON

"TERROR acts powerfully upon the body,
through the medium of the mind,
and should be employed in the cure of madness."

—BENJAMIN RUSH, M.D.
"The Father of American Psychiatry"
1818

One

WASPS, I'D DISCOVERED in my month of being a shrink, are notoriously hard to read. Their body language borders on mute, and their language itself is oblique, like those masters of obliqueness the English who, I had learned in my three years at Oxford, when they say "Yes, actually" mean "No," and when they say "No, actually," may mean anything.

Now, try as I might, coming at him from various different interviewing angles, much as my father the dentist would come at a recalcitrant tooth, Cherokee Putnam remained a mystery. It was six-thirty in the morning. I was bone-tired, having been on call at the hospital all night long. Cherokee had appeared at the admissions unit without calling in advance, and had paged the Doctor on Call—me. He said he wasn't at all sure he needed admission, but he hadn't been able to sleep and had to talk to someone "about a delicate matter," in confidence. The closest I had come to reading any feeling in him was when he told me how, at a dinner party at home recently, he'd gotten so furious at his wife Lily that he'd actually done the unheard of: picked up his linen napkin and thrown it down onto the tablecloth beside his plate.

To my probings, he denied that he was depressed. He denied suicide attempts, suicide gestures, suicidal ideation, and showed no signs of being crazy. He seemed like just the kind of guy the word "normal" was made for.

He looked normal enough. He was my age—thirty-two—my height and build—six-three and slightly fallen from slender. But while I was a lapsed Jew, he was a cornered WASP, in buttoned-down pink shirt and pressed khaki pants, with an excellent blade nose and blue eyes, a charming mole on one boyish cheek, and strawberry-blond hair combed back and parted off center. Tan and handsome, he looked like the young Robert Redford. He was rich, the father of two young girls—Hope and Kissy—and he admitted sheepishly to being a lawyer. A Yale graduate, he'd made a small fortune working for Disney in California, before coming back to his roots in New England eighteen months before.

"But you kill yourself at Disney," he said. "There's a saying out there, 'If you don't come in on Saturday, don't bother to come in on Sunday.' "

His wife Lily was also from New England. He'd spent "a million two" to buy a foothill and a horse farm nearby. He and his wife were into horses, she into show-jumping, he into polo. After a year of leisure he was now trying to figure out what to do next with his life.

"Is that what's troubling you?" I asked.

"No, no, not at all," he said, "but once in a while I wake up at three in the morning comparing myself to other people, successful people. I turn to my wife and say, 'I'm a failure.' That used to get her right up, but now she's so used to it she barely wakes up. She just murmurs, 'Take a Halcyon and go back to sleep.' Lily's heard it too many times."

"So there are problems in the marriage?"

"Oh no, no. Things are fine, actually. The normal disagreements, mostly around her being so neat, and me, well, y'see how neat I seem?"

"Very nice, um hm."

"Very. But in private I'm pretty messy. Nothing big, just socks on the floor, nothing hung up. She's very neat. We had a big tiff last week, when the help was off—I emptied the dishwasher and just threw the silverware into the drawer. Lily nests the spoons! Just the other day I said, 'Please, I beg you—give me the dignity of living like a pig.' " I laughed. He smiled, barely. "Lily's a stunning woman. If she were here, you couldn't take your eyes off her. She did the whole debutante thing, cotillion, the works. Even after two kids, dynamite body. Incredible, really. You should see her on a horse."

"It must be a great feeling," I said, stifling a yawn—thinking, Enough of this bullshit, how can I get rid of him and get some sleep?—"to wake up early in the morning and go for a horseback ride with your wife."

"She's never there early in the morning."

"Why not?"

"Lily's in psychoanalysis. Actually . . . her doctor is on the staff here. That's why I came here. A Dr. Dove. Do you know him?"

"I do."

"She sees him every morning at six A.M." He glanced at his watch, one of those mariner's, with nineteen dials. "She's there right now." His eyes met mine and then skittered away, as men's eyes do when they are about to try to make contact. "Look, I half think I'm crazy for thinking this, and as a lawyer I will deny that I ever said it to you, but . . . well . . . I think . . . no, it's crazy."

"Go on."

"I think . . . think that my wife is having an affair with Dr. Dove."

My mind recoiled. Talk about pigs. Schlomo Dove was one of the most unattractive and unappealing men I'd ever met. He was a man who, in the parlance of these times, would have to be referred to as "Beautifully Challenged." A fiftyish, short—five-five, maybe—fat Jewish man with thick, curly chestnut hair coming down over his brow like a helmet, tiny eyes sunken into slitty sockets, snaggly teeth still hoping for braces, and a nose that didn't look happy, he seemed to take pleasure in flaunting his homeliness, wearing suits that were rumpled and ties that were stained and loose around his neck like a series of slack, secondhand nooses. Despite this, or perhaps because of it—in the counterphobic way that some people, afraid of heights, become bridge painters—Schlomo was a performer. The fat little guy was always in your face, always dancing up to you bigger than life, in academic seminars or private supervisory sessions always rising up onto his tippy-toes like a bingeing ballerina to present some goofy Freudian stuff in the voice and gesture of a Borscht Belt comic, self-mocking in the extreme. Schlomo had a large private practice, and also was well known as one of a small number of psychiatrists you went to for a consultation to get yourself matched up with just the right therapist. He was an eminent psychoanalyst, on top of the Freudian pile in the institute down in the city, and Director of the Misery Outpatient Clinic, which lay at the swampy, reed-clogged end of a sausage-shaped lake that roughly split the hospital's campus.

Eminent, yes; appealing, no. How could any woman, especially a gorgeous WASP Ice Princess, go for Schlomo Dove?

So looking at Cherokee, I thought, No problem, this guy's crazy. Yet one thing I'd learned in my life so far, especially this past year traveling around the world as a doctor: as in human achievement, where no matter what you do there is always someone who has done it more, so in human degradation, there is always someone hurtling on down past you, down past what you can even imagine. And so I said only, "Really?"

"Yeah. It's been over a year now that she's been in therapy with him. We came back East, it was our dream. To take time off, together, to be with our kids, after the phoniness of Hollywood. Everything was in place. And then she feels a little down, you know, and goes to him for a consultation." He sighed. "She sees him every weekday morning, sometimes on Saturday, occasionally on Sunday too. Our sex life has dried up. But she looks more and more sexy. Not only to me, but to my friends too. Buys sexy underwear. Lotta color, lace, you know?" I nodded, my mind rolling into fantasies of lace and color and my girlfriend, Berry, and thanking God that one perk of being a shrink is that you hear some pretty hot sexy stuff. "It's not like her. Not since the kids. And she cut her hair short, like a boy. *Really* strange, that. Her long hair was her pride. Not like her at all."

"Have you asked her about this?"

"I've got no solid evidence. I ask her what goes on in therapy, but she says that Dr. Dove says it's confidential."

"But it's driving you crazy. You might just—"

"You think I'm *crazy*?"

There was a hint of crazy in this, given the reality of Schlomo, but just a hint. "No, no, you are not crazy."

"Oh. Good. You believe that he's . . . you know, screwing her in therapy?"

"I believe that you believe it."

"I don't, totally, I mean. But you say I'm not crazy?"

"Suspicious yes, crazy no."

"Not even, maybe . . . I don't know . . . a little paranoid?"

"Have you ever *seen* Dr. Dove?"

"No, why?"

"Look," I said, "you don't know the truth. You've got nothing to go on."

"And it's driving me crazy! Do I need hospitalization?"

"No."

"Can I come talk to you?"

"To start therapy?"

He grimaced, as if I'd just suggested we try a few root canals. "I wish you wouldn't call it that. Father—none of my people—believe in psychiatry. 'Stand tall,' they always say, if there's any trouble, 'stand tall, and call your lawyer.' Therapy's for . . . others."

"Too 'messy,' eh?"

He blinked, as if in strong light. He sighed. "You got me. Shit."

"I'd be glad to see you."

He paused. I felt him struggle with it. Then he loosened his tie and through gritted teeth said, "Fuck 'em. Let's make an appointment."

We set up an appointment for the next week. He stood, crunched my hand, and walked out as gracefully as, well, as a horse. I liked him and felt for him, and if I could get him to come to therapy, I could help him. Schlomo? Do I tell him about this? Better talk to my supervisor, Ike White, first.

My on-call night was over. I walked over to the administration building, the Farben, handed in my beeper, and walked on past the grand front stairway with its rosewood banister that curled up overhead to the right and left. On the landing two antique Chinese vases filled with silk flowers framed a landscape painting of fields and cows and a proud, lone tree. My feet sank into the carpet as if I were in slippers. As I opened the front door and went from air-conditioning to reality, the damp heat hit me like the fat palm of a Turkish masseur slapping me around in a steam bath in Istanbul. Squinting in the russet morning, I stood on the front steps, perched on the crest of a high hill overlooking the city. Feet on granite, head between soaring pillars, I felt like I was standing in the doorway of a bank.

Mount Misery was the name of this hill, and of the hospital built upon it. The hill had been christened first, in the early eighteenth century, by a band of hardy Puritan farmers tormented by the nor'easters that would whip the rough rock for four days at a time. The hospital had been founded later, in 1812, by a group of civic-minded Yankees who, having built a hospital in the city to treat diseases of the body, decided they wanted a matching set, and built one far out in the countryside, in the shadow of the mountains, for diseases of the mind. Their keeping the name Misery showed a measure of obvious delight, that perverse delight which comes with ironic resignation. By the late nineteenth century there were many of these elegant farmlike mental institutions, some of which still survive: Austin Riggs, McLean, the Brattleboro Retreat, Shepard Pratt, and Chestnut Lodge. The principle in the construction of asylums was denial: "Out of mind, out of sight." Misery had been protected from suburban sprawl by its natural boundaries: the high hill, several ominous ravines, and the swamp at the end of the lake. Its dozen or so separate buildings were surrounded by eighty acres of fields, woods, and streams, all rimmed by a high, iron-spiked fence.

Mount Misery soon became a teaching hospital affiliated with what was nicknamed "the BMS"—the "Best Medical School" in the world. Throughout its history Misery had been in the forefront of the latest red-hot treatment for mental illness. At first this consisted of shackles, purges, bleedings, and teaching proper table manners. Now Misery offered all the different treatments of late-twentieth-century psychiatry. Traditionally it had been the hospital of the unstable wealthy—it was at one time fashionable to be able to announce that one had "a son at Harvard, a father buried in Mount Auburn Cemetery, and a mad cousin in Misery." These days it attracted not only the wealthy, but also the insured. While welfare cases were rare, each of us new first-year residents in psychiatry would spend some time at Candlewood State Hospital, the state facility down the hill and across the swamp. At Misery there were artists, poets, folk singers, writers, and a steady stream of those tender young men and women cracked by the most ruthlessly prestigious colleges in America. Creative, interesting people who, it was said, made "great cases." The unofficial hospital motto was, "There's Sanity in Misery."

It was almost the end of July. The morning was already hot and humid, the dawn cool seeping out under the night's umbrella in smaller and smaller droplets, heating up, sizzling off, gone. To the north, mountains cooled their peaks with clouds. Before me, lining the roads and coalescing in peaceful woods, were oaks, maples, and, with their clusters of lilylike flowers, catalpas. To my right was the red-brick colonial of Toshiba, the Admissions Unit, with the windowless research wing sticking out of it just above ground level like a stainless steel prosthetic foot. High up on the hill to my left above a ravine nicknamed "Loopy Lovers Leap," peeking out from a clearing in the pine forest like eyes from a hiding place in a scary fairy tale, were the twin spiked towers of the two buildings named the Heidelbergs—replicas of the famous Bridge Towers that were the gateway to the real Heidelberg, "Birthplace of German Romanticism." Heidelberg West was the Misery Center for Psychopharmacology, the drug treatment of mental illness. Heidelberg East, just across the ravine, was Alcohol and Drug Recovery. An incessant, busy stream rushed down from the ravine, pooled in the sausage-shaped lake, and oozed off to swampy stuff where, amidst the cattails and skunk cabbage and forlorn willows, was the squat ivy-covered building that housed Schlomo's Outpatient Clinic. Farther down the hill, alongside the road leading to the wrought-iron gate and granite gatehouse, across the broad swath of the orphaned eighth fairway of the once-grand Misery Links, rose the towering Greek Revival structure of Thoreau, the Freudian Family Unit, its bubble skylight a cyclops eye staring back in transcendental defiance past me, up at the spiked, certain, drug-centered Heidelbergs. Far to my left, past the lake and out of sight in the deep woods, was Emerson, my current home base, which housed Depression, Borderline, and Psychosis, one on each of its three floors. Here and there on the lush green lawns an immense copper beech spread its branches like a hoop skirt sequined with metal.

I took off my suit jacket, turned left, and wandered along the narrow, twisting, and hilly main road that skirted the lake and crossed the stream on a narrow stone bridge. The ivied buildings could have been a college campus. What could have been students strolled peacefully along, none looking like patients. I had yet to learn how to tell the patients from the staff on sight.

I was one of five first-year residents in a three-year training program to become psychiatrists. This, our first year, was tightly structured. Every eight weeks or so we would move from one rotation to another, on a computer-generated schedule that we had been handed on our first day in Misery. Each of these Misery rotations was to teach us how to treat inpatients, those poor souls locked up in the various wards. Each rotation was with a group of patients with a particular diagnosis, each group housed in a different building—depressives on the first floor of Emerson, borderlines on Emerson 2, drug addicts on Heidelberg East, and so on. Each of the first-year residents did the exact same rotations, in different order, every couple of months moving on in a kind of equal-opportunity psychiatric musical chairs, with exactly enough chairs for all. I was a month into my first rotation, on Emerson. Next I would move to Toshiba, then to Thoreau, and, for the final part of the first year, to each of the Heidelbergs. In addition, all year long each of us was assigned to a different Outpatient Clinic Team, and would follow our very own patients as outpatients—not admitted to the hospital—in psychotherapy throughout the course of the year. And of course each of us first-year residents would be on call every fourth night, as the DOC—the Doctor on Call—the only doctor available to the 350 inpatients all night long.

Around the far end of the lake and up a last rise through the woods, I came to Emerson, where Ike White's office was. The center stairwell had spectacular woodwork, enclosing the stairs in wooden banisters and railings that were meant to prevent suicidal jumps. The light from the skylight at the top was chopped up by hundreds of slats. On the second-floor landing was a sign, EMERSON 2: BORDERLINE WARD, and a small handwritten note, *Split Risk*. I searched the twenty keys on my ring for the right one and opened the door. As I was trying to pull my key back out, someone shot out past me screaming, "Freedom!" He ran down the stairs and was gone.

Next came two large men running full-tilt. Feeling I'd made a terrible mistake, I walked into the large, well-furnished living room.

"Hey, dickhead!"

I turned, just *after* I realized that to turn and answer was really stupid. I found myself facing a sandy-haired, baby-faced man my age dressed in jeans, suspenders, and a white shirt and bow tie.

He smiled and said, "Dickheads Make Mistakes!"

In the nursing station there was pandemonium. Two people were on the phone at once, talking about how Harrison, a dangerous paranoid man, had split again.

"Nice work, Dr. Basch," the ward secretary said. "Split Risk splits again! If he gets at his wife, we'll all get sued to hell."

"Sorry. What time will Ike White be in?"

"He's been here like two hours already. Down in his office."

"Since five A.M.?" I asked. "Why?"

"Said he had some work to do."

I went down a flight to the first-floor ward, Emerson 1, Depression, and knocked on Ike's office door.

"C-c-come in," he said, with his characteristic stutter.

Dr. Ike White, Director of Residency Training, was a short, slight man of forty, with a slender face and light green eyes highlighted by delicate, long lashes. His dark hair was cut boyish, all the way to a cowlick he twirled with an index finger when deep in thought. Ike was the kind of person who always seemed glad to see you. His stutter made him sound vulnerable, and humble. He was my mentor, the reason I'd come to Mount Misery for my psychiatric training. I'd met him a year before, when he'd interviewed me for admission. It was difficult to get into Misery, ten applicants for every slot. Yet Ike had taken one look at my documents and said, "A t-t-terrific C.V."

"I look pretty good on paper."

He smiled. "How can we c-convince you to c-c-come?"

"You're accepting me?" I said.

"Yes. I don't b-b-believe in p-p-putting pressure on. Let's just t-t-talk."

I had been surprised. For years, applying to the best colleges and medical schools, I'd gone into these interviews on guard against deception, and intent on deceiving. Ike just seemed to want to make contact with me, hear about me, for no other reason than his curiosity. As if we were friends, we began to talk. And as we went on, I was even more blown away: Ike *listened.* I felt heard, responded to, suddenly more alive. We had a wide-ranging, leisurely talk—surprising in itself, for most other doctors who'd ever interviewed me for anything had been in a hurry, the goal of the interview being mainly to get it over with. When I asked Ike about himself and his work, he responded with clarity graced with humility. His expertise was depression and suicide. He treated patients, did research on the causes of depression, and was both a Freudian psychoanalyst and an expert in the use of drugs to treat depression. He loved to teach new residents. Ike was a rising star in the BMS sky.

"Is there anything you're *not* good at?" I asked.

He smiled. Gesturing to the floor-to-ceiling shelves on which books were haphazardly arranged, and to the piles of journals and notes on the floor, with a few paths threading through between desk and analytic couch and chair, and the desk buried under paper and heavy objects holding down other paper, he said, "I have a helluva t-t-time keeping my stuff in order."

I'd gone into the interview planning to do my psych training in a tough, competitive program at the inner-city hospital nicknamed "Man's Best Hospital"—"the MBH." My interview with Ike—set against the elegance of Misery, where not only the buildings and grounds but even the two tennis courts were immaculate, with bright white lines and crisp twiny nets—changed my mind.

"Okay," I'd said. "You convinced me. I'll come here on one condition."

"N-name it."

"That you be my teacher."

He smiled shyly. "N-n-nothing would make me h-h-h-*happier*."

So Ike had become my main teacher, or supervisor. Learning to become a psychiatrist was an apprenticeship system—you learned by being apprenticed to senior psychiatrists on the Misery staff. You watched them treat patients and received their supervision on your treatment of patients. Usually you would have an hour of supervision for every hour you spent with a patient in therapy. The supervisory session would consist of your telling the supervisor what went on in the session, either from your memory or, as some supervisors required, from notes you took during the session. Like most first-year residents, I had never actually done psychotherapy with patients. In fact I hadn't taken psychiatry as a medical student—it wasn't a required course at the BMS, and I, at that time more focused on the body than the mind, had never gotten around to it. Unlike most of my fellow first-year residents, I myself had never even been in therapy—I'd never felt the need until the experience of my medical internship, but then there had been no time, or money. I was a latecomer to wanting to be a shrink. It had kind of surprised me, as a career choice, toward the end of my internship. Most of the other first-year residents had been focused on becoming shrinks for a long time, at least from medical school on. As a result, I felt more naive about all this psychiatric stuff than the four others, and was always trying to catch up.

Ike White had helped me, immensely. My first month I'd spent with him on Emerson 1, Depression. During that time I had been dazzled, not only by his brilliance and integrity, but by his modesty and just plain humanness. Watching him interact with his depressed patients on his daily rounds, I'd seen his skill at listening and responding to them, and had tried to model myself after him. In my month with Ike, he had fulfilled all of my expectations.

Now, he nodded a welcome to me. He sat behind his large cluttered desk, papers piled to his head. His dark suit seemed too big, as if he'd lost weight. It was cold in the office, so I put my own suit jacket back on. I told him about the interview with Cherokee and asked what I should do.

"T-t-tell me more about his d-delusion."

"Is it just that," I asked, "a delusion?"

"So f-far it is."

"Should I talk to Schlomo?"

"What are your thoughts about t-t—"

"Talking to him? I think I should let him know—"

The phone rang, twice, then the answering machine clicked on, and then at a high volume came a strong, assertive voice:

"Dr. White, this is Hilda in the Misery Benefits Office. I'm returning your call from this morning, inquiring about your benefit package—"

Ike jumped up and turned off the volume. He sat down, smiling shyly, and with a strangely embarrassed look in his eye. It made me nervous, and to break the tension I joked:

"Congratulations. Ladies and gentlemen, we got a cure! Hilda's not depressed anymore, hell no!"

We laughed. Ike, dealing with depressed people all day long, had developed what he called his "Answering Machine Strategy." He set the pickup level on the machine so low that when depressed people called and spoke at the low, hesitant level of their depression, the machine would cut them off. To avoid being cut off, they had to speak up. As time went on they would learn to be more assertive, which helped them recover. I didn't know whether or not this Hilda from Misery Benefits had been depressed, but it had become a standing joke between us.

"Of c-c-course you can talk to him," Ike said, returning to my question about Schlomo.

"Do you know him well? I mean is this possible?"

"He was my a-analyst. I saw him five t-times a week for six years. D-do I know him well? No. But your p-patient, Cherokee?" He looked down at his hands. "B-being with sick people is sc-scary. You start to wonder, 'Am *I* s-sick? Why is he the p-patient, and I the d-doctor?' " He smiled at me. "Roy, psychiatry is n-not only a science, b-but an art. More than in any other medical specialty, you learn by working with others. Day after t-tomorrow, August first, I start my vacation. I've arranged for a t-terrific third-year resident, Dr. Leonard Malik, to t-take over and supervise you when you move to the b-b-*borderline* ward, and—" The intercom buzzed: "Mary Megan Scorato is here." Mary was a patient on our depression ward. Ike shrugged. "Sorry. It's urgent. She's ac-acutely suicidal again. Have to see her. Will you be at the seminar t-tonight at my house?"

"Sure will."

"Good. I'll save our g-g-good-byes till then."

"But it's impossible, isn't it? Someone like Schlomo? Doing this?"

"Our patients come in with seams," he said, "and they go out seamless."

"What does that mean?" I asked, amazed at the seamless flow of words.

But the buzzer buzzed again and I was history.

AS I FINISHED lunch and was taking my tray to the garbage, I saw Schlomo eating. Head down, fork up, it was not a pretty sight. The hell with it. But then I realized that, being a Freudian, he would vanish the day after tomorrow, for the month of August. I approached him. There was an empty seat on either side of him, and across the table too.

"Dr. Dove?"

He raised his head. Those tiny eyes popped out a little from under those slitty lids, and he said, "Call me Schlomo. Everybody else does. Including myself." He laughed. A trickle of red gravy from the Misery Lunch Special, a "Sloppy Joe," oozed from the corner of his mouth.

"Schlomo, can I—"

"Good. Schlomo likes being called Schlomo by cute young psychiatrists."

"Can I see you later today for supervision?"

"Oy what a joy! Schlomo Dove will see you at two."

Later that afternoon I found myself wandering through the wet heat down the hill and around the lake to the swampy end, wending my way through the mosquitoes and cattails reaching high overhead and the muddy path sucking at my shoes, to the Misery Outpatient Clinic, where I asked to see Schlomo Dove. His office was filled with fragrant plants—narcissus and jasmine—and bananas of all degrees of ripeness, some green, some yellow, some black. Schlomo, with a huge yellow plastic watering can in his hand, was doing his plants. He smiled broadly—showing teeth with severe gaps from a childhood where orthodonture was not an option, clenching a fizzled fat half cigar. He gave me a big "Hello, Dr. Roy Basch!" urged me down into a leather chair beside the leather Freudian couch, and said, "*Nu?*"

Schlomo was the kind of man who seemed happier to see you than you were to see him, and I was caught off guard. Given this reality of Schlomo, there seemed to be no way that Cherokee's suspicion could be true. I half decided not to tell Schlomo anything. But he stood there so open-faced, seemingly so anxious to hear and so able to hear whatever I'd say, that I plunged in, telling him that Cherokee Putnam thought he was having an affair with Putnam's wife Lily, Schlomo's patient.

For a second Schlomo just stood there, the oversized spout of the watering can arching at me like, yes, a big, thin yellow penis.

"What a great case!" he said. "Oedipal. Boy thinks momma is *schtupping* Poppa Schlomo, boy goes meshugge. Great case for you. Schlomo will supervise you on it."

"Wouldn't that be a conflict of interest?"

"*Nu*, so I won't supervise." He laughed. "If you can get another supervisor with balls instead of one of the goyim around here who think their shit don't stink, good luck."

"So there's no truth to what he's saying?"

"You *believe* the patient?" Schlomo said.

"I shouldn't believe the patient?"

"Never."

"Not even what they say in therapy?"

"*Especially* not in therapy. The patient is unbelievable. Someone like you is unbelievable too, because you haven't been analyzed. When you decide to do it, does Schlomo have the guy for you."

"Ed Slapadek, I know, I know." Ed was the analyst Schlomo always recommended to new residents. "So I shouldn't believe what my patients are telling me in therapy?"

"No Slapadek for you, *bubbie*. Better. Patients spend their time in therapy lying, and thinking they're telling the truth. Your job is to show them they're lying. When they stop lying, you terminate. Therapy is simple: they fall in love with you, they get disappointed—sad and lonely—they work it through, they get better. It takes chutzpah to be a shrink. Does Schlomo have it?"

"No question," I said, *chutzpah* reminding me of the rumor that Dershowitz the lawyer was a Schlomo patient, lying there lying and—

"Call me Schlomo."

"No question, Schlomo."

"Do *you*?"

"What are your thoughts about if I do?"

Schlomo laughed heartily and then suddenly threw his watering can into my lap, soaking me. I leaped up. Schlomo cracked up.

"Asshole!"

"I know, I know, it kills me." He took a terrible-looking hankie out of his pocket and tried to get at my crotch, but I was heading for the door. "Royala, Royala," he said, wiping the tears of laughter away, "you might have chutzpah too. Don't let 'em kill you here. In this Christian shithouse, somebody farts, they call the fire department. God's Chosen People meets God's Frozen People. You got a spark, a little outrage. Like Schlomo. Keep it. Schlomo can help."

This startled me. He was right. Already, after only a month in this buttoned-down place, I was feeling hemmed in. "Yeah. Thanks."

"Don't mention. Good thinking, about not believing that patient. I know all about that joker from his wife."

"You *believe* her?"

The slits of his eyes widened. Dark beads glittered in there. And then he recovered. "What a mensch! To fool Schlomo is not easy. See? You might have *chutzpah* too. Great case. Keep Schlomo posted. A cliffhanger. Bye-bye. Call Schlomo to make you a match, with that very special analyst, just for you. You got two choices: call Schlomo now, or call Schlomo later. When you're halfway into all that sad and lonely, you're halfway out too. Mmm—such a cutie. I'd like to sink my teeth into that tender little ego myself. Ciao!"

I left feeling like a few convolutions of my brain had been unrolled, not knowing whether I'd just met with a moron or a genius or if it mattered. This clown, Ike White's analyst? Sex with *this*? You'd have to be crazy.

Exhausted, I floated around the grounds and found myself at the tennis courts. I sat on an iron bench in the shade of an immense copper beech tree, watching two patients play. One, a white-haired man dressed in the long white pants and long-sleeved white shirt of gentlemen's tennis of Bill Tilden's era, stood at the baseline and hit smooth perfect ground strokes. The other, a thin man, young, with jet-black hair and black-framed glasses tinted amber, was clearly self-taught. He seemed manic, gifted with jittery quickness and speed. The older man would hit a shot deep to the right side, and the younger would run it down and take a mad swipe at it, starting his stroke as if his elbow were attached to his hip and then lifting like a man loading something onto a truck—say a fresh-killed turkey. The return would be deep to the left side, seemingly out of reach, but with fanatical effort the young man would be there, and back it would go again, for long, thrilling rallies, on and on. The older man seemed imperturbable, calm and businesslike; the younger tireless, never failing to run a shot down, making incredible saves. Diagnosis? The younger, manic-depressive, manic phase; the older, normal. The spot was so peaceful, the lowering sun muted to cool through the coppery curtain of leaves so friendly, the soft *phwop phwop* of the ball on the strings so soothing, I dozed off.

LATER THAT EVENING I got a lift out to the suburbs to Ike White's Freud seminar with another first-year resident named Henry Solini. Misery kept us new residents so busy, so isolated from one another on our separate wards, that I'd never had a chance to talk with Solini. He was a crooked-smiled little guy with dark curly hair ending in a short neat ponytail, mischievous eyes, and a thin gold ring in one ear. He dressed down, shirts and slacks instead of suits and ties, and had already been dressed down for this by the powers that be in Misery. In late afternoon I'd run into Henry in the hallway of the attic of Toshiba, when both of us had rushed out of our tiny offices onto the iron fire escape to stare down at a tremendous commotion on the Cyclone-fenced tennis courts three floors below. Solini was so tiny, he barely came up to my shoulder.

Six men had cornered Split Risk Harrison, the patient I'd let out. He was screaming, "You crucified Christ, you crucify sweet Bill Clinton, don't you realize who you're crucifying now?"

The six mental health professionals rushed him. He ran full-tilt and hurdled the net, only to find the gate locked. He turned, spread his arms against the chain-link fence, and said, "Listen. This relationship is not working. You've got to get to *know* your crucifixee, okay?"

They jumped him, tied him up, and carried him away.

"Wrong coast," Solini said, looking up at me.

"Wrong coast?"

"On the West Coast he'd be pretty normal, no problem. All my life I've been trying to expand the definition of normal."

As we drove out to Ike White's house, Solini hunched over the steering wheel of his brash red Geo with the North Dakota plate reading "Discover the Spirit: Peace Garden State," he told me about himself. He'd been born of Italian-Czech heritage and raised in Mandan, North Dakota, where his family ran Ideal Cleaners. "I grew up with wheat farmers and Lakota Sioux. My best Indian buddies would sit around town with their legs cut off from falling asleep drunk on the railroad tracks on their way back to the reservation in Fort Yates."

"Sounds pretty bad."

"No foolin'. I have this idea that the dry-cleaning fumes stunted my growth." With a sorrowful glance at me he said, "I'm only five-two."

He'd escaped to Reed College, then med school and internship in San Francisco. His medical internship, which he'd finished just the month before, had been every bit as horrifying and disillusioning as my own in the hospital nicknamed "The House of God," with the added hell of his caring for large numbers of AIDS patients. Many of his friends had died of AIDS.

"Man, I am worn out," he said. "Not only from the internship, but from singing at funerals."

"You sing?"

"Reggae. I'm the only white man who ever was lead vocalist in Jamaica Juice. I mean medicine is one thing, but Bob Marley and the Wailers is something else." He flipped on the tape deck and for a while we listened to the hard-driving revolutionary joy. I asked why he'd gone into psychiatry.

"I love working with crazy people," he said. The little guy rolled his hands around on the steering wheel, his rolling hands rolling his arms, his arms, his body, until he was almost dancing in the seat and I had to grab the wheel myself.

"But why'd you come to Misery? It's like the Wall Street of psychiatry."

"Misery's cool. I need a rest. Three thousand miles from my ex. I heard Ike White speak once, out in Berkeley. He was cool. I didn't get to meet him in person, just talked on the phone. I came here for him."

"Yeah, me too." Looking at his ponytail and earring, I asked, "But how did you get accepted?"

"Geographical distribution and good C.fuckin'–V."

"But what about the photo? The application photo?"

"No problem. Sent 'em one from my yearbook."

"Med school?" He shook his head no. "College?"

"Get real. I had hair down to my waist and *three* earrings. One in my damn nose. High school. The Mandan High Braves. Basketball. Crew cut. No jewelry. No problem. So what about you, Roy-babe?"

I told him that during my year in the House of God I'd gotten pretty cynical about medicine, feeling something was missing in my being a doctor, not to mention in my life. "I've had enough poodling around in diseased bodies. I can do bodies now. But I never feel I really understand. I want to understand people, that's all."

"Well, it's been a month. You understand anything yet? I mean really?"

I thought about this. "Starting to, a little, with Ike. But that's gotta be a good thing to do in the world, right?"

"Pretty noble, man. Pretty high hopes. Could be trouble."

Inside Ike's house Henry and I headed for the bar and poured bourbons. We met in a living room, which, in contrast to Ike's office at Misery, was tidy and formal, all urethaned hardwood and Laura Ashley, implying Mrs. Ike. Ike offered cigars. Henry and I were the only takers, aside from Ike himself. Ike leading, we walked into Freud.

I had read the evening's paper, "Mourning and Melancholia," during my medical internship. As I listened to Ike lead us through it, I was impressed. It wasn't only that Ike was brilliant, he was so damn modest. He almost apologized for even teaching us this arcane Viennese stuff in the era of high-tech psychiatry. Ike sparkled.

The monograph was about the grieving process. Freud dissected the difference between normal neurotic grief—"mourning"—and pathological grief—"melancholia," or depression. "The heart of the difference between normal and sick," Ike said, "is captured in a single remarkable line." With passion, Ike quoted, " 'The shadow of the lost object falls across the ego.' "

Between the bourbon and the sleep deprivation I soon had a buzz on and drifted in and out. My fellow residents soon were sounding very intelligent about this mourning, this melancholia, this Freud.

Saying good-bye to me, Ike seemed concerned. "Are you ok-kay?"

"Sure. Just a little wiped."

"That p-patient Harrison splitting—was that d-difficult for you?"

"No," I said, surprised that he knew about this. "Not really."

"Working with sick people is p-pretty stressful."

"Can't be more stress than doing straight medicine."

A slight delay—about two seconds—and then Ike said, "It's a different k-kind of stress."

Creeping home in the cozy red Geo, soon Solini and I were singing along with Bob Marley's "Them Belly Full (But We Hungry)."

After Solini dropped me off I stumbled roughly up the narrow and trickily reversing three flights of stairs to my loft on the top floor of an old turreted Victorian and found Berry asleep in a chair. I hadn't seen her in a few days. How lovable she looked, that long, tan Modigliani face tucked snugly into her bared shoulder, her blouse unbuttoned, the lace of her bra bulging bright and white against her deep tan, her short dark hair mussed and long black lashes two crescents on her cheeks. Her full lower lip was a pillow for her upper, both curled in a half smile, as if her dream was sweet. Knowing her recent pain, her struggle with self-confidence and her vulnerability, I felt glad for that half smile.

I'd been with Berry for almost a decade. After my hellish year of medical internship and her hellish one as a child psychologist at another high-powered hospital, we'd decided we needed time together, to get to know each other again, and to try to heal. We'd taken a year off and traveled around the world, beginning in southern France, ending just a month before in southern China. During our year of freedom, our relationship had deepened. We'd talked about getting married. Yet we each felt that first we had to see what it would be like back in the high-test rocket of America.

Berry too was trying something new, teaching four-year-olds in a preschool. Her internship in child psychology had crushed her, a few red-hot supervisors making her feel that she was "too sensitive" and didn't have the "critical discipline" to be an academic. She had rebelled against a central part of her training: doing psychological testing on kids, labeling them as "sick." For her refusal, she was constantly made to feel like a failure.

Yet she loved being with children. Wherever we stopped in our travels, I would volunteer as a doc, she as a teacher. She'd decided that when we got back she would work with "normal" children, in a preschool.

I bent and kissed her.

"Where've you been?" she asked, her half smile replaced with worry as she awakened. I told her. "You never said you had a seminar tonight."

"I forgot."

"Haven't you ever heard of telephones?" I said I had in fact heard of them, yes. "I've been worried. How was your day?"

"My day and night and day? Loved every minute of it. Being a shrink's a snap. It fits me perfectly: a Jewish doctor who can't stand the sight of blood."

"Sure, if you go through it drunk."

"I'm not drunk."

"Fine," she said, getting up, "and I'm not staying."

"C'mon, give an inch, willya?"

"Try me tomorrow."

"Wait, wait, how was your day?"

"One thing I've learned," she said, "is not to try to talk to a drunk."

"Hey, come on, I'm not your father, I'm your—"

"Tomorrow," she said, and left for her own apartment.

"Hey, I'm sorry," he called after her. Too late. She was gone.

In bed I read a letter from my own father, the dentist, one of the world's great optimists, a master of the conjunction. All his sentences were in the pattern of phrase-conjunction-phrase:

> . . . Glad you are done with your year off and it was a loss of a year's income and not normal. Psychiatry is a waste of your talent and you will soon find out and go back to real medicine. Dentistry was always an intellectual challenge and a secure income. I still hope that someday we can have our family foursome and Mom has such a smooth short swing. I am playing well and try to concentrate on keeping loose my arms like ropes . . .

Two

HUNGOVER AND RAW, the next morning at nine I trudged into the Farben Building and up the grand stairway to my secretary Nancy's office. The Cherokee-Schlomo matter seemed far away and phantasmal, like a faded dream. Nancy wore a cheery pink top, which exposed her tanned shoulders. Her eyes were red with tears.

"What's wrong?"

"Didn't you hear?" Her eyes widened.

"What? Hear what?" She started to sob horribly. "What?"

"Ike White's dead. He killed himself last night."

"What? He . . . he couldn't have. I saw him last night. We all did."

"After you left."

Things went blank. I heard her sobbing, but in the distance, as if she were one floor down. My legs were watery. I found myself in a chair.

How could this be? It was impossible. I was talking to him, shaking his hand. He was smiling. He was going on vacation, for Chrissakes. I mean he seemed a little burnt out, but basically he'd been cheerful.

"Are you sure it was suicide?"

"Totally." She sobbed even harder.

I felt a cold grinding in my chest, a metal fist around my heart. My whole body was heavy. Then I saw all over again as if it were yesterday the stain on the parking lot of the House of God where one of my buddies, a fellow intern named Potts, had landed from his leap from eight floors up, and tears broke, hot and sharp, searing my eyes. Ike? Not Ike.

Word spread, and by the time Solini and I pushed our way into the standing-room-only Misery daily report at nine-thirty that morning, everyone not only knew that Ike White had killed himself with an overdose of sedatives, but also knew the kind and rough number of pills, and that on that last afternoon he had called the hospital benefits office to check on his insurance coverage—the return call I myself had heard on the answering machine. He'd popped the pills at about eleven, not a half hour after he and I had grasped hands limply without eye contact and I'd told him to enjoy his vacation. He'd died in the emergency room of a local hospital, with his wife and his new psychoanalyst at his bedside, and with his psychopharmacologist in constant touch by beeper.

As we stood packed together at the back of the old auditorium, most of us knew the terrible truth. We were looking for help in how to handle it.

Dr. Lloyal von Nott stood up on the small stage, his funereal suit and dark hair and brows a picture of sad decorum. Here was a man not only in control, but in charge. He was the Chief of Misery, and like other chiefs of other institutions, he had that dazzling sincerity that meant you couldn't trust a word he said. The meeting was a daily half-hour report from various wards of Misery on the events of the past twenty-four hours, including new admissions and current problems. With the calm dignity of his high British accent, Lloyal handled the usual business of running the hospital, proceeding as if nothing had happened, right up until the grandfather clock in the corner struck the hour with ten mournful bongs. The last bong died, leaving an ominous hush. Lloyal cleared his throat. The tension was incredible.

"Thank you very much," Lloyal said, and started to leave.

Unreal. For a second no one said anything. Then the meeting started breaking up. Suddenly someone called out, loudly, "Excuse me. Dr. von Nott?"

Lloyal paused. The meeting coalesced. Heads turned to locate the speaker. A tall, gray-haired woman wearing dark glasses was standing, chin raised in that Stevie Wonder posture—clearly she was blind. "Dr. Geneva Hooevens here. We are all very upset about Dr. White's death. Perhaps you could give us some information?"

"We are sorry to announce the death of Dr. Isaac White. He died of a fatal disease. The new director of residency training will be Dr. Schlomo Dove. The time of the memorial service will be announced, anon."

Fatal disease? It was suicide. What the hell was going on?

"But," Dr. Geneva Hooevens said, "we are hearing a rumor of suicide."

"There is no truth to that rumor. Dr. White died of a fatal disease." Lloyal turned and left. The meeting ended.

Solini and I walked along slowly in the still, untroubled sunlight toward our wards on Emerson. With us was Hannah Silver, the only woman in our first-year resident class. I'd known Hannah at the BMS. She was a delicately featured woman with black hair spinning down to her shoulders, intense eyes set in a thin, Sephardic face, and a body that seemed to get more and more hefty as it descended, as if built low to the ground, for speed. A New Yorker with a sensitive soul, during an intense Upper East Side analysis she'd given up a promising career as a cellist, for medicine. She and I had worked together with Ike on Emerson 1.

"What do they mean 'fatal disease'?" Solini asked. "Are they talking existential? Or is it some medical disease the poor guy had?"

"He was in perfect health," I said. "He was only forty-one. Nancy spoke to a nurse friend of hers who saw the lab report: massive overdose of barbiturates. It was suicide, no question."

"Why won't they admit the truth? Why the cover-up?"

"I don't know," I said, feeling ghostlike, the grip of that small, stammering hand. It was stunning to think that while he was shaking my hand he had already put everything in place to kill himself an hour later. What had he said, so fluently? *They go out seamless.* I looked at Hannah. She too had chosen Misery because of Ike, had decided to specialize in Ike's specialty, depression and suicide. Now she was trudging along like a robot, in shock.

In my month with Ike, dealing with the most depressed people on the face of the earth, I'd come to believe in him, in what he said and what he did. He was always calm, never saying much or doing much, but giving Hannah and me the feeling that he knew what he was up to, that walking the walk with these poor depressed souls would bring them out the other side. Ike had been the wise, calm, all-knowing doctor.

Now something in me cracked open, calling into question who and what I could believe, or not believe. With Ike, I had believed in my own experience of him, and it was totally false. The ground under my feet took on the feel of gauze, the heat made my head spin. I said to Henry:

"But I thought psychiatrists are supposed to be able to *face* the hard feelings, help you get through them, you know, *alive*?"

"No joke, man. Maybe they're trying to teach us that we're better off mentally if we pretend that what really happened didn't really happen. That we *don't* feel what we *do* feel?"

"But if you can't even keep the doctors from killing themselves," I said, "how the hell can you keep the patients from killing themselves too?"

Henry scrunched up his face in puzzlement. "Good question man, yeah."

"I feel so *bad*," Hannah said, rolling her eyes up toward the sky. She often did this eye roll-up when she spoke. One day when I'd asked her about it, she was surprised that she still was doing it, and explained that it came from her being in psychoanalysis for so many years. She'd gotten into the habit, from lying there on the couch with her analyst behind her, of looking back toward him whenever she said anything she thought he'd think she should think was important. "I came here to work with Ike, and when I asked him to be my teacher, he said . . ." She started to cry, so that Ike's words came out in a kind of wail, " 'Nothing would make me *happier.*' "

Emerson's high walls and locked doors seemed sinister. On the first floor, Hannah unlocked the door to her ward, Emerson 1, Depression. Solini left me on the second-floor landing and continued up to his ward, Emerson 3, Psychosis. Noting the Split Risk sign, I opened the door to my new ward, Emerson 2, Borderline Depression, with caution, shielded the opening with my body, back-flipped in fast and threw the door closed. It shut with a tremendous *wham*!

"Dickheads Slam Doors!"

The same sandy-haired young man as before. I went into a slow burn, wanting to respond, but stopping myself. About twenty other patients were sitting around the living room, staring at me. I saw the two tennis players. The normal, older man, in a crisp summer suit, was reading the *Wall Street Journal*. The younger, thin man—the manic one—was reading a tabloid and eating a carrot. He took a bite. In the tense silence the crunch seemed enormous. No doctors were in sight. The patients—teen to senior citizen, dressed from high fashion to rags, many with bandages around their wrists or heads or legs, one in a neck brace riveted into her skull, one in a wheelchair—seemed like so many wounded, shell-shocked refugees, waiting for a war to end so they could move on. These were the dread "borderlines."

I asked the ward secretary where I could find Dr. Malik.

"The one with the carrot. Hall meetin's just about over."

This was a surprise. I stood and watched. He was speaking:

"Like I said, Ike White killed himself. Nobody knows why. Hard to take. But we gotta face reality. Game's over for him, but not for us. I'm here. You wanna talk suicide, I'll *talk* suicide. But *do* sports! Catch ya later."

Malik walked over to us. He was wearing a short-sleeve white shirt and a slender red tie, khaki trousers, and well-worn Nike running shoes. His wiry athlete's body seemed too small a container for his energy. He had jet-black hair, parted carefully and slicked up and over in front. In his long tan face, his hawk's nose was bridged by black-framed glasses whose lenses were tinted amber. We shook hands. His was large for his size, and, though tight with tendons, gentle. An athlete's hand.

"I saw you playing tennis yesterday. I thought you were a patient."

"So y'think there's a big difference between doctors and patients? Sometimes your patients are better than you." He fixed me with his eyes. I had a strange sense of being seen *into*. He glanced at my suit. "Boy, you got it bad."

"What do you mean?"

"You know what I mean, doncha?"

"Sort of," I said, sensing him sensing my discomfort wearing a suit.

"So if you know what I mean, you don't ask what I mean. To be a shrink you still got a lot to unlearn, like all us kids who went to med school. 'Specially us hot-shit high-achiever Jews."

I wanted to ask what he meant but stopped myself.

"You stopped yourself. Good." He took another bite out of his carrot, closed his eyes and chewed carefully, savoring it.

"What's with the carrot?"

"A carrot a day keeps colon cancer away." I laughed. "No joke. Studies have proved it."

"And just where is it you put the carrot?"

"Ha! Haha! Good. So. You play any sports?"

"Tennis, basketball, and golf."

"You do okay in psychiatry as long as you keep playing sports and use what you know from sports. Anything else before I show you what's what?"

"I was surprised you told them the truth about Ike White. I've been trying to figure out what von Nott meant by 'a fatal disease.' "

"That's bullshit. Lloyal means he was biologically depressed, but depression never *has* to be fatal. *Never*. All this fatal-disease bullshit is so they don't have to admit they killed him."

"They *killed* him?"

"Places like this kill guys like him right and left, and a lot of the dead don't even know when they're dead 'cause their souls die first."

"That seems pretty bitter—" I started to say, but then stopped, for Malik had tears in his eyes, amber-tinted wetness. One tear, escaping from under his glasses, ran down his cheek, translucent, losing form as it ran, leaving a trace behind, like a snail's. Looking away, he chomped his carrot mournfully, giving out several forlorn crunches. He gulped down sobs, his Adam's apple shuttling up and down his thin neck. I asked, "You must've known Ike really well?"

"Nobody knew Ike well." He removed his glasses, squinted like a mole in the light, and wiped away the tears with the back of his hand. "Nobody alive knows a suicide at all."

"Why'd he kill himself? Is there some dirt, some secret? Why?"

"Maybe, maybe not. 'Why' questions don't work too good in psychiatry. What can I tell you? Psychiatrists specialize in their defects."

"And Ike specialized in suicide?"

"Wrote the classic papers, yop. Maybe we'll find out more, with time, and the more you find out about a person, the *more* sense they make, never less.

Lloyal was crushing him. He died of death." He blinked, looked around in puzzlement. "Why'm I preaching to you? Jesus! C'mon—"

"Wait." He waited. "If the other shrinks are lying about him killing himself, and you're telling the truth, aren't you gonna get into trouble?"

"So what else is new? They don't like me teaching you new guys, 'specially not here on Blair Heiler's ward. Eleven months of the year Heiler terrorizes these patients, so nobody else wants to deal with the mess in August when he's on vacation in Stockholm. Sucking Nobel Prize butt."

"Terrorizes!"

"Yop. So. Emerson Two. Know anything about it?"

"It's the borderline ward," I said. Ike had given me a lecture on borderlines, patients who were on the border between normals—or neurotics—and crazies—or psychotics. The lecture was based on the DSM—the *Diagnostic and Statistical Manual*—the bible of psychiatric diagnosis published by the prestigious American Psychiatric Association. The DSM described borderlines as suffering from a pervasive instability in interpersonal relationships, self-image, and feelings. The official diagnosis of Borderline Personality Organization, or BPO, was defined by thirteen Krotkey Factors, created by the borderline world expert Dr. Renaldo Krotkey. Dr. Blair Heiler, local borderline expert, was a follower of Krotkey. Some of the Krotkey Factors were: impulsivity (BPOs were dramatically impulsive about sex, shopping, gambling, substance abuse, reckless driving, binge eating, etc.), fear of abandonment, unstable relationships, suicidal or self-mutilating acts, mood swings, feelings of emptiness, and a fierce, withering rage. Borderlines were emotionally labile, sometimes seeming completely normal, sometimes really crazy. They could change in an instant, seemingly for no clear reason. Most borderlines were women. Ike had painted me a dire picture, and now I quoted Ike to Malik, "Borderlines are hell. They make your life as a psychiatrist miserable. They're almost impossible to treat. Borderlines are the worst patients in all of psychiatry."

"Yeah, well, don't hold your breath, but borderlines don't exist." I laughed, thinking he was joking. "No joke. Problems with relationships, self-image, feelings, impulsivity? We *all* got that! Your job is to resist brainwashing as long as possible and just try to help these poor people. Being lied to about Ike's death has got 'em bullshit! All three floors of Emerson are rumblin', ready to blow! Try to help 'em and play *sports*! Listen up."

Heiler had left the ward full. Malik said that most of the patients would be better off out of Misery and that we would discharge as many as possible. Given the fact that insurance companies were now dedicated to not paying out insurance, this wouldn't be difficult. The ones who needed to stay, he'd go to bat for. He started dialing a phone.

"How do you get insurance to pay for them to stay?" I asked.

"Allora! Testa di catzo!"

I turned, and then realized once again who it was. I'd just been called a dickhead in Italian.

"Thorny," Malik said, "meet the new resident, Roy G. Basch."

I looked into the eyes of the tall, sandy-haired, baby-faced man. He wore jeans, suspenders, blue work shirt, and bow tie. A row of fresh sutures, like a tiny barbed-wire fence on his forehead, overlay other old scars. I shook his hand. It was as boneless as Ike White's had been the night before.

"What's that?" Malik asked, talking into the phone. "You ain't gonna pay for another day of Mr. Thorne's stay here in the hospital?"

"They gotta pay or else I'm dead!" Thorny said frantically.

"Yeah, well, he's extremely paranoid and dangerous and—" He listened for quite a while and then said, "How can we *prove* it? Well, Ms. Tillinger, he just told me that unless you let him stay he's gonna come right down there to your office with a gun and— That's right, a *gun*, and, in his words, 'blast them insurance fuckers to smithereens.' Now, where exactly are you located, dear?" Covering the receiver, Malik shook with laughter. He said, "Managed care, I love it. Basch, go talk to Thorny." I hesitated. Malik made shooing-away motions, saying, "Go, go. Move."

Thorny was glowering at me. He walked away and sat down. I felt a strange fear. Malik hung up. "What am I supposed to do with him?" I asked.

"Be human," Malik said. I stared at him. "Human? Human being?"

"But he's so pissed off, suppose I say the wrong thing?"

"Think these people are fragile? Just try 'n' change 'em. But hey, I know you're scared. I was too." His eyes locked in again. I felt a kind of rush, a "click"—he was the first person since I'd been there who had talked to my fear. "Weird, ain't it," he said, "to be so scareda just sitting down and talking to somebody? Image is a killer, and self-image is a *killer* killer! So listen up, if you need me, call." He squeezed my arm and walked off, stooping to pick up a piece of litter.

"Dickheads Save Planet!"

"Yeah," Malik shot back, "for assholes like you."

I walked over to Thorny, thinking about how to be human.

"So, Dr. Dickhead, tell me about yourself," Thorny said.

Uh-oh. Surely this was backward—*I* was supposed to be asking about *him*. "I'm the new resident." I felt a sharp pain in my palm. I was clutching my key ring so hard the keys were biting into the flesh. "You?"

"Got here a month ago from New Orleans. My daddy's rich, made a fortune burnin' trash down Cancer Alley. Calls himself the Burn King of the Bayous. I did okay till I was eighteen, 'n' got sent north to Princeton. Lasted but three months. You look kinda tentative, Doc. Scareda me?"

I was, but I wasn't going to let *him* know it. "Nope."

"Sure is sad Ike White killed himse'f, ain't it?"

"They say he died of a fatal disease and—"

"Oh, pleeeeze!" he said, disgusted, getting up. "Hey, patients! Hey, borderlines!" They all looked at him. "This new doc is *pitiful*! We got ourselves a real *loser* in this Roy G. Dickhead Basch!" He walked away.

Not a good start. If this wasn't a borderline, who was? Humiliated, I decided to interview another new patient of mine named Mr. K., whom I recognized as the kindly old gentleman who'd been playing tennis with Malik. I found him on the sun porch, finishing the *Wall Street Journal*. We had a wonderful talk. He was, he said, the last survivor of an old Yankee family. Only recently had things gone awry. His golden retriever, Duke, had died. His son had come out as gay. His wife was drinking again, and his daughter had run off with a drug dealer. He'd come to Misery a month ago for a rest.

"You seem so sad," I said, touched by all this recent misfortune.

" 'Tis cause for weeping, yes." He started to cry.

"We'll discharge you soon. Maybe even next week."

"That would be grand!" he said happily. "Thank you for your time."

Time that had flown by. I was excited at this, my first good interview of a borderline. At the nursing station I told Malik about it. The head nurse and social worker listened in. I said that Mr. K. seemed about ready for discharge. When I stopped, no one said anything.

"Ever hear of a mental status exam?" Malik asked. Someone giggled.

"Oh shit," I said. "I blew it?"

"Big-time. Let's go." He led me back to Mr. K.

"Gonna ask you two proverbs," Malik said. "Tell me, Mr. K., what do people mean when they say, 'A rolling stone gathers no moss'? "

"They mean that I have never been *happier*!" he said, and started to sob uncontrollably, on and on, in horrific pain.

"And, 'People who live in glass houses shouldn't throw stones'?"

Abruptly he stopped sobbing, began laughing hard, and said, "It's a big cry, a big big *cry*!"

"And who's the president of the United States?"

"Herbert Whoever."

With Mr. K. listening, Malik told me that when Mr. K. was six, driving with his mother, a car hit them and she was decapitated. Her head landed in his lap. "At ten he was institutionalized. From then on, because he's rich, he was assaulted by whatever treatment was at the leading edge of American psychiatry: insulin shock, cold water dousings, being strapped into the Benjamin Rush restraining chair and given emetics and whirled around till he puked his guts out, enemas and high colonic irrigations to get it out from the *other* end—"

"Woo-wheeee!" Mr. K. cried, shaking his head in amazement.

"—enough electroshock to light up Iowa, the most toxic drugs ever concocted, two first-rate psychoanalyses—one for each hemisphere, for the left, Freudian, for the right, Jungian—and a prefrontal lobotomy." Malik made a stabbing motion up through his own eye socket, and then a slashing wiggle. "An ice pick, stuck in his *brain*?"

Sickened, I said, "Thank God they don't do that anymore."

"Oh, it wasn't *that* bad," Mr. K. chided.

"Oh, but they *do*!" Malik said. "Lobotomy's making a comeback! Check out *Archives of General Psychiatry*, June 'ninety-one. Big article proving that lobotomy is the treatment of choice for refractory obsessive compulsives."

More sickened, I said, "But we had a great talk, Mr. K., didn't we?"

"Thumbs up!" Mr. K. said, putting his thumbs down, smiling sweetly.

"Yes, you did. Luckily, they botched his lobotomy. Left half a frontal lobe. Lloyal's his therapist. Fifteen-minute sessions, a hundred twenty bucks a shot. They talk finance. Mr. K.'s trust fund will keep him in Misery till he dies. He's been here forty years."

"But he was just transferred over here to Borderline yesterday."

"Heiler had an empty bed. Empty beds mean stalled careers. He 'n' von Nott agreed Mr. K. needed a trial of BPO with HFL—Half a Frontal Lobe."

"That's quite funny actually," Mr. K. said, chuckling normally.

"They can't *touch* you," Malik said. "As a shrink, Roy, you gotta be able to tell when something's organic—medically treatable—as opposed to mental. You don't treat brain tumors with psychotherapy. Proverbs can help find out which is which. Read Mr. K.'s chart. It's a memorial to the harm done by shrinks trying to fix people. Now we gotta protect him."

"From what?"

"This." He spread his arms. "All this. The more I see, the more I think that if all the shrinks in the world were to die of heart attacks at once, all the patients in the world would be a helluva lot better off."

"Including you?"

"If and when I act like a shrink, yeah."

"But you are a shrink."

"You gotta know it to let go of it. You tell me if and when, okay?" I nodded. "And when I'm gone in a month, protect him from Blair Heiler and you."

"Me?" I asked, stunned. "You don't know what you're talking ab—"

"Kid, you're gonna go for Heiler like America goes for stars! C'mon, we got Case Conference. Heiler set it up before he went on vacation."

Malik left, but I couldn't, yet. A cloud darkened the quiet porch. I turned back to Mr. K. In silence, he was weeping. Two glints of tears were running sadly down his old man's old damaged man's cheeks. I felt really bad. "I'm sorry, Mr. K.," I said. "Are you sad, hearing all that?"

"Hahaa!" he said, his laugh crackling and high-pitched, like a child finding a favorite toy, say a stuffed zebra. "Doctor, I've got some advice for you: always keep a low center of gravity sometimes."

"Deal," I said, relieved.

Laughing, he gave me a thumbs-down and a high five.

Case Conference was designed to try to get a fresh look at a problem patient by bringing in a world expert to talk things over. Waiting in the conference room was Dr. Errol Cabot, the world expert of the day, his world expertise being the drug treatment of mental illness. Errol was a chunky thirty-five-year-old man with a square-jawed flat face and eyes that seemed to bulge out of a sea of thyroid. This drug doctor was so restless and hyper he always struck me as being on drugs. His dark red hair was cut back like the helmet of Winged Victory, and he wore a long white lab coat.

With him was his protégé, a new first-year resident named Win Winthrop. I knew Win from medical school. Though fat, he was energetic and optimistic, with the keen intelligence I had always associated with people with his fiery red hair and freckled, alabaster skin. In med school he had been doing special projects on the uses of computers in surgery, and using the internet and medical telecommunication to bring surgical supervision to distant parts of the globe, even, once, to a needy hospital in Tierra del Fuego. Early in medical school he had discovered, for the first time, a sex life, stimulated by a hot web-site e-mail with a surgical nurse several years his senior, who turned out to be just as hotly optimistic as Win, especially in bed, where Win had had little experience. She was soon pregnant. They married and had a baby boy. Now she was pregnant again. Given his surgical bent, I'd been surprised when Win declared for psychiatry. He had explained that he would be combining fields, hoping to use computer-driven, stereotactic surgical techniques on the human brain, and, in his words, "using drugs with surgical precision, making surgical strikes against our common enemy, mental illness. You see, Roy, Mother has been bipolar for years, untreatable, much to Father's chagrin. I'm working on a cure." Win's father was a Boston Brahmin, a well-known lawyer at Hale and Dorr, and he had been disappointed in Win's choice of psychiatry, for he had been hoping against hope for the only honorable medical specialty, surgery.

After only a month, Win, like a dog with its master, had become much like Errol: both were hyper and manic with eyes wide as boys eyeing an electric train set; both had their red hair cut like Prince Valiant; and both were bulky under their long white lab coats. They were rocking in their chairs as we entered the room. I was to find that Errol—and Win too—had two traits that would prove remarkably useful as they threw drugs into people: unawareness of self, and unawareness of others.

That day the patient was Mary Megan Scorato, admitted several weeks before to Emerson 1. For those weeks, Ike had been her therapist. I remembered that she was the "acutely suicidal patient" Ike had needed to see the day before as I'd left his office. Mary Megan was one of those "salt of the earth" people whom everyone loved, a kindhearted woman of Irish descent married to an Italian who, in her weeks on Depression, had taken to "mothering" all of us, patients and doctors alike. Hannah had formed a special bond with Mary Megan. "I *love* that woman!" Hannah always said, rolling her eyes way up. "She's a great mother—prefeminist and unconflicted—and boy is it nice. Like eating whatever you want and not gaining weight. My mother, on the other hand, had a sign on the refrigerator: 'A Moment on the Lips, Forever on the Hips.' " Mary Megan baked cookies for us all, listened to other depressed patients' problems, cleaned countertops, and did laundry. Everybody loved her. How could you not?

Yet she herself remained hidden. A woman from a poor Irish family, she'd worked her way through secretarial school and had become an assistant to the director of admissions at Harvard, over an hour's commute away. Institutions like Harvard always have a warmhearted type on the front lines, protecting the hard-hearted higher-ups, and Mary Megan was it in Admissions. She had had her share of suffering: married at forty, she gave birth to a baby with Down syndrome. Now a six-year-old, the boy was severely disabled. Mary Megan was a hefty woman, but she had lost her appetite, begun eating very little, and lost a great deal of weight. People said, mistakenly, that she "looked good." Two weeks before, she had completely snapped. She was picked up by the state police on the side of the interstate, weeping hysterically, threatening to throw herself into the traffic. As they were coming home from vacation, the family's luggage had blown off the roof rack and her six-year-old's new parka had flown away and reappeared crucified on the front grille of a trailing ten-wheeler. Since then she'd been actively suicidal. But something didn't make sense. Why should luggage falling off a car and a parka on the front of a truck plunge a fine, by-all-accounts cheerful woman with lots of friends at work and home into suicidal despair? No one, not even Ike White, had been able to find out.

"Okay!" Errol said as we sat down, before Mary Megan was brought in. "Let's go. Win and I have read the chart, so we all know the case. First, diagnosis. It's absolutely clear this gal is a BPO with Ano—"

"First," Malik said, "we talk with her."

Errol's jaw dropped, as if this were incredible, for a doctor to actually talk with a patient.

Mary Megan Scorato came in. Her freckled milky complexion was marred by dark bags under her eyes and slack skin around her mouth. The edges of her lips turned down, as if she were on the verge of tears. Her auburn hair was unwashed and halfheartedly in a bun, ends escaping out and hanging despondently down, ends she didn't brush out of her eyes. Her clothes, usually neat and clean and perky in the way that an old-fashioned good mother's kitchen clothes are perky, were rumpled and too big for her thinning body. She nodded to Errol, Win, Malik, and me and sat down. Malik explained that we would talk.

"This morning I wrote a little poem for this conference," she said.

"What meds are you on, sweetheart?" Errol asked.

"Dr. White was so kind and good, I wrote a poem."

"What meds worked best in the past, gal?" Errol asked.

It went on like that, Errol talking drugs and Mary Megan talking poetry. Mary Megan got more and more subdued. I felt for her. Finally Malik said, "You okay, Mary?"

"No I am not! I came here to read my poem for Doctor—"

"What about anticonvulsants, honey?" Errol asked.

Mary Megan stared at him and then took a green piece of glass out of her sleeve and held it to her wrist. "Let me read my poem or I'll cut myself!" Her thin cheeks made her eyes seem huge.

"Read," Malik said. "We'll listen." Mary read her poem, ending with:

> *"We all imagined his hesitant, stammering manner*
> *Merely concealed his heart's strong core,*
> *But he had his misery, his hesitant stammering manner,*
> *And nothing more."*

Stillness. She'd gotten him exactly right. Errol and Win kept rocking in their chairs, but said nothing. Mary handed the piece of glass to Malik.

"Beautiful," Malik said, "and true. Can I ask you a few questions?"

"Yes. If you can be kind, like Dr. White."

"I'll try," Malik said. He talked with her for a while, and then the strangest thing happened. Later I couldn't recall how it came about, but after just a few minutes of their talking, talking as if they were old friends meeting after a long time, talking about her Down syndrome son and the parka crucified on the truck, Malik asked her something that seemed completely bizarre: "Tell me about your *other* son."

Mary Megan sat up in shock, her eyes wide. "My other . . . ?"

"Yes. The one you lost." I had no idea what he meant. Mary Megan had said nothing about another son. I felt a kind of "click." I waited.

"Oh God!" she said, and began to weep softly, and on her tears rode a story none of us had ever heard from her. Thirty-one years ago, when she was seventeen, she'd been forced into sex with a neighbor and gotten pregnant. She'd told no one but her mother, who demanded that she give the baby up for adoption. Finally Mary agreed, on one condition: that the Clarissan nuns taking the baby let her see it just once. The Mother Superior agreed. She gave birth to a boy. The nuns never let her see it. Every year, every single year on his birthday, she would think of that baby boy and wonder where he was, and what his life had become. "A year and a month ago," she said now, "on his thirtieth birthday, the phone rang. I picked it up. A man's voice asked, 'Is this Mary Megan O'Toole?' I knew at once. My heart seemed to tear loose inside me. I said, 'Yes it 'tis.' 'Well . . . I am your baby boy.' " She wept frantically, searching for tissues. Malik handed her a box. Calming down, she went on, "We met a few days later, and . . . he said he wanted to meet just the once, no more. I told no one, no one knows this, no one a'tall, not even my dear husband Joey. I never even told poor Dr. White. I was okay for a year, but then, this year, without him, when that day came 'round . . . I could not go on . . . I couldn't even eat."

"Anniversaries are killers," Malik said. "You had an 'anniversary reaction'—it's totally normal. And why didn't you tell Dr. White?"

"He seemed too . . . vulnerable? And he didn't ask, like you did."

"You feel okay about telling us?"

"I do. You have a kind face. Thank you."

"Now that it's out, we can help you to heal the wound."

She wept again, quietly. I felt moved, awed even, by Malik's way: so simple, so *there* with her. She sniffled. "That would be fine. Thanks."

Mary Megan left, shutting the door quietly behind her.

"Okay good great," Errol said loudly. "Now let's do some real *work*!"

He and Win then discussed the "case," fitting it brilliantly to Borderline Theory, concluding that the diagnosis was BPO with A and B—Anorexia and Bulimia—even though Mary had explicitly denied previous anorexia or bulimic vomiting. And wouldn't you know it but BPO with A and B was a particular diagnosis Errol just happened to be the world expert in! Not only that, but by sheer coincidence he was also the world expert in the drug to treat it! "The treatment of choice," he said, "is my experimental drug amyoxetine—brand name Placedon. Brought it back from Bangkok—in my backpack. Placedon makes Prozac look like popcorn. We may need to add my other experimental drug, Zephyrill." While these names were enticing, as if, if you did these drugs you'd be partaking in an encounter with two of Babar's lost children, I was appalled at this, a diagnosis and treatment totally at odds with her obvious and what seemed to me normal grief.

"The woman is going through a normal grief reaction," Malik said. "If we can keep her off drugs, she'll pull together just fine."

"This is for the benefit of the new residents," Errol said, glancing at me and Win. "There's never once been a controlled experiment that showed that talking to patients does any good at all. Any effect is placebo effect. You residents shouldn't waste your time learning how to do this mumbo-jumbo, 'cause there's no 'it' to do. So Malik got her to tell a story, so what? Won't help. Like pissing in the ocean. There are no 'psychosocial' factors in mental illness. If it's mental illness, it's biochemical, and vice versa. Save her a lot of grief—give her Placedon."

"Thanks for sharing, Errol," Malik said, "and now go fuck yourself."

"So," Errol went on, as if Malik hadn't said what he had said, "to get these experimental medications, she has to be in our new research study." He took out a lavender form and got up. "I'll get her informed consent."

"She refuses all drugs," Malik said, rising. "Thanks for stopping by."

"Don't worry, we'll get her to sign."

"She won't talk to you, guaranteed."

"We'll get husband Joey to sign."

"Not without her permission."

"She's not competent to give permission. She's a *borderline*!"

"And," said Win Winthrop, "bulimic. She deserves a trial of Placedon."

"After she's on it, we'll get some of her blood," Errol said. "When her level's in the therapeutic window, she will be competent, and then she can decide rationally about going off Placedon no problem thanks."

Malik picked up Mary Megan's chart and read aloud as he wrote, " 'Patient is mentally competent. Patient refuses all drugs.' "

Red-faced, Errol rose and said, "Know what your problem is, Malik?"

"Maybe that I think you're a neo-Nazi?"

"Your problem is you're nuts and you should be on medication!" They hurried out.

"Wait!" Malik shouted. "When are you gonna study drug *compliance*?" He turned to me. "Know what they don't do?" I asked what. "*Sports!* C'mon."

In the nursing station, as he changed into shorts for his morning run, Malik said, "Don't get me wrong, I'm not against using medication. I use it, if it's right to use. But all the studies of compliance show that patients don't take their drugs fifty percent of the time, and that the only reason they do is if they have a good relationship with their doctor. And guys like Errol are terrible at relationship. Which is one of the two reasons they specialize in drugs. Walk me out." I followed him outside.

"What's the other?" I asked, squinting at him in the bright sun.

"Money. Drug-therapy guys like Errol see six patients an hour, at seventy dollars a pop: four hundred and twenty dollars an hour. Talk-therapy guys see one an hour, at a hundred bucks." He stretched his quads, pulling a bent leg up behind his back so that, with those amber lenses astraddle his beak nose, he looked like a wise, hip stork. "Talk therapy is dying. The drug cowboys are taking over. They use drugs to stay away from being with people. It's easier than being human with that kind of suffering. Other than drugs, the only way to make a living as a shrink is to write some bullshit self-help book. I'm thinking of writing one called 'Anorexia Digest.' "

"But how did you know, I mean about the other son?"

"Dunno. When she talked about that parka, crucified, I picked up somethin', like 'lost son.' So I took a shot, got lucky. Sometimes people don't know that on anniversaries they crash. Just to name it helps a lot."

"It's so sad! Every year, for thirty years, on that day, she's wondering where he is? It blows me away."

"Yeah. Ike's suicide for her, for all of us, is a big 'Fuck you!' " He sighed. "So now you see all the bullshitology around 'diagnosis.' "

"Isn't diagnosis important?"

"In psychiatry, diagnosis comes last."

I felt confused and overwhelmed. Everything this fanatic was telling me was the opposite of what I'd been taught about psychiatry before.

"Here, sit," Malik said. "Listen up." I sat on the lush, close-cropped grass, staring at Malik's tank top, on which two lambs were holding hands over their heads in triumph, and the acronym LAMBS. "This is a BPO ward. But check out the diagnoses: BPO with A—Anorexia; BPO with B—Bulimia; BPO with C—Catatonia; BPO with D—Depression; BPO with M—Mushrooms."

"Mushrooms?"

"Just checking. So Blair Heiler keeps trying to fit people into BPO, but they won't fit. So he keeps adding letters. One of these days he'll admit an adolescent with BPO with Z—Zits!"

"Why does Heiler try to fit people into diagnoses?"

"Money and fame. He's a protégé of Lloyal von Nott, world expert in money. He gets Lloyal to give him a ward for BPO. He gets drug money to study the Krotkey Factors to diagnose BPO. He finds that BPOs fit the factors! Quite a coincidence, eh? He gets more patients, with more BPO. Becomes world expert in BPO. Fame, money, climbing the greasy pole of academia. Heiler's in a catfight with his rivals at McLean Hospital to corner the market on BPO. Meanwhile he terrorizes these patients—which makes 'em act like BPOs! He publishes, they perish. Lotta suicides on his ward. Which is another Krotkey Factor: BPO with SS—Successful Suicide. And BPOs don't even exist. They're just people, right? We coulda got any diagnosis we wanted outta Mary Megan, depending on which diagnosis the world expert we called in was world expert in. In psychiatry, diagnosis comes last."

"What comes first?"

He put a hand on my shoulder. "Roy, you're gonna think this is crazy. In psychiatry, first comes treatment, then comes diagnosis."

"That *is* crazy," I said. "It goes against hundreds of years of medical science."

"You think this is a *science*?" he asked.

I didn't know what to say. For a while I stared at a duck carving lines on the still lake. Finally I said, "I don't know, Malik. You sound pretty cynical."

"Think of Mary Megan, her face when she took out that piece of glass. That was the face of terror, right?"

"But this, you, what you're saying, it's nothing like my month with Ike. This is not what I expected."

"Good. That's the first real thing you said. Listen up: all you gotta do to learn here is keep your eyes open, your fly zipped, your feelings up front, and ask for help. Don't read any bullshit articles. Don't read, do. See. Feel. Do. And see everything in Misery in terms of Ike's suicide." He turned on his Walkman. "Aerosmith's 'Amazing'!" he cried. "Steven Tyler is my God!" He sang along and started to plug the earphones in.

"Wait," I said. He waited. "Why are all these experts denying their feelings about Ike?"

" 'Cause they mistake having no feelings for being smart." He trotted off.

"I'M SORRY IF I SOUNDED ANGRY yesterday when you called to set up our appointment," Christine was saying a few minutes later as we sat in my office in the attic of Toshiba, listening to the *phwop phwop* of tennis balls being hit three floors below. "I was feeling really bummed, and I kind of said all the wrong things."

She was sitting on the edge of her chair, her brown eyes fixed on mine. As I met them, she looked down into her lap. She was a thin thirty-one-year-old woman with hair the bleached blond of Madonna cut smartly mid-length, freckled white skin, a button nose, and small lips tense with dark scarlet lipstick, matching her dark scarlet nails. The white part in her scalp gleamed, a furrow between dark roots. She was all in black, as if in mourning—black sleeveless silk blouse with hints of black lace bra, short black skirt, the white of her kneecaps highlighting the pattern of black flowers of her black panty hose. Her perfume was musky. I had a hit of being attracted to her—and immediately felt it was wrong. I focused on putting it out of my mind.

"So what do you think about it, Dr. Basch?"

She was leaning forward intently, curious to hear my reaction to what she'd said. With a creeping sense of terror I realized it was a little difficult for me to tell her my reaction to what she'd said since I'd been trying to put the sensual part of all this black and fake blond out of my mind and hadn't heard a single word. Glancing into my lap at my wristwatch—and trying to conceal my glancing from her—I saw that four minutes had passed. I'd missed hearing an important thing she'd said, and because it was important, I couldn't admit I hadn't heard it. Could I ask her to repeat it? Suppose it was that at her mother's funeral she'd been gang-banged by fourteen Hell's Angels and left for dead, and I respond with, "Uh, did you say something, Christine?" She was staring at me expectantly. In desperation I found myself saying, "Do you mind if I ask you two proverbs?"

"Proverbs? I . . . I guess not."

"What do people mean when they say, 'A rolling stone gathers no moss'?"

She sat back. "If I *do* just keep on dating and don't find a guy—I'll keep on going in my career with IBM and not have a family—not have that white picket fence and dog and babies—and just be a career woman?"

"Um-hmm. And, 'People who live in glass houses shouldn't throw stones'?"

"Okay," she said, smiling guiltily, as if I'd had some incredible insight in choosing this particular proverb, "I'll tell you about my mom."

Her mom, the wife of an Indiana farmer, knew how to slaughter animals and fix trucks. The mother/daughter relationship was a real love/hater. Somehow talking about Mom led back to her last boyfriend, Rocco. She said, "So I called Misery because of trouble with men."

"What's the trouble with men?"

"You tell me! You're one of 'em. What goes *on* in there with you? Do men *feel*? If so *how*, and *what*? What happens between receiving a message and sending back your response?" I stared at her, unable to send back a response. "See?" she said, shaking her head in dismay. "I read all the books. Y'know the Women Who Run with Wolves? Well, I'm a woman who ran *to* wolves, 'n' now I like run *from* wolves! The sex has always been great, but the talk? Pitiful. Ever since Rocco walked out on me I've been drinking more and smoking more dope and getting suicidal." She glanced down. I peeked at my watch, figuring time was up. Only another ten minutes had passed? *Half an hour to go?* I looked up. She was staring at me.

"Is the session over?" She fluffed her blond hair, releasing scent.

"My watch must've stopped."

"Eleven twenty-one." She uncrossed and recrossed her legs—*slwish slwish* went the rows of black flowers. Leaning forward and looking at me intently, she asked, "What about *you*? Where'd you go to school?"

Feeling pressured, I said, as blankly as possible, "Around here."

"And this is your first year as a psychiatrist?" I said nothing. "You can tell me, it's *okay*." Oh God. Is she a hyperdemanding borderline? I nodded. "And will you be talking to a supervisor about your work with me?"

"No," I said, lying, and then, "wait a second—did you say 'suicidal'?"

She blinked, and sat back. Her face drooped in sorrow. She said that yes she was thinking of killing herself and had some pills stored up to do it. She didn't see why she should go on living after all the losses in her life, the latest being her father who had died just a few months before. "I can't stop crying. I cry for days on end! My heart is breaking!" She sobbed horribly, her body all scrunched up. I wanted to do what anyone would have done—put my arm around her shoulder, comfort her—but a wall seemed to go up and I tried to keep cool and figure out what to do to keep her from committing suicide.

"You got any Kleenex?" she asked, all stuffy-nosed and puffy.

"No."

"Well, why *don't* you!" she said angrily, and cried harder, the black mascara running down her cheeks, so she looked like a sad, lost clown. "How can you just sit there, so unfeeling?" Her accusing me of being unfeeling made me feel so unfeeling that in dread I drew away. "*Say* something! I'm about to kill myself and all you can say is *nothing*?"

Gimme a break! is what I wanted to say, but instead, sensing its lameness as it came out, I said, "You shouldn't kill yourself."

She stared at me in disbelief. "You're not doing anything for me." She picked up her handbag. "Because you're a cold fish!" She got up to leave.

"See you next week."

"You wish!" She grabbed the doorknob. "I *am* going to kill myself!" She walked out, slamming the door, and the room echoed with angry black-on-blond.

I sat there for a few seconds, and then I jumped up, opened the door, and found myself face-to-face with Arnie Bozer, another first-year resident, standing in his doorway across the hall, staring after my fleeing patient. I ran down three flights into the hot damp day, shouting, "Christine! Christine!" and caught up to her at the tennis court. She stared at me with contempt. "Are you all right?" She shook her head no. "I'll call you tonight."

"You better not. I'd rather talk to a mortician." She walked away, *slwish slwish*, around the corner. My heart sank. What if she did kill herself?

"*Oy gevalt.*"

With a sinking feeling, I turned around. Schlomo Dove. Still in his crumpled suit, he was wearing aviator sunglasses, carrying a tennis racket, and peeling a banana.

"She said she was going to kill herself. I followed her down here."

"You did *what*?" he cried, as if I'd just told him I'd converted to Islam.

"Followed her down to the tennis court. Because she—"

"You shouldn't even *think* that, much less *do* it! Get yourself an analyst, *bubbula*, fast." He finished peeling the banana. "Now Schlomo Dove will eat a banana, for Schlomo's heart." Chewing, he danced off up the path.

And Cherokee's going through hell about *this*? Maybe the cure would be to introduce them. Get a little reality testing going, why not?

Feeling bad about Christine, I headed back toward Emerson. What if she did kill herself? How bizarre. In any other setting I'd've been able to talk with her, easily, naturally, but in this setting, designed for talk, I was on an Alice in Wonderland trip where the smallest, most trivially natural things had become gigantic, laden with criticism, shadowed by the threat of death. "A cold fish," she'd said. Hey, she was right. *She'd* been the one able to feel things, and talk about them. Was she more normal than me?

"SO MAYBE SHE *IS* more normal than you," Solini said, sitting in Emerson 2 with me and Malik at the end of the day. "So big shit."

"So I don't know what I'm doing." I glanced at Malik, sitting there poking a wooden toothpick, a "Stim-U-Dent interdental cleaner," in and out of his teeth pensively. "I was trying to do what you said, Malik, act human, but—"

"*Be* human. I said *be* human. You wanna act, try Hollywood. Here we do real. C'mon, c'mon. Tell me about it."

Malik talked me through my session with Christine. He was curious about what had happened, asking good questions, nodding, giving me feedback on what had gone on. He tuned in not only to Christine, but to me, seeming to sense what I'd been feeling. Behind those tinty lenses, those eyes *got* it. Attended to intently, I recalled just about everything, word for word. I felt understood—the same feeling I'd had in my first interview with Ike White.

"Look," he said, "the thing that pissed her off was your not responding to her—not telling her where you went to school, that you'll be supervised in your work. Why didn't you?"

"It seemed unprofessional. I can't be totally open with her, can I?"

" 'Course not."

"So how do I know whether to tell her things about me or not?"

"Use the 'Asshole Criterion.' Key concept. When you're with a patient, to decide whether to tell her something, you make the decision based on whether or not you'd be an asshole if you didn't." We laughed.

"But she said she was going to kill herself."

"Her 'doorknob' comment? Nah, I don't think so."

"How do you know?"

"Same as you. Use the 'Corner of Your Eye' and the 'Afterimage.' What'd you see with Christine out of the corner of your eye? Quick."

"She was sizing me up, and was cool about it. Cool and calculating."

"And her afterimage? Quick."

"Intense. At the tennis court, really intense. Her eyes."

"See? That's real. Authentic. Her intensity scared you, she felt your concern, she got it. Low risk, okay?"

"And what about Ike White? Quick."

"Eyes off somewhere else. Not here. I never got to real with him, and boy did I try." He blinked. "I never realized that before, I mean that I never asked myself about *his* afterimage. That's good, Basch, to ask me that, yeah. You did good. Why doncha go home."

"Yeah, in a little while," I said. "Henry, I want to ask you a favor. Will you tell your patient Thorny to stop calling me a dickhead?"

"No problem. Let's do it." We walked out into the living room.

"*Achtung! Putzkopf!*"

"Hey, man, stop calling my buddy Dr. Basch a dickhead, okay?"

"Fuck you, you faggoty midget."

Henry's other patient, Split Risk, hearing this, limped off to his room. We walked after him. Solini and I entered the room. Harrison backed into a corner and crouched, shouting, "Are you guys gay? You crucify Ike White and now you wanna fuck me up the ass? Do you? Answer me!"

I froze, then turned to Solini, figuring that, as the therapist, *he* should have first crack at answering this. He too had frozen.

"Hey there, Harrison," I heard Malik say casually, and felt his hand on my shoulder, parting Solini and me. "Jill wants to talk to you, okay?"

A tall woman with long light hair came in. Outside the door were three big guys. They and Jill were "mental health workers."

"These two fags are negotiating to fuck me up the ass."

"Harrison," Jill said, "can I talk to you?"

"Only if you get these two fag doctors out of here."

We stepped out of the room. Jill, alone facing Harrison, said, "You're a little out of control, and you've got to take these meds, okay?"

"Who says?"

"I say, and Dr. Malik, who you know is a good straight guy, says. Here." She moved slowly to him and handed him the pills and water.

He started to take them, but suddenly Solini started coughing, big bullet-like coughs. With a scream Harrison threw Jill aside and charged. Solini and I ran. The three big guys covered Harrison with their bodies, but as easily as a housewife snapping the dust from a blanket, he lifted and scattered them. Jill ran out, her face bleeding. Again the goons pounced. This time, while they held him down, Malik pulled down his pants and gave him a shot in the butt. They sat on him until the trank took effect, then carried him away to the Quiet Room.

Malik led us back to the nursing station. Jill's scalp had been cut, and I volunteered to sew it up.

"Homosexual panic," Malik said. "People don't get more enraged than that. If you're male, you gotta stay away. Why didn't you ask for help?"

"He seemed friendly," Solini said.

" 'Friendly' don't mean shit around here. Any doubts, ask for help. The problem ain't not knowin', it's not askin'. Especially for us guys, like not askin' directions even when we're lost. Repeat after me: 'Ask!' " Henry and I looked at each other. "Go on, say it: 'Ask!' "

"Ask," Henry and I said, kind of embarrassed. "Ask."

"Louder!" Malik yelled. "*Ask!*"

"*Ask!*" we yelled out. "*Ask!*"

"LOUDER!"

"ASK! ASSSSSSSK!"

"AW*RIGHT*!" Malik said, giving us high fives. He opened up the sports section of the *Times*, working his Stim-U-Dent.

I did a slow, neat job on Jill's scalp, the light blond hair falling silkily away from the gash. From my position above her I was looking down at the swoop of her breasts, a long cleft descending, widening, blossoming to a fullness, the tan summer skin arrested by shy white skin above the peach-colored lace of her bra. Even the wound itself, the inner lips of tissue flaring a pulpy red, was sensual, an O'Keeffe iris, closing gradually under my fingers as I placed the sutures, first the subcutaneous amber catgut, then the black silk, and pulled it up into a healing pucker.

"Thanks," Jill said, her light eyes on mine, "I hardly felt a thing."

"It's nice to be able to do something right around here."

"It's a zoo," she said, "which is why Malik likes it, right, sport?"

"Spent half my childhood in the elephant pavilion of the Lincoln Park Zoo, Chicago. Loved the smell of elephant shit. Always wanted to be a vet."

Jill left. Malik and Solini and I sat there. It felt cozy and safe.

"You did good in medicine, did you, Basch?" Malik asked intently.

"Yeah, but it wasn't enough, and—"

"Yeah, that's important, to do good in medicine, yeah."

Solini was on call, and got beeped out. Before I left I asked Malik, "Why don't my patients cooperate with me?"

"Because they're uncooperative."

"So then why are they in here? Don't they want to be?"

"They wanna wanna, but they can't."

"Why can't they? All they do is hassle me."

"That's why they're here."

"To hassle me?"

"What you call 'hassle' is your job."

"Psychiatry is hassle?"

"The hassle that drives their families and friends and lawyers and regular doctors bullshit. Nobody knows what to do with 'em. *Somebody's* gotta, okay? We can't just walk away. That's what we get paid for."

"To deal with hassle?"

"Human suffering, yop. These people are in pain."

"I didn't go to school all these years to write orders for visits to department stores." Two borderlines had gone to Bloomingdale's that day, Heiler BPOs with BCCs—Bloomingdale's Charge Cards.

"Visits to department stores are important. Lotta hassles, shopping."

"But they all hate me."

"You want 'em to not be who they are? Like Lloyal and the rest of the dickheads running Misery want Ike White's suicide not to be a suicide?"

"You're not listening! I've got no idea what to do!"

"Good."

"Good?"

"Just don't terrorize 'em, okay? They're just human—more *like* you and me than not. Trust your gut, your *kishkees*. Don't believe what anybody tells you."

"Not even that?" I asked.

"Sweetheart! You asked! There's hope!"

I took my suit coat and walked out onto the ward toward the door.

"Dickheads Go Home to Momma!"

Feeling a slow burn of fury, I ignored Thorny and left. But I was surprised to find that Malik had slipped out behind me. The heavy door clanked shut. He and I were alone on the wooded stairwell.

"Look, I figured out why I'm preaching to you today. I'm fucked over by Ike's bein' gone. He was real important . . . y'know, to me?" His eyes glittered behind the amber. "I *got* to show you what I know, okay?"

"Sure."

"And bring your racket tomorrow? A *sport* a day, okay?" I nodded. "By the way, have you ever done any psychiatry, I mean before now?"

"Nope. It wasn't required in med school when I was there."

"Ever been in therapy yourself?"

"Never felt the need. I tend to just jump into things, and think later. So I just jumped in here, to try to understand people, as a shrink." His eyes widened. "Bad, eh?"

"Hell no! Good—even great!"

"That I don't know anything about shrinking?"

"It's a *gift*!" he said, and disappeared back onto the ward.

Walking away, I felt a wave of exhaustion, an inner exhaustion, as if from a vague lack, say of oxygen to my brain. I'd been punched around above the neck, but from within, and not allowed to punch back. As I walked the shaded road up the hill, the oaks lining it, the oak leaves, the actuality of the leaves whether or not they were named "oak," even things you'd think of as vague such as the heat, the humidity, the exhausted sunshine itself—all were a starkly real and actual comfort, compared to the world of Misery. In the haze of the exquisite twilight, the leaves of the grand high oaks moving gently, light-greenly in the breeze, seemed rock solid.

As relieved as I was to get out of the nuthouse, and as real as the outer world seemed, I found I was carrying with me a suspicion about the people in it. My fellow bus riders were subject to scrutiny. I studied their physical appearance—their body language, the barricades of their bus faces—and their overheard words for clues to their mental illness, realizing with alarm that I was making a running checklist of the Krotkey Factors for the diagnosis of Borderline Personality Organization, which Malik had said didn't exist.

At home, wiped out, I staggered to bed. As I started to fall out of exhaustion into sleep, I was horrified by the idea that I was killing myself to learn a profession that was supposed to keep people from killing themselves but that the world expert in how to do this had been shaking my hand at ten-thirty the night before and at eleven that same night that same hand was flipping enough pills into that world expert's mouth to kill himself, all of which was being denied by other world experts teaching me psychiatry. Having seen so much death in the world all last year I could understand how it was a helluva lot simpler to close down to this disaster rather than open up to it and the one guy who'd admitted the truth and cried about it had no explanation for it and while he seemed on the ball he was a definite flako a jock shrink of all things always jolting my mind telling me these slashed-up, suicidal patients were more *like* me than not, like the first time a baby stares out into space jolted by a first idea of a word or of a self which are maybe one and the same all the breathless red spices of summer, all in all so far except for Jill and her definite peach lace it was all so fuzzy you'd have to call it kind of crazy—and what the hell did those initials on Malik's tank top what was it what the hell was it oh yeah LAMBS what did they stand for anyway?

Christine! Shit.

I said I'd call tonight. Too tired. But what if she was sitting there waiting, what if my call might just make the difference in keeping her alive, like someone's promise to Ike White, unkept, had tipped him over? Or had my telling him my suspicion about Schlomo, his analyst, tipped him over? God. Christine might be sitting by the phone, pills in her hand. Was it too late? Midnight.

I picked up the phone. Dialed. Four rings. Answering machine, and Carly Simon's 'You're So Vain' came on. And then, *Beep*.

"This is Dr. Basch. Hoping things are all right and feel free to call me in the morning. See you next week at the usual time and please call tomorrow to confirm."

Putting the receiver down, I found that my heart was pounding. My anxiety was bringing out in me my father's gentle dental conjunctions. Was Malik wrong, could she too be lying there dead? Should I go over?

I poured a knockout scotch and lay down, my mind reeling back and forth, back and forth, shuffling fears and hopes till it could no longer take credit or blame for anything living, and died.

Three

"WATCHIT, BASCH, YOU'RE JIGGLING the napoleons!"

It was seven the next night. Malik and I were climbing up the manicured hill to the Farben Building. I was carrying by a loop of green satin ribbon a box of French pastries from Gourmet Misère, a shop in the nearby mall. The napoleons were, according to Malik, the key to an easy night on call.

The day had sped by. While most of my Emerson 2 patients had deigned to speak with me, the sessions had had a surface-level, lacquered feel, which, compared to their hostility, was a relief. My main worry was still Christine, the Lady in Black. She hadn't returned my call, my several calls. Despite Malik's reassurance, I was scared for her. But what more could I do?

That morning I'd seen Cherokee. He'd called and said he needed an appointment right away. He seemed worse, eyes red from another night without sleep, collar wrinkled, the part down the middle of his scalp ragged, his light hair falling to and fro like wheat missed in a harvest. Our first session, he said, had made everything worse, opening him up, setting his mind reeling in the terror of jealousy. But talking about it with me again seemed to calm him, and we did manage to move from Schlomo—whom he imagined to be "tall dark and handsome, like you, Basch"—to his deep sense of being a failure in his life and his work.

"I thought you did well at Disney?" I said.

"Disney is suspect, to *my* people. But the real killer, lately, is that I feel like a failure in my marriage."

"Tell me about it?"

He opened up about his sense of failure in feeling things, especially when his wife asked him what he was feeling. "The other day we were sitting on the beach after a marvelous picnic lunch. The girls were off with the nanny. We're both feeling good, okay? And Lily turns to me and asks, 'What are you feeling, hon?' Her asking seemed to paralyze me. I felt a sense of—I don't know—you'd have to call it a sense of dread, as if I were saying to myself, 'Nothing good can come of my going into this with her, it's just a matter of how bad it will be before it's over. And it will *never* be over.' "

I laughed at this, and he smiled. "I know," I said, "I've felt that too."

"Really?"

"Oh yeah. What happened then?"

They'd gotten into a terrific fight, ending up with his going off sailing alone, and her going home. Now, suddenly, he and I were working together, on the same team, trying to puzzle out his pain. It felt like we were friends. In my month as a shrink I'd never felt this before. At the end of the session he said he had forgotten to tell me they would be off on vacation for the month of August. "We always go to Via Cigno, our house on the Vineyard. Ever since I can recall, every August, Via Cigno. And I mean *every*. The rituals in WASPdom are carved in stone. August the first, go to Vineyard. Labor Day, come back. Hell could freeze over on August first, and the WASPs would still get to Vineyard Haven." We laughed. "But this year . . . I don't know." I asked about this year. "He—" He bit his lip, his brow and eyes twisting in jealousy. I realized that he couldn't bring himself even to say the name. "*He* does August at Wellfleet. She won't be seeing him, but it's just a short ferry ride—"

"Why not do something different?"

"Different?" he asked, as if I'd suggested he do something lethal.

"Sure. Go someplace else, someplace you and Lily love?"

"Genius! Basch, you are *un gènio*!" He laughed, clapped his hands, and let fly with a stream of Italian, voice ringing in that half-dopey, half-tragic lilt, hands pointing and waving like crazy. "*Toscana!* Our favorite place in the world. We'll rent a villa, with a pool for Hope and Kissy, and *cavalli*! Horses! Ha! I grew up there, honeymooned there. *Magnifico! Magnifico psichiatra, magnifico paziente!* As Hope says, 'Like awesome!' Ciao ciao!"

He did the Italian hand wave and trotted out. I felt great. His dread, his feeling a failure in relationship—I'd sometimes felt it too, with Berry. Maybe underneath we were similar? I remembered, then, a day riding the tube in London, as six English schoolboys entered and stood, each in a blazer and jacket and cap and umbrella, and you could see each as his life went on getting more tightly wound up in darker blazers and then dark suits with that dark vest for added tightliness and black hats and black brollies, the years accreting with terrifying certainty, darkening that boyish glitter. Decades on, you couldn't poke a pin underneath that suit, that black. Here, now, with Cherokee, we were starting to undo it. He'd gone out of my office boyish, yes.

Now, as Malik and I walked along toward the Farben, a stream of sensible cars flowed past us: mostly Volvos, Saabs, and those big American babies shaped like coffins. These safe, solid cars moved along in an orderly flow, most containing a man in a suit. One curly-haired little man in a big black Caddy turned out to be a honking, waving Schlomo Dove heading for vacation on the Cape, his bumper sticker reading: I'D RATHER BE IN THERAPY. Here were the "talk therapists" of Misery, each having finished their six o'clock at six-fifty, heading home in their safe cars to their thought-to-be-safe first wives and even-less-safe second wives and safe-but-perplexed children suffering from what Malik said was a disease called the "analyst's child syndrome."

With the exodus of the doctors came the liberation of the patients. Barred from the cafeteria during lunchtime, the patients were heading for chow in groups of about a dozen, each hall of Misery herded along across the broad perfect lawns by a mental health worker, the frozen trudge or shuffle signifying the dose and overdose of drugs, as well as diagnosis, which came last. Malik pointed out to me the hopping, skipping manics, the herds of trudging depressives, the paranoids darting and peering, tree to tree, the schizophrenics seeing in each bush a bear, in each dusky cloud a closet, the psychopaths trying to hustle the eager-to-be-hustled hysterics—even a rare agoraphobe, squinching down like a soldier running crazily to make the next foxhole. The group from the Child Unit was particularly heartwrenching, the kids in bright colors in one long linked chain, a many-colored crocodile, the last segments limping along spastically, trying to keep up. When the doctors went safely home to supper, Misery changed for the brighter and the wilder.

The weather too was changing. Ever since my arrival the Misery air had been that heavy, damp, polluted gunk that makes your lungs act like dehumidifiers and your head like the collecting tank. Now the sky was uneasy, with small bruises far off to the northwest where a first edge of the cold front sliding down from Canada was encountering the fat, couched heat from the Gulf of Mexico, billowing up over the south face of the mountains, clouding the shimmer on the oblong lake. The day, darkening as it went, seemed filled with portent.

We entered the Farben. Malik tapped on the bulletproof glass protecting the operator, Viv. She buzzed us in. Viv was a short plump woman of fifty with gray-blond hair in a beehive perched on her head, and blue eyes under plucked brows. Her voice—all clackety and tough—suggested a tenacious, working-class background. I liked her at once. She was just back from her vacation.

"Roy? Like Roy Rogers? Mind if I call you 'Cowboy'? It's not every day a woman like me is given French pastries by a handsome young doctor. Is he like you, Lucky?"

"Not yet," said "Lucky" Leonard Malik, "but he has potential."

"The human potential movement is one of my absolute favorites," Viv said. The switchboard squawked, a frantic voice asking to speak to the Doctor on Call, me. Viv put the caller on loudspeaker. With one eye on us she asked a few questions, found out that the caller already had a therapist but was hesitant to call him at home. "Doll, you're paying good money for his time—you call him right now, 'kay? Tell 'im Viv at Misery toldja to do it." A few more interchanges and the caller, calmed, hung up.

"Genius, Basch," Malik said, "genius. Did you catch it? I mean the first question you ask in the psychiatric interview?"

"The first question is, 'Tell me, how are things?' "

"Nope. The first question is, 'What is your insurance coverage?' "

"Didja tell this cowboy to be nice to me?" Viv asked coyly.

"Viv is the night operator. She screens all calls. This magnificent woman is all that stands between you and the mass of Great Americans seeing TV ads saying 'Unhappy? If so, if you want to feel better, dial 1-800-2MI-SERY.' Viv is your guardian angel. You promise to treat her accordingly?"

"I do."

"I hereby pronounce you man and operator."

We sat chatting in the bulletproof back room. Viv and I ate pastries, Malik broccoli.

"Broccoli?" I asked.

"Antioxidants. Best protection against prostate cancer."

"Uh-huh. And just where is it you put the broccoli?"

"Ooo-wee!" Viv cried out. "That can hurt!"

"You laugh," Malik said, "but you don't know shit. Let's talk organic, let's talk leafy greens."

Like many athletes, Malik was meticulous about what he put into his body. Now he waxed poetic about wax beans and soy nuts, kohlrabi and kale, and cabbage, red and white. He claimed to be able to actually taste the pesticides in nonorganically grown fruits and vegetables, and challenged us to test him. Vegetables were mostly revolting to me, and I soon tuned out.

Other night workers dropped by to talk. Viv handled incoming calls easily, as if talking to friends: a woman wanting to terminate with her therapist because he kept a live snake and a live owl in his office, a man wondering if it was possible to strangle yourself with your own two hands, and others. If there was no insurance, the caller was turfed to Candlewood State, down below the swamp.

A tap on the bulletproof glass announced the arrival of a well-worn, shabbily dressed older man who, from his battered nose spotted with red spider telangiectasia, I knew was a chronic alcoholic. My guard went up. I'd been abused by enough drunks and addicts in my internship to last a lifetime.

Viv buzzed him in. George had been Malik's patient two years before on Heidelberg East, Alcohol and Drug. Viv and Malik greeted him warmly. We all talked for a while. In two days with Malik I'd yet to see him leave for home. Half joking, I said, "What are you, Malik, a workaholic or something? Go home."

Silence. George and Malik and Viv exchanged glances.

"Not bad!" Malik said proudly. "Shall we, George?" They got up to go.

"Wait," I said. "What's 'not bad'?"

"If you need me," he replied, "I'll be at the meetin' down the hall."

"What meetin'?"

"Alcoholics Anonymous. A meetin' George here founded."

"The 'Misery Loves Company' meetin'," George said, smiling.

"George's my sponsor. We'll be just down the hall."

Malik an alcoholic? Dependent on an old drunk like George? I watched them walk off, the bulky, battered classic drunk and the thin trim doctor—also a drunk? Weird.

I began to be called out to attend to various problems around the hospital. The place was so big—350 beds—and so spread out, often I'd walk ten minutes between visits, my black bag pulling heavily at my arm socket by the time I arrived. Like a hired gunslinger riding into town, I'd walk in, feel the curious stares of the patients, be directed by a lone mental health worker or nurse to the problem, do my thing, write it up, and leave, beeped along to another gathering of humans quarantined by some shared diagnosis, which Malik said didn't exist.

Outside again on the freshly mown grass, looking up at the darkening sky, I had to struggle to see the normalness of this grass, this sky, as if there were a torque on my sight, a spin on the natural world, this grouping together of crazy people pulling the iron in my blood, my brain, into an afterimage that was warped, and weird. Them, not me. Not *like* me, no way José. These people are sick. They are the patients, I am the psychiatrist. *Prego.*

"FORGET YOU'RE A PSYCHIATRIST. Wake up!"

Malik. Pulling me away from the erotica of dreamland: Berry in a sari, four naked Thai dancers, an elephant, two happy macaques, and a—

"We got a hot one! This is your big chance, come *on*!"

Two A.M. I'd fallen asleep only eleven minutes before, trying to write up my fourth patient, a paranoid MIT student who'd seen a bug in his pizza and was sure it had been planted by the FBI.

"Big chance for what?" I asked, feeling grubby, my shirt all dried sweat, my underwear stale, my socks damp on my feet. All I wanted was a big chance for a shower.

"To *learn*. Zoe Bicker. Rich college kid. Dartmouth. Looks like she stepped out of *Town and Country*. Drove herself here. Won't say why. A mystery. And you and me and Primo are gonna solve it! Wake *up*!"

"Primo?"

"Live and off-color, Doc, y'get me?"

This "Primo" was a tall, bulky, uniformed member of Misery Security. My eye caught the glint of his badge, a bas relief of the Misery logo: a pine tree, a half-moon, and a duck rampant. Primo's face seemed to spread too far in all directions, and his thin dark hair was slicked, like Elvis's. Long black lashes shadowed dark eyes, a long large nose fell quickly to a smile where a Stim-U-Dent wedged itself between two scary teeth and one pink gum.

"We got some real doozies here tonight, Doc," Primo said. "Y'get me?"

"Forget you're a shrink," Malik said again. "You're sitting on a train. This Zoe sits down across from you. She's upset. You ask her about it. She tells you her story. An amazing story. You're totally absorbed."

"But I've got to get a psychiatric history."

"History comes from affect. Find the feeling, the red thread running through, you find out everything. What's the first question you ask?"

"What's your insurance coverage?"

"Bad news."

"Bad insurance?"

"Good insurance—she's rich. If we let her in, and she stays till Heiler comes back, he'll never let her out. And what are you gonna *be* with her?"

"Human," I said sleepily, "gonna be human."

Primo and he rolled their eyes. "Kid," Malik said, "you are on a roll."

Zoe Bicker sat forlornly in a corner, knees primly together, head lowered. She looked young, barely twenty. My "corner of the eye" take? Shame, and—from a man's red bandanna around her neck—love lost. She was slender, and her fine straight nose, hollowed cheeks, and thin lips gave her an aristocratic look. Her light brown hair had recently been styled in that windswept look of fashion models, but now it looked mussed. She was girlishly dressed in a crisp white summer dress with tiny pink flowers encircling her slender neck. In one hand she clutched a red teddy bear, and I flashed on Heiler's famous diagnosis of BPO with SA, Stuffed Animal. In the other hand was a letter. Her face was ashen. I thought, Sitting on a train, and asked, "What's going on?"

"I don't feel all that bad anymore. I don't want to be dramatic. Maybe I should just leave. I'm sorry to bother you at this hour of the morning."

"Bad?" I asked, really nervous that Malik was watching. "About what?"

Silence. Earlier in the day Malik had mentioned "the Eskimo Effect." Just as Eskimos have names for different kinds of snow, shrinks have names for different kinds of silence. This was a silence of fear. It was hard to wait for her to respond when all I wanted to do was finish up and get some sleep. But then she looked me in the eye, a look of desperation, and said:

"If Mother knew . . . I want to die. I want to kill myself."

Oh shit, I thought, I don't need this. My mind tugged at its tether, wanting to run. She was staring at me, staring really *hard.* Things got quiet and still, but the stillness was so intense it seemed loud. Her little-girl eyes searched mine, searched *hard.* Her pain was palpable, like a thing, floating right there between us, a new element created by this searching, a flash.

Suddenly I felt enormous pressure—from her, from Malik—to do something to help her, and I found myself asking, "What about your mother?"

Whatever had been there between us fizzled. She looked away, stood up and said, "I don't need to be here. I'll go now." She took a step toward the door. "Okay?"

"No, wait—" I said, realizing I'd blown it.

"Why? I'll be better off at home. Why should I stay?"

I glanced at Malik and Primo. Stim-U-Dents hanging from their lips, their faces were pursed in concern, sad for this poor young woman, and suddenly I felt it too. Turning back to Zoe, I said, "God, you look sad."

Her eyes widened in surprise, startled that she had been understood. "It's awful!" she cried out, with self-loathing and rage. "I'm so fucked up!"

It was like a dam had burst. Crumpling down into her chair, she began to sob so hard that the chair shook. I had to fight the urge, in the face of all this watery pain, to head for the high ground. Then she told us of being dumped a few weeks ago by her latest boyfriend, a Dartmouth student, and of how this rejection echoed with a string of others, one-night stands and brief flings fueled by pot and booze and degradation. I followed the red thread of sorrow through her life, a saga of purposeless wealth and empty privilege. With a few questions from me it led back to struggles with her older brother, past a cool, powerful father, a rich and famous Manhattan corporate lawyer, to an obese mother raised in high society.

"Whenever any of us felt bad, Mother would say, 'Now, now, children, back into your Happy Boxes!' I grew up thinking there really were these boxes! It was horrible! I never for one moment felt that anyone really loved me! I couldn't bear to live anymore. I decided to kill myself, tonight."

Her story felt complete. I said, "It's time to stop."

"Wait a sec," Malik said. He asked her a few questions about wanting to kill herself: how she'd thought to do it, whether she'd gotten pills and written a note, etc. She did have a bottle of pills—Xanax—which she handed me with the letter she'd been clutching, a suicide note. I'd failed to ask the one obvious question: Is she really suicidal or not?

"But maybe I'm not so bad?" she said. "All this doom and gloom. Maybe I shouldn't come into the hospital at all? Isn't it a sign of weakness?"

"Coming into a hospital on your own," I said, "is a pretty strong thing to do, don't you think?"

Silence, one of Watch Basch Destroy All He's Achieved.

Zoe turned to me. Her mouth was open, like a dazed sleepy child, her eyes puffy and red. Her red teddy, too, seemed dazed and sad, staring out at me from the fortress of her arms. "Are you just starting your residency?"

Thinking, Don't be an asshole, I said, "Yes."

"My cousin is too, in Texas. Will you be my therapist?"

"Sure."

Back in the office, Malik distributed fresh Stim-U-Dents to Primo and me. I was shaking. "Is it safe," I asked, "to leave her alone in there?"

"Now it is. So." He settled back. "You almost blew it."

"You mean when she started to leave?"

"Uh-huh." He worked an incisor. "Think back. Why'd she wanna leave?"

I thought back. "When I—because I asked about her mother?"

"Yop. She says she wants to kill herself, you ask her about her *mother*? Earth to Basch: 'Where *are* you?' Dincha feel the 'click,' when everything got still and you and her connected?" I nodded. "But then you ran like hell?"

"I didn't know what to do for her."

"For her pain? You thought you had to do something?"

"Yeah, to help her."

"Did it help her?"

"Oh yeah, Malik," I said sarcastically, "it really helped her."

"Exactly." He sighed. "It's so fuckin' hard to just face the pain. We get a hit of pain, we go, 'It's *her* fault, or *my* fault, or my *mother*'s fault or my *father*'s fault or *God*'s fault,' and we try to do something to it, to fix it—it all happens in a second! Pain—" He snapped his fingers. "—judgment! Push away that pain! Fight that suffering as if it'll destroy us, when the truth is, if we stay with it, it'll heal us."

"Like they say, Doc," Primo said, pointing his soggy Stim-U-Dent at me, " 'Don't just do something, stand there.' Key principle of Misery Security."

"Shit. It all seems so obvious now."

"Don't feel bad, Doc," Primo said. "The one thing I learned, in all these years in Security with all youse young docs? If there's one obvious thing that any man on the street woulda asked a patient about, you can be sure that's the one thing the first-year resident will *not* ask about."

"Even Malik, when he was first-year?"

"Malik was for shit."

"At best," Malik said, "for shit."

"So how'd you stop being for shit, Malik?"

"I was *so* for shit, I had a lotta room to learn. First, I got sober. Then, I married an Israeli. She was a doctor in the Israeli Army. Is she tough?" He and Primo rolled their eyes.

"Like the sweet pain of a toothpick," Primo said, "against a tender gum."

"It's all so clear," I said, "I think I've got it now."

"No you don't," Malik said.

"Well, I've got something."

"You got the *idea* that you got something. Remember that 'click,' kid, 'cause you may not feel it again for a long long time."

"Why not?"

" 'Cause when you're with patients from now on, you're gonna think about how to make that 'click' happen again, and if you're thinking about it, you can't be there with it and it won't happen. You're gonna psych yourself out. So listen up: just in case you do get to be Zoe's therapist, I'll do the physical. Once you lay your hands on a patient, therapy's over."

"What do you mean 'in case' I am?"

"She's rich. Even as we speak the Rich Patient Referral Network is humming—the worst shrinks in the world are gonna try to steal her. I'll do my best 'cause you'd be good for her. Put her on five-minute checks—she's at risk."

"Think we can help her?"

"Help her, hell," he said excitedly. "Cure her!"

"Cure? In psychiatry? Come off it, Malik, you can't—"

"No joke. People think that in medicine you can cure people and that in psychiatry you just foozle around. Fact is, it's the reverse. You don't cure heart disease or kidney disease, you palliate it. With a basically healthy young woman like this who wants to kill herself, if you can connect with her right now, at this shit-moment in her life, she'll probably never try to kill herself again! If that ain't cure, what is? I'm heading home. I live five minutes away. You'll do okay, long's you know when to *ask*. Ask for help."

"I can't believe I didn't ask her the main thing—"

"Lotta room to learn, Basch. See if you can do it without marrying an Israeli." He rolled his eyes. Primo rolled his eyes. I rolled mine.

"But it's like there's a whole other world," I said, surprised to see all at once how this work relied not on what I'd always been educated to do—

think logically and analytically to solve problems, to chop up the world into either/ors or if/thens—but on "ands," on subtle, intuitive hunches and senses, on messages sent from uninhabited regions, acted upon in realms beyond words or even beyond actions themselves. "Like there's a whole other way of being with people. Is it the world of the *kishkees*?"

"*L'intestini e testiculari,*" Primo said. "You get me, Doc?"

"Starting to."

Beaming like a proud parent, Malik sang to me, " 'Had an angel of mercy to see me through all my sins . . . ,' " and walked off, totally into Aerosmith.

While doing Zoe's write-up I took many phone calls, including one from a man saying, "Yuk yuk I'm a duck quack quack quack," another from a woman convinced that her cat was wearing a fur coat and fur gloves, and then my beeper went off and out came Viv's voice, for an emergency:

"*Emerson Two*, stat, *Cowpoke. I'll hold your calls, good luck.*"

As I ran down the road, my heavy black bag tugging at my arm socket as if it wanted to get away from what awaited it, I felt a rush of cool wind swooping up the hill and saw a jagged knife edge of lightning, and I counted the seconds till the crack of thunder—six miles off and coming fast. I ran into Emerson and up two flights and opened the door.

"Dickheads to the Rescue!"

"Fuck off!" I screamed back, losing it completely.

"Dickheads Lose It Completely!"

"What the hell is wrong with you?" I asked. He fell silent.

"Roy! Over here!" Jill said, down the hall, in the doorway of Mary Megan Scorato's room. I ran there and went in. Blood was splattered on the bed, the walls, soaking the towel that Jill and the night nurse were holding to Mary's wrist. Mary seemed dazed, glassy-eyed, a little twitchy. Somehow, despite being off sharps and on five-minute checks, she'd gotten a razor. I unpeeled the caked towel from the wrist. The blood started oozing—not spurting, which to my relief meant vein, not artery—and the sight, to my surprise, made me feel queasy. Having seen so much blood and gore in the past two years, why would I feel sick at this? I probed the wound, Mary jumped, nudging Jill up against me. I felt Jill's shoulder, her hip, and sensed a body that was big and pliant and strong. Our eyes met.

"You work nights too?" I asked, hungry for contact with sanity.

"The money's better. What a mess. How're you doing?"

Thinking, You are incredibly attractive, how 'bout we go out for a drink and talk? I said, "Fine, fine," and tried to focus on the blood. Jill and the nurse left. As I sutured, I asked Mary why she'd done it. She said nothing. Knowing her grief, I felt for her. How could you call this her fault? If I had been born her, I might not have done as well. Do people by nature do their best?

"You shouldn't cut yourself, you know," I said, feeling parental—she was, after all, someone's child. She didn't answer. I wrapped the soft, clean gauze around the prickly row of sutures, and did it carefully, thinking that the quality of my touch might determine something. "Didn't it hurt?"

"It hurt more t-t'feel d-d-dead," she said, twitching. "D-D-Dr. White d-d-dead."

"Yeah," I said, "he screwed us all." She stared, and twitched, in silence.

Jill and I sat in the muggy nursing station, at opposite ends of the large table piled with charts and styrofoam cups and Burger King wrappers and cans of Diet Pepsi and a woman's yellow tank top. I pictured us as husband and wife, dining in. "Well, darling, shall we ring for the help, to clear?"

She smiled, and reddened. "I blush easy," she said. "Look, I feel really bad—it's my fault—I was a few minutes late, on checks."

"I'm sure you did your best." Her blouse was wet with blood. Bumpy lace lay underneath. I was desperate to quit this on-call shit and touch her.

"What if that's not good enough?"

"My mother always told me," I said, wondering Why the hell am I bringing *her* into this now? "that if you do your best you can't be wrong."

"And my mother always told me to do what my father said—*and*, to watch out for men. Which, if you think about it, is pretty screwed up." My beeper. Viv's voice:

"Hate to do this, Cowboy. You got med trouble on Heidelberg West."

I groaned, got up, took her hand. The palm was rough. "Manual labor?"

"Horses. My passion."

"Lucky horses."

The thunder crunched and blasted above and the rain finally came. Being there with her was a comfort; we were fellow night warriors in Misery. I said good night. Thorny, standing in front of the door, said to me contritely:

"Wish I knew, Doc."

"Knew what?"

"What you asked—what's wrong with me. That I keep calling you a dickhead? Maybe has to do with my daddy polluting half of Louisiana and a lot of the Gulf—talk about a dickhead! Y'all can see how a successful guy like you, to me, well, I reckon you'd be a dickhead too?"

Amazed at actually having this talk, I said, "Sure, but I've got to—"

"I started askin' myself: How am *I* poisonin' things? And how're things poisonin' me? Man, you start askin' those questions, you see there ain't much out there that's not poisonin' the world. We're all dickheads, dickin' around with the planet. At Princeton, I did my first term paper on this shit, and got an F—'Off the subject,' the prof said. So I dropped out. Just when you was startin' to excel at ol' Harvard, right, Doc?"

"I'd like to talk now, but I've got an emergency. Tomorrow, we'll talk—"

"Damn! Wish I had a damn emergency somewhere. Or even somethin' to do."

"Volunteer. Get privileges, work for Greenpeace. We'll talk, okay?"

We shook hands on it, like real men, even like fresh new frosh in crisply fall Cambridge at the Princeton-Harvard game when, in football weather, you'd flow down from the Square across the bridge toward the stadium with a girl on your arm and a flask in your pocket and the world at your feet. I walked to the door, feeling good about him.

"Dickheads Take the Bait!"

I turned and stared at him in disbelief. He winked. I left.

The skies had cracked, and up there the lightning was dancing and the thunder was banging big kettledrums and with a whoosh the sulfurous cool air was sweeping up and was met by lowering curtains of rain, with fiery streaks of hail that popped off the roofs of the cars like oil off hot skillets. The hair on the back of my neck stood on end with the static electricity, and my drenched and bloodied shirt felt clammy, making me shiver. I had to get way up the ravine through the woods above the Farben to the Heidelbergs. To avoid getting drenched, I took to the tunnels.

I'd heard about the tunnels, a labyrinth under Mount Misery connecting all the buildings. Moving toward the Heidelbergs, the first stretch was long and twisting and going up and down like a roller coaster, badly lit and damp and smelling of sewage, the next section straight as a railroad and lit with the latest fluorescence and with that glorious scent of freshly fluffed laundry. Sometimes where bulbs were burnt out I would miss the signs telling me where I was, so that I lost my way, and found myself heading up toward a crest in a dark, scary aboveground stretch, the rain pouring in through a window, the thunder making it hard to concentrate on which way to go. Then, from over the crest ahead, I heard, of all things, a reggae band. Solini?

No Solini. Something Solini had told me about. A crazy black man who'd shown up the night before when Henry was on call, and who'd formed a psychotic attachment to Solini on the basis of their shared interest in reggae. The guy had no insurance, and Henry hadn't the heart to turf him to Candlewood State, so he gave him a map of the Misery underground. There he lay, on a piece of cardboard imprinted with "ogress Is Our Most Impo." From a small tape deck came some Bob Marley, but soft and fuzzy, as if Bob and the Wailers were lying exhausted and hungry on their own "ogress" cardboards in their own tunnels somewhere else. He stared at me, his face scarred and pocked, the hard gravel roadbed of the poor.

"Solini?" he mumbled, struggling up on one elbow, smelling of stale wine.

"No, no—no Solini," I answered, "go back to sleep."

On Heidelberg West, the Drug Unit, I patched up a drug mess that Win Winthrop had made. Back in Toshiba, while writing up Zoe, I took a few calls—"Storm calls, Cowboy"—and it was true—the storm had people under beds and in closets thinking cancer and AIDS and downsizing and gerbils.

As the sun came up, I found myself copying over, into the chart, a part of Zoe's suicide note:

> They say I've got everything but it's all plastered on my life like a smile on my face and inside I'm dying. Maybe, Mom, if you gave my diaries to some mental institute they could find what I couldn't and help someone else. People don't leave notes because it's hard enough to do it without making it so definite and thought-out—that's why I slept with the light on sometimes Mom, it wasn't like I was really going to sleep.

Strange, I thought, for me to write out these words calmly, words written in torment a few hours before. Same hand motion, same words, but now, words only. How light words seemed, riding the fire underneath. Ike had left no note. Suddenly I felt pissed. The fucker! He was a fucking expert in this, he knew the pain he was going to cause!

All at once I felt so alive! With Malik, with Zoe and Mary Megan and Thorny, there had been flickers of understanding, yes! I walked out into the fresh wet morning feeling powerful.

IT DIDN'T LAST. Exhaustion came down on me like solid thunder. The day was a blur, filled with fuzz.

I remember sitting with Solini and Hannah at lunch, staring dully at the way the mental health workers, nurses, social workers, psychologists, and Buildings and Grounds all intermixed with each other for lunch, yet the psychiatrists mixed with no one but other psychiatrists. They all sat together at two central tables, and as in a film, a black-and-white art film entitled "How Shrinks Eat," they moved like wind-up toys in dark suits and white shirts: fork-to-food, food-to-mouth, fork-to-food, food-to-mouth, fork-to . . .

Solini had been called in that morning by Lloyal von Nott and raked over the coals for his "looseness" on his admitting night. Now Henry said, "Y'know, when they accepted me here, I thought I was fooling them, by getting in? But now I know that they knew I thought I was fooling them, by getting in, and so they fooled me, by letting me in."

"I know," I said. "It's infuriating, the way there's so much crap and then, once in a while—like last night with Zoe—you really help somebody."

"Maybe, Roy-babe, the problem is you expect too much, and have to settle for less, and I expect too little, and have to settle for more?"

"So why the hell are you doing this, Henry?"

"Because it beats dry cleaning?"

Hannah took out a bottle of pills, extracted two and gulped them down. I asked what they were. "Zoloft. I've never been so depressed in my life."

"Does it help?" I asked.

"It's cosmetic," she said. "I'm putting all my patients on it too."

"What?" Henry said. "You're putting all of *them* on Zoloft?"

"Why not? They're all more depressed now, having me as their psychiatrist."

Arnie Bozer, the resident who'd seen Christine run out of my office, walked up. His bald head, full-moon face, chipmunk cheeks, and plump lips made him look well scrubbed. Arnie was a chipper fellow from the wooden Midwest, a young man who didn't seem to know the meaning of the word "unhappy," and who for all you knew might just be an ax murderer underneath. "I'd love to join you, guys, but I'm power-lunching with our chief. Jeez, Roy, I overheard the end of your session with Christine. God, you were in a tight spot, with her demanding that you disclose your personal feelings to her."

"You were eavesdropping?" I asked. Then, remembering I still hadn't heard anything from her, I felt a jolt of fear.

"You didn't close the inner door. I myself have a policy on personal disclosure: I tell my patients everything I'll allow them to know about me right away before they say anything. Then, that's it. I tell them that I will never tell them anything personal ever again. That's my policy."

"How can you have a policy, man," Henry asked, "when you haven't really had any patients yet?"

"Policy is my area of expertise. I'll be doing my third year at business school—the B.B.S. But that Christine is neat. Maybe I'll call her."

"To be your patient?" I asked.

"Gosh no. I'm a stranger in this neck of the woods. I'm from Indiana. Same state as her."

"You want to *date* her?" I asked.

He nodded, and blushed. He actually blushed, a dull pink bulb.

"Arnie, that's unethical!"

"Thanks for sharing," he said, and, whistling "Dream the Impossible Dream," he left.

Hannah was playing with her food, the lo-cal option, the Misery Catch of the Day. "I'm so depressed. I still can't believe Ike killed himself. And Mary Megan slit her wrist? I *love* that woman! It's like suicide's in the air, like it's contagious. I keep having the fantasy I'm going to a funeral tomorrow."

"Whose funeral, girl?"

"Mine."

Henry and I looked at each other.

"But you don't seem that bad, Hannah-babe," Henry said.

"Look at me funny, I'll start to cry. Do you know what it's like to be working on Emerson One now? A whole ward of severely depressed patients? And who was their hero, their only hope for living a normal life?"

I knew who their hero was, but I asked anyway.

"Ike White. It got so bad last night I called up my old analyst." She rolled her eyes up to the recessed lighting and said, "He said my problem is that I'm not being self-centered enough. 'Narcissism is good,' he said, 'a good good thing.' He's in L.A. now, head of the IHN."

And what was the IHN?

"The Institute for Healthy Narcissism. He was great: in twenty minutes he drilled out the unconscious forces under my depression."

"Sounds like a visit to the dentist," I said.

Hannah stopped chewing her fish. "Isn't your *father* a dentist?"

"Retired. So?"

"So you need a psychoanalysis, to work through your feelings about your father, your attitude toward authority figures."

"You mean my mother?"

"Your mother?"

"The authority figure."

"The authority figure?"

"Is there an echo in here?"

"What *about* your mother as authority figure, Roy?"

"Could someone as wonderful as me," I said sarcastically, "have a good mother, Hannah?"

"See? Work it through, or you'll act it out. Your unconscious is coiled down there—like mine, like Henry's—just waiting to attack! My only hope is that Zoloft keeps me afloat till after Labor Day, when Schlomo gets back and finds me just the right new analyst—and that there aren't any more disasters with my patients. I can't take another disaster with any of my patients."

ANOTHER DISASTER WITH one of her patients, in fact her favorite patient, Mary Megan Scorato, was awaiting her fifteen minutes later on Emerson 2. As the three of us walked in, Mary Megan was pacing back and forth in little shuffling steps like a robot, the budding twitchiness I'd noticed the previous night now blossoming into whole-body convulsions and tongue-flappings and slappings and—as if in mockery of Hannah's own eyes—eye-rolls up and down and around and even seemingly over, like egg yolks frantic to escape beating. Her white-bandaged wrist twitching up and down made her look as if she was directing traffic, or practicing samurai chops, or waving like Miss America in a convertible. Periodically she shouted out:

"ACCEPT! REJECT! WAIT LIST!"

Hannah's own eyes got big as yolks and her mouth fell open and I thought she was going to die. What we were seeing was something called TD, Tardive dyskinesia, a side effect of drugs. But what drug? Malik had written in the chart that Mary Megan refused all drugs. Hannah began trailing Mary Megan up and down the ward, trying to get her to talk to her, but all Mary would say was "ACCEPT! REJECT! WAIT LIST!" On one pass I asked Hannah if she'd put Mary Megan on any drugs. It turned out that yesterday Win Winthrop, Errol's slave, had convinced Hannah to try Mary Megan on their experimental drug, Placedon. He said this new wonder drug would cure her depression and that it had no known side effects, none whatsoever, whatsoever.

"But I broke the pill in half," Hannah said pleadingly. "And I broke *that* half in half. I gave a tiny dose!" She hurried off after Mary Megan.

"Unbelievable," I said to Henry, "a quarter dose, full-blown Tardive. That experimental Thai shit is murder."

Malik arrived, sized up the situation and got some Cogentin, which sometimes worked to relieve the symptoms of Tardive.

"She'll never take *another* drug," Hannah said. "I killed her!"

"People are pretty resilient," Malik said. "Let's check it out. Sit."

We sat together in the living room watching Mary pace and twitch and shout and flap her tongue like a frog. While it was bad enough that this sweet sad woman had been turned into a kind of amphibian, it turned out that Hannah had neglected to get her to sign the informed consent to be in Win and Errol's experiment and get the Placedon, and if she didn't snap out of it, everybody involved would get sued to hell. Malik talked about Tardive, about how in the fifties when the major tranquilizers came in, they were tested for a few years and then used on everybody, and how, as time went on—more time than they were tested for—it turned out that these drugs produced horrific side effects, this tongue-snapping frog-shit called Tardive.

"Tardive's a disease caused by treatment, but there's no treatment for Tardive!" he said. "And just you watch: if they find a cure for the second disease they caused by their failed cure of the first disease, it'll be a *worse* disease! All these new drugs—it's like the Drug of the Month Club, for Chrissakes—are only tested for a few years. The lifetime of a lab rat is only three years. For all we know, Prozac and Zoloft, five years down the road, are gonna turn people into lizards! All these nice housewives and teachers and bus drivers and pilots turning into lizards? Prozacians? Zolofters! It's sick!"

"ACCEPT! REJECT! WAIT LIST!"

Mary Megan was standing before us twitching and snapping and snorting, quite lizardlike, a Placedonian, why not? But she was listening.

"If you take this pill, this Cogentin, you'll stop twitching," Malik said.

"REJECT!"

"Okay," Malik said. "But are you hearing voices, Mary?"

"ACCEPT!"

"What are the voices saying?"

"ACCEPT REJECT WAIT LIST WAISTLINE!"

"Like in the Harvard Admissions Office, right?"

"AW GEE ACCEPT!"

"And then who calls? Your baby boy." Mary Megan twitched and stared. "Isn't it sad, Mary. To lose that little baby boy. It's not fair."

"N-not fair n-no," she said through gritted teeth.

"Yes, it's like death. So sad," Malik said softly, sincerely.

No one spoke. No one moved, not even Mary. For a moment we were still, like birds caught, still, in a pocket of wind. You could almost touch the stillness, as if it were alive. It's hard to put into words what Malik had actually done, because it seemed so obvious but it was in fact so magical.

Suddenly Mary Megan's eyes pumped out tears, big fat globules that her twitchy hands couldn't wipe away, and Malik took a fresh tissue out of his pocket and unfolded it and dabbed the tears away as best he could from her jerky cheeks and eyes. He put a Cogentin in her palm. She moved it toward her mouth but at the last second twitched and plastered it on her forehead, where it stuck in sweat, and its edges started to ooze. He picked it off and, timing it between tongue flicks, popped it into her mouth.

"I'm sorry, Mary," Hannah said, "really sorry."

"We regret to inform you that your application for admission to HARVARD! Has been denied Dr. HANNAH Silver you FUCKING ASSHOLE!" She shuffled away.

"Congratulations, Hannah," Malik said, "your therapy with her has begun."

"I care for that lady so much! I'm in agony."

"Good. People like Mary do good with young therapists who care in agony."

"But I have no idea what to do."

"Forget 'do,' Hannah," Malik said. " 'Be.' "

"Be what?"

"Basch? Solini?"

"Human," Henry and I said. "Be human."

"How?" she asked.

"Ever been in love?" Hannah nodded. "Ever lost the person you love?" Hannah said nothing, but her eyes teared up. "With Mary just now, when everything went quiet, dincha *feel* it?" We looked at each other. All of us nodded. "There it is, kids," Malik said.

" 'Love'?" Hannah asked with a touch of skepticism.

"Like us all. All this is, really, is a lesson in love." He smiled, and walked into the nursing station. We followed. He got a fresh carrot out of the fridge and started chomping contentedly. The ward secretary handed Malik a stack of pink messages, saying that they were from insurance companies and he had to call them back right away or else the patients on the pink sheets of paper would be discharged. She left. He threw them into the garbage.

Picking up Mary Megan's chart, Hannah asked, "One more thing, Malik. Medical Records is bugging me for a diagnosis on Mary Megan."

Malik chewed his carrot, picked up *Sports Illustrated,* and said, "Yeah, yeah, put down whatever bullshit you want."

"That is really really cynical, Malik," Hannah said hotly.

"Oh yeah?" he shot back angrily. "Did they make a perfect diagnosis on Ike White? Yop. Endogenous depression. Did they give Ike White perfect treatment? Yop. Industrial-strength drugs and world-expert psychoanalysis." His face red with rage, he was almost shouting. "And nobody got with that poor bastard's pain! Where's this lady's pain, Hannah? Fucking Ike couldn't get with it with her, now you're her therapist so you get a shot. *Be there!*" He breathed a few times. "We'll help. Pray that Placedon shit wears off."

"Oh God," Hannah said, staring at Mary shuffling. "It seems hopeless."

"Yeah, it may be the worst moment of her life. But think of your own worst moment. Go on, all of you. Think: What's the worst moment of my life?"

We did. Malik asked us to tell them. Mine was looking out the eighth-floor window of the House of God, seeing the body of my friend splattered on the parking lot below. Solini's was just last year when his best boyhood friend, a Sioux named Everett Chasinghawk, had run off with his wife. Hannah said hers was too terrible to tell.

"But if you think of your *whole* life, it's just a moment, right? And that worst moment, if someone's right there right then with you and there's a 'click,' is the moment you *move!*" He seemed to crackle with energy, all electric and jazzy, and even though I was dead tired I caught some, crackling a little inside, like a spark in the ashes. "So listen up. We gotta start to discharge these patients, 'cause a lot of 'em'll get worse with Heiler. We gotta empty beds."

"Man, how do we empty beds?"

"We keep the drug fascists away and we throw the insurance into the garbage and we discharge like crazy."

"But we can't just throw people out," Hannah said, "without aftercare."

"The LAMBS!" he said, that tight, slender face crackling with happiness.

We asked what was the LAMBS.

"The Leonard A. Malik Buddy System. Listen up. The big problem in society is that there's no more community. Parents don't live where their kids live, neighbors aren't friends. Where are your closest buddies? At least three hundred miles away, right?" We thought, and we nodded. " 'Member when you were kids at camp, the buddy system where, when you went swimmin', you had a buddy and you raised your arms and counted off? Felt great, right? So why don't we keep doin' it when we grow up? Each patient gets a buddy." He handed out computer sheets. "I matched 'em up by where they live. Matched you up too." Solini and I were buddies. Hannah and Arnie Bozer were buddies.

"Have you ever tried this out?" Hannah asked skeptically.

"Yop, on my group for depressed men, and it works! These guys were diagnosed depressed, tanked up on drugs, and now they're not! They threw down their Prozacs! They're *better*—their shrinks hate me!"

"Why, man?"

" 'Cause they're *better*! No more drugs, no more therapy, no more money!"

"And you really think," Hannah asked, "that it'll work with borderlines?"

"Borderlines don't exist. Will it work? It's *got* to. Eacha you, start calling up your buddy on the phone every day."

"Sounds simplistic," Hannah said, "and unorthodox. Freud would never—"

"Hannah!" I said, excitedly.

"What?"

"You! You're looking me right in the eye!"

"Mary Megan Scorato needs a trial of meds," said a voice in the doorway.

"To cure her Tardive dyskinesia," said another, beside the first.

Errol and Win, in their long white lab coats.

"Zephyrill," Errol said. "It's experimental." He held up a lavender sheet of paper. "She's just signed her informed consent to be in our study."

Hannah shot to her feet, eyes blazing now, and screamed, "I will *not* give that poor woman any more drugs! Placedon made her crazy and gave her Tard—"

"Because you gave her a low dose," Win said. "I said high dose."

"High dose would've killed her!"

"Wrong. Principle of Paradoxical Effect: the higher the dose, the lower the effect."

"Quiet!" Malik cried out, and then, his voice filled with reverence, he asked, "Errol, did I hear you right? You've found a drug to *cure* Tardive?"

"May well have done," Errol Cabot said modestly. "Yes."

"Fantastic. Think of the millions of people who have it. Roy, Henry, Hannah, this may be a historic moment. If this is true, this is—don't let me jinx you here, Errol—this is Nobel Prize stuff, wouldn't you say?"

Errol's eyes seemed to film over, as if he were going into a trance. "Yes, yes," he said dreamily, "if my clinical trial works. And Mary is—"

"*Perfect* to try it on," Malik interrupted. "Cure her, Errol, you're in."

"Zephyrill," Errol said dreamily. He took out a bottle of pills, handling it carefully. "Brand name for phenylisotonerylamine. Brought 'em back from Zimbabwe. Only pills in the West. High-tech psy—"

"Great," Malik said. "Nurse Hall? Handle that baby with care. Lock 'er up with the narcotics, understand?" The nurse took the bottle, handling it as if it were plutonium. "I'll stick that consent form in her chart."

Errol handed it to him. Chests puffed like chickens, he and Win left.

Malik took the pills from Nurse Hall and threw them into the garbage. He tore the lavender consent form into confetti and threw it into the garbage too. "We already got one drug treatment worse than the disease," he said, "why go for two? It's the NPT—the Nobel Prize Technique. Mention the possibility of the Nobel Prize and they go limp. Won't hear anything you say for five minutes. Everybody go home."

"To my *husband*?" Hannah said. Six months earlier, after her analyst had discovered healthy narcissism and moved to L.A., she'd impulsively married Billy ben Lube, a Lubavitcher Hasid, in a ceremony with a cast of thousands in Brooklyn. She had confided in me that the marriage was not going well.

"You can stay at my place tonight, Hannah," I said. She said she might, though I didn't believe she would.

My exhaustion-induced fuzziness had gotten even more fuzzy, and a while later I found myself pacing up and down in front of my secretary Nancy, saying, "I'm not normal."

"Oh come on, Dr. Basch, you are so normal."

"Not *so* normal," I said, transfixed by her vaccination mark, lying like a flattened flower, say a white poppy, on her bronze deltoid. "Call me Roy."

The phone rang. Nancy handed it to me.

"Dr. Basch," a voice said, "this is Christine. Your patient?"

"Oh *hi*!"

"What's *wrong*?"

"Why nothing, nothing, what's wrong with you?"

"I didn't say there *was* anything wrong yet."

"Are you okay?"

"No. But I would like to see you next week."

"Great." We set a time, and hung up.

"Of course she called," Malik was saying out on the lawn after I'd signed out. He was in shorts and a new LAMBS T-shirt, getting ready for a game of tennis with Mr. K., finishing an organic radicchio, and drinking coffee from a styrofoam cup.

"How'd you know?" He started juggling three orange Day-Glo tennis balls.

"She saw that your following her down to the tennis court was dumb for a shrink but basically human. Her feeling your caring helped keep her alive. Zoe too. *She's* the real suicide risk. She's gonna be tough. But if we can just stop acting like doctors, then they stop acting like patients, and things *move*. The potential in humans is amazing! An incredible mystery of nature!"

"Yeah, well right now I'm not into the incredible mysteries of nature."

He laughed. "Sorry, I get carried away. You did good. Go home."

I didn't move. Feeling exhausted and confused, I was reluctant to leave him yet. He noticed, and asked me what was the matter. "I'm feeling a little lost."

" 'Course you're lost, you're finding your way. It's called 'learning.' We all used to do a lot of it as kids."

"But can't you give me something to take home with me?"

"Hey, good asking! Listen close: stay on the side of the angels."

"Angels? You're crazy!"

"Y'gotta be crazy to do this, 'n' you gotta be *deft*. Like in *sports*!"

"Wait. Why'd you stay with me last night? You didn't have to."

"Gotta show ya what I understand."

"Okay, red-hot, what do you understand?"

"I understand 'psychiatrist' in Greek means 'Healer of the life-breath, the spirit.' And that maturity is a topspin backhand. Catchu later."

"But if shrinks specialize in their defects, what do *you* specialize in?"

"I'm eclectic."

"No defects?" He was doing jumping jacks, raring to go, and said nothing. I pointed to the styrofoam coffee cup. "Want me to throw that away?"

"Away? Cowboy, Cowboy—you still think there's an 'away'?"

"INTO THE GARBAGE?" Berry asked, amazed. "This Malik seems a little strange."

"Who isn't?"

It was later that night and I was lying naked on my bed in the seven-sided turret of my loft. I watched Berry reach around and unhook her bra and then shrug her shoulders to let the loops drop and free up her breasts, and my exhaustion was overcome by excitement. I thanked God that after all our years together our sensuality was still somehow mostly new. She quickly slithered down her panties and feigning modesty covered herself as best she could and lay down beside me, my *kishkees* echoing to that thick lush black triangle, a furry pillow for my cheek. Side-by-side skin-beside-skin, the air lush with her perfume which called up our time in France the Dordogne the previous summer tonight maybe even the anniversary of same the cemetery high above our hill village and river valley the headstones strewn with wildflowers wild poppies roses daisies, and the air tonight tingling with imagination, it was thrilling and I wanted it to last as long as death. I knew I was idealizing her and part of that was sexual but if an exhausted burnt-out man can't idealize a woman sometimes what is there to live for?

And so Berry and I lay side by side and naked in bed in the hot silky night, staring out the five windows of the turret, listening to the sounds of a suburban summer evening: TVs, marital strife, kids, cars, and the last malignant shrieks of power tools of many sorts.

"How was your day?" I asked.

"Great. I just love being with these four-year-olds, it brings it all back—childhood, the energy, the incredible curiosity! And they're so funny! This one little girl, Katie, she's so smart and she thinks she knows everything, and she was going on and on about something so I said to her, 'Katie, you're perseverating,' and she looks at me and says, 'Yeah, I know.' "

We laughed, but the laughter was shaded by our failure, two years before, to conceive. We'd even gone to a doctor—me, to a doctor!—but nothing abnormal was ever found. We'd stopped trying. We were living with the shadow.

"Sounds wonderful," I said, "being with normal little kids."

"The two things they learn in school are how to eat 'snack,' and how *not* to share. But they're so sweet!" She sang, "Will and Eva go wash your hands, Will and Eva go wash your hands, Will and Eva go wash your hands, ride, Sugar, ride!"

"Sweet, yeah," I said, trying to hide my cynicism, after having had my hands in slit wrists and my face in borderline rage for the past thirty-six hours.

"Okay, okay," she said, picking up on it—she could read me better than anyone in the world; she had that same sixth sense about me that Malik had about everyone. "Let's have it. *Your* day?"

I told her about Malik, about how he seemed to respond to what you said by putting a spin on things the reverse of what you'd expect, and how, as I kept telling him I didn't know what I was doing as a shrink, he kept telling me that my not knowing was terrific and to keep on not knowing for as long as I possibly could.

"At least," Berry said, "this Malik isn't accepting the Misery version of what's 'normal.' He sounds like he's been hurt pretty badly too."

"You're right." I told her about his being an alcoholic. My fingers were on the nape of her neck, caressing from the nuchal line of the occiput, along the trapezius, onto the deltoid insertion.

Berry sighed, and asked, "Where are you about Ike White's suicide?"

I stiffened. "Please, not now. I didn't really know him."

Outside, a siren wailed. We listened it down into silence. Crickets filled the vacuum, edging the silence with cellolike chirps.

"But you respected him a lot. Just tell me what you feel."

I froze. "I don't know."

"I know you know, hon. You can talk to me about it, it's okay." But it wasn't and I couldn't and said nothing. "Oh boy," she went on, shaking her head, "you've got that 'I work in mental illness' look. That's the way I used to look, trying so hard to make it in psychology, remember? It's so different now, so much easier, being on the opposing team."

"Opposing?"

"Mental health."

"Oh. Yeah."

"Can you talk at all?"

"I'm wiped out, fresh out of feeling, for today." I stroked her breast.

"But we need to get in touch, to make love."

"You know making love is *how* I get in touch."

"Can't you just talk to me a little first?" she asked.

Right then, this seemed like asking me to climb Mount Everest a little first. I had that same "I'm a cold fish" feeling I'd had with my outpatient Christine, and, tensely, I said, "Please, please don't spoil it."

"*I'm* spoiling it? All I'm asking is—"

"Damnit, lay off!" I shouted. She flinched, and her hands protected her breasts. Then, slowly, she sat back and stared at me, fear in her eyes. A rush of shame. Why the hell was I yelling at her? I felt horrible. "I'm sorry. I'm really tight."

"I'll say."

"This stuff is so weird. During my medical internship I'd blow up ten times a day, but when I got home I was okay. Now, no matter what happens, I have to bottle it up, not show any feelings—and I get home and explode."

"But I *want* your intensity, Roy."

"I know, but right now I want to get away from it. It's too much."

"You think that as a therapist you shouldn't let on what you feel?"

"If I do, people like Schlomo Dove tell me I'm sick and that I should be in therapy."

"You're not sick. But maybe it would be a good idea."

"Right. I'll go see Schlomo, he'll make me a match, with that oh-so-special analyst, just for me. 'Tell Schlomo,' " I said gooily. " 'Tell Schlomo about sad and lonely.' "

She laughed, I laughed with her, and the glass wall between us broke. We embraced, and like horny angels together we made that downstream journey where at best the notion of "Me, Roy, you, Berry" goes under, tumbling along under the death-defying notion of "us."

Four

DEAR BASCH,

We started out well enough in Tuscany but it soon turned into the vacation from hell. Lily left last week to go back home, saying she needed some "space." I accused her of needing to see you know who! She said I was *pazzo*—crazy—and that everything was *bravo*—fine. Tuscany felt tainted so the girls and I are doing Amalfi. It's beautiful but not when the woman you love can't share the beauty. Hope and little Kissy and I are having good fun, but there are moments—times when we're in the most breathtaking spots, like this "Terrace of the Infinite" in Villa Cimbrone, Ravello—when I sense them missing their mom so much my heart breaks. At times like that I try to joke. *Città Fiasco.* Failure City. We'll keep on doing the tourist thing. I'll call you after Labor Day.

Ciao,
Putnam

He had mailed a postcard in an express letter. The postcard showed a curved railing edging a sheer drop to the Mediterranean. The view south toward the boot was infinite: mountains, clouds, sea easing into sky. I had been in that exact same spot, with Berry. One step off, you're dead.

I was relieved that he was in touch with me, but worried about him. If there was one thing he could be sure of, it was that Schlomo Dove would *not* be seeing his wife while he was vacationing on Cape Cod. In much the same way that the august Pope was sacred to Catholics, the August Cape was sacred to Freudians. Having spent eleven months of the year in vicious gossip about each other and their patients, Schlomo and the other Freudian yentas had been spending the month in vicious gossip about each other and their patients while lying next to each other in floppy hats and baggy swimsuits on the bluntly narcissistic beaches of what Viv called "Misery East." Schlomo was said to be into nude sunbathing, airing those pits, those girlish tits, that pendulous belly, to the trade winds. Reading poor Cherokee's card, I worried again about his sanity, and hoped he'd call soon.

It was the day after Labor Day, and I was sitting in Malik's rounds chair on Emerson 1, awaiting the arrival of Dr. Blair Heiler. The day before, Malik had left to do Advanced Child Pathology in the Public Sector, the first of several third-year resident rotations that would take him away from Misery. His first rotation would be on the Children's Unit at Candlewood State Hospital, down the hill and across the swamp. His wife Bronia, the tough Israeli whose name was accompanied by an eye-roll, would be his boss.

The Emersons were in good shape. In my month with Malik, my work with patients had gone pretty much as he had predicted: to the extent that I had been able to stop acting like a psychiatrist and be a person to them—starting by discarding my suit and tie for shirt, slacks, and running shoes—they had responded not as patients but as people. For a month the ward secretary had presented Malik with piles of pink message slips from insurance companies. He always said he would get to them after a carrot or a run or tennis, and most of them went into the garbage. "Mental hospitals are hazardous to your mental health," he'd say. As their insurance ran out, those Emersonians who were ready were discharged, often in buddy pairs to the growing outpatient LAMBS system, which Malik called "my retirement." For us first-year residents, empty beds meant an easier time.

If a patient needed to stay, Malik would dazzle or threaten the insurance company into paying. Thorny and Zoe were on the runway, revving for takeoff. Mary Megan, recovering slowly from the single blast of Placedon, still twitched and shouted, but was talking to Hannah. Malik had always stressed just how sick sick people are, and it had taken all of our efforts to help the Emersonians deal with Ike White's suicide and get them back to a sense of basic safety, trusting that we their doctors would not kill ourselves too.

On his last day, offering us fresh packets of Stim-U-Dents, Malik had proclaimed, "The rip in the fabric, from Ike White's suicide, has been healed. Beware of Blair Heiler, and do more *sports*!"

That morning, as I was waiting to begin rounds, Heiler returned from his vacation in Stockholm. Given his reputation for terror, I was on guard.

Six feet five, with light blond hair, eyes the silvery blue of mica, a Roman nose and a movie-star chin, walking onto the ward in an airy summer suit and Liberty of London tie, Blair was a stunning sight, an image so clear and sharp that, set against the bizarre background of Emerson 2, for a second it seemed to fool the eye, and I found myself thinking: This guy can't be real. It was as if you'd been sitting in your living room expecting Jack the Ripper, and in walked the Boy Next Door. An alluring male cologne completed the package. Blair's manner was relaxed, modest and friendly. He had a charming habit of tossing his head to flick a blond forelock back out of his eyes, and then patting it down with long slender fingers. His eye contact was unwavering, and while his looking down at me was disconcerting, his easy laughter was disarming.

Blair was forty-two, happily married to an heiress of one of the major convenience store chains, and the father of a three-year-old boy. He had been born on an army base in Alaska, where his father was on the rise toward major general, and his education had been typical of military children—many different schools in many different cities and countries. As a young man he had gotten used to transience, to seemingly impulsive swings in and out of school systems and playgrounds. He had grown familiar with a life of unstable personal relationships and fear of abandonment, and had learned to handle the powerful mood swings and emptiness associated with repeated hellos and abrupt good-byes. In a sense, he had lived with the Krotkey Factors a long time. Now, Blair too was a guy on the rise, a happy, healthy member of the Misery family. Already an Associate Assistant Professor of Psychiatry, his high-powered research on borderlines was rumored to be about to lift him a rung higher on the academic ladder, to Assistant Associate Professor of Psychiatry. I stopped him on his way into his office and introduced myself.

His face lit up and he shook my hand warmly. "I've heard a lot about you, Roy—Rhodes scholar and all. The chief says you're a star."

Disarmed, I thanked him and asked, "Where do you hold your rounds?"

"In my office, right here on the ward," he said good-naturedly.

"You want me to bring the patients in there?"

"Only if there's a problem with insurance, Roy. I spend most of my time on the phone to the bastards in managed care, trying to give these borderlines as much time as they need as inpatients here. It's dirty work, but someone's got to do it. Later. Got some empty beds to take care of."

I was confused. This guy didn't match the guy Malik had described.

Later that morning Blair held his weekly Case Conference for the staff and residents of all three floors of Emerson. I volunteered to present Zoe, my rich young college student, to him. The conference room was packed. I took a seat in front of the crowd, to present the case, suddenly nervous. Hannah and Solini sat in the front row. Hannah smiled and Henry raised a clenched fist for support.

Heiler entered and sat facing me. Sound evaporated from the hot room, leaving that distilled, tight stillness you feel before a show begins. I presented Zoe's story, telling about her privileged Brahmin family, her sense of failure, her seeking out inappropriate men as lovers, her history of bulimia, her struggle at college and recent rejection, depression, and suicidal thoughts.

"She's done well in therapy," I said. "She's gained weight, plays sports, and she's just about ready for discharge. The treatment plan—"

"First comes diagnosis," Heiler said, "then comes treatment. Diagnosis?"

"Depression," I said, "reactive, to the loss of the man in her life."

"Great. Bring her in."

Stunned by the size of the crowd, Zoe flinched, and stumbled on the Oriental rug, murmuring, "I'm sorry—I'm so clumsy." She bent and turned down the up-flapped edge. Clearly, her self-esteem was rock-bottom. While she'd made an effort to dress up—crisp white sleeveless blouse and pressed jeans, lipstick and eye shadow—it was obvious from her scared look, tightly pressed lips, and clenched hands pressed thumb edge to thumb edge as if in a kind of petrified prayer, that she was feeling depressed and vulnerable.

Heiler rose, introduced himself, and then, smiling, flashing those gorgeous eyes, took her hand gently, as if he were about to raise it to his lips and kiss it. Seductive. Then he sat down and leaned back in his chair with hand to cheek and legs elegantly crossed. His loafers were dainty, pointy-toed, buffed a buttery dark. He flicked a blond lock and gestured to Zoe to start.

She blushed. "I didn't expect so many people here."

"You feel angry about that?" Heiler asked, his voice low, even husky.

"No, just a little surprised."

"Dr. Basch didn't tell you?"

"He probably didn't know."

"You look angry," Heiler said, his tone sharper.

"No, really, I'm not," Zoe replied.

"If it were *me*, *I* would be angry," Blair said indignantly, "damn angry, being put on the spot in front of all these people." Zoe glanced at me, puzzled. I smiled, to encourage her. Heiler gestured toward me. "You angry at your therapist?"

"No, I like my therapist. He's nice."

"Nice?" Blair said incredulously, as if she'd said that I was in fact not nice but a homicidal maniac. Sitting up in his chair, screwing up his face in distaste, he mocked her, "*Nice?*"

Zoe stared down at her lap, her face flushed. Tears eased out from her lowered lids, onto her cheeks. I couldn't believe this was happening.

"Anything that makes you uncomfortable," Blair said, again in his seductive, reassuring tone, "you don't have to answer, 'kay?" Zoe nodded. "Good. So tell me, Zoe," he went on, as if they were once again best friends, "what would you like to do with your life?"

Zoe hesitated, and then, with embarrassment, through her tears said, "After college, I'd like to become a . . . a social worker."

"A *social* worker?" Blair said, as if this were incredible.

"I don't want to talk about it."

"Why not?"

"It seems pretty pretentious, right now, being in a mental institution, saying I want to become a social worker."

"Tell us about wanting to become a—" He paused, and then, with obvious loathing, went on. "—a social worker."

"You said I didn't have to answer anything that makes me uncomfortable."

With a sardonic smile, Blair said, "Wanting to become a *social* worker?"

It went on like that, Heiler assaulting, Zoe withdrawing, like a turtle withdrawing into a shell, and the shell being ripped off, polygon by polygon, exposing the pink flesh. I felt terrible for her, and furious at him, and thought several times I should jump up and stop him. In other situations, seeing this kind of public cruelty, I would have. And yet now I—and the others—seemed paralyzed. Starting to weep, Zoe talked about her depressions and her trying to kill herself. Heiler, who didn't seem too interested in these depressions and these tryings, interrupted her:

"What's wrong with you? Why haven't you gotten better?"

"Dr. Basch says I am better."

"Isn't it possible that your idealization of Dr. Basch is a denial of your primitive rage at your bad-object mother and your hatred of men?"

What the hell does that mean? I wondered.

"What does that mean?" Zoe asked.

"You've been here several weeks! Why are you still so sick?"

"I don't know."

"C'mon, c'mon—you must've thought about it. Why?" Zoe said nothing. "Why?" Blair shouted, so harshly that I jumped. "*Why?*"

"Don't know! Leave me alone." Like a child, she pleaded, "Please?"

Heiler paused. With frank contempt he said, "A *social* worker, eh?"

"Asshole!" Zoe screamed, and jumped up and ran out, slamming the door so hard my teeth seemed to rattle. Stunned, I watched as Heiler turned to us, smiled, spread his arms wide, palms open in that kind of grand gesture that the star of the show uses at the last curtain call, and said, once again back into that charming, friendly, boy-next-doorish voice, "So, guys, what do you think? A seven?"

A few nervous chuckles. Not to chuckle seemed a definite risk—if you didn't side with this madman, you too might get attacked.

"I'm toying with the idea of another Krotkey Factor, Number Fourteen: TDS, The Door Slam. Independent observers could rate it on a scale of one to ten. I bet it would predict the diagnosis, and correlate with severity and prognosis."

The hairs on the back of my neck tingled: Surely he didn't think that this obviously depressed woman was a borderline?

"What diagnosis, Dr. Heiler?" a BMS student asked innocently. He was a frail, sickly looking boy, and seemed to be wheezing.

"Borderline. DSM 301.83. Textbook case. I was working on Krotkey Factor Number One: LNT—Latent Negative Transference. Let me explain."

Solini squeezed my knee in horror. In a cheerful, good-natured tone, Heiler explained that his technique, "confrontation," had evoked the anger that was "latent," or hidden, in each and every borderline. "She wasn't angry at *me*," he said, "it was her transference to me. She was distorting her real relationship with me based on early infantile experiences, with her bad mom, in the first year of life."

"But she *was* angry at you," I said. "Anyone would be."

"Not that angry," he said, "not borderline angry."

"How do you know she's a borderline?"

"Because of that incredible anger."

"But she didn't start out angry—you provoked it."

"Who says?"

"*I* do. It was obvi—"

"*You?* You, who've been a psychiatrist two whole months? You don't know diddly-squat about treating borderlines. Your so-called 'concern' is going to be a real problem—you're already overinvolved, imagining that you can rescue her. To you, what I did seemed cruel, right?"

"It was cruel, it was vicious, and I won't—"

"My friend, you'll get used to it. We all start out oversensitive. These darn borderlines *make* us oversensitive, make us feel sorry for 'em. Beginners like you always get drawn in—overconcerned, trying to rescue them—these gals are *seductive*. The things they get us to do for 'em—give 'em meds, find 'em places to live, even loan 'em money! This one—Zoe—she's the kind who'll even show up at your *home*! You unlisted?" I shook my head no. He shook his head too, as in *You poor bastard*. "Seduce the pants off us, given half a chance. Incredible talent they have, to somehow pick up your weakness and go for it—like they have a special radar or something." He shook his head in a kind of humble admiration and dismay, a dismay over male helplessness in the face of a female sexual expertise that would make Cleopatra look like Mother Teresa. "But hey—armed with the theory, it gets a lot easier."

Heiler got up, turned to the blackboard and wrote in big capital letters THE THEORY. Then for several minutes he outlined the Borderline Theory, listing the Krotkey Factors for diagnosis and then, with the aid of circles and flowcharts and line diagrams between stick figures that crisscrossed and darted into their stick brains and through their stick armpits like sword thrusts faked onstage, and even into their tiny stick crotches, focused particularly on Factor Number 3, "Projective Identification." This, spelled out with the kind of certainty you get from accountants and surgeons, showed borderline rage as so horrible that it couldn't be contained in the borderline's stick body, and so was projected onto the therapist's stick body, which then, in a kind of carom shot back, made the therapist, to the borderline, seem enraged at the borderline, which then made the borderline afraid of the therapist, and hence depressed.

I didn't understand much of this, but I had to admit that it did seem kind of brilliant, as if, if you could understand it, it would explain, brilliantly, a lot of the things you didn't understand.

"Which is what we call empathy." Blair Heiler wrote, in big caps in the nexus of lines and circles that looked remarkably like a child's try at a house, or perhaps a cat: EMPATHY. Turning to us, he said: "What you saw with Zoe was her and my projective identifications overlapping, which is called—" Here he underlined the word. "—EMPATHY."

"But isn't empathy putting yourself in another person's shoes, in a feeling way?" Hannah asked tentatively. "Isn't empathy subjective?"

"Exactly," he said, "which is why we're going to be completely objective about it." Heiler turned to the blackboard and wrote SELF, and then OBJECT. Solini crunched my knee. I crunched Hannah's. "The world is divided into the SELF," Heiler said, "and every other person, or, the OBJECT." He drew a vertical line between SELF and OBJECT. "There is a wall between them, a kind of movie screen for projective identification, or *EMPATHY*, which is key in working with these gals. Freud didn't know shit about borderlines—there weren't any in Vienna in 1890. Hell, Freud didn't even *charge* his patients. My teacher, the great American pioneer in"—tapping the blackboard—"SELF-psychology, and OBJECT-relations, is Dr. Renaldo Krotkey, a true genius." Reverentially he repeated this while writing the equation, "RENALDO KROTKEY = TRUE GENIUS. I am a Krotkeyan. Questions?"

Silence, one of "How Could We Nongeniuses Even Think of Asking Questions of Even a Protégé of the Great Renaldo Krotkey?"

"But Roy and I have been thinking," Hannah said bravely, "that Zoe fits the criteria for depression?" In a shaky, hesitant voice, Hannah retraced the genetic and personal history, along with the vegetative signs—loss of appetite, bulimia, change in sleep pattern, etc.—and the suicidal ideation. "And besides, she's really responded. She's incredibly better."

"Ah yes," Heiler said, nodding, "so all you new residents are being quote 'nice' to her and she's getting quote 'better'?"

"We're not just being 'nice,' " I said, "we're trying to be human."

"Being human is being *totally* human, which, for your information, isn't very 'nice,' and isn't even all that human. Christ, when I walked in here I thought I'd wandered into some kind of, I don't know, some kind of love nest or something. It's phony. It's Leonard Malik's New Agey-Wagey sentimentality, and with borderlines *it does not work.*"

"But ever since Ike White's suicide," I said, "we've—"

"Ike White's *death.* Believe me, Ike was one angry mother. Never got his anger out. If I'd been here to drill out your LNT, your rage at his death, you'd've been over it a lot sooner. What's Malik's theory? Having a buddy? What's his technique? Holding hands? The Borderline Theory and Technique have been proven scientifically, accepted by the toughest referees in the toughest journals in the world." His voice softened, and he went on, "Look. I know that the first time you see it, this theory seems strange—it's counterintuitive. If just being nice to borderlines worked, don't you think I would do it? Of course I would! In fact, I tried, way back, at first. But it's like dealing with difficult children: you've got to be firm. Everybody knows that if you don't dig up the Latent Negative Transference in these gals, next thing you know you've got people killing themselves, or killing other people. For fifty years people have been trying to cure borderlines by being 'nice and human' to them. Everybody felt better, nobody *got* better. It's easy to act nice, it's hard as hell to stand firm and confront the rage locked up in borderlines. Borderlines are hell. There aren't too many of us left who have the guts to treat 'em. I've specialized in borderlines for years and years, and I've seen what works: You go through that rage to the truth, to their miserable pain and suffering, and, believe me, they get better."

"But," Solini said, rolling his hands and squinching his face, "I mean, but everybody agrees that the lady *is* better?"

"In this case," Blair said, "better is worse. She'll have to get worse—which is in fact better—in order to get better, which will still be worse. If she gets a little worse, she won't get a lot better, but if she gets a lot worse, she may get a little better. Not smarmy-'nice' better, really better. *Borderline* better." He looked at his watch. "Daily report."

"Blair?" I said. He looked at me. "Isn't it about time for your vacation?"

Everybody cracked up. Blair too laughed. From his great height he stared down at us. "I'll be filling Ike White's slot down on Emerson One, and Dr. von Nott has converted Emerson Three to a borderline ward too. I'll be supervising all three of you residents. Dr. Errol Cabot and I have just gotten a two-million-dollar Department of Defense grant to study the use of medication on borderlines. Most Emerson patients will be on randomized double-blind trials of Placedon or Zephyrill or placebo." He smiled. "Don't worry, Roy, your overinvolvement with her is normal. Sick, but normal. Gals like her are experts at getting guys like you entangled. Read my paper: 'Rescue Fantasies in the—' " He opened the door. People were screaming out there. " '—in the Naive Resident.' " He left.

Solini, Hannah, and I walked onto the ward. Henry reached for his key to open the door out of Emerson 2. Suddenly Zoe was in my face, eyes wild, arms raised and fists clenched, screaming, "How could you? I'll never talk to you again!"

My arms went up, for protection. "I'm sorry, I didn't know."

"You're incompetent! I hate you! Hate hate hate you—"

Primo Jones materialized and started standing around between us, shifting his weight bulkily to counter Zoe's moves, rolling his eyes. I left. Shaken, I followed Hannah and Solini down through the woodwork forest of the stairwell and out onto the lawn, heading toward the lake. The day was clear and hot, with that perfection of summer that reminds you of picnics and swimming holes set amidst protective rock and straight, tall pines. From the rows of locked, screened windows of the second floor of Emerson came screams, shouts, and other desperate sounds of the first liberation of our patients from their getting better, which, according to Heiler, was their getting worse.

"That was insane," I said.

"Maybe not," Hannah said. "Dr. Renaldo Krotkey is the world expert in SELF-psychology and OBJECT-relations. 'Confrontation' is an accepted interview technique with borderlines. It really helps them get clearer. It did make some sense."

"Leveling her? And then saying it was *my* problem, being too sensitive?"

"Maybe you are—maybe we all are—like the first time you see real blood in surgery."

"You're defending that jerk?"

"Shhh," she said, grabbing my arm, nodding toward Emerson. "Here he comes."

Blair Heiler had come out of Emerson and was walking up the road to Misery Daily Report. He glanced at us. He was well out of earshot, but I stopped talking, as if he too had borderline radar. His gait was peculiar. As if contact with the ground stopped at his belly, each leg shot out of its own blind will, each step pivoting his hip seductively. The walk of a stick figure.

As he disappeared over the rise in the road, Hannah said: "Look, Roy, I kind of agree with you. While it was going on, I was appalled. But then, when he explained it, it was incredibly brilliant. I mean he really woke Zoe up—she was acting really *real*—wasn't she?"

"You understood it?"

"No, it's way too complicated to be understood by beginners, people who don't really understand. Malik's a sweetheart, but what's his theory? If he has one, it's kind of fuzzy and . . ." She fell silent, drifting off.

Standing there in the moment's sun, the slight breeze stirring the fresh chlorophyll scent up from the lawn clippings, I saw what she meant. Heiler had gotten to Zoe, flipped her into a hyper-real rage. He'd been able to justify everything he'd done. The theory rang true. "Henry," I said, "what do you think?"

Solini thought. He thought so hard he gave the impression of having lost his train of thought. He tugged his earring; his brow furrowed like a basset's. Henry too had flourished under Malik, finding a support group of Jamaicans in Dietary, jamming with them in the music room of the Recreation Building. "Malik was cool," he said, "but for the next few months we're like three white mice, man, running the Heiler maze. Maybe we gotta just chill?"

"How can it be right to treat a person like that?" My question hung there without answer, like a dead branch of a tree, caught in other, live branches. Like the ghost of Ike White.

"Got to go," Hannah said. Smoothing her skirt over her thighs, she did something she'd never yet done in her two months of psychiatric training.

"Solini, look," I cried out. "A smile."

"Holy shit. Far out, Hannah-babe. Go for it."

Hannah smiled more, in embarrassment. "But the thing is . . ." She trailed off again, an index finger caressing a corner of her smile.

Solini and I waited. No luck. "What, Hannah?" I asked. "What?"

"Oh." She seemed surprised that we were still there. Blushing, she said, "It's just that he's so brilliant and . . . and God is he handsome."

HANDSOME HE WAS, and as is often the case with great Americans, his handsomeness solidified his power.

From that morning on, the Emersons changed. With Malik there'd been a sense of all of us—residents, nurses, social workers, MHWs—working with the patients, walking a path beside them at their pace, trying to match their gait. But Zoe's door slam was like the starting gun of a fierce race with no clear course and no clear finish, everyone for him-or-her-SELF. From that day on the patients started to turn against us. It was what Blair had drawn on the board: SELF versus OBJECT, with a wall in between.

That first day set the tone and the pattern: Blair would do his "Insurance Rounds," crunch a patient or two on the way out, and spend the day in his office in Farben. There he would see his private patients, many of whom were exquisite and sexy BPOs with HF (Hysterical Features) from Misery's wealthiest families. He would supervise his research lab and tend to the banks of computers that were crunching up complex and confusing raw data from the Emerson patients, spewing out intricate permutations of the Krotkey Factors, encoding the spew into diagnoses of "BPO with (LMNOP)," and wadding the encoded spew into an even more complex and confusing Borderline Theory for publication. With Blair gone from Emerson, the crunched-up patient would try to crunch up the staff.

Blair moved swiftly to take over Emerson 3, Psychosis, rediagnosing almost everyone as BPO with P (Psychosis); and Emerson 1, Depression, rediagnosing almost everyone as BPO with D (Depression). The small sign on the doorpost of Emerson 2—"Borderline Ward"—came down. A big sign went up over the main entrance to all three Emersons:

BORDERLINE HOUSE

He took most patients off their antipsychotic or antidepressant drugs, and with Errol and Win began the two-million-dollar Department of Defense drug study. At random, without any of us knowing which patient was being put on what drug, most Emersonians were put on Placedon or Zephyrill or placebo, and except for Henry and Hannah and me, never spoke to a doctor in person again. Abandoned by their doctors, they were left with feelings of abandonment. This, Blair said, was nothing but our old Krotkey friend the LNT, Latent Negative Transference.

Heiler couldn't have been happier. Day after day he would unlock the massive hall door at nine sharp, wearing yet another from his collection of stylish summer suits and ties with tiny and bright flowers, graced by what seemed yet another alluring cologne. Closing the door behind him gently, he would turn and face the Emersonians. They, knowing that this would be their only chance to try to talk to the guy controlling every aspect of their fate, would eye him fiercely, as if they'd like to kill him and eat him. It was a moment of incredibly high voltage. Blair would look down at them from his safe height and smile sardonically, shaking his head in dismay at their plight. This provoked more rage. As his stick-figure legs kicked out machinelike from his hips, carrying him through the clawing underlings with the imperturbability of a shooting star through empty space, they would try to get through to him, asking for privileges, begging for a personal meeting with him, demanding discharge or transfer to another unit.

Before disappearing into his office for insurance rounds, he would turn and face the snarling patients. There would be a hush. Then Blair would smile, shake his head with disgust and contempt, say loudly, "These darn borderlines," and close his door quietly. The place would go bananas.

The Emerson staff too would try to corner Blair on these stick-figure drive-bys, trying to make him understand that the atmosphere on the unit was so bad that no one was getting better but in fact everyone was getting a lot worse.

"Good," Blair would say, moving away. "Good work."

"But they all hate us," said Vijay, a Pakistani mental health worker.

"Great," Blair said. "That's just great."

"They think we're all assholes," the head nurse said.

"Assholes?" Blair said pensively. "Assholes?" He considered this. Nodding his head sagely, he said, "Yeah, they're right. You are."

This would infuriate the staff further. I soon realized that this was perfectly in line with his being an orthodox Krotkeyian: Focusing his attention on his SELF, but for a tiny sector for every other person as an OBJECT, was the theoretically correct technique for infuriating. Expertly, in the name of EMPATHY, he treated us as OBJECTS.

Zoe, enraged at me, kept pointing out my incompetence. Her bulimia blossomed, her weight plummeted. She conceived a passion for thinness. I was appalled by this, and stuck to my Malik routine, sitting in his chair out in the living room for rounds, available to anyone who wanted to talk to me, trying to keep on being human. This seemed to make my patients even more enraged. Rather than talk to me, they shouted at me. The LAMBS died. I didn't know what to do.

Solini and Hannah were having just as bad a time as I was. The next Case Conference, Solini presented his therapy patient Thorny. Since my night on call when I had screamed back at him, Thorny had been doing better. Coming from Cajun country, Thorny was a fan of zydeco music, which was close enough to Solini's reggae for them to form a bond, if not a band. Henry and his nascent band of Jamaicans would sometimes allow Thorny to join them on drums. Thorny had been sent to Misery because of his uncontrollable temper. Under the influence of alcohol or other drugs, he would pick fights in bars with men who were bigger and tougher than he, leaving a record of scars, which had finally made his father, as legal guardian, commit him to Misery. I'd been in touch with his father—the "Burn King of the Bayous"—and we were on the verge of discharging Thorny to a halfway house nearby.

But somehow in the conference, Blair not only provoked Thorny to an enraged door-slam that measured at least eight on the Krotkey Scale, but provoked tiny Henry Solini himself. Towering over him, pointing to Henry's earring, Blair accused him in front of everyone of being "a fag."

"You better start working on your latent homosexuality, Dr. Solini," Blair said, "because that's what's making your patient sick—your not being honest about wanting to fuck him up the ass."

"Homophobe!" Henry shouted, fists clenched. "Fascist homophobe!"

Blair paused, then smiled. "Good. Work on that gay little Latent Negative Transference of yours, will you?" He walked out, the others following. Hannah and I went to our small friend, who was trembling all over.

"C'mon, Henry," I said, "let's take a walk."

"How'd he know what Split Risk said to me, about 'up the ass'? Did you tell him, Roy?" I said no. "How'd he know that? Radar?"

"Unreal. Accusing you of that, in public."

"Yeah, but the thing is, maybe he's right. The theory, I mean."

"You, gay?"

"Latent gay? Gay-latent? Like they say—'there's a kernel of truth, in every Wheaties flake'?"

And yet Blair's assaults on Solini and me were fairly benign compared to what he did the next week in Case Conference to Hannah Silver.

Hannah was having a terrible time downstairs in BPO with D. Her patients, still devastated by Ike's suicide and its denial, taken off their anti-depressants and put on God knows what, had gotten more depressed. Hannah and the staff were stretched to their limits, trying to keep suicide attempts to a minimum. Hannah was unskilled at drawing bloods for the Department of Defense study, and whenever one of her depressed patients, arms bruised the color of ripe plums, saw her approach, all hell broke loose. She insisted that Win Winthrop draw the bloods. He readily agreed, but the combination of his butcher's touch with his preacher's zeal sent Hannah's patients spinning even more quickly down that ever-constricting spiral through depression toward suicidal despair.

There was one bright spot in Hannah's world: Mary Megan Scorato. She had mostly recovered from her blast of Placedon. Malik had called in a lawyer and written an ironclad document to prevent her from partaking in the Placedon-Zephyrill drugfest. With Malik's help, Hannah had formed a strong, empathic bond with Mary. Depression was familiar to both of them.

Occasionally I'd see them together walking the grounds, and if I hadn't known them, I would not have been able to tell which was the doctor and which the patient. Their lively chatter back and forth was warm and friendly. The weekend before the conference, as a trial run before discharge, Mary Megan had gone home on an overnight. Hannah, concerned about her potential for harming herself, had had Mary phone her on Saturday and Sunday to let her know how things were going. Hannah had high hopes that the Case Conference would help Mary plan for discharge.

In the conference, Heiler, trying to mobilize the latent rage in Mary, failed miserably. No attack provoked anger. In fact, his escalating assaults brought an enshrouding silence. She sat there still as a stone. Finally Blair said, "Yeah, and I hear you were knocked up when you were seventeen."

She jumped, and then settled. Picking at the red scar on her wrist, she said, softly, "That is a private matter."

"Why?" No answer. "*Why!*"

Mary was silent, but her knuckles were white. She seemed paralyzed, imploded into a psychic hell. The slight smile on her face resembled the illusion of a smile you sometimes see, if the muscles clench right, on the face of a corpse.

Blair said Mary Megan could leave. With the gait of a marionette, she did.

Pissed off, Blair attacked Hannah. "Your being 'kind' to her," he said, "isn't fair to her. Don't you get it? This is a BPO with USA!"

"USA?" the BMS medical student asked in a wheezing voice.

"Unsuccessful Suicide Attempt. Because of you, Dr. Silver, that sweet lady's about to go down the tubes. You had her call you on the *phone*?"

Hannah looked down at her own clasped hands and nodded.

"That's the worst thing you could have done. Let's talk phone calls."

At the blackboard, Heiler wrote BORDERLINE PHONE CALL, with stick figures of patient and therapist—SELF and OBJECT—holding tiny telephones to stick ears. "You tell your borderline to feel free to call you at home." He wrote:

A) FEEL FREE TO CALL ME AT HOME.

"When they call you at home," he went on, "you say"—and he wrote:

B) WHY ARE YOU CALLING ME AT HOME?

"When they say 'Because you told me to call you,' you say":

C) YES BUT WHY ARE YOU CALLING ME?

"When they say 'Because I'm upset,' you say":

D) YES BUT WHY ARE YOU CALLING ME?

"And continue," he said, "until they hang up. Not only is this getting them to take responsibility for themselves, but remember—you never know what these borderlines are doing while they're talking to you on the phone."

"What could they be doing?" the BMS student asked innocently.

"Masturbating. Talking to you, and masturbating like crazy."

The med student began wheezing uncontrollably. He reached frantically into his pockets. His face got red. Shit, I thought, we're gonna have to do mouth-to-mouth. But then he found his inhaler and, pumping it, he left.

"In short, Dr. Silver," Blair said, "you suck." He left.

Solini and I thought Hannah would be devastated, but she was calm. "He's the expert," she said. "Studies have shown that SELF psychology works. I guess I'm not getting anywhere with her, really."

"But that's crazy," I said. "If you were his patient, and you were upset, would you call him for support?"

Immediately her eyes rolled up to the recessed lighting. "Of course not, Roy, that's the whole point. Now that I'm in analysis again I understand." Hannah had had a consultation with Schlomo Dove, who told her: "You are like the sun, giving your warmth away to others, leaving yourself cold and empty," and then hooked her right up with the perfect analyst, Dr. Ed Slapadek, rumored to be so tough that he made Blair Heiler look like the Easter Bunny. Hannah smoothed out her dress. It was light cotton, and covered with the kinds of tiny and bright flowers that often graced Heiler's Liberty of London ties. There was new lift in the zone of her breasts, as if one of those postmodern Wonderbras was lifting flesh all the way from those hips.

"New dress, Hannah-babe?" She blushed and nodded.

"Gotta run," she said. "I've got supervision with Blair."

AFTER A FEW WEEKS of the Borderline Theory, our patients were doing their best to act like borderlines. They were all worse, much worse—cutting, slashing, smashing, bashing, and sexualizing with a celestial fury which, turned on the Heiler spindle, meant they were better. It was Borderline City.

My most difficult patient was Zoe. Continuing to binge and purge and jog in the ravaging heat, in therapy she would point out how I'd missed the point and that the real point was that I was too distant, cool, and incompetent. "I want a new therapist," she'd say to me. "I want Dr. Heiler."

The worst was one day, as I was sitting in the living room, she assaulted me in front of the other patients, screaming, "Asshole! Hey, everybody, see this guy? He's my therapist and he's an *asshole*!"

I sat there fuming, not knowing how to respond. Then I noticed Blair Heiler, watching from the doorway. He took a first kick-step into the jungle of borderlines, and all hell broke loose. He reached his office door, turned, and said, "You poor sonsabitches," and closed the door behind him.

Later that day, with Henry and Hannah in supervision with Blair, he smiled at me and reached his elegant, long-fingered hand across his power desk to mine.

"Glad to see you're finally getting the hang of this, Roy."

"But she hates me," I said, surprised at his being so nice to me.

"Great, just great," he said, pointing out that while Zoe had often called me "jerk" and "incompetent," this was my first "asshole."

"Easy for you to say. She loves you. Hates me, and loves you."

"She's splitting."

"What's 'splitting'?"

"Krotkey Factor Number Four." He went to a blackboard and did stick figures.

Splitting was so complex that I was soon lost in the childlike scribbles. In the center, with bald head and glasses, Blair wrote DR. RENALDO KROTKEY = BORDERLINE GENIUS. On either side were a tiny stick figure with diapers, labeled BORDERLINE BABY = SELF, and a large, strangely imposing stick figure with comically large breasts, who turned out to be BORDERLINE MOM = OBJECT. Blair took the eraser and split MOM vertically into two parts, which he labeled GOOD MOM and BAD MOM. I didn't understand much of this, except that it was classic KROTKEY and that BABY SELF could not contain all the rage it felt in its stick body at OBJECT MOM, and so, in order to achieve OBJECT CONSTANCY and keep MOM in *one* piece, it had to split MOM into *two* pieces—GOOD MOM and BAD MOM—and love GOOD MOM and hate BAD.

"I'm the GOOD MOM," Heiler said, "you're the BAD, you poor bastard."

"Why?" I asked, using Blair's favorite confrontational word.

"*Good* question. Because the MOMs of borderlines are so screwed up."

"Why are these MOMs different?" Hannah asked.

"Oh God," Blair said, as if this were the dumbest question ever. "The sicker the person, the earlier in life the damage was done. The damage done you two guys—your being so 'nice'?" Solini and I looked at each other. "You got to about age three before you took the hit. Borderlines are so sick, they take the hit earlier, in the first year of life."

"How do you know that?" I asked.

"They *had* to be damaged that early, to be so sick! Whose fault is it?" He drew a box around MOM. "MOM's fault. MOM won't let the borderline separate from her, become a SELF-sufficient SELF and treat others like OBJECTS. The borderline tries to suck MOM's tits dry."

"Which is why Zoe treats me as BAD MOM and you as GOOD MOM?"

"That, and because you're doing a terrible job with her by being 'nice.' "

"But what do I do about it?"

"Treat her worse."

"And she'll like me better?"

"Ahh, women," he said, staring at Hannah as if she were a specimen. "Treat 'em worse, they love you better. An eternal truth. Stop trying to be a nice guy and she'll split the other way."

"I'll be GOOD MOM and you'll be BAD?"

"Guaranteed."

"That's crazy!"

"No, that's Krotkey." He sighed in admiration. "A man who never took a hit. Totally undamaged. A genius."

"But Malik says that—"

"Malik finishes training in July. Do you know where Malik will be then?"

"No, where?"

"Neither does he, and neither does anybody else. But it won't be here at Misery. Malik's a pussy." An Asian woman came in and placed a ribbon of computer sheets on Blair's desk. "Preliminary data on Placedon and Zephyrill."

"Already, man?" Solini asked.

"You've got to publish the preliminary before they beat you to it. Borderline work is dog-eat-dog. Lotta sonsabitches. You guys'll want to join my research team, get your names on my papers, start those careers."

"But about Zoe," I said, "I don't think I can be nasty."

"Sure you can. It's in you, and it's fun. To think only of your SELF? To get out your anger at OBJECTS? It's the greatest. Mind you," he said, with a wink, "healthy narcissism can be hard for some OBJECTS to take."

"But won't my being SELF-centered get in the way of relating to others?"

"No. Relating to others will get in the way of your SELF. Get a SELF, then get yourSELF a sexy OBJECT." On the blackboard he wrote: SELF = SEX. *MORE* SELF = *MORE* SEX. He chuckled. "Yes, yes, narcissism is what made this country what it is today." His eyes shone proudly. For a second it seemed he might cry, with pride. "My dad, a major general, taught me that."

Jesus, I thought, the guy has a heart after all.

"Healthy narcissism, Renaldo Krotkey. The American Dream."

It was all I could do to keep from saluting.

"Now then," Blair said, snapping back from pride and glory. "Solini?"

"Sir?" Henry sat up, expecting to be reamed out as a gay-latent all over again. But Blair reached over and shook *his* hand. "Glad to see that Thorny your dickhead is doing worse."

"Thanks, sir. But he thinks he's doing like better?"

"Never accept a borderline's reality as real."

"But I'm worried. He's talking pretty well to OBJECTS like me and Roy."

"Maybe he is," Blair said, "to *real* OBJECTS. I'm talking *internal* OBJECTS, people inside his head. We physicians are smarter than that. The more intelligent the person, the higher the graduate degree, the less concerned with reality. Don't quote me on that, but as a rule of thumb. So don't be 'nice' to him, eh?"

Solini pledged that he would not, and we waited for Heiler to turn to Hannah and her great work down in Depression where all her patients were so terrifically worse—especially her favorite, Mary Megan Scorato, who was on five-minute checks for suicide—that we thought that rather than a handshake she'd get a small medal. To our surprise Blair totally ignored her. Her face fell.

"Because you guys are getting the hang of this," he said, "I'm going to teach you the most important and delicate matter in all of psychiatry—harder than borderlines, more intellectually challenging than research." He walked to the blackboard and drew a stick building. "Pick a city—say Boston. What are the two biggest buildings in Boston?"

"The Prudential," I said, "and the John Hancock."

"INSURANCE," he said, writing it in caps. "INSURANCE bastards. Biggest buildings, biggest profit margins on earth. The cocksuckers."

Heiler proceeded to give his most complex lecture. Stick figures represented DOCTORS, PATIENTS, and, in the stick building, stick INSURANCE executives with dollar signs ($ $) where their eyes should have been. Basically it was about how, for each patient, you had to make up multiple DSM diagnoses to dupe INSURANCE and transfer some of the dollars from the INSURANCE executives' eyes to the DOCTORS' pockets. He concluded, "Every single day, we doctors have to make sure our patients are sick enough to stay in the hospital, but not so sick that INSURANCE says they're not improving and have to be discharged. Sick, but getting well. Getting well, but still bad. Bad, but getting better."

"Which is worse," Solini said.

"Which is," I said, "in fact better." Blair laughed. That charming laugh.

"So we have to keep them acutely chronic?" Hannah asked.

"No, chronically acute," Blair said coldly. "Welcome to mental health care in America, folks. It sucks, and I want you guys to start doing it."

"Doing what, man?"

"INSURANCE rounds. Stop talking to patients, start talking to INSURANCE."

"You want us to not see patients?" I asked pointedly.

"Not seeing them *is* seeing them—part of Borderline Technique. Think *I* don't know how infuriating it is for them to try to catch me to talk? Drives 'em nuts. They go ballistic, start acting like they're guzzling rocket fuel. Which lets 'em stay here longer, long enough to shift from BAD

OBJECTS to GOOD." He flicked a blond forelock and downshifted to his Huck Finn aw-gosh mode. "Look, guys, *I* know that sometimes I seem uncaring. But it's because I really *care* for these borderlines. For them to get better, I have to confront them all the time, and to do that I have to keep them here as long as possible. It's hard to change a borderline. Most psychiatrists won't even try. They hear the word 'borderline,' they run like hell. There are only a few of us left who are fighting to take the time and energy to do it right. Think I like spending four hours a day on the phone to these high school dipshits in fucked-up places like Omaha and Toledo telling me they're gonna discharge my borderlines because they're not sick enough? I do it to give these borderlines the time they need. I do it because I care."

Oh my God, I thought, underneath all this, he's *nice?*

"*I* care enough," Blair went on, "to let these darn borderlines stay here and take all the time they need to get worse."

"But most of them don't want to stay," Hannah said. "They want out."

"Of course they want out," Blair said derisively, "they're borderlines."

He dismissed us. Henry, Hannah, and I stood dazed in the lobby.

"He's crazy," I said. "And cruel."

"It seems cruel," Hannah said, "but he's an expert in cruelty to this kind of patient. What do we know? I've got to believe Blair knows what he's doing. Don't you have the sense that underneath it all he's a sweetheart?"

Neither Henry nor I said that we had that sense.

"Well, I do. He comes on tough in public, but behind the closed doors of an office, no one knows what goes on. I bet his patients adore him."

"No foolin'," Solini said, "he's probably fucking 'em all on that desk."

"Lucky them," Hannah blurted out. Then she blushed and said, "Oh gosh."

WHY DO MEN FOLLOW LEADERS?

Without realizing it, trying all the while not to try it, as gradually and inevitably as the turning of summer toward fall where from day to day you can't really see the changes but one day you wake up chilled, your throat scratchy, the air crisp, chilled, not only almost fall but even containing the seeds of winter, we began to be affected by the Heiler machine.

How could we not be? Given the ferocity of the patients, and the vagueness of psychiatry in dealing with such definite ferocity, we felt constantly under attack, constantly criticized, constantly made to feel we were failing, that compared to Heiler and a lot of other experts we were simply *inadequate*, as psychiatrists and as human beings. Faced with these violent, raging people, what were we supposed to do? It wasn't like treating someone with a broken bone, where you took an X ray and saw the crack and followed the manual on how to set it. Here there were no white bones and black cracks. Here there were spectra of color with no edge between one color and another, and if you took an X ray you'd see pitch-black. In the chaotic gray of emotional pain, we needed something definite, something that would show us what to do.

Blair Heiler, in the hell of Emerson that he had created, was strangely comforting.

Especially after Malik, after the vagueness of Malik who gave us no THEORY except to be human and who was always asking us to keep asking questions and telling us that our innocence was our power and our way of empowering our patients who were not OBJECTS *to* us but much *like* us, in being, basically, human beings—it was comforting to have some certainty, for the one thing you could say about Blair was that he was certain. There were no shadows in his sun. Follow Heiler, and you knew what to do. You never had to think. Heilerized, we could be certain of ourSELVES. Certain of ourSELVES, what did it matter that our patients, our OBJECTS, seemed so uncertain, so stuck? Given Heiler logic, stuck could be unstuck, could it not? Heiler was marching music, stirring up feelings of high school glory when I, trombonist in the Columbia High Fish Hawk Marching Band, would blast out "The Dominator" and kick my legs out and move swiftly through "Semper Fidelis" up from the river to the cemetery for the Gettysburg. Heiler was Sousa; Malik was all Ravel.

Blair assured us that once we got out all the Latent Negative in each borderline, we'd ride out the storm of rage, and the adjustment of borderline character to normal character would be profound. We'd sail off into a sunset of mental health, a sheaf of published papers under our arms, our patients safe and sound and married to appropriate OBJECTS and each secure in a healthy SELF. Like each of our own SELVES, yes.

To drive this point home, Blair would often quote from the historical figure he revered above all others, the man he said was the beacon to which all men aspire, the greatest American of all, who else but Ralph Waldo Emerson:

> "*Star by Star,*
> *world by world,*
> *system by system*
> *shall be crushed—*
> *but* I *shall live.*"
> (Emphasis, Blair Heiler)

Hearing this, how could you help but think of poor Ike White? Hadn't Malik told me that Lloyal von Nott, Heiler's mentor, had been "crushing" him?

The goddamn thing was that when you were with him, being scanned by that radar of bedroom-blue eyes, and blond forelock and Huck Finn grin, it all felt so right that it immediately brought up the idea that it was in fact so wrong you'd be a dickhead to buy it, all in all confusing as hell, as if you'd shown up for some pain-relieving but terrifying dental work only to find a sign on the office door reading "Dentist Dead."

Confusing, yes, for the harder I tried not to try it, the harder I seemed to be trying it. Or it me.

Five

SCHLOMO AND DIXIE DOVE were the twin constellations in the New England Freudian firmament, a kind of Big and Little Dipper of neurosis. The Doves were almost public figures, so out front that everybody thought they knew them. They had been born of immigrant Jewish parents, and in both were nurtured the seeds of a cultural hunger to "make it," a hunger that blossomed to indulgence in him, denial in her. Trim and tight as a fighting fish, Dixie was called by him, in public and with all good humor and even a twinkly affection, "the Barracuda."

They'd met on the Grand Concourse in the Bronx and worked their way through college in Manhattan—he CCNY, she Hunter—and then on to Boston, where he made it in Tufts Medical and she at MIT, in astrophysics. Both were analyzed by men analyzed by Freud, he by the pathetic Nash (né Nischgedankberg), she by the bellicose Bebring. Nothing unusual in all this, I thought, driving up the hill to their mansion one afternoon in early October. Except for the psychoanalysis, they were much like my own parents, yes. But then something else had happened, something essential to the perverse self-promotion at the heart of the American Dream, and in a life-move of sheer implausibility, which in hindsight seemed inevitable, Schlomo parlayed his vulgar wit to a prodigal power. Without anyone knowing quite how he did it, everyone woke up one morning to find that the good Dr. Dove had captured a share of the market on fixing up neurotic people with neurotic therapists. It was brilliant, for suddenly many of the therapists in the area were dependent on Schlomo for patients, and thus money. Schlomo was ballsy on money: you paid in advance, in cash only, a hundred fifty for twenty minutes—"Gratuity included," Schlomo would say, laughing—after which he'd guarantee you the right shrink. If you didn't like the one he sent you to, he'd send you to another, and another, until you did. For no extra charge. He'd keep for himself the patients he wanted.

They were an outrageous-appearing couple, Schlomo's sloppiness countered by Dixie's being a florid fashion rack, all colorful dresses and blouses and skirts and pants with tropical flowers, with her signature floppy hats, real flowers pinned amidst the fake. Notorious for never refusing an invitation, they went to all social functions and always seemed to have a good time, Schlomo's laughter bouncing up from the center of the room, Dixie's commentaries on Schlomo slashing in from the corners. Not that everything had always gone well. One reason, everyone said, for their good cheer and impulsive social functioning was the matter of the swimming pool. Growing up in the searing and cindery summers of the city, Schlomo and Dixie had always dreamed of having their own pool. Finally, with the money from his booming practice, they bought the mansion and dug the hole. And swam. Swam and swam. Swam for years, until one day their two-year-old son was found facedown just below the surface, dead. It makes sense, I thought, parking under an elephantine copper beech. All this hyper humor is the frantic eruption of that immigrant hunger denied, the slow starvation of their outliving their only child. You had to feel for him, yes.

I was at Schlomo's house for a supervisory session. I knocked, went into the kitchen of the mansion, and was face-to-face with Dixie, in a housedress that could have passed for an advertisement for a cruise up the Congo. "Wrong door," she said. "He's in the carriage house."

"Sorry. I'm Roy Basch, how are you today?"

"You should be," she said. "It's diagnostic."

"Of what?"

"How the hell do *I* know? When he finds you a therapist, you'll find out."

"No, no, I'm not a patient, I'm on the opposing team, the doctors?"

"Big deal. Carriage house. He's there."

Since my one talk with Schlomo about Cherokee, I hadn't gone to see him again. I knew that my avoiding him had something to do with my loyalty to my patient Cherokee. Schlomo had taken over from Ike White as Director of Residency Training, and he seemed to be everywhere at once around Misery, constantly running outpatient groups, giving lectures, eating those bananas, wandering the grounds as if he had all the time in the world. He saw most of his private patients here at his home office, starting with Lily Putnam at six in the morning. I'd often come upon him schmoozing with one of what he referred to as "the Great Unwashed," sometimes Buildings and Grounds, more often, as he noshed on some horrible dish, Cafeteria. Solini and I had nicknamed him "the Oily Schmoozer of Misery."

Ike White's colossal lie, his suicide and its colossal denial, had cracked open something cynical in me, leaving me with a deep sense that you couldn't believe much of anything you were told at Misery. While I had settled into a healthy respect for just how possible it was that a shrink could be screwing his patients, every time I would run into Schlomo in the flesh it seemed absurd. Blair Heiler, with those long fingers and boyish smiles, yes. Schlomo no. Schlomo had noticed my avoiding him, and whenever I'd run into him, he would badger me to come see him for supervision. "You never call," he'd say, mimicking a Jewish grandmother, "you never write, not even a postal cart!" Finally one day he'd cornered me at the vending machines in the tunnels. "Look, I got duties too, as Residency director. Make nice. We'll meet outside this goyish country club. Come to the house." He reached into a horrible inner pocket and handed me a map. We set a time.

I walked down the path to the carriage house and sat in the waiting room. An obese man dressed in a light gray jumpsuit came ponderously down the stairs and into the room, weeping as if his heart would crack. He clomped past me, cowlike, and out the door. Schlomo yelled for me to come up.

The second floor of the carriage house was a large open room under a mansard roof, one whole side of which was skylight. In the light Schlomo looked worse, in shirtsleeves, baggy slacks, his chin grizzled, and his eyes, deep in there, red-edged as if from lack of sleep. As in his office at Misery, here was a leather couch and in back of it a leather chair, and a tidy desk and other chairs. The decor was fragrant plants and bananas in all stages of ripeness. Here at home the cigar in his mouth was lit. He puffed happily. In his hand was that yellow plastic watering can with the penile spout.

" 'Enter to Grow in Wisdom!' " he shouted joyously. "Inscription over the Harvard Gate."

"Throw that in my lap again," I said, "and I'll kill you."

"Deal. Sit, sit. Sit." He gestured me to a chair in front of a desk. "Y'look good. Things agreeing?"

"Fine, fine," I said, realizing that suddenly my mind was spinning with questions and fantasies about his patient Lily Putnam.

"Good, good. So why don't you ever come to see Schlomo for supervision?"

"Just because you're now director of training doesn't mean I have to subject myself to you."

"Training's for horses or seals, boychik, not for persons. Why so nasty?"

"So what do you want?"

"Schmooze. Just to schmooze. Outrage, remember? I got it, you got it, the goys don't got it. So how's it goin'? Tell Schlomo."

He waited, smiling, puffing. I thought of the drowned kid. Finally I told him something of what I'd been going through, with Heiler.

"Oy *gevalt!*" he said. "That's it! That's why you're so nasty lately—you've been Heilerized! All that borderline crap. Little Blairey Heiler! The *putz*. Yeah, he's like you. Never came to Schlomo, never analyzed. Anger? Oy!"

"You're saying that anger's not important?" I said angrily.

"Fifty years ago he'd be gassing you and me and laughing. Never mind him, c'mon c'mon, let's go deep. What's doin' in there? Tell Schlomo."

"Nothing."

"Oh boy!" he said, delighted. "C'mon. Spill."

Those eyes waited, glittering dark crystals. I checked out the watering can, and then glanced away at the couch. Schlomo had been Ike's analyst. Six years, Ike had lain on that couch. I could almost see him, stuttering there, hoping it would help. "You were Ike White's analyst?"

For a second he seemed startled. Then he sighed, puffed his cigar to a rose red, and said, "Yes. His first one. Poor Isaac."

I remembered that Ike's "new" analyst had been at his bedside when he died. "Why'd he need a second one? Didn't the one with you take?"

"You have feelings about him?" That ugly face softened, the eyes kindled.

"Not really."

"Tell Schlomo," he cooed, "tell Schlomo about sad and lonely."

"Nope. No feelings. Gone."

Schlomo nodded his head slowly and then abruptly threw the lit cigar into my lap. Sparks flew. I jumped up and threw it back at him, brushing my pants frantically. The ash had stained the fabric, bits were burning through.

"Asshole!" I screamed. "You ruined my suit! Three fifty in Oxford and you ruined my suit! Are you *crazy*? Are you a fucking *imbecile*?"

"I know, I know, it's terrible. Here—" He was heading toward me with the watering can. "—hold still, I'll put it out—"

"No! Stay away, you jerk!"

"Send the bill, send the bill." He sighed. "No feeling, eh?"

I was enraged. But then something strange happened. All at once Schlomo seemed to crumple and half fall to the floor, where he sat cross-legged, as if at a dying campfire. He started crying softly.

"What?" I asked. That repulsive body shook. "What happened?"

"Isaac, poor Isaac." He chanted a riff of Hebrew, then translated, " 'Take your son, your favored one, Isaac, whom you love, and go to Mount Moriah, and offer him there as a burnt offering.' " He sighed. "Six years. Good work. Boom. Dead. Suicide."

"Suicide?"

"You believe these pinheaded goyim with eyes so close together you can't get a pencil between? These Lloyals and Heilers who think their colons are filled with cologne?" He fell silent, rocking a little, in grief.

"I met with him the day he did it," I said. "It was the day Cherokee told me about his suspicion about you and his wife. I keep thinking that, maybe, just maybe, that was the final straw."

"Nah. I called Isaac later that day, after you came to see me. It was okay. You didn't do it. Poor little guy."

"Why did he kill himself?"

"Because of *this*," he said, looking up at me with a pitiable sorrow.

"Because you were always throwing things into his crotch?"

Schlomo sat up, even bounced. His eyes widened, black buttons in pink cloth. "And because he maybe never got as angry as you? See? You *got* it."

"Got what?"

"Get *more* of it—make nice with Schlomo. Gimme a hand up." I did. His hand was damp. "So," he said, again cheerful, "come for supervision, come kibitz. Better yet, let Schlomo analyze you. I'll give you such a deal!"

"Me, analyzed by you? I don't *think* so!"

"*Nu*, so I won't analyze. I'll farm you out."

"I don't want any part of you," I said. "Life's too short for Schlomo."

"And Schlomo's too short for life!" He laughed. As I walked out, he called down the stairs after me, "Bye-bye, bye-bye. Don't forget to write!"

I walked up the flagstone path and stopped to see the damage to my pants in the slanting October light. Two burn holes. The fucker would get the bill. Looking up, I saw the pool, the blue not of water but of paint. It was empty. Shit. I walked on again to my car, and as I drove away on down the hill, I started to put the fragments together, as if my brain, unrolled, were rolling back up convolution by convolution, gyri and sulci snapping back into place to make some sense of this phantasmagorical shrink. The bizarre thing about Schlomo was that his outrageousness left no room for pretense. He seemed real, but it was a reality like everybody's Uncle Irving, the schnorrer at the cousin's wedding who was funny but turned out to have been embezzling from the business for thirty years. It was real, but was it true? Fuck Schlomo! Stay away. In the jungle of the Doves, you see a snake, you don't grab it.

CHEROKEE HAD CANCELED several times. Each time, he'd left a message, in pleasant tones, that he was too busy and things were going well. I felt bad, for I liked him and felt that in our two meetings when he was in crisis we'd really connected. I figured that given his WASPdom, where any opening up is followed by a more harsh closing down, he was ashamed to see me again and had, to use Zoe's phrase, "gone back into his Happy Box." Later that week when he walked into my office all tan and fit and relaxed and aglow from having healthy horses under him all summer, I smiled, as did he. Like old friends catching up, we began chatting.

Italy for him had been "transforming," bringing back childhood memories of living there from age seven to fourteen while his father was in the American diplomatic corps. His Italian had come back easily, the underpinning grammar snapping up the remembered words. The beauty had been overpowering.

"One night in Tuscany we took a walk in a field, and suddenly there were fireflies! Hundreds of fireflies—*lúcciole*—like shooting stars in the dark field, just as in my childhood! It was so exquisitely beautiful!" He sighed. "Where are they now? Did you see a single firefly this summer? Even one?"

With surprise, I realized I had not. "No."

"No, they're gone from here. Compared to Italy, we live in a dump."

He talked about his childhood in Rome, summering near Siena, his brilliant, reserved, diplomat father, whom he loved terrifically until his slow death a few years before; and his stern, crazed mother, whose life in Roman society circles had ended abruptly with the family's transfer back to the States, now a recluse in Sun Valley, Idaho, never having seen her grandchildren.

"Narrowness of mind," he said, "seems a Putnam family trait."

"Except for your name. Where'd it come from?"

He lit up and with transforming animation told me that it came from a great-grandfather, Honor Putnam, a descendant of the brothers John and Thomas Putnam, two of the elite of Salem, Massachusetts, villains of the Salem witch trials. It turned out that Honor, having taken part in the massacre and resettlement of the Cherokees from their home in the Appalachians to the reservations in Oklahoma, had a vision of the hell he might face and named his next-born son Cherokee. "I'm actually Cherokee Putnam the third," he now said, "and for a while people called me 'Trey.' Never met Honor, of course. Funny, I dream of him, sometimes."

He fell silent. There was a sense of peace in my small office under the eaves. Yet I was troubled. But for his enthusiasm for the fireflies, there had been no feeling, no affect, in anything he'd said. It felt surface level, phony. The sense of peace turned to a sense of stalling, like when engines cut out on a small plane. Our time was almost up and there had been no mention of Lily.

"So what's going on with your wife?"

"Oh, things are better now. I feel a bit sheepish, actually, getting so upset. I think we can stop these meetings. Thanks for all your good help." Pleasantly he talked about the resurrection of his sex life with Lily. The rift in Italy had provoked a cliff-edge despair in both of them that had led to the most romantic of reconciliations, a long weekend "*sans enfants*" at a hotel called the Summerhouse in Nantucket, a weathered mansion overgrown with roses, fireplaces, and moonlight on the Indian summer pacific Atlantic, and lovemaking to the sunrise. "I just wanted to stop by and say so long and thanks."

You'd think I'd've been happy for him, and shaken his hand and said, Good work and good luck, but no. It all seemed too nice, especially given the vulgarity of Schlomo. After weeks of Heiler I could not help but hear, in his "things are better," the negative, and said, "So things are worse?"

"No, no, Basch, I said things are better."

"Are you sure?"

He paused. "Yes, I'm sure. That first weekend in Nantucket she was hotter than she ever was with me before, and it's kept on since. She's been an animal. Almost like analysis with . . . with *him* has freed her up."

"Him?"

A shifting in his seat, a chagrin on his face. "You know who."

"You won't say his name?" He stared at me. I could sense anger there, maybe even a borderlinelike rage, and felt that if I could just get to it with him, we could get to the reality, break open that narrowness of mind, yes. "What about her underwear?"

His jaw clenched. "She had . . . a red garter belt."

"A red *garter* belt?"

He looked at me suspiciously. "What the hell are you implying?"

"You angry?"

"No, I'm not angry, I'm wondering what you're trying to do here."

"*I'd* be angry, if it were *me*."

We stared at each other, his beautiful blue eyes narrowing, as if looking out from a cottage into a sunset turned harsh. Then he abruptly got up and left.

I felt a hit of dismay and rose to go after him, but it was as if I felt Heiler holding me back, warning me not to blow it. I opened the door and looked down the hall. He was striding away, gesturing to himself. Suddenly he slammed the wall in fury with a clenched hand. What the hell had gotten into me? I was going to lose him! I took a step out into the hallway, feeling guilty that I had provoked him, that I'd driven him away, that he wouldn't be back.

PROVOCATION, Blair had chalked on the board the other day, = ENTICEMENT.

Bullshit, I thought, but immediately came a second thought, that in fact a few simple questions from me had tilted us from pleasantries to connection, from well-bred niceties to rage and suspicion. He had gotten angry, and he was really *there*. Sadly, I sat back down. One or two tiny comments from me, and his paranoia and rage—all that Latent Negative Transference toward me—had blossomed. Maybe he was a BPO. BPO with GE—Gorgeous Eyes. The Borderline Theory said that soon Negative would turn Positive, and he would heal.

"WHAT'S *THAT*?" Berry asked, grabbing me by both ears, so my head felt like a jug held by its handles. It was a few days later, and we were naked in my turret, making love.

"What's what?"

"What you're doing. Grunting like an animal, using dirty words."

"That's Krotkey."

"Krotkey?"

"Renaldo Krotkey, the borderline expert. Krotkey came out the other day in the *Times* saying we don't use enough animal sounds and obscenities in sex."

"Are you crazy?"

Berry and I had been having a rocky time. Our lives were so different, mine with sick adults, hers with happy kids. As I'd gotten more into Heiler, she'd gotten more guarded. Our flare-ups, for me, were provoked by her astonishing ineptitude with real objects—dropping things, losing things, things flying out of her hands. Berry had grown up with a terror of taking action in the physical realm and this had been transformed into a carelessness that had almost killed us several times as we'd traveled the world. Now her carelessness was merely irritating—she left dishes and coffee cups in the bathroom and piled up in the sink, keys and books and clothes everywhere; her cat, when he visited, habitually vomited in the turret at night, so that I'd sometimes get up and step in squishy cat vomit on my way to the bathroom. Things were rough. Yet we both knew that the rigors of "health care training" didn't last forever.

The phone rang. It was my patient Zoe, calling me at home, again. True to Heiler's prediction, I was paying for not being unlisted. She had gotten in the habit of calling me late at night, screaming at me and refusing to get off the line. This time I'd had it. Berry could overhear the conversation.

"I'm feeling pretty desperate," Zoe said.

"I told you not to call me at home."

"Oh, too good for me, are you?"

"It's not that—"

"In the middle of something unusual? Like sex with your wife?"

How do they do it? I asked myself. How do they know? I said, "Why are you calling *me?*"

"Because I'm *upset.*"

"But why are you calling *me?*" She screamed and hung up.

"What the hell were you doing?" Berry asked.

"It's the only way to stop her."

"If *you* were in trouble, would you want to be treated like that?"

" 'Course not. I'd take responsibility for myself—I'm not a borderline. Day after day she's on me. It's good to get my anger out, okay?"

"You've been getting a lot of it out lately. It's like you're angry all the time."

"And you don't like it?"

"If we can talk about it, yeah. But we haven't been able to lately."

"*I* can, why can't you?"

"Goddamnit, because you're so into yourself! It's getting hard to take!"

She sat naked on the edge of the bed, staring at me. I sat, braced, staring back, suddenly having that same incompetent feeling I'd had with Zoe and Christine. Berry, a BPO? With what? I used to think with ALOE—A Lot Of Empathy—but right now I wasn't so sure.

"Y'know," she was saying, "it'd make all the difference in the world if you'd just smile at me."

"I'm trying," I said, "I really am, but it's not happening."

" 'Kay. All I want, sweetie, is to be close to you. Feel you *with* me."

"*I* feel close. I'm just trying to focus more on myself."

"What?" she said, eyes widening. "You, *more* self-centered? Are you joking?"

"Heiler says it's healthy."

"Okay, okay," she said, trying to calm herself, her hands in front of her breasts moving back and forth, their palms pointing toward me. "I'll give you the benefit of the doubt. Maybe there is something in SELF-psychology for you."

"But not for *you?* Is that what you're saying?"

"Not for *us*. God!" She gathered up her clothes. "I'm going home." I tried to stop her. "Fuck off," she said. As she turned she dropped a heavy necklace and a roll of panty hose. "I've tried hard enough to carry 'us' for one night. It's like moving heavy furniture. Without help."

I said I was sorry and tried to convince her to stay, but she left.

The next morning she paged me, from the preschool. I was at the nursing station on Emerson, suturing up Thorny's face. The Lady Who Ate Metal Objects, now officially a Heiler BPO, had tried to get at Thorny's Rolex. A struggle had ensued. She'd coughed up a penknife and slashed him. Now, in the background, the kids were singing:

"It's cleanup time in the classroom,
It's time for girls and boys;
To stop what they are doing,
And put away their toys."

"Last night," she was shouting, over this sugary off-key din, "makes me think that things are more screwed up than they seem."

"No, no," I shouted back, trying to get Thorny to hold still, "it makes me think that things seem more screwed up than they are."

"Everything I say, lately, you immediately say no to."

"No I don't."

"See?"

We fought. The kids sang. I said we'd talk more on the weekend. She said she was busy on the weekend. We said good-bye.

Busy? A hit of jealousy. I picked up the phone to call her back. But no, we'd just start arguing again. I put the receiver back down.

That Friday, I came home from Misery feeling bad about facing a weekend without her. I got the mail—including a conjunction-filled letter from my father that I devoured at once.

> Hope you're back in your relaxed routine and know you will be the best resident in your class. Mom and I argue alot and it is normal for retired Jews. Had an 86 with two three-putt greens and my game now is all set . . .

Could this be BOP with HSD? High Speed Drill?

I was taking in the garbage cans for my senescent retired woman doctor landlady when an old dark blue car drove by, stopped, and backed up. A woman looked at me and called my name. She looked like Jill the mental health worker, but couldn't be because Jill had blond hair in braids down her back, and this woman had blond hair cut to a fuzz but for a cockscomb on top, a punk cut.

"It's me, Jill."

"Oh, hi." I crossed the street to her, noticing the rusted-out rear parts of her blue Buick. She was wearing a sleeveless tank top and shorts. An open can of Bud was sweating cold between her thighs. "What happened to your hair?"

"Cut it all off."

"Why?" I asked, smelling beer on her breath.

"Had to do something. I broke up with my boyfriend and had to move out and I lost my job—my other job, not the one at the nuthouse—and I lost my horse because the boyfriend owned the horse and I've got no money, and yesterday I cut off all my hair."

"Looks great," I said, stunned by her good cheer in the face of these catastrophes. "Must be cooler, right?"

"And winter's coming—figure that one out. I'm getting just a little tired of these 'growth-promoting experiences,' know what I mean?"

"Yeah. But what are you doing here?"

"I'm living with friends for a while, up the street. You?"

"I rent the top floor. Up there. With the turret."

She followed my gaze. "Bet it's nice up there." I felt the sweat bead on my forehead, and thinking maybe I shouldn't do this because of Berry, I said fuck that who knows what Berry's doing, and so I asked Jill if she'd like to have dinner sometime. By coincidence she was free that very night.

At seven I picked her up and we went to a fish restaurant nearby and ordered martinis. We talked hilariously about Misery being so weird and we maybe ate our fish. I invited her back to the top floor and then, showing her my loft when we got to the bedroom in the turret, as easily as a fish in water with another watery fish I kissed her and she me, opening her mouth, and then, lingering as if in sad parting, all scented with cherry blossoms and suntan oil, she said, "Your lips are so *soft*!" I started to caress her. She said, "Wait."

"What?"

"It's gonna happen eventually," she said, pulling away and crossing her hands over her chest and grasping the bottom of her tank top, "So let's get it over with, okay?"

"O-*kay*!" I turned down the dimmer of the chandelier. She stood there in just her bra and jeans, the bands of pink satin alternating with bands of nothing, forming complex whorls on the roundnesses of her breasts like on seashells. I shivered. With straightforward innocence she stared at me and pursed her lips. I got aroused but somehow I didn't dare move because the moment was sacred in the way when you're drunk so many things seem sacred and you have a dim sense that the chandelier in your head is so dim that you might not recall much the next day. As if in prayer, she brought her hands together at her sternum, and like a curtain opening her breasts fell away, jouncing a little, the bra hanging down lacily, as if it had disintegrated into pink ribbons. Her tan highlighted the white of her skin, and popping out on the white roundnesses, her nipples were, of all shades, lavender. She stretched, so tall that her fingertips wiggled the chandelier. I started toward her.

She said, "Wait a sec."

She brought her hands down to her jeans and undid the metal button and slowly unzipped the metal zipper and then carefully, so as not to disturb her panties, rolled back the denim edge and carefully pulled them down her thighs. Stepping out of her jeans, she turned to throw them on a chair, her thong bikini straining in and up against her buns. The chair tipped under the weight, then righted itself. Turning back, she peeled the bulging white lace triangle down, revealing her untanned pudenda frosted with a lace of light brown hair.

"Now," she said, smiling mischievously, "you."

Next thing I knew she was on top of me, but all at once I felt whirly from booze and thought of Berry and felt a killer guilt. Things stopped dead.

Into my head floated a phrase from my father's letter:

> Hope you are being conscientious and know you will soon be on top . . .

Silence, a silence of Uh-oh.

"What's the matter?" she whispered. "Am I too wet?"

"No, I'm just a little nervous."

"How sweet! How really sweet!"

"Maybe it's the booze."

"Sweet!" She bent and kissed me as she had that first time, all cherry-blossomed and suntan-oiled and with the sweet sorrow of lovers parting, and then she drew slowly away and led my hands to her breasts, and I caressed the tips with my fingers and then my lips and lay back again sighing. She sighed and said with hearty appreciation, "God your lips feel so *good*!" and that did it and we did it and it was wild and hot and blond and wet and fantastic.

Walking her back to her house up the street in the moist dark of a moonless night, I felt so appreciative of her, of her frankness and suffering and not needing to psychologize it and of her passion and of the way the pungent wet lace of light brown hair when it dried had fluffed up like the punk cut on the crown of her head, well, it felt a little like love. We parted with another tender kiss, soft as a baby's cheek, a baby's tongue.

"I never had a martini before," she said sleepily, boozily.

"I love that whirling underwear," I replied boozily, sleepily.

Each into our healthy SELFs, sex-OBJECTs to each other, we parted.

The next Monday afternoon she and I met on Emerson, and she had a few questions: Was I married or engaged or in a relationship? I hesitated. "Hide it and you're dead," she said. So I answered the questions about my relationship with Berry. "You gonna tell her?"

"I don't know." Guilt rushed up, spilled all over. I thought to myself that I'd better not see Jill again, and if so why should I even think of telling Berry? I'd loved Berry for a long time and with a terrific intensity and depth. Things were rocky, but they would smooth out, as they had in a small way in a phone call the night before, at the end of the weekend, although we'd both avoided asking the terrifying question, what we'd each been "busy" with. Jill was new. The sex had been great, our selves big and hot and able to move wetly hard against each other. The love was new, shallow, with little momentum, and could be stopped now with little loss. I said, "I haven't thought about it."

"You better." She sighed. "It's tough for me too. But I've been through the ringer with men, and now with all this other stuff I don't want to get hurt in the near future. I'm really attracted to you."

Despite my feelings about Berry, and realizing that if I wasn't going on with this I'd better not rev it up, I revved it up with the truth, saying, "And I'm attracted to you. Like a damn magnet."

"Yeah. Guys make me feel so frisky about sex. But don't hold your breath. It may never happen again."

"Who said it would?"

She smiled, her eyes sparkling with mischief. Punching me playfully on the deltoid, but so hard that I winced, she said, "*Me*."

LATE ONE CRISP AFTERNOON in mid-October I sat in my cramped office up under the eaves of Toshiba with Christine, my blond Lady in Black. I would be on call all night long. That morning as I had driven the country road in my old Mustang convertible with the top down, under the pleached arbor of seared red sumac and blared yellow birch, acorns falling amidst the squashed squirrels, I felt angry that I couldn't be out playing in this day so full of chilled hope and possibility but had to be locked up with 350 lunatics. Cherokee hadn't called back, and I found myself thinking that this was not only okay but good, that his Latent Negative Transference toward me was maturing, and that he'd show up again when it was ripe, starting to turn to Latent Positive. Shimmering in and out of possibility was the helpfulness of the Borderline Theory. Not the clearly ridiculous stick figures, no, but rather the idea that, as with a spoiled child, you had to be cruel to be kind. Being nice to borderlines hadn't worked; Heiler firmness had started to.

Autumn was the debut of a series of international borderline meetings. Blair had flown off to Frankfurt for a conference on the psychopathology of immigration into Germany, entitled "Borderline Germans and German Borderlines." He'd left Solini and me in charge of Emerson. Before he left he had done stick figures for us and Hannah, figures and an equation: SELF

= POWER. *MORE* SELF = *MORE* POWER. Looking down at Henry and me, Blair had said, "Don't be pussies. Just Do It." Clearly Blair's own power in Misery came from a pristine and relentless SELF-love.

Since my first session with Christine, when she'd threatened suicide and I'd chased her to the tennis court and she'd said she'd rather talk to a mortician, things had gone well. Using Malik, I'd been more or less human with her. She'd stopped talking about suicide, dumped her boyfriend Rocco, and was taking tennis lessons. I'd asked her why she always dressed in black, as if in mourning.

"I *am* in mourning. For my father, and for men in general."

"Men in general?" I'd asked.

"My problem is I see the *potential* in men. I never only see what's there, I see what *could* be there. In every relationship, I try like hell to help men to fulfill that potential, and I'm always disappointed. Like with you."

By the time Malik had left, she had gotten a lot better, and since she was a lot better, her insurance had started to hassle me. I kept getting calls from a young-sounding woman—a girl, really—her "case manager" in Tulsa who demanded to know increasingly personal details about Christine: Was she having sex with her boyfriend? If she was depressed, why wasn't she on drugs? Couldn't it all be PMS?

On the basis of my answers, the teenybopper in Tulsa would authorize another two sessions at a time. It was infuriating. One day I said to her:

"You're making it impossible for me to do psychotherapy with her."

"Yeah, I know," the girl said, her chewing gum snapping loudly. "We don't like to pay for psychiatrists to talk to people anymore."

"What do you mean?"

"We onny pay psychiatrists to hand out drugs."

"Well, who the hell are people supposed to talk to?"

"Gotta putchu on hold."

I fought; the girl in Tulsa won. Christine's insurance no longer paid for therapy. She paid Misery herself, a reduced fee. If patients knew how much their insurance companies knew about their personal lives—their spouses and children, their sex lives, their finances, everything really—and how all this data was just lying there on big computers available to millions of great Americans, would they allow it? Which is why, Malik said, lawyers never used their insurance to pay for their psychotherapy and insisted no record be kept of their visits—which, of course, was against the law.

Therapy with Christine was hard. She was a fantastic weeper, like my mom. She'd spend the first five minutes sizing me up, and then talk about her newly dead father and other men and start to weep. She would weep for at least the first half hour, two lines of mascara streaking down her cheeks as if in a sad race. Five minutes from the end the weeping would stop, the makeup would be blotted into raccoon eyes and, knowing we had only five minutes left, she would demand to know why I wasn't helping her. Every time she left, she made me feel like a failure. She was my last patient on Tuesday, and the rest of every Tuesday I spent awash in guilt that I had let her down. Tuesday nights were hell.

I'd resisted seeing Christine in terms of the Borderline Theory. It would be like applying Heiler to your child. Yet now, staring at her, a bleached blond Madonna sitting there dressed all in black—from the tip of her black pointy shoes through her black skirt and suit jacket and up to her black beret aslant over her freckled face, encircling her bleached blond hair like a hellish halo, her black mascara and dark lipstick and nail polish, and her legs in black tights not only crossed but recrossed toe-under-ankle—watching her go in an instant from rage to tears and back to rage, it was hard not to notice that she fit many of the Krotkey Factors, hard to resist the idea that here before me was no normal neurotic but a BPO with HF—Hysterical Features—and also with the classic Borderline Sign, BTP—Black Toenail Polish.

"I'm totally stressed out!" she cried. "Why won't you give me Valium?"

"You smoke pot and drink every day, and you think I'd give you Valium?"

"I smoke dope because you won't! Why?"

"Why yourself?"

"I just asked you that. What's wrong with you today?" Suddenly she smiled coyly. "I've started dating Dr. Arnold Bozer. Your colleague?"

Arnie Bozer was the optimistic blockhead from the wooden Midwest who'd asked me for Christine's name and number. Just that afternoon in Resident Support Group, Arnie had announced, excitedly, "I've started my psychoanalysis with Dr. Schlomo Dove. I went to his home office for the first time this morning and lay down on his couch. Holy moley, you shoulda heard my first associations!"

None of us asked to hear Arnie's associations.

At the end of the Resident Support Group, Arnie had taken me by the elbow, like a guy trying to sell you a chicken or something, and said, "Roy, I just wanted to tell you you're doing a great job with your patient Chrissy."

"How do you know that, Arnie?"

"I'm dating her. A really nice gal."

Now Christine was stroking the outside of her thigh with an index finger whose nail was the dark shade of venous blood. "Arnie and I made love last night for the first time. *Fannn*tastic. I'm used to guys who just want to fuck, but he kisses great. Said he wanted to make love *with* me, not *to* me."

She stared, challenging me. I felt that radar, scanning my weak spots. Classic borderline. Tightly, I said, "So what did you do?"

"Do?"

"Sexually." She smiled. I blushed.

"You're blushing!"

"Am not." A bead of sweat slid down my forehead into my eyes.

"Think I don't know that you're attracted to me? That first day, the sexual vibes in the air?" I said nothing, sensing now the fierce hunger of the borderline. "Can't you say *anything*? You're acting so weird today. *Why?*"

Okay. It's every man for himself. *I'm* not sick, *she* is. Be firm. With a cut of Heiler anger, I said, "Why are you always trying to manipulate *me*?"

"Me manipulate *you*? Jesus Christ!" She uncrossed her legs. "I'm leaving." She got up, went to the door, and grasped the doorknob. "And this time I won't be back. I'll get what I need from Arnie. He has potential. You don't. Your heart is a block of ice." She turned quickly and opened the inner door and marched out. Or tried to, for she forgot that there was an outer door too, to soundproof us from the Bozers in the hallways. She bashed her face into it, and cried out in pain. She put her hand to her nose, checked her fingers for blood, and found it. "Terrific—a bloody nose. And still no Kleenex!" She stormed out, slamming the door behind her, about a three on the Heiler scale.

Should I chase her? No. She's not ruining *my* Tuesday night, hell no.

My night was hellish nonetheless, in all the ways that humans can be hellish around their health. It's nerve-racking to be alone in charge of a mammoth mental hospital at night, all the while sensing that something is deeply amiss in nature and not quite knowing what. For several hours Viv had me running all over the place tending to emergencies, doing admissions, and answering phone calls from anyone on the planet who, as they sensed in their bones the sinister darkness of autumn and saw with more fear than romance the full moon rise, heard the murmur of mental illness and dialed toll-free to Misery. Finally, some godless hour long after midnight, as I was walking through the parking lot outside of the Farben, Viv beeped me:

"Emerson-Two, Cowboy. Zoe pulled out her feedin' tube."

Zoe was in bad shape. Blair Heiler had restricted her from jogging. In retaliation, Zoe had cut herself and tried to throw herself through the plate-glass window between the living room and the nursing station. Without telling her, Blair replaced the glass with Plexiglas so that the next time Zoe jumped into what she thought was glass, she just bounced, much to his satisfaction. From that humiliating bounce on, Zoe had refused food entirely. Blair had force-fed her through a feeding tube. Her weight had plummeted to seventy-three pounds. Her electrolytes were so screwed up that she was dazed and vomiting and in danger of kidney and liver failure and death. I still felt a special link to Zoe—my first inpatient—and was scared for her. I'd urged

Blair to transfer her out to a medical hospital. He had refused, and laid down the law: force-feedings by feeding tube. Now, for Zoe to miss even one feeding might be catastrophic. The tube had to stay in.

Reluctantly I turned around, and slowly, heavily, feeling really pissed off at the huge effort that replacing her feeding tube would require, I started walking back through the woods toward Emerson.

"Tough night?" said a voice at my elbow. I turned. L. A. Malik, in white short-sleeve sport shirt and khaki pants, munching soy nuts. He looked fit and tan. His tone was concerned.

"What are you doing here?" I asked.

"Hung around to talk to the guys, after the AA meeting." It was almost two. The meeting ended at nine.

"That's a long hang-around."

"Not when you're with your buddies." He was not smiling. The only time I had seen him since being with Heiler was a few weeks before, when he and I had played tennis. I was the better tennis player, but his persistent, energetic style pissed me off, and somehow he beat me in straight sets. Afterward he'd been somber, even distant, and had started to just walk away.

"Wait. You're not gonna ask me how things are going with Heiler?" I'd asked.

"Don't have to. See you around."

"What do you mean?"

"Y'can tell everything about a guy," he'd said, "by how he plays a *sport*."

"Gotta go," I said now. He asked if he could come with. I said okay.

We walked down the winding road, several arms' lengths apart and in an awkward silence, our cartoon puffs of breath empty, past the handsome nineteenth-century brick buildings, mostly quiet and dark, around the head of the lake, which was calm and yet, in its moonlit, quicksilvered dark, ominous. As we came over the last hill toward Emerson, the sheer surface of the night was broken, first by screams, and then, as we turned the last corner at the edge of the lake, by light, for many windows were still lit up. In the chill autumn moonlight the new brass plaque over the lintel gleamed: BORDERLINE HOUSE.

As we climbed up through the wooden-railed stairwell, the enveloping shouts and screams made it feel like we were in the warp of a nightmare. We stopped on the landing of Emerson 2. Sounds of shouting, angry people surrounded us, slipping out under the door, raining down from Psychosis above, blasting up from Depression below. The Split Risk sign, previously a temporary thing made of cardboard and stuck to the door with tape, was now a small brass plaque screwed in. Carefully I unlocked the door. The living room was packed with my patients, pacing, growling, shouting, threatening.

"And now, folks, the Dickhead of the Decade, Doctor Roy G. . . ."

Silence, one of, Could It Be?

"Dr. Malik, I presume?" Mr. K. asked.

"Malik!" Thorny cried. "Hot damn!"

As the patients flocked around him, I walked to the Quiet Room. A pathetic sight. Zoe was faceup on the mattress, tied down in four-point restraints, moaning. She was so emaciated, barely hidden by a loose tank top with a picture of Snoopy, that I could see, as if on X ray, the clavicle, acromion, the coracoid process. The fatty breast tissue had been mostly reabsorbed, an attempt by the body to find sustenance.

All at once I felt immense fatigue. I was tired of dealing with all the shit of the night, and angry and disgusted at having to put a new feeding tube down.

"Sorry, Zoe, but I have to put a feeding tube down."

"No!" she cried. The struggle began. The mental health worker held her head still; I put Lubafax on the green tube and put it into her nose. A feeding tube is easy if the patient will swallow it down; if not, it's hell. The tube popped back out. I put it in. Out. In. Amazing, her strength. Out. "You can control yourself, you can eat—why won't you?"

"Because!"

"Why?" I shouted, losing it. "*Why?*"

Suddenly she quieted, looking past me, as if stunned. I turned.

Malik was in the doorway, staring at us.

Looking at him, I too was stunned, and fell silent. His face was filled with sorrow. He glanced at me. I felt a rush of shame. Not that he made me feel ashamed for what I was doing. Rather, I had a sense of him taking in the scene as a whole. Not Zoe and the mental health worker and me, but, somehow, the squalor of one human being tied down like an animal in a white harsh box of a room, in pain, part of the pain being inflicted by two other human beings, untied, but just as sorrowfully caught up in the squalor. He seemed to have entered full into the scene, and yet to have stepped back from it too. In his sorrow I could see his seeing it in every particular, and yet as part of a whole world that had somehow against its natural inclination gotten perverted.

He stood there, still, for the longest time—the other Emersonians were standing, still, behind him—his stillness not only making this perverted piece of reality whole, but his still center like the mystery called "the eye of the storm," being a center of reality, drawing everything to it, expanding everything from it, making every everything, from the storm to the mystery, more real. Muffled screams came down from above, and up from below.

"Mind if I come in, Zoe?" he asked.

"No."

Malik came in and stood against a wall. "Mind if I sit down?"

"No."

He slid down the wall and perched on his heels, in that universal posture men take when they are finally ready to talk. "Pretty rough, eh?"

Her lips trembled. Her starved eyes filmed with tears. It was that "click" I'd seen him have with people—the one I too had had with Zoe that first night on call. I realized that I'd never seen Blair Heiler have this "click" with anyone. With alarm, I realized that since that one time with Zoe, I'd never had it again. Zoe clenched her teeth and said, "Tell them to leave."

Malik looked at me and the mental health worker. We left and walked through the clustered patients, back to the nursing station. For the first time in a long time, there was not a sound on Emerson 2.

"ARE YOU SAYING that Blair willfully mistreats patients?" I asked Malik.

It was almost four in the morning. We sat in the nursing station. Zoe had eaten and was asleep. The hall was quiet.

" 'Course not. Heiler believes the theory—that's his problem. Deep down he feels trapped in himself, an object to others. He doesn't feel things much, so he provokes intense feeling in others, to feel a little. He never feels *with*. Theories about people are great, to protect you from being with people. The poor guy thinks that the way to be loved is by what he does, not who he is. The report card, not the kid bringing it home. The Nobel Prize, not how his own kids don't know him. It's classic American, it's Ike White, and man it is deadly. There's never a reason to treat patients cruelly. *Never*."

"What happened?" I asked, picking up on something.

Our eyes locked in. He nodded. "Good, *real* good." He sighed. "My first year, when I worked here with Heiler, I got into myself and Heiler big-time. He hooks people like us—competitive, high-achiever types. I was still drinking, treating people pretty bad. And then, this one patient of mine—" He choked up, closing his eyes, breathing deeply to get control. "One day in my office, I trashed her. She ran out, slammed the door. On the way back to Emerson, in the tunnels, well . . . she looped her belt over a pipe and hung herself."

"Oh my God."

"Yeah. Still hurts. Bad." He wiped his nose and took off his tinty glasses, squinted like a mole in the light, and wiped the tears off the lenses with the tail of his sport shirt. "Haven't had a drink since. But it's hard to make amends to the dead. So . . ." He reached out and put his hand on my shoulder. It felt hot. "Your patients are worse, a lot worse. And worse is worse, not bullshit better—you know that now, right?"

Suddenly I saw it: Zoe was worse and Thorny was worse and Mary Megan was a lot worse and Cherokee and Christine were worse—worse than worse, maybe gone!—and Berry was going, and the only ones not worse were Mr. K., who was a half-pint low on frontal lobes, and Jill, who was high on temporals. "Yes, I know that."

"Sure you do." He rubbed my shoulder, then let go his grasp. My shoulder felt warm, as if he hadn't let go. He put his amber glasses back on.

"But what can I do about it?"

"Lie to him."

"Lie to him?"

"Lying to supervisors—key concept in learning psychiatry. Listen up: You've been lying to patients and being truthful to doctors, right?" I nodded. "Reverse it. Lie to the doctors and be truthful with the patients. What a radical idea, eh?" We laughed. "And when he's off at one of these bullshit meetings, discharge like crazy."

"Into the garbage!"

"There you go. Jeez, it's late. Bronia will kill me. Tough?" His eyes rolled. "We're flying to Tel Aviv tonight, for a month." He stretched, and looked out at the living room. About a third of the patients were sitting there, wide awake. "What the hell are they doing up at this hour?" I told him about the big Department of Defense study, which caused insomnia in some Emersonians and narcolepsy in others. Malik said, "Stop the drugs. You gotta."

"I can't. The nurses give them their meds."

"Yeah, well, I betcha Mr. K.'s doin' good though, right?"

"Yeah. It's strange, but he's doing great."

"Let's go." We went to see him. He was sleeping peacefully. Malik woke him up, took out a mother-of-pearl pillbox and asked Mr. K. to take a pill. Mr. K. opened his mouth and Malik popped it in. Mr. K. swallowed it, and smiled. "Open your mouth." Mr. K. opened his mouth. Malik gestured me to look in. Nothing. "Tongue up on the roof of your mouth." Mr. K. put his tongue up on the roof of his mouth. Nothing. "Pill." Mr. K. produced the pill. Magic. Malik asked him, "Ever try to teach that to other patients?"

"In the fifties, when the major tranquilizers came in, I taught a lot. I enjoy teaching. Shall I take it up again?"

"Talk to Dr. Basch." We walked out. "For decades he's tongued pills, avoiding every major assault of the drug docs. Get him to teach the others."

"Heidelberg West, Cowboy. The Lady Who Eats Metal Objects just swallowed the charge nurse's car keys and you gotta get her to throw 'em back up."

Our walk back up the hilly moonlit road to the Farben retraced our steps geographically but felt profoundly different—we were buddies once again. Malik's meticulously restored antique VW bus sat in the parking lot. Under the harsh argon its dents stood out in high relief.

"So," I said, yawning, "we tell the truth to patients, lie to Heiler, and get Mr. K. to teach everybody to tongue their meds. It's not going to be easy."

"Yeah, but because Heiler's got all different kinds of people under one roof in the name of 'borderline,' they can come together as a real team! Once they sense you're with 'em, once they're less foggy from the drugs, they'll start to play off their differences, and there's a lotta good energy in that! They'll pull together and do good. I bet you can even do LAMBS again without that jackass noticing. Talk about exciting!"

The puffs of his breath seemed alive, the words in them exciting the molecules to dance the fine edge between water and air. How excited he was, his sharp eyes blinking, his smile broad! How he loved people! I could see, in this thirty-some face, the shy thirteen-year-old Chicago kid who—locked up in math and science and isolated from his family and from girls, his only real friends being the elephants and their keepers in the Lincoln Park Zoo—had found a way to be with others as buddies and had gotten so excited about it that all these years later he was out under a full moon just before dawn in a forlorn parking lot of a mental hospital hopping up and down like a lunatic.

"Lincoln Park Zoo?" I asked, realizing that I had just felt that "click" with him, my own radar locking in. The words seemed to hang there, condensing in the crystalline puff of my breath before dissolving in the solution of the air, easing away with all the languorous freedom of a sleepy baby's sigh.

He "clicked" back. "Sleep tight, sweetheart, and lie like hell tomorrow."

"Can I?"

"Can't not. Once y'sense the truth, kid, the false loses its grip on ya."

He picked a piece of litter off the asphalt and put it in his pocket, climbed up into the bus and rolled down the window. Leaning an arm on the sill like a friendly trucker, he offered me a Stim-U-Dent and stared down at me for a second. Nodding, he asked, "Authentic?"

"You mean my authentic self?"

"No, the opposite."

"What opposite? There is no opposite to self."

"There you go! 'Self' is made up of all the non-'self' stuff."

"Like what?"

"Like, for instance, all this!" He swept his arms around the landscape, from the dark west toward the glint of sunrise in the east. "The whole damn world! Haha!"

"I'll try."

"You do better if you don't," he said, grinning, "like in *sports*!"

"Pray for me in Israel, Malik, will you?" I said sarcastically.

The only sound was the hum of the argon lights, high over our heads.

"I will, Roy. None of us are here for long."

He turned the key. The old bus cleared its throat and rolled off down the hill out of Misery, and for the first time I noticed his license plate:

BREATHE

What the hell does that mean? I wondered as I stood there working the beveled edge against my gum. The stretching sensation and crisp mint taste fit the still-clear realness of my friend, freeing up from metaphor the actual autumn night, the actual strength of the sun.

Six

"LYING TO SUPERVISORS?" Henry Solini shouted.

"Learning psychiatry!" I shouted back over the loud music.

"Learning psychiatry?" he cried out.

"Lying to supervisors!"

It was the next day, after work. Solini, Hannah, and I were sitting in The Misery, a funky bar down the hill from the hospital. Henry and I were sharing a pepperoni pizza. Hannah was picking at a Greek salad without feta. Shouting over Marley's "Natty Dread," I told them what Malik had said.

Ever since Heiler had accused Henry publicly of being "gay-latent," he had gradually imploded. Like a time-lapse film of a flower packing back up into its bud, Henry had gotten compacted in on himself: shoulders more hunched, head tucked between, nose and lips and eyebrows somehow squinched down and tucked into the face, as if for protection from a rain of blows. Now he sat blinking his eyes, moving his hands slowly, like a cat its paws at the end of a long run of purring, and asked, "Telling the truth to patients?"

"Exactly."

He blinked again, and his eyebrows seemed to unfurl from the creases of his brow, his chin lifted, lifting his nose, and his eyes seemed to blossom, bright and mischievous, as if suddenly he had the idea of planting a bomb under Ideal Cleaners in Mandan, North Dakota. "Enough of this shit," he said. "We got no choice. We're getting killed, and the patients are worse."

"Which, of course," Hannah said, "may be better." She tucked a stray lock of raven's hair back over an ear, an ear graced with a diamond earring that turned the sorry bar's light into rainbows darting here and there. Of all of us, Hannah had been treated worst by Heiler. Her patients down in Depression were doing astonishingly badly, her marriage to Billy ben Lube was borderline violent, but Hannah was doing astonishingly well. Day after day she almost glowed. "Psychiatry," she said now, "is built on truth. There's no way I could lie to him. Those eyes. They see right through you. Like radar. Could you look him in those eyes and lie, Roy?"

I realized it would be difficult. "Maybe, maybe not."

Her own eyes rolled up to a fake Tiffany with a Clydesdale marching around it. "Even if I could lie to Blair, I couldn't lie to Ed Slapadek—and they're tennis partners, so he'd tell him. You should see *his* eyes. He not only knows what I'm thinking now, he knows what I'll be thinking next!" Her eyes stayed up. I winked at Henry.

"It's a good thing Malik was just joking," I lied to her.

"Joking?" Hannah asked.

"Lying to supervisors? Who wouldn't think that was a joke?"

"No one," Solini said, getting my message. "No one at all."

"Truth is, Hannah," I went on, "Malik must have been using the concept of lying unconsciously, as a kind of reaction formation to show how we have to be absolutely scrupulous about telling the truth."

She pondered this. I could almost see the words clicking into place, little keys fitting little locks in the labyrinth of the Borderline Theory in her mind.

"Yes," she said weightily, "that does make sense. Besides, even a little white lie cripples me with guilt. Ed Slapadek is excellent on Jewish guilt."

" 'Guiltiness,' " Solini sang out, danced over to the jukebox, and put on the Marley song of that name. Out on the dance floor, shuffling his arms like the pistons of a steam train, his face squinching up in delight, he lip-synched the words.

Solini's new girlfriend Nique Nique came in and joined him in dancing. She was a tall, powerfully built, ebony-black Jamaican he'd met through the Misery cafeteria workers he jammed with. I felt relieved that he and I had easily lied to Hannah, but I also felt sad that she'd declared so clearly against what I now saw as the inevitable ambiguity of the merely human, and declared herself for the Heiler machine. Holding my beer, I joined the two dancers as we, white, white, and black, transformed our chilly and insular bar into a warm, sun-filled one alive with revolution, decades back, in Trenchtown, Jamaica.

. . .

AS THE CHILL of October congealed into the cold of November, as Solini and I would walk *sschlwoosh! sschlwoosh!* through the fallen leaves of Misery, kicking them up in puffs of snapped bright colors into the crackling sunlight, while we might have felt some fear, we felt little doubt. We had no choice. While we might not yet know what to do with our patients, we knew what not to: we would not be cruel to them. Feeling choiceless, we felt free.

Heiler was away the rest of that week at meetings of the International Dissociation Association, first in Germany doing "Borderlines on the Autobahn" and then on to Israel doing "Borderline Jews and Jewish Borderlines"—the same lecture he'd given in Germany but with the word "German" changed to "Jew" throughout—so we had a whole week of telling the truth to our patients without worrying about lying to him. It started with Thorny's untied shoelace.

Thorny had been threatening to kill me. Now, as I sat with him on Emerson, his scarred face looked particularly nasty. Even his teeth looked scary. I was on guard. He bent to tie his shoelace. Tying a shoelace is not something you think about—thinking about it makes it harder. Thorny tied his shoelace painstakingly, thinking about each loop and bow and pull. When he finished, the lace was loose and clearly wouldn't hold. Looking up, he saw me staring and he flushed.

"My parents never bothered to teach me. I learned by watchin' other kids, in gym class 'n' such. I tie 'em like I'm lookin' in a mirror . . . dickhead."

"Want me to teach you?"

He stared at me suspiciously, wondering if this was a Heiler technique. Then he nodded. And so I taught him. Or tried to, for with him sitting across from me, mirroring me, I started trying to mirror him, which didn't work. We had to sit beside each other. Trying not to think, I made the ties and he followed. We did it over and over, making those child's rabbit ears of bows, then making them vanish, like magic. With each success we chuckled, sharing the child's sense of wonder at this tight but slippable knot. He sat back, looking with satisfaction at our work. We were sitting side by side facing out the window at the lake, the woods, the mountains alive with dying leaves, chlorophyll receding, revealing the husks of fire. He started to talk. It was pure Malik: two passengers on a train.

"Imagine what that was like, Doc, goin' to Princeton without bein' able to tie your damn shoes? Freshman year was hell."

"Yeah, I know. I felt that way too, my first year at Harvard."

"You too?" he asked. "A red-hot like you?"

"You bet."

"That ain't too convincin', Doc."

"Dickheads Ain't Too Convincin'."

He burst out laughing, but then his face fell. "Yeah, but that was the fork in the damn path. I went down. Guys like you went up."

"Why?" I asked, realizing as I said it that it was a Heiler word, one I'd used with viciousness on Thorny before. But now I'd said it sincerely. He went on in the same friendly tone. So it's not the word, I thought, it's what the word travels on. Heiler, on guard, put his patients on guard. If I stayed authentic, I needn't be so careful about what I was saying. A relief.

"Compared to guys like you I felt so damn inferior—Princeton took me 'cuz Daddy was rich—so I tried to find somethin' where I could stand out. I joined the Appalachian Mountain Club, rock-climbin'—all so's I could pound six pitons into the ceiling of my room and hang my bed from 'em. Things fell apart."

"Tell me about it."

Easily, honestly, and in a way that soon had us both laughing at the absurdity of it all, he did. He'd gotten into booze, then narcotics. Opiate in cough medicine was his drug of choice. He'd learned to cough. When he'd run out of emergency room doctors to dupe, he bought a dog and trained *it* to cough, duping veterinarians for dog cough medicine. All along the way picking fights with bigger men, continually getting beaten up, thrown out of bars, finding himself at dawn lying in desolate parking lots, in ditches.

Listening, I asked myself: Why him and not me? Why, at the end of the day, do I take my keys and let myself out, locking him in? Our histories were not dissimilar—good genes, busy, battle-weary, obsessive fathers and bored, battlewise, depressed mothers, bright boyhoods of sports and girls and A's on report cards—similar until we hit college and I dug in and he flipped out. Years later I'm locking him up for the night. Had I myself made myself "succeed"? Had he himself made himself "fail"? Was he defective, I not? Born and raised him, would I be him? The Borderline Theory would say that his sick SELF was his fault, my less sick SELF my triumph. What horseshit. All at once I saw Thorny not as basically sick, but as basically healthy.

My rotation on Emerson would end in six weeks, just before Thanksgiving. My final week, Heiler would be away in Kuala Lumpur doing "Borderlines of the Pacific Rim." Thorny and I agreed he would leave before I did. He'd have to find a buddy, a place to live, some work.

"A job? Who'd hire a dickhead like me?"

"Not necessarily a job. Work. You don't need money. Volunteer."

"Like my *mom?*" He blinked, ran his thumbs up and down his suspenders, and then, shyly, revealed his secret passion. "Toxic waste?" I nodded, knowing he was thinking of his father, whom he referred to as "the Great Polluter." He licked his lips. "Ozone holes!" He was grinning. His face looked open and powerful. But then fear drifted in. "Shit. Leavin' here scares me."

"We'll work on your fear, together. Like your shoelaces. Deal?"

"Dickheads Make Deals!" He opened the door. "But you gotta take me off the meds—they make me crazy—like all my goddamn narcotics or something."

"Talk to Mr. K. He's running a Department of Defense Drug Support Group."

"Him? You jokin'?"

I looked down at his shoelaces, as did he. I looked back up at him, meeting his eyes. I asked, "Still tied?"

"Still tied." And then he got it, that now we were rebels together. "Mr. K.?"

"A great American. Send in the next victim."

The next Emersonian came in, and the next, and while I still didn't know what to say to them that might help, I focused on not using Borderline Technique, trying to not be cruel to them, to not do much of anything to them. It helped. Their radar picked up my trying hard to do nothing to them, and they tried hard to do nothing to me. We shared a sense of relief.

Last, I went to see Zoe in her room. She had been doing better recently and eating solid food, but she refused to see me. I felt ashamed at the way I had screamed at her in the Quiet Room that night with Malik. He'd suggested I apologize. In my many years of medical training, no one had ever suggested that I, a doctor, apologize to a patient. Zoe lay on her bed in jeans and a sweatshirt with Nelson Mandela smiling against the colors of the African National Congress. Knees up like a teenager, she was reading *Catcher in the Rye*. She stared at me skeptically.

"I'm sorry, Zoe. I lost it, and was cruel to you. I made a mistake."

"Get out."

Feeling hurt, I did. Had I lost her? Lost Cherokee and Christine too? Berry? I drove home overwhelmed with a weird exhaustion, as if to be a shrink were an unnatural act, a movement decidedly against human nature. The lines on the road home wavered as I tried to keep my lids up until I crashed into bed before eight and fell through that membrane to the sleep of the dead.

Phone. I struggled up from the deep, not knowing which country I was in, France or Turkey or China, let alone in what bed.

"Zoe wants to talk to you," the night nurse on Emerson said. It was eleven that same night. I said okay, to put her on. "She won't talk to you on the phone. Afraid you'll hang up. She wants to talk to you in person."

Heiler would have slammed that one out of the park. "Be right there."

Zoe sat in the living room, ashen and scared. "I . . . I just wanted to say . . . that . . . I accept your apology. And that we can start to work together again."

"Great. Glad to hear it."

"Your cruelty wasn't your fault. I mean you've only been a psychiatrist a few months. You're still learning, struggling with incompetence, right?"

"Who isn't?"

Startled, she stared at me quizzically. "Really." She yawned. "Anyway that's all I wanted to say. Go home to your wife and kids."

NO ONE KNOWS what a shrink is doing behind closed doors. Solini and I found it easy to be not cruel to our patients without anyone knowing.

The week that Heiler was away, we worked hard to un-Heiler. It was astonishing to see just how quickly we and our patients shifted from adversaries to allies. Soon our patients, no longer under attack, no longer attacked; no longer humiliated, they no longer humiliated; treated more humanely, they acted more humanely. It was all so obvious—but what Malik called "the elusive obvious." Henry and I soon had a sense that we were riding some pretty strong unseen forces, much like, as we walked toward Emerson those bright crisp fall mornings, we'd see the last fugitive leaves spinning in scarlet and gold whirlwinds, riding the unseen breeze.

That Friday afternoon Heiler was due back from Germany. I was scheduled to see him at six that night, to report on the three wards of Emerson. As the time approached, I realized that, face-to-face, under pressure from those blue jolts of eyes, I might not be able to lie. At six sharp I called him in his office. My heart was racing. I said, "I can't make it to supervision."

"*Why?*"

"I'm beat, and Berry and I are leaving early tomorrow morning to hike."

"To *hike*?" he said derisively. "You realize that while you're out hiking, other psychiatry residents will be in their labs, working? Getting ahead?"

"I need to take care of myself, that's—"

"Have a 'nice' hike," he said and hung up.

The next afternoon Berry and I were taking a break from our day-hike up nearby Mount Jackson, in the Presidential Range of the White Mountains. The view was exquisite, the long bright rainbow of autumnal color stretching west at the bottom of the clear cold sky, the stretch coalescing the spectrum into a smudged pastel and then into an imagined smudge over an imagined Lake Champlain and, even, an imagined curve of the planet itself. Having been stuck behind the long caravan of Winnebagos and Airstreams fighting their way up the Kancamagus Highway to "see the leaves," having found a break in the caravan of hikers clomping up the mountain, we were finally getting a small hit of nature. The air was that chill mountain variety. Our sweat soon cooled.

As had our relationship. Each of us was more edgy and guarded, neither mentioning what we were doing in the increasing number of nights when we were no longer seeing each other. I had seen Jill a few times more, at home and, with Viv's vigilance, in the on-call room, and it had been the same hard run of martinis or champagne lubricating frank, wild, mutually self-centered sex. The gap between Berry's days singing nursery rhymes and mine shouting down borderlines had widened. But this weekend was a chance to heal. So far, so good.

I had told her about Heiler, and now, sitting side by side in the nostalgic lift of the vista, I said, "But I don't think I *can* lie to him, face-to-face. When I'm with him, I get so damn flustered, I feel totally unsure of myself. I can't lie to him, but I can't tell the truth, either. I'm screwed."

"Who is?" Berry asked.

"I am."

"Who?"

"Me. What do you mean who? Me. Myself. I."

She smiled. "So that's what you've got to do."

"What?"

"Get him to talk about himself, and you won't have to lie. If he's into himself, he'll never even get around to you."

"HimSELF! Of course."

" 'Male station-identification.' Once he settles into using the word 'I,' you've got him. Like I was just doing with you."

"With me?"

"Asking you about yourself, about how you're going to deal with Heiler—your hopes, your fears. Taking care of this relationship. Being curious about your experience, drawing you out. How often do you do that with me?"

"But you always seem so *interested* in hearing about me."

"See?" She smiled and got up, brushing off her jeans. "Let's go. We've got another hour or so to the top."

"Wait. You're *not* interested in me? It's a lie?"

"Who's asking?"

"What do you mean 'who'? *I* am!"

The personal pronoun came out like a bullet, echoed off a rockface and dropped. I shivered, sensing that maybe she was right, that there were depths of self-centeredness in me invisible to me, coming not only from my own decades of life, but from millennia of manhood. Depths of self unseen by self? Unable to be seen by self? Was this what Malik had meant?

Staring at her, I sensed that for once I was taking in who she actually was, from the purple bandanna tied around her hair, through her brown eyes set in her long face and her plump lips and swan neck and purple Pendleton work shirt and patched jeans, to the leaf-red laces on her hiking boots and the searing yellow of the birch leaf stuck to one sole. Startling, how new she seemed right there right then—new yet known, like an old friend you haven't seen in years.

"I get it," I said. "So tell me about yourself."

"Maybe I will," she said coyly. "But now we hike." She smiled, took my hand, and pulled me to my feet. We started off up the crowded old trail.

Later that night, after a dazzling dinner at the Wildcat Inn in Jackson, we hiked, aching, up the narrow tilted stairs to our room under the eaves. The floor slanted in one direction and the ceiling in another and the mattress in a third, but we were happy and tipsy and full. I undressed her, unbuttoning, unclasping, nuzzling, overwhelmed by how newly attractive she seemed, her eyes wet with love, her body full and soft. I was careful not to Krotkey.

Lying side by side, cooling in the cooling evening, listening to the sound of sawing wood coming from the other side of the thin wall—a rickety bed being severely tested by romance—and despite her carelessness with a match and candle, which had set fire to a doily—I said, "You're wonderful. I love you."

"It's so easy," she murmured, snuggling in, "when we're both just here."

I got to Emerson extra early Monday morning, and sat in the Malik rounds chair. The patients were friendly, even cheery to me. The cheerier they were, the more apprehensive I became of Heiler's seeing them so cheery.

Heiler entered and stood for a moment inside the door, staring down at us all with palpable contempt. A dismayed shake of his head seemed to set his pelvis in motion, and one leg kicked out from his hip, and then another, as he marched toward his sanctuary to masturbate the INSURANCE executives.

Suddenly Thorny was in his face, screaming—"All you are is a life-support system for a dickhead"—and Zoe too, and then all the others. To their rage, his reaction was a cruel smile. By the time he'd shut the door behind him, the ward had once again been transformed into two dozen Borderlines from Hell, the worst patients on earth, proving the Borderline Theory.

I relaxed. When Heiler was with patients, no matter how they really were, they would act toward him like classic Heiler borderlines, lurching into rage, fear, projection, and all the other Krotkey Factors. It was like the Heisenberg Uncertainty Principle: Heiler's observing destroyed the observed. Not only do psychiatrists specialize in their defects, I thought, they evoke them in their patients, creating patients whom they can then doctor, and make a good living off of. Had Ike White done that with depression? He'd given the impression of being calm and happy, interested in us, his residents, his patients, interested in living. But his calm, orderly attention had been amidst the piles of debris of his office, the buried shit of his life. The most sensitive of his patients, like Mary Megan Scorato, may have sensed it, and his lie may have depressed her more than his depression. The sonofabitch had been lying to us all. We could've taken his misery; the killer was the lie.

"THORNY'S DOING BADLY," I lied to Heiler, with Solini, that day in supervision. Hannah no longer met with us. She had supervision alone with Blair.

"Good," he said coolly. "Pretty well on schedule."

"Can't even tie his own shoes."

"Bet you had a ball, confronting him on that one." We all laughed, that hearty man-to-man laughter that Blair was really good at. "You're not being too 'nice' to him, are you?" he asked suspiciously.

I was staring down at my lap, and realized that if I looked back up into his eyes I might not be able to hide my lying, so I decided to try a Berry and ask him about himSELF: "We heard that you really kicked ass in Germany."

"You did?" he said, perking up. "From whom?"

"*Everybody*," Solini said, in on it. "It's all over Misery, what you did to Gunderson and the rest of the McLean Hospital borderline boys." These borderline researchers were Heiler's rivals, from Harvard Medical School. He was crazy with envy of them.

"Yeah, it was a dogfight, but I beat the hell out of those Harvard jerks."

"That's exactly what we heard," I said. "And Renaldo Krotkey saw it all?"

His face fell. "No. Krotkey was a no-show. Which, as far as *I* was concerned, was a brilliant way of showing his latent hostility. He sent a paper. It was so brilliant that *most* people there couldn't understand much of it."

"How much did *you* get?" I asked expectantly.

He closed his eyes. "Thirty-five percent? Maybe thirty-seven percent?"

"Incredible! You hear that, Henry?"

"Thirty-seven percent?" Henry said, awed. "I never *heard* a percentage like that."

"I know," Blair said, nodding off, eyes half closed in admiration for himSELF. But suddenly he came to and sprang back, asking me, "What about Zoe?"

Startled, worried he might find out she was eating again, I stalled for time. "She met with me twice this week."

"Too soon. Too soon for her to fall in love with you, activate the Latent Positive Transference, and get erotic. What's going on, Basch?"

"Hey, wait a sec, Roy," Solini said. "Blair, is it true that you and Renaldo Krotkey are going to be on the same borderline panel together? In Lima, *Peru?*"

"Krotkey's not a definite," he said modestly, "Krotkey's a maybe."

"Quite an honor, though," Solini said, "even to be on the same brochure?"

"Have you seen it?"

"Hey no, babe. Do you have one?"

"Do I ever." And did he ever. He rose and with that legs-shooting-out-from-hips stride crossed the office to a stack of full-color brochures. With pride he handed us each one, then two. Machu Picchu was on the cover, and in fake Mayan script was the title: "Borderline Pre-Columbians; Psycho-pathogy Among the Peruvian Indians." Heiler's photo and endless C.V. were inside.

"*Nice* photo," I said admiringly, "isn't it, Henry?"

"I never *saw* a photo like that!" he said with awe, as if at a sighting of a life-sized photo of the Virgin Mary hovering somewhere over North Dakota.

"Has to be. In the borderline field, appearance is everything. I went all out on that photo. Professional photographer. Cost a grand."

"That's all?" Henry said. Blair nodded. "Well worth it."

I noted that, while Heiler's photo was underneath Renaldo Krotkey's—Krotkey's bowling ball head covered with shocking red hair, his big bent nose, pendant lower lip, warped white collar, and severe bow tie making him look like nothing so much as a waiter in a kosher deli—it was not directly underneath. In fact, directly below Krotkey, directly above Blair, were the McLean borderline experts. With sick delight I employed Heiler cruelty:

"I didn't know that the *Harvard* experts would be there too?"

"Those fuckers. I'm going to blow them away with my drug work."

"You're presenting it?" I asked.

"Presenting the preliminary."

"But no one knows which patient is on what drug," Henry said.

"*I* do. I broke the code, for the preliminary. I call the paper, 'Being "Nice" to Borderlines: Random Blind Trials of Placedon and Zephyrill.' " He smiled. We smiled back. "I made you guys fourth and fifth authors."

"Thanks, big fella," I said, knowing how much he valued his height, which, he had informed me, was one inch greater than the tallest other borderline researcher in the world, the seemingly kind, and yet, for all the seeming, dreaded Shneero.

"Big fella, thanks!" Henry said. "I never *heard* of being an author like that."

"*I* wanted to," Heiler said. "My students' careers reflect on *me*."

The rest of the session was spent on his research and his SELF. Attuned to the word "I," we were amazed at how often Blair used it. I's popped up like little flags to stand tall in front of us, one after the other until the stuff in between got lost, as when, on Memorial Day in a cemetery, you get distracted from the graves by the flags and the flowers.

Many of the Emersonians got better, and Heiler either never noticed or figured that better was worse. It was amazing to Solini and me how, even on a matter as concrete as Zoe's gaining weight, Blair could be so blind: He never saw it. Whenever we were with Heiler, we'd massage his ego and he would fall into a narcissistic narcolepsy, a SELF-stupor, and forget about us or the patients. Occasionally we'd have to use heavier weapons. Upon his return from Peru, his SELF seemed a little damaged. We went right for it.

"No Krotkey?" I asked.

"No Krotkey. He sent another paper."

"Bet you got almost forty percent this time," Henry said, "eh, big guy?"

"At *least* forty percent, yeah." But then he attacked. "Solini. You were on call last night and you refused to admit a borderline? Great INSURANCE? A charismatic leader of a Satanic cult? Ritual *sacrifice*? Publishable! Why?"

"I don't do body parts, Blair."

"You do gay little dicks just fine. And you just hung up on her?"

"Nope, I turfed her to an Angelic cult. Down the street from McLean."

"McLean" hit Heiler hard, and he attacked me: "And you, Basch. You turfed out a borderline too? It says here she was three hundred fifty pounds. At *least* three fifty! Violent and hypersexed? Came in overdosed on Prozac?" He was almost drooling at this, the Mother of all borderlines. "Why?"

"I cured her."

"Bullshit. How?"

"Sent her home on a low-Prozac diet. Cured."

"Bull*shit*!" he cried, and picked up the census sheet. Enraged, waving it at us, he screamed, "Empty beds on *my* unit? Why?"

"These darn borderlines!" I sneered angrily. "They terminate too soon!"

"*Way* too soon!" Henry said. "Never *saw* soonness of termination like tha—"

"What's the matter with you jokers?" Heiler said suspiciously. "Solini?"

Heiler stared hard down at Solini, as if accusing him of conduct unbecoming an Armenian or something. Solini fidgeted silently. We were going under.

"INSURANCE!" I cried out. "Those INSURANCE fuckers stopped paying!"

"I never *heard* INSURANCE like that!" Solini cried.

"Don't give me that shit—I taught you guys how to do INSURANCE—"

"But when you left," I said, "they changed the payment protocols."

"What?" Heiler asked. "WhatWHAT*WHAT*?" He was screaming.

It was true. INSURANCE was fighting back. I hesitated, deliciously, letting him twist in the breeze. "Changed the protocols. Payment for borderlines is down. Payment for dissociatives is up."

"They can't do that!" Blair cried out, apoplectic.

"Life's full of little surprises," I said.

"Little surprises, yeah," Henry echoed, "and this is one."

"Get out of here, you idiots, I'll straighten those assholes out mySELF."

"That's cool," Henry said, and we left.

After that, Solini and I got more and more bold. Playing Blair like an instrument, time and again we were amazed at how sightless those blue eyes could be when focused in on himSELF. Whenever he seemed to come out of his stuporous nod and hone his razor eyes in on us, one or the other of us would play the trump card, the NPT—Nobel Prize Technique. After mentioning that we'd heard his work was Nobel Prize quality, we'd watch as he tuned out for at least five minutes and talked totally about himSELF while Henry and I floated, as nearly invisible to his mind's eye as those tiny flecks that come out in summer on the beach, coalescences in the vitreous humor, unseen but in the brightest light.

Many Emersonians were discharged. Lloyal made sure that Heiler's beds refilled quickly, so that Henry and I would be presented right away with yet another poor person labeled BPO with SOO, Something Or Other, or DD (Dissociative Disorder) with SOO. But such was our freed-up excitement, our rebelliousness, and our daring, and such was the support we felt from each other and from the spirit of Malik and from the just plain good feel we had with our patients, that we actually found ourselves looking forward to new admissions. Working like crazy, we learned to encounter a person in emotional pain, all of our senses and mainly our "sixth" on alert for what Malik had called "a mutual encounter with the psychological facts." This, according to him, might in some cases bring a "click" of understanding, that understanding prompting further understanding which would prompt still further until—like a skier leaning out over the tips of the skis—moving through and toward our understanding would generate a momentum which he called healing. Of course, a lot of our patients were out of reach of this healing—Malik had a healthy respect for how crazy, and unreachable, some people were, and for them he suggested that "if you can't help 'em, at least don't hurt 'em. Don't spread more suffering around." But with many of the others, as long as we were open to something happening and free of thought and not too focused on chasing that "click," sooner or later the "click" would be there. Then we would see that what a person in the solitude of terror had always thought of as his or her secret and unique sickness—what psychiatry labels "psychopathology"—is in fact, when opened up to plain view, not such a terrifying sickness at all and not even all that unique, but more or less commonly held, and just a part of being human. These people might tap into their childish yearning for life, might even start moving toward vitality. Then we would see that better is better, yeah.

We hadn't seen all that much healing yet, but Malik had yet to steer us wrong, and besides we'd be damned if we'd follow Heiler's orders, ever again. Not that it was easy. We were still having a bitch of a time moving out Zoe and Thorny, who were reconstituting from cruelty slowly, in fits and starts, and Mary Megan Scorato, still acutely suicidal, and of course Mr. K., who, thanks to the buoyant surgeons, was always sinking just that one little frontal lobe shy of discharge.

MARY MEGAN SCORATO was being presented by Hannah to Heiler at the final Case Conference of our Emerson rotation. It was mid-November, and in a week the three of us would be leaving Emerson, for various other rotations in Misery: I would be going to Toshiba, the Admissions Unit; Henry to Thoreau, the Freudian Family Unit; and Hannah to Heidelberg West, Psychopharmacology. Now, sitting beside each other in the conference room, Henry and I were reading a memo each of us had gotten that morning from Lloyal von Nott:

Misery Capital Campaign Luncheons

> Mount Misery is embarking on a capital campaign. Each of you will have a luncheon with Dr. Lloyal von Nott to identify any of your patients who are potential donors. You will not be asked to solicit your own patients for monies. Rest assured the contacts will be made by us.

"Give them the names of our rich patients?" I said. "Isn't that unethical?"

"So what else is new?" Henry answered.

Into the garbage.

I had been on call the night before, and at some ungodly hour I'd been called to see Mary Megan Scorato. In a panic about Heiler conferencing her the next morning, she was having fantasies about hanging herself. Staring at her, at the bags under her eyes almost as black as her grandmotherly sweater, watching a vestigial Placedon twitch slither across her cheek like a dim recollection of her beloved therapist Ike White, I sensed how deep her depression was and how far she'd fallen since Heiler's reign of terror had begun. I liked her immensely, and felt immensely sad. I wanted to help her.

"What's your worst fear about tomorrow's conference?" I asked. She sat quietly, wringing her hands, and did not answer. "Are you worried that Dr. Heiler will be nasty to you again in public?"

"No, I know from Dr. Hannah Silver that he's just trying to do the best for me."

"What, then?"

"That Dr. Heiler will discharge me."

"If there's one thing you can count on," I had said, patting her hand, "it's that he won't discharge you. You've still got plenty of time left on your insurance." This had comforted her. She thanked me as I left.

Now, we sat in the jammed conference room as Hannah presented the case. Mary Megan was brought in. Heiler took a tack I'd never seen him use before:

"Why are you still here?"

"I . . . I don't know."

"You've been here over four months, for a simple depression. *Why?*"

"I'm not feeling better. I'm thinking of killing myself."

"I doubt that. How do I know you're not just manipulating me?"

"I've never manipulated anyone. I don't want to live. I want to die."

"Sounds like manipulation to *me*." They went on like this, Heiler accusing Mary of manipulation, which made her try harder to convince him that she really *did* want to kill herself. Finally he said, "I'm discharging you tomorrow."

Silence, one of, What? Before Her Insurance Runs Out?

"Please," Mary Megan said, "please don't. I'm not ready. Hannah, please don't let them do this. It is wrong, and I'm afraid. Hannah, please?"

Hannah, shaken, said, "Oh Mary, I'm really sor—" but then she glanced at Heiler, and, a good soldier, went on, "Dr. Heiler is in charge. I'll continue with you as an outpatient, when I get back from my vacation next week."

"No!" Mary Megan shouted.

"Now, now," Heiler said. "Now, now. It'll do your SELF-confidence a world of good to get out of here. I'll write the order myself. Right now. Good-bye."

Crushed, Mary Megan was escorted from the room. Solini and I couldn't believe what had just happened.

"But she still has insurance!" I said.

"Nope. Yesterday her HMO changed the protocol. Payment ran out today."

"And you're not gonna go to bat for her?" Henry asked.

"When she's actively suicidal?" I chimed in.

"Suicidal, hell. Manipulative. Think *I* don't know when a borderline is manipulating *me*? Read my article: 'Thirteen Ways of Looking at a Borderline.' " Heiler kicked out over to the nursing station and wrote the order himself.

An hour later, with many hugs and kisses and best wishes and tears, all of us Emersonians said good-bye to Mary Megan Scorato. In her eyes was terror. I unlocked the door and helped carry her suitcases downstairs. Her husband Joey and six-year-old Down syndrome son Tommy—in that shortened face, those epicanthal-fold eyes streaming tears of joy—helped her to the aging

Isuzu whose defective roof rack had started her trip into Misery. Waving bravely, she left.

Heiler flew off for his week conferencing in the rain forest near Kuala Lumpur, where Krotkey's status had been upgraded from a "maybe not" to a "maybe." Hannah flew off for a week in Sun City, Florida, with her Holocaust survivor parents.

Solini and I, appalled and enraged, went into high gear, discharging as many of the healthier Emersonians as possible before Blair returned. Our mission was to leave as few patients as possible at Heiler's mercy after we were gone from Emerson.

By now we'd learned a great deal about how to discharge people, how to prepare them for the terrors of freedom—learned just how pragmatic an art psychiatry was—how getting someone back to the "real" world was not a matter of THEORY or TECHNIQUE or SELF or OBJECT but of the nuts and bolts of where will they live and how will they eat and what will they do all day long and who will they have for support to keep them from the killer isolation and thoughtless savagery that we have numbly come to call "civilization." Malik's LAMBS network was a blessing, and by the end of the week we had discharged almost half the Emersonians, each hooked up with a buddy.

Our greatest coup was Zoe and Thorny. Having been on Emerson so long, they were stuck tight to it. They were too opened up, too human for "normal" life: too kind to fight through traffic, too compassionate to pass a panhandler by, too believing around salesmen, not to mention religions. Their day passes into "normalcy" had made them realize how unpracticed they now were in the cruelties of daily life. Henry and I had tried everything to pry them loose. No luck. Finally I saw that to leave Mother Misery felt, for each of them, just too damn lonely.

"Henry, I've got it. Thorny and Zoe as buddies."

"Cool. Let's ask 'em."

We did. Sitting on the half-deserted ward, we watched as they turned their radars on each other, sizing each other up as potential buddies. We saw them suddenly see each other as sex OBJECTS, what Heiler had labeled the TET (Total Erotic Transference) in each of them sizzling, like meat on adjourning barbecues. Having sizzled, it quickly fizzled. Zoe said:

"I'll room with you but I won't fuck you."

"Dickheads Off the Hook!"

"If you promise to protect me from other men," Zoe said, "I'll try it."

"And I'll try it," Thorny said, "if you promise to protect me from other men too. And help keep me away from dogs and cough syrup?"

"And you've both got to find work," I said, "either for pay or volunteer."

They agreed. The deal done, they got on the phone to find an apartment.

The two of them walked out triumphantly the next morning, to cheers from us all. Henry and I called them that night at Misery Garden Apartments. Behind their dead-bolted door and barred windows, they were eating pizza and watching *Star Trek* reruns. When I asked Thorny how it was going, he said:

"Dickheads Make Great Americans!"

THE DRUG BLACKSHIRT Win Winthrop was sitting with Solini and me a few days later in the nursing station on Emerson. Win would be rotating in to take my place with Heiler in a few days, and was telling us all about "psychiatric infomatics," some computer bullshit or other that he thought was going to make him rich.

"Outside call, Cowboy. Urgent. From a psychiatrist in Kansas."

It was a staff psychiatrist at the Menninger Clinic in Topeka, Kansas.

"I believe you recently discharged a patient named Mary Megan Scorato?"

"Yes."

"She was admitted here yesterday. I'm sorry . . . there's bad news."

"What?"

"She hung herself last night."

"What?" I cried out, feeling the same sick punch in the gut I'd felt with Ike White. The Menninger psychiatrist repeated the news. Feeling sicker, I asked a few more questions, and then said, "Wait a second. Her insurance had run out. How did she pay for admission?"

"Her son paid for it, out of his own pocket."

"Her son?" Her son was six years old and had Down syndrome. Then, suddenly, I saw it all, saw all thirty-one years of it, and a chill ran through me. "You mean the son she gave up to the nuns—put up for adoption—when she was a girl?"

"That's right. She spent the day with him here, before she was admitted. He lives just outsida Topeka. I'm sorry. She seemed like a real sweetheart."

"Yeah. She is. I mean was."

I hung up. In shock, I told Solini and Win. By the end I was crying, hard, really shaking with sobs, as was Henry. We'd kind of loved her, and we were crying for her and crying with rage, at Heiler and her Health Maintenance Organization, for murdering her. We just sat there in that ridiculous cruddy nursing station and cried.

"Really rough, Roy," Win said. "Death is so final. Can we have her brain?"

"What?"

"Her brain, for the Misery Brain Bank. Errol and I are doing a new study on brain changes in borderlines on Placedon and Zephyrill. Can you get us permission from the next of kin—I guess it's her husband?"

"Get out of here."

"It may seem insensitive but brains go to mush real fast and we have to get online and tell them how to preserve it in Kansas."

"Hey, man," Solini said, "don't you have any fucking feelings at all?"

"Exactly. Feelings have no place in the science of psychiatry."

"Go fuck yourself," I said to Win. "And get the hell out of my face."

"If you won't talk to her husband, we will."

"After what Heiler did to his wife, you think the husband would give you jerks permission to grind up her brain? Are you insane?"

"Errol's an expert in permissions for brains for the Brain Bank."

"No way, man, and fuck off."

"Errol's incredible. The toughest cases, the man brings home the bacon."

THE FUNERAL WAS held in the Scoratos' own church, the Most Holy Redeemer. A memorial service, to give those who knew her on the Misery campus a chance to say good-bye, was held in the Misery Chapel, a small stone replica of a famous Lutheran church in the Ruhr. The chapel was packed with those whose lives Mary Megan had touched while she was at the hospital, mostly patients, some staff. I sat with Solini. Heiler had been notified in Kuala Lumpur, and was due back, but we hadn't been able to get in touch with Hannah in Florida. Music was played. Mary Megan's husband, their misshapen six-year-old son beside him beneath the cross which was hung on invisible wires from the nave like a solid gold plus sign, read a poem filled with rage, which segued into "All Things Bright and Beautiful," which my sick, numb feeling did not allow me to actually sing. Deaths echo deaths. Ike White was right there.

At the end, the husband and son rose and walked slowly up the aisle to the exit in the front, the father's hand a dead white on the son's dark suit coat shoulder. People were filing out to pay their respects to them at the door when all at once a sense flickered through the crowd that Heiler was there. Everyone turned. There he was, standing alone at the business end of the chapel, arms akimbo under the suspended cross, as if he owned it.

Then a strange thing happened. Without anyone initiating it, everyone began standing aside, opening a long aisle from the front entrance all the way back to Heiler. In silence we stared at him. He was presented with a choice, either to stand there under everyone's gaze or to walk the silent gauntlet to the front, to get out. He did the latter, those legs kicking out as if it were the most normal thing in the world to walk through a community of people who hate you and blame you for the death of someone they loved. As he walked through, the line closed in after him. Solini and I were too far back to see what happened when Heiler came to the husband and son on his way out, but we heard a sharp curse, and then a deformed wail, before we began moving slowly forward again, to pay our respects to the survivors of this tragedy.

That afternoon Heiler called us three Emerson residents into his office for a last meeting. Hannah had just returned. Despite her tan she looked bad. Heiler, despite his tan, looked worried. Could it be? Could he be hurt by having driven Mary Megan to suicide? Seeing what I took for pain about the tragedy in his face, my heart opened to him, a little. Maybe Solini and I were wrong. Maybe in the privacy of his office he wasn't so vicious, he really was human, maybe even a good therapist. Patients did keep coming back to him, did they not? Their Mercedeses and Porsches and limousines rivaled Lloyal's own.

"You three are leaving my service tomorrow," Heiler said, "and there are things we need to talk about."

Good, I thought. At least, before we leave, we'll talk about this mess.

"You've done a fairly bad job. Solini and Basch especially have fallen off lately, discharging patients too soon. Zoe and Thorny? Paying out of pocket and you discharge them? I've never had so many empty beds. Why?"

Solini and I looked at each other in disbelief. He was upset about *beds*?

"You're the one who discharged Mary Megan," I said, "not us."

"Borderlines kill themselves. But you're right—it always looks bad."

It was vile. Heiler was less hurt by the death of the patient than by the insult to him. He would be seen as having failed—by his Harvard rivals, by Renaldo Krotkey. His SELF had gotten hurt. It was sickening to see, so close up, how for Heiler being a great psychiatrist was more important than helping a patient. I said, "I hear there's going to be an investigation."

"Who said *that*?" he asked, startled.

"It's all over Misery," Solini said. "They got the transcript of your last interview with her. We've been talking to lawyers and shit."

"With me away?"

"You were away, big fella, what did we know?"

"It wasn't just *me*," Heiler said, with the slightest hint of fear. "Very wise men are making these decisions."

"Who?" I asked.

"And like about what?"

Heiler got up from his desk and stood before Solini and me. He thundered down on us, "Something's fishy. What have you two been doing?"

"Did Krotkey make it to the rain forest?"

"Shut up." He stared at us. Hannah recrossed her legs. Heiler's laser eyes bored in on us. "Have you two little pricks been being 'nice' to me?"

Silence, one of: Well, You Found Us Out.

"Have you two little pricks been *lying* to me?"

"Go fuck yourself, Heiler!" I shouted, jumping to my feet. "Fuck you!"

"Asshole!" Solini cried, jumping up at my elbow. "You zygotic oaf! Up yours!"

Heiler moved closer. I saw what looked like bite marks on his neck. He stood over us, like a pile of rock. Then he nodded. "Good, good. Even if you two little dickheads did discharge them all too soon."

"ON TIME?" I cried out. "Heiler said they were discharged on time?"

"Quite on time, as per Heiler Theory," Chief Lloyal von Nott was saying that afternoon, in that high British accent. We sat in his office in the Farben. Henry was next. It was the first time I had met with Lloyal alone. In person he seemed reptilian, his office cool, he cooler, so that I actually shivered. His blackish eyes, set as narrowly as a red setter's, were unfathomable. The lines of his skin revealed him to be older than he tried to appear. "Blair said that you and Dr. Solini had worked through the LNT so efficiently that your borderlines were discharged quite on time. Good work."

"It was nothing," I said, startled at Heiler's neat lie, wondering suddenly if all along he'd assumed we'd been lying and had been lying right back.

"It proves Borderline Theory and Technique work rather beautifully on borderlines. The downside risk is empty beds. Half our beds on Emerson are empty. McLean Hospital, today, has no empty beds. None. How can I run my hospital if people like you insist on discharging patients?"

"It does make trying to treat patients difficult."

"We don't treat patients anymore, actually. We process them."

"It's good to know."

"Dr. Heiler's evaluation says you are too self-centered, too confronta—"

"I was upset about a patient's suicide, a woman named Mary Megan Scorato."

"Yes, and I called you in here to talk about the luncheon."

"The luncheon?"

"The Misery Capital Campaign Luncheon. You have yet to respond."

"You see, Dr. Heiler abused Mary Megan Scorato in front of all of us, and three days later she got admitted to Menninger's and killed herself. As chief you need to know about it. Here's the report."

"Yes," he went on, dropping it onto his desk, "and as her administrator, she was your responsibility. Now. About the luncheon—"

"Dr. Heiler says that since I reflect on him, he's responsible for me."

"Yes, quite. He informs me that he takes full responsibility. So—"

"He can't."

"Why can't he?" Lloyal said, with the British pronunciation, "cahnt."

"Because he reflects on you, and you reflect on Misery, and Misery—"

"Yes, yes," he said, narrowing those red setter eyes even further. "Now, about the luncheon—"

"You see, Heiler is so vicious to patients that people won't refer patients to him anymore—which means empty beds. I've heard there's a movement to ban him from seeing patients or teaching residents and med students at all."

"Ah, but he publishes. The Zephadon/Placeryll data are rather smashing."

"I thought the preliminary data were inconclusive," I said.

"Quite—the preliminary. But about a month ago the patients on Emerson Two and Three began improving. Not on Emerson One, though, Depression. These medications work—though not in depression. Because of our work—Blair's, mine, and yours—borderlines all over the world will soon be put on these medications."

"Which *one* worked?" I realized that Mr. K.'s taking everyone off the drugs on Emerson 2 and 3 might result in everyone being put on the drugs worldwide.

"Both. Both worked equally. An elegant study."

"And both worked better than the placebo?"

"Slightly. The placebo effect in borderlines is quite strong. Dr. Errol Cabot is doing a more sophisticated statistical analysis to heighten the difference. I don't understand these maths. I was born in Luxembourg and—"

"*Were* you?" I said, as if impressed, trying male station-identification.

"I am European," he began, his eyes drifting toward a coat of arms on the wall that looked like nothing so much as a Rorschach of two birds of prey joined at the waist clawing each other to shreds, "born in Luxembourg, raised in—" But then he caught himself, and I saw that he hadn't risen to the top of Misery by falling for such blunt flattery. Lloyal specialized in psychopaths and money. He was so skillful in slipping the knife into your back that you didn't know you had been stabbed until a few days later, when, as if a fuse had burned down, your balls fell off or guts plopped out onto your shoe tops and you realized that what you thought of as a benefit to you was in fact a detriment, a promotion a demotion, a rise a fall, a good a bad, and the most skillful part of it was that you couldn't remember who did it to you, and at the top of the list of suspects would not be Lloyal von Nott. Your memory of your interaction with him might in fact be pleasing. You would gladly pay his astonishing fee. "But more of that some other time," he said. "Just think: all over the world, borderlines will soon be put on these medications, and Misery will get the credit. All over the world. Just think of that."

I just thought of that and felt slightly ill, and slightly nodded.

"Yes, psychiatric disease is every bit as predictable as medical disease."

"Medical disease isn't predictable," I said.

"Who says?"

"In my year as a medical intern, nothing was predictable. Mostly the ones who ought to have died lived, and the ones who ought to have lived died."

"Sounds quite predictable to me. Yes, psychiatry is a medical science. Ordered and predictable. Like a healthy self. Like America itself."

Did these guys really *believe* this shit? In order to rise to the top of the Mount Miserys of the world, did you have to leach out your heart of care and concern, your head of doubt, so we're left with ventriloquists' dummies for leaders in business and religion and government and education, leaders with an eleven-year-old boy's sense of what matters in life? What do all our chiefs have in their heads—Swiss cheese?

"Actually I called you in to address the luncheon. The Capital Campaign Luncheon. You've not signed up for a luncheon."

"My lawyer says it's unethical to reveal the names of my wealthy pa—"

"Your lawyer?" A startled reaction. I wanted to laugh.

"Ever since you and Misery lost that malpractice suit to the tune of 3.2 million, we all have to be extra careful, don't we?"

"We have paid out nothing. It is under appeal. Chief Counsel to Misery, Nash Michaels, has it well in hand. Misery is robust today. Robust."

Nash was a noted sleaze. "Good. Quite a guy, that Nash Michaels."

Von Nott turned away and looked out the window at a beefy man clad in combat fatigues who had just started cracking branches off a bare bush. "When one is chief," he went on, "people are always trying to rape you. Not only insurance executives, not only staff and residents. Even Buildings and Grounds are raping me." I had an urge to say, *The trees raped you? The bushes and trees raped you?* He turned back to me. "Trying to unionize. Dr. Basch, I went to your file today, pulled your papers. Your behavior is so different from your papers. On paper you look so . . . so strangely promising. Frankly it's as if, perchance, there's been some mistake."

"A mistake in Misery, sir? In a robust institution like this? Could it be?"

"None of this goes any further, Doctor, understand?"

I did not say I understood.

"Dr. Heiler," he went on, "concurs."

"I'm sure he does. He wouldn't want to jeopardize his career."

"You needn't fret about *his* career. He is on the verge of being promoted from Associate Assistant Professor to Assistant Associate Professor."

"Quite an honor. But then why does he seem so insecure? One of the best borderline experts in the world, and still he's insecure?"

"Precisely. Blair's one of the best, but not *the* best."

"Like Misery's one of the best but not *the* best either?"

"Cut the crap, Basch!" he shot back, his British accent cracking. "Or else!

We are watching you—we know all about what you're doing, even about your little trysts in the on-call room. Is your brain in your dick? Eh?"

I had an urge to laugh. I smiled, with a sense of triumph.

"If you're not impotent yet, you will be. Believe me, I know."

"Oh I do believe you, Lloyal," I said, "just about as much as I believed you when you told us that Ike White died of a fatal disease."

"GONNA GO BACK TO THE HOUSE, *cut my wrists a bit;*
Take a buncha pills, call my stupid doc,
Borderline . . . ya-da-da-da, da-da-da-da-daaaa,
Borderline . . ."

Later that night Solini and Nique Nique and Jill and I were driving toward Misery in Solini's red Geo, singing these lyrics at the top of our lungs to the tune of the rock-and-roll golden oldie "Get a Job." We'd come from Henry's reggae gig in the city. Solini had been terrific—his hair in dreadlocks, his voice full, his body free. When he came down from the stage, I hugged him and kissed him.

"Gay-latent!" he said, kissing me back. "Cool!"

Tipsy on rum and pineapple juice in the way that it sneaks up on you in the shade, we drove through the late-November rain toward Mount Misery. Solini, wearing his rainbow woolen Rasta cap, was hunched over the steering wheel peering out at the wavering roadway. Nique Nique was in the passenger seat, a warm scent of jasmine. Jill and I were scrunched up in back.

We parked at Emerson. A misty rain was falling, the kind you can't help but like. Henry and I stood side by side peeing on the front lawn, humming "Borderline." I kicked at a soggy clump of brown leaves, raising the scent of earth, the image of healthy decay that would fuel the distant spring. We stared at the big brick building. Over the lintel was a new sign:

DISSOCIATIVE HOUSE

With insurance now paying more for dissociative than borderline, Heiler was changing most of the diagnoses. Looking back, historians would be astonished at this shift of mental illness to an epidemic of "Dissociative Disorder" at the end of the twentieth century and draw all kinds of conclusions—correlated with the shifts to Placedon and Zephyrill as the drugs of choice for these illnesses—when in fact it was the clever work of an ace accountant someplace in the dull underbelly of America—Bozerland—coming up with something that might just make his rich insurance boss richer.

Emerson 2 and 3 were quiet. From Emerson 1, Hannah's ward, came the usual bedlam, crazed screams and counterscreams, echoing like gunfire.

We stared as if at a war memorial. We were finally done with Heiler.

Not quite, for who should come out of the main door but Heiler and Hannah. They walked down the granite steps and headed toward his BMW. Hannah was talking to him passionately, pleading with him. He just kept on walking, those stick legs almost kicking her aside. At his car, as he raised his key to shoot the lock; she got between him and the door, blocking the infrared ray gun. He stepped back and tried to shoot around her. She blocked him again, standing in his way and gesturing to him, both palms up and shaking as if weighing two fruits. He shook his head no and went up on his toes to try to shoot down past her. At that she leaped up at him, threw herself upon him, but he seemed to turn even more rigid, and say something to her that caused her to go limp. She slid down him to the ground, like snow sliding off a mountain. Heiler stepped gingerly out of the ring of her arms, aimed his key and shot his car, which answered with a cheery chirp. He got in, turned on the ignition—soothing music came on—backed away from her, and drove off.

"She's been like gettin' it on with him?" Solini asked.

"In Kuala Lumpur?"

The four of us went to Hannah. She was lying in a puddle, weeping.

"He called me a borderline," she cried out. "BPO with SM."

"Sado-Masochism?" Henry asked.

"Survivor Mentality! My parents survived Auschwitz. What'll I do?"

"Please don't lie there in the wet," I said. "C'mon."

We helped her up. Her legs and arms seemed stiff. A stick figure.

"When did this start, Hannah-babe?"

"After the first conference on Mary Megan."

"When he humiliated you?"

"Ed Slapadek, my analyst, said humiliation was good, a good good thing, and would make my SELF strong. But Blair called me a . . . a *borderline*!"

"Takes one to know one, babe," Solini said. "Tell him that."

"Maybe, honey," Jill said, "you should give him up."

"Ed Slapadek said that would be a cop-out. Prove my SELF weak." She started crying again. But soon the chill sank in, and it seemed to sober her. Calmly, she said, "Please don't tell anyone. Please?"

"But we're worried about you, Hannah," I said.

"Oh I'm okay. Just got a little hysterical. Billy ben Lube would die if he found out. And I wouldn't want to damage Blair's career. Promise?"

Solini and I rolled our eyes, shrugged, and promised.

"Good night." She walked through the mist to a new BMW of her own.

"*Quelle malchance*," Nique Nique said, "*quelle femme malheureux!*"

Winding down, we wandered around and found ourselves on the top floor of the research building, looking through the long glass window over the other buildings of Misery, the faint glow of the faraway city reflecting off the underside of clouds, lighting up a dark hint of mountains. I stood with my arms around Jill, my hands clasped on her tummy, her head in the crook of my neck. Henry and Nique Nique were humming nearby. The scent of formalin. Many jars like those used for canning fruit, but larger. In each jar was a brain. We realized we were in the vault of the Misery Brain Bank.

"Yeck!" I said, feeling squeamish. "Let's go."

"My mother's brain is here somewhere," Jill said. "That's why I came here to work. She was manic-depressive, here for years. It really helped her a lot. My dad and I used to call this place 'Heaven on the Hill.' "

I stared hard at a brain resting by its stem in a jar, marveling at the intricacy of the convolutions, the sulci and gyri, the arteries and nerves, at the emptiness of it now and the irony of its donating itself to science, given what I knew of the artlessness of brain reps like Errol and Win.

"Hey, Roy," Solini called, holding a jar up to the light. "Look."

We gathered around. The jar had a brain that seemed pinker than most.

The label read: SCORATO, MARY MEGAN.

DRENCHED, JILL AND I climbed the flights to my apartment and stripped to our underwear. At first our lips on each other's were cold. We lay side by side on the bed in the turret, hearing the rain drum on the copper dome above. As I lay there the room began to spin, from all the rum in my cerebellum. I put a foot down on the floor. Next thing I knew Jill was lying on top of me, her back on my front. Then she was reaching around under her rump for my underpants, helping me to slip them off.

> . . . Florida is great and with great weather. We were at a dinner dance at the club last night and it was very nice. My new woods are great and they have a low swing weight . . .

With a severe contortion of all of our legs, the underpants were dangling off my ankle, her purple satin ones off hers.

"Look, Roy. This would be me as a boy!"

I peered over her neck and saw, rising from between her legs, my penis. I reached to her back to unhook her bra but couldn't do it, and then realized it was a front hook. Away the halves fell like, yes, cleft hemispheres of a brain. I rolled those plump grapes. We both sighed.

> . . . which is the new theory and that low swing weight means club head speed will rise . . .

With a twist Jill eased me in and led one of my hands away from her boob to the tiny sailor standing in the prow of that furry rowboat, I a passenger. For a moment we lay still together, on that edge between shore and water, enticed by wanting to push off but not pushing off.

"Roy, do you believe in E.T.s?"

"E.T.s?"

"Extraterrestrials?"

I didn't know if I did or didn't but what the hell so I said, "Yes."

"You do?" she cried.

"You bet."

"Me too. That's why I love this room—I can keep watching for 'em. When I was a girl, my mother saw one and told people, and they laughed at her. They teased me in school. I'm always on the lookout for 'em. Whenever I get to a place with a view, I look hard. Like in the brain bank."

"Did you see any?"

"No, but I'm keeping my eyes open."

"And this?" I asked, touching her.

"Open," she said, "wide open, buddy, to you."

> . . . so work hard and I know compared to the rest you will be the best at your chosen profession and even if it is not what I expected for you this will be true . . .

In the warm wet hum of us together with the rain drumming not so much on the roof as on us and in us, I found myself thinking of my time so far in Misery where if you tell the truth they kill you and if you face the truth you kill yourself, winding up with your brain in some gunk in a jar in a lab in a damn bank. I'd learned nothing much about how to do psychiatry but had learned what not to do, how not to harm people by using the tired old descriptions of the world written by men whose hearts were dried up by ambition and whose minds were twisted by dreadful secrets they lied through their teeth about like Ike White, whatever his secrets were. Schlomo would know, Schlomo, Ike's failed first analyst, and why had he failed anyway? This stuff is dangerous! I thought of Christine who was probably okay as okay as you could be with Bozer and Berry who was okay except for us being disconnected and then of Cherokee who I doubted was okay. I had a vision then of Cherokee floating out there somewhere, floating like a spacewalker in the subzero black tethered by a threadlike lifeline not floating happily oh no floating in that deathly isolation of terror—but what could I do? I'd called often and left messages, written him notes—he hadn't replied. The only thing I hadn't done was show up at his house like a dread borderline, tromp through his stables yoo-hooing, or with mallet in hand and jodhpurs and Teflon cap appear at his polo field looking for a game, I guess I could try that, but what I actually did try right then was to kind of pray for him imagine that, trying to call through that lifeline to him, "Hang in, Cherokee! Be well! Call or write a postal cart! Come back!" How Schlomoesque and what had Schlomo actually *said* to Ike anyway, that last afternoon maybe that fat little creep had tipped Ike over? And then I recalled what Solini and I had said a little while ago, on parting:

"This is a helluva way to learn to be a psychiatrist," I'd said.

"Yeah, but it beats dry cleaning."

"Still?"

"Are you kidding? Standing there breathing carbon tet fumes, staring up the skirts of these big Lakota Sioux women doing the pressing?"

"Hm. Doesn't sound so bad right now, does it?"

"Hm. Y'know, right now it doesn't, does it?"

"Least you could keep your ideals."

TOSHIBA

You've studied it and studied it and decided that it's turning bits on and off! And it's a BRILLIANT INSIGHT! . . . And then there's this relationship with Hewlett-Packard that we KEEP SCREWING UP! . . . .What about this bullshit thing with no definition!"

—BILL GATES
Microsoft
1991

Seven

AS IF HALFHEARTED PRAYER had worked, a few days later there was a message from Cherokee Putnam to give him a call as soon as possible. At the sight of that pink memo slip, my heart whirred on its spindle like a happy top, the way it does when you see something that reminds you of the person you love, the way I'd feel whenever I'd see Jill's rusted-out Buick parked in back of the house up the street where she was staying, and the way I used to feel with Berry. I still loved Berry, more than I loved anyone else in my life, but lately we'd both gotten guarded and careful and fighting the touch of nostalgia. The sight of her Volvo driving up the hill toward my turret brought less a whir than a worry that Jill, driving by, would see it and get pissed. Did the zing of Cherokee's note mean that I loved him? Well, kind of. I called him back at once. He picked up at once. We met in my office almost at once.

"I was damn furious at you," he said. "We'd had two such good meetings, and then, in that one session, you were acting like such a creep. It was unlike you."

"I'm sorry," I said, noticing how frazzled he seemed—Eddie Bauer twill pants wrinkled, pullover sweater stained, hair uncombed, eyes tired.

"Nothing to be sorry for. In fact you set things moving again, set me thinking that maybe that jerk actually was screwing her after all. I was miserable, but I thank you, for that." I nodded, wondering if, now that I'd vowed never again to use Heiler cruelty, there was something useful in it after all? Terrific. "And so yesterday morning at six I followed her to his office."

"You did *what?*"

"Followed her there, thinking I'd go in with her. But I couldn't, I just couldn't bring myself to. I sat and watched her get out of her Jeep and go in there, but it seemed, somehow, too . . . just *too*. I sat there imagining, fuming, and then decided to confront her after the session, when she came out. At six-forty I walked down the path to the carriage house and into the waiting room." He shook his head in amazement. "Oh boy."

"What happened?"

"This . . . this total imbecile was waiting there, for his appointment." As I listened, he gave a perfect description of Arnie Bozer. "And he wanted to talk. Like we were pals, he started asking me who I was, what I was doing there, that there must be some mistake because he was next—all in the most sickly-sweet, waffley way?" I nodded. "And in the middle of this she came out, crying hysterically. Seeing me, she stopped, as if she'd been shot, and then ran out. I wanted to run after her but then I heard *him* shout down from upstairs, and this cornball starts up the stairs and, well, I don't know what got into me but I shoved him aside and went up there myself. The imbecile fought back, tried to elbow me out of the way so that we both were standing there in front of this . . . this . . ." Words failed him. He shook his head, eyes widening, mouth agape, like a man who has seen a bad accident. Then he turned to me. "You've seen him?"

"I have."

"So my first thought was 'No way, absolutely no way.' There I stood, with this advertisement for flapjacks beside me, and he . . ." With difficulty he said the word, "Schlomo says, 'This your lover, Bozer?' And cracks up! This Bozer goes bananas—by the way, what's with these bananas?"

"He says they're for his heart."

"Heart?" His face turned thoughtful. "Father died of heart failure. Anyway, this cornball shouts out, 'No! I never saw him before in my life! He's got the wrong time, tell him to go!" And Schlomo turns to me and says, '*Nu*, and you?' I tell him who I am, and his face lights up like a kid's on his birthday. 'Oy what a joy, come in, come in.' Bozer goes ballistic, and Schlomo shouts at him, 'Arnold, sit! Go downstairs and *sit*!' And like a dog, he does. And then I sit down with . . . with my enemy, and . . . and . . ."

"Yes?"

"It was quite a trip." Cherokee smiled, then laughed, and then told me how, starting out ready to rip out Schlomo's heart, he wound up charmed: "That man could charm a moose into a hat rack." More than charmed, feeling like he'd learned something about himself. He'd confronted Schlomo about Lily. Schlomo had responded with the most humble and abject curiosity, saying, "Tell Schlomo, tell Schlomo Dove, about betrayed." Gradually, somehow, with an implied, pathetic self-denigration, which Cherokee said had really cracked open when Schlomo said, "Compared to Schlomo Dove, you are gorgeous!" they'd shifted the focus to Cherokee's own concerns about feeling like a failure as a husband for Lily, and as a father for Hope and Kissy, until, finally, Schlomo asked how Cherokee's therapy with me was going. "I told him it was over, because you were inexperienced and had acted like a jerk. I asked him if he could refer me to an experienced analyst. Know what he said?"

"What?"

"He said you were young but a 'mensch,' a terrific therapist, and I should stick with you. So I thanked him and called you right up."

I was so stunned by all of this, I couldn't say anything.

"And I left, after an hour, and thanked him, and you know what he said?"

"What?"

" 'No charge.' " Cherokee shook his head in amazement. "One look at that guy, you know how much he's suffered. He knows what it's like. I told Lily about it—for the first time I told her about suspecting her of having sex with him. She was mortified, and didn't want to talk about it. The only thing she said was, 'The one thing I have that's totally my own, and you barge in and try to take it away. After all I sacrificed for you and this family? How could you?' I was feeling reassured, flying high, looking forward to working with you again, but now, telling you about it all . . ."

"Yes?"

"Well, it's strange—and this is really crazy: his being so ugly, and his being, well, so damn human with me in the face of that ugliness, made him appealing, you know what I mean?"

"I do. Like an underdog is appealing."

"Exactly. But then I start thinking that if I, given all the reasons to hate him, if *I* can like him, doesn't that mean that there's something there that *she* could like, even love? I mean if he's human, she could fall for him, right?" I nodded, having gone through these same thought processes myself, about Schlomo. "But then again, he's *so* goddamn human, so up front about who he is and what he's like, it's like . . . like looking at a hot pastrami sandwich or something—what you see is what you get—the meat, those little specks of spices, the mustard, the kaiser roll—you look in those ink-dot little eyes in that wide-open mess of a face, with no trace, not the slightest trace of duplicity—and believe me, I've spent my life in my family and in lawyering dealing with duplicity—and you figure there's no way he can be lying to you . . . especially about sticking his pitiful little pecker into your wife! But then, that thought brings up the opposite—what a perfect body and face and demeanor for a lie! It's mind-boggling! I don't know what to think now. But the guy's a charmer, I'll give him that."

A charmer he was. Schlomo had done his number on Cherokee, as he'd recently been doing on me. After our meeting when he'd thrown the cigar into my crotch, and before I'd had a chance to send him the bill, his tailor had shown up at my office door. Reginald was his name and gaiety was his game, not only in terms of homosexuality but also in terms of manner. He was as neat and perfumed as Schlomo was sloppy, as glancingly funny as Schlomo was blunt. Caricaturing a gay tailor measuring a straight man for a suit, he measured me for a suit—the tape-touch on the inner thigh first a challenge of denial and then a hoopla of giggles, reminding me of my parents dragging me down to a cousin in the garment district for a wholesale bar mitzvah straitjacket in dark wool—and then brought out thick books carpeted with swatches of fabric in a myriad of textures, patterns, and hues, telling me his life story and then assuring me with fond farewells that I would receive the finished product in no more than one week and that it would fit "*perfetto*." Sure enough one week later there it was at my office door and I tried it on and it fit *perfetto*.

Since then Schlomo had been on his best behavior with me, helloing cheerfully from various sectors of the Misery campus, oily schmoozing with me when we chanced to cross paths on a path or a quad or in a tunnel or a hallway, and flattering me to high heaven through third parties, letting me know in various ways that "Schlomo's door is always open." I'd even attended a few seminars where he'd performed, brilliantly and yet earthily—like a college professor somehow *not* mummified by academe—up on his tippy-toes in that sloppy grand opera without music or slides or notes or overhead projections or computer printouts, seeming to be telling everyone the down and dirty about psychiatry, including his outrage about the ones neglected by Misery, "the Great Unwashed." He was fascinating, and brilliant—and funny. You had to laugh, first at him, and then, since he was laughing at himself, with him in laughing at himself, and then at a world that had created him and you laughing. Laughing with him, it was hard not to like him. Liking him, it was hard not to believe him. I didn't know what to think anymore.

"So now, I don't know what to think," Cherokee was saying as we were ending the session. "I feel better for having confronted him, and I feel that sex between her and him is absolutely absurd, but his making me feel better worries me more, about him and her."

"You and Lily have to talk about this. But you may not be able to do it alone. I'd be glad to see the two of you together, to try and help."

"Good point," he said enthusiastically. "I'd do it, but I doubt she would. Anyway, it's impossible for a while. We always do Thanksgiving with her family in Philadelphia, and then we always do December in the Alps—Gstaad—and then the Rockies—Aspen. I won't be back until after New

Year's." I was disappointed, and must have shown it, for he said, "Hey, don't feel bad, when I come back we'll really get down to work. That little fart opened up some damn good stuff, about Father and me. 'Oedipal,' Schlomo said, 'even for a goy, you got major Oedipal. Go deep. Tell Roy G. Basch I said to go deep, poppa and momma and boychik Cherokee the American Indian prince.' " Cherokee shook his head. "You gotta laugh, right?"

"Gotta. But you wouldn't want to try to meet, even talk on the phone?"

"Hey—you suggested I try 'different' once, and it was disaster. Why do a different different, and double the disaster?"

"But how can you go on vacation with Lily for six weeks with this hanging over you and she not willing to talk about it? Won't it be unbearable?"

"It's called 'normal.' Father and Mother did it for fifty-one years. In their generation—and all the ones before it—men and women *never* talked to each other, right? Unless, maybe, it's different with Jews?"

I smiled. "A lotta screaming and crying," I said. "Not much talk."

"So, hotshot, have a fun holiday. See you in the New."

"Why don't you keep in touch by phone, or fax or e-mail."

"Keep in touch?"

"Check in. I think it would be a good idea. Like weekly?"

He thought this over and smiled. "If you need me to, sure."

We shook hands. This time my grip was stronger than his. He winced. "Oh," he said at the door. "When I went back downstairs, that moron, that Future Farmer of America, was still waiting, whistling something from *Man of La Mancha*. Where do they find these guys anyway?"

"Disneyland."

"Ha! Haha! Yes!" We laughed hard, together—that "click." "And you know something, Basch? When I worked there, *I* did my best to create them! God! *Ciao ciao*."

He left, leaving a smile still on my face, but as it too left, I was surprised that his afterimage was, for all that wealth and determined good cheer, unpressed, rough-textured, faded from pink, and sad.

BURNING GREEN BEANS filled the air, and then, when Berry rushed to the pan and threw it in the sink and turned on the tap, the sizzle of steam.

We were at Berry's apartment. She'd decided to cook us dinner, a green bean and tofu stir-fry. Ever since we'd gotten back to America, we'd mostly eaten out or done takeout, cultivating a kind of United Nations of restaurants, each of which reminded us of a place we'd been. We'd started the evening guardedly loving, but everything seemed intent on going wrong, much in the way that, when things start to break in a house, the reign of breakage continues until most major fix-it men have been called. Little things were irritating me: the knot and tangle in the curly phone cord, which, when I picked up the receiver to answer a page from Viv, sent the whole phone crashing to the floor; the piled dishes in the sink and jungle of makeup, tops off, in the bathroom; and finally her cat, a pedigree Russian Blue named Keejer. Berry's family had always had cats and dogs; my family, owing to my father's fear of unanesthetized animals, had had no pets but guppies. The smell of stale cat food and the pieces of cat litter between my bare toes had always been irritating, and now even the cat himself, sitting like a fake cat staring at the kitchen cupboard where Berry said there must have been a loose mouse, the castrated cat himself turning to stare at me with a terrorizing disdain, bothered me. I stared back at him, suddenly understanding that if our sizes were reversed, he would long ago have killed me and eaten me.

Tonight he seemed even more disdainful than usual, and I couldn't help wondering who else he was disdaining, when I wasn't around. Cherokee's suspicion, and my thing with Jill, had made me more suspicious of Berry. I'd said nothing about Jill, nor had Berry about anyone else. I felt torn and in torment, keeping a secret from the woman who'd always been the one to whom I told my secrets. As the evening went on I'd felt—like when you're swimming off the cold coast of New England and suddenly you're embraced by a warm thread unraveling from the sensual weave of the Gulfstream—the twin currents of rising joy and rising sadness, dreams done and dreams deferred. Things between us felt as fragile as nostalgia. Fragile not only from our other hidden lives, but from the gap between her healthy work with kids and my warped work of becoming a shrink.

"Shit!" Berry said, staring at the burnt tofu and beans in the pan balancing on the pile of dishes in the sink. "Sorry."

"It's okay. Let's go out to dinner."

"Fine. Where shall we go?"

"Let's go to Miguel's."

"How about Pentimento?"

"Okay," I said, not really caring, "let's go to Pentimento."

She paused, studying me. "But it sounded like you wanted to go to Miguel's."

"No, no, it's okay—let's go where *you* want to go."

"But I want to go where *you* want to go too." She considered this, and asked, "Why *don't* you want to go to Pentimento?"

Feeling more tense, I said, "I just want to decide."

"We *are* deciding."

"We're not getting anywhere. Let's just make a decision."

The phone began ringing.

"Why are you yelling at me?"

"I'm not yelling!"

We stared at each other. The answering machine picked up.

" 'Hi, Berr, it's Chandra, just checking in. Are we on for tomorrow night? Call me. 'Bye now.' "

Berry and I stared harder and longer at each other.

"What?" she asked.

"Who's that?"

"A friend. She's a divinity student, working part-time at the nursery school."

"A friend?"

"Yes, a good friend. Someone who really understands. You know what it's like when you meet someone like that?"

"A woman?" The specter of gender floated across the room, cutting through the acrid scent of beans ruined, beans deferred. Our eyes met, did a little dance of unspeakable loss, and then disengaged.

"Doesn't have to be. We're going to the movies tomorrow. C'mon."

"What a world!" I said. "Men like women, and women like women too. We're doomed!"

We fought our way through the slicing cold wind and got into her car. The heater was broken and we shivered the whole way to the Hunan Haven, a good choice because it was so plain and bad it reminded us of the Xiang-xiang Hotel restaurant in Changsha, China. We'd worked together in Changsha during a flood of the Xiangjiang River the past spring, the last stop before we'd come back to the States. Now we parked in back of a car whose bumper sticker read:

MY KID BEAT UP YOUR HONOR STUDENT

Back from the trip we'd been startled at how America had become a nation of bumper stickers, and by now we were desensitized, but this seemed particularly ominous.

The bare tables and the waiters speaking a dialect of Chinese that sounded like nothing so much as a bunch of spoons jangling together in a bag, and the food-memory—simple, fresh, with scary spices that made our tear ducts well up like ripe lichees—lifted us back to our time in China, before these Chandras and Jills and shrinks and the thug who bought the bumper sticker, and I felt a dreadful burden of guilt. The owner's daughter, a three-year-old girl of meticulous and dazzling beauty, brought us our check. We both stared at her in awe, caught suddenly in the trap of our infertility.

"Hey, buddy," I said, "I'm sorry." I reached out my hand, palm up.

"Me too. Everything in the world seems so precarious right now."

My love for her rushed in. I squeezed her hand, meaning it. She squeezed mine.

"Thanks," she said, her eyes tearing up. "Are you thinking about Changsha too?"

"Yeah. Working together at the orphanage during the flood—was it only last May? Seems years ago now, doesn't it?"

"Ages ago, yes."

"Seeing the rows of cribs with the newborns," I said, "all girls—and then realizing what it meant. It was the closest I ever felt to you."

"And I you," she answered softly. "All those abandoned baby girls, five to a crib, with just a date of birth tacked up over each head, in a little plastic packet. Five to a crib, all five under the same red and gold quilt. The parched light. Coal smoke."

"We fed them bottles of soy milk and rice."

"And when they cried," she said, "no one came to comfort them."

"Except us."

"Yes, we did," she said, almost whispering.

Now tears came to my own eyes. Hand in hand, we left.

Out on the street we were struck by a blast of icy air and stinging sleet that knocked us both back a step. We had to clutch each other to keep from falling. It was the first real hit of the cold that every November clenched its fist around the heart of New England.

"I hate this climate!" I shouted, leaning into the gale.

"Me too!" she shouted back.

"Let's move to China!" I shouted, thinking palm trees and dim sum. "We've got enough money to live out our lives like kings!"

"And queens! Deal!"

We stayed the night together, feeling like together we'd survived a grave threat. Jill was in my mind, but in a different compartment. I slept restlessly, Berry soundly. I awoke at three in the morning to find her cat had placed the bloody head of a mouse neatly in front of my face.

The next morning Berry was off to Child Place Cooperative School and I off to my first day of my new rotation—Toshiba, Admissions. As we were leaving, just before opening the front door and facing the howling snowy wind, Berry asked, "Remember what I said about the holidays?"

"They're the worst."

"The absolute worst. Holidays are hell for people. Admissions to mental hospitals go way up. Brace yourself. Thanksgiving to New Year's is the worst time of year."

. . .

"OUR BEST TIME, the whole fiscal year!" said Nash Michaels, M.D., J.D., Director of Admissions at Misery. "Admissions go up severalfold. In parallel with the holiday boom in retail stores. Thirty percent of our gross profit per annum arises in this single five-week period."

It was later that morning, and I was sitting in the luxurious Toshiba boardroom. Nash Michaels was a real "maybe" kind of guy. Maybe he was more a doctor than a lawyer and maybe he was more a lawyer than a doctor; maybe an honest lawyer who'd help you out of your jam, maybe a smiler who'd wind up owning your house; maybe fifty, maybe forty; maybe those turtle-lidded eyes hid something smart, maybe something unalterably stupid; maybe his first name was a sign that he was from the proud lineage of Schlomo's first analyst the pitiful Nash, or maybe he was named by a kooky mother after an extinct automobile; maybe that dark wavy hair and five-o'clock shadow were sinister, maybe dextrous; maybe he'd lost that forearm now replaced by a hook in a terrific war, maybe in a suburban wood pulper; maybe he'd gotten a good education, maybe not—when I'd asked where he'd gone to college, he had put a hand over his mouth and slurred it so that maybe he said "Harvard" and maybe he said "Harpur"; maybe all in all he was a Brahmin from Boston, or maybe just as all in all a little *pisher* from Brooklyn. The one thing he was not maybe about was the future. As clearly as seeing a razor in a mirror, Nash Michaels had seen the future of American psychiatry. It lay between his legs, in his laptop computer.

Yet maybe not, for he was not the *only* director of Toshiba. With us was Jennifer Tunaba, a tall young Japanese woman whose English was peppered with techno-cybertalk. Jennifer was an M.B.A. Her father, a wealthy industrialist, was said to have told von Nott, "You hire my daughter, I promote Misery in Japan." So Mount Misery had become *the* mental hospital in the world for those rich Japanese whose minds had been crushed by the same culture they had been taught to revere. Once admitted, they were spirited away to a bilingual ward upstairs called The Golden Path.

I soon learned that this arrangement, cochiefs of Toshiba, was a stroke of genius on Lloyal's part. In the flowchart on the wall before my eyes, both Nash Michaels, M.D., J.D., and Jennifer Tunaba, M.B.A., were trapped in little rectangular boxes connected by a line and then, like a mobile, the line suspended from other boxes and lines suspended from Lloyal. The suspension was done with immaculate equality, so that, given both Michaels's and Tunaba's blasting desire to advance upward, their frantic contortions to get ahead only caused their little boxes to bang into each other and carom back to an uneasy distance. Nash hated Tunaba for her lack of medical knowledge; she hated him for his lack of business knowledge. Each constantly tried to knife the other in the back, though given the flowchart, it had to be clear to each that if one box were emptied, the other, like a seesaw suddenly unbalanced, would throw its occupant up into the no-man's-land below Lloyal, to dangle. And not dangle neatly, no. The dangle would be at an angle, and for a flowchart, ruled and balanced, an angle was cancer. The empty box would soon be filled. If the body filling it was not of the same weight, appropriate weight would be added, to balance again, like when you buy and balance new tires. Aligned, the chart would flow along to nowhere once again.

These thoughts were prompted by the chart lying open before me, of a patient who was to be admitted that day:

> This is the 4th Misery, 7th psychiatric admission for this 22 y.o. [year old] s. [single] w. [white] C. [Catholic] m. [male] with a CC [Chief Complaint]: "The angle of the dangle equals the heat of the meat if the mass of the ass remains constant."

"You will be responsible for doing admission interviews, physical exams, and write-ups for every patient admitted between eight and five, Monday through Friday," Nash was saying. "Any patient arriving between five and eight is the DOC's. You stay as long as it takes to finish your write-ups and orders. I leave at five sharp. Almost all admissions are scheduled. We have rare emergencies. Anything to add, Jennifer?"

Jennifer smiled. She was a willowy woman in a smart, dark dress. Her smile distorted the olive oval of her face, one side tardy and limited in its ascent. Jennifer said, "No."

"Volume," Nash said. "We make it on volume. I'll show you the operation."

Behind a bulletproof door as sturdy as a bank vault was the Admissions Unit. It was clean and bright and cheerful, with a Japanese leitmotif—rice paper screens; Toshiba TVs, VCRs, and computers placed as strategically as rocks in gravel gardens; and signs done in those letters with ballooning bottoms and slender tops that can be "seen" by computers. Nash explained at length the physical layout. He said nothing about the patients.

"What about the patients?" I asked.

"The patients?" he asked.

"The patients," I repeated.

"The software?" Jennifer asked.

"Oh, the software," Nash said. "What about it?"

"Will you be supervising me on them?" He stared at me, uncomprehending. "Or will Jennifer?" She stared at me, just as uncomprehending. "*Super-vi-sing?*" I said deliberately, loudly, as if to someone who doesn't speak your language. "So I can learn about patients?" More incomprehension. "You know, *learn?*"

"Learn?" Nash repeated, and then went on, "Admissions Unit is short-term. Maximum stay seven days. After that it's discharge back out, or transfer further in, to Inpatient Unit. You better start. So long."

My first admission was a fireman named George who, several months before, had been the sole survivor when, as he was driving over a snowy pass, his car had crashed head-on with a drunken driver's. His wife and three children—including a five-month-old baby—had been killed. An emaciated man with eyes sunken in horror, he was obsessed with its being his fault: "The baby gave out this happy squeal—she was in the car seat in the front, and I looked down at her for a second and heard my wife scream—'George, look out!' and then . . . glass everywhere, and flames. All dead. It was my fault. If only I hadn't looked at her." He looked up at me, and I felt his pain and his isolation in it. Overwhelmed, he looked away.

"That's horrible," I said. "You poor guy."

"The irony is, my two older kids always called me a 'bumblefuck.' "

"What's a bumblefuck?"

"A slow, overly cautious driver. I haven't been able to talk about it to anybody. All I see is glass. Glass everywhere. I'm feeling hopeless, Doc."

"You've been cutting yourself with glass?"

A look of horror and shame crossed his face. He nodded.

"Tell me about it?" He was reluctant. I understood—he felt trapped. But I also understood that my vision was larger than his and could hold his pain. His feeling trapped was normal, and, if opened up, was an energy for healing. I used the skills I'd learned from Malik to coax us along that tricky path of talking about the trauma and the time since. It was hard work. He'd open up, then shut down. But we were getting somewhere, until suddenly Nash Michaels burst in. He dragged me out into the hallway. Jennifer was waiting there.

"You've been in there forty-three minutes," he said. "You can't take that long. These days, no health care provider can. Length of stay is down; beds are empty; admissions are doubling every year, but the daily census is falling."

"But he's in real trouble and—"

"You have seven admissions to do today by five o'clock. Seven, and we'll try to squeeze in two more, thanks to the run-up to Thanksgiving. The key to success in Toshiba is to always stay one step ahead of yourself. At least one."

"But he's desperate. He needs to talk."

"Not now. Admit him. Talk to him on your own time, before eight or after five. You can't open things up on admission—it does more harm than good. Including physical exam and write-up, you should take fourteen minutes for an admission."

"Fourteen minutes? That's impossible."

"Dr. Bozer did it. Best resident we ever had. C'mon. I'll show you."

"But this guy is desperate—a cutter. I'm getting a really good history—"

"For admission, you don't need much history. The girls on the phones in preadmission get enough usually. The goal of Admission is to admit."

"But even to admit, I've got to think about him, about his treatment."

"We do no real treatment on Toshiba. There's not enough time."

"Well, then for diagnosis. I've got to give it some thought."

"Ah!" he said, as if solving a challenging episode in charades. "*That's* your problem."

"Diagnosis?"

"Thought."

"What's wrong with thought?"

"Thought plays no part in diagnosis."

"You mean go more with my feeling?"

"Feeling?"

"Feeling. What the patient feels, and what he makes me feel, what I feel with him? Affect?" He stared at me. "*Go with the affect?*"

"No, not the affect. The decision. Don't think, decide. As soon as I stopped thinking as a psychiatrist, everything went a helluva lot better."

"But isn't thought essential in order to decide?"

"Thought *gets in the way of* deciding. If you think, you leave room for doubt. If you doubt, you can't decide. Like the college boards. If you put down your first impulse, the first shot out of the box, you usually got it right, right? If you thought, you doubted, and the other multiple-choice answers started to look better and better, so you got paralyzed, right?"

"But this isn't multiple choice; there are feelings involved here."

"Take your feelings to your therapist. We don't do feelings here. Do you know how to make Decision?" I said I did not. "Decision Tree."

"Algorithms," Jennifer said. "Technical name."

"You get raw data from the patient. You look in the back of this." He held up a well-worn copy of a small green book, the size of a child's first reader, the kind with the animals with real wool the child can touch. "*Quick Reference to the Diagnostic Criteria from DSM-IV*. You look in the back." He looked in the back. Sure enough there were many treelike charts, where you start at one branch and you come to a fork and decide which of those to go to, and another fork and another until you find yourself out on a limb with a single leaf and no more forks, which is *Diagnosis*. "The computer will do it all for you—diagnosis, medication, date of discharge. Let's go."

"Toshiba computer," Jennifer said proudly.

We went back into the room with poor George, who sat hunched over, staring at a wall. "Hi there!" Nash said, loudly and cheerfully, and pumped his hand like a politician. "Mind if I ask you a few quick questions?" Before George could answer, Nash was asking him a few quick questions.

It was astonishing. Starting with the Chief Complaint—"It's my fault"—Nash would ask a question—"You feel guilt?"—and George would start to answer. Nash was interested only in yes or no answers. If George started to explain, he'd cut him off with another question. At first they seemed to be talking at cross purposes, but soon George got into the rhythm. Wanting to please his doctor—and perhaps feeling relieved that he didn't have to confront the painful feelings that had brought him into Misery—he barked back, sprightly "Yes" and "No," moving swiftly and neatly through Decision Tree in the back of DSM-IV until his doctor smiled, rose, pumped his hand again and said, "You have 'Mood Disorder, Major Depression, Recurrent, with Melancholia, 296.33.' Your insurance will cover seven days in Misery. We'll start you on antidepressants. If we find you are suicidal or psychotic, we will rediagnose you and your insurance will cover more. Any questions?" It looked like George had a lot of questions, but before he could start, Nash was saying, "Thank you very much Dr. Basch will do your physical and have a pleasant stay in Misery," and was gone. Jennifer and I followed.

"Four minutes," he said, back in the boardroom. "Have a nice day." He left.

Jennifer remained. I sensed in her face a kind of contempt for what we had just seen, and I asked, "It seemed incredibly cold, didn't it?"

A pained look came across her face. I felt that I might just have an ally here. She walked silkily around the rosewood table to the thermostat.

"It's sixty-nine, precisely." She rushed out after Nash.

I was appalled. This technique was the classic "medical model" I'd learned in the House of God. Starting with a live human being, you asked a lot of quick questions to funnel the human down into a diagnosis and a treatment. You cut off conversation, for talk meant less time for sleep. Malik had shown me that being a shrink was doing the opposite: turning the funnel upside down, opening things up in order to connect. It was delicate, meticulous, intuitive work, and I finally had a sense that I was learning how to do it, and now— Viv's voice burst out of my beeper:

"Number One's ready for a physical, Cowboy, and Numbers Two, Three, Four, and Five are waiting, and Number Six is the Lady Who Eats Metal Objects and she ate her hairdresser's wedding ring and is on the way in too so don't think, honeypot, decide."

I did the physical on George the bumblefuck driver. When I asked him if the scars across his chest where he'd cut himself with glass were attempts at killing himself, he refused to open up to me again and said only:

"Y'know, I really *liked* that guy, Doc Michaels. A real pro. Got straight to the point. Guy like you could learn a lot from him, y'know?"

When I went to do George's write-up I found it already done, laser-printed and in the chart. Nash had given the computer the *Yeses* and *Noes*, and the computer had given back a terrific Admission Note, in the medical model that made poor George's catastrophe look as bloodless and manageable as any medical illness—though he'd missed the glass-mutilation question suicide gesture, which I wrote in by hand.

"I'M BRAIN-DAMAGED BUT I don't think so," was the Chief Complaint of Number 2, a twenty-two-year-old woman whose heart-wrenching story included being hit over the head with a pipe after being raped in the parking lot of Misery Mall. I did what I thought was a terrific interview, but it took until noon and Nash was on my back to hurry up. As I escorted Number 2 through the lobby waiting room, I was accosted by Numbers 4 and 5 and their families—the "angle of the dangle" man was Number 4—as well as Number 6, The Lady Who Ate Metal Objects, who, when she recognized me, started screaming, "Your watch! Hey big boy, gimme your watch!" Primo Jones was standing next to a man dressed as a woman holding two grapefruits for boobs. This was Number 5.

"Thanksgiving's comin', Doc, and the turkeys are gatherin', y'get me?"

I typed poor Hit Over the Head with a Pipe Number 2 into the Toshiba and it climbed Decision Tree out to the limb called "Organic Mental Disorders Arising in the Senium and Presenium 290.13." This seemed too cold, given what I'd felt with her, and too damning, labeling her forever as "brain-damaged" when in fact her organic sequelae were minimal and she was reacting normally to a terrible trauma. I tapped in, for diagnosis, "Depression, appropriate." I listed no DSM code.

By the time I got to Number 3 it was way past lunchtime and I'd had no time for lunch. I was so overwhelmed with work that I decided I would try to do the Number 3 interview the Toshiba way—strictly multiple-choice medical model—but Number 3 was just about the saddest story in the world, an imploded fourteen-year-old boy who'd tried to hang himself in his mother's walk-in closet.

Interviewing him and his parents—parents who seemed decent, concerned, caring, and mystified, and who'd done everything right as far as I could tell—I was drawn in, thinking of my own parents and of my too being a mystery to them. But at a particularly delicate point in the interview Viv paged me stat to the waiting room where Number 5, the Grapefruits Man, and Number 6, the Metal Lady, were rolling on the floor fighting. I told Primo to bring the Grapefruits Man into the other interview room and I'd be there in a minute.

When I went back to the boy who'd tried to hang himself, it was strange: he and his parents were still where I'd left them—opened up, ready to try to understand—but I was not. Frazzled and pressured, my mind elsewhere and my heart closed down, try as I might I could not get back to where I was, and things were going badly. Viv paged me that my patient Zoe was wondering why I hadn't shown up for her appointment. I realized I'd completely forgotten it. I cut to the physical with the poor suicidal kid and locked him up in Toshiba and went to see the Man with the Grapefruits.

The Lady Who Ate Metal Objects, Number 6, took me until late afternoon. I was exhausted. There were at least four more patients to go. How was I going to make it through the day?

I shifted my mind-set, away from the hard, subtle work of being human with patients, to distance, diagnosis, and treatment. Don't think, decide.

Sweet relief. Admitting Number 7, a gay man, hearing his plaintive question to me—"Do you know what it's like when you're a kid and every other boy is out playing baseball and you're in the basement playing Cleopatra?"—I smiled, ran the symptom checklist for depression, and hit 296.20, Major Depressive Disorder, Single Episode. With Number 8, a woman who kept saying, "This life is a test. It is only a test. If it were a real life you would have been given instructions on where to go and what to do"—I cut things short, sealing her up in 295.40, Schizophreniform Disorder. And when Number 9, a Heiler Anorgasmic Dissociative, started screaming at me, "You fucking doctors don't know what this fucking Prozac you give us does!"—I hardly flinched as the future of psychiatry in my lap popped out "300.15 Dissociative Disorder."

With the burden of trying to help lifted, I cruised, filling in the blanks of the medical model, doing the physicals, tapping into the toy Toshiba, hitting "print," snapping the Admission Note into the three-ring binder.

Number 10 was a 44 y.o. rural rabbi of the Reform movement with a Chief Complaint of "I'm gayogenic and I'm abusing suckinols."

"Gayogenic?"

"I turn women gay. A year ago my wife left me for a woman, a few months ago my female cantor left the temple for a woman, and just after Succoth the head of my temple's Haddassah made *aliyah* to Israel with my cousin's wife. My faith in God is shaken. How could God do this to me?"

"Good question and shalom," I said, locking him up. I sat with my cute little Toshiba Satellite Pro, with 90MHz modular Quad-Speed CD-ROM and 810-million-byte hard drive, watching admiringly as it did 305.41, Barbiturate Abuse (Seconal) in living color, and thinking, Hey this is almost fun.

"Fun, eh kid?" said a familiar voice.

"Malik?" He was in a blue and white sweatshirt emblazoned with a line of

Hebrew, translated as "It's Better in Israel," and twirling a basketball in his hands. With him was Henry Solini, in baggy gym shorts, red, green, and black Marley T-shirt, and rainbow-colored wool Rasta cap.

"Let's play some *hoop*!" Malik shouted. He was eating a carrot.

"When'd you get back?"

"Yesterday. We do Thanksgiving in Chicago. My family. I *need* Chicago, after a month in the Promised Land with Bronia. I got the gym for an hour."

"Don't have time."

"C'mon c'mon—you can't make any real contact with these patients, there's no time, right? Don't get involved. C'mon out 'n' play with Henry 'n' me."

His words went against everything he had taught me so far. "I know what you're trying to do, Malik. It won't work."

"Yeah, these suckers are *doomed*! So feed some shrink bullshit into that bullshit computer and we'll choose up sides. This weather makes me want to shake and bake!" He wiggled his hips, dribbling the ball, and I sensed the "hoop fever," so familiar to me—a hum of vitality in my body and head every November, my pulse quickening, happiness sparking in my palm with each *tap tap tap* of the ball on the pavement on my walk down to the gym. "Over to Jordan!" he cried, throwing it to me.

I had played basketball in Columbia, in fact had been co-captain with the immortal George Konopski of the Columbia High School Fish Hawks. Basketball had been my one-way ticket out of the foreign country of my family, my ticket into the life of buddies and bodies and girls. In one smooth motion I caught the ball in one hand and spun it easily up onto my index finger, then "walked" it down each finger in turn, keeping it spinning, until, spinning it on my pinkie, I popped it back to him. *Years* to learn this.

"Hey hey hey!" he said. "You play hoop!"

"Saved my life."

"Me too!" Malik said. "Come on."

"Me three!" Solini said.

"You too?" I asked, startled, given his minuscule size.

"Point guard, Mandan Braves. Unbeaten, my senior year, till we played the Fort Yates Warriors, in their gym down on Standing Rock Reservation. Everett Chasinghawk, their point guard, stole me silly. Same dude that stole my wife last year. We were doing okay till they got out their war drums for their fight song, 'On the Warpath'—we crumpled."

"C'mon, Roy," Malik said, like a little kid dying to play, "c'*mon*!"

"Can't. I'm way behind." Shaking their heads, they started to leave. "Hey wait a second, Malik. What do you mean they're doomed?"

"Once they come into the Misery system, they gotta hope they run into guys like us, who are out of it, to help 'em out of it. Tell you what. Gimme the name age sex address occupation religion and Chief Complaint of each of your admissions. I'll give you back the DSM diagnosis."

I did.

And then he did. He hit every DSM diagnosis, ten for ten. Every damn one.

"But doesn't that just mean," I asked, "that the diagnosis is right?"

"Nope, it just means that it's bullshit. If you ask the 'normal' status quo questions, you get the 'normal' status quo answers. Like cancer. In the last fifteen years overall cancer rates are up twenty percent! *Everybody's* gettin' cancer! *Kids*, for Chrissakes! Don't you have friends who have cancer? *Think*." Reluctantly I thought, and realized that I had gotten a number of phone calls since I'd been back, from friends, and friends of friends, sudden terrified calls announcing melanoma, pancreas, breast, asking me for help in finding them good medical care. I nodded. "We all know somebody. I got two cancer calls already since I got back—one's my nephew, who's only three—leukemia! People our age—lymphoma, ovarian—this didn't happen to our parents! When they look back, this is gonna be known as the *Age* of Cancer."

"Yeah, man," Henry said, "but what's that got to do like with this?"

"That's what I'm *telling* you. Getting cancer is 'normal' now."

"So what do we do?" I asked. "Give up?"

"The hell! We open our eyes, we take it all in. We fight the 'normal' bastards putting all the shit in our water, earth, air—the air we *breathe*, do you believe it? And we take care of business in here." He tapped his chest, in the zone of his heart.

I'd forgotten how intense Malik was, volcanic, a force of nature wrapped in tinty glasses and sports mania and dumb-jock talk.

Malik wiped his brow, and finished his carrot. "Jeez, you get me going, Basch—how do you *do* it anyways? I was so peaceful in Yisroel." He bounced the ball and pivoted smoothly away. Then he stopped and turned back. "Look," he said. "These people coming in here are sick of a sick world. They're the canaries in the mine shaft, kid. Just like us."

"Us?"

"Who else? Right, Solini?"

Solini juked and jived, and sang some Marley.

"Just remember, Roy," Malik said, "when you're all computer-literate 'n' cold? Like they say in Hollywood: 'You meet the same people on the way back down.' "

"But I don't have the time it takes to connect with these people."

"Schmucko, schmucko! You still think connecting is a matter of *time*?"

"Okay, then—I don't have the energy."

"The energy ain't *in* you, like a little battery; the energy *comes from the connecting*! Like in tennis, taking a ball on a short hop, using its own momentum to fire it back harder over the net, or—" He threw a no-look pass at Solini, hitting him in the nose. "—making a touch pass in *hoop*!"

THE SIREN'S WAIL rose in pitch. It was almost five o'clock, and I saw Nash heading out the front door, with Jennifer following close behind. With so much unfinished work, I felt I needed to talk to him. I ran out and caught him just as he was getting into his black Lincoln Continental Town Car with tinted windows.

"I need to talk to you," I said. The siren came closer.

"You can't. It's five o'clock." Jennifer was getting into her car, a black Lexus.

"But if they stay for only seven days, what the hell are we doing to help them?"

"Toshiba keeps them safe, gives them meds, I'm out of here." He got in. I stopped the door from closing with my foot.

"Seven days of safety and meds doesn't do fuck-all for most of them."

"So after seven days they go back out, and then come back in, sooner, sicker. They get sicker and sicker sooner and sooner till finally their insurance company can't legally *not* send them further into Misery, for longer stays on Inpatient Unit. Now get your damn foot outta my door."

"But what about—"

Suddenly the siren was close, and then closer, and it was heading right for Toshiba, and, seeing it, Nash shouted—"Get away!"—and I thought it was so he could get out to tend to this emergency but in fact it was so he could slam the door and get out before the emergency emerged.

I watched him peel the Continental off and down the hill and watched the Lexus tail him down and then I was caught up in the emergency. The EMTs rushed the body of a young woman into the lobby. Reflexively I slipped into real doctor mode, asking the medics what they knew—"OD, barely breathing when we found her, maybe barbiturates, maybe heroin, she was scheduled to be admitted here tomorrow"—and started doing all the brutal, desperate medical things to get a heartbeat and a breath.

Solini arrived and joined in—he was the DOC. We tried everything, nothing worked. Finally, exhausted and scared—for she was young, younger than Henry and me—we pulled the sheet up over her face and retreated to the boardroom, where we slumped down into our chairs.

"Sorry, Cowboy, it's rough. Shall I send in the next of kin?"

Henry looked at me sadly. I said, "We do it together?"

"Cool," he said.

Her husband came in, a solid-looking young man with a blond crew cut and a colorful work shirt. He sat down and turned to me. "How bad is it, Doc?"

"Bad," I said, trying to keep my voice steady. "She's dead."

He stared at me for a second, then at Solini, then turned away. And then he screamed, "Bitch! Fucking bitch!" threw his chair down and stormed out.

"Not what I expected," I said to Henry.

"No joke. In psychiatry you've gotta have no expectations about patients and no interest in them."

"What?" I said, startled. "Who told you that?"

"Dr. A. K. Lowell, the chief on Thoreau, the Family Unit. She's classic Freud. I started my rotation with her today. She was totally silent the whole day, and then at the end she said that. She's weird, but maybe about that she's cool?"

AS IF WEIGHTS WERE ATTACHED to my feet, I trudged out of Toshiba sometime after nine at night.

A neat thin man in a tweedy sport jacket and Woody Allen glasses stopped me, asking, "Are you a doctor?"

My guard went up, like an off-duty pediatrician is on guard around kids.

"Yes."

"My name's Sedders. I think I need admission to the hospital."

I clicked on what I'd learned to be the first question of any psychiatric interview, and as empathically as possible asked, "Do you have insurance?"

"Yes, that's the problem."

"How's that the problem?" I asked, framing a Chief Complaint of *I have insurance*.

"It's managed care, an HMO. 'Healthycare Incorporated.' Admission has to be approved by two doctors from the HMO, and none will return my calls. I've been trying all day. Most of the time all I get is a busy signal. The office is in Washington. State."

"Keep hitting 'redial.' "

"I do. When I do get through I get a secretary, never a doctor."

"Is it an emergency?"

"That's what the secretaries all ask. I'm not sure. It's certainly urgent. I'm thinking seriously of killing myself."

"How seriously?"

"I'm not sure. I have no standard of comparison."

"Tell them it's urgent. Be a little more self-assertive."

"You think if I say that, they'll get the doctors to call me back?"

"It's worth a try. Keep redialing."

"Thanks muchly, Doctor—" He read my name tag. "—Basch. You're the first doctor who's taken the time to talk to me. I feel a little better already."

"Good."

When I got home there were three messages on my machine:

"What a boffo session, Doc. Nothing Mickey Mouse about you. I feel better. Good luck with that sweet family of yours on Thanksgiving. I'll try to keep in touch. Putnam."

"Don't worry, buddy, I love you."

"Me. Call *me. Now.*"

Eight

FLORIDA IS WHERE my parents are dying and living.

"Roy?"

Florida is where a lot of great Americans die.

"Quick or you'll miss them!"

I opened my eyes and it was still dark. Florida. In a hotel with Jill. I followed the tropical breeze toward her. "What time is it?"

"Just before dawn. Look."

She was standing on the balcony, wearing nothing. Her back was to me. My eyes went from her punk thatch over her muscular shoulders down the line of her spine and then to the incurling of her rump, one leg straight, the other hiked up on the railing of our balcony, like an explorer sighting a shangri-la. I walked over, leaned against her, and clasped my hands over her slightly rounded belly. "What?"

"E.T.s—Extraterrestrials."

"Again?"

"This time for real. See that? What do you think *that* is?"

I followed her finger and there, across the long flat surface of the Gulf of Mexico, were four ovals of light, hovering in the breaking sky. "Airplanes," I said. "We're not that far from Tampa, and the flight paths to Central America and the Islands."

"No way," she said, and, as if in answer to my skepticism, the ovals dipped down toward the surface of the water, not in the unison of some kind of reflection, but each a little differently, and then seemed to bounce, two, three, four times on the mirror of the sea, before, hovering again for an instant, they waggled once and were gone. "You never saw airplanes do that!"

As we stood there I could feel the tension in her body, her tight tummy, her sporadic breathing.

"I'd give anything to go up," Jill said quietly.

"Up?"

"With them. People have, you know. People do."

"You believe those stories?"

"I've met people who have. Lots of people. In Montana last summer." I stroked her tummy. "Mmm, nice. I've thought, a few times this year, that they followed me back. I'd wake up and feel them there, by my bed."

"You saw them?"

"Sensed them. I have something to tell you, Roy." She turned to face me, pivoting like a ballerina on one leg, hiking the other leg, which had been on the railing, over my hip. "I think they were here."

"Here?"

"In our room. Around the bed. Last night when we were making love."

"The little perverts."

"They were just curious, that's all." She put her palm to my cheek, looking into my eyes. She was taller than Berry, almost my height. "Do you think I'm crazy? Are you clicking away with your little DSM diagnoses?"

"Nope. That was no airplane. Do you think they're dangerous?"

She shook her head no, put her chin down, and leaned into me, forehead-to-forehead. I felt wetness on my eyes, and realized she was crying. I asked what was wrong. "My mom saw UFOs, and when I was in high school they had her picture in the paper—it was a small town—and when I got to school the next day the other kids really got on me—called her a loony and all. So it means a lot that you accept this in me."

"And it means a lot to me that—" I was cut short by her gesture of appreciation, which was, by stepping up on a low cast-iron balcony table, hiking herself up to straddle me.

"Think you can handle it?" she asked coolly, as if she were asking whether the guy wires to the main pole of a tent would hold.

"I'll die trying."

"Hmmm," she said, encircling my neck with her arms. "Know the difference between fucking and making love?" I said I did not. "In making love, you kiss." Putting one finger under my chin, she looked into my eyes and smiled, and I smiled, and then slowly, maybe a millimeter at a time, she moved toward me, her mouth opening, her tongue lying in it like a pink cushion on a purple couch, and kissed me.

. . .

LATER THAT THANKSGIVING morning we drove to my parents' condo. I had switched coverage with Arnie Bozer, he taking my Thanksgiving Day, I his Christmas. He was still dating my former outpatient, Christine, who, after my Heilerizing her, had never come back to see me again.

"This is a very special Christmas for me, Roy," he'd said. "I'm taking Chrissy home to Indiana to meet the folks. Thanks so very much."

I usually spent Thanksgiving with Berry at my family's house in Columbia, New York, but in the past year my father the dentist had retired to Naples, Florida, and had invited us down here, to celebrate with my brother and his family, who were flying in from Phoenix. Berry was going to her parents' in Maine, saying that she didn't feel comfortable being with my family with me right now. Although I hadn't told her explicitly about Jill, I had a sense that she knew. Jill had no family nearby. She had no money either, and I had paid her airfare. Misery had paid my airfare, for me to be its representative at a conference entitled "Is Psychotherapy Dead—or Just Mismanaged?"

"What did you tell your parents about me?" Jill asked as we parked the rented cobalt Saturn carefully in the lined box marked Visitor Car in the condo lot.

"That we worked together, and we both were down here for a conference."

"Uh-huh. And they've met Berry?" I nodded. "They like her?"

"They love her."

"Okay. Just like to know what I'm walking into."

"It won't help. No preparation helps." An hour before, I had found an index card in my wallet, written by Berry and me after our last visit here:

How to Survive a Trip to Your Parents'

1) Live Through It; 2) Breathe and Smile; 3) *Primum Non Nocere*: First, Do No Harm; 4) Get Out of the Condo—Change the Setting; 5) Pray; 6) Try to Surprise Them, Without Hostility; 7) Get Set to See Yourself at Your Very Worst.

Family and Berry. They seemed to go together. Recently she'd said to me, "It's as if we grew each other up. You and I were each other's ticket out."

"Out?"

"Of our families."

Now, her image rising up in my mind's eye like a dental X ray rising up out of a developer in that eerie red light of the darkroom in my father's office, I felt torn. Why was I doing this? Being with Jill could be a big mistake. I stared up at the four-story concrete-block building, identical to another beside it. Each condo had a railed balcony protected by green screening, giving each a lime tint. The lot was full of huge American luxury cars. I spotted my father's Chrysler New Yorker. "The biggest car Chrysler makes and it has the most trunk space." He would say this with pride. I would feel irritated, and then guilty. Why should a man's love of his big car irritate his son?

How flat the whole scene seemed. Even the sunshine felt two-dimensional, flat slabs of light slapped up against white walls, and against the flat chlorine kidney of the Cyclone-fenced pool. We got out, staring at a sign:

POOL RULES

> Swim at your own risk. Shower before entering pool. No radios without earphones. Bathing load 15 persons. No food, glass, or alcoholic drinks. No floats. No pets. Toilet-trained infants only. You must shower before entering pool. After using chairs and lounges, please replace in proper position. See other rules on bulletin board in Pool Hut.

"Control is big in Florida," I said. A well-tanned woman and man, dressed in shorts and banded T-shirts like members of Team Senior, rolled up on tricycles. Only as they passed was their age apparent. "It's a utopia for second childhood."

"It doesn't say you can't go topless."

I laughed, remembering my father telling me about his recent reaction to the French Riviera: "They go topless and it doesn't bother you that much."

We turned and walked toward the building. Through the gap between the two buildings we could see the flat green of the golf course, a lone geriatric palm, and, on the horizon, the Gulf of Mexico. A fishing boat was heading across the flat blue, a cloud of gulls pluming up in its wake, an ever more chaotic white wedge against the flat blue sky. The sea was so still that the plume of gulls was reflected in the darker blue. I saw this as a hint of entropy, a break in the square flat concrete of the condo world where the fifties generation had gone for golf and tennis and concerts and restaurants, with clear rules, clear sightlines, and protective netting, like around a playpen. The unruly plume of gulls was like a rip in a Norman Rockwell. I wanted to be on that boat, heaving fish over, feeding the chaos of those gulls.

Hold it. My parents were basically good people. Dad had stayed in the same office on Washington Street for thirty years before retiring the previous year, filling cavities, hauling out molars, going home to my mother's hot lunch, meeting with the Jolly Jews, his investment club, and golfing, always golfing. In his golfing prime he had an admirable tail hook, and got a lot of roll. Once he and I had contested the Hendrik Hudson Club Championship. It escaped me who had won. Mom too had slogged it out—slogged, hell, lived her dream: a ranch house a big car two kids one a doctor even if a psychiatrist one a wealthy banker. I stared up at the green balconies. This was their dream come true. A little generosity was required. I felt a rush of sadness, then tenderness. This would be my only day with them all winter. Make it good. As Malik said, "None of us are here for long."

"Maybe," I said to Jill, "this time will be different. One thing: under no circumstances go into a room alone with my mother."

"Why not?"

"In a room alone with you, she'll destroy anything between us."

"Hey, if there's one thing I know about, it's 'the boyfriend's mother.' "

"Yeah, but not mine."

We were buzzed in through the heavily locked door and up to the third floor and then down the hall to where my parents stood in the spotlight of their open condo door. As I approached, seeing the hope light up in their eyes, the memory of how I had been as a college student, a teenager, a boy, a baby, hope lit up in me too, the hope for the return of the imagined remembered, and tears came to my eyes. When I was almost to them, seeing them so much smaller than recalled, I felt ashamed of my suspicion, and felt a rush of joy, like a young boy's.

"Hi, bud, and welcome," my father said. His voice trembled as he took my hand, as if he would cry. He wore a pink sport coat and polka dot tie clasped high on his belly, the belly itself straining hard against a big brass cowboy buckle on pants pulled up almost to his chest.

"Hello, dear," my mother said, kissing me on the cheek. She was dressed up, as if for a night at the opera, all cantilevered silk, diamonds and pearls. "You've come casual," she said, "as usual." I was wearing clothes I'd bought with Jill in Tampa—Italian shirt with the greens and browns of Tuscany, baggy Italian pants. "Have you gained weight?"

Boom. First hit. Righting myself, I introduced Jill. My father was friendly to her, as if greeting a new patient with the potential for some expensive bridgework. My mother was a little too friendly, as if doing Heiler Opposites. We went in.

The condo was meticulously neat, ordering a constricted space for utility and purpose, the purpose being order. The wall-to-wall facing mirrors gave the image of doubling the space, fooling the eye and then fooling the fooled eye, and the beige shag rug and beige furniture gave a sense of soft welcome.

My brother the banker looked good, tan and fit, his athletic body filling out a suit. His wife, a Realtor, looked healthy too, tanner and fitter. Their cute little girl wore a shimmering dress labeled "Baby Dior." My father offered us drinks. "I myself have never been drunk, and people drink more in Florida."

Jill and I took Jack Daniel's.

"Let's have a toast," my father said as we sat down to eat, "and to my two successful boys."

"And to our parents," my brother said.

"To Mom and Dad," I said, raising my glass. We drank, and started to eat.

"The achievements of my boys make me proud," my father said, "and when I'm asked, I always comment that even though my younger boy is more successful in money and the other is successful as a physician, they're both successful."

"He talks about you both so much," my mother said. "Talks a blue streak to strangers. But as soon as we get in the car to come home, nothing. Why won't he talk to me?"

"Stupid bitch," my father said under his breath.

Jill grabbed my knee. I looked at my brother and saw the alarm in his eyes. My father's words hit me in the gut. I started to sink.

"His mother never talked," my mother went on, not having heard it, for she was deaf in one ear, the ear toward him. "Except to Ga-Ga, her maid. She never cooked a meal herself, ever. Ga-Ga cooked."

"Stupid idiot."

"More stuffing, Roy dear?"

"So how's the golf, Dad?" my brother asked. I appreciated this, his trying to pull us all back onto the shore.

"Not so good, and I always say it doesn't matter how you score as long as you can keep playing. They keep the course in great shape—it's lush and the greens are fast—but they've got a few peasants as members and there's nothing I hate so much as a refugee on a golf course. You should see Mother's short swing and the way she is hitting the ball is just great."

"It hasn't been that easy," my mother said, "to make new friends."

"Moron!"

I felt paralyzed, wanting to confront him on this, but on the other hand not wanting to bring it to my mother's attention. What should we do? Pretend we didn't hear what we heard? Say something? What? We all kept silent, paralyzed and guilty, accomplices in the denial. It was hell.

Luckily my niece soon rescued us, first making a big pile of all of our bamboo napkin rings and then suddenly hurling them one after another at each of us in turn. We tried to duck and weave out of the way, but in the infinity of the facing mirrors and with the wine boosting the high from the bourbon it was hard to figure the angles. Jill and I thought it was funny, my brother and his wife were less amused, and my mother and father were upset and tried to control her. As we gathered the napkin rings, my niece plopped a golf ball into her melted chocolate ice cream, splashing it on the beige carpet, and was taken to the TV room to chill out with Barney. My brother then did a smart thing, bringing out the latest photos of his daughter. Everyone was enthralled, poring over the images.

Soon it was almost nine at night. Fearing that Berry would call and find out that Jill was there, I excused myself and called her in Maine. We talked about our Thanksgivings. Her friend Chandra was there, something Berry hadn't mentioned before—in my mind, it helped justify Jill. Sixteen people, total—her mother and father were good at making friends. There were artists and musicians, Chinese students, and people who were still working at the liberal causes that had started in the thirties. I loved her family. In comparison, Thanksgiving with my little nuclear group seemed lonely, and sad.

"I'm sorry, Roy," Berry said.

"For what?"

"Your pain. Wish I could be there to help. Give everybody there my love."

"I will. And mine to everybody there." We hung up. I felt like a rat.

My father suggested we call his father in a nursing home in Connecticut. First my father talked to him and then I, the oldest son, talked to him. I'd always loved my grandfather, a tough old guy who'd come from the old country and made it as a grocer in New York. But now I hardly recognized his voice, it was so shaky and faint, like a scratchy old record.

"I'm dead," he said.

"*What?* Who's dead?"

"Not dead, bed—b-a-d—bed. Dey just keep you here and let you die."

"I'm sorry, Gramps."

"Can you get me out of here?"

"How?"

"Tell your pop."

"I will."

"Why you never come visit me?"

"I will."

"Promise?"

"I promise. Soon."

"Berry dere wit' you?"

"Yes."

"Good. You'll marry her, I know. Nice goil. Did I tell you that when I proposed to my wife, she said no. So I got a gun, and went over dere—Washington Heights, Magaw Place—and I said, Geiger, marry me or I'll kill you. So she did. When dey moved finally, you know dey found dat gun in the chandelier?"

"I love you, Gramps." He told me this story every time we talked.

"You need a permit now, don't you?"

"A wedding permit?"

"A gun permit. You didn't need 'em, back den. So long." I handed the phone to the next in line, my brother.

While I had been on the phone with my grandfather, my mother had cornered Jill. She'd tried to edge her toward the guest bedroom. Forewarned, Jill had faked toward the bedroom and cut toward my sister-in-law. My mother nabbed me and took me into the guest bedroom. As the door closed I heard my father say:

"Stupid idiot."

"Where's Berry?" my mother asked.

"With her parents in Maine."

"You're not breaking up with her? Not after all this time?"

"I'm not thinking about it in that way," I said, suddenly feeling a surge of love for Berry and my mother, wanting to be close to both.

"I've always before stayed out of it, but this! This girl, Roy?"

"She's a friend."

"This kind of girl is not a friend. Don't you think I love you?"

Boom. Another hit. "Of course you love me, Mom."

"Yes, I do." She sighed. "I don't know what happened to you. I remember once, you were about six, and you were late coming home from school, and you walked in and I could see that you'd been crying—something had happened—and I said, 'What's wrong, dear?' and the strangest thing happened—I could see you wanted to tell me, but then it was like a wall went up, and you didn't. You said, 'Nothing,' you turned away and walked out. Do you remember?"

"Yes, I do." I had gotten beaten up at school, and, walking home along the railroad tracks crying, I couldn't wait to tell her. But then, as I walked into the kitchen and I saw the concern in her eyes, and as she'd asked me, something happened in me and I stiffened and made my face stiff, and said nothing. I had felt caught, frozen in the spotlight of her love.

"So what was it?" she asked expectantly, as if my telling her now could set everything right.

"I'd gotten beaten up by some kids at school, that's all."

"And you couldn't tell me? Why not?"

"I don't know," I said, feeling, all these years later, the same thing—caught, frozen, full of dread—like Cherokee with Lily on the beach: dreadlock.

"It's a shame," she said, "the way that wall went up. It never has come down. Like with your father. And now? What's going on now?"

"Just trying to learn to be a psychiatrist, Mom."

"But this girl? I am your mother. Can't we discuss things anymore?"

"I'd like to, but it's really hard to talk."

She started to cry. "You've gotten like your father; you don't talk to me. How often do I see you? Three times a year? Your visits are never long enough. I feel, Roy, that you've gotten into total selfishness. You don't smile. You need to grow up and settle down. And not with this one, no."

"I hear you, Mom. But it's late and we've got an early flight tomorrow."

"Any words of wisdom? Any words of wisdom, Doctor, for your mom?"

As used to her quick switches as I was, they always caught me off guard. Now, I tried to hang in. I felt for her, and wanted to say something—say a million kind, wise, funny, generous, empathic things to her—but could not.

"Stupid bitch," my father said outside the door.

A toy crashed against a wall.

"Nothing?"

"Gotta go. It was a wonderful dinner."

"You all ate it so fast. Six hours to cook, six minutes it disappears." She sighed. "Maybe, if you'd stayed a doctor, we could talk?"

"A psychiatrist *is* a doctor, Mom!" I said, trying to hang in, hang on.

"You know what I mean—a *real* doctor. You keep hurting me but it's all right." She started to cry. I felt such pain. I moved to her, put my arm around her to comfort her. She seemed small, her shoulders fragile, as if the bones were precariously connected, the flesh full of doubt. Guilt tore at me.

"I'm sorry, Mom, really."

"Yes, I know. Don't worry about me. Worry about your father."

"My father?"

"He's gotten so bitter lately. He always wanted this and now that he's gotten it he's angry all the time. He loves his golf and is playing well, although for the first time ever, yesterday, he quit on the fifteenth hole."

"He didn't finish the round?"

"Said he was tired. But he's so bitter. Maybe you, Mr. Psychiatrist, can understand." We walked out.

I found my father in the bathroom, guzzling Maalox.

"Hiatus hernia and it's killing me. Every night and three bottles a week."

"Every night?" I said. This was alarming. "Have you had it checked out?"

"What's to check? A lot of the Jewish men have it and the professional men especially seem to have it. There's something I want to talk to you about and usually I do it in the dental chair but there's no chair anymore."

"You miss it?"

"No. So." He took out a list.

When I was an adolescent, into sports and girls and rarely home, my behavior had driven him nuts, but he would never say anything about it at home. Only on Sunday mornings, under the guise of working on my teeth, would he talk to me directly. We would drive downtown to the old grain-and-feed building that housed his second-floor office. Is there anything more bereft than a dentist's office on a Sunday morning? There, with the sweet fermenting scent of hay and grain mixing with the acrid antiseptic scent rising from the sterilizer, he'd put me in the chair and, as the Novocain froze my gums then my mouth and even my lips and tongue, he would sit beside me on his stool and take out a list and read me, one after the other, my failures. At his mercy—and fearing that if I protested, the drill would do its work with a lot less mercy—I listened, enraged. Finished, he would drill. I'd always thought this normal. Always felt he was a good father.

Now, referring to his list, he said, "It was a waste when you took all those years off and I hope now you'll go straight through." His words, without the anesthesia, hit me harder. "Three years on the Rhodes in Oxford and another year off last year, and each year off is a year less of earnings and so forth. Don't mind your mother and she's just upset. Her side of the family is always upset and they're too sensitive."

"Is there something bothering you, Dad?"

"What do you mean?"

"You seem so bitter, so unhappy."

"No, no, I'm happy, very happy here and the weather's great."

"Maybe retirement's not living up to your expectations?"

"It's great and the fairways here are so lush. My golf could be better but otherwise there's a lot to do with concerts and so forth and I'm very happy."

"But what about the cursing?"

"What cursing?"

"The cursing under your breath at Mom? It's terrible to hear."

"I don't curse under my breath at your mother and why would I?"

"You do. She can't hear it, but we can."

"I'm not aware of my doing that and if I do I'll stop."

THE LIT-UP CONDOS in the muggy night seemed like mausoleums. Jill and I sat in the car outside. The old people were out on their lime-tinted balconies, but I had an image of the three floors of screened balconies as cages. From somewhere came a tune from *Fiddler on the Roof*, and from somewhere else came a woman's voice saying, "You never talk to me it's like living with a dead man and I can't stand it!"—followed by jagged sobs. The night seemed polluted. I started driving. Slowly, aimlessly.

"He-lo-oh," Jill said. "Hi there. Remember me? Where are you?"

"I feel like I failed, totally."

"It was intense. That cursing is something else. But hey, at least it's a family. Mine's gone."

"I remember once—or think I remember—sitting at the kitchen table with my father and brother, and my mother screamed and next thing I knew there was a knife sailing through the air at us, and it stuck in the wall above our heads. I thought it was normal. It was crazy."

"Mine was just as crazy. Except for the UFOs."

"My father used to be a photo nut, took thousands of pictures, and there's not a single picture of me as a kid that shows me smiling. How can he live, with all that bitterness? What's eating him up? Her? Lousy golf? Me? Does he miss dentistry? What? And whatever I do, it's never enough."

"Never 'normal' enough?"

"Yeah."

"So maybe they're helping you break out."

"No joke. Being with them makes me want to be totally outrageous, totally crazy, risk everything, self-destruct! Makes me want to run, leave the country, leave the whole damn planet!"

"*Now* you're talkin'. Kiss me here." She led my hand to her belly.

"I can't do that while I'm driving."

"No foolin'. C'mon. I need handling."

"Handling?"

"Women need handling, like horses."

"Now? Can't you wait till we get back to the hotel?"

"No. Hot weather makes me hot." She grabbed the steering wheel and ran us up onto a shoulder, in the lee of a stone wall around a low barracks of condos. Across the way was an empty lot, with a sign announcing that another nine holes were coming soon. A Winn Dixie glowed in the distance. We went backseat and were soon doing what was sure to be illegal on this public thoroughfare, and in my mind was a question:

What is all this perfect order, this utopia of houses and cars and weather, a denial *of*?

At first I thought it was a denial of dying and death. But no, death was familiar to these senior citizens; in fact it brought out their best in terms of funeral arrangements and shipping bodies back up north and the widows banding together to adjust to the good life alone. Then I realized that with everything on the physical level having been taken care of as meticulously as making a house safe for a baby, what was being denied was whatever else there was after every material object including luxury items had been satisfied. Malik might say—and say with sorrow—that here alas was a denial of purpose, a denial even of joy, under the guise of the pursuit of happiness.

. . .

MISERY WAS A GHOST MOUNTAIN the next day, deserted by shrinks, except for me in Admissions. Not having Nash and Tunaba around made it easier. Compared to dealing with my family, dealing with people with severe mental illness was easy, for I had the authority of being their doctor. Some of it was even fun, like my Number 3, the new young editor of *The Town Crier*, Toby Updike. Immobilized recently by a broken leg—he'd slipped on the freakish ice outside the barbershop one afternoon as he was hustling along to a tryst with the wife of the town treasurer—he came in psychotic, with a Chief Complaint: "Someone sent me a memo saying: 'Name all your employees broken down by sex.' "

Viv and Primo were there, and the day took on a kind of festive tone as we worked together to handle the holiday horrors of all the happy families. I started enjoying myself, rocking and rolling along to the tune of whatever insurance would pay for, in terms of what was normal mental illness. But then, late in the day, I got a shock, in the form of my buddy Henry Solini.

He had been doing his scheduled rotation on Thoreau, the Family Unit, run by the classical Freudian psychoanalyst A. K. Lowell. Now he appeared in Toshiba to evaluate Toby Updike, for transfer to Thoreau. At first I didn't recognize him.

Henry Solini, the Henry Solini whom I'd last seen dressed in Rastafarian-cool, was now wearing Misery-tight: a new, three-piece suit and a red tie with dark blue regimental stripes, which, as I looked closer, I saw were in fact row upon row of Misery logos—half-moon, pine tree, duck rampant. His ponytail and curly hair had been shorn to an ominous fuzz, accentuating his male-pattern baldness, and he was growing a goatee and moustache. His earring was gone, and in his breast pocket was a thick cigar.

"Solini!" I cried out. "What happened?"

He stared at me blankly. Two seconds. "What makes you ask?"

"You look all Freudian!"

Two seconds. "I had a consult with Schlomo Dove? He said I had to drill down to the roots of my 'gay-latent' and the only way to do it was to go under psychoanalysis? I started last week with Dr. Edward Slapadek?"

"Oh," said Primo. "Is he outta jail now?"

Solini jumped.

"Just kiddin', Doc."

"Hannah's therapist?" I asked. "What is this? Is Schlomo getting a kickback?"

Two seconds. " 'Kick . . . back'?" Solini said, his brow furrowing like a schnauzer dog's. He was taking my joke seriously. Often before he'd seemed to space out by focusing past me onto a scene in the distance, but now he seemed to have turned inside out, and focused on a scene somewhere in a vast inner distance, shutting out me and the real world entirely. It made me feel as if I didn't exist.

Two seconds. "It's like an A-bomb has exploded in my belly?—what an association?" He reached into his inner suit-jacket pocket and whipped out a small, leather-bound notebook with the kind of brass clasp you see on a girl's first diary, unclasped it, slid a Cross pen from its leather loop in the binding, turned the point out, scribbled down the association, turned the point back in, slid the pen into its loop, closed the notebook, reclasped it, and whipped it back into his inner pocket. Noticing me, he asked:

"You got an analyst yet?"

"No way."

"Yeah," he said, walking away, "I hear he's pretty good?"

Nine

KEEPING IN TOUCH turned out not to be Cherokee Putnam's strong suit. Since the day almost a month before when he'd told me about confronting Schlomo Dove, I'd only heard from him once, an e-mail haiku:

Mountains misty,
Kids nifty,
Wife nasty.
Cher, Gstaad

I had pored over this, trying to decipher his emotional state, as one tries to unpack a love letter. There was a certain airy lift to the message, a Heil-eresque health in that "nasty," and a startling new intimacy in that "Cher." And yet the "nasty" was nasty, and the overall compression, however poetic, seemed a shadowed resignation to ongoing pain, like the throb of a toothache with your dentist still dead.

A few days before Christmas he had called me at home, something he'd never before done. The family had just flown in from Europe, and was just about to fly out the next afternoon to Aspen. He wanted to see me the next morning. "She's seeing . . . seeing *him*," he said bitterly, "so I might as well see you."

"I'd be glad to."

When I saw him, the torment in his eyes made my heart hurt, and hurt all the more for his appearing so healthy. Winter-suntanned, every hair in place, navy-blue sweater framing his face like a Brooks Brothers ad for a handsome face in a crew-neck sweater, he was gorgeous. He said he felt like shit.

"You were right," he said. "Not talking was hell. The only way we communicated was in bed."

"Bed?"

"Yeah, do you believe it? The sex was . . . *animal*." He stared at me, and in his eyes was a terrific abjection. "It wasn't making love. It was fucking. Made me think of . . . of *him*." He sighed. "And here's the worst part." He gulped for breath. I waited. Nothing. "Ah, the hell with it. I'll just go."

"What? You can tell me."

His eyes shifted—he wasn't about to tell me. "Christmas is a bitch," he said. "Ever since I can remember." He went on to talk about the Putnam Christmas ritual, where every December in Europe his father would move the clan to the Alps and conduct a series of drunken visits to drunken friends, all the terrified blond kids sent off with German nannies to run the gauntlet of the ski slopes until sundown when they'd run the gauntlet of the family dinner. Sensing that we were off track, I asked him how he'd first met Lily. He was startled, suspicious. But then I saw the startle reverse, back past his anger and suspicion, and as it moved all the way back past the birth of the first child, Hope, back to the real hope of Lily and him in love, it softened, and he smiled.

"It was an arranged meeting," he said. "I had finished Yale and was living in Boston, doing Harvard Law, bored and floating. Her mother's sister-in-law, Happy Borgmann—two *n*'s—knew my father's Final Club roommate. I hated those arranged things, they never worked out, but . . ." He sighed. "When I saw her, I was awed. She was so . . . innocent. Innocently lovely. Lily. Like a moist orchid." There were tears in his eyes. "Someone had given me tickets to Symphony. That night, I knew she was having the same intense attraction to me, and all the way downtown we talked and talked and we went into Symphony Hall and the lights went down and these four men in referee shirts and twirled moustachios came out and started singing four-part harmony. It was 'Barbershop Quartet Night' at Symphony. With anyone else I'd've been mortified, but with Lily it was exactly right—we laughed and laughed, talked about what a hoot it was, how unacceptable it would be in both our families. Magic. Like a dream."

We sat, still, the "click" between us a third element in the room. What he couldn't know was that I'd met Berry in much the same way. Our parents, golfing acquaintances, had fixed us up, each pair bringing their child with them to Tanglewood, the summer home of the Boston Symphony. I had reluctantly agreed to this, as had she. Then, that first moment, well, it was love. That sheen of innocence, yes. Cherokee looked at me, and in his eyes I saw the cloud of all the years since—the kids, Los Angeles, the Disney Studio in godforsaken Burbank with a corner office in a grand sandstone-colored building with a facade modeled after the Acropolis, each of seven columns being one of the Seven Dwarfs, crowned by a gargantuan Snow White, and now this—all this loss, of all this innocence. I felt my own looming loss, of Berry, asking myself—

A knock at the door. We both jumped. Another knock, and then we heard the outer door open, and then the inner, and standing there was a slender woman with light brown hair cut short as a boy's, with one eye bruised and swollen shut and the other glittering with fear and rage. Despite the black eye she was radiantly beautiful, delicately featured, a girlish face, lined. She wore jeans and boots and a fashionably worried leather jacket. A string of opalescent pearls was around her swan's neck, a riding crop in her hand.

"What the hell are you doing here?" Cherokee cried.

"He hit me," she said to me. "Did he tell you?"

"You have no right to just barge in on my therapy."

"You did it to me."

"I waited until after."

"And then spent an hour with him, with *my* therapist?"

"Yeah well I'm not fucking mine!"

"Oh God!" she said, holding on to the doorknob for support.

"Hold it!" I said, like a referee, standing between them. "I'm Dr. Basch."

"Lily," she said, holding out a hand with a diamond mine on it. Her hand was slight, tentative, lost. Brave but lost.

"Why don't you sit down with us," I said, "and talk?"

She struggled with this. Then she shook her head. "No. I can't."

"Come on, Lily," Cherokee said. "It's a chance. Go for it with me."

"Dr. Dove said it would pollute the transference. No. I can't."

"That smelly little Jew is brainwashing you!" He looked at me. "Sorry, Basch, I didn't mean—"

"Before this gets still more out of hand," Lily said, "I need to say to you, Dr. Basch, that I don't mind that he hit me—his father hit him, with a belt, quite a lot actually—but I do mind what he's doing with the children."

"What? I'm doing nothing with the children!"

"That's the point. You're withdrawn from them. And that's the way you were with me—more and more withdrawn—before you hit me."

"I would never—never ever ever—do them the slightest harm." He had tears in his eyes. "How could you possibly think that of me, Lil?"

She looked at him, feeling, clearly, his moving toward her. I knew, as did they, that her slightest movement toward him, even the slightest sign of her intent to move toward him, might tilt their lives toward each other, maybe for a long time. Such moments can, and do. I was rooting for her, hard.

She turned and left.

Cherokee slumped down, hands over his eyes, as if to not see what he did see. I waited. He said nothing. I said, "Okay. Tell me."

"I was drunk, she was drunk, we argued about—God knows what now—and I hit her. I hardly remember it. I'm totally ashamed. Father never really beat me, just whacked me once or twice with his belt."

My father too, more than twice. Talk about terror. To be at the mercy of an enraged dentist? "Did he hit your mother?"

"When they were drunk, sure, some."

"And your children? Hope and Kissy?"

"I swear to you, never. Never in this world. Lily's the one who loses it with them, lately. She gave Kissy quite a shake, in Italy—that's one reason she left to come back here for therapy. You do believe me, don't you?"

"You didn't tell me about hitting her."

"I was afraid of what you'd think of me. I would have told you, before I left. That's why I called. I *want* you to know these things, Roy. But you've got to believe me, about the girls? *Never*. Do you?"

I considered this and realized I did. "Yes."

"Thank God. Didn't I tell you Christmas was a bitch?"

"I don't think you should go to Aspen."

"Got to. There's a party at Eisner's house, all my old Disney friends. Remember Eisner? Three hundred fifty million, in one year? His house is incredible—perfect—looking up a valley into the mountains, all hand-hewn wood, a mix of Adirondack Lodge and Rocky Mountain. The best house *ever*. The man has taste."

"This isn't about houses, it's about your life. And your family."

"Yeah, but Aspen is Aspen. It's only another ten days. I'll be back."

We parted with a sense of the tenuousness of our link, as if all this talk were well and good, even a serious dalliance, but Aspen is Aspen, Gstaad Gstaad. He may be getting easier to read, I thought, but—and maybe even *for* his sense that he's being read more easily—he's getting harder to change. Like us all. I was scared to let him go, to let him out there, but what else could I do, lock him up? Against his will? Fat chance.

CHRISTMAS ADS FOR MISERY were running daily in the *Crier* and on TV—late at night or early in the morning to catch those with the buzz of high anxiety preventing sleep, or those with the fuzzy early-morning awakenings of the depressed. Each ad ended with "Our operators are standing by." The weather was a gold mine for the hospital. As if to mock the TV image of

Christmas—those soft pillows of snow, that squeaking of new boots on the packed roadbeds, the crisp chill wishes for Peace on Earth Goodwill to Men—it was unseasonably warm. Primed for temperatures in the twenties and thirties, we got forties and fifties. It was screwy. The big banks of November snow went all runny. There were floods. Things pretty much turned to mud.

At Misery, Buildings and Grounds were confused, splashing through the muddy lawns to hang decorations on droopy, overheated pines. With the weather so crazy—and with the ad campaigns suggesting that it was a person's right if not duty to have a Happy Holiday—people were having a harder time staying sane. Global warming was in the air. The snowcapped peaks of the impassive shadowing mountains seemed to mock the foothill dwellers, for snow lay only on inaccessible slopes. The nearby ski areas were barren, but for a trail or two of fake snow, as tattered as the pots of pooping poinsettias in the malls.

People flocked to Misery. The number of admissions, already high, went higher. My daily admissions moved up from an average of seven, to nine, then to eleven. In response, health care insurance denials of health care payments went higher still. Protocols were altered, loopholes in policies appeared. The daily discharges moved up from an average of eight to ten, and then to twelve. Like a parasite in the bowels of the hospital, health care insurance was making sure that, no matter how many of the mentally unhealthy were fed in, many more were purged out. A voracious animal, Misery needed constantly to be fed.

Nash and Tunaba fought back. They spent hours huddled over the big Toshiba in their shared office, reading from right to left—from the dollar amount of the latest health insurance payments to whichever DSM diagnosis was now bankable. If suddenly insurance was paying top dollar for, say, 301.13, Cyclothymic Disorder, the big Toshiba would be reprogrammed to reprogram all the little Toshibas, so that for data I typed in that previously had led to my sweet little Toshiba laptop spewing out, say, 302.90, Atypical Paraphelia, now it would spew out, time after time like a run of luck at craps in Vegas, 301.13, 301.13, 301.13, and—wait for it—301.13: Cyclothymic Disorder.

On the day of Christmas Eve, I was sitting behind the bulletproof with Viv—they'd built a new bulletproof for the holiday season in the Toshiba lobby—looking out at the crush of people trying to get into Misery. The lobby was packed with people fleeing the normal world, seeking asylum. Primo Jones was doing some serious nothing, standing around, trying to control the crowd.

"I ain't so sure Christ died for this, Doc, y'know what I'm sayin'?"

All day long, tormented by nonstop Christmas carols on the Muzak system, I had been clicking along, admitting patients to McMisery as efficiently as a kid flipping burgers at McDonald's, making diagnoses spanning the "Slee-eep in Heavenly Peace" sky from 313.21, Avoidant Disorder of Childhood, to 293.82, Organic Senile Hallucinosis; from 302.72, Inhibited Sexual Excitement, across the street to 302.75, Premature Ejaculation; and from 295.70, the dire Schizoaffective Disorder, over to the strangely enticing 312.33, Kleptomania.

Now, with Primo for security, I interviewed a violent middle-aged Italian bricklayer with a Chief Complaint of "I am God."

"How do you know you're God?" I asked.

"Because I was chosen."

"Why were you chosen to be God?"

"Because I was in hell. You want proof?" He unbuttoned his shirt. On his belly was a magnificent tattoo of *The Last Supper*. Clearly it had been done many years before, when what was now his belly had been his chest, and when he'd been thinner, for now it had expanded, so that Christ and the Apostles were all wearing broad grins.

"What'd you think, Doc?" Primo asked after we'd locked him up.

"298.80. Brief Reactive Psychosis."

"Youse don't think he's God."

"He may be, but it's not reimbursable."

I went to see an adolescent carrying what seemed to be a vacuum cleaner—indeed it said "Panasonic"—but it was covered with aluminum foil and had a fur coat on it. Instead of the standard attachments it had a huge metal funnel which the kid kept pointing at the ceiling as he jumped around. Primo came up and started standing around, to protect me. I asked what the thing was.

"Orgone accumulator," the kid said. "To catch the orgone particles. It's homemade, but it works. I took a welding course to make it. Lotta particles during Christmas. I carry it everywhere."

"And what do people say when they see it?"

"They say, 'Oh I see you've got your orgone accumulator with you.' What the hell do you think they say?"

Primo and I rolled eyes, and Primo said, "I got the diagnosis, Doc. What you got there is a WEFT."

I asked, what was a WEFT?

"Wrong Every Fuckin' Time. What that kid needs is to stick 'im in a clothes dryer and keep feedin' in the quarters."

In the waiting room was the kid's shrink, a Reichian. I thought he might help me to understand what was going on, but he too was holding a vacuum cleaner, in this case with the funnel reversed, so that the narrow end was pointing at the ceiling like a gun. "It's a cloudbuster," the man said. "Whenever I see that kid, my body armor tightens up. I've been getting Rolfed, myself."

"Now I can die happy, Doc," Primo said. "Now I've seen everything."

Not quite, for next was a dazzling young woman wearing a "God Made the Irish Number One" button, dressed provocatively for the heat of summer, her Chief Complaint: "Insurance put a rider on my breasts but Jesus never fails."

I finished her up and headed off to the Farben for Lloyal von Nott's Christmas reception. On my way out I was buttonholed again by the Woody Allen look-alike in the tweed sport coat and tie, the man named Sedders who didn't know how suicidal he really was and who was trying to get in touch with the doctors of his HMO—Healthycare Inc.—to certify his admission to Misery.

"I finally got through to a doctor!" he said excitedly.

"Great. I knew your persistence would pay off."

"I said that if he didn't authorize my admission to Mount Misery before the end of the year—next week—that I was going to kill myself, and that my lawyers were aware of this fact."

"Good thinking. When you mention lawyers, doctors start listening."

"That's what I thought, but then he said, 'You've been saying the same thing to our allied health professionals for several weeks now, and you haven't even made a suicide gesture, let alone an attempt. It doesn't sound all that much like an acute emergency anymore.' I told him that it was, but he said, 'I have to put you on hold.' I waited for almost half an hour, but he never took me off hold. Now what do I do?"

"Call back, start out sounding rational and then start screaming."

"Okay. Merry Christmas! Oh God! Now I've offended you, I'm sorry!"

"How have you offended me?"

"You're Jewish, right? You don't believe in Christmas."

"Who does anymore, I mean really?"

"Yeah." He squirmed and looked away, the way men do when they are about to try to make contact. "Dr. Basch, you're turning out to be my only friend."

DIXIE "THE BARRACUDA" DOVE loomed over her man in the receiving line, her holiday dress and hat sporting such luxuriant fruits that she seemed a living advertisement for a Chanukah cruise up the Amazon. The Misery Christmas reception was traditionally held in the Danebiel Ballroom, named after a former chairman of the board of Misery who had the IQ of a paper clip and a fortune made out of nothing, in stocks and bonds. Lloyal von Nott had been his therapist, from midlife crisis and divorce through an Alzheimer's so fierce that for years he referred to Lloyal as "Dear Uncle Caleb." Such was his love for Lloyal that upon his death he left a pile of stocks and bonds to Misery, on condition that his name be put on a ballroom.

Everyone was there, from the olive-green-clad Buildings and Grounds clustering around the vodka punch, through the red-clad and broad-beamed nurses and secretaries and social workers grazing on the jumbo shrimp and prime rib, to the black-suited shrinks and administrators huddling in the corners as if their lives would be in danger if they actually talked to these lesser ones adangle in the flowchart below them.

This class division was obliterated only in the receiving line, where you got to balance your crumpet and jumbo shrimp and bloodied rib and drink in one hand and have the other clasped damply by Lloyal von and the sycophantic Nash and Jennifer T. and Blair "the Handsome" Heiler and the drug brownshirt Errol Cabot and then the Doves—ah, those Doves!—the world's most charming analyst-astrophysicist tag team, these Doves trying hard, at least at this party, to put a little *oy* back in goy.

After a few quick glasses of the vodka punch, things got rosy, and rosier still when Jill appeared in a dark pink jumpsuit unbuttoned a touch too far, showing the edge of a lighter pink brassiere. Her underwear never ceased to amaze me. Like a good therapist, in every meeting she gave you something, in terms of glimpses of her underwear. I poured her a punch. Jill was the kind of woman who, when she enters a room, everyone stares, as if she had sparkly dust sprinkled over her like that glitter at parties, a dust of fame, so that you felt that, by being with her, some of the glitter couldn't help but sprinkle off onto you, and even the morning after, rising from your tired bed and getting dressed for work, you'd find little pieces of glitter on your wrist or your neck, and all during the day come across more pieces stuck in weird places—behind your ear, in the webbing between your fingers, on your thigh.

"I've got a clinical question for you," Jill said. "I'm feeling—"

"Wait," I said. "First, I've got a clinical question for you."

"Yeah?"

"What's your insurance coverage?"

"No, really. I'm feeling kind of blue, you know, with the holidays and all, with no family. So just tell me, is it like going to go away?"

"What *else* is it going to do?" I asked, thinking 309.00, Adjustment Disorder with Depressed Mood. She thought for a second.

"That's just what I wanted to hear," she said. "Do you take Visa?"

We went through the receiving line. The Chiefs of Misery gawked at her, especially Lloyal and Nash and Errol and Blair Heiler, who took Jill's hand with the somber lasciviousness of a world-expert lecher, and then confronted her by raising it to his lips as if she were a DD with RHS—Dissociative Disorder with Really Hyper Sexuality.

Things started to have that fluid feel where you think you're being witty but you have a niggling sense that you're not being as witty as you think. Hannah and Henry appeared in dark suits like twins dressed exactly alike by an oafish mother. With them was a tall woman with chiseled features, cropped hair, and walled-off eyes, also dressed in a dark suit and wrapped in a demonic silence. This was the woman who had replaced Bob Marley as Henry's hero, the classic Freudian psychoanalyst, A. K. Lowell. With each of my attempts to engage any of the three of them, Dr. A.K. would pull her haunted silence more tightly around her, and Hannah would roll her eyes up to her Great Analyst in the Sky and talk about her latest workshop, a Jungian Rodeo Quest in Boulder, and Henry would peer inward, his face twisting in terror at what he saw.

Malik swam in, wearing a ridiculous plaid sport coat over a sweat suit, mopping sweat from his face with a remarkably petite Israeli Army towel. With him were his former patient and now AA sponsor George, and Mr. K. They'd just come from a half-court three-on-three basketball game in the gym.

"So tell me, Malik," I said, nodding toward Mr. K. and George, "how come these patients of yours are always so interesting?"

"Easy," he said. "I've developed a sliding scale, based on how boring they are. You do a *sport* today, Basch?"

"I'm about to."

He glanced at Jill. "I mean *aer*obic."

"More punch?" Jill asked me. I handed her my glass. She left.

"Watchit, Basch," Malik said. "Sex in Misery is tricky."

"Uh-huh. So what's with the sliding scale?"

"The more boring they are, the higher their fee. Every month we evaluate it, and if they've gotten less boring, their fee goes down."

"Who decides how boring they are?"

"We do it together, right, Mr. K.?"

"Yes, er, no, I hardly pay anything anymore."

"Pretty soon I'll be payin' him," Malik said. "Gotta go, Basch. Can't be around all this booze."

"There's a Christmas Alkathon," George said, "and a new meetin'."

"It's called 'the Brain-Damaged Group,' " Mr. K. said, laughing.

"The thing about bein' sober," Malik said, watching Jill walk toward us, "is that for better or worse you grow a conscience." He winked.

Before I could figure out what the hell he meant, he was rocking away, again singing that same damn Aerosmith song. He disappeared into a thicket of social workers, just as Jill arrived with my punch.

Then suddenly, there before me and Jill, was Berry. I felt myself go hot around the ears, the neck, the throat.

"Oh hi!" I said way too loudly.

"Hi, Roy," she said. "I was driving by and thought I'd stop in."

"Berry, Jill," I said, tightly. "Jill, Berry."

"Heard a lot about you," Jill said.

"Oh?" Berry asked.

"Roy and I worked together on Emerson."

Small talk was made. I felt drunker, in a world all afloat. Things turned glassy, glassine. Sweat pooled in the hollow of my back. We three made weird talk with several shrinks.

Jill went for more punch and Schlomo Dove came over, sloppily dressed and looking particularly ugly, his jowls pressing down on the wilted collar of his white shirt, open at the neck so that gray hairs sprouted out over the loose, nooselike knot of his necktie. It was a stained number sprouting the same kinds of tropical fruits that currently graced the Barracuda's dress and hat for her Amazon outing.

Schlomo started hitting on Berry, so shamelessly that her eyes popped in amazement. She shot me an "Is this a joke?" look, and tried to repel him. Things turned pitiful. Luckily, Viv cut in:

"Four more admissions, Cowboy, one the Virgin Mary."

"Gotta go," I said.

"I do too," Berry said. "I'll walk you out.

"When can we talk?" she asked when we were alone in the hallway.

"How 'bout tomorrow?" I said.

"How 'bout tonight?"

I hesitated. Jill and I had plans. "Fine. Come over at eight."

"These shrinks!" Berry said, at the door. "What a bunch of losers! They're like twelve-year-old boys, looking at your tits before they look into your eyes!"

"Twelve's pushing it. I'd say about nine."

"This brings it all back—the way they demoralized me, in my training. The men who run these places are pitiful!" She stared at me. "Maybe *that's* it."

"It?"

"For you. We've got to talk."

"All hell's breaking loose, Cowpoke, so c'mon!"

"At eight."

I did my admissions, the last the Virgin Mary with a Chief Complaint of

"Three times in the Bible Jesus said 'I'm going to die' and nobody even stayed up with him and talked with him they all went to sleep and if there'd been any women among his disciples you can bet they'd try to comfort him by suckling him with these two gorgeous thirty-eights."

296.44, Bipolar Disorder, Mania, with Psychosis and Exhibitionism.

At quarter to five I went up to my office in the attic of Toshiba to pick up my stuff. A woman was waiting for me. Her hair was bleached platinum and she was dressed all in black. On her lap was a wrapped Christmas present, all angels. Who could this be? She turned.

"Christine?" I said, surprised. My blond Lady in Black had gone platinum?

"Oh, Dr. Basch, thank God you're here!" She blew her nose loudly. Her eyes were red with weeping. "Can I see you?"

"Sure. I've got a few minutes. Come in."

I hadn't heard from Christine since she'd announced for Arnie Bozer and walked out into the door, bloodying her nose. Since I, Heilerized, had Heilerized her.

"I've got a headache to die from. Aspirin won't touch it."

"What's going on?"

"Arnie. That prick. I was supposed to go to his home in Indiana with him for Christmas today, to meet his family. Last week I went skiing with my girlfriend in Colorado. The day before I came back, Arnie sent me a dozen red roses at my hotel. No one had sent me flowers since high school. They were lovely. When I came back I was psyched. I mean he had said . . ." she was overcome with weeping, and shouted out, "he loved me." Again her black mascara ran down her cheeks, diffusing in her rouge, in a lethargic gray. "So my first night back—last night—we get together for dinner, and I'm in such a loving mood. I've been thinking Arnie is it, Mr. Right, right? So at dinner he starts talking about himself and his analysis with Dr. Schlomo Dove."

"I thought he wasn't supposed to talk about what Schlomo and he did."

"He never did before, but for some reason last night he starts to tell me everything. On and on about his childhood on the chicken farm. It was sort of interesting, but only sort of. I mean how interesting can a childhood with chickens be? And we were *eating* chicken too, wouldn't you know it? It's like he's talking to a mirror. I start feeling I don't exist."

"Yes?"

"So I go—in the kindest, most loving voice—'Arnie, that's fantastic, but I haven't seen you in a week and, maybe, before we get into all that we can make a little contact with each other?' " She looked at me imploringly. "Nothing wrong with saying that, is there?"

"Nope."

"Well, he goes apeshit. He goes, 'I thought you were truly interested in *me* and here I'm telling you the most important thing going on with me and you don't want to listen? You just want to talk about yourself?' So I go, 'No, I don't want to talk about me, I just want to talk a little about us, okay?' He goes more apeshit—like he's going to smack me. I hold up my salad plate, for protection. And he goes, 'Us? There is no more us. I'm out of here.' And he gets up and starts to leave. So I go, 'Please, Arnie baby, please stay and talk. I need to talk to you.' And so he stares at me and with like incredible contempt he goes, 'That's a borderline dissociative response,' and walks out. Now he won't return my calls." She lost it again, sobbing hard.

Bozer was at the moment rotating on Emerson. His "borderline dissociative" comment came from his Heilerization. I didn't mention this to Christine.

"Is there something wrong with me?"

"No."

"I mean he seems fine. I must be the one who's screwed up."

"Arnie's got problems," I said, "big-time."

Startled by my frankness, she stared at me. "Y'know, they ought to have some kind of licensing board for men, some way they could look men over and check out all their wiring and connections and all, so they come out certified."

"Certified?"

"To be in a relationship with a woman."

I burst out laughing, as did she. She gave me the wrapped Christmas present. It was a blue sleeveless sweater.

"I knitted it myself," she said. "I've spent so much time looking at you, I've measured you in my mind. I'm sure it'll fit. Go ahead, try it."

I slipped it over my head. It fit perfectly.

"Thanks," I said. "It's really nice. Regular time next week?"

She nodded, got up and went to the door. With her hand on the doorknob she said, "You're a real sweetie. Better than two Bayer aspirin."

"Merry Christmas."

She started to cry. Waving bravely, she left.

Jill was waiting for me at my car, with a bottle of cheap champagne.

"I'm glad I met Berry," she said, "and that she knows everything about us."

"Everything?" Jill was drinking from the bottle. She nodded. "But how? You didn't tell her. I heard every word between you."

"You heard but you didn't. We did it girlwise—too high a frequency for guys to hear. I really liked her. It's worrisome."

"How's it worrisome?"

"If a guy like you couldn't even make it with a girl like her, it makes me wonder what the hell I'm gettin' myself into. It's not that I don't like sensitive guys, but give me a choice between a sensitive guy and a guy who's great in bed and I'll take in bed, every time. Like now." She kissed me. She tasted like vodka and cherry.

"I'm not sensitive?"

"I didn't say that, *you* did. Let's make crazy love all night long."

"I've got to see her tonight, at eight."

She was quiet for a while, as we drove along. Then she said, "I'm feeling pretty good right now. For the first time in a long time my self-esteem isn't being affected by real-life disasters."

"It's that low, is it?" I said, trying to lighten things up.

She didn't laugh. "What's with you guys and jokes? I mean really. What?"

"Grief."

"Oh yeah?"

"Yeah. Everyone's got their own grief, sucking away at their heart."

"FLAKY, BUT NICE," Berry was saying guardedly a few hours later in my turret. "She seemed flaky, but nice."

"Yeah," I said, just as guardedly.

She paused. "Roy, I think you're depressed."

"I'm okay."

"You're not—I mean, don't take this the wrong way, but . . . but you're not thinking of suicide, are you?"

"Are you crazy?"

"No, I am not cr—"

"Don't you know me at all?" I said, irritated, coming down off the alcohol high.

"That's what I'm asking. I don't feel I do know you very well right now."

"No, I am not thinking of suicide. It's just tough right now, seeing so much grief coming into Admissions every day, and doing nothing much to help."

"Roy, please—*you* need some help. I think you should get into some therapy."

"Therapy? After seeing what it's done to Solini? To Hannah? Hannah's in fourteeen different kinds of therapy and she's worse than ever. When she talks to you, she stares up at the light fixtures. Because of therapy she left a great career as a cellist—to become a therapist! Not to mention my models as therapists: Heiler? Schlomo? Lloyal? *Ike White!* Gimme a break."

"There are other therapists, out in the community, not caught up in all the academic stuff, more commonsense people. I've found one."

"Hey—I'm not that complicated a person. I just want to stop thinking so much. All I want is to do my job till five, go home, not think."

"I thought you went into this *to* think, to understand?"

"Right now I'm stressed out. I just want to have a little fun."

"And I'm not fun?"

"I love you, but this, this is not fun, no."

"So you want it nice," she said, "but I want it real?"

"All I want," I said, feeling more and more trapped, "is to be free."

"And if the only real freedom is in relationship?"

"Real freedom is like climbing Mount Everest. You do it alone."

She took this in, then said, "Nobody climbs Mount Everest alone."

"Here we go again."

"Fine," she said, rising, her voice shaking. "Good night and good luck."

"No!" I said, feeling as if some bottom were falling out. "I'm sorry, I'm really sorry. It's just that, with you now, everything seems so damn hard. Like gravel or something."

"And I'll bet that with her everything seems easy."

I hesitated. "Yeah. Like for you, with whoever you're with—Chandra . . ." I paused. She said nothing. "Or some red-hot nursery school teacher or something." She smiled. "What's funny?"

"If anyone, it would be my car mechanic."

"You're making it with your car mechanic?"

"I wish. If I were, my car heater would be working, wouldn't it?"

We both smiled. All winter her Volvo had been ice cold. The texture of the stuff between us went to velvet.

"I just want you to know, Roy, that whatever I'm doing now, I'm not jeopardizing this relationship with you."

She waited for me to respond. Things turned, velvet back to gravel.

"I don't know," I said finally. "I just don't know."

She stared at me, and I saw the realization hit her, the horror in her eyes of our losing each other. I felt it too. She started to cry. I moved to hold her, wanting to comfort her. She cried harder. I felt her ribs expand and contract around her sobs, all edged, jagged.

"Hey, come on," I said, "don't cry."

"Why not? If I don't cry over this, what am I going to cry over?"

"I can't stand you crying."

"If you can't stand a person crying you're in the wrong business."

"Patients I can stand. This is different. You're not my pa—"

"Terrific—you're empathic with strangers, but not with your . . ."

"My *what?*"

"Whatever it was, it's not anymore!" She was furious now, her eyes afire, the pupils harsh, like pins. "You need help! And I'm sick and tired of trying to give it—without getting anything back."

"Nothing I do is ever enough!"

"Forget it!" she cried out, grabbing for her coat and hat. As she got up, she knocked over the lamp, and the bulb smashed, so that the only light was a hellish shaft from the bedroom. "Shit," she said. She started to bend to pick it up, but then straightened back up and kicked it as hard as she could across the living room, where it brought down a small table and a bottle of George Dickel sippin' whiskey. She walked out, slamming the door. Her footsteps fell away down the stairs, one flight, two, diminished, diminished, died.

Devastated, I sank to the floor, numb, desolate, hoping against hope that she'd come back, listening for her footsteps rising toward my door instead of falling away.

Then I heard them. A knock on the door. I opened it.

Jill. Her face was tense.

"I saw her leave, and I couldn't stand it. I need to see you."

"Come on in."

"No. It's not safe. Let's go for a ride in my car."

We went out. It had suddenly turned cold, freezing everything. We drove in the full moonlight along the mountain valley roads, the reflection off the ice on the fields making the night brighter than the day, which had been overcast with low clouds. The rare cloud was now like a child's fuzzy animal, say a polar bear, or a white whale, filmed with silver from above. I felt cold and numb.

"I have a real fondness for power lines," Jill said as they dipped and rose alongside us, in one long straight clear stretch beside the White River. "They're beautifully designed—almost like Chinese characters. I'm having trouble right now, with you and her. She's so intelligent, so educated—it makes me feel really inferior. I'm at a turning point in my life, I know that, but I've never had a real turning point before. I mean if you've never gone to college, or got married, or been in the armed forces, you never had turning points. I don't do them all that well."

"Yeah, well, if it's any comfort, I've had a lot of 'em, and I don't do all that well either." We meandered along, not talking much, really.

"One thing I've learned," she said. "A guy's truth in bed doesn't translate to truth in talking, but mine does. But I liked what you said before about grief. It was like from your heart."

"Thanks," I said numbly.

We got back to where she was staying up the street. I got out. Jill sat there. I went around to the driver's side. She rolled down the window. It was freezing cold and it was hard to keep my footing on all the ice.

"You really love her, don't you?"

"I have, and in a deep way I still do. She's like family. But it's pretty much over, I think."

"I know what I'm up against now. Something about actually meeting her, seeing her really real, woke me up. So good-bye."

"Please, don't—"

"Let's not drag it out. It's gonna be a disaster for me if I keep on with you, I just feel it. Just leave."

I tried to talk to her, but she rolled up her window. I tapped on it, to no avail, and tried to mouth words to her—"I love you"—but my breath crystallized to ice, obscuring her face and, to her, my lips. Finally I gave up and turned around, but my feet slid out from under me and I had to grab her side rearview mirror.

She rolled down the window. She was sobbing, and she clutched my hand clutching the freezing mirror and said, "I don't care if it's bad for me. I can't give you up. I love you."

VIOLENCE, DEATH, AND MUTILATION were the Father, Son, and Holy Ghost of Misery after Christmas. In my five weeks on Toshiba, I had gotten used to people being crazy. I was having a hellish time with people being violent.

Insurance, under pressure to pay out more money, was paying out less. The only ticket into Misery was violence, violence toward yourself or to someone else. People tried, tried damn hard. Ever since Christmas the weather too had turned violent, first an infernal mix of snow and drizzle, and then a relentless arctic wind that seemed to knock the breath out of your lungs and fling your testicles up toward your spleen. An ice pack had slid down off Canada, quick-freezing everything. The world turned to ice. Ice coated car windows and locks, front steps and front walks, sidewalks, roads, runways. Men ventured out to chip and chop and sand and salt it away. Chippers snapped, choppers split, sand got into everything—the ice was like iron. Giving up, returning to the house and being asked by the wife why the walk was still icy, the car stuck, the boots shedding sand on the rug, the man might snap, or start chipping or chopping at the wife or house-bound kids. Someone would call Misery. Misery would call Insurance. Insurance would turn them away.

Yet some of them, the Walking Worried, would just show up. They would sit in the lobby of Toshiba, hoping to talk to a doctor. Each day by midday they were spilling out onto the front walk and frozen lawn, trying to get a foothold on the ice. When I or Nash or Tunaba would walk by, they would clutch at us. We would try to escape, slipping and sliding away. Some camped out in cars and vans. Some held up pill bottles like petitions. It was heart-wrenching.

My last day on Toshiba, the last day of the year, was hell: a run of horrific admissions, the sequelae of violent, mutilating acts. By admission Number 21, I was fresh out of compassion, for the day, the year, and maybe even, I realized with alarm, for the rest of my life. Number 21 was a 31 y.o. heroin addict with a CC: "I'm in withdrawal, I need detox, and this is the only place in the state that will take me." Unfortunately, while he'd been waiting in the lobby, the last bed on Heidelberg East, Alcohol and Drug, had been filled. I had to refuse him admission.

"What the fuck am I supposed to do!" he screamed. "I'm in withdrawal, I feel like shit, I gotta get a fix."

"Do whatever you've been doing. Maybe a bed will open up tomorrow."

"What I been doin', Doc, is knockin' over little ol' ladies in the street and snatchin' their purses. Is that what you, in your professional opinion, are tellin' me to do? Go out right now and knock over another little old lady?"

"Christmas is history. We're all in full-catastrophe mode now."

That morning the *Boston Globe* had published a list, in chronological order, of every woman and child killed by a man during the past year. It averaged out to one woman or child killed every five days. A woman had been killed every nine days. A child had been killed every fifteen days. Many men, after killing the women and children, killed themselves. A week before, the upper half of the torso of a Swedish au pair had been found in a Dumpster. Terror turned to horror.

The latest murders had been just the day before in a "safe" suburb; a family named Quist. Norman Quist first slit the throats of his two small children and dumped their bodies in a river, then came back home and bludgeoned his wife Colleen to death. He then shot himself dead.

I had just admitted Colleen's sister, with a Chief Complaint: "I was the one who found my sister's body. Her head was split open by an ax and her brains were all spilled out and blood was soaking everything. Everywhere I go, I see her lying there, the ragged white of her skull, the dark blood, the pink brains. And he slit the throats of his children? They were angels, little angels. How can I live with this?"

When I came to giving her a DSM diagnosis, my mind got stuck. She wasn't crazy, she was what anyone would be: crushed. But she needed time to heal, to be safe. The hospital wasn't a bad place to stay for a while, for her. But her insurance wanted her treated as an outpatient. I gave her the most innocuous DSM for which they would pay, "296.20, Major Depression, Single Episode," and she made it in.

I felt sick. Sick not only at the carnage, but at being a man. For most people, who learn about a killing by watching TV, the killing fades as quickly as anything on TV, basically gone by the next commercial and helped along to oblivion by the commercial itself and the fake TV killing that soon follows, leaving no residue. But in Misery I had to live with the aftermath of the carnage, the enduring reality. What most people looked at from a couch as a flat run of pixels, I *saw*. Saw what it did to real live human beings, how it lasted not the six minutes to the next commercial, not six hours six months six years, but a lifetime. More—how it echoed down the generations. For weeks I had been having nightmares. I walked around enraged, sick at heart.

I wasn't totally alone. One potential admission that day was a 32 y.o. assistant district attorney with a CC of "I'm supposed to get married next week but after seeing all the killing and things done to the kids I keep thinking over and over that if I do go ahead and get married and have kids I might wind up doing the same. Four out of ten American households have a gun. I have a gun. I've lost my faith, I guess. Is that crazy or what?"

"I've lost my faith too. You'd be crazy not to. Insurance won't accept it. Go home to your fiancée."

I went on, on autopilot, my heart as hidden and numb as the tiny silicon one hidden somewhere inside my laptop—except for a jolt when I remembered Lily Putnam's black eye. Could Cherokee, out there somewhere on the loose, turn even more violent and turn up in tomorrow's headline, something like WILD WASP WASTES WIFE, KIDS, PROMINENT SHRINK S. DOVE, SELF. In an icy sweat I called Aspen information. No luck. I left a message on his home machine to call at once, knowing I wouldn't sleep easily until I heard they were all safe.

"YOU STOBBED CARING about me and I don'wanna *live*!"

This was the CC of my next to last admission that day, Number 23, none other than my patient Zoe, who had come in totally drunk.

Since her discharge from Emerson, she had done well in therapy with me, helped along by her LAMBS partner, Thorny. They had continued to live together in Misery Garden Apartments. Thorny was going to NA—Narcotics Anonymous—and volunteering at a local recycling and alternative energy company.

Zoe and Thorny had decided, since they were doing well, to show their near and dear ones just how well they were doing. Wouldn't it be cool, these good buddies thought, to spend the holidays visiting each other's families? Big mistake. The trip to Louisiana to meet "the Burn King of the Bayous" had gone badly, given Thorny's new focus on cleaning up his father's mess. They left early for Palm Springs, California, where Zoe's family wintered in Rancho Mirage, an armored enclave of the rich set between Bob Hope Drive and Frank Sinatra Way.

I hadn't seen Zoe in a few weeks. Now I was stunned by how she had changed: her tall, slender, college-girl frame was no longer in jeans and blouse and Reeboks, but in flowery dress and gold lamé shoes and fake red fingernails, her light brown hair now in a garish fading perm. She was heavily made up, the makeup so messed up that her aquiline nose seemed stuck in her sun-reddened, feverish face. The Rancho Mirage look. Having used booze to come down off a long run on cocaine, she was totally exhausted, drunk, sniffing and blowing her nose, and slurring her words.

"She's been fighting with her mother and father," Thorny said, "and scorin' coke since Christmas. She's up to almost a fifth of scotch a day. Her parents wanted her to go to Betty Ford, but I got her back here to you."

"I'm glad you did."

"Better the dickhead you know than the one you don't. Even though she can't talk to you right now, Doc, when we talked about you last night she told me she thought you were smart. Smart, but cold." He considered this. "Me, I think you're warm. Warm, but stupid. But hey—you're miles ahead of Solini."

"Are you still seeing Solini in therapy?"

"You gotta be jokin'. Seeing Solini, now, is useless as stirrin' shit."

I tried to make contact with Zoe. Crashing from the coke, out of it from the booze, she said, "Youbeen disdracted 'n' distant," and slumped into sleep.

"Shit," I said, feeling bad about her relapse, and my part in it.

"*Sono tutti catzi*, Doc," Thorny said.

"Which means?"

" 'Everybody's a Dickhead.' But we're all doin' our absolute best. Even me. Later."

I started Zoe on a detox program, and called Heidelberg East, the Alcohol and Drug Unit, to see if I could transfer her over there. They still had no beds. I admitted her to Toshiba for the time being.

My last admission of the day—which would fill all the beds in Misery for the year—was a 16 y.o. Hispanic-American woman brought in by her parents. Her father was the CEO of a supermarket chain, her mother a pediatrician. Her CC was: "My boyfriend dumped me life sucks I want to die." Such was the family wealth that Nash himself did the admission interview, Jennifer and I watching. The parents were not allowed to participate.

It was a masterpiece of efficiency lasting a mere five minutes, but as Nash finished her off and got up to go, out from her boot came a carving knife. She lunged at Nash. I froze. Jennifer crouched in a tae kwon do stance. Nash screamed "Help!" grabbed me between one arm and one hook and threw me out of his way and toward her. He opened the door and ran out.

I tripped over Jennifer, rolled toward the young woman's feet, and as I saw Jennifer run out the door I thought, My life is over but I've given it to a worthless cause trying to deliver quality mental health care to this unfortunate rich young woman, and then I saw the glint of the blade and raised my hands to protect myself and had another thought, which was, Oh shit!, but suddenly someone barreled in and tackled her and pinned her and the knife dropped soundlessly to the thick carpet and I was saved.

"Close call, Doc, y'get me?"

Shaking all over, I couldn't speak, but nodded.

"I wasn't fuckin' after you," the young woman said, "I was after him."

"Who, sweetheart?" Primo asked.

"That motherfucker who only gave me five minutes of his time. It took a lot for me to come in here, and that cocksucker gives me five fuckin' minutes?"

In another five minutes she was escorted back out and released to the icy windy night, too dangerous for a mental hospital. I was bleeding from a scratch from Nash Michaels's hook. I put a Band-Aid on. My problem now was that there was one free bed. Two were on the waiting list. I read their charts.

The first was a Vietnamese refugee named Ngo, who, on finding his four-year-old daughter raped and strangled in an abandoned apartment, had flipped out and gone stalking the streets, searching for Henry Kissinger. He was totally psychotic and dangerous.

The second was one Grasci and his lawyer. Grasci was the creator of a hot new NASDAQ hit called Softi Serv, which was some software that linked with some other software and that in fact would turn out to do little or nothing except hook a few more million computer nerds and suburban male obsessives and make him rich. He was paying out of pocket and desperately wanted to be admitted. It turned out that he'd just beaten his wife silly with a pool cue. His Chief Complaint? "Why the hell was she putting on sexy underwear when we were getting dressed to go to court for our divorce, when she'd never wear sexy underwear when we were married?" He was here to create a legally binding defense.

It was musical beds. Nash Michaels was at the keyboard. It was no contest.

"They tell us America is best country!" screamed Ngo the Vietnamese man as Primo led him out the front door and pointed him toward Candlewood. "They say here you have chance. What chance my little girl have? I kill them all you wait and see!"

I sought out the sanctuary of the bulletproof.

"Terrific," I said to Viv, taking her Christmas bottle of Chivas out of the drawer and sipping. "We admit someone who is sane, and we send someone who is insane and dangerous back out into the world. What's wrong with this picture?"

"Yeah, Cowboy," she said, "it makes you wanna puke."

"Makes you want a law banning men from women and children."

Hannah came in, to take over as Doctor on Call. She'd just gotten back from a trip to Philadelphia to give a dissociative lecture at a hospital, and was distraught.

"On my way down there this morning, at the Philly airport, when the cab dispatcher asked the cabbie if he knew how to get to the hospital, the cabbie said no, so the dispatcher motioned me to the next cab in line. But then the first cabbie and the dispatcher started arguing, and the cabbie pulled a gun and shot at the dispatcher and drove off! So the dispatcher says to me, as if nothing unusual happened, 'Take the next cab, young lady.' So I jumped into the next cab, who said he knew the address, but after we were going he said, 'I don't know the address either but I wasn't going to lose the fare.' He was stoned, going eighty miles an hour, and we ended up in some deserted park. I thought he was going to kill me! But we finally got there and it was forty-five dollars! And then I got out and went to the psychiatry department, and I'm white as a sheet and I told all of them what happened and no one said anything to me, no words of comfort, nothing!"

"No one said anything, dear?"

"None of the psychiatrists. The secretary did. She was very nice. She said to me, 'Oh you poor girl,' and got me a cup of coffee. She was very nice. None of the psychiatrists said anything. I mean I've taken cabs all my life in New York. There used to be some morality; now there's none."

"People out there are seethin' with rage, dear," Viv said, "seethin' with rage. Everybody feels they're not gettin' what they deserve outta life."

"But this is America," she cried, her eyes rolling up to the fluorescents. "I mean it's not like this isn't it—*this is it! This is normal life!* This is where we live! What are we supposed to do? Stay away? Away where? How?"

"You need some support, dear. Where's your family?"

"New Guinea."

"Funny, dear, you don't have a New Guinea accent."

"No, no, they're visiting my sister and her husband in New Guinea for Chanukah. The successful sister."

"There are some good people in life too, dear."

"Sure there are," I said. "Where's Blair Heiler?"

Hannah's eyes rolled down to mine, widened with terror, and then rolled up again like shades. She said loudly, "Shhhh!" She didn't want Viv to know what Viv and everybody else at Misery knew, much as von Nott hadn't wanted everybody to know what we all knew about Ike White's suicide. "You're right, Viv," she went on, "I've met somebody new."

"Good for you, dear. Who is he?"

"He's in the field, a psychiatrist."

"What antidepressant is he on?" I asked.

"I . . . I don't know. He didn't say."

"Is he happy?"

"No, he's not happy."

"Not Prozac, then. Is he peaceful?"

"No, I couldn't really call him 'peaceful.' "

"So he's not on Paxil. How 'bout breezy?"

" 'Breezy'?"

"Breezy."

She thought a few seconds. "Yeah, he is kind of 'breezy.' "

"Zoloft. He's on Zoloft. Aloft, like the balloons in their ads? Breezy."

"What happened to your husband, dear?"

"We're separated. He's so boring you could die. Now his whole family's on my case. The ben Lubes are restless. It won't be easy. But it's nothing compared to a trip to Philadelphia. Unreal."

A call came in for Viv. Hannah whispered that there wasn't any new man at all and that although things were rocky with Blair and her, they were still very much on. Hannah left to take her first call. I was off duty at last.

I chatted with Viv until Primo came back. "More bad news, Doc."

"Yeah?"

"They found a body, way way back in the woods, frozen solid. And on the body was a letter and it was addressed to youse."

He handed me a letter the size of a Christmas card. I opened it. A handmade Christmas card. Within a crude, child's outline of a Christmas tree was written:

Life
Is Tough
Life Is Hard
Here's Your Fucking
Christmas Card.
Mandy

On the reverse side was a message for me:

Dear Dr. Basch,
My wife Mandy made me this card. You tried hard but Healthycare kept putting me on hold. In my safe deposit box is all the information, which our lawyer will use to sue the pants off Healthycare. My wife and kids will be taken care of. Thanks for your help.

Sincerely,
Sedders

"You know him, Doc?"

"Not really."

"Died of exposure."

"Don't we all," Viv said, "in the end?"

"Yeah, well," I said, "we should give the guy a medal."

"Why's that, Doc?"

"He killed himself first. *Before* killing his wife and kids. Yes, my friends, this man was a great American. I'm off duty. Happy New Year."

Feeling a terrific thirst, I went downstairs into the tunnels and along to the soda machine under the Farben. I put a dollar bill in and nothing came out. Then I noticed that the light said: Will Not Make Change.

Underneath this someone had written: Change Is Very Difficult.

Upstairs again, I stared out the locked front door at the crowd—maybe twenty poor souls. Having been told that there was no chance of getting in, the crowd had turned nasty. Wild-eyed people were banging on the bullet-proof glass of the front door. How would I make it to my car?

Primo materialized to escort me.

We battled our way through, trying to stay on the sanded and salted walk, the crowd slipping and sliding on the ice on the lawn. It was pathetic, all these people sick of normal life, wanting in to a hospital for the mentally ill. They were downstream from something. We were hauling them up out of the water, but nobody was looking upstream, for whatever that something was.

My car was blocked from backing out by a small family—father, mother, baby. The father came over to my window and shoved a sign in my face:

UNEMPLOYED EXECUTIVE.
WILL WORK FOR FOOD.
CAN YOU HELP?

I thought of Malik. Once during the summer, walking with him toward a sporting goods store in the village, we'd passed a drunk asking for change. Malik had given him a dollar. I'd given nothing. The panhandler had said to him, "Have a nice day," and then turned to me and said ominously, "and a *safe* day, you."

"Why'd you do that?" I'd asked him. "He'll just spend it on booze."

"It's just my way," he'd said, "of betting on the Divinity."

Outside my car window now, the man was joined by his wife and baby. I started to dig into my pocket for change.

But then I saw the children, all the children mutilated and killed by men, and though I heard Malik's voice telling me that these were cries from the mine shaft on behalf of us all, I was filled with despair. How could a God, something Divine, do this? Hannah had said it: "This is America, this is it. Normal life. What are we supposed to do? Stay away? Where? How?" Divinity? Don't talk Divinity to me. If you're going to talk anything, talk Hell.

I looked at the man and shook my head no.

He gave me the finger and moved away, the harsh wind hitting him, sliding him back, his legs working hard to stay up on the ice, and to keep his wife and baby up too.

The sun was a red teardrop in the notch of a mountain, leaving a darkness over our low hill. As I pulled away, the klieg lights went on. The crowd, somehow beaten down by them, shrank back from the front door. Illuminated over the portico was brand-new graffiti, spray-painted in Day-Glo orange:

IN TOUCH WITH A SHITTY TOMORROW.

"Exactly," I said out loud, "better than being in touch with today."

THOREAU

"I have found little that is good about human beings. In my experience most of them are trash."

—SIGMUND FREUD

"The mass of men lead lives of quiet desperation."

—HENRY DAVID THOREAU

Ten

CHEROKEE WAS OBSESSED. "I can't get it out of my mind," he said a few days later in my office up under the eaves of Toshiba, "that he's fucking her in therapy."

He looked worse than ever—strawberry-blond hair mussed, gorgeous blue eyes shadowed by lost sleep, lips set in a firm line. As if giving in to the grunge look his daughter Hope had copied from her cousins on the family vacation in Aspen, he had a week's growth of reddish beard, his shirt collar had lost its snap, and his shirt itself was stained with a reddish blotch shaped remarkably like South America. His jeans seemed baggy, as if he'd lost weight. His hidden messiness had gone public. He had gotten a little Schlomoesque.

"I can't get it out of my mind!" he said desperately. "The last thing at night, when I close my eyes to go to sleep beside her, there it is, a tiny voice, like a devil sitting on my shoulder whispering in my ear, 'He's fucking her in therapy.' And when I wake up—at five when she gets up—I feel okay for a few seconds and then—bam: 'He's fucking her in therapy.' I lie awake in bed from six to six-thirty, imagining. It's like I'm there with them, like I can almost see them."

"What do you see?"

"He's sitting in his chair behind that couch. She gets up off the couch and lifts her dress and shimmies down her underpants. She bought new underpants in Aspen. White satin, with a lot of lace?"

"No fooling."

"No. And not for me. I don't like white all that much. Ever since I hit her in Gstaad, no sex. Nothing. Everything is worse and . . ." His eyes glazed over. "There it is again: 'He's fucking her in therapy.' I was just then seeing her holding out her hand and leading him to the couch and going down on all fours and hiking her skirt up to her waist. It's so vivid, almost as if I'm right there watching, peeping through a crack in the door."

"Have you and she talked about it?"

"Not a word. I tried, she won't. It's killing me. It never goes away. In Aspen, there I am with Hope and Kissy at the top of a mountain, looking out over a view you could die for, ready to start the run down, and I hear a whisper in my ear: 'He's fucking her in therapy.' At Eisner's party, there I am with the two Michaels—Eisner and Ovitz—on either side of me, and boom: 'He's fucking her in therapy.' It's like a secret I've got inside me. Like a cancer or a crime I committed or something. It's driving me *crazy*!"

He did seem a little crazy—eyes wild, lip twitching, hair askew, and foot twitching like poor Mary Megan Scorato's after Hannah hit her with micro-dose Placedon. Whether or not Schlomo was screwing Lily, Cherokee was in trouble. And the strange thing was that as Cherokee was seeming more crazed to me, Schlomo had started to seem more normal. No matter how much you despised him, you had to admit that his performances at his Outpatient Team Meetings and at the Misery Academic Seminars were brilliant. Not only brilliant, but human. Whenever he interviewed a patient, or supervised me on patients, he seemed to be able to get it, get with it, zoom in on what was really going on, and despite his Yiddish *tummler* style, I always came away with more understanding of the person I was trying to deal with. I would sometimes sit with him in the cafeteria as he mangled some mystery meat and dazzlingly talked shrinkery. My custom-made suit was a dream. Schlomo hadn't repeated his "in your lap, boychik" maneuver, which he claimed was part of a recently diagnosed illness related to his heart disease, a kind of hand-twitch-specific Tourette's syndrome. His sloppiness I had started to see as a well-known sign of depression, that child facedown in the pool. Sometimes Schlomo would even talk about Ike White's suicide, as a tragic event befallen a rising star. While every fiber of my being wanted to see Cherokee as basically a regular guy who was being tormented as any man would be by his wife's behavior, and Schlomo as at best sick if not criminal, more and more I had perched on my own shoulder a devilish doubt, whispering, *Maybe not.*

"What the hell am I gonna do about this? C'mon, Basch, aren't you going to help me?"

It was the fourth time that session he'd asked me the same question. He'd talked for almost thirty minutes nonstop. What could I do? I knew something was missing in my work with him. No matter what I tried, I couldn't shake him out of his obsession. If I asked him about the obsession itself, he obsessed. If I tried to lead him away from the obsession, finding small openings with which to widen the scope, to other people in his life, he would talk briefly about these others but then—bam: "He's fucking her in therapy."

Again I tried to shift the content, asking him bluntly about the first thing he'd told me, back in July when he'd appeared at the Admissions Office at six in the morning: "Tell me about feeling like a failure."

This led to his talking about his father's disdain for his not joining Putnam, Weld, Umbeshrein, Sanchez, and Brown, his father's Wall Street firm, and his going instead straight from Harvard Law to Walt Disney.

"Father always taunted me about that. 'Working hard, are you, Cher?' In fact I was working hard, a lot harder than him. People think Disney is all sweet mice singing and dancing with ducks and carefree retarded dogs and bad guys portrayed as fags or blacks, but it's as tough as they come. I busted butt for Disney, and it paid off. I . . . um, quit last year, got my golden parachute, retired. But he never respected me for it. 'It's Mickey Mouse,' he'd always say, 'Mickey Mouse.' "

"You have some feelings about your father?"

"Yeah yeah, but what am I going to *do*? Tomorrow morning when she gets up and I hear the water run in the shower and she comes out looking like a million bucks and goes off to him? I half think of getting a gun and blowing him away. Don't you have any ideas?"

"You have a gun?"

"You think I should get one?" he said, eyes sparkling with a sudden manic energy. "Good idea!"

"No! No, no. No."

"Shit. Well, do you have any other ideas?"

I was out of ideas. Everything I said, he said "Yes, but" to, and went back to his obsession. Despite my training, I felt stuck. I knew how to interview people, but I had no idea how therapy worked, of what happened to bring about change. I had learned how to do things in the short run, but had no idea how to make things happen in long-term therapy. Maybe if I myself had ever been in therapy, I might have had some idea of what to do. Even Arnie Bozer, the lunkhead from the Land of Lincoln, had learned from his therapy with Schlomo, talking proudly of how he used Schlomo's interpretations to him in his early-morning sessions word for word on his own patients all the rest of the day, regardless of their diagnoses, gender, therapy issues, or anything else.

"Schlomo says," Arnie would say, " 'the unconscious is timeless.' This means you can say anything to anyone at any time. That's my policy, Roy."

My own long-term therapies with Zoe and Christine, and intermittently with Solini's ex-patient Thorny, had been haphazard rough trips, with rare promising moments that later seemed not to "take." Zoe was back in Toshiba being detoxed, and Christine was back seeing me only because of Bozer's Heilerization. How did therapy work? How do people change? Do they? Did it?

Cherokee's jealous obsession was like a wall around a city. I'd tried all my techniques to get in, and nothing had worked. I had no idea what else to say. I feared that if I didn't help him now, he wouldn't come back for another session. Failure loomed. His eyes met mine.

"Great," he said, eyes wildly flailing around the room, "I'm a failure at this too! This is not working. Ever since that day I came in, everything has gotten worse: no sex, no relationship with my kids, no fun—"

Suddenly the door opened briskly and in walked a platinum-blond woman. It was my outpatient Christine, the Lady in Black.

"Dr. Basch—" She looked past me and saw Cherokee. "You're with someone?"

"Yes." She looked dazzling. Madonna hair, black tights.

"Don't we have an appointment at four?"

"Four-fifteen."

"I thought you said four."

"Let me check." I went to my desk, leaned over my appointment book. I felt behind me their crisscrossing stares, interwoven with their feelings about me, felt it like an electric blanket thrown over my shoulders, set on high. I straightened up and said, "Four-fifteen."

"Sorry," she said. "My mistake."

"Look, I can leave early," Cherokee said. "I don't mind."

"No, no, it's your time," she said. "I can wait. My name's Christine."

"Cherokee."

"A Native American?" She smiled, a dazzling porcelain event despite the glitter of a gold bridge tied to a rocky canine, or maybe even more dazzling because of it—a postmodern smile, a kind of deconstructed dental reconstruction. "Enjoy, *Cherokee*." She glanced at me. "*Nice* sweater, Doc. Whereja get it?"

I was wearing the sweater she'd knitted. "Thanks." She shut the door.

"Can I ask who she was?" Cherokee asked, eyes wide.

"You can ask but I can't answer."

"Does she always come at this time?"

"I can't tell you."

"What a knockout," he said. "I love black."

"You have some feelings about her?"

"Yes. I feel . . . compared to her, I feel ugly." I was stunned by this. He was about as handsome a man as I'd ever seen. "Every comparison I make," he went on, "I come up short. She's something else! But I even feel ugly compared to you."

"Me?" As he'd been talking, I had been doing my own comparison, feeling really ugly compared to him. So I figured that this was transference, a distortion of our present relationship from his past, and asked, "And who have you come up short to in the past?"

"Don't let it go to your head, Roy," he said, ignoring my question, rising. "I'll give Christine the rest of my time. See you next week."

He shook my hand and left. I waited. And waited. Obviously they were talking. At 4:45, a half hour late, in she came, flushed with excitement.

"What was *that*?" she asked, waving a limp hand before her face, as if to cool down after a workout.

"You know I can't tell you, Christine."

"Nothing?" I smiled and shook my head. "And I thought *you* were hot?"

She talked about Cherokee, Cherokee, and more Cherokee. It was startling to hear how he'd presented himself to her: a normal happy relaxed young guy coming in for a few sessions of therapy in the same spirit he would come in for a few golf lessons to tune up his game, to find out—his words to her:

"What I want to be when I grow up."

"He's incredible," she said, leaving. "I mean talk about a man with *potential*."

"MALIK?" I BLURTED OUT.

"Thoreau!" he answered.

"Thoreau?" I yelled.

"Malik!" he said.

"Shhh!" said several voices in the darkness. "Shush!"

It was the next morning. I was settling into a chair at the back of a dark room on the second floor of the Family Unit on Thoreau, my next rotation in Misery. There he was, a high-voltage generator next to me in the dark. He had a basketball. He held it under my nose. "Take a whiff."

The smell—crisp, pungent new leather spiced with the acridity of vulcanized rubber seams—brought back memories of the new balls we Fish Hawks were handed on game days at Columbia High as we burst out of the locker room led by Konopski and Basch, the co-captains dazzled by the bright lights and cheers of the packed bandbox gym. "Ahhh!" I said, breathing deeply, my nose on the pebbly skin. "Converse is my *madeleine*."

"Hey, me too! Stim-U-Dent?"

"I took one, and felt the familiar minty sharpness between my teeth. My eyes were accommodating to the dark. A dozen people were there, facing a curtained wall. "What the hell are you doing here, Malik?"

Heads turned, in hostile silence.

"SHHHH!" Malik said, as loudly as possible.

"SHHHH?" I said, just as loudly.

"Five, four, three, two—-play ball!" Malik said.

Bong bong bong bong bong bong bong bong bong.

A grandfather clock, snaking through a loudspeaker system. The curtain parted. A semicircle of chairs faced us, an empty chair at each end. We were behind a one-way mirror, staring at the Family Olaf, farmers from Missouri, who were about to have their first session of Freudian family psychoanalysis. Their teenager, Oly Joe Olaf Junior, had just been admitted to Thoreau for doing badly at Simeon's Rest, a special boarding school nearby for students doing especially badly at other schools. Oly Joe, in psychoanalysis with Dr. A. K. Lowell, had regressed to an oral stage, and had been spending a lot of time at school in his room curled up under the covers sucking things, refusing to come to Misery for his analysis. He'd been brought into Thoreau so that he could be forced to see A.K., and so that his family could get involved. The family had been flown in for this meeting. Oly Joe Junior sat curled up in a chair looking scared, wearing a baseball cap beak backward and a T-shirt reading "No Fear!" Oly Joe Senior was in an ill-fitting suit, Mrs. Olaf in, believe it or not, a calico dress. Six-year-old Betsy, also in calico, sat in her mother's lap as if camouflaged, clutching a fuzzy yellow duck.

At the last bong, A. K. Lowell entered, wearing a dark suit in a mannish cut and carrying a cigar. Following her was an anxious middle-aged woman in plain dark skirt, blue sweater, and sensible shoes. This was Faith Baltsburg, a social worker who was a world expert in money anxiety. A.K. and Faith took their seats. So far it reminded me of a daytime talk show, say *Jenny Jones*.

"They're all transvestites," I said to Malik.

"Ha! Hahaha!"

"Shh," hissed someone in front. "They're starting."

Well, they were and they weren't, because A.K. was laying out silence. The silence persisted. The Olafs looked at each other and at A.K. and Faith.

"What's supposed to happen now?" Mrs. Olaf asked of Faith.

Faith said nothing.

"Are we supposed to start talking, Faith?" she asked again.

Faith seemed chiseled out of granite, and said more nothing, although I saw an anxious flick of her eyes over to A.K., as if asking for guidance.

"Doc, you want us to tell about Junior?" Mr. Olaf asked A.K.

A.K. said nothing.

"I said you want us to tell 'bout Junior?" Mr. Olaf repeated, loudly.

A.K. said more nothing.

"AIN'T YOU GONNA SAY NUTHIN'?" Mr. Olaf was now yelling.

A.K. said about as much nothing as humanly possible.

"Sheez. We come all the way from Missoura 'n' you ain't gonna say nothin'?"

"No, they ain't sayin' nothin', Pa," Oly Joe Junior said. "*We* have to talk."

"About what, son?"

"Like whatever comes to mind."

"Oh," the father said, "okay." He settled back in his chair, placing his hands flat on his thighs the way farmers will do when there's no internal-combustion engine present and they don't feel really alive. He wrinkled his brow and proceeded to say what was coming to mind. Nothing.

"Faith dear," Mrs. Olaf said, "yesterday you told us that there was hope, for Oly Joe, for him goin' back to school. What did you mean, 'hope'?"

Faith looked like she'd just been shot, her eyes darting quickly to A.K., who scowled at her and lit the cigar. Faith looked at the wall and said nothing.

"Isn't that what you said, dear? *Hope?* That there's *hope* for him?"

Everyone was looking at Faith, who, shaken and trembling with anxiety, in a voice devoid of anxiety, said, "And what are your fantasies about me?"

"I'm leavin'," Oly Joe Junior said, slowly uncurling from his chair.

"Honey, please," his mother said, "if you walk out now, I feel you'll never come back."

"To this place? Hell no."

"No, honey, to us." She began to weep. The little girl with the fuzzy duck started to cry too. The mother held her, rocking. It was really sad.

Oly Joe curled up in his chair once again and fell silent. He and his father listened to Mrs. Olaf and the little girl crying together.

Suddenly A.K. cleared her throat. I looked at my watch. Eight minutes gone. "And is it your fantasy," A.K. said, in a tone of impeccable neutrality and to no one in particular but rather to a figure up near the ceiling which the smoke from her cigar had formed, say a heifer, or perhaps a hog, "that if your father were dead, you would love your mother more?"

Oly Joe seemed stunned. He uncurled and started crawling toward the door.

"Oly Joe?" Mrs. Olaf cried. "Oly Joe? Don't crawl out the door!"

Oly Joe crawled out the door.

Mrs. Olaf handed the little girl and her fuzzy duck to Mr. Olaf and walked out the door after Oly Joe.

Mr. Olaf and the little girl sat there for a while. So did the duck.

"Pa," she said, "I have to go to the bathroom."

"Okay, sugar," Mr. Olaf said, and turned to Faith. "Pardon me, ma'am, but where's the bathroom?"

Faith was dying to tell where the bathroom was, but a quick, anxious glance to A.K. solidified her resolve to keep this information strictly to herself.

"We're simple folk," Mr. Olaf said. "We don't understand this." He carried the little girl and her fuzzy duck out. A.K. and Faith sat there as if everyone who wasn't there anymore was still there.

Silence, one of Surely They Won't Sit There Till The Hour Is Up?

Silence, one of They Sure Will.

I heard soft snoring beside me from Malik. Soon I slept too.

Bong bong bong bong bong bong bong bong bong bong.

I awoke from a dynamite sleep to find the lights going on on our side and going off on their side and people shifting their chairs into a circle.

"Solini?" I cried out, surprised that the little guy was there, even after his rotation with A.K. had ended.

Startled, he jumped up in his loose-fitting dark suit, shaking his head in a "Don't talk!" gesture. He recinched his Misery tie. I felt sad.

A.K. and Faith entered and sat down and led us with masterful authority into nothing happening.

Malik played with the basketball, spinning it, fondling it, bouncing it twice. In the small room it made a big sound. No one said anything.

"The projective identifications onto the son," someone said, "were not introjected by father or mother, despite their being offered the Oedipal interpretation. The projective/introjective Oedipal Oscillator was the primary defense against the pre-Oedipal dynamic: the fuzzy duck."

What the fuck, I thought, does *that* mean? Malik rolled his eyes.

The others seemed to know what that meant. There ensued a laborious discussion about this Oedipal Oscillator. It was impossible to comprehend what they were talking about. There were quotes from Freud and much mockery of the "simple folk" who had been doing so badly as a family right before our eyes. Mockery turned to blame. The group was split about evenly: half blamed the mother for Oly's psychopathology ("She's an engulfing/intrusive mother"), and half blamed the father ("He's a distant/sadistic father"). Just before the hour was up, A.K. cleared her throat again. Everyone got tense, as if an order had gone out: "Cover your crotch!"

A.K. fixed Faith with a muscular stare, and said, in an incredulous voice, "Your fantasy is there's *hope*?"

Faith, skewered, shook with anxiety. A wallet dropped from her hands, spilling credit cards, cash, and coins, which rolled, whined, and settled.

Bong bong bong bong bong bong bong bong bong bong bong.

Quickly the room emptied. Solini rushed past without a word.

"What the hell was *that*?" I asked Malik.

"Psychoanalysis."

"But that family, they were really hurt. Why didn't you say something?"

"Deft, Basch, you gotta be deft." He sneezed. " 'Nother Stim-U-Dent?"

I started working it between an incisor and a molar. "But what are you doing here, Malik? I thought you were on an elective."

"Yeah, and I elected to do this. I'm the resident in charge of the ward for three months."

"You?" I said. "But you despise this stuff!"

"Yop. Analysis goes against everything I have faith in. Take every AA slogan, then take the opposite, you got psychoanalysis: Keep It *Complicated*, *Last* Things First, *Hard* Does It, *Don't* Ask for Help. What bullshit."

"So why are you here?"

He looked me straight in the eye. Behind those tinty lenses, the voltage went up. "Of all the people who supervised me my first year as a resident, A. K. Lowell did the most damage, to me and my patients. *She is the worst!*"

"Worse than Heiler?"

"Heiler's a sweetheart compared to her. Heiler's scared of her."

"But why? She doesn't seem that bad. And everybody says she's brilliant."

"That's why. She *seems* brilliant. Seems to know what she's doing, so that if only you could learn it, you'd be brilliant too. I hate her."

"I thought you don't believe in hating people."

"I don't. But I hate her. That's why I'm here. Big-time challenge."

"She knows you feel this way?"

"Yop."

"And she's letting you take charge of her ward? Why?"

"She thinks it shows how great an analyst she is. Thinks she's being completely neutral and nonjudgmental, not taking a stand. 'Course, not taking a stand *is* taking a stand: that you're not taking a stand. Not responding to a person is a cruel response, an evil response. Nothing drives a baby as crazy as a 'stiff-faced' mother. Like those sweet Viennese being completely neutral as they watched the Nazis round up the Jews. A.K., and analysis, is about as judgmental as they come. When people look back, they'll see Freud as one of the most destructive jokers of the century."

"Wait a second. You may not agree with him, but Freud was a genius."

"Destruction is not genius. *Never*."

"But look at his discoveries—the unconscious, dreams, childhood sexual—"

"He stole most of 'em. Check out the reality, the facts coming out on Freud now—he lied, made up data, denied real data—harmed his patients more than he helped 'em. The worst thing is the Freudian view of the world: self self *self*!" He wiped sweat from his brow. "How's that for humility, eh?"

"Sounded a bit more humble than usual, Malik."

"I don't know how you do it, kid, get me going like that? Anyway, I'm here on a kind of humanitarian relief effort—tryin' to prevent her from doing too much harm."

"To the patients?"

"And to you."

"Me?"

"Look what she did to Solini." He bounced the ball. "How 'bout a quick one-on-one?"

"Is there time?"

"Lots. That's another reason I'm here—for a three-month rest. I'm feeling kinda tired out."

"You, tired?" I asked. It seemed unthinkable. And then for some reason I started thinking of Berry, about its being over, at least for now, because when I got that it was really over, it felt awful. I wasn't sleeping at night and was constantly exhausted and wondering should I call her up again and try to patch it up again, but nothing had changed, so how could I?

"Burnt out," he said, "yeah. So this place is a chance to rest. See, there are only eight beds on Thoreau, and right now only four are filled. A.K. can't keep patients in therapy."

"Why not?"

"Basch, Basch, you just *saw*! C'mon."

I followed him downstairs and out the door into air so January it was like inhaling slivers of ice, and over to his VW bus with the license plate reading BREATHE. We drove out of the valley that retained the ghostly shape of what it had once been—the eighth fairway of the Misery Links Golf Course—a tricky dogleg par four to an elevated green, the second shot over the dank cattails of Schlomo's Outpatient Clinic in the corner of the lake—and then on top of the hill around the back of the Farben to the gym. Malik told me about the Family Unit. It had been funded by a federal grant from NASA, steered to Misery by an astronaut who'd come to A.K. happily married but claustrophobic. Through analysis, while remaining claustrophobic, he had left his wife and kids for a nineteen-year-old dancer and a new red Porsche. A.K. got the grant based on a paper in *Anal. J.* in which she argued the cost effectiveness of applying Freudian concepts to an entire family at once. Her famous paper was entitled: "The Freudian Family Driven by a Projective/Introjective Identification Oedipal Oscillator." The Oscillator was so abstruse a concept that it was said that if anyone other than A.K. understood it—and it was commonly doubted that A.K. did, entirely—it was the magical analyst whom Blair Heiler worshiped, Renaldo Krotkey. It was also said that Krotkey, struggling with the Oscillator, had said, "The only person who can understand this shit is Frau Kernberg." Frau Kernberg, a mythical figure in the analytic canon (said to have once met Freud), was old and wheelchair-bound in a continuous care facility called Conquistador, in Boca Raton, Florida. Only Krotkey, her disciple, was granted admission to her nursing home chamber.

Now, with Malik, I asked, "What is it, this Oscillator?"

"What is it? It's horseshit, is what it is. Horseshit. It's A.K.'s reach for fame. Shrinks specialize in their defects. A.K.'s is empathy."

"You've got to be joking."

"You're not laughing. Primo and Viv told me all about A.K. Listen up."

It turned out that A. K. Lowell had grown up as Aliyah K. Lowenschteiner, the daughter of fine, upstanding kosher butchers in Queens. She'd been a terrific young woman of immense promise and even, in Viv's words, "that certain something," until midway through her first year of psych residency here at Misery when she had gone under analysis with the head of the Freudian Institute—one Dr. Schlomo Dove. Aliyah and Ike White had both been analyzed by Schlomo. In fact they had been in the same class in the institute, and the best of friends. During her years on the couch with Schlomo, Aliyah had been transformed totally: Loewenschteiner became Lowell, Jew became Episcopal, hooked nose became straight, long dark hair became lightened to chestnut-brown and cut short; she divorced her Jewish gastroenterologist husband and put her son under child Freudian analysis. "And she changed her personality," Malik said, "from—according to Viv—terrific, to this. Now she does it to others."

I wondered about this. Compared to the imbecilic DSM revolving door of Toshiba, A.K. didn't seem that bad. At least she was *trying* to understand people, in long-term therapy.

"You're thinking, after Toshiba, she doesn't seem all that bad, right?"

"Jesus Christ, Malik! How the hell do you *do* that?"

"Easy. *I* don't." He winked. "*She's the worst*. Wanna play H-O-R-S-E?"

We started shooting baskets in the deserted century-old gym, where the yellow pine floor and walls stirred images of women in black bathing costumes and men in curled moustaches throwing medicine balls. We eased into that fluid ballet permitted to men in the presence of a hoop, and the *whap whap* of the ball on the hardwood echoed down through my adolescence of glory to the loneliness of my childhood and that first day of winter running up and up out into the crisp air toward the gym feeling light and free, free from the dusty sad rooms of my family, free to find a life with others, as buddies, on teams.

After a while Malik called it quits. He was sneezing, out of breath. "Chest cold," he said as we sat on the floor cooling down. "The NASA grant—which, by the way, has CIA written all over it—lets teenagers get admitted to the Family Unit for free. The CIA must be trying to figure out how to crush the violence and drugs or something. Those bozos think Freud can help. Imagine! They oughta stick with psychics. Anyways, our job is to help these kids learn to live, play *sports*. Get that Oly Joe out for some *hoop*. Rough 'im up under those boards. So how y'doin, kid?"

"Bad."

"That good, eh? What's up?"

I told him about Berry and Jill, and he listened in that electric way that made me feel, Okay, it's just part of the human condition and you'll walk through it and maybe learn, but when I went on to talk about my dilemma with Cherokee and Lily and Schlomo, he wasn't so reassuring.

"Why didn't you tell me about this before?" he asked.

"You've been away. And he's been doing okay, up till now."

"This is bad," he said. "Maybe real bad."

"Is it possible?"

" 'Course it is. Studies show that at least ten percent of shrinks are currently fucking their patients."

"A pig wouldn't fuck Schlomo."

"But Schlomo might fuck a pig. Never underestimate the power of ugliness."

"Do you know him well?"

"No. Funny, about me and Schlomo. I've always kept my distance, and so has he. Like we both know it'd be bad news. There's no way of knowin' the truth yet. So we have to keep our eyes peeled, keep tryin' to get him and his wife to meet with you again. But all you can do is try 'n' help *him*, Cherokee."

"But I'm not getting anywhere! I feel stuck. I can't move him from his obsession—I don't know how therapy works."

"Therapy's like life, therapy works like life works—no road maps, no instruction manuals. What moves therapy along is what moves good friends along: you like each other, feel understood by each other, know each other better. You can do more things because you feel your friend with you, and you want to see each other more. That warm feeling you carry, even when you're apart. Zesty, y'know?"

"Like now?"

"Yop. Want me to see Cherokee?"

"No," I said quickly.

"Oh," he said, nodding his head, sensing my protectiveness. "I get it. Maybe you and I see him together?"

"No, not right now." I felt that Malik was so, I don't know, so immense, I didn't want to be, in comparison, diminished. "Maybe sometime."

" 'Kay. But be careful. With a guy like this, you never know. Let's keep talking about him. And *don't* go pawing around in his past, his childhood."

"Isn't the past important?"

"Only if it's so present you can taste it," he said bitterly. "The past is self. The past is an excuse. The past is why I can read you like a book." He sighed. "Not my strong suit, humility. But listen up." He fixed me with his eyes. "Any obsession is a turning away from really living your life."

"So?"

"So in therapy you gotta look at the life, not the obsession. If you're really into living your life, in connection with others, living your life to the hilt—hey, you can't obsess. Whatever the obsession, it starts to look foolish, irrelevant, like when you're totally in love, talkin' on the phone all the time, the phone bill's irrelevant. Think of your own obsessions, okay?"

What came to mind first was Berry losing Berry losing Berry, but then it was Jill and her satiny underwear. I was wondering how this could be "a turning away from really living my life" when suddenly I felt strong arms lock around my neck and a searing pain on the top of my head.

Malik had jumped me from behind, grabbed my head, and was grinding his fist into my scalp, making it burn. I struggled to get away, but his arms were like steel bars, and he hung on, grinding harder. My scalp felt on fire. We fought, hard, until I was sweating and he was sneezing and he let go, laughing, sneezing, coughing, laughing.

"What the hell are you doing, you jerk?"

"Giving you a noogie. Remember noogies?"

"Yeah, but why are you giving me a noogie?"

"To get you in tune with the kids here. You did good today, you played a *sport*! The key concept, these three months, is: we stick together. Say it."

"I'm not gonna—don't!"

He was lunging at me again. "Say it."

"We stick together."

" 'Cause the risk, now, with old A.K., is immense."

"FASCINATING CASE, YOUR CHEROKEE."

She was talking? A.K. was talking!

It was later that afternoon in her office high up under the skylight in the dome of Thoreau. I was in supervision with her. As I'd talked about my work with Cherokee, up until that moment she had said nothing. A.K. was the kind of woman who, given the choice between being true to her gender or being true to her ambition, had jumped wholeheartedly into her ambition. She had outmanned men in a man's world. She had learned the power of silence. Backed by her power over me and by the emblems of Freud placed strategically around her office—much as the CEO of a corporation might be backed by the company logo and slogan and sound byte and web site and, out the window behind the desk, the smokestacks—A.K. held silence like a stick. As in one of those grade-school games where you try to outstare the other guy, trying to make him blink first, she outsilenced me. Her cropped light brown hair was mannish, as were her high cheekbones and fixed nose and dark and unmade-up eyes. Her lips were the only feminine touch, plump, inviting, as if they were about to giggle at all this muscular silence, at the power suit and the tight, tall body, and shout out, "Hey, come *on*—lighten up!"

Unable to hold her silent gaze, I had inspected every inch of her office. The decor seemed of the century past, reminding me of my immigrant grandparents' apartment on Magaw Place in New York City. Heavy velvet drapes, weathered leather chairs with grandmotherly doilies, fringed lamp shades, and in the corner a massive analyst's couch covered by a heavy multicolored drape reaching to the Persian carpet. Behind the couch was a high-backed leather chair, winged for a nodding head, and a fringed ottoman. My eye caught a black-and-white photo showing another draped couch, chair, carpet, ottoman—a replica of the office I was sitting in! The caption informed me that this was "S. Freud's Office, 19 Bergasse, Vienna, the Birthplace of Psychoanalysis."

A small framed photo sat with its back to me on A.K.'s desk. In a locked glass cabinet behind A.K. was a row of leather-bound ledgers like you used to see in accountant's offices, each with initials on its spine.

As I told A.K. about my session with Cherokee, she wrote furiously in a crisp new ledger. Each page had a vertical line down the middle. On the left-hand side, A.K. wrote what I said Cherokee said and what I said back to him. For each phrase on the left-hand side, she wrote her own phrase on the right-hand side, as if doing a crossword puzzle.

"Fascinating case," she repeated, and glanced at her watch. She lit her cigar. Then she reached to the left-hand side of her desk next to the small framed photo where there were two perfectly sharpened yellow number 2 pencils, grasped one in her sculpted hand, and slid it slowly across to the right-hand side of the desk, where it joined two other perfect yellow number 2 pencils, in strict alignment. This meant that we were now at the three-quarter mark of the supervisory session. When I had entered, there had been four number 2 pencils on the left. As I had sat down, she had slid number 2 number one left to right; at the fifteen-minute mark, number 2 number two; now, number 2 number three; when that sinewy forearm reached for number 2 number four, I gathered, the session would be over and I would be history.

"Deep down it's penis," she said, reading right to left.

"Penis? But he's obsessed with Schlomo fucking his wife."

"No, he's paranoid."

"Suppose it's true?"

"Paranoia," she went on, as if I hadn't asked what I'd just asked. "But paranoia is surface level, a defense against a deeper homosexuality . . ." She paused, blowing out a diabolical silence.

"Homosexuality?" I said, as nonchalantly as possible, but all of a sudden seeing how attracted I was to Cherokee, how much I liked, even loved, him. I started to sweat, and said nothing more.

"Homosexuality which is a defense against the Oedipal struggle, which is, at its deepest level, a defense against castration anxiety. Penis."

"Penis?"

"Penis. Your patient Cherokee is a classic case of what Freud describes in his classic on cases like this, 'Certain Neurotic Mechanisms in Jealousy, Paranoia, and Homosexuality.' " She nodded to a bookshelf on which were several feet of books in light blue dust jackets, as strictly aligned as the pencils. *The Collected Works of Sigmund Freud.* "Read Freud. Cherokee is a classic case of homosexuality, disguised as paranoia." She then gave a brief rendition of the classic paper that sparkled and shone with clarity, even with a flicker of wit. It was not all that hard to understand, although my attention was split: part of me was listening to the content, part of me was astonished by the process—she was so damn chatty. She seemed to care about teaching me how to work with my patient. This, after Toshiba, seemed bizarre. She stopped, laying out silence.

"But what about Schlomo fucking his wife? You don't think it's true?"

"There is no truth, there is only the individual perception of experience."

"Wait a minute. The truth is that I'm taller than you."

"That's not the truth, that's your transference to me."

"We can measure it. To see who in fact is taller."

"You think 'taller' can be 'measured'?"

I saw her point. She wasn't only aware of the objective fact, she was also aware of the deeper meaning psychologically. "But I'm stuck," I said. "With Cherokee, I don't know what to do."

"You're not doing badly." This stunned me. Except for Malik, my supervisors at Misery were constantly telling me just how badly I was doing. "You even asked about the father-transference, his feeling ugly compared to you."

"Yeah but he wouldn't talk about it."

"Of course not. He had resistance to it. You should have asked about the resistance, the defense. You say, 'What *gets in the way of* your talking about your father?' In analysis there's a correct response to every situation."

"A road map?"

"With limited routes. Roots. Like a towering tree. They come into our consulting rooms with seams, we psychoanalyze them, they go out seamless."

They go out seamless. Ike White's phrase. Her friend, classmate, and fellow Schlomo patient. Was this some kind of secret Freudian password?

A.K. lit her cigar, puffed, and stared at the shape. A banana, perhaps a cuke. Could, of course, be a penis too. "This hospital is a travesty of psychiatric care. Money, insurance, DSM diagnosis to five digits, drugs. No one listens to patients. No one gives them enough time to heal. Here on the Family Unit we are lucky. We have time, money, and Freud. Freud is the only complete, cohesive, scientific theory of human development, pathology, and treatment. In fact we today here are much like Freud in fin de siècle Vienna: radicals, rebels, even revolutionaries, trying to increase human knowledge in spite of the distortions of the biologists and the bankers. In the consulting chamber, we use the powerful tool of psychoanalysis to help people change and grow."

"Psychoanalysis cures people?"

"No, no," she said with a smile. She actually smiled! "We wouldn't stoop to cure. As Freud put it, 'Much will be gained if we succeed in transforming your neurotic misery into common unhappiness.' "

"But Cherokee won't talk to me about his feelings, or his past. He just talks about his obsession."

"You have to go deeper into his obsession, find the deeper meaning, the roots of it in his childhood, his past."

This was exactly what Malik had warned me against doing. Suspicious, I asked, "How?"

"If he talks feeling, you talk thought. If he talks thought, you talk feeling. If he talks past, you talk present. If he talks present, you talk past. You the doctor talk constantly about what he the patient doesn't want to talk about. This is the analysis of the resistance. Then, when he starts distorting his relationship with you and calling you a sonofabitch for not talking about what he wants to talk about, then you do the analysis of the transference, telling him he's treating you like his father, his mother, his aunt Sally, whatever. On a deeper level still, you can analyze the resistance to the transference, and the transference to the resistance. Not to mention the countertransference to each—but that's way beyond you at this point."

Finally I felt I was getting some concrete advice about what to do in therapy, and I scribbled this down on the back of a bank stub. "But how do I do that?" I asked. "How do I get him to talk about his feelings?"

"You use the Three Techniques of analysis. One, free association. You ask, 'What's the first thing that comes to mind?' Two, dream analysis. You analyze dreams. Three, fantasy analysis. 'Tell me your fantasies about x.' You explore."

I saw her arm twitch. Fearing she was thinking number 2 number four, I felt an urgency to ask her about Christine, with whom I was also stuck.

"Can I ask you quickly about Christine, the one who—"

"You followed down to the tennis court."

"How do you know about that?"

"The one who gave you that sweater you are wearing."

"How . . . how . . . ?" I was stunned. "Who told you?"

"If you were analyzed, you would no longer blush. Be careful, Dr. Basch. All you have in this field is your reputation. You just *raped* that patient."

"What!"

"Seduced her. By taking her sweater as a gift. Gifts are never just gifts, but parameters—uncontrolled events influencing the analysis."

"But it's just a sweater."

"A sweater is never just a sweater. You slip your 'head' into it. What comes to mind?"

"Penis into vagina. But I don't believe it."

"Freud said, 'Women's strongest motive in coming for treatment is the hope that they might somehow still obtain a penis, the lack of which is so painful to them'—'Analysis Terminable and Interminable.' " Again she opened the new leather-bound ledger. "Go on."

I told her about my work with Christine, leaving out the meeting with Cherokee. Why ask for trouble?

"She said, 'You're better than two Bayer aspirin'?" A.K. shook her head. " 'Two bare-ass prin'? And you don't believe it's all about the penis?"

"At first maybe, but the last session, she said, 'You're turning out to be a real friend, helping me. I can see you helping people in your family. I see you rushing in, like the Red Cross, healing the cholera in your family.' "

A.K. nodded and then seemed to grow larger, head larger, eyes larger, pupils dilating as if in astonishment, dark brown, even black. I felt transfixed by her, as if caught in headlights at night. Finally she said:

"But deep down, with your family, you feel that *you* are the cholera."

Boom! A bomb went off in my gut. Boom! Shrapnel rained down. A vista opened up inside, a vista of me in my family, my feeling that I never satisfied them, that I was always disappointing them—those accusatory tears of my mother, those puzzled stares of my father from the dental chair—always bringing sadness to them and leaving them with sadness, like that last trip to Florida with Jill, the sadness of my aloofness, of Jill not being Berry—my father hadn't written to me since!—the first time he hadn't written in all the years since I left for Harvard. Feeling that I was always letting them down, I had tried harder and harder to achieve things, starting every conversation with my latest achievement, bringing prizes home—like my boyhood friends who hunted on the Polish Sportsmen's hunting preserve out by the Lone Star and Universal Atlas quarries would bring home first squirrels and rabbits and then deer, first a doe and then, finally earning their manhood, a buck—as if, if I brought home big enough prizes my achievements could win their love, and yet gradually it dawned on me that no achievement can win love—

"All you have in this field," A.K. was saying, grasping the fourth and final yellow number 2, "is—"

"Your reputation."

"And your penis."

Boom! Shrapnel rained down.

"Explore," she said firmly, the pencil almost aligned with the three others. "Listen in the material for the penis envy."

"I will," I said, trying to rise from my chair but suddenly feeling so weighted down that at first I failed. It was as if I'd been sitting on a planet of a lot greater gravity, say Jupiter. With immense second effort I hoisted my leaden bulk to my feet—which felt far away. "I will explore."

"You can't, fully."

"Why not?"

"You haven't been analyzed."

"I have to be analyzed to explore fully, to treat my patients fully?"

But the four pencils were now strictly aligned. I was history.

"Thanks," I said, feeling a strange gratitude of such bizarre intensity that it seemed to be controlling my mind and my legs, so that it was all I could do to resist the urge to make a slight bow of obeisance, like a slave to a kind pasha. I staggered out.

"YOU'RE SO LIKE *INTO* ME TONIGHT!" Jill said that night as we lay on the rug in front of a dying fire in the house up the street, cuddling. She was back from a UFO conference in New Jersey. The couple who owned the house was away. Their dog Muffie, a big mutt, lay nearby. I was treating my heartbreak about Berry with alcohol and sex and love. If I thought of Berry with a man, my obsession with Jill helped me feel I had no right to be jealous, and if I thought of Berry with Chandra, my mind went round and round. At first I would feel happy for her for being with someone she described as so solid and sensual and spiritual, and then I would feel a panic of envy and wish I could find someone like that and sometimes with alarm I would realize that that someone might in fact have been Berry.

"You have some fantasies about that?" I asked. All evening long I had been trying out the Three Techniques A.K. had taught me.

"Shhh!"

"What?"

"Shush!" She looked around. Muffie whined pitifully.

"Is someone there?"

"Them."

"Who?"

"From the UFO." Tail between her legs, Muffie waddled out.

"They're here?"

"In a ring around the rug."

"Shit."

"I just knew they would follow me back from Newark."

I stared right and left and tried to struggle up. Nothing.

"Don't stare at them, dum-dum," she whispered. "Just act normal."

"I don't see anything," I whispered back.

" 'Course not. You can't *see* 'em. C'mon."

"With them watching?"

"They're here to learn. C'mon."

With a little coaxing, I did my part as an earthling to demonstrate the use of what A.K. had referred to as "the powerful tool of psychoanalysis."

At some point and to my alarm, as if implanted in my hetero head as an experiment by aliens, I found myself thinking of Cherokee.

ELEVEN

"IT'S NOT WORKING. This therapy's not working. Let's just forget it."

It was a week later, halfway through my session with Cherokee, and I was about to lose him. I had used the Malik approach, first trying to persuade him to bring Lily in with him for a meeting. No way. Then I had suggested that his obsession with Schlomo fucking her was a turning away from his life.

"What life? I've got no life. You don't get it. This overshadows everything. Focusing on it with you has made it worse. It's there constantly now, just below the surface: 'He's fucking her in therapy.' Today, the only thing I'm looking forward to is seeing your patient Christine again after my session's over. In fact, I might as well leave early. Spend some extra time talking to her." He started to rise from his chair. "Let's just forget it. I guess I'm just a hopeless case."

My heart sank. And I'm just a hopeless case as a therapist.

The past week had been a weird, conflicted time. There were only four patients on Thoreau, and so I had had time to read and think. And play basketball. Malik had organized a LAMBS game for the four adolescents, and I'd joined in. Even Oly Joe had uncurled once a day to play. But I had also started reading Freud, the papers A.K. had suggested: for Cherokee, paranoia; for Christine, penis envy during interminable analysis.

The paranoia paper was incredible. In a scant twelve pages Freud managed to describe the neurotic mechanisms in the normal condition, jealousy, the pathological condition, paranoia, and the reason for both these conditions, "a defense against homosexuality." I'd been struck by how perfectly

Cherokee fit Freud. I'd copied out a few quotes, which were now lying before me on my desk:

> Delusional jealousy represents an acidulated homosexuality, and rightly takes its position among the classical forms of paranoia. As an attempt at defense against an unduly strong homosexual impulse it may, in a man, be described in the formula, "Indeed I do not love him, *she* loves him!"

According to Freud, Cherokee's paranoia about his wife fucking Schlomo was a defense against his own homosexual impulse to fuck Schlomo. And what did Freud say was the root of this homosexual impulse?

> The high value of the male organ and the inability to tolerate its absence in a love-object . . . Attachment to the mother, narcissism, fear of castration—these are the factors.

Cherokee had mentioned his penis once before. He'd called it his "blue steel throbber," yes.

Yet now as I stared at Cherokee rising up from his chair and about to walk out of my office for the last time, I had no idea how to *use* Freud on him. Desperate not to lose him, frantic to do something, I decided to go with the practical things A.K. had mentioned, the Three Techniques. So I said:

"Wait. What are your fantasies about being 'a hopeless case'?"

"My fantasies?" he said, stranded halfway up out of his chair.

"Your fantasies."

"I did fantasies at Disney. You want to turn this into Fantasyland?"

"Put it another way: What's the first thing that comes to mind?"

"Oh. Father," he said, lowering himself distractedly back down into the chair. "Father always gave me the feeling I was a hopeless case. When he was hospitalized in the Peter Bent with heart failure, I went to see him, and he looked so horrible—puffy, blue-lipped, wasted—I was overcome, and I blurted out 'I love you, Father' and went to hug him. And then, with his last bit of strength he held up his hands and said, 'Don't act like a puff, Cher, not at this late date.' " He paused. "That was the last time I ever saw him."

I found myself tingling with excitement. Homosexuality. For the first time in my training I had a sense of a frame around a person, a method of making sense, finding the deeper roots of the scraggly neurotic growth sprouting up haphazardly like suckers from a dead stump. I saw him now not only as a person, but as a person informed by a theory. I had in my power a way of leading him through. This was what Hannah had meant by "making the unconscious conscious." Free him from neurotic suffering by being a kind of Ross Perot of psychology, "getting in there under the hood." Suddenly I saw A.K.'s silence as a commitment to this exploration.

But now Cherokee had gone silent again, and was fidgeting.

"You have some feelings, in thinking about your father?"

He looked at his hands. Large hands, long graceful fingers. Sadly he said, "Father loved my jazz piano. I'm a failure."

"And what *gets in the way of* talking about your feelings for your father?"

"I feel ashamed."

"You have some thoughts, about feeling ashamed?"

"I loved Father. The one time in my life I tell him, he calls me a fag. That must have been Hollywood to him. Chock full of fags."

I glanced at my watch. A minute left. I glanced at Freud. Go for it.

"In your family, there was an incredibly high value placed on the male organ," I said, "and anyone without one was suspect."

Boom. His eyes popped open, then his mouth. I felt the ripples. My interpretation had hit home. Go for it again.

"And so you keep thinking she's fucking him because *you* want to fuck him."

Boom. Boom. He seemed to rock back in his chair.

"I . . . Doctor, I'm stunned."

" 'Doctor'?"

"My uncle—Father's brother—the only warm body in the family—he was a doctor." Cherokee looked directly at me, gratitude in his eyes, and then glanced away. "A . . . a . . . this is ridiculous . . . a rectal surgeon."

"It's time for us to stop."

He, as I with A.K., now seemed to be having grave difficulty rising from his chair. Mopping his brow with his shirtsleeve, he walked out.

I mopped my own brow with my own shirtsleeve. Then I scribbled furiously, as word-for-word a recounting of the session as possible, racing to finish in the ten minutes before Christine came in.

She never did.

> Fidelity, especially that degree of it required in marriage, is only maintained in the face of continual temptation . . . He projects his own impulses to infidelity onto the partner to whom he owes faith . . .

Exactly. And written with the touch of the poet, besides.

FREUDIAN FAMILY ANALYSIS of my patient Zoe began first thing next morning. Zoe, finally detoxed from her run on coke and booze in Rancho

Mirage, had been transferred from Toshiba to Thoreau the day before. Malik had tried to transfer her away from Thoreau, to the Alcohol and Drug Unit, Heidelberg East. No luck. Zoe had insisted on being where Malik and I were.

Now I was sitting with Zoe on the patient side of the one-way mirror. With us were her father and mother and their assigned couples therapist, Faith Baltsburg. Zoe's siblings, an older brother and sister, had refused to participate.

In therapy Zoe had said, "My parents are total opposites, and I take after both of them." She'd described her father, Zeke Bicker, a New York corporate lawyer, as "a lion, a really strong athletic person with a mind like a steel trap, but good fun too." Her mother was "a warm, caring, beautiful person who'd devoted her life to her family and volunteer work—I just love her to death!"

Meeting them now was a revelation. The "lion" was a frail old man hard of hearing, his mind less a trap than entrapped, by age. The "beautiful person" was a slovenly, obese elderly woman smelling of sweat, beer, and gastrointestinal distress. Sitting there with them, Zoe herself seemed much different.

The first time I'd met her, on my first night on call with Malik when she'd come in clutching a bottle of Xanax and a red teddy bear, she'd been "the good little rich college girl," all crisp white summer dress with tiny pink flowers encircling her neck, wearing a red bandanna, her light brown hair styled in that windblown look of fashion models. Her suicide note had talked about a fake smile plastered on her face, hiding the reality. The night of the feeding tube was the low point. Over the months with me she'd gotten more real, gingerly picking her path along her own life, wearing her own kinds of clothes—casual, cool—letting her hair grow, forming relationships with me, Malik, and Thorny. She'd done well until her trip back to her family over the holidays, the stress of which had revved up her "disease"—Malik's word—of substance abuse, and she'd come back in, as Thorny put it, "coked to her tits." Now she sat in the session as "good little rich college girl" once again. She again wore white. Her tall slender frame and short light brown hair made her seem boyish.

My cotherapist Faith had been silent the whole session, often staring down into her open purse. Faith was at the low-water mark of her analysis, four years in. She had that scared-rabbit look that I knew from Solini and Hannah was a sign of dire associations, a kind of perverse commercial for Freud's "The Psychopathology of Everyday Life," where even the most innocent-seeming object (a checkbook), when fed into the Freudian machine of fantasy and dream, loomed monstrous (a blue penis flattened by a truck). Nothing meant only what it meant; everything had a deeper meaning from the past, as if the corporate slogan were: IN TOUCH WITH YESTERDAY. FREUD.

Now, on the business end of the one-way mirror for the first time, I felt intimidated, and as the session had gone on I too had said little. Zoe's father had been as puzzled by our silence as had Farmer Olaf. Zoe's mother, a veteran of years of hard-core analysis in Manhattan, had learned to chatter distractedly for fifty minutes at a clip and carried us along on her beery and biliary breath. From time to time she was joined by Zoe. Finally, like a dancer picking up the beat, father too jumped in, and in a voice trembling with the love of a father for a daughter, said:

"Zoe, we're behind you and Dr. Basch one hundred and ten percent."

I felt a sense of real warmth among them all. We ended with Zoe saying:

"Thanks, guys, for this." She started to cry. "I love you both so much!"

Her father cried. I felt teary. Faith and the hepatically challenged Mrs. Bicker stared at us with sympathy. The session ended in silence, one, I thought, of reconciliation.

We joined the group on the see-through side of the mirror. The discussion turned on how Zoe's alcohol and drug abuse was a symptom of deep depression which was in turn a symptom of deeper childhood conflicts—our old friend the Oedipal Oscillator, whatever that was. Once her depression was analyzed out, her drinking would stop.

"No way," Malik said. "Never. You got it ass-backward. She's an alcoholic. Once she stops drinking, she won't be depressed. We gotta transfer her over to Heidelberg East, Alcohol and Drug. Hook her up with AA. None of you Freudians have any idea how much damage you do tryin' to analyze out depression, leaving behind a hopeless wet drunk. Wake up, okay?"

No one said okay. What was really strange was the bluntness of this assault from Malik, who'd always told us to be deft. He didn't do "strident" well. He looked tired, his energy damped down. Strange. I figured that this attack on analysis would provoke a strong, clear counter, but no. A.K. and Faith and the others reacted to Malik's insults with silence, as if Malik had not said what he had just said.

Then the silence was broken by enthusiastic talk of what else but the Oedipal Oscillator. Everyone else in the room, including poor, imploded Henry Solini, were into their own guesses about the Oscillator, vying for A.K.'s attention, as if, when that clock bonged out at the end of the hour, A.K. would be awarding a prize for "Freudian of the Day." Sure enough, just before the end, A.K. cleared her throat. We all looked up at the clock. Thirteen seconds. A.K. fixed first me, then Faith, in her high beams, and said, with immaculate scorn:

"What the hell were you two *doing* in there?" A wad of cash fluttered to Faith's feet, many twenties, one fifty. I trembled, my hands, I realized, covering my nuts. "That whole session you were helping your patient deny her sexuality."

"How can you tell that, Aliyah?" Malik asked pleasantly.

"I can tell," she said coolly, "because she failed to turn me on."

Bong bong bong bong bong bong bong bong bong bong.

I sat there feeling skewered. I had failed totally. Everybody but Malik filed out.

"Ah, don't sweat the petty stuff," Malik said to me, "and don't pet the sweaty stuff neither. You coulda talked more, sure, but in terms of protecting Zoe, you did good. Y'helped that family today. A *lot*. Let's go. Hoop."

We went to Oly Joe Olaf's room and uncurled him from his fetal position. We picked up a few other psychoanalyzed adolescents and went to the gym.

My game was off. I couldn't put the ball in the ocean.

"A TERRIBLE JOB with Zoe," A.K. was saying to me that afternoon in supervision. "All year long you've been doing a terrible job. Subjecting her to Heiler treatment damaged your alliance with her, led to her feeling abandoned, and made her try to kill herself with alcohol and cocaine." We were almost at the two-pencil mark. As I'd described my work with Zoe, A.K. had been writing at withering speed, finding clues in the left-hand column and writing the answer in the right. Now she stared intently at the page, like an oracle reading entrails. Finally she asked: "Has she spoken to you about her fantasies of you?"

"No."

"Get her to tell you what, in bed, she imagines doing with your penis."

"How do you know her fantasies about me are erotic? Maybe her fantasies are just ordinary things, like where I live, or what kind of car I drive."

"Those *are* erotic."

"But won't talking about my pencil make things too hot?"

"Your 'pencil'?"

"I mean my penis."

"A slip. Impressive. You are concerned about inflaming the erotic transference?" I nodded. "Good. But you've been colluding with her denial of it far too long. Her drinking and drugging are symptoms, sublimation of repressed erotic wishes. You've got to drill them out."

"How do I do that?"

"What's the first thing that comes to mind?"

"Porpoises."

" 'Porpoises'?"

"Came to mind, yeah." A.K. rubbed her eyes, as teachers do when dealing with slow learners. "But what should I do?"

"Put lead weights in your pants."

" 'Put lead weights in my pants'?"

"You do nothing. Let her do the work. We are all just messes, trying to deal with bigger messes. She is sick. You, hopefully, are less sick. You separate her sickness from your sickness and throw yours away. Try silence."

"Silence?"

"Shut up."

I shut up.

"Not *now*." She stared at me intently, as if I too were entrails. "So many people who seem happy go home and cry into their pillows at night."

I felt a rush of cold air. "But when she was on Emerson," I said, "with Dr. Heiler, she went through a phase of acting kind of sexy when she came to see me."

"And did you explore her fantasies?"

"No. No one told me to."

"So you colluded with her in denying her erotic fantasies about you. You probably even colluded in denying your own erotic fantasies toward her."

"I didn't have any."

"Oh, so you didn't *have* any, eh?" She wrote this down. "Heiler," she said, with revulsion, "Heiler. See my analytic couch?"

"I see your couch."

"That couch cost me $250,000. Remember Heiler's couch?"

"I don't remember it, no."

"Because Heiler doesn't have a couch. He has only *chairs*. Heiler failed his analysis. Not good enough. Too much the sadist. As I'm sure you noticed." I nodded. "Good." She flipped to a new section of her ledger and said, cheerily, "Next case?"

I took out my notes on Cherokee. As I spoke, describing how Cherokee fit Freud perfectly, A.K. wrote at great speed—thirty-four across, sixteen down—with each new clue saying "Good, good, good, very good." I couldn't believe it, all this approval. But at the very end, when I told her about my using Freud on Cherokee directly, she suddenly scowled and said, "Bad, bad, very bad."

"What do you mean? It was great. I can't wait to see him next week."

"He won't be back next week."

"*What?*"

"He may not be back at all. You may have ruined the therapy entirely. You made one of the worst mistakes in the book: premature interpretation."

"But I used Freud, word for word."

"Because you used Freud, word for word. *You* can't use Freud. One has to filter Freud through one's own understanding."

"I did."

"You can't. You're neurotic. You haven't been analyzed."

"B-b-but what should I do?"

"The lead weights."

"In the pants?"

"If he comes back, get him to talk about your penis."

"Him too?"

She glanced down her page to about fifty-six across, and read, " 'Father loved my jazz piano. I'm a failure.' If that's not castration anxiety, what is?"

"I get it," I said sarcastically. "Piano and everything else equals penis."

"You're terrified of your *own* homosexuality."

Boom. Dark sweat at the Boy Scout meeting in the basement of St. Peter's Church after the Scoutmaster had gone home, Jimmy Gora and Ralphie Grzyb saying, "C'mon, let's see that kike cock," my standing there pants at my ankles aroused as they inspected and ridiculed me. "Hey," I said now, "I'm hetero. *Totally*."

Silence, one of, Well If You Are, Why Insist You Are?

And then all at once A.K. seemed to puff up like an adder. Her pupils widened. I braced myself. She said:

"And why are you trying to be such a good little boy with him and me?"

Boom. Through the curtain of metallic rain I heard the harsh chanting of men swaying back and forth and saw the hazy red and gold lights of the candles in the synagogue way down below and a man in black with a funny cap like a pillbox pointing up into the balcony at my mother and me and screaming, "Out out get dhat childt out of chere" and my mother laughing but the man screamed louder and someone next to us hissed at us and my mother stopped laughing and roughly she picked me up turning carrying me screaming out saying, "Be a good little boy a good little boy, Roy, be a good little boy. . . ."

IN ZOE'S INDIVIDUAL THERAPY the next day, I got stuck again. She was still feeling great about the family therapy session, talking about what "great guys" her father and mother were and how it had all been "good fun" and "healing." Part of me felt it had been a good session, yet part of me saw A.K.'s point, that we hadn't really drilled down to the deeper roots of the problem. Malik had said that the issue was alcohol and drugs, from which all else followed; A.K. had said that the issue was sex, repressed, from which alcohol and drugs followed. So far in the session I'd tried to take the Malik route, working on her suicidal drinking and drugging in Rancho Mirage, but she minimized it:

"It's not that bad. Thorny tried to get me into this AA stuff, but I can't. It's way too religious for me."

Nothing I tried would move her from this position. I felt stuck.

"So, Doc," she said, cheerfully, "what's on your mind?"

"What comes to mind, about what's on my mind?"

"I dunno. I feel so good now. Like I don't need to be in the hospital anymore. You've helped me. Knowing you were here made me come back. I feel now that we're more equal, like I'd like to know more about you."

"Like what?"

"Little things, like what kind of car you drive, 'n' stuff like that."

"And what's the first thing that comes to mind about my car?"

"That it's big and powerful, one of those big new Beemers."

"You have some thoughts about my car?"

"I think, I dunno, that you must like it."

"You have some feelings about my liking it?"

"Why all these questions, Doc?"

"Our shared task is to explore, and these questions may help."

"Okay. I'll do whatever you want. Within limits."

"Limits?"

She squirmed, adjusted her legs, lifting her skirt briefly, showing her thighs. "I've been having a lot of . . . like funny feelings about you lately. And I had a dream. I just remember a piece of it."

"A piece?"

"Your car—it was a big black Beemer—turned into a . . . a . . . I can't say it."

"A penis?"

"Uh-huh."

"My penis?"

Nodding, she stared at her bare feet, then curled them up under her thighs, flashing white panties. "This isn't . . . wrong, is it? Is this okay?"

"Better than okay. This is psychoanalysis."

"Far out." She blushed. "Okay, Doc. You're the boss."

"GOOD, GOOD, EXCELLENT," A.K. said in supervision that afternoon as she wrote down what Zoe and I had said, until we came to my penis and she said, astonished, "You said *what*?"

"You told me to explore the erotic transference."

"*She* didn't bring up your penis, *you* brought up your penis. You made one of the worst mistakes in the book: countertransference distortion."

"Which is?"

"Your shit gets in the way of her shit. Let's see if it can be saved." She worked the right side intently. With each pencil stroke and frown I felt myself fade, lose bulk, like an astronaut too long in space. I waited and waited. Finally she put down her ledger and said, "She will run away."

"How do you know that?"

Her answer was to reach for number 2 number four.

ZOE RAN AWAY THAT NIGHT.

The next day I went to supervision with A.K. and said, "You were right. She's gone. And she won't be back."

"If you now make the correct interpretation, she will be back."

"Now?"

"In her scheduled session."

"But how can I make the correct interpretation to her if she's not there?"

"Every time someone leaves," A.K. said, "it's as if they take with them a little piece of our heart."

"What's the correct interpretation?"

We sat in silence, a proclamatory silence, for the rest of the session.

AT THE TIME of Zoe's session the next day, I sat in my office and left the door open in case she showed up. I free-associated to her, running through her whole history, from our first stormy meeting when I'd felt a "click" of connection with her, all the way through to her fantasy of my "big black Beemer," which was really not a marvel of German engineering but my penis. As I sat there letting her fill my head with her self wherever she was, I felt—like a cloud coalescing from thin air solidly enough to cast a shadow—a coming together of her life, and I saw her as a girl desperate to engage her mother, and then as a baby hungering for love but being fed privilege, and suddenly I saw the present, all the men and sex and drugs, in terms of this past, and I whispered an interpretation to where she would have been sitting: "You'd like to mop the floor with your engulfing mother, for not giving you enough."

ZOE WAS BACK THE NEXT MORNING. I was amazed.

In our session she was hungover, apologetic, and weepy. She'd gotten drunk and picked up a guy and gotten laid and robbed. I felt horrible—it was all because of my mistake.

In supervision with A.K., after I'd finished recounting the session, she kept on scribbling on the right side like a car motor kicking over after the ignition has been turned off, the pencil making loud *scritches*. She said:

"You *seem* bright, but you keep making bad mistakes."

"But today I said almost nothing."

"Because you said almost nothing, when you should have. You failed to ask the crucial questions, to explore her acting out by running away."

"I did ask her about running away."

"Oh?" She took up her pencil again. "And what did she say?"

To my surprise, I drew a blank. "I don't remember."

"You do remember."

"No, I don't."

"You do, but you're blocking. Your memory is repressed, buried under tons of unanalyzed garbage. You blocked out the most crucial part of the session."

"Why?"

"How do I know? It's *your* neurosis, not mine. You *seem* bright, but intelligence can take you only so far in this field."

"Are you saying I need analysis?" She smiled. "Look, I'm getting more and more confused. I don't know when I should be silent with her and when I should talk. I never know what I should say. I don't know when to explore, when to interpret, when to have the lead weights, when to weigh in. How do I do this, anyway?"

"It is an art. It is very hard to learn, to be good at. Even a genius like Freud had trouble learning it." She puffed up, her eyes got big. I grabbed the arms of my chair. She said:

"You might not be good enough."

Ka-boom! A blow to the head, my ears ringing my mother standing there looking down at me her eyes red with weeping and asking, "Can't you help me, Roy?" and I not knowing what to say but saying to myself, "Stay like this and don't show anything on your face and it will be over," feeling iced by her love and as she turned away her shoulders shaking with sobs hearing a voice inside saying, "Compared to a normal boy certainly compared to that nice boy Mitchell Cohen down the street you're not good enough not good enough you're really not good enough. . . ."

LIFE WITHOUT BERRY suddenly was unthinkable. That night I spent alone at home, obsessing about all the ways I had blown it. I felt lonely and desperate. Jill was at a UFO symposium; Malik was away in Akron, Ohio, on an AA retreat. I hadn't seen Berry since that night she'd walked out saying, "You need help!" Another example of my not measuring up. We'd talked on the phone a few times. At the start of each conversation we were both so relieved to be back in touch that we'd said we ought to get together, but as we'd talked, our rapt yearning for what was had been overwhelmed by the stark differences of our current lives, and we'd hung up with more coolness than when we'd started, with no further plans. In the wake of these phone calls I'd always felt shattered, having realized what I was losing. Do men only know what they've lost when they've lost it, when it's too late? In hard times, especially in the House of God year, Berry had always been there for me. So that night, in the hollow echo of desperation, I picked up the phone and called her.

Machine. Her voice on the machine was a comfort, until she said, ". . . and I won't be back until Monday." Monday? It was only Wednesday! Without leaving a message, I hung up, feeling terrible. Compared to Chandra—or another guy?, a hellish thought—I felt unimportant to her. If I loved her, why was I running from that love? Neurosis City. I got a glimpse of just how deep my psychopathology went. A long, scary night.

The next day I felt shaky. A.K. ran a Resident Support Group for first-year residents. I had gone to it a few times but then stopped, because she ran it as she ran everything, saying nothing until the last few seconds. Now, understanding her silence, and feeling that I needed some support, I went. Seeing Solini and Hannah, seeing that "scared deer in the headlights" look in their eyes, I now got it: they too had glimpsed the sickness deep down in their psyches, the big diesels of the unconscious driving behavior that was neurotic. I understood their sense of doom, their need to be careful in what they said or did, knowing that the unconscious was always humming down there. If each of their analyses was making them worse, well, wasn't it what Malik said, that you had to walk back through the heartache to heal?

Of all of us, the drug fascist Win Winthrop seemed to be doing the best. He was always confident and smiley, making me feel that compared to him I was doing really badly. Whatever Misery rotation he was on, he kept up his drug work with Errol Cabot. He'd had several articles on psychiatric infomatics accepted for publication, involving drugs, computers, and rats. His home life too seemed to be soaring. His wife had just had another baby, a second boy, a gender that delighted him. Through some tax cheating and a drug company scam, he was making a ton of money. He'd bought a big old house in a quaint old town and had a full-time English nanny, Guatemalan housekeeper, and Thai cook. Lately, he'd told me, the three loves of his life were the Internet, drugs, and male bonding. He was often jetting off to Robert Bly–Sam Keen warrior camps, the latest being up in the wilderness outside Saskatoon with a "tribe of Iron John Wildmen, steaming our balls off in sweat lodges and then rolling naked in the snow. It's the burden of masculinity, Roy. We men are the real victims now. You think white men aren't angry? You bet your butt!"

Thinking of himself as a man who was a victim, Win was constantly alert to being victimized as a man. The other big change in Win over the course of the year was how he'd bulked up. Having started the year fat, now he was all muscle. With Errol Cabot, he worked out at the gym, and had that basted look of a man on anabolic steroids. Watching him now, brawny and threatening, I wondered if he himself was on drugs. Specializing in his defects? He exuded what he called "warrior" power.

Hannah, noticing A.K.'s cigar smoke hovering in an elongated shape right in front of Win's eyes, associated out loud, "Looks like a penis, doesn't it?"

"Hey, lady," Win shouted, "don't denigrate *my* genitals! If you're going to call it something, call it what it is: call it a *cock*."

That day, even Arnie Bozer made me feel that, compared to him, I was a flop. Heilerized, he talked openly about breaking up with my patient Christine, saying, "*I'm* doing fine, thanks to Dr. Blair Heiler, and to my psychoanalysis with Dr. Schlomo Dove. The thing that I really miss after breaking with Chrissy is the sex." He talked about the sex in a hip, healthy way. Once again the subject was penises. God.

A.K. cleared her throat. Our eyes hit the clock. I could have sworn she was looking directly at me as she said, "You have failed in your task, which is to talk about your erotic fantasies about *me*."

I walked out with Solini and Hannah. Henry was rotating in Toshiba. I asked him how it was going.

"Going?" he said, startled, like a man in a daydream crossing a street, awakened by a blast from a truck. "Bad?"

"Yeah, I know. Toshiba is the pits."

"No, no, I mean my analysis with the Slapper? I'm one sick dude? I thought it was the fumes from my old man's Ideal Cleaners in Mandan? Turns out it's my old man himself? Five-foot-six, little fucking Napoleon? Wherever I look I see pricks? And I'm only five-five?"

"You too?" I said, realizing that I too was seeing penises. Once you start looking and listening for them, you see and hear them everywhere.

"You? You're six-three if you're an inch?"

"I'm feeling pretty bad, Henry."

"Still seein' what's 'iz name?"

"I never was, Henry!"

"Yeah, I hear he's big on castration? Goes right for your nuts? It's balls-to-the-wall time, babe, Oedipus City—hang tough?"

"Why are you talking in questions, Henry?"

"Am I?"

"Yeah."

"No I'm not?"

"See?"

"Gotta take it up with Ed Slapadek, the Slapper will drill it out?" He wandered down the hall, grazed a wall, stared at it, and stumbled out.

"How are you?" Hannah asked. Previously dark-haired and hefty, she was now bleach-blond and thinner. She'd even bleached her eyebrows. Rather than a dress with tiny flowers like Heiler's ties, she now wore a beige cashmere sweater.

"I'm bad," I said. "Depressed." I told her about what had been happening on Thoreau.

"Could be worse. You could be me. I'm really *really* down. I'm rotating with Errol Cabot and Win on drugs, Heidelberg West. They're Nazis."

"Loss of appetite?" I said, seeing her thinness as a symptom of depression.

"No, no, I did this for Blair."

"Really? You look terrific."

"Blairey says I look awful." She started to cry. "Got a Kleenex? I'm all out." I handed her one. Her eyes rolled up to the chandelier over the staircase. "Last month at a meeting in Dallas, he was ogling all these thin Texas blondes in cashmere, so I worked like hell to lose the weight at the Dr. Brownburn's Eat It Off Diet Clinic, and I did my hair. I even did my eyebrows."

"And he hates it?"

Crying, she nodded. "And then one of my patients—she'd lost both parents to cancer last year and her brother OD'd on heroin and she was a real mess—but she was doing *okay*, okay?" I nodded. "I really liked her, and she had this chance to go on vacation, a free mileage thing, to Hawaii? Well, we talked it through and she seemed okay and I said, before she left, 'Have a nice vacation.' And she—" Hannah sobbed hard, clutching my arm.

"She killed herself?"

Hannah pulled back. Horrified, she asked, "How did you know?"

"Just a guess."

"Blair told you?" I shook my head no. "It's all over the hospital?"

"It was a wild guess."

"You think that's the kind of shitty therapist I am?"

"No, you're a terrific therapist."

"Liar. None of us is a terrific therapist yet. We don't have enough experience being therapists to be even adequate therapists, let alone good."

"I guess I just picked it up, from your upset."

"Oh. That's pretty neat, Roy. But you think it's my fault?"

"Of course not. Nobody would."

"Blair did. Said it was because I told her to have a 'nice' vacation, that I laid a heavy expectation on her that she should have a nice vacation, that other people would and why not her."

"You mean you should have said to her, 'Have a shitty vacation'?"

"Blair said that might have helped. I think I'm toxic to patients."

"How's the analysis going?"

"I'm really really depressed."

"Sorry to hear that."

She stared at me. "You still don't get it, do you?"

"Depressed about Blair?"

"Blair is not 'Blair,' Blair is 'Daddy.' " Saying this had a profound effect on her. She dropped to the floor in a faint. Not wanting to let her just lie there, I caught sight of a ladies' room. Picking her up under her armpits, I dragged her in. She came to and groggily murmured, "In my purse . . . the Eat It Off bar . . ."

I found a giant-sized candy bar in her purse. On the space-age Mylar wrapping was printed, "Eat It Off Very Nutritious Brownburn Bar." I gave it to her and sat down on the tiled floor with her, leaning against the stall, her open purse in my lap, listening to her voracious crunchings that sounded like a dog on a bone. Dazed, she sat cross-legged, her skirt up to her waist, her cashmere sweater riding up over her bra. I looked at the label. Every ingredient was synthetic except for one: "A hundred percent refined sugar?"

"The Brownburn Method," Hannah said. "You constantly eat food that has no nutrition value and that your body can't possibly use, which makes you hypoglycemic. So you have to get to your Eat It Off Very Nutritious Brownburn Bar before you go under."

The door opened. Faith Baltsburg walked in. She stared.

Silence, one of, So You're a *Pervert*, eh?

Wordlessly I left.

AS A.K. HAD PREDICTED, Cherokee Putnam failed to show up for his appointment a few days later. I was amazed. How had A.K. known? For the whole fifty-minute session I sat there associating to Cherokee and his perfect fit to Freud's homosexuality—and freeing up a few of my own homosexual associations, which involved first a round of golf with him and me bare-chested and then hugging him and burying my rough Jewish cheek in his smooth Episcopal one, all of this really scary—finally whispering to his empty chair, "You feel inadequate in this therapy and you felt inadequate for your father."

I ended the phantom session on time, closed the door, wrote up my associations in the ten free minutes, and then opened the door for Christine.

She too was not there. She hadn't shown up the week before either. My fantasy was that she was getting it on with Cherokee in a motel. As Freud said:

> For the development of femininity, the unsatisfied wish for a penis should be converted into a wish for a child for a man, *who possesses a penis*. (emphasis, S. Freud)

Feeling silly, I did another phantom session, ending with a whisper, "You feel you are not enough and your seduction of Cherokee is an attempt to fulfill your wish for a child and a man, for me and your father."

I hustled downstairs out into the rarefied mountain air, and down the hill through the cold to Thoreau. Malik was coming out of his office with a woman wearing a gas mask attached by a hose to a box slung over her shoulder. They parted. I asked him what was going on.

"Environmental distress syndrome. She's so sensitive to the toxins, her immune system's gone crazy. That box purifies the air, lets her breathe." He looked at me intently. "Ohhhhh, shit."

"Go easy on me today, Malik," I said, "I'm feeling kinda shaky."

"Me too."

"You?" I asked, first surprised, but then remembering how he hadn't been himself lately, sneezing and coughing, sounding strident and intolerant.

"Yeah. I'm feeling really tired. C'mon in." In his office, action posters of pro athletes graced the walls. Spinning a basketball on his finger, he asked what was going on. As always when I was with him, I soon felt embraced by his attention, his energy, and his concern, and I opened up, telling him about Zoe and Christine and Cherokee, about how scared I felt, how confused.

"I'm worried about this guy Cherokee," Malik said. "You try his wife?"

"She won't come in."

"He's depressed. Think he's suicidal?"

"No."

"You asked?"

"Not recently."

"Ask. You gotta *ask*. Maybe he needs meds, a little Prozac?"

"I thought you didn't like meds."

"I don't, but I use 'em. How 'bout we see him together?"

"Nope."

"Don't be a hero, Basch."

"Don't worry."

"Ask for help, okay?"

"Okay." He coughed and blew his nose. "But right now," I went on, "hearing myself talk this way to you, all this Freud stuff seems, I don't know, kinda silly."

"It's bullshit. Worse—it's abusive. It's driving your patients away."

"But Zoe came back. And it fits. Perfectly."

"That's why it's bullshit—*because* it fits. Human beings are so complex, any theory fits. By fitting, the theory excludes the complexity, so you lose what's 'human.' Theories that fit exclude other theories, and so don't fit.

Like religions excluding other religions, preaching peace, leading to war. What fits can't fit. The 'perfect-fits' fit the worst."

"That's crazy."

"Nope, that's Gödel. Kurt Gödel, Gödel's Theorem. Paradigm shift, 1931."

"But the things A.K. is teaching me allow me to go deeper."

"You think people are like holes, where there's a deeper, and deeper is better?"

"You're the one always talking about 'understanding.' "

"In the present, not in the past."

"But the thing is, I feel it in myself! If I could only drill down to the roots of my behavior, in my past, I'd understand what I'm doing, and I'd be better. All of a sudden my mind is buzzing with the past!"

"See? That's it. A.K. gets you to think that if only you were good enough to see through the present to the past, you'd be really good, maybe almost as good as her. Analysis reduces one thing to another—this is not this, but that; the real is not real, but fantasy; the present isn't present, but the past. Kid, I got news for you: healing happens now. Nobody's healed in the past."

"Freud did it in the 'now.' In his cases, when the unconscious is made conscious, it's like a flash of light—a catharsis. Bingo. Better!"

"Never happens, catharsis. Never seen one yet, in three years here. And I don't know anybody who's seen one yet either. Freud lied, you know. A *lot*."

"Isn't it possible, Malik, that you're so anti-Freud because you've never been analyzed?"

"Whaddaya mean not analyzed? I tried it, okay? With an all-star analyst."

"Really?" This was a surprise. "What happened?"

"Stopped in the nick of time."

"Why?"

"My jump shot tailed off. And then someone I admired told me to stop."

"Who?"

"Ike White."

"Ike?" I said. "But he was an analyst himself."

"Right. So he *knew*. He lived it, he died it. With his brand-new analyst at his deathbed." He sighed. "Look, kid, I'll put it to you simple: analysis says that the way out of the old is the old. But it doesn't work. Going back over the old just grinds that needle down deeper into that groove. Round and round we go."

"What's the alternative?"

"The way out of the old is the new."

"I don't need aphorisms, Malik, I need help! I'm losing control! Down in the swamp of my mind my old man is drilling away on my molars, muttering curses, and my mother is throwing knives and crying her heart out and it's all there, right in front of my eyes, all the fucking time! I constantly feel I'm not good enough! Compared to you, I'm one sick puppy!"

He squeezed my shoulder, like he used to do. "There's nothing wrong with you, kid. You're fine." I felt a warmth, under his hand.

"But I *feel* sick, Malik. And you're not *with* me in it!"

"Okay. You're right. I don't know what's wrong with me today. Talk."

"Look—all I want now is to learn to use psychology to help people."

"Psychology doesn't help people."

"I'm outta here."

"Wait!" He clutched my shoulder. "What helps people has nothing to do with psychology. It's not what theory you use, or what words you say."

"What helps people, then?"

"When a person feels *seen*, and you *sense them feeling seen*, and you feel seen by them. Right then, in that moment, there's a touch of the spirit. That's it, that's all. Spirit. Healing in psychotherapy is an act of spirit."

"I don't know from 'spirit.' I know you can't prove it, but I still—"

"Of *course* I can prove it. Psychology you can't prove, but spirit's easy to prove." He smiled. "Want me to prove it?" I nodded. "You're breathing, okay?"

"You want me to answer that?"

"Yes."

"Yes, I am breathing."

"Good. So'm I. Now, next step: stop breathing."

I held my breath, as long as I could, and then breathed out.

"No, no," Malik said, "I said, 'Stop breathing.' "

"I did."

"I mean stop breathing period."

"Don't be ridiculous."

"Try 'n' stop breathing, see how far you get. Are *you* doing the breathing? Or is the life-breath something beyond you, something we call 'spirit'?"

"But I'm not there, Malik, I'm on real shaky ground. I need some real, concrete guidance. Freud and A.K. have it. Why are you bugging me, why?"

" 'Cause I care, kid, and I feel like I'm losin' you, fast."

His words hit home. A warmth spread through me, over me, all the way up to my ears. No matter what, he had stuck with me, through the year. "Yeah," I said, "I care too. It's just that I'm feeling a little lost."

"I'm with you, Roy."

"Lost?"

"Feeling a little lost too, yop." He smiled, sadly, those dark eyes glistening. He coughed back tears, once, twice.

"Why?" I said. "What's wrong?"

"Just life," he said quietly. "Life as it is, life as it could be?"

The rest of the afternoon I was in a funk, a gloom so murky that I was barely functioning, tripping over wastebaskets and bumping into doorjambs. On the way out I passed A.K.'s secretary, who'd once been my secretary, Nancy.

"So long, Nance, see you tomorrow. If I'm still alive."

"Look at you! Your clothes are all rumpled, your eyes look like, I don't know, black eyes or something. You look terrible."

"You should see it from this side."

"Remember, Roy, you're not crazy."

"From where I am, crazy's a step up. At least it's a definite."

"Hey, you'll make it. She likes you, you know."

"Who?"

"Dr. Lowell."

"Me? She told you that?"

"She'd never say it, but I can tell. She like *really* likes you. G'night."

Enlivened by this, I walked out. As I bundled up to meet the cold, suddenly there she was beside me. If I looked terrible, she looked terrific, the soft fur collar of her stylish black coat pulled tightly up to her cheeks, framing her closely cropped head of light brown hair, which at that moment shone like a corona against the golden happenstance of a fake gas lamp. Hearing me, she turned. The gold light made her face look bright and fresh.

"I don't get it, Dr. Lowell," I said. "I listen to one or two patients a day and wind up a total wreck, while you listen to patients and supervisees all day long and you look as fresh as ever. How do you do it?"

"So who listens?"

I stared at her.

She laughed. She actually laughed! "That was a joke. Don't be so stiff all the time, Roy. Laugh a little."

"I will."

"Good evening."

"Good night. Yes, yes."

I watched her disappear into a sexy black Oldsmobile Cutlass Supreme. The door closed with a powerful *thunk*. Despite the inhuman cold, I felt a glow in my chest, a warmth. Might I just be good enough, after all?

TWELVE

WAS IT CYNICAL OF ME, or idealistic, to give Freud a chance with Cherokee, Christine, and Zoe?

Despite myself, despite everything I had learned about what was crucial to being with other people, as the deep-freeze of January was iced over by the cruelty of February, I tried it. How could I not? If I resisted, A.K. told me I was resisting because of my neurotic, unanalyzed resistance. And what alternative was there? Heiler's SELF-psychology? Toshiba's imbecilic *Diagnostic and Statistical Manual*? The druglords, Errol and Win? Which left Malik—Leonard A. Malik with his buddy system and his humble power of example of how to connect. But day by day in the virtual Vienna of Thoreau, Malik seemed to be fading, his voltage dimming down. I loved him and was in awe of his gifts, but I had started to feel a niggling suspicion that he was just that: a gifted man, one of a kind who, despite his scorn for theory of any kind, was able, through sheer bigness of heart, to work magic with the suffering of others.

Compared to him, I wasn't much gifted. It was a relief to stop trying to be Malik and to realize that I, not great at this and maybe not even all that good, had to rely on a theory. Much like my father who, realizing that compared to other golfers he was no pro and would never be, scoured *Golf Digest* every month for theories—"The Waggle at Address," "Freeing up the Left," "What *Not* to Think About on the Backswing," "Three Lessons on Bad Lies"—and then bought the latest equipment, the Big Berthas and Miracle Wedges that promised long balls and exquisite touch.

Was my reliance on theory an act of cynicism or idealism? Working my way around the world the year before, I'd met many men and women who at first seemed cynical or idealistic, but who, as I'd gotten to know them, had confounded categorization. In July in the Dordogne, the cynical farmer next door turned out to be a Resistance fighter who had held the line against the Germans, the line being the very farmhouse we were getting drunk in as he told me. Eleven months later in Changsha, China, the idealistic young woman working nonstop to rescue the rows of girl babies from the rising floodwaters threatening the orphanage in Social Welfare Center Number One, when asked about the neglect of fifty less hardy newborns in a back room, shrugged and said, "Bad luck." Telling the faithful from the nihilistic was as hard as telling the truthful from the liar. Ike White, who had seemed so authentic and humble, had all the while I knew him been living the arrogance of a lie.

Just that month *Consumer Reports*, having surveyed thousands of great Americans about psychotherapy in much the same way they surveyed them about vacuum cleaners, announced that talk therapy *worked*—worked whether or not drugs also were given, eat your heart out, Win—and the more therapy, the *better* it worked. Freudian analysis, the most, was by implication the best.

And so, in this, the most vain season—dark when I awoke for work and dark when I left Misery for home—whether from resignation or brave hope, I started the psychoanalysis of my patients. A.K., upon hearing that Cherokee was rich, had worked the entrails and said, "Regress him. Take him up to five sessions a week. Deepen his transference to you, as I'm doing with Oly Joe Olaf." Oly Joe, the teenager who had been carried into Thoreau all curled up in Oral Stage Arrest, under the five-times-a-week onslaught of A.K. had now regressed even further into orality. Sometimes he lay curled up in bed with his "blankie," sucking his thumb, chewing gum, babbling baby talk and sipping a Mountain Dew—all at the same time. While regression didn't seem much like progress to me, I knew that I didn't know enough to know that for sure.

Seeing Cherokee Putnam five times a week was making a profound difference. Suddenly things started happening just as A.K. had predicted. In late January I had bought my first bound ledger with a line down the middle of each page, and a supply of yellow number 2 pencils and an electric pencil sharpener that honed them to perfect points. This was my ledger entry for the end of a session in early February:

"I dreamed I was lying in Father's arms—ah, forget it."	O.K., this is the Oedipus Complex. God I'm hungry! Maybe tonight I'll do take-out Chinese?
"Yes, and what comes to mind?"	Technique 1: The Free Association.
"He was squeezing the life out of me. That's all I remember."	Castration anxiety and unconscious resistance to talking about it.
"And what is your fantasy, hmm?"	Technique 2: Fantasy. I'm starving!
"He's fucking her in therapy. I feel horrible."	His Oedipal wish to "fuck" his Mother/wife is being projected onto his "fucking" his Father/Schlomo.
"And what are your thoughts about her fucking him in therapy?"	Technique 4: Ask the Opposite: if he talks feeling, you talk thought.
"I think it's true."	Projective Identification. Hey, could this be the Oscillator?
"Hrummpht!"	Technique 5: The Psychoanalytic Grunt. But I feel a little like Thai. Hm, wonder why I associated Thai?
"Last night we went out to dinner and afterward in her purse I—"	Dinner? Now you're talkin'.
"Where'd you go?"	
"The Gandhi, but afterward—"	Oh yeah, that new Indian place yeah.
"How was it?"	Maybe I'll try it?
"It was good, but afterward I found a pack of condoms in her purse. And I've had a vasectomy."	Hm. Maybe she *is* fucking somebody after all.

"Yes, and what are your feelings about your thoughts that he's fucking her in therapy?"

Technique 4: Ask the Opposite of the Opposite You Just Asked. No, better stick with Chinese.

"I still hear that voice inside, but ever since I started my affair with Christine, it doesn't bother me as much. I worry about getting in too deep with her, but . . ."

God I love hearing the sexy bits of their affair! More!

Fear of his Engulfing/Intrusive Mother.

"And so you feel better?"

Shit—a mistake. Erase it.

"I feel like crap and it's *your* fault! Now, not only am I paranoid, but you've got me cheating on my wife!"

His Oedipal rage at my mistake. Erase this too.
He thinks I'm his Father.

"*I've* got you cheating?"

Father-transference interpretation.

"She's *your* patient, isn't she? It's so embarrassing! I'm acting just like Father—all of his slimy affairs. And now I'm hearing his voice all the time too: 'Don't be a puff, Cher'!" I'm so depressed I could scream!"

You mean your Mother.

Identification with Father.

Projection of his homosexual wish. Oh, such a *punim*!—why do I sound so much like Schlomo? A sign that I'm comfy with my own homosexual wishes. And hey it hurts to have your cock cut off.

"Ahem."

Thirty seconds left. Hit him with a final interpretation, one to grow on.

"Time's up already? Please, Doc, don't hit me too hard today, O.K.?"

Castration Anxiety. He sees me as his Distant/Sadistic Father, great.

"Hey, it hurts to have your cock cut off."

Silence. Stunned look in eyes.

Got him. Great! Go for it again.

"You are hungry for your Father's love and starve yourself to get it and Christine can't feed the hurt of feeling 'I am not good enough.' "

Not bad, but why all these "ands"? Just like my father, and why do all my Freudian interpretations sound like his letters? And why has he stopped writing me letters?

Silence. Panicked look in his eyes.

Maybe tonight I'll order chicken with cashews?

More silence. His look changes to gratitude and admiration.

And Szechuan spicy pork.

"Gotta hand it to you, Doc, you're good. You beat me again."

Oedipal Rivalry: I, the Father, win, he, the Son, loses.

He staggers out, closes the door.

Chow down!

Cherokee's Father-transference to me now was so intense it was almost palpable: his hunger for my approval, his identifying with me, trying to be friends with me, asking about my car, my wife, my house, my kids, fearing my wrath, complying with whatever I said, putting himself down—all because he wanted to kill me.

It was incredible to see, in Cherokee's childhood Genital-Stage arrest, how well he fit Freud: at age five his unresolved castration anxiety had backflipped into a killer Superego now perched on his skull like a hawk, peering down at the dove of his Ego in his brain, both dove and hawk pecking at the lizard in his groin, his Id. The unconscious forces behind his behavior were being made conscious. His affair was, deep down, a way both of identifying with his distant/sadistic Father and of making love to his intrusive/engulfing Mother (to whom he had a strong attachment, the root of his homosexuality). His trying to "kill" Father by shunning Wall Street for Walt Disney deep down was a way of loving Father homosexually. He'd been afraid to "be bigger" than Father and had "cut myself down" in love and work (*"lieben und arbeiten*"). Day after day we'd been drilling down through the swamp of his obsession to the bedrock of his childhood until finally, today, he'd gotten relief from his symptom:

"I still hear that voice—'He's fucking her in therapy'—but you know something, Doctor? It doesn't bother me as much."

If this wasn't turning his neurotic misery into common unhappiness, what was? He still hadn't owned his homosexuality, but the love between us was almost palpable and I had every confidence he would. It was dynamite work.

As was my work with Christine and Zoe. A.K. had suggested I regress these cases as well, but Christine could only afford to come once a week. She too fit Freud like a glove. That harlot-blond hair, those black weeping tights and short skirts, those grand swings of mood from elation to despair, her using sex as bait—here was a classic case of hysteria.

> Our hysterical patients suffer from reminiscences. Their symptoms are the remnants and the memory symbols of certain [traumatic] experiences . . . They cannot escape from the past, and neglect present reality in its favor.

And why, deep down, do they do this?

> Every hysteria is founded in repression, always with a sexual content . . . Envy for the penis—the striving after the possession of a male genital.

A.K. said that since I was seeing her only once a week, I had to hit her with harder interpretations. This I did. In a session a few weeks before, she'd offered a dream fragment:

"I dreamed that I floated out of my bed and into the arms of a woman in white standing tall, and as I went to her we both burst into flames."

"White standing tall" was obviously a penis, and "burst into flames" an ejaculation. I said, "You have the wish to suck *my* penis?"

"Yeah. I'd like to turn off the lights and give you a blow job."

"As you wished to do with your distant/sadistic Father."

"Yeah," she said cheerfully, "and as I'm gonna do in about ten minutes, with Cherokee, in the Jammer Motel just down the road."

Failing to get my interpretation, she was "acting out" sexually. Freud's "economic" theory of repressing libidinal energy was hydraulic, like trying to stuff a fat lady into a tight bathing suit: if you got one part in, another part would pop back out. Repressing her desire to suck her Father's penis, she sucked any man's penis she could find—even, for a while, Arnie the Lunkhead Bozer's.

After my dream interpretation she "cut down" on "giving head" but started having migraines. I interpreted this hysterical conversion symptom as repressed penis envy for her distant/sadistic Father—"Giving head gives you head-*aches*." She stopped having migraines and started blacking out at work—"hysterical blindness," as in nineteenth century Vienna. She'd always wanted to be a painter. In the last session we'd analyzed this right out: She'd held herself back from painting because her Father was legally blind. "Canvasing men" sexually was a symptom of her inability to "hold a paintbrush to the canvas without shaking"—penis envy, big-time. It was exhilarating work.

But my most challenging case was Zoe.

Zoe had money. Living on the Family Unit and seeing me three times a week, she was regressing like crazy. The erotic transference was like a good fastball: high-inside and hot. The previous week A.K. had quoted me this, by heart, from Freud's "Observations on Transference Love":

> "One motive at work, connected with falling in love, is the patient's efforts to reassure herself of her irresistibility, to destroy the physician's authority by bringing him down to the level of a lover."

"Yes," I said excitedly, "that's exactly what she makes me feel."

"You want to fuck her?"

"No. Well . . . maybe a little."

"Fuck her a . . . 'little'?" She smiled. "Or do you want to suck her?"

This too seemed appealing. I nodded. She smiled again, and suddenly I had the fantasy of getting up and unpeeling A.K. herself from that dark, manly suit. What was *under* there? I blushed. "What's the difference?"

"You want to suck me?"

"Well," I said, trying to make a joke, "you found me out."

"Like you always wanted to suck your mother because you were not enough?"

Boom. A curtain parted like in the Columbia Movie Theatre and I saw my mother in a summer "playsuit" and my father's gentle dental hands and I myself playing right field in Little League behind the Elks Club—my father always said their initials, BPOE, stood for "Best People on Earth"—needing glasses and not having told anyone I couldn't see and suddenly there was a high fly ball to right and with everybody yelling "Catch it catch it!" watching it sail over my head for an inside-the-park home r—

"Fuck is Oedipal," A.K. was saying, "Genital Stage. Suck is pre-Oedipal, Oral Stage. 'Guck' is Anal Stage. We won't get into *that*, yet. Penis Equals Breast. Deep down—when she talked about your 'big black Beemer'?"

"She wanted to suck my penis, yes."

"No," A.K. said, dismayed, and blew out a lump of smoke which before my eyes seemed to go from penis to turd to long nipple, recapitulating nicely the Freudian regression A.K. said was the Holy Grail of analysis. "She wants to suck your breast. Suck Penis, Suck Breast. Bite Penis, Bite Breast. She's regressing down through the Genital Stage to the Oral Stage. The transference will soon turn maternal: She will see you as Mother, engulfing and intrusive, and will want to suck you and bite you. Take her up to five times a week. Regress her more."

And so I did. But I must have been doing something wrong because rather than talking about her mother, she talked about her older brother, Butler:

"When I was about twelve—I'd just gotten my period, and my boobies—I loved my boobies so much! Anyway it was summer. We were at our camp in the Adirondacks—we own like four hundred acres—it was really really hot and I was swimming under our dock in the lake. And my brother Butler swam over to me under the dock, I think my mother was up on the dock, and he said, 'Let me stick it in there' and I said, 'No way José,' and he said 'Just once' and he kind of trapped me up against a slick piling and the sunlight was coming down in slits and he pulled down my bikini bottom and he said 'Here feel this,' and he took my hand and his penis was hard as a rock and so big! And I said, 'Hard as a rock,' and he said again, 'Just let me stick it in to feel it a second' and I felt this huge thing splitting me open and screamed but his hand was on my mouth so I just let it happen and he came and then I bobbed under and wanted to drown myself and he hoisted me up and said, 'You tell on me I'll kill you.' "

She sat there, one leg curled under her, the heel rocking back and forth in her genital zone, breathing hard. I said, "Your *mother* was overhead?"

"Yeah, and it hurt, but it was exciting too. All that night I cried to myself, but . . . my hands were between my legs—God I'm so embarrassed to tell you this—I never told anyone this before. And it went on from there. We did it a lot, under the dock, in the boathouse, in his room, his bed . . ."

I found myself feeling enraged at this brother, this incest. I burst into my next session with A.K. and said, "I'm going to get that sonofabitch Butler to come to Family Analysis and confront him in front of everybody!"

"Fantasy," A.K. said.

"Fantasy?"

"She wasn't abused in reality; she has the fantasy of being abused. Freud's greatest discovery was to see reality as less important than fantasy, to see that the so-called reality of the 'real' world is in fact fantasy."

"But Freud said"—I quoted, from my notebook—" 'Their symptoms are the remnants and memory symbols of certain (traumatic) experiences.' "

"*First* he said that, but then he took his step of genius: these memories were fantasy." She quoted, from memory:

> "Analysis had led back to these infantile sexual traumas and yet they were not true . . . Hysterical subjects create such scenes in fantasy . . . to cover up the autoerotic activity of the first years of childhood, to . . . raise it to a higher plane . . . When their mothers gave them enemas or rectal douches they used to react with fear and screams of rage . . . This is why, in fantasies of later years, father so regularly appears as the sexual seducer . . . but the seducer is regularly the mother."

"Freud moved the world," A.K. went on, "from out there"—she pointed number 2 number one directly at me, at a point between my eyes—"to in here." Number 2 number one swiveled so that it was pointing directly between her eyes, above her beautifully done nose. "The world is not the world out there," she said. "The world is within us."

"Like Christ? As in 'the Kingdom of God is within you'?"

"Spare me," she said coldly. "God is sublimation. God!"

"What should I do about it?"

"Do nothing. It's Oral. If she talks fucking, you talk sucking."

"And if she talks sucking, I talk fucking?"

A.K. stared at me as if I were mentally challenged. "The goal of regression-analysis is to regress her," she said. "If she talks sucking, you talk *more* sucking."

Which I did. But my technique must have been off, because it didn't work. The more I talked sucking, the more she talked fucking. She seemed to blossom, appearing in the office renewed and glowing, popping with sexual energy. She got a flashy haircut—light brown hair cut even shorter—and wore tasteful makeup and tenacious perfume. Her clothing seemed to be having trouble staying buttoned or snapped or hooked or down over skin or up over skin. She'd come in with a blouse unbuttoned down past Thursday, revealing a red satin bra, and sit with her legs crossed high up, a long length of thigh whooshing up into a bulging triangle of red satin. She would smile at me and ask: "Do I turn you on?"

She did. Stiffening my face so that it had all the responsiveness of a stone, I used the Three Techniques to try to shift her from Genital to Oral. She revved up, filling our sessions with her erotic history: from childhood masturbation to rubbing nipples and "matching snatches" with girls at Miss Schader's Boarding School, through first sex with a waiter in Grand Cayman and dozens of sordid drunken affairs with both sexes and group sex on boats in trains crossing Austria under tables or over oceans embellished one day with a dream of "flying in a big pink balloon over the Matterhorn and through a dark dirty tunnel to Germany and diving into a river of beer"—clearly a regression from Genital to Anal to Oral—and on up to the disastrous affair at Dartmouth College that had led her to that edge called suicide and then back a step, into Misery.

Once, leaving my office, she slipped and fell into me. By reflex I grabbed her around the waist, and my palm, I swear unintentionally, found a breast. As she straightened up she turned to me and suddenly we were a man and a woman and there was a jolt of sex between us.

The erotic flew between us, like a confused bird.

I turned brick red and backed away clumsily, pushing her gently toward the door. I locked it and sat there sweating, seeing just how easy it would be to seduce her in my office. The door would be locked. No one would know but us. Neither of us would dare tell. That night I couldn't get her out of my mind.

I called up Henry Solini, told him about Zoe, and asked what I should do.

"Don't do anything?" he said. "At times like that I hear my old man's voice, the one time he told me about the birds and the bees? 'Remember, Henry,' he goes, 'flies cause disease. Keep yours zipped.'?"

"Thanks."

"Don't thank me, man, thank your analyst? He's doing a great job?"

When Zoe came into the office the next day she brushed against me. As she crossed in front of the low-angled February sunlight slipping in through the window, I saw she was wearing nothing under her flimsy shirt. When she sat, I saw she wore no panties either. If ever I wanted to do it, now was the time.

No way. Something in me, something like what you feel when a child is with you, a sense of her vulnerability, her waiflike fragility, filled the space between us. I felt a wave of revulsion. It would not only be wrong, it would be evil. Her offering herself to me was offering me a chance to groove on myself. It wouldn't be sex, it would be power. Like rape. It would be rape. I the therapist had the power. I could use it. If I were desperate or empty or into power, I might just use her to fill me up. What did this say about Schlomo Dove? If anything, he seemed full—too full. Cherokee was the empty one, the thin dusk of moneyed twilight as opposed to ten shouting Jews. And while Schlomo was ultra-analyzed—President of the Freudian Institute—Cherokee, so far, was just getting a handle on his paranoia.

I responded to Zoe that day by being more theoretical than ever. Rejected, she screamed, "You are a royal pain in the ass!" and stormed out.

I wrote up the session for A.K., who praised me for using the theory but pointed out that I must be using the theory wrong because while, even if I were to be given the benefit of the doubt and her "pain in the ass" were a regression from Genital Stage to Anal Stage, there was no hint, no hint at all, of any Oral.

"I'll try harder."

"That's the worst thing you could do."

"I'll try less hard."

"You can't."

"Until I'm analyzed?"

Number 2 number four.

Work with my cases was intense and exhilarating. I looked forward to seeing them, spending hours the nights before going over my ledger and reading the relevant Freud, and then after each session transcribing for supervision with A.K. Now I had a vision of how therapy went. As I held to this vision with my cases, except for Zoe they mostly went that way. I'd float out of sessions light-headed, full of ideas. With my associations, dreams, and fantasies, my inner life was rich, a garden of unconscious delights. No wonder so many analysts had creative hobbies like sculpture or painting or basket-weaving. In terms of my cases, it was the best.

But in terms of myself, it was the worst.

On Thoreau, surrounded by Freudians, I felt watched constantly. Feeling watched constantly, I came out constantly with words and actions that were bizarre, a sign of my deep psychopathology. Tapping a pencil on a desk was guess what? Fondling a basketball while waiting for Malik? Eating a banana in public?—the stares of Faith and other Thoreauvians soon made me stop, fold it up, hold it down—more stares—"What is he going to *do* with that banana?" It was astonishing how any object or action could be seen, deeper down, as sexual. At first it had only been penises. Now it was also breasts. Breasts and nipples were everywhere! It was remarkable just how many breasts you could see and hear, if you kept an open mind. Lunchtimes were hell, with hot dogs and melons—once, with Faith, a taco transformed itself before my eyes into a vagina.

It was a vicious cycle: the more I started to feel that my every move and my every word were being analyzed, the more wary I became, and the more utterly stupid things I seemed to say or do. Worst was my seeming to be happy—say, about my cases—which deep down meant I was unhappy. The happier I seemed, the deeper down was my unhappiness, the more miserable I must be. The present became mythic, almost Jungian! It was hard to take.

My own worst psychopathology came out around A.K. herself. I began to show up for supervision either too early or too late, at the wrong time or on the wrong day. One day I barged in on her during a session, interrupting a well-dressed woman, knees up, weeping on the couch. Humiliated, knowing I had set the analysis back several weeks if not months or years, bowing my abject apologies, I slunk back out. Suddenly I seemed in possession of a trick appointment book, its pages now porous, unable to hold my writing, or acidified, so as to render my ink invisible, or even with whole days missing. My mind seemed made of mud. My everyday life was pure neurosis. My head felt like a bog, my stomach raw hamburger. My life felt jinxed. I was a nervous wreck.

Then, soon, I got paranoid. Was it our old friend homosexuality? I walked Thoreau on eggshells, when I wasn't hiding out behind the closed door of my office. When in public, I was as silent as possible. I was living under a kind of Freudian Miranda warning—"Anything you say can be used against you." I shut up. But when I did speak, Freudian slips abounded. My efforts to cram my words down into silence seemed to make my actions burst out in ever more bizarre ways—the Fat Lady in the Bathing Suit theory. Everyone seemed to be wondering when the hell I'd get myself into analysis.

When I told A.K. about Cherokee finding condoms in his wife's purse and being vasectomized, so that she *was* fucking someone, A.K. said nothing. Then I told her about Cherokee dating Christine, and she was furious. "You fixed them up with each other? What the hell are you doing, running a dating service?"

"I happened to leave the outer door open, she came in early, and they just happened to meet."

"You didn't 'happen' to, and nothing is 'just' something. Your repressed wish to fuck her came out in your 'leaving the outer door open' so *he* could fuck her. It's Oedipal. Primal Scene." Her eyes widened. I braced myself.

"And do you imagine that you saw your father fucking your mother?"

Boom. Pitch-dark, and on the other side of the thin wall of my bedroom a grunting, a muffled crying . . .

"Are you going to go on?" A.K. was saying.

I fought back tears, and said nothing, my head hanging down. I felt her staring at me, slats of heavy winter light through venetian blinds. Childhood.

"When you're ready," she said, in a kindly tone I'd never heard before, "you're ready." I looked up. There was kindness in her eyes. "There's a lot of pain in there, waiting to be let out."

Astonished and touched by her concern, I went back to talking about the found condoms in Lily's purse and Cherokee's vasectomy. When A.K. reframed this, saying, "The reality of the condoms in her purse is less important than the deeper meaning of 'the condoms in her purse,' the dreams, fantasies, and associations to the condoms," I nodded my agreement. Somehow I managed to stumble through the session until she grasped number 2 number four and said:

"You're not doing that badly. You're bright, and even though you're only a first-year resident, I've been giving you third-year-resident supervision. Perhaps it is beginning to pay off."

I floated out of her office on a pink cloud, as if tipsy, or in love.

. . .

" 'BEWARE OF ALL ENTERPRISES that require new clothes,' " Malik was saying, staring at my new Schlomo suit and rainbow-colored Jackson Pollack tie, the first suit and tie I'd worn since the day I'd met him on Emerson, lifetimes before. "A quote, from Henry David Thoreau."

It was late Thursday afternoon February 25; the talons of winter were hooked so deeply into the year that you could almost feel the horny cartilage all icy against your ribs. Malik was standing outside his office on Thoreau, and beside him were an elderly woman and a seeing-eye dog. I wanted to talk to Malik about Cherokee.

The woman, like Malik, was wearing orange-tinted sunglasses. She carried a red-tipped cane. I answered Malik with silence.

"Dr. Roy G. Basch, meet Dr. Geneva Hooevens, and her dog Yoman."

She was the blind woman who, at the meeting after Ike White killed himself, had stood up bravely and asked Lloyal von Nott why he was denying that Ike White had killed himself. Geneva was a large, broad woman with rich chestnut hair in braids. In her handshake I felt a delicate, iron sensitivity.

"Geneva," Malik went on, "practices in the community, and also has an office here, as a member of the Attending Psychiatrist Staff. She saw one of our Thoreau patients a few times in therapy, until the parents heard how terrific the Family Unit was and stuck the girl here against her will. I was just going over her impressions."

"Yes, won't you join us?" Geneva asked.

I did, and in silence listened to them discuss the case, thinking that they were talking much too pragmatically, about the manifest symptomatology—promiscuity—rather than the deeper developmental arrest around the pre-Oedipal Mother, who I knew, from family therapy, was engulfing and intrusive. I drifted downstream on my associations, until Geneva got up to go.

"I guess her family saw me as not high-powered enough," she said. "And maybe they're right. Out there in the community, in daily practice, you're just flying by the seat of your pants—theories don't matter much. A girl like this, well, I start to feel I'm not doing it right, just stumbling along, and that I should be reading more—but what seems to work best is just trying to create a kind of friendship. Seems to help some of them, even though it's not in the books. The books are always written by the analysts."

Startled by her humility, I asked, "Have you been analyzed?"

"Oh yes!" she said, laughing. "I trained here in the sixties—it was all the rage. I even became an analyst myself. Funny you should ask. Just yesterday my husband and I went to our periodontist for some gum work. And who should I meet in the waiting room but my old analyst? And he didn't remember me! Seven years with him, five days a week, and he has no memory of me! I was drinking at the time, but still. And as I'm lying down in the dentist's chair—like on the couch—my mouth full of blood, I think:

'Geneva, you've finally found something that's more painful, less effective, and costs more than psychoanalysis!' " She roared with laughter, as did we. "When I was in your shoes, analysis was like the final merit badge: you had to do it, to prove you were really serious. But when I saw the analysts in action I said to myself, 'Geneva, this is ridiculous. They must be *joking*!' But then, I found people here, good people, who believed in these theories. So I started believing in them. You have to believe in something, right?"

I looked into her blank orange glasses. "Yes."

"Now I see it as 'The Emperor's New Clothes.' There are good therapists who are analysts, but they're good in spite of being analysts. The good ones unlearn it all. But you're luckier than I was. You've got Malik. Good-bye."

"Are you available for supervision?" I asked.

"Me?" She seemed surprised. "What have I to teach? I just try to keep it simple now. But sure. Call me if you like." The dog led her away.

"She's amazing," I said to Malik.

"Terrific person, terrific therapist. How's it going?"

"Fine," I said guardedly, not wanting to open myself up to his criticism.

"You haven't been to the gym. You avoiding me?"

I said nothing.

"Okay. Listen up. You gotta stop doing this bullshit 'regression' on Zoe. She's going down the tubes."

"No, she's going back to her childhood—"

"And she may never come back out! *You don't play around with people's heads!*" He coughed, sneezed, blew his nose. "A.K. is a mindfucker. Period."

"You've been making a lot of mistakes yourself lately, Malik. Double-booking patients, forgetting appointments—the time you locked yourself and your patient inside your office so it took Primo half an hour to pry you out? You've got a few little flaws too, Malik—"

"Flaws? I got character defects up the wazoo! I may be one of the most defective kids who ever tried to do this shit! I mean look! Look at me! Would you trust a guy like this with your *mind*?"

I looked. Slicked-up black hair, orange glasses, sharp features—he seemed even more tight and wiry lately, sneezing and coughing, unable to shake his winter cold and yet even in winter wearing a golf shirt with a polo player with raised mallet over his heart, jeans and black Nikes. The fire was still there, but so, I associated, were the ashes. Oedipal, yes. "No way I would trust you with my mind, no."

"And that's why I'm trustable."

"Because you make mistakes?"

"Because I hang in with the mistake *after* the mistake. Things go wrong in therapy, so?"

"So mistakes pollute the transference."

"Oh jeez. Things go wrong in life, kid. Remember 'life'?"

"Therapy isn't life."

"In therapy or in life, it's not just what you do, it's what you do *next*. It's not the screwups that screw up a life, it's what happens *around* a screwup. We never get it right, first shot outta the box, but gettin' it wrong and hangin' in, we get so we care about each other. Like ballplayers on a team? Those Columbia High Fish Hawks? Blowing a big lead, and hangin' in, hangin' in, and then, like magic, startin' it rollin' and beatin' 'em at the buzzer?"

"Therapy's different. The doctor has the experience; the patient comes for that experience—even, that wisdom. You taught me that."

"I taught you that what works is gettin' in touch, feelin' that 'click'—"

"Freud says we can never really get in touch. Because of the unconscious distortions of childhood, we're always shouting across an unbridgeable gap."

"There ain't no gap, kid, and you know it. You 'n' me have 'clicked,' a *lot*. Theory creates a gap, theory *is* that gap. A.K. uses the idea of a gap to justify the gap her analysis created in her—she's a shit therapist. All her patients have terminated, except Oly Joe—who I'm trying like hell to save."

"I don't know what you're talking about anymore, Malik."

"Hey, Roy, I'm your buddy, remember?"

I tried to remember, to focus on what he was asking and respond, but my mind veered and filled with a dream fragment—standing there in front of Zoe and Christine and Cherokee, totally naked, a giant erection in my hand, and—

"Okay," Malik said, "we can't do this anymore. You're gone." He left.

I stood there, feeling a pain in my chest, and coughed. Malik came back.

"Look. I'm having a lotta trouble lately, in this bullshit environment. Seeing you go through this, after all we've been through together, is rough. I'm gonna protect Zoe from you. You're gettin' totally into yourself, kid, you've got a taste of that psychoanalytic joy at being miserable, you're thinking you ought to go under analysis yourself, and . . ."

Total selfishness my mother said Roy you've become totally selfish and you don't have any idea how much it hurts your father and me and she turned away weeping and my father snapped me up by the nape of the neck with an iron grip and wrassled me down to the basement smelling of rats dead for a while under the woodpile and with a rat-trap grip on my neck ripped down my pants and started to whack me with his open hand which stung but didn't hurt all that much and my mother on the cellar steps cried out and down, "Not with your hand, Stu, you'll ruin your hand for your dental practice!" and so he whipped out his belt and whaled away and that hurt like hell like fire and despite myself and through gritted teeth I screamed and cursed him which made him whale away harder and part of my screaming was with pain and part of me was drifting off away to a place past where the clouds were to a sense of something else . . .

When I came back from my associations, Malik was gone. If we'd talked about Cherokee Putnam, the talk was already repressed.

"YESTERDAY WITH CHRISTINE I couldn't get it up!" Cherokee was saying an hour later, in therapy. "All your talk about castration has ruined me. You understand? I couldn't get it up!" He stared at me, as if I could get it up for him. "She was great—'Happens to a lot of men,' she said—which made me feel worse, thinking of all the men she'd had, who I couldn't measure up to. She tried to help—her hand, her mouth, her vagina—it just made it worse. Finally she fell asleep with her cheek on my belly. I was mortified. Staring at my limp dick lying there across my thigh and every once in a while I'd look at her—her tits, that curve where her ass rolls into her vagina?"

I nodded, as analytically as possible.

"And it would wiggle a little, like a drunk trying to get up off a sidewalk. But if I tried to do it? Soft as an old banana. 'He's fucking her in therapy,' and I can't get it up. Makes me want to kill myself."

Incredible case. I proceeded to explore his impotence, his associations, fantasies, and dreams leading back through castration anxiety to oral rage at Mother and his sadness at seeing a just-issued postage stamp with a cowboy, in his words, "riding a stallion hot and heavy, a whip in his hand next to a covered wagon with his wife and kids to commemorate 'the Cherokee Strip Land Run.' " Such was the intensity of our work that time ran out without my offering an interpretation. I said, merely, "Time to stop."

"But what about my limp dick? My manhood? What should I do?"

"Your limp dick is a symptom of your deep conflicts. We'll analyze them out and your symptom will vanish. See you tomorrow."

"But I never had a *problem* with my dick, before I met *you*! I'm obsessed with *his* dick, *my* dick has finked out, and I'm a worse failure than ever! Now I'm not even good enough in the saddle! If it stays soft, I'm sunk." He sighed. "You sure this is the way to go?"

His question hung on a hook in the air, like a magician's hankie on a finger, or a penis why not?, as my own number 2 number four slid to the right.

After he had gone I wrote on the right-hand side of the ledger:

> "Finked out in the saddle" equals homoerotic oral transferential sadistic rage at distant/sadistic Father and engulfing/intrusive Mother, both.

OLY JOE OLAF was a kid on a mission, the only problem being that none of us knew what that mission was. Since his disastrous family therapy where Faith Baltsburg first made the mistake of telling the father and mother that there was "hope" and then wouldn't tell anybody where the bathroom was, his parents had refused to come back to therapy, and in fact had been petitioning to have him released from Thoreau, claiming that his being curled up in a fetal position was a sign of his being hurt by therapy. A.K. had used all her Freudian authority as a professor at the BMS to argue that Oly Joe's being curled up in a fetal position was a clear sign that the therapy was working and that it would be a crime to interrupt it at such a crucial stage. Furthermore it would be impossible to let him leave Thoreau, for how could anyone survive out there in the world curled up in a fetal position? The court had awarded temporary guardianship to Misery, and A.K. was continuing her regression of Oly Joe.

On call that night, I was paged at about eight to Thoreau, where Oly Joe Olaf, uncurled and furious, was standing at the door, threatening to run away. He looked somehow both frail and dangerous, his blond hair tentatively in a ponytail, his pasty face pimply, ugly but for his eyes. Everyone has beautiful eyes, and his were exquisite: the light blue-green of a Caribbean sea. His stocky, powerful body was ready for action, tight with Oral Stage Rage, ready to bite the breast that fed him. The door to Thoreau was never locked, which at first had seemed strange to me, since the one thing these hyperspaced adolescents needed was clear limits. But after a while I'd seen the wisdom in A.K.'s insistence that the limits had to be set inside their heads, not outside.

"I showed up for therapy with Dr. Lowell," Oly said. "She said I had the wrong time. I checked—turns out I was right—*she* had the wrong time. But she wouldn't admit it. She wouldn't like say anything! And even though she didn't have another patient then, she wouldn't see me. She just blew me off! She's making me crazy! Gimme one fuckin' reason I should stay here?"

"What are your fantasies about why you should stay here?"

He stared at me, and then said, quietly, "To wait for my ammo to arrive."

" 'Ammo'?"

"Fuck it. I'm out of here!" He turned to the door, but before he could run downstairs and away, he was met by Malik.

"Yo, Oly Joe!" Malik said happily, as if meeting a long-lost friend. Malik was wearing a stupid red and black lumberjack cap with the earlappers up like Sherlock Holmes and carrying that same old basketball. "Runnin' away?"

"Yeah. This place sucks!"

"Sucks *bad*!"

Oly Joe seemed startled to hear this from Malik. "Y'think so too?"

"*Wicked* bad! Fuck it's cold out there! Cold as a witch's tit in a brass brassiere! Got a place to stay?"

"Nope. Kin I like stay with you?"

"Nope. The cops would kill me for that. How 'bout we shoot some hoops?"

"How's that gonna help?"

"Helped me when I wanted to run when I was your age. We'll talk."

"I don't wanna talk, I wanna run."

"Good idea. This place is for shit!"

"Yeah. But I got no place to like go?"

"Bummer. Hey—you can always run from the gym, right?" Oly Joe nodded. "And I *gotta* shoot some hoops—this place has got me nuts! 'Kay? C'mon!"

They left.

Shortly before eleven I was sitting with Viv and Primo behind the bulletproof in Telecommunications, communicating with them through silences and interpretations.

"Nice suit and tie, Doc, y'get me?" Primo said.

"You have some feelings about this suit?"

"Toldja," Viv said to Primo, as if I weren't there with them. "Used to be fun too, this one. Lotta fun, Primo, remember?"

"They start out fun," Primo said, "and they fall for Freud 'n' wind up with the personality of a platypus."

"This one was such a great cowboy too! Holy cow—Hannah?" Hannah Silver was walking slowly past on the other side of the bulletproof, looking lost and sad. "Why, hello, dear! What are you doin' here at this hour?"

"I'm just, um . . . catching up on some paperwork?" Hannah said.

"Jeez, you look down, Hannah, y'get what I'm sayin'?"

"I am down."

"Love life or life itself?" Viv asked.

"Both." She looked at me. "I feel so alone."

"Cup of tea, hon?" Viv said. "I've got herbal."

Hannah shook her head no and started to walk away slowly.

"I'll walk you to your car," I said.

We walked along in silence. The night was brutally cold, the north wind a jillion invisible sabers, slicing up our bodies through our coats.

As we passed the gym we looked in through the old wire-mesh windows. Malik and Oly Joe were playing basketball, one on one. Oly was awkward, Malik graceful, but the game, clearly, wasn't about the game but about the invisible threads spinning chaotically between the two of them. Oly threw up a wild shot that missed everything and then crumpled to his knees and started sobbing. Through the window his sobs were silent. Malik retrieved the ball and came back over to him with it. Then he knelt with the boy and put his arms around him. The boy leaned against him and then into him, sobbing, like a son finally connecting with his dad, as if a big hand had drawn all the invisible threads together.

I felt touched, but conflicted. It felt "right," but would it hurt the therapy? Was Malik acting out of his own need as much as the boy's?

Hannah turned and looked up at me, her dark eyes despairing beneath those ridiculous bleached brows. "That's what *I* need, Roy." She bowed her head. I put my hands on her shoulders. "Blair broke up with me today, for good. Said he never wants to see me again. Never. What should I do?"

"Want to talk about it?" I asked, but then my beeper went off:

"Earth to ex-Cowboy, call home."

"Yes, I'd like to talk, but you've got to go."

"Yeah, I'd better. What about your analyst?"

"Ed Slapadek?" She stood still, and I could see the struggle in her eyes, between wanting to ask for his help and fearing his response to that asking, his telling her to take responsibility for her SELF. "No. You better call home."

"And you *go* home, Hannah, y'hear?"

"To nobody? Yeah, I'm going . . . home. You're a good guy, at heart." She kissed me on the cheek and then clutched me and started sobbing.

"Platypus, call your mom in Florida."

Hannah pulled away and fumbled with the keys to her new BMW with a bashed-in front light, making it look like a woman with a black eye.

"What about calling Solini?" I shouted.

She stopped, thought, shook her head no, started the engine, and drove morosely down Mount Misery toward the river valley sprinkled with the lights of villages, which, in the clear arctic air, seemed like jewels in a twisted necklace.

I ran to the on-call room, where Jill answered my knock. I was about to call my parents in Florida when she, in her peach-colored bra that held up her boobies like eggs in satin baskets, encircled me with her arms and slipped her tongue into my mouth. My fingers slipped in under the thong of her matching peach bikini. I was about to enter her when the first thing that came to mind was Cherokee's soft dick and the second thing was A.K.'s voice saying, "You're not enough," and the third thing was Lloyal von Nott's voice saying, "If you're not impotent yet you will be" and my penis plummeted as if shot, a dying quail.

The harder I tried, the softer it got. I lay over her, my belly sagging onto hers until my back started to ache. I rolled away, humiliated.

What followed was at every step haunted by Cherokee and Christine. Jill tried everything. Nothing helped. My penis, like his, would occasionally struggle up from its hairy pillow like a drunken sot, only to flop back down.

Lying beside me, staring with me up at the accusatory ceiling, Jill asked, "How are you feeling, Roy?"

I stiffened—all but my penis—and said, "I don't know."

"Come on, Roy, I love you—you can tell me."

"I told you, I don't know," I said, feeling testy.

"You don't have to get angry at me."

"I'm not angry."

Sighing, she slipped her tiny bikini up over her rump and adjusted it so it made a satiny "snap." She slipped the silky whorled bra onto her shoulders, bringing both sides around her boobs like hands around fruits. Her red-lacquered fingernails met at her sternum and latched the bra shut, like closing the store for the night. I got a little hard, but was afraid to try it again and fail.

"I feel sorry for guys. I wouldn't be a guy for anything in the world. Let's just chalk it up to a bad night and a weird rotation."

"Weird rotation?"

"Analysis, babe. *Hard* on the significant other."

The next morning in supervision with A.K., I told her about Cherokee Putnam's impotence. She read the entrails and sometime after the three-pencil mark her eyes enlarged. I braced myself and she said, "And *you?*"

My face got hot. How had she known? "Last night I was impotent too."

"Uh-huh. And I notice that you're now scratching your arm."

Mortified, I looked down and noticed that I had in fact been scratching my arm, just inside the elbow, a red patch over the olecranon. "Yes, I am."

"V.D.," she said.

"Venereal Disease?" I cried, thinking, It's already gone from my dick to my arm?

"*Vagina Dentata.* Classic. You have the fantasy that vaginas have teeth and will bite off your penis."

"I'm a wreck!" I blurted out. "I'm feeling really really down!" And I told her about myself as I never had before. About Berry and Jill and about my family. As she wrote this down there was, again, a kind look on her face.

"You need outside help," she said. "You need to take this to an analyst."

"So you think it's time for me to take the plunge?" The obvious unconscious referent, to my limp penis, made her smile, and I smiled. "Can you suggest someone?" The itch was incredible, and I tried to rub it as nonchalantly as possible on my new suit coat.

"It would pollute the transference. You have to find your own."

"Go to Schlomo?" She said nothing. "Your old analyst, Schlomo Dove?"

But the fourth number 2 was in that big beautiful hand and I was history. I got up and trudged to the door and grasped the doorknob.

"Dr. Basch?"

I was not history? A countertransference doorknobber? "Yes?"

"Would you like to play tennis sometime, and come over for dinner?"

I turned, tears of gratitude in my eyes. "Yes!" I said, wanting to add but catching myself, *darling*.

"Keep it up," she went on, smiling, "and you too may someday be good enough to be a candidate at the institute."

I left, floating on air, feeling that I was very very special.

"YOUR FATHER DIED TODAY," my mother said on the phone that night from Florida.

"What? Grandpa's dead?"

"No, no, your father, your father. He had chest pains last night and I called you but you didn't call back and then today in the hospital suddenly he just died."

My father is dead. No more conjunctions.

"The doctor said it was painless."

"That's good."

It was Friday evening, the twenty-sixth. We talked about the details but I was in shock. The funeral would be on Monday, March 1, at home in Columbia.

I hung up feeling lost and guilty, and needing to talk to someone. But who? Berry? I still hadn't talked to her and felt estranged. A wave of desolation broke over me. She was family, my real family. I needed her with me in this, the first of our four parents to die. Yes. I called, praying to get her, not her machine.

I got her machine. Worse: ". . . and I'm out of the country until Tuesday."

I felt horrible.

Who else to call? Malik? Jill? I thought about it. With each, right now, there seemed to be too much old baggage, they would be too demanding. Solini? Hannah? Forget it. And then I thought of A.K. She would not be intrusive, no. I called her up at home.

"My father died today, suddenly."

Two seconds. "I am sorry."

"What should I do?"

Two seconds. "Listen for it in the material."

"Material? You mean my cases?"

Two seconds. "Yes and in your own material. At the funeral. You might also try 'Mourning and Melancholia.' " I could have sworn I heard the *scritch scritch* of a pencil. "Father dies. Son is impotent. Impressive. Good night."

So to prepare for the funeral I read Freud's classic. I hadn't looked at it since the seminar, after which Ike White had shaken my hand, wished me a nice vacation, and gone upstairs to kill himself. Now, reading it, I was impressed. Here was genius. It was absolutely clear: the healthy response to the death of my father would be "mourning," and the pathological response would be "melancholia." The crucial difference seemed to be the matter of ambivalence, where, if you had mixed feelings about the dead person, or "object," in Freud's words, "The shadow of the lost object falls across the ego." When Ike had quoted that incredible phrase, I hadn't understood; now I did. This falling shadow was big trouble, leading to insomnia, loss of appetite, self-reproach, even suicide:

> The tendency toward suicide makes melancholia so interesting—and so dangerous . . . It is true we have long known that no neurotic harbors thoughts of suicide which are not murderous impulses against others redirected upon himself.

Ike had failed to work this out. I certainly had mixed feelings about my father. I'd have to be on guard.

The night before the funeral, as I sat in our living room in Columbia listening to the local rabbi, one Goldfarb, a chubby pink-cheeked young man with bright red hair, recently moved to Columbia from Nebraska, ask my mother and brother and me about my father so as to be able to compose the next day's eulogy, I was on guard. Any ambivalence about my father would have to be nipped in the bud, analyzed out, and kept merely neurotic.

"And what did your husband like to do?" Goldfarb asked my mother.

"Golf. Golf was his first love." She paused. "I mean after the boys."

" 'Golf.' " The rabbi scribbled this down. "And where did he golf?"

"We golfed all over the world." My mother and brother, like me, were numb. Dry-eyed. As my mother talked about golf, the rabbi, feeling he now had enough information about golf, turned to me, the oldest:

"You know, Doctor, Columbia is the *pupik* of America. You know *pupik*?"

"*Pupik?*"

"Yiddish for belly button. And you know what a belly button collects?"

"You have some thoughts about what a belly button collects?"

"*Schmutz*." He stared at me expectantly.

"And you have some feelings about *schmutz*?"

"Yes, Doctor, I certainly do have some feelings, yes. This congregation is unreal. *Schmutz*. Now. What else did your loving husband like to do?"

It went on like this, the rabbi writing in a little notebook a little, and then turning to me again and telling me how terrible Columbia was:

"I was in New York not long ago, having a bite at a deli, and the waiter asked where I was from and I said Columbia, New York, and he said, 'Still got the whores up there?' This place was famous for its red-light district!"

"Yes," I said, "everybody knows that."

"*I* didn't, when I took this job. Now, Mrs. Basch, what did he belong to—I assume B'nai B'rith, but was he an Elk, a Lion, a Moose?"

After he left, my mother and brother and I had a chance to talk.

"He loved you boys, you know," my mother said. "Do you know that?"

"Yes," I said. My brother said yes too.

"And in his own way he loved me. These last few years, he didn't really show it. He was so bitter. But you should have seen the cards he wrote me, for birthdays, and anniversary. Wonderful, wonderful cards."

"Why was he so bitter, Mom?" I asked. "He'd always dreamed of golf in Florida."

"I think it was money," she said.

"He had plenty," my brother said. "His own, and what we gave him."

"Not plenty compared to some of the others down there. And especially some of the less educated men, the building contractors, the businessmen. He felt superior to them, being a professional man, and yet they had more money. Some had millions, so he said. He said it wasn't fair. I think he felt that he wasn't a great success."

We talked on, numbly, into the night.

The next day the funeral was held in what used to be a childhood friend's home that had become a funeral home. It was a freezing cold day and we were all still in shock. There was some question whether they could break ground at the cemetery.

I cried twice. Once, when my grandfather arrived from his nursing home in a wheelchair, his eyes filled with grief and rage at God for taking his only son first. Then, as I was being offered condolences by my father's dental assistants and by Bill Starbuck, the aged town doctor, and by an old high school buddy who'd just lost his own father, and I saw in their eyes the pain they felt and thought I was feeling, the pain of the loss of a father—rather than my feelings for my particular father—then I really sobbed, recalling the good golf games, swept by guilt that I had been cool to him the last time, with Jill, and that I'd missed the diagnosis: the hiatus hernia pain was not his stomach but his heart—one clue in hindsight being the astonishing fact of his quitting golf before the eighteenth hole—and maybe I could have saved him if I had been a better real doctor.

As I sat in what used to be my childhood friend's romper room and listened to the rabbi's excellent eulogy, which made it sound like my father had been not only his trusted dentist and devoted congregant but also a dear friend, I thought: Is this split—between the idea of losing a father and the actual loss of my own father—the seed of a killer ambivalence? I was dry-eyed through all the Hebrew at the grave and the lowering of the coffin and the dance of the pebbles on the coffin lid, which completed the journey from strong potent man to dirt, and then, back at home, dry-eyed at the buffet. My mother and brother were just as dry-eyed; all of us seemed to be taking it as neurotically as possible.

"Are you sick?" my grandfather asked, bending me to his wheelchair.

"Yes," I said, thinking of myself as neurotic.

"Yeh, me too. Sick at heart. And God must be sick too, to do dis—the Big Fella needs a psychiatrist—*nu*? I should be foist. Den him. Den you. Here—take dis." He handed me a fifty. "Where's dat nice goil, Berry?"

"We broke up."

"Nah, don't be stupid. Get a gun, like I did wid mine vife. Show her who's d'boss."

I hugged him. We both wept. Was this the last time I would ever see him?

At sundown the rabbi returned. He did a quick riff of Hebrew, blessing the bread and wine, and then buttonholed me again:

"And *cheap*? To get a raise here is like pulling teeth. If you hear of any openings where you are located, Doctor, think of me, will you?"

"It's not that much different there. The reality of 'location' is less important than the fantasy."

"No, no. No. You remember your anatomy, Doctor? One *pupik*, and this is it. Shalom."

I said my own sad shaloms to all and drove the three hours back, alone, free-associating, fantasizing, analyzing it all out.

The next morning, preparing for my cases, some unconscious motivation made me pick up Freud's classic, "Jokes and Their Relation to the Unconscious."

A wife's like an umbrella: sometimes one takes a cab.

I made a note to try this one out on Cherokee Putnam later that day.

SOLINI APPEARED at my office that evening. He seemed more worried than ever, and now sported a tic. His right eye twitched like crazy, as if trying to mate with his right ear.

"How are you, Henry?"

"Depressed?"

"Good."

"You?"

"Me too."

"Good? I'm worried about Hannah?"

"What's wrong?"

"She didn't show up today for our meeting? We debrief our sessions with the Slapper every Tuesday? And she's never missed, not once? I asked around? Win said she didn't show up at the drug unit—didn't show up at Misery today at all? So I called her condo and there's no answer?"

I felt a chill. "Let's go."

We drove together in his red Geo, which churned through the flat iced-up planes of the night, laboring badly, as if the planes were being stacked before its beak in ever-more-foreboding succession. Solini hunched over the wheel as he had that first day driving out to Ike White's. Now, instead of Bob Marley, there was Silence, one of Jesus I Hope She's Okay.

At the concrete bunker that served as the outer walls of her condo, we got out and, either from cold or fear, started running across the parking lot, our breaths hanging in the air behind us like cartoons of choo-choo trains. We knocked on her door. No answer. We stared at each other wondering what to do. Henry had a key. Gingerly we entered, walking as if on foam, though the floor was uncarpeted. I'd never been inside, and now realized why she hadn't wanted me to see her place: it looked unlived-in, boxes still unpacked, nothing on the walls except an announcement of a conference in Kuala Lumpur entitled "Borderlines of the Singapore Boom" with Heiler's name highlighted in yellow Magic Marker. In a corner, in its case, was her neglected cello.

We called, softly, then louder, "Hannah? Hannah-babe? Hannah?"

No answer. The first thought that came to mind was that she'd hanged herself in her closet. We rushed into her bedroom and I threw open the closet door. Nothing. We rushed into the bathroom. Yes.

She lay naked in the half-filled tub, a plastic Wonder bread bag over her head. The bag was misted from within with moisture that hid her face. Time stopped and my mind expanded to fill the vacuum with crazy and shameful thoughts like, She's dead and it's my fault, and What a wonderful body she has from the waist up, and What's that on the floor is it really a yellowed clipping from the *New York Times* headlining a "Young Cellist's Stunning Debut"?

"Shit!" I cried out and was at her, Henry beside me, ripping the bag off, feeling for a pulse and—hurrah!—finding it! She was drugged and drunk but she was not dead. Henry and I took the moaning Hannah out of the tub and dried her, the towel snagging on her puffy skin. We fed her full of coffee and brought her back.

"Christ," she moaned, "I can't do anything right."

We sat up with her all night long. She talked about losing Blair's love.

"But the final straw was when I was on call Sunday night. I got a ride with Security way over to Geriatrics, in the Rokitansky Building, to see an old woman who'd fallen out of bed. The guy from Security—the Ukrainian with the lisp—he tried to kiss me, and I said no and he kept on and on—I thought he was going to rape me or shoot me. I finally broke away. So yesterday I went to talk to Lloyal von Nott, to make an official complaint, and you know what he said?" She paused, and then went on, bitterly, " '*Be a man*,' he said, 'If you can't take it here, get out.' "

"Shithead!" I said.

"Let's kill him, man?" Solini said.

Hannah was staring into space. Then she clicked back in. She looked around the bare-walled room as if seeing it for the first time. Suddenly her eyes came alive. "That's it! All these men, all my life—fucking me over. And I try to kill myself? Kill *me*, for *them*? For these pricks, these Nazis? Give up my cello, for *psychiatry*? I must have been insane! In-fucking-sane!" She stood up. "That's it. It's over. I'm out of here. No more psychiatry. No more *men*!" She picked herself up and, with a fresh energy, got out her Vuitton valises and started packing.

"What are you going to do?" I asked.

"Wyoming." She looked around. "Now where did I put my cowboy boots?"

"Wyoming, babe?"

"Wyoming, yes!" Full of fire, full of life, she suddenly seemed bigger, more beautiful, even incandescent. "My old college roommate Gilda lives there. On a sweet little ranch. *No men*. Gilda's a musician too—viola—we used to play in a chamber group. She did law school, for a while she was a criminal lawyer. Now she's mostly a rancher. She's always wanted me to come out there. I'm gonna do my music in Wyoming!"

She swore us to secrecy about her suicide attempt. As the sun pulled itself up out of its cloud cover, she wondered why she hadn't died.

"The Wonder bread bag lets air in," I said.

"I thought it was airtight, to keep the bread fresh."

"In the bread section of the supermarket," I said, "what do you smell?"

"Fresh bread."

"So how can you smell it if the smell can't get out?"

"Christ. *Another* lie. That's been it, hasn't it, here, I mean right from the start, with that sonofabitch Ike White! But then what keeps it fresh?"

"Chemicals, babe," Henry said, "killing us all, just like Malik says?"

Before we left, Hannah thanked us. Looking us each, in turn, directly in the eye—no more eye roll-ups now—she said, "Guys, you better get out while you still can."

"Of Misery?" I asked.

"That too," she said. "I was thinking of your psychoanalyses."

I stared at Hannah. Despite her near disaster, I was not feeling much really. For a second, I worried about that. Yet wasn't my not feeling much a proof of my deep repressed feeling, of the severe psychopathology in me, which in fact *demanded* my going into psychoanalysis? So I said to her, "I'm not in it, yet."

But Hannah was staring at Solini now. She took his hands, and, eye-to-eye, in a high, Joan Baez voice, she sang to him from Bob Marley's "Trenchtown Rock."

Henry used to lead off his act with it.

"I hear you, H-babe? I'll be thinkin' of you in Wyoming, and we'll see which way it goes?"

LIKE THOUSANDS OF OTHERS before me, I went to Schlomo Dove the next day to make a match for me with the right psychoanalyst.

We met in his office in Misery, just down the hall from the office of Lloyal von Nott. Seeing him in person, so runty and ugly, dressed in a rumpled old suit and stale shirt and no tie and wearing a big button that read, TRUST ME I'M A DOCTOR, I felt more certain about what I realized I'd finally settled on in the Cherokee matter: there was no way that Lily Putnam, the tall, auburn-haired, and beautiful WASP princess, could have allowed herself to be fucked even once by Schlomo, in therapy or anywhere else, the confirmation of this being the way that Cherokee's paranoid obsession was playing out exactly as Freudian theory dictated, at its deepest level being simply the repression of homosexual desires for the penis of Father and the fantasied penis of Mother and of the screen memory of catching Aunt Vic and Uncle Hap going at it on a tattered rug in the servants' quarters of the Putnam chalet in St. Moritz at age six, which happened to be the exact same age as little Kissy, when Cherokee first wandered into Misery last July. It was like in golf when, once in the middle of a miserable round, you hit a shot dead-solid perfect.

"It's about time!" Schlomo said, putting down the watering can. "*Nu*, Schlomo is putting down the watering can, and Schlomo is not smoking the cigar. Place your money nice on the desk and let's *kazatsky*!"

I plunked down $150 cash for the twenty-minute session, sat across from him and told him about myself, my impotence, and my father's death.

"And what do you *feel*, Roy G. Basch?" Schlomo asked, picking up a rather black-skinned banana and starting to peel it.

Rather than feeling what I was feeling and telling Schlomo, I found myself watching him peeling and then looking away at all the other bananas in the room, bananas at all stages of ripeness, from a green bunch on the windowsill to perfect yellows on his couch to some yucky black-splotched babies on the floor under his desk like the one he was messing with.

"Tell Schlomo Dove what you feel, hmmm?" He took a bite. It was obscene.

"To tell you the truth, I feel scared you're gonna throw that banana in my lap."

"Ho ho," he said, "ho ho. No, no, Roy Basch, for to build the therapeutic alliance, Schlomo will now put his banana on his desk. See?" He did so. "*Nu*, so let's do some feelings?"

I tried to come up with feelings but came up dry. "I'm coming up dry."

"Not even Roy Basch sad and lonely? Tell Schlomo, about sad and lonely? You can tell Schlomo."

"Nope."

"You're like the sun, giving out your warmth to other people, leaving yourself cold."

This sounded good, but I remembered that it was word for word what he had told Hannah at her consultation with him.

"For this," I said, "I'm forking out a hundred and fifty bucks?"

"Oy, do you have Oedipal!" Schlomo said. "You got early infantile up the wazoo! And does Schlomo Dove have the guy for you!"

"Please, not Ed Slapadek. I can't take the Slapper!"

"No, better."

"Tougher?"

"Tenderer. Adolf Zement Shaper. Former head of the Boston Institute. You'll love him. Then hate him. Then love him maturely and terminate. Have fun. And watch that erotic transference! Here's his number. Bye-bye now!"

Despite everything revolting about Schlomo, I left feeling a little sad. Unlike Arnie Bozer, unlike Lily Putnam, Schlomo had not offered to keep me for himself. Compared to Arnie Bozer, I'm a reject? It was surprisingly hard to take.

A few days later I found myself on the couch on the top floor of the institute in Boston, talking about my dick and my father—my not having feelings in one, or about the other.

Adolf Zement Shaper was a roly-poly old man with a round face and hair so white it looked like a photo negative of what he must have looked like as a young man. He greeted me warmly with a dynamite silence and motioned me to a couch. I lay down and started free-associating. Suddenly I heard him clear his throat. My eyes hit my watch: only fifteen seconds left? Where had time gone?

"You come in with seams," he said, "and you go out seamless."

Thirteen

CIVILIZATION AND ITS DISCONTENTS presents a bleak vision of human life. Freud says that we humans are beasts, driven by sex and aggression. These bestial libidinal drives are barely and poorly sublimated to "civilized" life. Bestiality is the best we can do. Bleak, yes, but accurate. Read the newspaper, see what birds of prey we are. I now understood the depression I saw on the faces of those in psychoanalysis. Bleakness demanded it.

Henry took Hannah's departure hard. He was completing his rotation on Toshiba, the Admissions Unit, and he was deeply depressed. He walked around with the kind of trudge that I'd noticed in the schizophrenics medicated to their eyeballs in the Heidelbergs. He now had tics in both eyes.

"Isn't Ed Slapadek helping?" I asked one day.

"The Slapper's digging into my gay-latent, but I don't feel gay—don't feel nothin' below the waist? I'm digging into gay-latent with all my patients?"

"What? You think *they're* all gay-latent too?"

"Why not? They're all very terrified of gays, having me as their therapist?"

Was Henry going crazy or just going through a normal psychoanalysis?

One day he exploded. He assigned each of his twelve Toshiba admissions a DSM diagnosis from the section on "Psychosexual Disorders," starting with 302.50, Transsexualism, through 302.10, Zoophilia, and 302.90, Atypical Paraphelia ("Telephone Scatologia—lewdness"), ending with 302.00, Ego-Dystonic Homosexuality. Nash Michaels and Jessica Tunaba found him diagnosing a Saudi prince, reading back to him as he copied out from the DSM:

> "There is a sustained pattern of homosexual arousal that the individual explicitly states has been unwanted and a persistent source of distress . . ."

Primo brought Henry to my house. We drank and talked all night long. I said that in my own analysis I too was feeling depressed.

"Yeah, analysis kills your health, physical and mental?" he said. "I'm hangin' on by a threat?" He stopped, and stared inward, in horror. "Holy shit what a slip? Man, I am deeply *deeply* depressed?"

In the morning he insisted I drive him to Slapadek's house for his regular appointment, to—his words—"fight fire with fire." I waited in the car for him to come back out. He never did. I rang the bell but no one answered.

The next day Henry did not appear. Lloyal von Nott met with Win, Arnie, and me. We assumed it was to talk about Hannah's and Henry's being gone, but he ignored this and talked about the Misery Capital Campaign Luncheons. Later we got a memo from Schlomo Dove, Director of Training, saying that Henry Solini and Hannah Silver were both taking leaves of absence and we three would now be on call every third night, to fill in.

Soon I was exhausted, even more irritable and vulnerable. But my patients continued to respond to my psychoanalytic method. I continued to see Zoe and Cherokee five times per week. Like me and as expected, they were both deeply depressed and following A.K.'s predictions perfectly, though they refused to regress from Genital Stage to Oral Stage, clearly a problem of my technique, not Freud's theory. A.K. said that it was because I was still so neurotic and only beginning my analysis that they were still stuck, holding on to their genitals: Cherokee not being able to get it up, and Zoe not being able to give up trying to seduce me. In general they were doing Freud. It was Oscillator City, and I'd begun to think I'd started to understand it a little. Listening in the "material" for my patients' unconscious perception of my father's death, I heard all kinds of referents. It was astonishing to me, just how clearly they unconsciously were picking up my unconscious.

My sessions with Christine, only once a week, seemed shallow, skimming the surface of Cherokee and his flaccid penis.

A.K. was warming to me even more. She talked about her own work with Oly Joe Olaf, using it to give me helpful hints such as, "If, for a long time, you don't say anything at all, then when you actually *do* say something, you have incredible power."

"Slashing in like a Cutlass Supreme?"

She smiled and nodded wisely. "With Oly Joe, I am trying to build up a stronger baby version of himself. I send him fond letters and write him nice notes in children's books like *Goodnight Moon* and *Where's Spot?* She took down one of her dozens of leather-bound ledgers, opened it and took out a Hallmark greeting card, with a note in it:

"An analyst is like a mom,
Read this over and you'll feel calm."

"Wonderful," I said. "Very creative."

"Yes. In those locked-up binders are my notes on the case. Six hundred seventy-one pages of process notes so far. Sex and aggression. Understand?"

"Do I ever," I said. "I am one sick puppy."

"Good. Last weekend I myself went to a Tavistock workshop in the Allagash Wilderness and . . ." She paused, then said, with pride, "I was *psychotic*!"

"I'm half psychotic all the time! And now I've got all these symptoms too." I told her how, after only a few weeks of analysis, I had developed scary psychosomatic symptoms: exhaustion, splitting headaches, recurrent flu, a booming flatulence, and night terrors. "I've never been so depressed in my life."

"Good, good," she said, nodding wisely. "You're getting warm."

She invited me to come as her guest to the annual New England Regional Defense-mechanism Congress—NERDCON—held every April in Boston and always on the same topic, "Me, Myself, and I: Psychoanalytic Theories of Yourself." A.K. would be presenting a new paper, "Goldilocks and the Three Bears and the Oedipal Oscillator." We also made a firm date, at the end of the month, during my last week rotating on Thoreau, for tennis and dinner at her home.

Most incredible to me was not her warmth and openness in our supervisory sessions, but rather how she still treated me like shit in public, with silence and contempt. Our secret was being kept within the four walls of her office, held by us both. No one knows what goes on behind that therapist's closed door.

My own analysis with Adolf Zement "Poppa Doc" Shaper—my nickname for him—was going like gangbusters. I would come in, he would nod me toward the couch, I would lie down and begin to free-associate and fantasize. He would say nothing until the end. Then he'd utter soothing phrases like, "We are all messes, trying to help bigger messes," or "It's amazing how many people go home and cry into their pillows at night." I looked forward to my sessions and felt incredibly worse when I left them. Things were going extremely well.

POOR BLAIR HEILER. All those months chasing around the world to be at a conference where Renaldo Krotkey would actually show up, and now while Blair was off in South Africa—"Black and White Borderlines After Apartheid"—listed on the program just below Krotkey himself, Renaldo was sitting right here on Mount Misery, watching a Family Analysis on Thoreau.

He had appeared by surprise, a short fireplug of a man with a head like a bowling ball covered with shorn red hair, and a horribly pocked face. He wore a European-style suit with a bow tie that made him look like a waiter in a kosher deli, and he had a German accent. He had come with a European-style woman whom he referred to as "My amanuensis, Pensilena Teiche." She wore a short black leather slit skirt and matching leather vest over a bare chest. Her hair was as blond as my hysteric Christine's. Despite the prominent No Smoking signs, both chain-smoked Gitanes from black and silver holders.

There was an electricity in the room as Lowell greeted Krotkey, a jolt, I associated, much like the moment Freud met Jung. I felt nervous as hell, for Krotkey would be observing my Family Analysis of Zoe. Malik was there too. A.K. herself would be taking the place of Faith Baltsburg, who, regressing hard, had been found the day before weeping hysterically in the safe-deposit vault of the Rank Bank. A.K. now had a lot of free time, for all her therapy cases had left AMA—Against Medical Advice—except for Oly Joe Olaf.

Bong bong bong bong bong bong bong bong bong.

A.K. and I entered the room and took our seats at either end of the semicircle of Zoe's family—father, mother, and, for the first time, her siblings: older sister Marion, a mother of six married to someone at Morgan Stanley and living in Darien; and older brother Butler, a senior vice president at Chase, living in the East Eighties, and still single. The first part of the session went well, as her sadistic father joined her engulfing mother in saying how much worse Zoe was. She wore her petite flowered dress, and was rocking seductively in her chair.

A.K. had been puzzled by Zoe's not regressing from the genital. Finally she solved it. Zoe's old friend Thorny was visiting her every day after work. They talked about—in Zoe's words—"everything!" including what was going on with me in her therapy. A.K. said that my allowing Thorny to visit her on Thoreau was diluting the transference and I had to prohibit their meeting. I had mixed feelings about doing this. Thorny was doing well, going to AA, working at a recycling plant. All year long they had helped each other out. They were best friends. But A.K. had insisted, and had written the order herself that prohibited Thorny from entering Thoreau. Ever since, Zoe had been enraged with me—which A.K. pointed to as a glimmer of movement toward the oral, the "tit tucked away."

Now, Zoe's brother and sister, Butler and Marion, joined the happy chatter of the family, which all of them, laughing, described to A.K. and me as "just us Cranky Yankees." They chatted and laughed as if they were sitting not in a mental hospital but a private club, laughing and chattering easily in those polite shallow deflections of thousands of cocktail parties and balls and benefits the family had absorbed to make sure that nothing deeper or even deep ever got said. A.K. and I held to a tight, top-drawer silence.

Finally Zoe said, "Butler, you fucked me when we were kids."

Butler's hand went to his neck. "What?"

"You fucked me—first under the dock, and then all over. Don't deny it."

"You're crazy. You are nuts."

"What'd she say?" asked Father, who'd forgotten his hearing aid.

"Nothing, darling," said Mother. "Children? Quiet."

"Prick!" Zoe shouted. "You ruined my life! There's a child buried in our backyard up in the Adirondacks! Dr. Basch? Tell them!"

All eyes were on me. Pressured to speak, I was terribly conscious of the great Krotkey and the awesome Pensilena and the rest of the team watching from behind the mirror. I glanced at A.K. She was glaring at me, sending a clear message to me: Don't Say Anything. I gritted my teeth and crossed my legs.

"What's wrong with you? You never stick up for me anymore? You prick!"

"What'd she say?" the father asked. No one said what she'd said. "Dr. Lowell?" he said, turning slowly toward A.K. "Might you not give us some advice, on the method to best handle her, at this time?"

"She won't say anything, Daddy," Zoe said. "She's the biggest prick around!"

A. K. Lowell cleared her throat. I glanced at the clock: eight seconds to go!

"And is it not possible that Zoe's rage at you is *your rage at her*?"

"What?" the father asked. "I didn't hear. Could you repeat th—"

Bong bong bong bong bong bong bong bong bong bong.

I followed A.K. out. Zoe screamed, "Cocksuckers! Assholes!"

"What?" Father asked, and then, louder and louder, "What what *what*?"

I felt good about my not saying anything, and about A.K.'s saying only one thing. I sat next to A.K. in the conference room, expecting to be showered with Krotkey's praise. Sure enough, the little fire hydrant rose immediately, his face red. He shouted:

"What the hell were you two *doing* in there?"

My heart went ga-thunk. I looked to A.K. Her face was ashen.

"You have to *intervene* with these people, you have to interpret everything, at every juncture. You can't let them get away with that kind of aggression. *Gott in himmel!*"

"They are here," A.K. said, voice trembling, "to listen to each other—"

"The hell they are! They are here to listen to *you*. Like you are here to listen to *me*. You can bet that Professor Blair Heiler wouldn't have sat there like a . . . a . . ." Krotkey's eyes went back and forth between us, and then settling on my own eyes, he said, "like a *weich putz*! Blair Heiler would have *confronted* them, gotten all that anger out sooner, worked it through better!"

"Are you telling me," A.K. said angrily, "that there are empathic breaks in *my* therapy?"

"You betcha!" Krotkey seemed to have only one volume setting: high.

"Have you been talking to my ex-husband?" A.K. said.

"Cunt," Krotkey averred. One of his famous crudities. He handed his spent Gitane in its holder to Pensilena Teiche for reloading.

Others now joined in. To my surprise there was no talk of the Oscillator but a lot of talk about our failure to confront the aggression. Heiler Theory of Confrontation was held up as a model of what we should have done.

"Dr. Krotkey?" It was Malik, standing up. Krotkey swiveled his bowling ball head, like the turret of a tank. "I wanted to ask you about the abuse?"

"Speak!" Krotkey shouted, rising to his feet.

"Zoe says she was sexually abused by her brother. In private, her sister has corroborated this to me—she witnessed it, and the sisters talked about it years ago. Studies by Judy Herman, Diana Russell, and others show that over seventy percent of female inpatients have been sexually and/or physically abused."

"So?"

"So what do you make of this?"

" 'I make nothing of this,' " he shouted. "To quote Frau Kernberg, private communication."

There were gasps of admiration—Krotkey communicates with Frau *Kernberg*?

Malik went on, "Are you saying, as Freud said, that this is not reality, but fantasy?"

"Freud said," Krotkey shouted, " 'If in the case of girls who produce such an event (seduction) in the story of their childhood their father figures fairly regularly as the seducer, there can be no doubt either of the imaginary nature of the accusation or of the motive that has led to it. . . . We have not succeeded in pointing to any difference in the consequences, whether fantasy or reality has had the great share in these events of childhood.' "

"You're saying that *it doesn't matter* whether it happened or didn't?"

"What matters is how the girl negotiates the Oedipus conflict."

"It does matter," Malik said heatedly. He coughed. "It matters profoundly to the girl, and to her treatment when she—"

"The girl? Girls don't even know they have a *vagina* till they're twelve!"

"How do you know that?"

"I am a *physician*! I am publishing a book—'A Newer Psychology of Women.' That's how, cocksucker! *Hasta la vista*, motherfuckers!" He started barreling through the crowd toward the door but became entangled in one of our tricky NASA folding chairs. Cursing in German, he tried to extricate himself from its Space Age hinges. Pensilena Teiche, the woman with the leather breasts, tried to help. Malik said something, but too softly to hear. Krotkey leaned toward him and screamed, "What?" Malik repeated it, but so softly that Krotkey had to lean even farther toward him. "What?"

"You really hurt people," Malik said quietly.

"It takes balls to stand up to all these girls claiming abuse! Try it!"

"I work for FEMS," Pensilena said, "False External Memory Syndrome. Most memories of abuse are concocted. Quote: 'We cannot logically assume that memories of childhood sexual abuse can be repressed.' Reference citation, Harrison Pope and James Hudson, McLean Hospital and Harvard Medical School."

Throwing chairs and cursing like what he'd told us we needed to do while fucking, Renaldo Krotkey, and then his amanuensis, crashed out.

In silence, A.K. and I walked upstairs toward our offices together. As I turned down the hall I heard a familiar voice call out:

"Hey, asshole."

I turned. A skinhead stood there. He was pointing a gun at A.K.

Oly Joe Olaf. His ponytail was gone, his head was completely shaven. His T-shirt read "No Fear." His hand was shaking. His eyes were wild.

Paralyzed, I stood there watching. A.K. froze too. Then she said:

"Yes, and how does that gun *feel* to you, Oly Joe?"

"Fuck feel. I'm gonna blow you away."

"Yes, and you have some *thoughts* about that gun, Oly Joe?"

Oly Joe cocked the trigger, and paused. Then he threw the gun down on the floor. It bounced, as if it were made of plastic. Oly Joe ran out, his combat boots echoing down one flight to his room.

A.K. stared at the gun, and at me. I picked up the gun.

"It's not real!" I said. "Did you know that?"

"Biting the breast. I'm discharging him. For acting out."

"Even though it wasn't real?"

"Biting that breast was real."

I left for my analyst's home office.

Fascinating session. Poppa Doc nodded me onto the couch. As usual I associated freely without his saying a word. As was unusual, he didn't snore. In fact I hardly heard him breathing. Impressive. When I left I glanced at him in the dim half-light, and he didn't look too happy. I figured this was his empathic response to my being deeply deeply depressed.

By the time I got back to Thoreau, Zoe had signed out of the Family Unit, AMA—Against Medical Advice.

. . .

"CHRISTINE BROKE UP with me. She said I'd failed to live up to my potential. I still can't get it up, but she said that had nothing to do with it, that it wasn't my dick, it was me! Which is even worse! Not only did you take the starch out of my cock, you took away my . . . my . . . my potential! And my wife too! What the fuck is wrong with you? I am a total failure. Fuck!"

It was the next afternoon, and Cherokee Putnam was finally curling up in the chair in my office in Toshiba, knees clasped in his hands, rocking, heavily into what I knew, with relief, to be his Oral Stage rage.

"You ruined my sex life. All your analysis of Schlomo fucking Lily in therapy has just made it more real. My obsession is worse. And last night Lily said to me, 'I'd almost think you're having an affair, Cherokee, but I figure you can't be, because you're too depressed. You'd be happier if you were.' " He glared at me, his paranoia almost palpable. "I'm starting to think you're in cahoots with Schlomo. You talking about me behind my back?"

I glanced at the Freud on my desk:

> The clinging to the condition of a penis in the object as well as the retiring in favor of the father, may be ascribed to the castration complex.

"Are you? Answer me."

> The enmity which the persecuted paranoiac sees in others is the reflection of his own hostile impulses against them.

"You have the fantasy that Dr. Dove and I are in cahoots, against you?"

"Yeah! You and Lily and him—all in bed together!"

"Yes, and your anger at me is your lost love for Father?"

Boom. He wilted. I could almost see his inner vista open up, of Father, hated and loved, and Mother, with no "dick"—or, rather, with a dick so soft as to be invisible.

"And," I went on, "your keeping secrets from Mother?"

Boom boom. He wept quietly. "I do have a secret. I never told anyone else this." I braced myself, ready for incest, beating, murder, zoophilia. "You remember when I told you that I quit Walt Disney?"

"I do."

"I didn't quit, I was fired. Last Christmas in Aspen, I . . . wasn't even . . . invited to Eisner's. I'm a failure, a total failure. Nothing I do is ever enough. My severance pay is just about gone. I'm just about broke—a secret I've kept from Lily. I always tried my best, but now, it's like my whole life is spread out before my eyes like a patient on a table or something, and I'm looking down on it and I can see that all the while I was trying my best at the wrong things." He sighed. "Listen. I love this:

"Get all the gold and silver that you can,
Satisfy ambition, animate
The trivial days and ram them with the sun,
And yet upon these maxims meditate:
All women dote upon an idle man
Although their children need a rich estate;
No man has ever lived that had enough
Of children's gratitude or woman's love."

I knew the poem, and loved it too: "Vacillation," by W. B. Yeats. My impulse was to tell him I loved it too. But A.K. would rip me to shreds if I did.

"Yeats," he said. "Guess you don't know it. I was Class Poet at Groton. Always wanted to be a poet. At Yale my senior year, I was in a poetry seminar—very select—run by a poet who'd been in a seminar with Anne Sexton? My teacher said I had promise. Said he would help me apply to creative writing programs?" He shook his head. "I chose to make money instead. Not even law, Disney. Mickey Mouse was my big rebellion—some rebellion, Disney's more the Dow Jones now than GM or GE. Now, I'm out of money. But in two days, a big note comes due, 'a rich estate.' " He stared at me, a dissonantly calm look in his eyes, curious, even quizzical, as if wondering how I would respond. Again I felt torn, wanting to respond but fearing A.K.'s critique of both my wanting and my response. There was something chilling here. I compromised.

"You have some feelings, about your 'big note'?"

He got up and walked to the door. There were still ten minutes left. His hand was on the doorknob. "And now," he said, "I've even failed with you."

"You're leaving early?" I said with alarm, feeling that if he walked out and never came back, I too would be a failure. Once again, compared to good therapists like A.K., I was coming up short.

"Do you care?" Cherokee asked, his voice again curious, calmly probing, as if from above his life, probing the body below.

"You mean care if you leave early?"

"I mean . . ." He gave me a sorrowful look. "I mean, just, you know, *care*."

I did. Despite our differences, at that moment I saw his struggle as much like my own. I too felt that no matter what I did I was a failure. I sensed, then, that he was lonely and desperate and needed me to be with him right there, and that I should simply say that to him, say "Yeah man, I do." But just as the Y of *Yeah* was pushing off from my silence it was as if a shot of

Novocain had hit, freezing my jaw and my tongue and setting my lip atingle. In that instant—what Freud called "the procrastinating mechanism of thought," which cools our libidinal impulses and assures man's superiority to beasts, the beasts out there in nature and the beasts within our skulls—into my head marched A.K., stern, and Freud sterner if not sternest—that enormous uncut beard hiding any sign of his lips, those thick steel-rimmed glasses hiding any real sign of his eyes—and before I could figure out exactly what to say to Cherokee, he was gone.

Sitting there free-associating until time was up—he might come back, might he not?—I felt scared. Was I scared for him or scared for me? His shit or my shit?

I wanted to run after him, chase him down all the way to the tennis court and beyond, hound him to his house, his barn where he kept his horses, his office in the hayloft off limits to Lily and the girls because it was the nerve center of the phone calls and faxes of his doomed thing with Christine, wanted to take him into my arms as Malik had taken Oly Joe in that old yellowed gym that night, as any caring father would a frightened son, yes. But I felt the lead weight of psychoanalysis, the flowering of Western civilization, pressing me down on my chair, as if all the Freudians on earth were a species apart, men and the rare woman of greater gravity and—

A knock on my door. My heart did a flip-flop. Hope. "Yes?"

"Any dickheads in here?"

Thorny. In a crisp white shirt and bow tie and the kind of suspenders the Generation X bankers were now wearing. He came in as if this were his TV room at home and sat down casually and said, "You're in deep shit, Doc."

"How?"

"Your head's messed up. I couldn't believe what you did to Zoe. And then not even lettin' me into Thoreau t'see her? *Bad* move, Doc, wicked bad. She asked me to deliver this to you. Personally." He handed me a letter.

> Dear Dr. Roy G. Basch:
>
> I am firing you as my therapist. You are brainwashed. I can't take it anymore. I had a secret consultation last week with Dr. Schlomo Dove. He said that I was a person with all the warmth of the sun, but that I give my warmth to everyone else and it leaves me feeling cold and empty—like to you. He is taking me on as his own patient. Maybe you should find another profession, one that rewards heartlessness, like law.
>
> Have a nice life.
>
> Zoe
>
> P.S. Butler abused me. *Really*. And there *really* is a dead child buried in our backyard in the Adirondacks. I could have shown you where to dig.

I was shaken by this and furious at Schlomo, so shaken and furious that it took all my skill to hide it from Thorny.

He scrutinized me. "Anything you want me to tell Zoe, Doc?"

I wanted to say to tell her that I cared about her and wanted her back as a patient and I'd tried my hardest but I said, only, "Like what?"

"Like, 'Hey, all is forgiven come home let's try again, kid'?" He waited, much like a good analyst would. "Tell you a secret, Doc—she'd kill me if she knew I said it: she really wants you, you know, as a therapist. You've helped her a lot this year. She knows you care. All you got to do is *ask*."

Ask. Malik's main word. Everything in me consciously wanted to ask, but I had seen, through A.K. and Poppa Doc, just how untrustable my conscious mind was, given my monstrous unconscious, and so I knew I'd better not.

"Dickheads Get Shrunk," Thorny said, rising. "It's pathetic."

VIV BEEPED ME that night, when I was on call, for a phone call from Lily Putnam, Cherokee's wife. Lily had never called me before. Something was up.

My instinct was to talk to her but again I heard A.K.'s voice: "You did *what*?" So I thought of telling Viv I couldn't talk to her. But that didn't feel right either. Then I thought that, since A.K. was supervising me on Cherokee and was ultimately the person responsible, I'd call her at home. I asked Viv to tell Lily I'd call her back. I called A.K.

"Lily Putnam wants to talk to me. Cherokee's wife. I'm worried about Cherokee. He left today's session ten minutes early."

"Wait," A.K. said. The receiver clunked down on something. I heard a key unlock something. A.K. was back. "Tell me about the session."

I told her. I heard the *scritch scritch* of her pencil, doing the crossword in the ledger as I talked. When I finished, A.K. said, "Tell his wife to call her analyst."

"Schlomo Dove?"

"We can't all be lucky."

"*What?*" I said, thinking, This is a strange way to talk about your former analyst. "What do you mean by that?" Silence. "But you think Cherokee is okay?"

"Work it out on the couch."

"You mean in another phantom session, if he doesn't come back?"

"Not him, *you*. In *your* analysis."

"With Poppa Doc?"

Scritch scritch. "Who?"

"Never mind."

I hung up and called Viv. I told her to tell Lily Putnam to call her analyst,

Schlomo Dove. I felt bad, but I knew that I'd done the right thing by calling my supervisor, and I was relieved now that A.K. was taking responsibility for deciding that Cherokee was basically okay. I couldn't wait until the next afternoon, to tell Poppa Doc the news.

JILL WAS HAVING a party that night, in her new apartment on top of a converted factory. One wall was all window, offering a panoramic view of the sky, perfect for sighting UFOs. She had invited friends who were into aliens. The lights were off inside, so that everyone could see outside. Interesting reversal of psychoanalysis. The talk was about the latest news from Fyffe, Alabama, of cattle mutilations. The cows had been found dead, parts surgically removed as if by a laser beam, with no signs of trauma, struggle, or blood.

Each conversation felt slightly askew, for the eyes of the UFO-watcher were continually moving in a nystagmus—flicking from me to the night sky, from the sky back to me—the kind of eye wobble I'd seen at parties where real stars were present and people were always looking past you at them.

"Great party," I said to Jill after everyone had left, as she stood at the sink washing the last dishes. I put my arms around her and stroked her tummy. Since that night on-call when my dick had "done a Cherokee," we hadn't made love, but now I felt ready. "I'm dying to make love to you!"

"Uh-huh. C'mon." She wiped her soapy hands and took my hand. We lay down on her bed facing the wide milky night. "Talk to me, 'kay?"

I found that I was blocking.

She rose on an elbow and stared into my eyes. "Don't you understand? Talk to me, and you will get laid great. I will fuck your brains out, 'kay?"

"I thought Eduardo was interesting." Eduardo was a handsome young man from Ecuador who was a guide for tours to the Galápagos.

"Yeah? How?"

"It was interesting how his interest in plants and animals was an identification with his mother."

Jill stared at me anxiously. "He thought you were weird. He asked me, 'Are all psychiatrists so weird?' "

"Only the unanalyzed think we're weird."

"Y'know, when people find out I work at Misery, they ask me that same question. I used to say, 'Some are a little weird, and go into it to understand themselves'—which *is* weird when you come to think of it since you should go into it to help people—'and some want to stand back and observe people'—which is *also* weird, since that doesn't help anyone either. But now, I just agree with them. Eduardo said that his last tour group was all doctors—

about twenty of them. And six of them were really strange. Like quiet? Scrunched up, faces all scrunched up? Into themselves more than into the Galápagos? Guess what? He found out five were shrinks, and one was a pathologist."

"Interesting."

"Roy, come on!"

"You're getting upset."

"You're damn right I'm getting upset! And you're going to listen!"

"I am listening."

"Well, then respond! If you don't respond to me right now I'm going to rip your eyes out!"

I was blocking even worse. She stared at me as if I were a giant lizard of the Galápagos, and then she got up, went to the window, and scanned.

"See any?"

"Look," she said, turning to face me, "I've stuck with you all year, through the Heiler bullshit and the crap on Toshiba, but this is the worst. You are so weird! There's no 'now' for you now—you're either fantasizing about the future or remembering the past—five minutes ahead or five years behind—you are never here anymore! I have no idea what's going on with you, in the rest of your life! And I get the feeling there's lots. You back with Berry?"

"No way. I'm free."

"So why aren't you here? I stuck around for the first three rotations, but I don't know if I can take the fourth! I have no idea who I'm dealing with!"

"Don't worry. I'm done with surprises. Psychoanalysis is it."

"Roy. I've worked at Misery a lot longer than you—I've seen what it does to people. Being a shrink is a very unnatural act! Humans aren't designed for it! Please—there's still time—this is it, right now—you can't wait for it to change, or for something different to happen tomorrow, because I'm going to feel this way tomorrow too. Don't go blind on me."

She was right in my face. I felt overwhelmed with dread. She sighed.

"God save me from a guy who sees me as his mother. Maybe the only sensible position to take is that guys are aliens. I mean if you start there, you don't expect them to change—you can't expect to change a dog into a cat, right? You stop trying. There are a few mutants—I thought you might be one, that first day you walked onto the ward the wrong way—you seemed wild, rebellious—but now—"

"Psychoanalysis is rebellious."

She stared at me in disbelief. "Maybe there are mutants and I'm just not meeting them? Some guys you can have bridge conversations with, at first. But sooner or later you find yourself beating your head against a wall. Know what I've learned, from all these guys?"

"Yes?"

"You have a lot of energy when you break up with them, because you stop trying to make a dog into a cat. I mean you reach a point—like now with you—where everything stops, like when you're pedaling along on a bicycle and the chain slips off and all of a sudden you're pedaling air, too fast, and alone, and going nowhere. That's us now."

"You have some feelings about 'us now'?"

"Go home. With you gone, I'm gonna feel like incredibly depressed, but I won't feel as alone." She stared. "You didn't even loosen your tie."

I got up and started out.

"Roy? I can't stand you right now. But I still probably love you?"

Boom. I thought of telling her that my dad had died and that I needed to cry and that I loved her for her straight unleashed humanness but then I was a child standing at the top of our stairs in Columbia my mother at the bottom and I was bored stiff stuck inside on a sunny day hearing myself asking my mother, "WhadamI gonna do *now*? WhadamI gonna do *now*?" as if she knew and suddenly I felt wetness in my eyes. Jill saw it and came and hugged me and there were tears in her own eyes as she asked:

"What? Can you tell me?"

Everything in me wanted to tell her but the harsh chorus in my head turned my tongue to stone—stone tongue stone mouth stone teeth teeth teeth—and I felt my heart if not break then attack a little like my pop's and I shook my head and two more tears popped out and feeling her squeeze my hand really hard I just left.

CONSTANT FOUL-SMELLING RAIN was driving people crazy, but my inner world was warm and dry. I awoke before the light that next morning, a Sunday. Feeling an early-morning chaos of loneliness, I decided to go in to Thoreau and read some Freud. The Family Unit was now deserted. All the patients had left Against Medical Advice. It was just after seven when I walked upstairs to the office I was using next to A.K.'s, unlocked my door and went in. The empty rooms in the magnificent old building, the unambivalent woodwork and brick, and the silence were a comfort. I sat free-associating, and then took down one of my crisp new robin's-egg-blue volumes of *The Collected Works* and turned to "Totem and Taboo."

"Dr. Basch?"

Startled, I looked up. A tall slender woman was standing in the door. Her light brown hair was cut short. She was all in black, and despite her terrified eyes she was stunningly beautiful.

"Yes?"

"Lily Putnam, remember?"

"Sure."

"Cherokee shot himself."

"Oh God! Is he dead?"

"Yes."

"Shit!" In shock, I stared at her, trying to see her but failing. She walked to a chair and sat.

"I . . . I just had my session with Schlomo, and I saw your light on here, thought I'd tell you in person. I know how much he cared about you. Thought the world of you, actually."

"What happened?" I said loudly, as if she were a long way away and I had to shout to reach her.

"He and I had been more and more distant. Yesterday afternoon he came to me and asked, 'Do you still love me?' 'Yes,' I said. He said, 'But not enough. Or maybe it's me, my *core ingrato*, my ungrateful heart.' I asked what he meant but the girls came in—they were late for a swim meet—I had to drive them. He said he'd be out for a while. I left. And then . . . I got a call . . . he'd driven the Jeep to the ocean, out to his favorite wildlife refuge. And . . . and then . . . and put a gun in his mouth . . . shot himself."

"He had a gun?"

"I told him I did not want a gun in the house, and he'd promised he wouldn't, but I knew he'd gotten a permit. I thought it was all part of his flirtation with suicide."

"Suicide?" Suddenly I felt sick. Lies! All these lies! What else had he been lying about?

"As you know, he was obsessed with suicide. Talked about it all the time. For years, really. Talking about driving into abutments and calculating which hotel rooms he could jump from and not land on anyone below. Even though you were working on it with him, it didn't get any better. He seemed even more obsessed about it lately. Schlomo reassured me—I mean that he was in good hands, as far as trying to deal with his suicide, with you."

I felt a wave of nausea. Words and phrases sprang to mind—signs of his secret, which he had never told me, in fact had denied, early on when I'd asked him, before A.K. had started to supervise me. Since then, whenever I'd brought up the question to A.K., telling her that I wanted to ask Cherokee directly about whether he was suicidal, A.K. had told me not to. "*Don't ask!*" she'd said firmly. "Listen for it in the material." I'd blown it. I felt devastated.

"Did he leave a note?"

"No. Just his life insurance policies, and instructions how to collect."

"Life insurance?"

"Two policies. Worth a million each. And each had the standard clause, that the policy has to be held for over two years or there is no payment if you die by suicide."

"Two years?"

"Was—" She stopped, the reality catching her by the throat. She cried, and cried out, "Was yes—"

"Yesterday?" She nodded, sobbing. After a while she quieted. We sat still.

She sighed. "I'd best go. Lots of things to do." She made no effort to move.

"I . . . I'm so sorry. I'm in shock. I'll call you. We'll talk."

"We . . . you and I . . . we both tried as hard as we could. I was more worried about him the other night, that's why I called you. . . . Viv said you were busy. That you would call back."

"I . . ."

"No matter. Wouldn't have helped." She got up and walked slowly toward the door.

"Wait." I went to her and put my arms around her and hugged her. Her short light brown hair brushed my chin. She was sobbing. I was too shocked to cry. I felt the heightened sensuality that floods us in those moments when death is all around, when we feel that big callused fist.

"Thanks," she said, easing away. "I'm sure you did your best. He always talked about you with such fondness. I'll let you know about the funeral."

"How are the girls?"

"Hope, the eldest, says she hates him. Little Kissy isn't saying anything." She turned away quickly and, weeping, hurried out.

I sat there stunned, going over every piece of the disaster, feeling sick to my stomach at my failure to dig out his secret. "A note comes due," he had said. "Their children need a rich estate."

Terror. I felt like I was suffocating, as if my breath were coming in through a needle-thin tube. I had to get out of there! I grabbed my coat and hat and ledgers and left my office, for some reason turning the other way down the hall, past A.K.'s office. The outer door was ajar. So was the inner. I knocked. No answer. I went in.

On her ornate couch was a body. Sprawled, legs adangle down, head tilted back so the face was out of sight, the white jaw raised above the slit throat.

Time slowed down. I clicked into real doctoring, found myself at the body, searching for a pulse, hoping for a pulse for poor Oly Joe. Beside his cheek was a fuzzy yellow duck, blotched with blood. Thready pulse. His kid's heart was trying hard. He'd gotten both jugulars, but had missed the carotids—novice throat slitters tend to tilt the head back to cut, so the carotids retract in, becoming harder to hit.

I stopped the bleeding and breathed him and did all the other medical things to save what was left of his life and called Security, stat. Oly Joe hadn't been bleeding all that long, and looked like he would live, although his breathing was ominously shallow, as if from primitive regions of his brain stem. He must have sneaked in on this sleepy Sunday morning, knowing that no one would be around.

My body felt all watery. One of my mother's most powerful superstitions was that deaths come in threes. I had often heard from my inpatients how, in a particular life—inexplicably and seemingly chosen by a malevolent God—deaths had piled upon deaths, tragedies upon tragedies, all within a short space of time, sending even the most seemingly solid people spinning down to insanity, or, as in Toshiba at Christmas, violence and abuse. This is the kind of thing we go crazy from, or die slowly with.

As I waited for help, sitting next to him on the couch, I saw how the blood had run out all over A.K.'s prized Freudian couch and tapestry, and Persian carpet. A bloodied straight razor lay on the floor. Then my eyes were drawn to a leather-bound ledger, lying open on the carpet. I bent to the ledger and read the last right-hand side entry:

> Oly Joe jumps off the couch, grabs me and rips off my skirt my panty hose spreads my thighs sticks his tongue into me. Then I take his sweet little boy farmer's prick in my hands, cup his balls and . . .

Below, scribbled in big adolescent letters and spattered with blood, was:

> She fucked me so fuck you all! Oly Joe.

Gingerly I picked up the ledger, closed it, put it in my briefcase, and waited.

Soon Primo arrived. With him were two members of the state police. They had been looking hard for Oly Joe Olaf because the night before he had stolen a car and driven to his old school, Simeon's Rest. He was carrying with him an assault rifle and ammo, and had killed three people apparently at random. Two were students, a seventeen-year-old girl and a nineteen-year-old boy. The other was a professor of English literature. Others had been wounded. Oly Joe had vanished.

We sent Oly Joe in an ambulance to Timmons General Hospital.

I called A. K. Lowell. I told her what had happened. I said nothing to her about the ledger. She said nothing to me about anything.

The governor of the state, questioned later that day at a boar hunt on a private game preserve about how a seventeen-year-old boy who had just been discharged the day before from a mental hospital for threatening violence could walk into a gun shop and purchase an assault rifle and ammo without a hitch, said:

> "There will always be people who are crackers, who do these things. The problem isn't not having better gun laws, the problem is not having the death penalty."

By the next evening it was clear just how brain-damaged poor Oly Joe Olaf was, and most likely would be for the rest of his life. His breathing centers were in fact only up to the level of amphibia, and so he was on a respirator. The MRI of his brain showed damage that in all probability would forever keep him from speaking or reading or writing or walking or standing trial. His family asked that he be transferred as soon as possible to a chronic care facility that happened to be located near them, out in the farm country of rural Missouri.

MY LAST DAY on Thoreau, a few days later, I was about to leave my turret for my tennis-and-dinner date with A. K. Lowell when the phone rang.

"Roy?"

"Yeah?"

"Lenny. How are you?"

"Bad."

"Yeah, me too. I been out of town, and just heard. Unbelievable."

"It's the worst," I said numbly. I had been in shock ever since Lily Putnam had told me that Cherokee was dead. In shock, feeling nothing.

"The absolute worst. We fucked up so bad!" He started to cry, and then had a fit of coughing. "Look," he said, "I need to talk. I'll come over."

"Can't. I'm on my way out."

"No, no, you don't understand. It's our fault. We're to blame. I shoulda picked up, more, how you wouldn't let me see Cherokee—and hell, you shoulda asked me to see him too. We both fucked up. We gotta talk."

"Sorry, but I can't." I felt frozen, below zero, too low to feel anything. I knew I should see him and that not to see him now would be sick, but to actually face him, to face into all the feelings, at that moment was incomprehensible.

"What's so important?"

"You don't want to know."

"C'mon, c'mon."

"I'm going over to A.K.'s."

"You shittin' me?"

"No. How 'bout tomorrow?"

"We gotta talk *now*."

I felt a tiny opening, like the unwilling opening of an eye to an eclipse. But to see would be to burn, and I closed down harder. "Sorry."

"That's it?"

"For today."

"Tomorrow's too late. I need to see you now. If we talk a little, you can help me with this, and I can help you too." He sounded desperate. "It's now or never."

"Aw c'mon, Malik."

"Okay," he said, suddenly matter-of-fact. "Got a pencil and paper?"

"Wait a sec." I got a number 2 and a Misery envelope. "Yeah."

"Write down this number: 555-0100. Got it?"

"What do you mean got it?—that's your home number, Malik."

"Right. Y'got it?"

"Yeah, but—"

"Now burn it."

"What the—" *Click.* The phone went dead.

TENNIS WITH A. K. LOWELL was infuriating; she was a topspin lobber. I would smash a forehand down the line and rush the net, and she, on her own baseline, would get to it and lob it back high over my head, with enough topspin to bounce even farther away from me than I had expected. She parked her tall, muscular body on her own baseline, and even when I tried to dink it softly just over the net, she would either anticipate me and be there and lob it high back, giving her enough time to settle back in on her baseline, or not even bother to try to get it, conceding the point rather than losing her baseline dignity.

At first it was a challenge to try to adjust to her game, but then, after hitting a few perfect shots that rifled low over the net and then watching the ball sail up off her racket with lazy ease and plop down near my own baseline, its topspin making it hard to return with any control, it was less a challenge than a cause. As I tried harder and harder to penetrate her maddening system, it became less a cause than an irritation, a perversion of the spirit of the game in the name of her winning. I lost the first set 5–7, the second 2–6, and in the middle of the third—after I hit a particularly vicious smash down the backhand line that I knew she could never get to, and just to make sure rushing the net to protect the angles, to see her with an almost lazy backhand flick lob it high high high over my head as if daring me to try to chase it, and I gauging to see is it going out or not and figuring yes but wanting to make sure to be there, racing back, back, seeing it come down just on my baseline and then, because of its height, carom off even farther back so that I had to chase it right to the edge of the bubble dome of the indoor court and with a wild flail backward over my head manage to hit it before I crashed face first into the mesh fabric, only to see it drop short on my side of the net, her point—in the middle of the third set I lost it completely and just tried to finish the set without going psychotic. "You can tell everything about a person by how they play a sport." Love–6.

Thank God for dinner. We sat at a massive oak table in a massive room paneled with dark wood which, in the candlelight, looked as impenetrable as ebony. The house was a castlelike Tudor. The neighborhood, the yard, the house, the furnishings—all were High Episcopal suburban. A.K.'s new husband, Robert, was much younger than she, and a hairdresser. He cooked, served, poured wines—white and red and dessert—cleared, and did the dishes.

Strange, all of it. Strange too the way that A.K. seemed no different at home than at work. She used the Three Techniques and complex silences on Robert. Strangest of all was how she treated her five-year-old son Mo Ali—short for Moishe Alistair. Mo Ali seemed a delightful boy, dressed in Oshkosh jeans and kid Nikes.

"I saw ducks flying in the sky today," Mo Ali would say.

"And what are your fantasies about ducks?" A.K. would ask.

"The ducks are going to Disney World."

"Yes, and what are your thoughts about Disney World?"

"I think I want to go there can we please Mommy Robert said we could."

"And what are your feelings about Robert?"

"I want to stand on his head in the pool till he drowns," Mo Ali said cheerfully, "and be with you all the time in bed. When someone's depressed, Mommy, how come some of 'em kill themselves and some of 'em don't?"

A.K. would nod at me knowingly. I would nod back, feeling appalled.

" 'We're three happy chappies,' " Mo Ali sang out, " 'with snappy *serapes*.' "

"Three," A.K. said, nodding, "is Oedipal." I nodded back.

Finally Robert took Mo Ali up to bed and A.K. invited me into her home office up under the skylight. The furniture was arranged to replicate as exactly as possible her office on Thoreau, with the same couch and chair and big desk with, on the left-hand side with its back to me, the same small framed photo and the four sharp number 2's. We sat in silence.

"I've always wondered," A.K. said finally, "how a man could walk to his own execution." Two seconds. "And why people cry at happy endings."

I stared down at the carpet for a while, an expensive antique Persian. I wanted to talk about all the disasters on the Family Unit, but I hesitated—to bring up something as "hot" as suicide and murder would be like my hitting a scorcher crosscourt, then rushing the net only to be lobbed over, then scurrying back, breathless and sweaty and pissed off. Finally I said, "I'm rotating off the Family Unit. I won't be having supervision with you anymore."

"You could pay for it, privately."

"I don't know if it would be worth it."

She jumped in her chair as if shot. I, as surprised as she at this blast from my unconscious, went on, "I'm sorry about Oly Joe. We've both been having a helluva hard time. We both really screwed up."

" 'The relation between analyst and patient is based on a love of truth, that is, on the acknowledgment of reality, and it precludes any kind of sham or deception.' " She smiled. " 'Analysis Terminable and Interminable.' "

"I . . . I don't get it." She said nothing. For some reason I thought about how I still had her Oly Joe ledger hidden away, and how she must have missed it and wondered who had it, but had never asked me about it. Strange.

"Cigar?"

I nodded. She rose and went to a table-high humidor, searching for a key in her pocket. I too stood up, and took a few steps to her desk.

For the first time I saw the small framed black-and-white photo: Schlomo Dove stood in front of the Farben, short, fat, and rumpled, flashing his snaggly-toothed smile, seeming about ten years younger. Next to him on one side stood a woman taller than he, a slender young woman with a Jewish nose, light brown hair cut short, and wearing a silky summer dress. This must have been A. K. Lowell when she was still Aliyah K. Whatever, before she'd had her nose job and bulked up and started wearing men's power suits. Analyst and patient.

On the other side of Schlomo, with a gap between them, stood Ike White. Slender, smooth-cheeked, with a cute cowlick, he too seemed young. His face looked pained. I recalled Viv telling me that A.K. and Ike had been best friends, classmates at the institute, and that both of them had been analyzed, at the same time, by Schlomo Dove.

Then my eyes chanced upon a few papers on her desk: two bills, on her embossed stationery. The first bill was to the NASA grant for Oly Joe Olaf's sessions—at $200 per fifty-minute session—for the month of March: $4,000 and 00/100 dollars. With astonishment I saw that the last billable hour was the very Sunday on which I had found Oly Joe on her couch. The second bill was to Mr. Olaf, Oly Joe's father, "Prairie Home Farm, Tipton, Missouri," a bill for "expenses incurred in replacing psychoanalytic couch and Persian carpet after damage caused by your son's suicide attempt: "$4,534 and 59/100 dollars."

I looked at A.K. She glanced at me and then at the bills, offering me a cigar. Numbly I took the cigar, cut it, lit it, and puffed it silently. I sat back down.

"It's hard for me," I said finally, "thinking of Cherokee. All during your supervision, I never asked him more about whether he was thinking about suicide. Before I started with you, I did ask him, and he denied it. But whenever I brought it up with you, you told me *not* to ask him directly, that it would pollute the transference. I did what you told me. But he was obsessed with suicide. He talked to his wife about it all the time! I blew it. You blew it. That night when his wife called me and I called you, you said not to talk to her. Maybe, if I had . . . ?" I stared at her. "I thought you knew what you were doing."

Silence.

"I keep *seeing* him, how it must have been for him, knowing he was about to kill himself, the loaded gun already in his Jeep, asking his wife Lily that last time, for help—'Do you love me enough?'—seeing her and his sweet little girls for what he knew would be the last time, ever!—and then driving away from his house, his kids, for the last time, getting out of the car, walking out into the beach grass, putting the gun into his mouth—what was he thinking, actually taking the gun and actually putting it in his mouth? The taste of the metal on his tongue? Did he pause? He was smart, clear-headed—and he was really putting a loaded gun *in his mouth*?"

I started to cry, seeing the little girls, the gun in the mouth, being with him as he wondered whether or not to pull the trigger; finally I was starting to cry, thank God! "The gun . . . the barrel in his mouth, his lips, his *teeth*?" My body shook with sobs, but as I stopped I heard a *scritch scritch*. I looked up and was stunned to see that A.K. was writing in her leather-bound ledger.

" 'Teeth'?" she asked. "And are you thinking about your dead father the dentist?"

"Are you *joking*?" I said. She looked up, and then began writing once again, first on the left-hand side, then on the right. "Can't you say anything, I mean, like from your heart?"

"Yes, and when someone leaves they take a piece of your heart with them."

Poppa Doc's line. Do they learn those lines by rote, like child's rhymes?

Then it was as if my vision cleared. I saw her as totally empty, so empty that if I had my old House of God stethoscope with me and put it on her chest to listen for signs of life, I would hear nothing, nothing except the echo of my own breathing. I had the impulse to leap the desk like a net in tennis and plunge a number 2 into her chest.

"You killed him!" I shouted. "You kill them all! You don't know fuck-all what you're doing. You haven't got a clue. Because you haven't got a heart! You mind-fucker! It's sick, what you do—*you're* fucking sick!"

No reaction, none at all.

I took as deep a puff of the cigar as possible and thought about throwing it at her, but then I knew what would hurt her more. I took another long puff, until the tip glowed red, and then threw it down on the head of her Freud couch. Ashes scattered all over it. At that she rose and I crushed it in, smushing the ashes around. Then I turned and walked out, slamming the door as hard as I could behind me. It echoed through the barren house like a gunshot.

As I passed the child's room on the second floor I heard her little boy crying. As I passed through the family room, all dark wood and gloom and dark leather and Robert smoking a pipe and reading *Town and Country*, I said, "You poor bastard!" Robert said nothing. I found myself out on a suburban street.

I breathed in the cleansing sorrow of the rain and stared back up at the castle, its two lit windows—bottom left and top right—like the eyes of a huge warped face, and I saw clearly how through psychoanalysis you could know every nook and cranny of yourself and have no idea how to be with anyone, the seeming dazzle of the self blinding you to the connections with others. I remembered Berry saying once that what we need in the world isn't an analysis of ourselves, but to live with a lot of examples of good relationships.

And I knew then that I had once been in touch with people, with Berry and Malik and Solini and Jill, and that it wasn't inevitable that we are always shouting across an unbridgeable gap, but rather that the gap was in Freud and monstrous fabrications like A.K. herself who followed after, bereft souls floating untethered in pools of self like lilies in sepsis, the gap was in them, not in the essence of humans, nor in the essence of the whole world.

I stared up at the vigilant street lamp, the cone of glittering sleet in the winter night reaching toward me like a beacon, showing me as clearly as if it were the moment's sun that the real perversion of Freud and analysis was to take the essence of something and reduce it to something else—the present to the past, love to hate, joy to misery, life to death—and to do it under the guise of understanding and yet, let's face it, all the while doing it to escape from what Malik kept saying life at heart actually is—being, without description of that being.

For A.K. and the armies of obsessive scared kids like her, any other thing was better than eye-to-eye and heart-to-heart, anything was better than having someone else see your own sightlessness, or feel your own not feeling the beat of your heart in your chest, or sense your own insensitivity to your soul—anything was better than seeing that you were blind to the essence of love.

I needed to be with someone right then, but the ones I loved were gone.

Were they? Berry and Malik maybe were gone and maybe not. Maybe I could go home right now and call them up and they would answer, and we could make plans to get together, talk, puzzle this all out, and . . . Yeah, and then what?

With alarm I saw that what was gone was something else. To move toward them was not possible. My mind had been set spinning by A.K., and it would not stop spinning just because I wanted it to. It was spinning in the same way that poor Cherokee's had been spinning—his about suicide and his wife fucking Schlomo—round and round, the needle digging deeper into the groove. Eyes open, eyes shut, it didn't matter—the same record was playing and it was the record of me myself and I.

I saw myself trapped in a monstrous cell of myself, a cell so vast that from where I stood on the cold stone floor in the center between the execrable toilet and hard steel bed, even the bars were as far off as the edges of the world, beyond the edges of my vision, so that even if there were any other humans out there, they were out there out of sight over the horizon, not even remotely close to being in here with me.

Nor could I in good faith let them try.

They were too far away and it was late, too late, too late, not because they were gone but because what was gone, in spite of its bloated enormity and the damage it had done—to Cherokee and Zoe and poor Oly Joe and the kids Oly Joe killed and to Henry and Hannah and Jill and Malik and Berry and my father, caring and concerned all—what was gone was any semblance of the person who had the potential to be with others. What was gone was not at all the opposite of this ravenous self of mine but something else, something other even than any possible me, something else essential for being with others, something categorically else which, to my dismay, I realized I had no idea how to name, or what it could possibly be.

THE HEIDELBERGS

"It's one thing to desire a person's happiness,
it's another to deny them their pain."

—BERRY, CLINICAL PSYCHOLOGIST

HEIDELBERG WEST

"They [social deviants] behave like monkeys in the wild."

—DR. FREDERICK K. GOODWIN, FORMER DIRECTOR,
National Institute of Mental Health

Fourteen

". . . I CALLED CHEROKEE'S WIFE and told her that he and I had been having an affair. Maybe it was the wrong thing to do, but I was so upset, and felt so alone, I had to talk to someone. A real person, not someone in the helping professions, like you. It's so sad! He was a nice guy, a real nice guy. *I* didn't care that he couldn't get it up. It was even kind of nice, in a way, him being soft. . . . That first time I met him I said to you, 'He's too good to be true'—remember?" I nodded. "And he was! He had everything—a nice wife, two terrific kids, money, me! Why wasn't it enough?"

"Enough?"

"To keep him alive? What's with him? What's *with* you men? I mean it got so that anything I said, he took as criticism—last month he got a new car, a Jeep Cherokee Limited Edition, and I said, 'Hey, that's a great nickname for you, hon: *Jeep* Cherokee'—and you know what he said?"

"What?"

"He said, 'Cherokee *Limited* would fit a lot better with the state of affairs.' " Christine shook her head, and reached for her black hankie. "It's so sad . . . so damn pointless . . . and sad." She lowered her platinum-blond head and wept, sobbing hard, all that black of hers finally appropriate to the occasion, mourning his lost potential. "I feel—" She raised her face to me, mascara streaking all the way to the corners of her scarlet lips. "—like I did when my father died, when I first came to see you. . . . God, it seems like so long ago. You wanna . . . wanna know the first thing that comes to mind?"

"No, I'd like to know what Cherokee's wife said, after you told her."

"You would?" I nodded. "Well, for a long time she said nothing, and then she said, 'Did he talk about me?' And I said—maybe I shouldn't've, but I did—'Yes. He was obsessed with your having an affair with your shrink, Dr. Dove.' And then I didn't hear anything and I said, 'Hello? Lily? You still there?' And then the line went dead—she hung up on me. I tried to call back but she wouldn't answer. Was it a mistake?"

"I don't know. We've got to stop. We'll talk about it next week."

" 'Kay." She went to the doorknob and turned. I braced myself. "Funny, but I don't feel that bad. Not like killing myself. Not like at first, when my dad's diabetes got him, and he went legally blind, and lost both legs, and then died. You helped me a lot today." She looked at me quizzically. "You must feel like shit? I know you won't answer me but—"

"I do feel like shit."

"Yeah?" Startled, she stared at me. "I hope your wife can help you, I mean with it." She shook a finger at me, like a schoolmarm. "Don't *you* think about suicide, or else! I mean it is *not* a viable alternative." I grinned, a little. "What I mean is that I need you, Dr. Basch. Bye-bye now."

Suicide was a thought, but merely a thought that existed somewhere far away from the cramped low-ceilinged room in which I was now trapped with my guilt and shame. I was thinking about Cherokee all the time. Even when I was not consciously thinking about him I was startled to find him underlying all that I was thinking. My mind would snap back to him, my work with him, replaying our sessions over and over, replaying my supervisions with A.K. about him, trying to understand how much of this tragedy was me, how much was my fucked-up thing with A.K. As Malik had said, I was to blame, we were all to blame. I had learned in medicine that the main way you got into trouble with patients was when, if you were not sure what to do, you tried to go it alone and did not ask for help. This time, with A.K., I had asked her for help, all along the way. But I had been asking the wrong person. Like asking Mickey Mouse for empathy.

Deaths echo deaths. Ike White, Mary Megan Scorato, the Man Who Froze to Death to Sue His HMO, my father, and Cherokee. Where were they all now?

Nowhere except with me. Death was always there with me now, but I was rarely there with it. Numb, in shock from all these deaths, I was seventy percent there, at most. I was thinking that I was a jinx to live people, as if too much contact with me would put them at grave risk. On the lookout for their fragility, I treated them gingerly.

Now, with Christine gone, I picked up the phone and called Cherokee's number, to talk to Lily. It rang and rang.

. . .

"THERE ARE NO psychological or social factors in mental illness!" Errol Cabot yelled over his bulky shoulder at me, outshouting the perverse April wind. "If it's mental illness, by definition it's biological."

If I had heard these words at any other time in the previous nine months of my training to become a psychiatrist, I would have laughed, thinking, They must be joking. But nine months of Misery had shown me that if I thought they were joking, they were probably dead serious.

"The patient is psychotic until proven otherwise!" Win Winthrop screamed. "Which means," he went on, "everybody in the West."

" 'The West'?"

"Heidelberg West. Psychosis. The worst psychotics on the face of the earth. Treatment failures elsewhere. Referred to us."

Win and Errol the celluloidal redheads were carrying a lead box filled with tubes of blood and urine up the steep hill from Emerson, where they'd just finished bleeding Blair Heiler's patients in the name of the Department of Defense. Virtually all Emersonians were now officially on Placedon and Zephyrill. The small differences from placebo had been analyzed all the way up to "significant." Heiler and Errol and Win were rushing full-blast into publication in the most prestigious journals on earth.

Win and Errol were manic. They moved fast, talked fast, and thought as fast and dirty as if life were taking place in the locker room of a men's gym. They had been up since five—after about four-hours-a-night of sleep—jogging around Misery with Lloyal von Nott and "Beef" Telly, the short, tough Security chief who always clutched a walkie-talkie tightly to his heart. Beef, who Primo had told me was manic depressive and who for the past two springs had tried to kill himself, first with roach poison and then with rat, always jogged last, protecting their rear. Now, despite the chill mountain morning, both Win and Errol wore open-necked summer shirts under their long white lab coats. Sweat glistened on both men's brows. Their necks and torsos and arms and even fingers seemed bulging and bulky, with that fatty sculpted look that you see only in men and women using anabolic steroids. The thick gold chain around Errol's neck seemed too tight, as did the class ring the size of a Placedon capsule not in his ring finger but on his pinkie. Around Win's porcine neck was an amulet of bone and feather, with a dog tag:

Warrior-Wildman Camp Key West.
Do or Die for Keen and Bly.

If psychiatrists specialized in their defects, did that mean that these drug jocks were pumped up on drugs?

They dumped the blood and urine on the lab tech in the Farben. As they turned to race out, Errol bumped into me. "Do you have a dog?"

"No, I don't have a dog, why?"

Throwing me aside he put on a burst of speed and tried to catch Win, whose white lab coat was already flapping, deer-tail-like, far ahead up the road. I ran after them.

The road from the Farben to the Heidelbergs first went down toward the lake but then took a sharp left turn along the stream that fed it, north up a ravine into the pine woods, twisting and turning, up and down, although the grade—always one step ahead of the racing drug mavens—kept going up and up, until there was a fork in the road, and there, on facing bluffs across the scary ravine, were identical three-story stone buildings, the Heidelbergs. The side of each building nearest to the ravine was a massive, five-story white-washed stone tower, with nine orange-red rings around the bottom half, four fortress-style windows rising one to a floor, and each tower capped with a dark dome out of which protruded a grand spike, from which sprouted a golden ball and then a weather vane shaped like a blunt-nosed fish, or maybe a whale, crested with a tiny pineapple. These were the famous replicas of the twin bridge towers at the gateway into the real city of Heidelberg. They had been built on Mount Misery at the start of the century by the mother of a male patient, who had been conceived when Mother had "left her heart in Heidelberg," as well as her virginity, on a grand tour of Europe. The Heidelbergs were linked, across the ravine, by an exquisitely arched wrought-iron footbridge, the delicate ironwork faux-crenellations spoiled somewhat by the high steel fencing recently built to discourage suicides from this bridge, nicknamed "Loopy Lovers Leap." Heidelberg West was Psychopharmacology, or drug therapy; Heidelberg East was Alcohol and Drug Recovery.

Panting, I followed Errol and Win into the foyer of the West. Rather than going in the main door, they turned right through a door marked STAFF ONLY, into the nursing station. I found myself staring through the open top half of a Dutch door, out at the ward. It was packed with patients and was filled with that tomblike quiet you feel under significant water.

Dozens of patients were either lying down asleep or trudging around the thickly carpeted floor or twitching horribly from Tardive dyskinesia, the incurable disease caused by the drugs each had been given to cure them of their curable disease. All wore long white nighties with the Misery logo—pine tree, moon, and duck rampant—as if they were players on a team. The nursing station was a space-age bubble where a nurse in a white uniform stood framed by the open upper Dutch door, a tray of drugs beside her. She would call a name, a patient would rouse him- or herself, come up, get drugs, and go away. No other staff were to be seen. The nurse smiled at me. Her whites were starched. Her teeth glistened amidst lipstick as red as Jill's. Ruffles fluffed down the front of her nursing costume. She seemed immaculately cheerful.

"Welcome to the West, Doctor. I'm Deedee. There's fresh coffee inside."

Inside, instead of the usual steel table and those uncomfortable plastic airport chairs, was a gleaming mahogany table and stressless leather chairs.

"Hello, Doctor," said another nurse, also in a white uniform, one that seemed to be covering her body only with reluctance, unbuttoned a touch too much at the top and stretched a touch too tight in the bust and raised a touch too high on the thigh and all in all reminding me of my medical internship where such uniforms were a statement of life and sex in the midst of disease and death. "Welcome to the West." Her voice was calm and soothing, as if she were taking the same drugs Win and Errol were on, to bring them down closer to human. "I'm Gloria, the head nurse."

"Roy Basch. Call me Roy."

"Roy. Call me Glo. Shall I brew you a fresh cappuccino?"

"Cappuccino?"

"Courtesy of Pfizer Chemical. And a fresh-baked croissant, courtesy of DuPont?" I nodded. "*Chocolat* or *amande*?"

"*Chocolat*." I noticed that her uniform was Courtesy of Dista.

"Good choice. Now. In your cappuccino—cinnamon or cocoa?" I chose cocoa. "Chocolate addict, eh?" she said, and played a big copper espresso machine, making steam hiss. I sank down into a stressless chair (Upjohn) and stared into an inner chamber (Glaxo) where Win and Errol were ripping quickly through charts, Win signing notes, passing them to Errol, who signed and tossed them down onto a table. In another room other nurses and mental health workers sat around, chatting softly or reading magazines. Stressless.

PROZAC, declared the cup Glo handed me. She raised hers in salute: RITALIN. I took a sip. Excellent, bringing back a memory of long mornings sitting with Berry in the Piazza Navone in Rome, now in another lifetime. The DuPont croissant was delicious—fresh, crisp, and with a slippery ooze of butter and fine dark chocolate.

"—tricyclics!" Win cried, crashing out of the back room with Errol.

"Dialing for Dow dollars!" Errol answered. "Let's fucking *move*!"

"Are we doing rounds?" I asked Errol.

"I don't do any goddamn rounds."

"Not even insurance rounds?" He said no. "Well, what shall I do?"

"Just stay outta my way. We just got burned by that quitter—what was her name, Win, that women's libber who ran away to Wyoming? What was it, 'Francine'?"

"Hannah."

"Yeah. Once burned, twice shy."

That whole first day I stuck close to Errol. His pace was frantic, the myriad aspects of his empire making my head spin. He first ripped through the charts on the West 2 and 3, above. These two wards were also packed full of patients. Most showed ritualistic behaviors—hand-rubbing, hair-pulling, one lawyerly-looking man scratching his rump incessantly. Finished with the charts, Win and Errol blasted past me, out. Cornering tightly on the stairs, Errol elbowed Win to his knees. Helping him up, I asked about the ritualistic behavior.

"OCD," Win said. "Obsessive Compulsive Disorder. A psychosis."

"But obsession has always been a neurosis, not a psychosis."

"Now it is. As of last Monday it's official: they're nuts. Insurance pays for thirteen days. Since last Friday eighty percent of our admissions have OCD. We're getting in on the ground floor. Obsession is biological. With drugs it gets better."

"Which drug?"

"*Drugs*, the plural. Six drugs. Read our paper."

"You've published already?"

"Got to." Win raced outside, into the harsh dazzle of the April day, but instead of trailing Errol down the ravine toward the Farben, he peeled off into the dark and muscular Misery woods, motioning me not to follow. I watched him crash through brush where there didn't even seem to be one of those nature trails a grateful Misery alumna had donated for birding.

I tailed Errol down into the basement of the Farben, to "Computer Lab," and then to "ECT Suite." Errol ran the ElectroConvulsive Shock Therapy concession at Misery. Donning a space suit outside something called PET Lab, he asked me, "Do you have a dog?"

"No. Why?"

"This is a PET scanner."

"You scan your pets?"

"Positron Emission Tomography." He vanished into a room with a huge tubelike chamber, the size of a coffin for a dolphin. Dry ice vapors misted up. Errol and a lab tech in a space suit banged on it, tapped it, shouted at each other across it. In response it emitted a purple glow like you see in movies when the aliens arrive. Nearby I heard pitiful barking and whining, and peeked around a corner at row upon row of dogs in small cages.

Suddenly we were moving through the lunch line. Errol took enormous portions of all the worst foods—hamburgers and french fries and fried onion rings and Schlomo's favorite, "Misery Mystery Meat," and Swiss cheese and cheesecake and refined sugar. He seemed to be on a high-fat, high-cholesterol, high-sugar diet. I started to follow him to his table but he said he wanted to eat alone. As he ate, he made call after call on his cellular phone. Gloria sat down with me.

"Who's he calling?"

"His private patients. Drug consults. A hundred bucks a shot."

"But he's eating lunch!"

"Awesome, isn't it? You make good money, in drugs."

As we talked I was amazed at Gloria's healthy outlook on life in Misery. Despite having worked with the most violent and psychotic people in the harsh world of the hospital for many years, she seemed peaceful, appreciative of life. After barely nine months here I was cynical and worn. I asked her how she managed it.

Her eyes flickered away. Malik had said that this was a sign of a person about to tell you a lie. "To tell you the truth, Roy," she said—another sign of lying— "I guess I'm just a pretty happy camper."

After lunch, Errol let me sit in on his private practice. His office was on the top floor of the Farben, with a fantastic view of the panorama unrolling to the north, where the line of white smudges on the horizon was maybe snow on the mountaintops, maybe clouds. The office too was a kind of museum of the drug trade, everything "Courtesy of" somebody, from the Brazilian-leather couch and chairs courtesy of Ciba-Geigy/Brazil, through the immense rosewood desk courtesy of Smith-Kline/Thailand, to a tiny working model of the blood supply to the human brain, bubbling and gurgling bright red cartoon blood in through the arteries and draining sludgy blue venous blood out through the veins, the lips contorting, seemingly at random, into kisses or smiles, with a flashing sign that said, "Zoloft Keeps You Aloft."

A series of well-heeled patients marched in, one after the other. Errol spent at most ten minutes with each and treated each exactly the same way: asking about their drugs—usually they were on three to six drugs—side effects, improvements, and then adding or subtracting drugs before saying good-bye. He asked a question or two about their symptoms. He asked nothing about their psychological state. The patients were treated with a courteous benevolence, like, say, good dogs.

It was astonishing to see how, being treated with total, authoritarian objectivity, they responded with total, submissive gratitude. Errol gave the impression of being absolutely *sure*. While he was sure about everything, he addressed but one thing: drugs. If his patients wanted to talk diagnosis, he talked drugs. If they wanted to talk symptoms, he talked drugs. Stress? Drugs. Suffering? Drugs. Family problems? Drugs. Job? Drugs. The love, yes, the adulation his patients felt for Errol was palpable. How could they love him? They could love him because not only did he convey to them that he was sure about their drugs, and, by implication, about all the other things they mentioned—diagnosis, symptoms, stress, suffering, family, job—but in addition he always said to each patient at the end of the ten-minute interview:

"This will make you feel wonderful and make you *better.*"

Most patients loved hearing this and thanked him.

A rare patient might ask, "Are you sure?"

"Absolutely. This will make you feel wonderful and make you *better.*"

Virtually everyone got an antidepressant, often Prozac, and a pseudoamphetamine, often Ritalin. Errol regarded these drugs with contempt. "Placedon makes Prozac look like popcorn, Zephyrill makes Ritalin look like Rice Krispies. *Family* doctors prescribe Prozac—a 'mood brightener,' Clairol for your brain. Cosmetic psychopharm, like nose jobs. Prozac's like pissin' in the wind, and Ritalin's like vending machine coffee." Most patients also walked out on Placedon and/or Zephyrill, giving a baseline total of four drugs. Not that Errol was dogmatic. As long as a patient wanted a drug, he didn't much care which drug it was. Many patients, having heard of drugs other patients were on—family or friends, or patients they met in Errol's waiting room—would come in and ask Errol for a prescription for the same drug they'd heard of. Errol congratulated them on the wisdom of their choice and wrote them a "scrip." As a fiercely cheery Lilly saleswoman had once told me, "Prozac sales topped two billion last year!"

The most heart-wrenching were the children.

Parents would bring their children in.

The children would always go out on Ritalin, and sometimes on Prozac.

Errol was doing his best to add to the 1.5 million American schoolchildren who were now on Ritalin, in a way a kind of speed, to treat something, some "disease," that hadn't even much existed five years before.

Over the course of the year, especially by working with Malik, for most people I'd come to see many of the lesser psychiatric drugs—especially Ritalin and Prozac and Zoloft and the other serotonin-uptake inhibitors—as symptoms. They were symptoms of the disconnections in the society, symptoms that in fact increased the disconnections, which led to more Ritalin and Prozac and newer versions of the same. Especially with kids, it was obvious that the cure was in creating the connections, not in giving them drugs that disconnected them further, and destroyed them. But that was more difficult, and hey—Errol was considerate: for the really young ones, he gave them their Ritalin in an elixir.

Finished with his private practice, Errol shot to his feet and bolted for the parking lot. Trying to keep up with him, I screamed out, "But a lot of them come back from their last visit with you *not* better."

"And then I give 'em a new drug and it makes 'em feel wonderful and *better.*"

"But what if it doesn't make them better?"

"I try a newer drug. Let's go!"

"Don't you ever run out of drugs?"

"You never run out of *mixtures*. Principle of 'the Drug Cocktail'—c'*mon*!"

The gull wings of his red Ferrari spread up and out as if just dying to catch the alluring spring breeze. A bumper sticker read:

RESEARCH TAKES BRAINS,
DONATE YOURS. CALL
1-900-BRAIN BANK.

"Nice car," I said. The seat welcomed my body like a perfect orthotic a foot.

"Ferrari Mondial. Sterling/Italia cut me a deal. Only 197 K."

"Still a lot."

"Not if you maximize your billability. Everything you saw, I bill for. Ten minutes, a hundred bucks. Ten bucks a billable minute."

"It's mind-boggling."

"No, it's modern psychiatry. Your little 'talk therapy' is now a minor subspecialty. A hundred twenty an hour, tops. Chump change. No cars like this. Managed care and insurance won't pay for talk. They pay for drugs. Pretty soon they won't even bother to teach you residents how to talk anymore. I sit on the President's National Health Care Task Force. The government doesn't believe in talk. It believes in drugs. If my patients want to talk, I send 'em to a social worker. Cheaper, and better. Placebo effect. No cars like this. Drugs aren't just a career, they're a lifestyle."

He slipped us into gear. The Ferrari growled along at the Misery 15 mph limit angrily, as if there were a hundred hungry Italians under the hood, late for their *primo piatto*.

"You bill for everything?" I asked.

"Everything," he said, dialing his car phone.

"Even the patients on the wards?" He nodded. "But you didn't see them."

"I saw them. You saw them too." He was talking into a patient's machine.

"You saw them, but you didn't meet with them, or talk with them."

"Saw enough to bill 'em. Saw their charts. You want to see something? See my alimony. I'm working on the wife from hell number three."

"But it's illegal," I said as we crept growling up to the wrought-iron gate out of Misery, "to bill insurance without actually seeing the pa—yeow!"

He'd hit the accelerator and suddenly the occipital lobes of my brain seemed to have flattened against the back side of my skull. My eyeballs flattened back against their sockets. The road blurred. I caught a whiff of swamp gas. Suddenly he downshifted and I was thrown forward. My frontal lobe crashed against my maxillary sinus, my eyeballs against my lids. Nausea.

We were passing under a falling-down arch and growling along again through the neglected mud and debris of the grounds of what looked like a medieval fortress: all turrets, walls, and pointed spires in stark relief against the suddenly lowering sky—we were in Candlewood State Hospital. Errol also owned the drug and shock concession at this state facility and was in charge of our first-year resident Misery rotation there—one morning a week for a month—which Schlomo Dove had demanded, as a token gesture to the Great Unwashed.

The contrast with Misery couldn't have been more stark. In place of manicured grounds and pointed fresh brick, here were crumbling walls and dumping grounds. I raced Errol into his office, the desk and furniture classic public sector, cheap alloy and imitation wood, the air thick with the stench of stale overtime, which brought back the memories of my long nights on the graveyard shift as a toll collector on the Rip van Winkle Bridge over the Hudson, back in Columbia. Errol was furiously signing a pile of state documents, in triplicate. I asked what he was doing.

"Signing discharges. The governor is cleaning this shitbox out."

"Discharges to where?"

"To wherever. Nobody cares about these people anymore."

"But you haven't even seen them."

"What the fuck's with you with this *seeing*? Take these keys to the wards. Get an education in the public sector. I leave in one hour."

I wandered long corridors, peering into empty wards. At first the doors were labeled ACUTE MEN'S 1, or ACUTE WOMEN'S 3. As I walked farther into the fortress, suddenly I was in CHRONIC. I peered into a ward that seemed full, CHRONIC WOMEN'S 9. I unlocked the huge door and went in.

It was like walking into a nightmare, a ring of hell. Filling the ward were forty women in ratty, stained hospital johnnies. Some were twitching and walking. A few were smoking, and a line of women trailed after each smoker. As I watched, one smoker finished and threw the butt on the linoleum. The other women dived for it and fought over it. The smoker turned and watched the scramble. Her fingers, where she had grasped the cigarette, were stained by the nicotine—not tan, or brown, but black, pitch-black. Lying on ripped couches, some women were masturbating. An old woman was repeatedly taking her nightie off over her head, as if getting ready for the day, and flashing pendulous withered breasts and a scraggly thicket of gray pubic hair before putting it back on, as if getting ready for the night. Several women were praying, crossing themselves, and another was blessing them.

The room was filled with a stench of feces and urine and sweat. Four staff members, all women of color, were sitting at a rickety table playing cards, occasionally glancing at a soap opera on a TV set screwed high up on a yellow-green wall and protected from assault by thick wire mesh. As I watched I heard, "In a moment, back to *One Life to Live*."

Seeing me, some of the chronic women shrank back, but some came toward me, so that I caught the stench close up. Their eyes were both dull and wild. A few clutched at me, or picked at my clothes like starved but wary birds at a blueberry bush. I fled to the nursing station. A broad-beamed, gray-haired woman, dressed in a plaid skirt and white blouse, looked at me with a startled expression on her wide friendly face.

"Who are you?" she asked.

"I'm a doctor."

"What are *you* doing here?"

"I'm from Mount Misery, doing my rotation here. One morning a week."

"Doctors never come back here, to Chronic. Except for one other young doctor, a few years ago, from Mount Misery."

"Malik?"

"Yes! Wonderful person. He had us all doing *sports*!" I laughed with her. "His wife Bronia works here, on Ironwood, the Children's Unit. I'm Mrs. Kondrath-Robb." We chatted. After a while she said, "Some of these women have been here forty years. No one comes to see them anymore. They can't survive anywhere else."

I glanced at my watch. "I have to go."

"Come back whenever you want. These aren't animals. These are people too." She walked with me through the clutch of insanity to the door. Once out of Chronic, I took deep breaths of the less fetid air of the corridor, and ran all the way back to Errol. I was utterly demoralized, not only by the sight of the patients but also by Mrs. Kondrath-Robb's reply to my "I'm a doctor":

"What are *you* doing here?"

Good question.

"YOU GOTTA DOG?" Win asked me, at the end of the day in his office in the lower bowel of the Misery labs, in the basement of the Farben. A big, aged, Siberian husky lay amidst the piles of papers and journals, licking his hock repeatedly. He looked sick. An old mainframe computer filled one wall, its two fat tape spools like the eyes of a cartoon clown. A desktop computer was clacking under Win's sculpted fingers.

"No," I said, "why?" I peered over his shoulder at the computer screen:

> Dogs were sought with chronic ALD for an 11-week drug treatment study. Notices were placed in veterinary newsletters. Dog groomers were also alerted.

"We need dogs for our study, on chronic ALD—Acral Lick Dermatitis. Where they lick themselves silly, causing lesions. See? Hey, Van Dusky!" The husky raised his head. Where he had been licking was red and raw, ulcerative and oozing. "ALD happens mostly with big dogs, like Van Dusky here."

"Your dog?"

"My nephew's. We're sure ALD in dogs has the same biological cause as OCD in humans. Got two grants to prove it. NIMH, National Institute of Mental Health, and Glücksspiel Apotheke Ltd., Düsseldorf."

"Why study dogs?"

"Because they have no psychology. Prove it in dogs, you prove it's biological. Prove a drug in dogs, you can use it in humans, especially kids."

"Kids?"

"OCD is big in kids. Biological. Besides, you can get their brains."

"Kids?"

"Dogs. Coupla weeks of Placedon and Zephyrill, Van Dusky here is *better*."

"That's better? He looks awful."

"Better. My nephew says, quote, 'He seems like a puppy again.' We count the licks." The clown eyes on the mainframe spun and numbers rolled out. "Win, you hot shit you!" he cried, and sprinted out the door and down the hall. I followed. A sign on a door cried out: STEREOTACTIC BRAIN SURGERY. KEEP OUT. The room was tiled on all six surfaces. There was a big sucking drain in the floor. "Why all the tile?"

"Used to be used for 'hydrotherapy,' " he said, his words echoing hollowly. "They used to throw lunatics in here and hose 'em down with water. Back then they knew nothing. They thought that the hosing helped. Fools."

He sprinted out up the tunnel. I sprinted after.

Back on the West, as I tried to catch my breath, he ripped through charts as fast as possible, one after another, signing his name to new drug orders. As I watched I heard screams behind me, breaking the sepulchral stillness of the ward:

"I'm a kernel of corn you're chickens you want to eat me you killers ahh!"

A wild-eyed man was running toward the Dutch doors, which Deedee the nurse adroitly slammed in his face so he went splat against the Plexiglas wall, although he kept trying to rip at it with his fingernails as if it were chicken wire. Quicker than I would have thought possible a goon squad of four anabolic mental health workers—three men and a woman—pounced on him, stabbed him with a hypodermic, and carried him away to the Quiet Room.

Beside me a door opened and Gloria poked her head out to check on the commotion. She was half out of her nursing uniform, going off shift. A white bra, a tiny pink bow in the cleft. Covering herself, she said, "Oh hi, Roy. He's a chicken farmer from Maine. Delusional. Thinks he's a kernel of corn, and that we're all chickens. Talk about crazy. We're using drugs and behavior modification. He'll stay in the Quiet Room till tomorrow."

"Good to know."

"See you around the campus, Roy."

On the ward, the other patients stared after their lost member briefly, and then continued sleeping or pacing or twitching, as if what had happened was a slight petulation far out on a sea, nothing to do with them, and now that it was done, something that had not ever happened at all, really. Like a child in a night-terror, screaming lucidly at you, who will remember nothing you or she said, in the morning.

Win took no notice of any of this. As he worked, he sang the Scarecrow's song from *The Wizard of Oz*, ending with the wistful line: ". . . if I only had a brain."

Finished with his paperwork, he popped up to his feet and ran out. I followed.

It was raining softly, the kind of rain that reminds you of the optimism of tulips and the fearlessness of daffodils. In the parking lot Win clicked open a big, new, silver Porsche and got in.

"Wait!" I called out to him.

"Don't have time. I moonlight at a shockbox upstate. Ring the doorbell, get your first shock treatment. Ha ha. Due at the shockbox in an hour. I bury the needle at one fifty on the interstate."

"But it's about OCD."

"Now you're talkin'." He stopped dead still, all ears. "Fire away."

"What about love?"

"Love?"

"You think that being in love is biological?"

"You bet. It's an obsession and a compulsion."

"Love is OCD?"

"And we're about to prove it, thanks to Glücksspiel and NIMH."

"With dogs?"

"Y'got one?"

"No. Thank God you're not working on monkeys."

"Yeah, I know. Monkeys cost the earth!" He drove off.

I stood there, the rain drumming harder on my bare head, noticing that I'd been staring at a red Geo. Solini's car. It had been vandalized, the tires taken, the eyes bashed in. Where was he? It was so sad!

I shivered. It was as if I'd been slipped a drug cocktail, mostly horror, but with a twist of delight. Horror at what I'd seen, but delight at how easy my rotation with the drug boys could be. As a doctor, I knew how to use drugs, how easy it was even to throw the *right* drug at a problem, let alone the wrong one. Using drugs in psychiatry was easier than using drugs in medicine, where you had real effects to measure—blood pressure, cancer cells in bone marrow, heartbeat. In psychiatry there was nothing much to measure with certainty, so you didn't really know what you were treating, and couldn't know if the treatment worked. All year long I'd prescribed drugs for my really depressed or psychotic or manic patients, often with good results. There were only about six kinds of drugs that helped psychiatry patients without hurting them. Drug therapy in psychiatry was mostly a no-brainer. The West would be a rest.

Despite all the death on my mind, just then the rain was a spring rain, soft and promising.

But then I heard the sorry wail of an ambulance approaching. It came in fast and stopped nearby, sliding off the gravel onto the grass.

The doors popped open. White-clad men got out, the last Dr. Errol Cabot.

They started hustling a stretcher out, one man holding an IV bottle high like on a TV show. Unlike on TV, the IV tube snagged on something, and someone shouted "Stop, you asshole, stop!" The stretcher stopped in its movement out, and the head slid off the edge, tipping down, jaw up like Oly Joe Olaf's on that couch. Fearing the body would slide off and plunge onto the gravel, I ran to it and clutched it. I saw the ghost of a face I knew.

"Lily Putnam?"

"You know her?" Errol asked.

"Her husband was my patient."

"Oh yeah, the suicide, okay."

Lily seemed hardly to be breathing; her face looked like stone.

"Hey, retards!" Errol was screaming at the flustered meditechs. "Get the lead out! I'm late!"

"She looks horrible!" I said. "What happened?"

"She's suicidal. She's an involuntary admission. I pink-papered her."

"Did she make a suicide attempt?"

"Not yet. Dr. Schlomo Dove said she was about to. He called us, and signed a ten-day paper, committing her to us."

"Schlomo, an analyst, signed her in for drug treatment?"

"Which is what she needed all along. The gal's endogenously depressed. Needs meds. Live better pharmaceutically."

"She looks terrible."

"Yeah and soon she'll feel wonderful and be *better*. I'm running in drugs now. IV, Placedon and Zephyrill. Principle of synergism. Two drugs better than one, three better than two, and so forth. Magic bullets."

"But she's totally zonked out."

"Better than being totally dead. Okay, men, ready? Move 'er out."

I watched them wrassle the stony body up the granite stairs into the West. My heart turned sharply on its spindle, fruit pecked at by crows.

My father's dead.

His face in his coffin, compared to his face in his life, looked better. Calmer, yes. He looked more alive, dead. All these deaths. I had a hit of pain that took my breath away.

I hesitated to breathe in again, for it seemed that any real breath in would break my heart.

Fifteen

LILY, THE NEXT DAY, was still too drugged up to talk to me.

In her chart was a brief note written by Dr. Schlomo Dove saying that ever since the suicide of her husband Cherokee, she herself had been threatening to commit suicide. Thus when she refused hospitalization, he had enlisted Dr. Errol Cabot to go to her home with an ambulance and a ten-day paper to commit her involuntarily to Mount Misery.

Dr. Errol Cabot had diagnosed her as "296.34, Major Depressive Disorder, Recurrent, with Psychotic Features which are Mood-incongruent." He noted that she met seven of the eight criteria, including depressed mood, insomnia and hypersomnia, decrease in sex drive, feelings of worthlessness or excessive or inappropriate guilt, psychomotor agitation and retardation, diminished ability to think and concentrate, and recurrent thoughts of death. The one she did not meet was weight loss when not dieting or weight gain, which I noted was the only symptom you could actually measure on a real scale.

To me, these symptoms were appropriate. The woman's husband had just blasted his brains all over a bird sanctuary. She'd just learned that he'd been having an affair, and maybe killed himself because he thought *she* was. Who wouldn't think of suicide, given all that? Yet she had never made a suicide gesture or attempt. Something didn't fit.

Under "Treatment," Errol had inserted into the chart a Xerox copy of his standardized drug protocol, or "algorithm." I was to learn that he inserted the same protocol into every chart, since he used it on every patient. The protocol was a diagrammed drug flowchart decision tree, developed by NIMH and IPAP (International Psychopharm Algorithm Project), which looked, to my eyes, remarkably similar to the flowchart I had seen on Toshiba where the computer led you out onto thinner and thinner branches until you were out on a limb alone with the correct DSM diagnosis, or the flowchart for Misery itself, where the pathetic Nash and cute Jennifer were enboxed and dangling by a thread somewhere below Chief Lloyal von Nott, making the hospital seem like nothing so much as a Calder mobile made up of real live human beings in cages. And are there flowcharts of every institution, I wondered, and, in the Oval Office, a Flowchart for America?

Errol's chart showed the flow of a total of thirty-four drugs to be used, alone or in cocktails, one after the other, flowing into each patient's body until something worked, or didn't.

I was soon to see just how simple this treatment was. In addition to Placedon and Zephyrill, Errol and Win would give each patient drugs that were either antipsychotic, anti-anxiety, antidepression, or anti-the-side-effects-of-the-other-drugs drugs. If one drug failed, they'd move on to another, or add another on. Almost every patient ended up on a six-drug cocktail. Since the six drugs had to be given on different schedules—from once a day to five a day—there was always a nurse in the Dutch door handing out drugs. She would check the mouth to make sure the pill hadn't been tongued, and then say, "This'll make you *better*."

What if, by the end of the six-drug bingo up to a grand total of the thirty-four drugs the patient was *not* better? There, in the lower-left-hand corner of the protocol, in a small box in print you needed a magnifier to read, was:

Discharge to social worker, for Placebo Talk Therapy.

Taped to the cover of Lily Putnam's chart was a handwritten sign: NARC.

"Narcotics?" I asked Errol as he raced out the door to shock people.

"Not A Resident Case. Stay the fuck away, Frank."

"My name is Roy."

"Learn the name of one more resident," he said, "you forget the name of one more drug. Stay away."

"Why? Why can't I see her?"

"*See?* What the fuck is this, a residency in ophthalmology? Go away."

"What about the other patients? You mind if I go see them?"

"Why?"

"To listen to their stories, to try to understand them."

"Oh Jesus." He nodded at Win. "He wants to understand 'em. To listen."

"OH JESUS!" Win shouted.

"These are psychotics. These brains are neurochemical theme parks. But hey, you wanna sit there and listen to 'em talk bubble bath? Be my guest."

I TRIED TO TALK with the patients. Someone had to. It wasn't easy. Either they were too crazy-hot to talk, or, doused with drugs, too cool.

Lily Putnam had been hit hard by Prozac and Ritalin and Placedon and Zephyrill, and she lay in her bed in her private room, not exactly sleeping but not exactly awake. She rose from the horizontal only to go to the bathroom and to drink liquids and take drugs. When I introduced myself, while there was a flicker of recognition, it quickly slid away under a molecular coverlet, like an ember underneath ash. No chance of suicide in Lily on drugs, no way. Nor of anything much else.

My attempts to talk with other patients were pretty much as unsuccessful. People hallucinated every imaginable thing—Christ, Hitler, the Pope, Elvis, cockroaches, dildoes, apple pie—and had tried to kill themselves in every imaginable way. Some patients were known to me. The Woman Who Ate Metal Objects was back after her last abdominal surgery, and quickly asserted her omnivorous self by eating the prosthetic pinkie of a gay psychotic plumber admitted for "phantom limb pain" who had the delusion that his real pinkie was poking up the rectum of Richard Milhous Nixon.

The patients, drugged at arm's length by their doctors, seemed less people than objects. Drugs had thinned out the essence of being human and had left them both heavier and lighter than human beings ought to be, as if a human on drugs blocked the light and yet was way too insubstantial to hold any light, to be at all luminescent, even to cast a clear shadow. It was as if you could pass your hand through them, only your hand making the shadow. But you couldn't pass your hand through them, they were so powerfully opaque. The vitality of the human had been diluted out all the way to the poverty of the translucent, leaving the steel shell of the opaque, all in the name of "better." It was appalling.

Even more appalling to me was that it was pretty much how I felt too.

What could I do? I felt so vulnerable and lost, so guilty about Cherokee and Lily, so isolated and alone, I felt myself sinking rapidly, trying my hardest merely to get out of bed in the morning and function, slipping into "full-catastrophe" mode, that is, trying to keep myself alive, and not psychotic.

ONE BEDAZZLING MID-APRIL MORNING I was sitting in the doorway of Lily Putnam's room with a Pfizer cappuccino and a DuPont brioche. Lily was asleep. I was waiting until her next dose of drugs, which would be the lowest concentration of the six drugs in her system. It was at these times that she was slightly more alert. I felt I had to make contact with her. Cherokee's delusion that she was being fucked by Schlomo was gnawing at me.

From time to time I would tune in to the Behavior Modification therapist, a short solid woman with a body like a van, a face like a hubcap, and a mind like a gearshift. Her name was Cynthia Krabkin, and she was pacing back and forth beside the psychotic chicken farmer, making him repeat over and over:

"I am *not* a kernel of corn, I am *not* a kernel of corn, I am *not* . . ."

Cynthia Krabkin's philosophy was that his repetition of this phrase a million times combined with the reward of her company might condition the chicken farmer to think he was *not* a kernel of corn. Sitting there on the quiet ward, I found this strangely comforting, a hymnal to the farmlands where men were men and women were women and animals were slaughtered and people ate red meat.

"Lily Putnam?" the nurse called out. I signaled I would bring her over.

"Lily," I said, shaking her gently. "Wake up." Startled, she stared at me. "It's me, Dr. Basch? Do you ever think of killing yourself?" She stared at me dully, and shook her head slowly, no. "Have you ever?" Another shake of the head no. "Have you ever heard voices telling you to kill yourself?" A shake of the head yes. She got up. Puzzling. Disturbing.

"Hey, Dr. Dickhead!"

I turned. Thorny? He was strapped to a stretcher being wheeled in. His clothes were in rags, his body was covered with fresh cuts and bruises, and he looked emaciated. His eyes were wild and his mouth was blaring, nonstop, a stream of consciousness sometimes making sense, mostly not:

"This dickhead's still clean Doc Zoe's in deep shit my old man is turning the Gulf to shit my mind is solid toxic waste haste makes—"

He was in the throes of a manic episode, totally psychotic. Deedee the nurse was moving toward him with a syringe, and I jumped up and got my body between her and Thorny. "Hold it," I said. "What are you doing?"

"Using the SPERT."

"What's a spurt?"

"Sub-Protocol Explaining Rapid Tranquilization."

"Which drugs?"

"I . . . I'm not sure. The SPERT drugs."

"All right. I know him. I'll take care of him myself. No SPERT."

"Yes and I'm using the SPERT—"

I grabbed his stretcher and wheeled him into the Quiet Room to talk.

It was impossible. Thorny's mind was racing, driven by a big motor, without much regard for whoever it was running at:

"Toxic Henry Solini's gone Zoe's gone to *Ecce* Schl-*homo*! Basch's in it for cash when I was up on my daddy's refinery tank down in Paradis Loosiana I heard God say 'the Dickheads Shalt Inherit the Earth.' "

Staring into his eyes, I saw myself unseen by him. As he continued to blast along, thrashing against the restraints, I sat on the floor, my back strangely comfortable against the harsh smooth white wall, and read his chart. He'd been arrested in Shreveport, Louisiana, after a fight in a music joint in the poor section called Ledbetter. His family had been after him ever since he'd been seen splashing fake blood on his father's refineries near Paradis, Louisiana, on the Mississippi south of New Orleans, and then had shown up at his trust-fund executor's house in the Garden District, badgering him for cash, having spent forty grand in ten days on a car and clothes and, they guessed, though Thorny denied it, on drugs. He'd broken into the Strand Theatre in Shreveport, a national historic opera house on whose facade was carved the motto "Progressive Amusement for Progressive People," and had recited from the stage the storm scene from *King Lear*. His father had been called, and had gotten a court order to commit him back into Misery.

While it wasn't clear what had flipped Thorny out—Zoe's abandonment of him, maybe—it was clear that he needed meds. If, as he swore on the Bible, he had not used drugs or booze on his manic trip, I knew from Malik that I had to be careful not to give him any drug that would rev up his addiction. At the minimum he needed Thorazine to cool down the manic engine, Cogentin to counter the side effects of Thorazine, and lithium. Of all the drugs I'd used in psychiatry, I had the most faith in lithium. It was a safe, natural salt that had been used for almost fifty years, and worked miracles with manics.

"I'm going to give you lithium carbonate," I said to Thorny.

"Toxic sweetheart I'm still clean and sober so don't fuck me ober!"

"Lithium's not toxic. You need it."

"No Department of Defense babies *volare* that killed that sweet lady Mary Megan Scorato?"

"No, none of them. Will you take the pills by mouth?"

"Only from a fellow dickhead check out them shoe-zers?"

I followed his glance to his feet. His Reeboks were tied tight, the rabbit ears lying peacefully across their double knot.

"You taught me that so I'm your patient you red-hot dickhead red on the head like a dick on a dog—deal?"

"Deal." He took the pills by mouth, and I left.

WELCOME TO THE

***

BEAT THE IRS PARTY

***

YOUR EXPENSES ARE TAX-DEDUCTIBLE

***

DOOR PRIZE IS A ZEPHYRILL-POWERED CHEVY NOVA!

This sign greeted Jill and me at the entrance to Errol Cabot's seaside estate. The long winding driveway through the lumpy red-streaked rocks was lined with cars, and we squeezed my old Mustang in between two tattered, seasick bushes. Loud drumming got louder as we walked toward the house, which, appearing suddenly against the empty sky, seemed as huge as an ocean liner, all wings and porches and decks and dormers and gables, shingled perfectly even over the tough angles, in classic New England fashion. The huge old mansion had been newly renovated, and the inside was less classic New England than postmodern Los Angeles. There was already a crush of people there, and Jill and I were greeted in the vast foyer by Errol and Win and two women, one a teenager of heart-wrenching beauty—Errol's newest girlfriend—the other a plainly dressed fortyish woman whose face spoke of many battles with kids and the laundry—Win's wife. Errol wore a baseball cap that read: MY WIFE RAN OFF WITH MY BEST FRIEND—AND I'LL MISS HIM!

Errol greeted us with enthusiasm, running his eyes over Jill's body, and saying, "Women are good for two things, and one thing is for lying to."

The place was packed, the drumming so loud that the talk had to be louder. I couldn't hear Jill very well, which was just as well, for the drive over had been rough, emotionally. Ever since my "weirdness" at her party, Jill had been more wary of me. My impotence had continued.

"Know what really bothers me?" Jill had said in the car. I asked what. "You seem so sure of yourself. You always have an answer for everything."

"I don't feel sure of myself at all."

"You know, Roy, most people aren't like you; they're like me—unsure of themselves, feeling, deep down, that they deserve better than they're getting in life, feeling that their life is a failure."

"Your life's not a failure, mine is."

"Look, I kind of love you, but I keep getting myself into these jams with guys, these incredible love nests that empty out in the most bizarre ways."

"Have you thought of antidepressants?"

"Yeah."

"If you want, I'll write you a prescrip—"

"But instead I'm going to the Galápagos. I leave tomorrow."

"What?" Even with my Prozac on board, said to block the brain receptors for Rejection Sensitivity, some receptors must have still been working. "With that guy?"

"Eduardo, yeah. It's a great place to see them."

"The aliens?"

"Just a bunch of rocks in the sea, and sky all around. Everywhere you look! And no one yet has been 'up' from there!"

"Don't go! I can't stand it, everybody going!"

"How sweet!" She took my hand and slipped it up her thighs smooth as a baby's bottom up and up to her panties but there were no panties and the tangle of welcome stuff was like an oasis and I flashed on how once in Morocco, south of the Atlas in the high Sahara, Berry and I had chanced upon an oasis called Source Bleu du Meski, all palms and shade and blue water that tasted of copper.

The drumming was coming from the living room. There, at least ten men, big and small, were crouched over drums, big and small, beating the shit out of them. Some men were bare-chested, some wore feathers. A few I recognized as the muscular mental health workers of the West. Against the panorama of an ocean leading all the way to Casablanca, these men seemed savage, their beating these long things between their legs a savage masturbation ritual. Coming of Age in Heidelberg? Why not?

"Robert?" shouted someone in my ear. I smelled perfume. Gloria, the head nurse of the West.

"No, Roy!" I shouted back over the drums.

"No, Robert Bly! He says men have gotten too 'soft'! They need to become 'warriors.' " Her hand was on my chest. "Robert says men need to get hard."

"By drumming?"

"That's one way. Want to take a look around the house?"

"Yeah." I searched for Jill, but she was lost in the crush of bodies. I was pulled along by Gloria room to room, a lot of body contact between us.

The house was incredible, looking out on and being looked in at by sea horizon and reddish rock. The party was not incredible at all, more frat bash than anything else. There were a lot of men in uniform—what seemed a whole destroyer full of sailors who were ripping at the women as if they hadn't been ashore for a year. The drug company reps were out in force, not only the lackeys passing out pills and pens and even condoms with the Glücksspiel Apotheke logo—a rose and two pointy-nosed dogs biting a crest—but also the corporate bosses, sacks of flesh with those fatty jowls and ears and blubbery necks and slits for eyes. Arnie Bozer was there with Blair

Heiler, the latter with his new flame, a red-haired young social worker. The pitiful Nash and the cute Jennifer were there too, sticking close together.

I followed Gloria upstairs and then upstairs again, the old steep stairs and her short steep skirt giving me full view of exactly what she wanted me to see. We stopped a few times to get drinks and eat things, then we stopped in the attic to catch our breath. A few others were there—several men and women were on the padded floor, embracing. The drumming, funneled up and bouncing around the sharply canted walls, was deafening.

"Want some chocolate cake?" Gloria shouted.

"Whose?"

"Union Carbide. It's good!"

I did, and it was good, and we shouted at each other for a while and then wandered out onto the widow's walk, where only a few other couples were. The drumming was insistent but lower down, as if in the pit of my stomach, and the view of nothing but half-moon and half-moon reflection in dark water seemed to freshen me, lighten me, and then overlighten me, for suddenly I felt light-headed and the banister seemed to become balsa wood in my hands, friable as dead skin, and the drop down to the rocks and water scary and I backed away and Gloria backed with me and I found myself, head spinning, entwined with her in a corner under the sharp elbow of a gable, her mouth an ocean her tongue a half-moon and her hands all over me and me all over her and I felt funny not funny ha-ha but funny high from the cake.

"WHAT'S THAT RACCOON doing out in the daylight?" I asked, finding myself in an overbright chilly morning, walking arm in arm with Glo along the main road of Misery. She was pressed tightly against me, and where she pressed, her body felt hot, like a feverish baby. The raccoon was stumbling along, stopping now and then to snap at something imaginary.

"He's an insomniac," she said.

"Or rabid," I said. "Or psychotic."

Like a hallucination, Lloyal von Nott, Erroll Cabot, and Win—with Beef Telly of Security protecting their rears—ran toward us, stared, ran past.

What had happened? I had only sensual memories, of Gloria stripping quickly her breasts seemingly pumped up like muscles with 'roids the nipples hard as if her spare job were as a wet nurse to a day care center and then before I could make a move she was rolling her leg over mine so that I was in her almost before I knew it was her—I had the sense that she had learned this as a preemptive strike against an impotent male since you'd have to deflate quick to avoid being in there—and the rest being bliss but for its lightness, as if it never made it to the engram stage of my biochemical memory. Where this lovemaking had taken place or how we had wound up in Misery I had no idea. I must have been slipped a drug, probably in the chocolate cake. Now my brain biochemistry was having trouble clicking back in, and I tried hard to remember who had just passed us and then said out loud, "Von Nott and Errol and Win and Mr. Telly?" and turned and saw I was right.

And where was Jill?

We came to the Heidelbergs. Glo, now demure, said, "Gotta go, Roy."

"I'm going home to bed."

"Sleep tight. Can't wait till you come in."

Suddenly there floated into my mind a bumper sticker I'd seen just a little while before when Glo and I had been driving up to Misery:

A TISKET, A TASKET,
A CONDOM OR A CASKET

Floating away from Glo, I realized that I had taken no precautions with her. Then with horror I realized I wasn't at all horrified about contracting AIDS and being dead.

Sixteen

ONE EARLY MAY EVENING, the kind of misty evening whose soft twilight and scent of moist earth and easing sky makes you feel that despite everything life is worth living, I was on call. Spring brought back memories of spring the year before, with Berry in Lago del Orta in northern Italy, and the memory challenged any notion that in a year I had made progress in my life. At this very moment lovers were rowing out to the island—the tiny island with its fairy-tale castle and cobbled lanes and no cars—but I was alone, and let's face it, when I felt anything through my drug cocktail, I was feeling so lonely and isolated that I wondered whether death could be any worse than this washed-out version of life.

That night I was taking a shortcut through the basement to pick up my beeper at Viv's when I passed STEREOTACTIC BRAIN SURGERY: KEEP OUT and noticed that the red light was on and the sign "Operation in Progress" was lit. I eased open the door and peered in at the operating room in the tiled cube that had once been a chamber of hydrotherapy.

Win Winthrop was dressed all in green, but for a red forelock thrusting out from under his shower cap like a cockscomb on a cartoon rooster. He was drilling a hole in a skull. His lips were pursed, either in concentration or because he was whistling. I went in. The sound was revolting, both because of the volume at which it sang off the tiled shower walls and because it was drilling into bone. There was a smell of burning flesh and bone that reminded me of my father the dentist. Win Winthrop, doing brain surgery on people?

But no. There is a God. Twitching under the green sheet was a leg, a dog's leg, with a raw lesion on it, licked down to bone, festering. A dog.

Win saw me and stopped drilling. "Go away."

"What are you doing?"

"Psychosurgery."

"On your nephew's dog? On Van Dusky?"

"Gonna make him *better*."

"But what does your nephew say?" No answer. "Cutting into his brain?"

"Stereotactic. You drill just this one little hole. Needles and electric current and gamma rays. No knife. No blood. No blood that you can see."

"But where did you learn how to do this?"

"Got this book." He pointed the drill at a big book open on the dog's back: *How to Do Brain Surgery. Volume I: Dogs.*

"What does your nephew say?" He fired up the drill. "Lobotomy," I shouted, "is a crime!"

"The Nobel Prize!" he screamed over the scream of the drill.

"You think you're gonna win the Nobel Prize for *lobotomy*?"

"Somebody already *won* for lobotomy, in 1949. We'll win it for Placedon and Zephyrill, you watch!"

SITTING WITH VIV behind the bulletproof, at eight-thirty that night, I was handling calls from the outside world, and talking. Rather, she was talking. I was too depressed to talk.

"You are really really depressed, Cowboy."

"You should see it from this side."

"Hey, I have." She smiled and took my hand. "Don't worry, it's just a passing phase. Those bozos in drugs would make anybody feel depressed."

"What are you on?"

"On?"

"What drugs?"

"None, Cowboy, why?"

" 'Cause you're happy."

She stared at me, those blue eyes under those long false lashes under that slick forehead and beehive bouffant seeming far away. This may have been a side effect of my new drug cocktail for the night: I'd added a hit of Ritalin to my Prozac. And one of those Placedon capsules big as the class ring on Errol's pinkie. Everything seemed tropical.

Then, there he was, gliding along on the other side of the glass, like a fish in an aquarium tank. "Malik?" I said.

He glanced at us. His eyes were red. "Got the flu. S'long."

He looked pale and gray. His black hair was less slicked and less sharply parted than usual, his face was glistening with sweat, and his white tie lay loosely on his purple shirt. He seemed exhausted, and for the first time ever he was moving slowly.

"Have you seen a doctor?"

He stopped and turned back to us. "Y'really know how to hurt a guy."

"C'mon in, Lucky," Viv said, "have a cup a tea?"

"Tea?" He licked his lips. "No thanks." He floated away, past the edge of the bulletproof glass. I thought about going after him, but he'd told me to burn his number. I was afraid I'd be opening up something too big to ever close down, so I just sat there.

"You two have a fallin'-out?" Viv asked.

"Yeah."

"What about?"

I tried to get my brain to sort this out so I could tell her but it seemed stuck in neutral and I just said, "Hard to even remember, right now."

"Yeah, well it's a bad sign, Cowboy."

"My brain?"

"I was thinkin' more of Lenny. I never once saw him leave the Misery Loves Company meetin' early. Never the once."

THE LONG NIGHT on call had been hard and easy both. Hard for the number of frantic people out there calling in who, like me, seeing the splendor of the year's May, felt mocked, still stuck as they were in the hellish February of their lives. Easy because of my Prozac'd distance from their pain. To sleep, I'd added a couple of Valium.

At four-thirty in the morning I was beeped awake to suture up a cutter on Rokitansky, Geriatrics. I felt so fuzzy from the Prozac-Placedon-Valium cocktail that to start my engine again I popped two more Ritalins as I walked up the hill past Toshiba through the dewy promise of a dawn. The Ritalins snapped me to attention long enough to suture the facial gash of the fallen geriatric, but as I walked back to the Farben I felt really weird, as if in my high Prozac cloud an alien from the planet Ritalin were speeding along creating a turbulence. My attention was deficient, my perception askew and spinning, like at a carnival when you first get off the Tilt-A-Whirl.

I found myself approaching Schlomo Dove's door and saw that it was open a crack. I looked at my watch: five-seventeen. What the hell was he doing here?

Ever since Ike White had died and Schlomo had taken over the prestigious position of Director of Residency Training, Schlomo had always told us residents that "Schlomo's door is always open." It never had been, so this time I pushed the door all the way open.

Across the room on the analytic couch was a naked woman on her hands and knees, her breasts hanging down, her back arched like a cat, and behind her pumping away against her so that his belly made slaps against her rump, was a naked Schlomo Dove. For a second he didn't see me. She turned her head. Our eyes met. It was Zoe. Seeing her turn her head, Schlomo turned his. In her eyes was horror. In his, rage. The two of them seemed frozen together, a pornographic ice sculpture.

Zoe collapsed on her belly, hiding her face in her hands.

Schlomo, penis encased in a condom and hanging below his belly like a surgical afterthought, jumped up and slammed the door in my face.

A dead bolt was thrown. The door was locked.

I stood there, head spinning, even in the first few seconds asking myself, Did I really see what I saw?—already doubting it. I knew full well what I had seen, but I didn't know if I could bear seeing it, or knowing it, really.

That night I spent with Gloria the head nurse. Glo fit my mood perfectly, as she was not particularly interested in it. Our lovemaking took place in pitch-black, soundlessly, on drugs. I got up to go to the bathroom in the middle of the night and found that her medicine cabinet was as chock full of drugs as a suburban freezer is with food.

After she left for work, I got out of bed and went to the medicine cabinet. Many of the drugs were easily lethal. I pocketed a bottle of barbiturates—phenobarb 30 mg.—and left. When I got home I took one pill.

TWENTY-FOUR HOURS LATER I awoke from a dreamless sleep, my best damn sleep in the eleven months since I'd come to Misery. It was like that blissful sleep of childhood when one moment your head is hitting the pillow in the scary dark and next thing you know there's your mom pulling up the shade and it's light.

Is this like death? I wondered, searching through the fuzz for coffee.

It took a whole pot of coffee and three Ritalins to burn off the fuzz.

In my mailbox from the day before was a postcard featuring a turtle—one of those bow-legged turtles that look like cartoon cowboys—being ridden by a girl in a bikini. The caption read: "Galápagos Giant Turtle of Pre-history."

In Jill's schoolgirlish handwriting, all loops and circles, was:

Weather here, wish you were beautiful.
Seen nothing yet but trying to see.
Love and XXX Jill.

Who cared.

My father is dead who cared.

Seventeen

"THEY GO OUT SEAMLESS." Ike White and A.K. and Poppa Doc had told me that.

"What makes one person kill themselves and another not?" This was the question that Mo Ali, A. K. Lowell's little boy, had asked.

Now I knew the answer: It's this, this big disconnect.

I was not in good shape. I was taking a phenobarb before I went to work and taking two at night. Already my liver enzymes had revved up to metabolize the barbiturate so that I needed a stronger dose for the same effect, the essential feature of an addiction. I needed the higher dose now to sleep. To forget my failures, to try to deny what I'd seen. I was still in shock at having seen—or thinking I'd seen—Schlomo and Zoe. It was too heavy, and I was too depressed to try to do anything about it. I thought of confronting Schlomo, or calling Zoe, or telling someone else, but it was just too heavy. It lay there in my mind next to Cherokee, with all the surprising weight you feel when for the first time in your life you try to lift up a dead body. Deadweight.

There were some successes on the West. If a patient was lucky enough to have bad insurance and got out quick, discharged to a local psychiatrist or a family doctor who had some common sense, things might go well. Patients who stayed any length of time were doomed. The further into the topiary maze of six-drug Marienbad they traveled, the harder it was to find their way back out. Errol and Win killed a lot of patients, in a number of different ways, and they didn't seem to care.

One of the worst drug runs, for me, was Thorny.

Errol quickly ran him through the drug protocol, thirteen drugs one after another, with no luck—what Thorny, in a rare lucid moment, called "Thirteen-drug Mardi Gras." Then, because he had failed drugs, Thorny was deemed "a good candidate for shock." He and I were both against it. His legal guardian, the Burn King of the Bayous, was all for it. So one day, after adding a Valium to my war chest, I went with Thorny down to Errol's ECT concession in the Farben basement.

I expected ghoulish, but got garish. The shock room was like a spare bedroom of a split-level ranch, with silk flowers and prints of red-coated men riding to hounds. The shockbox itself was disguised to look like a stereo receiver.

"They gonna kill me?" Thorny said, lying down, clutching my hand.

"Nope. This is safer than street drugs."

"Gonna turn me into psychobroccoli?" I said not. "If I die, tell Zoe I love her. And tell the Burn King that too?"

"Deal."

Dr. Miles Wucov and Nurse Wic slipped in an IV and placed electrodes sweetly on his temples. Then they ran in Pentothal, a barbiturate.

"Holy shit," Thorny said, "what a fantastic high and—" and he was out.

When he was out everything changed. Wucov and Wic, Argentinians, clattered on in Spanish. Cheerily, they paralyzed him with succinylcholine, pumped oxygen into his mouth, and whipped big leather horse straps down across his body. They shoveled a tongue blade between his teeth. Wucov hit the button once, twice. Thorny, drugged up, didn't convulse as much physically as, it appeared to me, he convulsed in his aura. It was as if he too had been made suddenly translucent and one hand of death had passed through him quickly, taking stock for the future, weighing what was now lost and how much would be left, throwing a shadow. Quicker than I'd expected, it was over and he was coming to.

I sat with him in recovery while other "good candidates for shock" got theirs. He was so dazed he didn't remember what day it was or what month. The thing he did remember was the Pentothal. Thorny's first words to me were:

"What a high! Gotta get me some mo'a that shit! Catch ya later—"

"Hold it." It wasn't hard to keep him from leaving, as his body seemed to have lost substance, some vital stuff stolen by that hand passing through.

But from that morning on, all Thorny could talk about was his craving for drugs. Downers had been his drug of choice. He'd been clean for nine months, but now the barbiturates had revved up his addiction. His insane craving, coupled with his loss of memory, put him at tremendous risk, if he were to escape. Well, I thought, at least they'll end it here, with Thorny a failure at both thirteen-drug lotto and electroshock therapy. Now he fits in the little box for turf to social worker, for Placebotalk. They won't try anything else to harm him, like changing his diagnosis and shipping him upstairs.

They changed his diagnosis and shipped him upstairs. Thorny's obsession with the drugs he'd been given for shock treatment soon got him diagnosed as Obsessive Compulsive Disorder, the newly fashionable OCD. He was turfed upstairs to West Ward 2 with the handwashers and the famous financier who scratched his rump incessantly. They started him on a new OCD six-drug roulette, at which he soon failed. Now, I thought, surely he'd be turfed to social worker, to talk. Even they would not shock him some more.

They shocked him some more. Now it was against his will, and not allowing me to come with him. Thorny resisted with maniacal strength, but six steroidal mental health workers wrassled him onto a stretcher and tranquilized him and wheeled him along to the Farben, where Wucov and Wic did their fandango on his brain. Thorny was on a once-a-day schedule for these blue jolts, and so rather than have to cart him back and forth, they converted part of the dog lab into a Quiet Room, and he lay there between toastings, tied down in four-point restraints, the horror of his isolation made monstrous by the reverberations off tile of the whining, barking, caged sacrificial dogs. They blasted him with enough watts to light up Mandan, North Dakota, Solini's hometown. I took it on myself to be his medical doctor, making sure he was physically all right. Sometimes, after a particularly vitriolic shock session, I stayed with him most of the night. The only tangible result of all this wattage was an increase in his barbiturate craving. When he spoke, all he said was, "I gotta get out, and get high."

All this was orchestrated by Errol, who never once talked to Thorny in person. Errol billed Thorny's father for these daily nontalks at $150 per thirty-minute session. It was a perfect scam: Thorny's memory was shot. He never remembered who came to see him, or when. Errol pulled the scam with psychotics as well. He could always claim that since they hallucinated him when he wasn't there, they could hallucinate him not there when he was. As Malik had said, "They cheat on everything: billing, taxes, research data, and wives." I focused my attention on doing the minimum, keeping Thorny safe, waiting until he was a clear treatment failure and they turfed him to talk. My only worry was that Thorny would escape. I bugged Errol about this incessantly. Mindful of being sued by a rich Burn King, Errol wrote orders for incredible surveillance of Thorny. Errol said, "One thing you can be sure of, Frank: Thorny will *not* escape."

Thorny escaped. There was no sawing through bars with a sharpened

Misery knife, no bedsheets out a window, no slow crawl through a heating duct, no tunneling under, no Hollywood horseshit, no. Rather, one of Solini's Jamaicans whom Thorny had jammed with, when asked by Thorny to let him out to get some cigarettes, obliged. Without a memory, without money, and with a revved-up addiction to barbiturates, Thorny was sure to use street drugs, and meet disaster.

It was only after he had escaped that I understood how lucky it was that he had. The next day, next to the cappuccino machine, I found a thick, well-worn book: *How to Do Brain Surgery. Volume II: Humans*. On a pink Post-it note tab stuck into the chapter on "Thalamic Lesions and OCD" was:

> Errol: It says here cingulectomy is the treatment of choice for irresponsive *[sic]* OCD. It worked on Van Dusky, why not with ole Thorny? Let me know. Win.

I had no idea what I could do about any of this. I buried my care in silence. You'd have to have a heart of stone, to see all this and not feel it. I was not feeling it much. My heart may well have been stone. I had told no one about my seeing Schlomo fucking Zoe. Since then I'd begun to doubt myself even more. Did I really see what I saw? Could there be some other explanation? Fatigue? Side effect of one of the drugs I was on? Could it have been not Zoe but a Zoe look-alike whom Schlomo had been dating without the Barracuda's knowledge?

But of course seeing Zoe being fucked by Schlomo in therapy made me realize that in all likelihood Lily Putnam was being fucked by Schlomo in therapy too. Cherokee had even imagined the same position I'd seen: doggie style. I knew that I should do something about it, but what? I had to talk to Lily, but she was still too wigged out to talk. So far it was my word against his, and I was enervated totally from being on barbiturates. Everything was an effort. My fuzz made it harder to think and to act.

Then one day I forced myself to go to my Outpatient Team Meeting, in the clinic at the swampy, sulfur-scented end of the sausage-shaped lake. I watched from behind a one-way mirror as Schlomo did his "down and dirty" *shtick* as the leader of an outpatient group therapy. After the group was over I filed in with the rest of the Outpatient Team for discussion, and watched Schlomo do his up-on-his-tippy-toes dance of celebration of himself as the mensch of psychotherapy.

I said nothing, sizing up my enemy. His piggy slits of eyes seemed to be avoiding mine. By the end of the session my heart was racing. The pulse in my temporal arteries cut through my barbiturate fog like the bell on a buoy. To wake up I ate a Ritalin. I followed him out and waited as his disciples peeled off gradually to their own offices. I found myself standing behind him as he unlocked his office door in the Farben, the door I had opened to my glimpse of hell. He turned and saw me standing facing him.

"Royala!" he cried out happily, as if we were old friends. "*Nu?*"

"I've got to talk to you."

"Schlomo is delighted."

I followed him in. Bananas were everywhere, in various stages of decay. I faced him, again dazzled by the actuality of his ugliness. Doubt rolled in, crashed over.

"I—I—" I stammered. "What I saw you doing, when I came in here that morning, with my patient Zoe . . ."

"You came in here with your patient Zoe?"

"No, no, I opened the door, and *you* were with Zoe."

"You came in here?"

"You know I did. You were . . . having intercourse with Zoe."

"What?" he said.

"Fucking her. I saw you having sexual intercourse with my patient Zoe."

His eyes widened from their porcine slits and his jaw dropped as if the jowls had gotten just too heavy for the fat-ridden masseters and buccinators. His teeth looked fierce, and I spotted a clumsily capped incisor and a badly rotated bicuspid. "What?" he cried out again. "Schlomo Dove having—look, Schlomo can hardly mouth the words—*sex* with a patient?"

"Yes. I saw it. I'm going to do something about it. It'll be easier if you admit it."

His eyes narrowed again. The masseters not only pulled that jaw back up but clenched, wobbling those cheeks, those jowls. His mouth closed hard, to a line. "You never came in here. You never saw Schlomo with a patient in here."

"I know what I saw."

"No you don't. Schlomo's door is always closed and locked. The consulting chamber is a sacred place. A safe place for one and all."

"I saw it. And I believe, now, that you've been fucking Lily Putnam too."

"You are confused, Roy Basch. Confused and deeply *deeply* depressed."

I felt an enormous weight, as if he were a block of strange metal emitting particulate metal from those eyes, that mouth, coating me, confusing me with weight, pressing out of me anything I might know for sure. The full weight of accusing him, the top analyst in town, one of the guys who matched tens of thousands of poor souls to other analysts, came down on me. I tried to speak. My tongue had gone metallic, it was too heavy to move.

"Roy," he said in a kindly tone, "to have a father die, and a patient die, all in the same month? Who wouldn't be depressed and confused? Why, no one wouldn't, no one wouldn't at all. You'd be *crazy* if you weren't, right? Schlomo understands. Now, Schlomo has another patient waiting. Good-bye, Roy, and be well."

My body felt as heavy as a dead man's. I got out.

I NEEDED HELP. Whom could I ask?

That's the hooker, I thought, over and over when I roused myself from my despair and lethargy to think at all—*whom* could I ask? It was astonishing to me that in almost a year in Mount Misery, surrounded by people who were allegedly the ones you would most want to go to to ask for help with your despair, I could think of only two people I could turn to: Berry and Malik. Berry seemed too risky. "Ask!" Malik had made us say. It had to be Malik. But he'd told me to burn his phone number. Could I call him?

One rainy evening a couple of days later, after finishing up with my patient Christine, who was responding to Prozac and Ritalin by not obsessing as much about Cherokee's suicide, I phoned Malik at home.

No answer. No tape. Strange.

Maybe because of my depressed haziness I had the thought that this meant he must be with his wife over on Ironwood, the Child Unit at Candlewood State Hospital. I climbed down from my office in Toshiba and walked toward my old Mustang, but I'd been eating more phenobarbs and my feet weren't making great contact with the ground and the cool wet drizzle felt so good on my feverish dull face that I decided to hike through the swamp to Candlewood.

It was one of those damp cool dusks where you can't tell if it feels ominous because winter is coming or liberating because it's about to be summer. The damp cool felt good. Leaving Misery was always easier than entering, and I moved quickly downhill and then farther downhill to the long straightaway through the marshland. The road was two-lane only, a rarity, and soon on either side as far as the eye could see there was nothing of civilization, for the land was too wet to build on, and by some miracle in these rapacious times, still too protected to drain. The lowland, set in a natural bowl of hills with thinning forests, was misty and hazy like the inside of my head. In the marsh there were no real trees, but bushes and cattails and swamp grass, last year's brown mixed with this year's green. The smell of skunk cabbage hit me, sharply as smelling salts, and opened my eyes wide.

The dim sunset was reflected in jagged pieces of pooled water, broken by hummocks. The only sounds were my feet on the blacktop—the reassuring *thunk thunk* reminding me of my many other solitary walks over the years, from Aranmore off the west Irish coast to Buyukada south of Istanbul in the Sea of Marmara, from the thin ancient paths boxing the rice paddies at

Mao's birthplace near Changsha to the Cotswolds, where I'd spent years alone learning not to be lonely—I'd thought, at the time, for good.

Deeper into the swamp I heard birds, and saw, like a ghost or a goddess, a lone white heron, beak poised like a sword, still as my father's face in death. I could have sworn I heard a flute, and stopped, still. Lonely lilting notes tore up from the far edge of the marsh, seemingly from one direction, then another, sad, desolate notes, held long, moving not in major steps but in chromatic elisions, making me feel cold and sorrowful. I hurried on.

In the wasteland of the state facility I skirted the main building, feeling guilty remembering my trip to Women's Chronic 9, for I had never been back. Ironwood, the Children's Unit, was a lone brick building on a small hill in the back. I used my keys and entered. A pounding came at me, rhythmic, through a wall: *Whrrr-thwak! Whrrr-thwak!* I searched out the door to this room and went in.

It was a large white box, with a ceiling twenty feet high. From the center of the ceiling was suspended a swing. In the swing, swinging hard, was a child, a boy. He would pump—*whrrr*—and pound his two feet into the wall—*thwak!* and pump back—*whrrr*—and kick the other wall—*thwak!* Where he kicked, the wall was black, and eroded, as if he were a prisoner who would kick through and then fly through and out and up and up. His body was rail-thin, and his face was demonic, focused only on the spot he was kicking ahead of him. I watched for what seemed a long time. He took no notice.

"Hey, man, can I gitchu somethin'?"

An African-American man, with keys. I jangled my keys, in the universal I'm-in-mental-health-too greeting. "I'm Dr. Basch. From Mount Misery."

"Frederickson," he said. "Pleased to meetchu."

"I'm looking for Dr. Malik."

"Bronia or L.A.?"

"Either."

"Bronia's back in Israel. Don't know where Malik hisse'f is. He usually be stoppin' by, every week or so. Ain't seen him in a while. The kids are askin'. Them that can."

"This one?"

"He cain't ask. Not even Malik be reachin' him."

"He can't talk?"

"All he can do, Doc, is swing. Goin' on a year. He eats and sleeps some, but it's all makin' a deal so he can do this."

"This is all?"

"There it is, Doc."

"It's sad."

"It's the worst thing in God's world. There are fi'ty others, as worse as him. Leastwise what they call God's world, you know what I mean?"

"I used to. Good-bye."

A BUTTERFLY NEEDLE, IV tubing, and a small bottle of normal saline had been easy to steal from the dog lab. I had hoarded plenty of phenobarb. For several nights in a row I had stayed alone at home drinking and playing a kind of horrific game, assembling the pieces of a successful suicide. A few nights before I had tied a necktie around my biceps, pumped my fist, and watched the vein swell up out of the antecubital fossa like a lavender pill buried just under the skin. Then I had untied the tie and put it back with the others in my closet. One night I had played with the little butterfly needle, grasping the two cute wings between thumb and index finger and bending them back over the spine of the needle till they touched, readying the point to puncture the vein. Another night I'd laid it all out like a child's jigsaw, the kind where an exquisitely cuddly cat is sawed up into only four or five pieces: the bottle of normal saline, the pills, the tubing, the needle. I'd unplugged the phone from the wall jack and stared at it, sipping George Dickel. So tonight was just another dalliance with the possibility, a variation on the theme. I knew, from all the suicides I'd seen this year in Misery—which, Lloyal von Nott had informed us all in a recent memo, were "in fact slightly below the mean for a fiscal year"—that playing with the lethal made it easier, just as practicing anything makes it easier, but that kind of rational thought had lost meaning, lately, for me.

Now, as if percussing a diseased chest, I tapped the wall behind my bed, sounding the stud. I hammered a nail into the wall above the bed, slipped the wire hanger from the IV bottle over the nail, ran the tubing down, and attached the butterfly. I dissolved the tablets of phenobarb in some saline, drew it up in a syringe, and injected it into the hanging bottle. The necktie lay beside me. I sat on the bed, trying to cut through my haze to remember.

One of the stars of my Rhodes class at Oxford, a gifted writer and quarterback whose perfect spirals hurt your hands when they hit, a terrific guy whom everybody wanted to be with, a young man who would dare anything and who had by the age of thirty published two acclaimed novels, the last, *Balliol Missed*, set in our years in Oxford, a man all aglitter with success, had recently filled an IV bottle with drugs and put the line into himself and lay down and opened the cock and floated out to death. Went to sleep. Now I knew something of that sleep. Nice. Dreamless. Barbs kill REM-sleep. I hadn't dreamed in weeks. Seamless. Ike too had gone out seamless, on barbiturates. Zoe's suicide note said, "A smile plastered on my face dying inside."

Now I understood. I was living a secret life. Plastering a shrink's sureness on my face, underneath doubting everything. Eating drugs to deny what I was seeing. A secret, double life. Not sharing my pain with anyone for fear of reprisal. Not sharing how I, like Cherokee, awoke every morning feeling okay for fifteen seconds until something hit that he called "Dreadlock!" and a little voice whispered, "How the hell am I gonna make it through the day?" Pop my wake-up Ritalin. Hoist my body to the vertical. A walking illusion. Over my year in psychiatry, instead of living a life more truly, I'd come to live it more falsely.

Now I sipped from my George Dickel, feeling bone tired, longing for sleep, even that curious sleep of death. I felt totally alone. No one was fit to be with me, and I was fit to be with no one.

"Who are you?"

"I'm a doctor."

"What are *you* doing here?"

"There it is. God's world."

"Why do some people kill themselves and others don't?"

Because of this, little boy, this big disconnect. Because of this yearning to ask for help and this loathing of the yearning. Feeling trapped, not wanting to be here but with all the usual refuges gone, even in the self, so that a retreat into the self feels like falling off the edge of the world. Not because of feeling, but of not feeling. Because "because" becomes bullshit. The Big Disconnect. Should I tie that necktie around this arm?

"Soul-death," Malik said, "their souls die first."

Now I understood. I felt, as if it were just last night, Ike's last boneless handshake, saw his averted eyes. Something had been missing in—

"Dr. Basch?"

A voice in the living room, 12:34 A.M. A feather of hope, then fear.

"Be right there."

I hid the bottle and tubing and needle and walked out into the living room.

It was Zoe. Her tall slender frame was bulked up by a heavy sweater, and her light brown hair, even though cropped short, was disheveled. Her face was as pale as that ghostly heron I'd seen in the swamp.

"Zoe?" I said, flashing on, of all things, Heiler's *They'll even show up at your home*.

She bent her head. "Sorry. But if I stayed alone in my apartment one more minute, I'd've killed myself." She bit her lip. "Dr. Basch, I need help."

"Sit down."

"Thank you."

My heart beat fast—*whrrr-thunk*. I felt wide awake, alert.

"That moment, when you saw me—" She stopped, and I thought she would cry. But then I saw that her shame and grief had gone way past crying. As had my own. Suicide is way past crying. She looked down into her lap. "That was the worst moment of my life. Worse than when I tried to kill myself. Dr. Basch, I am so ashamed."

She looked up, and our eyes met. Our vision coalesced around the vision of our eyes meeting when Schlomo was humping away, and then around a vision of shared shame, of both of us having hurt the other. I held her gaze. We were together in sorrow.

She sighed. "Thank you."

"For?"

"I don't know—I guess I feel like I'm really seeing you, and I feel really seen by you, that's all."

"Yes. Me too." I felt a flicker of excitement. We were seeing together. Was that what Ike White—and A.K. and the drug rats too—were afraid of? Being *seen*? Being seen as inadequate?

"Your face right now," Zoe went on, "is like that first time I saw you, that night I came into the hospital—so open! And now . . . you're hurting too, aren't you?"

"Yes, I am."

"That bastard! How could it happen? He's so pathetic!"

"How did it?"

"Partly, I guess, because he *was* so pathetic. Said his marriage to Dixie was miserable, celibate. That whole like tragic thing about his child drowning in his pool. I thought I could help him, maybe even save him—that's how crazy it got. I always choose the jerks, the abusive guys, right from high school I went out with the assholes, seeing the good in them, hoping . . . trying, I guess, to save them." She sighed, fidgeted. "And he was powerful. Pathetic and powerful both. I felt special to him. He was the best around, and that first session, after I left Thoreau AMA and went to him for a consultation, and he said that even though he almost never did it he wouldn't refer me to someone else but he would keep me for therapy himself?" Her eyes widened. "Do you know what that meant, to me, to someone who had no self-esteem left? I was honored. Talk about feeling like *special*. So special, I floated out of there like on a magic carpet." She shook her head, as if to clear her thoughts. "He seemed so *into* me! Put his hand on my shoulder as I left the office, patting my shoulder like a . . . like my father did, a few times. 'Tell Schlomo,' he'd say. 'Tell Schlomo Dove about sad and lonely.' And then, in the session, he'd pat my knee, and then he'd hold me. One thing led to another, like he hypnotized me with love or something, with those weird, slitty eyes, you know?" I nodded. "And he said he'd never done this before with a patient, that I was the only one."

"You believe that?"

"I felt it. But now . . ." Her eyes narrowed to fury. "He's scum! I hate him! He wouldn't even buy condoms himself—told me to buy them, '*You* buy the condoms, to learn to take responsibility.' He kept them in a Ziploc bag under the head of the couch. And . . . I mean, bananas? His fetish with bananas? I feel so . . . dirty."

"When you went to see him, you were incredibly vulnerable, and—"

"Yeah, but I'm a big girl, I knew what I was doing. *I* did it." She sighed. "Can I . . ." She paused. "This is really hard to ask . . ."

"Go on."

"Can I come back? See you again in therapy? I think maybe now, after all this, you could help me. Don't you think?"

"Yes, I think so. Sure."

She let her breath out in a whoosh, as if she hadn't been breathing for a while. I too breathed out fully, unclenching a breath from around my ribs.

"Thank God. I was sure you wouldn't." She fell silent. Neither of us knew what to say. Finally she went on, "I . . . I'm afraid to be alone tonight. But it feels weird to be here too. Can we just keep talking a little longer?"

"Sure. Maybe we can do something about him."

"Who would believe me?"

"We would file a complaint together."

"Who'd believe *us*? I could never go through it in public, no way. Maybe he just lost it this once, with me, right?" I thought about telling her that she wasn't the only one, but it seemed, just then, too brutal.

We sat. For a rare few moments in the suburbs, things were still.

"Amazing," she said. "When I was a girl, my aunt Bev always said that this kind of stillness, at this time of night, means that there are angels passing overhead." She smiled, shyly, and I smiled too. "I'm okay. I'll leave now, okay?"

"I'll walk you out."

MY FIRST CALL the next morning was to the information operator in the 701 area code, North Dakota. I got the number for Ideal Cleaners in Mandan, and dialed it. A woman with an accent I'd never heard before answered. I could barely hear her over the intermittent hisses of what sounded like big steam presses going full blast.

"Solini!" I shouted. "I'm looking for Henry Solini!"

"One minute," she shouted, and then shouted even louder out into the cleaning establishment, "Hey, Little Hawk! LITTLE HAWK!" The phone went *clunk*, and I waited for Henry "Little Hawk" Solini. The phone was picked up.

"Yeah?" a voice shouted.

"Solini?"

"Yeah? Who's this?"

"Roy."

"Roy?" he shouted, astonished.

"Little Hawk?" I shouted back.

"That's my Sioux name, out here. You know how it is. How the hell are you?"

"Bad."

"Sorry to hear that, man."

"How are you?"

"Cool. Everything's cool. Lemme get on the cellular phone and go out back in the alley so we can have some privacy."

We talked for a long time, about everything. I asked him what had happened after I'd dropped him off at his analyst Ed Slapadek, the last time I'd seen him.

"I was in rough shape, man, with Hannah tryin' to kill herself and the Slapper telling me I was gay-latent. I flipped out on Toshiba and I went to Ed needing some help. But he just kept confronting me about how I felt about *him*. So I tell him he reminds me of my father. He goes, 'Let's work on the father-transference,' and I go, 'No, you really *are* like him, short and authoritarian and bigoted.' So he calls me 'gay-latent.' That did it. I go, 'This is ridiculous!' He goes, 'What comes to mind about "ridiculous"?' I say, 'What comes to mind is "Fuck you, Ed!" ' I get up and veer off into the kitchen and go out the back door and run into the woods. I had my wallet—he demanded a hundred twenty dollars cash at the start of each session—and I used my Visa to get back to Mandan, back to Ideal Cleaners. And y'know what I found out, right back here in Ideal Cleaners?"

I said I did not know what he'd found out back in Ideal Cleaners.

"That there's nothin' wrong with me! Or my old man! Or Ideal Cleaners! Nothin'! We're all cool! It's rough, man, when you shine the high beams of analysis on reality. Everything looks different, and a lot worse than it really is."

"Good for you, Henry Solini!"

"Roy-babe, I am gonna make my *move*!"

"Aw*right*! And what's your move?"

A pause. "Dunno yet. The market for white reggae singers in the Dakotas is a little slow this time of year. I'm a little bored here already. What's up with you, babe?"

I told him what I'd been going through, about Schlomo and Zoe and Lily, and said I really needed his help and maybe he could come back to Misery, at least till the end of the year, and help me figure out what to do.

"Cool, Roy," he said without hesitation. "Von Nott put me on a leave of absence, so I can still come back, yeah. Yeah," he said, considering, "maybe before I quit shrinking, it'd be cool to stick it to those assholes. Yeah. Okay. I got a few things to clean up out here, with Everett and my ex and a motorcycle, you know how it is, but I'll be there, babe, maybe like next week."

"Great."

"Yeah, see if you can find my car, okay?"

"It's still where you left it, in the parking lot up in the Heidelbergs, but the tires are gone. I'll get it fixed up for you."

"Cool. One thing, though. I'll call Hannah, in Wyoming. She needs to get some damn closure on this Misery-shit too."

"Cool," I said. "Love you, Little Hawk."

"There it is. Hang loose."

I TRIED AGAIN that same morning to talk with Lily Putnam, but she was still too out of it, lying there with those same stuffed-animal eyes as all the others on the West, stuffed not like a child's fuzzy toy but like a taxidermist's dream. I realized that somehow I had to get her completely off drugs.

I searched out Mr. K. One night on call I brought him to the West. He showed Lily how to tongue her pills. She watched him, mute and confused, but maybe she understood.

Two days later on the hall, the Man Who Thought He Was a Kernel of Corn came up to me. He looked less weirded out. To my surprise, he actually talked.

"Just one more test and I'm going to be discharged," he said. "Dr. Cynthia Krabkin says I'm ready to go back to my chicken farm in Bangor."

"Congratulations. There must be a lot of pleasure in farming."

"I know now," he said, firmly, "that I am *not* a kernel of corn."

"Good luck." Lily Putnam, with a lifeless trudge and blank stare, came up and slipped me a note:

This is fake. I'm better. Meet me in my room tonight.

That night, without drugs, she was pretty much back to her usual self, alert, bright-eyed, appropriately sad. And angry. "Get me out of here!"

"Are you suicidal?"

"No. I've never been suicidal. I've got my children to think of. That maniac Dr. Cabot showed up at my house with a pink paper and a syringe full of hell and I've been in la-la-land ever since. I'm worried to death about my children. Can you get me out?"

"Let's go."

"Now? Right now?"

"I'll sign the discharge order myself."

"Oh." She hesitated. "I . . . Is it quite okay, I mean to do this?"

"I'm with you. Get your things. Walk like you're drugged up, to the door."

"But how will I get home?"

"I'll drive you."

I went to the chart rack, worried that someone would notice. The night staff were relaxing with glossy magazines in the stressless chairs behind the glass booth, eating and drinking and reading. Nonchalantly I wrote the discharge order and closed the chart. It would be a while before it was read.

As I came back to the Dutch doors, Lily was walking past, faking a drug-trudge toward the door. I went out onto the ward, as if going to talk to her. I talked. She, shuffling her feet, pretended to take no notice. As we neared the door, Deedee the nurse glanced up. Our eyes met. I froze.

But even from across the room and through the glass, her eyes showed a glaze—from whatever drug she was eating. I rolled my own eyes as if in frustrated resignation at trying to actually talk to one of these "psychiatric theme parks." She smiled, and walked away. My key slid smoothly into the worn lock. I led Lily out.

We drove silently through the crystalline starry night along a loud spring river and up into a declivity of the mountains and then down again to a valley and to the horse farm poor Cherokee had bought with his severance pay from Walt Disney. I felt Lily's fragility, and was reluctant to speak. She too was silent. The farmhouse was dark. Her parents, who had been taking care of the children, must have been asleep, as were the children. I went with her into each child's room, and heard her crying softly at the sight of these two damaged angels, sweetly asleep.

"I can never thank you enough," she said, saying good-bye at the door.

"There's one thing more. At some point I need to ask you what the truth is about Schlomo Dove."

Fear slithered across her eyes. She looked down at her feet. "We've been having sex since last summer. Come back tomorrow. We'll talk."

IN THAT HORRIFIC basement of the Farben the next morning, May 15 and my last day on the West, I found myself walking past the stench and pitiful whining of the dogs, which reminded me how worried I was about Thorny, wherever he was out there. I walked into Win Winthrop's office. Win sat at his desk playing with his keyboard. Van Dusky the husky, recovering from his brain surgery, was lying at his feet whimpering and licking his hock without cessation, without, one might say, "missing a lick." A note written in red Magic Marker was posted over the computer:

Arch. Gen. Psych. Wants Our Dog Study For Their Lead Article!

"*Archives of Genetic Psychiatry?*" I asked.

"Not Genetic, General. Published by the AMA: 'Physicians dedicated to the health of America.' They want our dog study for their lead article."

"Van Dusky?" I called out. The husky wagged his tail and got up, sort of, for only two of his four legs now worked. He tried to hop toward me on the good two, the bad two sticking out spastically. With a whimper Van Dusky fell on his face. He began licking his hock with his tongue.

"I just want to tell you, Win, that you'd've made a great Nazi."

"Yeah and you got no balls. Hey—stop that!"

I was ripping the tape spools off the two cartoon clown's eyes on the mainframe computer and stomping them into Van Dusky's wet dog chow. As Win bent to save them I kicked as many manuscript pages as I could all over the place and stomped those into the dog food too and then bent down and picked up Van Dusky and carried him out.

"You're psychotic!"

"Tell it to the ASPCA."

He chose to save his manuscripts rather than his dog. The dog was heavy, but I struggled upstairs to Telecommunications and shut the bulletproof behind me. Laying Van Dusky gently down, I told Viv what was up and she dialed the ASPCA hot line. I told them that it was an emergency with an abused dog in need of shelter and that the Misery dog lab was a torture chamber, right out of the Dark Ages.

While we waited, I talked with Viv about the atrocities I'd seen among the drug fascists on the West, and about how depressed I'd been. Soon the ASPCA men in their white coats were screaming at Errol and Win in their white coats. Mr. Beef Telly, head of Security, was shouting into his walkie-talkie for help.

As we watched this tragicomic pantomime on the far side of the bulletproof, I said to Viv:

"Those guys almost killed me."

"Yeah. If you was drowning, those jokers would throw you a rock."

When I went to pick up my things on the West, I passed the Quiet Room and saw the Man Who Thought He Was a Kernel of Corn, plastered up against the wall, terrified. He was staring at a real live chicken that was walking around clucking and scratching and pecking.

"What happened?" I asked him through the slit for speaking. "I thought you knew that you're *not* a kernel of corn."

"*I* know I'm not a kernel of corn," the man said, eyes riveted on the chicken, "but how do I know that that *chicken* knows?"

A nurse arrived, to scatter a few drugs.

How had this happened? How had the received wisdom gotten so far from the human heart?

HEIDELBERG EAST

"Identify, don't compare."

—ANONYMOUS

Eighteen

"YES, HE SEEMED REPULSIVE to me too, at first," Lily Putnam was saying later that night, lighting another cigarette.

We were in Cherokee's study, up over the horses in the barn. Dusk had turned to dark, and the roof, all skylights, showed the first stars faceting the night. The horses below were snorting and stamping, as if impatient for the man to reappear. We were sipping tea. She had offered drinks. I wanted a nice sharp bourbon, but I felt that in this middle ground between life and therapy I should abstain. I was trying to detox my way out of the beauty parlor of drugs I'd wandered into on Heidelberg West.

"I was ripe," she went on, "for someone to take a real interest in me. The years in California, away from both our families, in such a bizarre, hedonistic, rather fake place, had taken its toll. It was Fantasyland, really. Not only on Cherokee, on me too. Back here, poor Cher started to feel like such a failure. He withdrew from me. And from the girls. Even though he put in a lot of time with them, he wasn't really there for them either. I tried to get him to get some help, but he wouldn't. It went against his grain. I don't know how you did it, I mean get him to come to see you, it was marvelous, really. And so I was getting more and more isolated, more desperate, doubting myself, my attractiveness as a woman, doubting everything. I felt I needed help, though it went against my grain as well. Well, one day a friend told me about Schlomo, who could sort of match you up with the right therapist. That first appointment, he said, 'You're like the sun, emanating warmth, giving it away to others, leaving yourself cold and empty.' And then he said that although he didn't often do it, he would keep me for his own patient. I was thrilled." She sighed, and went on, "I believed him. Over time, I began to have strong feelings for him. I could see the person living in that repulsive, rather forlorn body. A powerful person. Those strange eyes, you know?" I nodded. "It started innocently enough. He'd touch me as I was leaving the office, first on the shoulder, a friendly pat, then my lower back . . . and so forth. Then he'd touch me when I was in the office, and then, well, when I was on the couch. And he isolated me from Cher and my family. Told me that analysis only works if you keep it secret. He was especially strict about my not telling my husband. One thing led to another. New underwear. Perfume. He had this thing about hair. I prided myself on my long light brown hair, but he said he liked it short, boyish. One day I cut it all off. For him? God damn!" She blew a plume of smoke, and looked around Cherokee's office as if for the first time, taking it in.

"I feel so guilty," she went on, "but it seems so strange now, to think that I would go in there at six in the morning, he would nod, we would undress, have sex, and then we'd smoke a cigarette together and talk, as if it were the most normal thing in the world, a kind of 'Hi, how are you? Okay, you? Okay.' I started smoking again, after having a bitch of a time quitting. And then, as time went on, we'd talk less and less about me, and more and more about him. Telling you about it now, it all seems like a bad dream. How could it have happened? At first I felt so ashamed. He analyzed it out. 'It's your WASP upbringing,' he said. 'People aren't naturally monogamous. This analysis will free you up. Affairs are good, a good good thing, as long as you don't tell the one you're cheating on. Get in touch with your grief, your *tsouris*.' I started to feel sorry for him. He told me about his little boy drowning in his pool. He complained about his miserable marriage—no sex with Dixie—about his heart condition—he was on diuretics, and kept bananas around, for potassium. Sometimes . . . we'd even use the bananas. . . . It got so I felt I was *his* therapist, imagine?" I nodded. Again she sighed. "Now, it seems like he had me in a trance, as if he somehow, without my knowing it, hypnotized me. When I would say I was ashamed, he would analyze it as my 'tight-ass WASP hang-up, a transference to your father. Tell Schlomo.' I would cry, and he would listen. Seemed to listen, anyway."

"And after Cherokee died?"

Pain came to her eyes. "I . . . I said to Schlomo that I wanted to stop. But he . . . more or less forced me. . . . He really got into it."

"And then you said you were going to report him?"

She nodded. "I don't know if I meant it, really. But that same day I got a call from your patient Christine telling me about Cherokee and her, and about how obsessed he had become, with Schlomo and me. That hit me hard. In a way, it motivated me to try to get clearer. I was sitting at the kitchen table, writing out a list of what to do about all this, and the next thing I knew that madman Dr. Cabot was there banging around the place shouting at me and waving a pink paper, and then I refused to leave and he injected me with something and I didn't really wake up until you got that sweet old man to teach me how to tongue the pills and you led me out." Her hand ruffled her short, light brown hair. "Thanks so much."

We sat in silence, together. Occasionally she would glance up at me, and I would hold her eyes for a second, and glance away. It was hard to face her. Not so much for her shame, as for mine. The horses snorted and stomped.

"Schlomo said that he had never done this before, with a patient, that I was the only one. He said that I was special to him."

I thought of A.K., making me feel special, to her. "I understand, Lily, how good that feels. But I have something to tell you."

"Yes?"

"You were not the only one."

She stared at me. "I . . . I don't believe that."

"I'm sure of it. There's one other woman he was abusing. At least one."

"I refuse to believe that."

"The things he told you—'the warmth of the sun' line, the 'keeping what you say and do in therapy secret'—I've heard the same things from her."

"What else? That I haven't already told you?"

"That he made *you* buy the condoms? 'To learn to take responsibility.' That he kept the condoms in a Ziploc bag hidden in the head of the couch?" Her jaw dropped. "Would you meet with the other victim? To see about taking action against him? I'll be there with you, or, if you would prefer, not?"

"No, I couldn't do that. I . . . I've had enough. As have the children. I'm quite exhausted. Barely hanging on, as is. I just want to pretend it never happened."

"Will you think about it?"

"Yes. No. No, I want it to go away, to not be."

"That's the mistake we both made, with Cherokee."

She got up and walked around her dead husband's office. Her body seemed slight and frail. Night birds chirped outside. The sophisticated horses kicked and whinnied under our feet, the aloof soft sounds a comfort. The silence was that expectant, big silence of night in woods on mountains.

"There are no pictures of me here in Cher's office," she said. "One day I noticed that, that he'd torn up every picture of me, even pictures which contained me, in his office. I never said anything to him about that." She stared at a picture of Cherokee in midair on a horse sailing over a fence. "Schlomo was my fault. I did it, of my own free will."

"No way."

"What?"

"Schlomo raped you."

"That last time, but not at the start. I wanted him to . . . to 'fuck' me."

"His words, right? 'Deep down you want Poppa Schlomo to fuck you'?"

She blushed, and nodded. "But I felt chosen. It got so I couldn't wait for morning—I'd dress up, put on perfume—don't you see?—I *liked* it."

"Yes, I do see. But being a therapist, I know how much power we have, how easy it would be. Will you think about meeting the other woman?"

"I can't very well not think about it now, can I? But I have to think of the children too. How could I put them through that? No."

I got up to go. "You okay, though? No suicidal thoughts?"

"No. I'm not one of those who walk out on their lives. Good night."

"YOU'VE HAD A DIFFICULT TIME here this year, haven't you?"

This question was asked me by Malik's friend, Dr. Geneva Hooevens, the blind woman analyst who had spoken up at the meeting to ask about Ike White's killing himself. Now, her question surprised me. It was the first time it had ever been asked me that whole year, with the exception of Malik, who seemed always to be asking me, one way or another. Malik. Where was he? Bronia, back from Israel, had called me, asking if I knew where he was. Worrisome.

Geneva Hooevens was temporarily in charge of Heidelberg East, the Alcohol and Drug Recovery Unit, where I would spend the rest of my first year. We were sitting in her office off the nursing station, which, Geneva told me, had once been the kitchen of the stone mansion built in 1812 as the home for the "Keeper" of the lunatics of the Mount Misery Asylum. Remnants could still be seen: labeled bells for ringing the servants, gaslight fittings. The large living room now served as a common room for the drunks and addicts who were the "clients."

I felt awkward with Geneva. I had not spent much time with blind people, and seeing her while unseen by her, I felt I had to be more aware of my movements, my sounds, even my glances, for I sensed myself being attuned to more acutely by her other senses. My doctor's eyes told me that this was not a blindness from birth, but one more recent and gradual: her skin, the truth-teller, was mottled and scarred from recurrent infection, the nails pale, suggesting a circulatory failure of the small vessels, most likely severe diabetes. She wore glasses tinted that same amber as Malik's, and her seeing-eye dog Yoman and her cane seemed naturally part of her. I found myself staring into Yoman's alert, patient eyes, as if they were hers, thinking, Thank God,

Win and Errol never got this one. The cane leaned on her chair akimbo, as if needing a cane itself.

"Yes," I answered, "it's been a nightmare."

"Oh dear," she said, with what sounded like genuine concern, although I had so often heard similar "genuine concern" from the shrinks at Misery—"genuine concern" that turned out to be the opposite, either "phony" concern or "genuine" attack—that despite myself I was suspicious. "What happened?"

"I went into psychiatry to learn how to be with people in a real, human way. I thought psychiatrists did that. But what I've seen here is the most inhumane treatment of people ever. It's worse than medicine. My father was a dentist and I'd always feared becoming a dentist. This may even be worse than dentistry."

"Yes, I know. Much of what I've seen here is perverse. Most large institutions evolve to perversity, to power-over systems, where someone always has power over you, and you have power over someone else. But here we do things differently. It's a whole new model of disease and recovery."

"How's it different?"

"Ever been to an AA meeting?"

"No. I don't know much about self-help programs."

"AA's more a 'mutual'-help program, in fact. A power-with program. The best way to learn is to spend time on the unit, working with the staff—most of them are recovering alcoholics and addicts. They have to be at least two years sober."

"And they'll tell me?"

"Show you. One tells a person some bits of knowledge; one shows a person something that leads to understanding. Remember organic chemistry, the premed course?" I nodded, realized she couldn't see me nod, but she seemed to sense it, and went on, "Do you remember much of your organic chemistry?"

I drew a blank, seeing vaguely a toy model of a carbon ring that could flip two ways like an umbrella in the wind, the two forms named . . . blank and blank. I had busted my ass to make an A in organic because they said if you made an A in organic at the Best College you were sure of admission to the Best Medical School. How crucial it had seemed, how hard I'd worked, and how worthless organic had proved in medicine. What a waste of that dazzling young energy, to memorize all that crap. And would all this training prove a waste too, looking back? "Nothing," I said. "I don't remember a thing."

"Nor do I, of mine. A waste. You forget knowledge. You never forget what you understand." She smiled, a Stevie Wonder smile directed up and out beyond us, yet to ourselves. "I'm a recovering alcoholic, eight years sober. My blindness came on gradually, from diabetes, exacerbated by my drinking."

"And you drank because?"

"Because I'm a drunk." She clasped her hands in her lap, over a bright red sash with tiny bells. Berry always said that if you look hard, you can see, in anyone, a touch of the Divinity. Berry! My heart twisted on its spindle, in pain. Geneva sat quietly for a few seconds. Then, in a firm, soft voice, as if she were placing each word like a seed in a row, right spacing, right depth, she went on, "Perhaps it would have been better if I had not gone blind. And yet, at some point, through my blindness I saw that seeking the easy and comfortable way was no longer my path. I've come to understand that one way to live is to run hard shouting against some fact of your life, and that another way is to surrender to the life force, to opening up, to learning the value of the situation in which you find yourself. The ego is insatiable, and will fight tooth and nail against surrender, against its own limits. Which is what makes surrender so valuable. Remarkable, is it not?"

"I . . . I guess I'm all out of 'remarkable' for today."

"Good for you!" she cried excitedly, clapping her hands like a child.

"Good?"

"Perhaps you're ready for something new!" She stroked Yoman, who responded with that happy "Hooray" whimper that dog owners love. "Feel free, here, to do as much or as little as you wish. I shall be most curious, given how you've been treated this year, to hear what you see."

"Thanks," I said, getting up, not knowing whether to shake her hand.

"Thank you!" she said enthusiastically, holding out her hand. I extended mine. She clasped it solidly, as if our hands were all of us, yet so much beyond us as to be small, almost comic or incidental parts of everything larger.

"For what?"

"For hearing me into speech. Good-bye." I said good-bye and walked to the door, but just as I opened it she said, "One more thing?"

"Yes?"

"Have fun!"

"Fun in Misery would be radical."

"Wonderful word, 'radical,' is it not?"

"Maybe," I said gloomily, not wanting to go along with all this hope. "Look—I'm really suspicious of religion, okay?"

"AA isn't religious, it's spiritual."

"What's the difference?"

"Authority." She pointed to the wall, where a framed photo hung. "See that photo?" A mob of Indians in turbans were being mowed down by rifle fire from a line of British troops in pith helmets. The commander of the British troops stood at attention, arms crossed over his chest, his face curious, as if he were judging a race.

"Yes?"

"The soldiers, firing, take no responsibility, for they are just following orders. The officer, having given the order, takes no responsibility for the actual killing. In a power-over system, violence is the inevitable result. But listen to me," she chided herself, "I'm telling you what I just told you no one can tell you. Good luck."

I walked out into the living room. Something big smashed into me.

"Outta da fuckin' way, Jack," someone shouted in my face, "don't ever get between a man and his beer." Stench, of sweat and beer breath. A bloated flesh balloon with yellowing skin and puffy red slits for eyes. A drunk, wearing a T-shirt that proclaimed: GOD MADE THE IRISH NUMBER ONE. He walked away.

I realized why I had been so reluctant, with Geneva, to go along with all this smarmy hope, this AA propaganda. In my medical training, drunks and addicts were the worst. I'd learned to hate them. They were admitted deathly ill. We fought tooth and nail to take care of them. When they were better they said "Fuck you!" and went out to drink and drug again. Drug addicts, in addition to being unreachable, had learned a hundred ways to dupe you, to get drugs out of you, one scam after another. The feeling is that you are working flat out using all your years of education and all your mental discipline and manual dexterity to help people who will not help themselves, who in fact seem hell-bent on destroying themselves and making you and their families suffer in the process. Eighty-five percent of violent crime is committed by people on alcohol or drugs. Every morning's newspaper tells another horrific tale. Ask any doctor: these are not human beings; these are monsters.

Watching this cretin assault the coffee, I was filled with loathing. I drank too, and I'd taken some phenobarb, but I had stopped. *I* wasn't driving boozed up full-speed down the interstate the wrong way, smashing into good folk doing everything right, killing whole innocent families like the Bumblefucks and walking away with a few scratches, soon to drink and drive and kill again. If I could control it, why couldn't they? Because I had some moral fiber, and because they were the scum of the earth. So don't give me this "I've got a disease" bullshit. You're still responsible. Me, help them? You must be joking. Where was the touch of the Divine in this shitbag?

I fled, driving down the hill with the windows open to the chill daffodil breeze, directly to The Misery. My detox from the phenobarb had left me feeling shaky, and two vodka tonics in the comfortable "morning in a barroom" ambience put me right. I bought some sugarless breath mints and drove back up the hill to Misery to see my patient Zoe.

. . .

WHO DID NOT SHOW. I sat there waiting, sucking one mint after another, staring out the window down to the tennis court. Finally, with only a few minutes left, Zoe arrived.

Ever since she had shown up that night at my house, she had avoided meeting with me. Now I saw her with new eyes: tall, slender, straight-nosed, light brown hair cut short—all tending toward boyish. She looked like a young Lily Putnam. She was dressed in rumpled jeans and a bulky sweater. She was embarrassed to be there.

We spoke like slight acquaintances, about the weather, about her concern for Thorny, who seemed to have vanished off the face of the earth. "It's hard to see me again," I said, "is it?"

"Uh-huh."

"Can we talk about it?"

"Not much time left."

"I can stay later."

"Oh great," she said sarcastically. "That's how Schlomo started out too. Gave me extra time one night. Because I was 'special.' Puke City. Look, I know that you think I should do something about him, but like it's not that easy. I'm a big girl. I can take responsibility for what I did."

"You were incredibly vulnerable, after what happened on Thoreau. A. K. Lowell made us all vulnerable. For my part, well, I want to tell you that I'm sorry. I owe you an apology."

"Accepted. Time's up." She got up and went to the door. "Everybody makes mistakes," she said. "So Schlomo made one. Big deal."

"Not just one."

"What?"

"Since we talked, I've talked with another woman patient who told me that he sexually abused her." Zoe stared at me, her mouth open in a little O. "Will you meet with her?" I asked. "I'll be there, if you want."

"No."

"Why not?"

"I don't believe you."

I took out a notebook in which I'd written down what Lily Putnam had said, and started to read. " 'Schlomo told me, "It's your WASP upbringing. This analysis will free you up. Affairs are good, a good good thing. Get in touch with your grief, your *tsouris*—" ' "

"Stop it!"

"Will you meet with her?"

"No way," she said. "If I can't feel even a little special, with a little self-respect, I might as well be dead."

She walked out. I sat there feeling defeated, staring at the tennis court covered with billowing curtains of rain. I glanced down at my junk mail:

Sanctuary of ISAAC and RACHEL *for Above-Ground Burial*
Act Before July 1 and Avoid the Price Increase
"If not now, when?"
Why wait to go shopping on the worst day of your life?

Shouts, screams, bangings outside my door. I ran out. Down the hall, Mr. Beef Telly and another Security man had cornered Solini's reggae man. He was huddled in a heap, one arm wrenched behind his back in a half nelson being tightened by Security. He screamed in pain.

"Solini?" the man cried. "Solini!"

Little Hawk opened his door, took in the situation, looked at me and winked. We ran down the hall.

"Let him go," Henry said to Mr. Telly.

"Trespassing. Eviction from Toshiba. I have my orders."

"He's a patient of mine."

"No he ain't."

"Henry," I said, "let's go for it!"

"Far out!" the little dry cleaner said, crouching into a judo posture.

We piled on top of Security, hitting at him and throwing him off Solini's reggae man. I heard Mr. Telly at my elbow calling into his walkie-talkie for reinforcements. I turned and smashed into his lapels with my two fists and lifted him up bodily and ran him across the hall and slammed him against the wall, knocking the breath out of him. His walkie-talkie fell squawking to the rug. I drop-kicked it down the corridor. Henry had karate-kicked out the other Security, who was lying there groaning, cupping his nuts.

We raised up the reggae man and walked with remarkable slowness into the restless lively rain.

"So what's up, Carter-babe?" Henry asked.

"Doc Malik," he said. The smell of cheap wine on his breath hung in the moisture all around us. "The doc needs help."

"Where is he?" I asked.

"Follow I." We did. Carter plucked his boom box. Out came Bob's "Cornerstone." He sang along using his own translation from Psalm 118: " 'The stone which the builders refused is become the main cornerstone.' "

We walked into the Misery woods, and were soon sheltered from the hail of rain by the high spruces and cedars and pines. The wetness freshening the pine needles brought to my mind the image of the suburban Jewish bathrooms of my youth. Under our feet the dirt was springy and welcoming. Watching the tiny scion of Ideal Dry Cleaners jiving along in front of me, the gold earring back in his ear, his hands and feet rolling to the Marley, made me mimic him, and in my jiving I realized how dull and dead I had become in these months, renouncing dancing, denying mere life and mere woods and mountains pulsing with streams and rivulets. My obsession with shrinking and myself had been a weird denial of the act of living my life.

We walked on, the trail that mossy and riverly flow over rock and roots embracing rock like claws, where fallen decaying trees nourished new red roots, spicy leaves, leafy ferns, and serious mushrooms, up hills I hadn't known were there and through miniature valleys with streams overflowing their banks and even a waterfall, ionized and resplendent. I hadn't realized Misery was so immense. Like settlers fearing animals and natives, I and other shrinks had stayed close to the buildings. Soon we were soaked through. Seeing Solini's thinning black hair plastered to his bulging skull, his shirt plastered to his back so that his black hairiness showed through like fur, watching him sing and dance along happily, I joined in, feeling happy too. " 'The stone which the builders refused is become the main cornerstone.' "

We danced down the spongy path into another stretch of old-growth forest, and there, amidst the high spruce, was a dead campfire banked up with litter: empty beer and wine bottles, styrofoam cups and spoons, chicken bones, a Saran Wrap box, discarded empty bags of Korn Curls, Mars bars. Beside the campfire was a snappy bright blue tent with a Hebrew logo in white upon it.

Carter the reggae man stood aside, nodding toward the tent. We went in.

A stench of stale clothes, whiskey, beer, old vomit. Curled in a corner was Malik. He was wearing a filthy short-sleeve white shirt and jeans. One foot was bare and on the other was a muddy Nike. He was snoring.

"Malik?" I said. No response. "Malik."

"Yo, Malik!" Henry said, louder.

We bent to him and shook him, and with disturbing slowness he awoke. He stared at us as if in disbelief, coughed once, and closed his eyes again.

"Come with us," I said to him.

"Get out of here."

"Hey, man, you can't do this."

"Get away."

"Listen to us—"

"Get outta here!" he snarled, sitting up and throwing us both back so we wound up sitting on our butts, facing him, our shoulders curved in by the canvas of the tent, our heads close. He was a horrible sight: thin, dirty, his eyes bloodshot and his cheeks streaked with lines that may have been dirt or may have been the tracks of dried tears. He squinted at us, and coughed again.

"You need help," I said.

" 'Help'?" Malik stared at me. "You don't know the meaning of the word." He lay down and covered his head with his arms. Henry and I looked at each other, got up, and went out through the tent flap. We stood in the clearing.

"Think we can like carry him back?" Henry asked.

"No. Not with him fighting us. There's got to be another way."

"What, man?"

"I don't know. But Viv will."

With Carter as our guide, we walked back out through the woods.

VIV KNEW TO CALL Malik's sponsor George, who called right back and came right over. George was Malik's ex-patient who'd founded the Misery Loves Company meeting.

"We've got to twelve-step him," George said.

"What does that mean?" I asked.

"Go get him."

"Fine," I said, and we got up to go.

"But I gotta get someone else to help," George said, dialing a number.

"Aren't us three enough?" Henry asked.

"I need another drunk," George said. "You never go and try to bring back a drunk alone. You go with another drunk."

"Why?"

" 'Cause if you're alone with an active drunk, you may just join in. I'll call Frankie. He's workin' on the East. He'll come right over."

George called Frankie and he came right over. He was a heavyset man who looked like armies of bottles and cigarettes and frying pans and women and policemen and lawyers had marched across his face, for many years. George and Frankie popped up their umbrellas like popping open beer cans, and as the light was fading from the rain we all walked silently back into the woods, to the campground, and up to the tent.

George and Frankie went in, and Henry and I waited with Carter. We waited so long that even the Marley got stale, and we turned it off. It got dark. We lit the campfire. Carter sucked at a bottle of Red Dog. Through the rain sounds we sat quietly, listening to the strangely gentle murmurs of men's voices inside the tent and the songs of bedding birds and maybe even an owl.

Finally, Frankie came out, and then Malik, and then George. Malik was unsteady on his feet, swaying and bumping up against the two big men, like a boy with tribal elders. He seemed surprised at the sight of the three of us sitting around the spitting campfire on our haunches like assimilated Native Americans trying to recall a few lost tribal rites.

"How are you?" Malik asked.

"Not bad, man," said Solini, "and you?"

"Not good. I'm dying."

"What?" I cried out.

"Shit!" Solini said.

"I've got lung cancer."

"How bad?" I asked, knowing that lung cancer is all bad, just death, and goddamnit it wasn't fair—Malik never even smoked.

"Bad enough," Malik said. But then he smiled, he actually smiled, and went on, "But not bad enough to drink over. Let's go."

"Where to, man?"

"Heidelberg East." He took a step, and fell down into the mud. It was pitiful. We rushed to help him to his feet. He was too weak to walk. We carried him out of the woods.

INSURANCE COVERAGE FOR MISERY residents-in-training reflected the hatred Lloyal von Nott had for having any residents at all, and was as bad as was allowed by law. With a DSM of 305.02, Alcohol Abuse, Malik would be able to stay for only eight days. If we could make up a few more DSM diagnoses and slip them past the flunky docs and pimply drones of insurance, Malik could stay longer. For a stay in a psychiatric hospital, cancer didn't count. For a stay in a real hospital, cancer was a pretty good diagnosis to have. As Malik put it, crumpling into a chair on the ward that night:

"I could probably stay till they treated me to death."

"Be with you in a second," I said, leaving to make up a chart for him.

"Yeah, sure. You doctors are all alike."

As I put together his chart, I had a sense that something was terribly wrong: I would be Malik's doctor? How could I make the shift from seeing him as my teacher to seeing him as my patient, and in a mental hospital that he had taught me was dangerous to your mental health? I stared down the hallway at the little group: Malik was sitting between George and Frankie, his head in his hands, his whole body shaking. From a chill? Fear? Could he be weeping? Solini was in motion before them, rolling and dancing, wiping his eyes as if crying. Something about the four of them, sitting there together in the dark lap of grief in a corner of that brightly lit hallway, helped me to move.

I stood in front of Malik and said, "I'll have to admit you."

"Shhh," he said, holding his head as if I'd shouted at him. "Whisper, 'kay?" I nodded. He paused. "I ain't sure I'm gonna stay."

"Malik," George said, "you are gonna stay. Right, Frankie?"

"Right. Turn it over, Malik. Right?"

Malik grunted something that did not sound like agreement.

"Where do you want him, Doc?" George asked.

"There's no need to do a formal interview," I said, "just bring him—"

"You gonna be my doctor?" Malik said savagely. "Or you gonna fuck around? 'Cause if you're gonna fuck around I'm outta here."

"Okay, let's go. Bring him into the examining room."

They hoisted him up. He stopped them. "Listen, all of you." He coughed pitifully. Solini blew his nose wetly. "I'm scared. My life is shit. I have no idea how to deal with this. I'm asking for help. From all of you." He looked from one of us to the other, his eyes, coming to me, seeming dull, low wattage, as if he'd been unplugged. "Forget I'm a doctor. Treat me as if I were someone you really cared about—a family member, or a good friend."

"You are," I said.

"Yeah, man," Solini said.

"A good friend in shit shape. I'm turning my life over to you."

Alone with him in the examining room, I sat for a few seconds, trying to adjust my "set" to being here with a new patient, but a patient whom I really cared about. Distance and closeness flickered back and forth, like one of those drawings that seen one way is an urn, seen another, two faces. I asked, "What happened?"

In a quiet voice riding on bitterness, punctured by dry coughs that seemed to tear at my own chest, he talked about his desperation on Thoreau, trying to care for people who were being destroyed by A.K., his desperation at seeing me being destroyed, the guilt he felt for not being able to protect Oly Joe or Zoe, his starting to withdraw from Bronia. "And from AA. Remember the night you saw me leave my meetin' early? I was 'budding.' "

" 'Budding'?"

"Getting ready to drink. You missed it."

"Missed what?"

" 'The Malik Sign.' Talking to you that night, when you offered me tea, I thought of drinking, and I licked my lips. A drunk who's gettin' ready to drink will always lick his lips the first time in a conversation he thinks of alcohol—an addict too, with his drug of choice. I got isolated. Didn't call my sponsor. Bronia went to Israel—again! Finally I went to see my doctor, got some tests. Coin-sized lesion, left lower lobe. Fingerprint of death. Had a long talk with my doc, going over alternatives. Then I went out."

" 'Out'?"

"Drinkin'. Took Bronia's tent and headed for the woods."

"What about the cancer? What'd they say?"

"C'mon," Malik said angrily, "c'mon! Stay with me where I *am*. I'm telling you I was trying to destroy myself, going into the woods!"

"But I thought that was why you 'went out,' and—"

"There's no 'why'! I drink 'cause I got a disease."

"You really believe that?"

"This isn't about what I believe or what you thought, this is about life 'n' death. Can you get with me or not? 'Cause if you can't, if *you* can't stand it, *I* can't stand it, and I'm gone. I'm such a smart tough miserable sonofabitch that anything less than reality is gonna fail! Let go of the shrink bullshit and just reach! Be with me! Yes or no?"

"Yes," I said, holding out my hand, palm up, to him.

He stared at it, and then put his own on it, his hand filthy and raw against the clean pink of mine, dirt making black rings under every nail but one that was purple, half torn off, his hand trembling from the few hours without alcohol in it, his skin dry from dehydration, the tremor stirring up a sickly sweet scent of ketone and a flashback to the derelict drunks of my internship. I squeezed his hand, the watery thinness of it a shadow of our first handshake on Emerson last July, when the tendons had felt like wires and the muscles like pliant steel—an athlete's hand.

"Maybe you are," he said, taking his hand away, "and maybe not."

He went on to talk about his pattern of drinking before I met him, and of his drinking during his residency. Two years before exactly, when his Heiler patient had hanged herself after a session with him, he'd gotten sober.

"My second anniversary was hell," he said. "We drunks, deep down, have such a shitty opinion of ourselves, that all the good things that happen when we're sober don't seem to fit, so we sabotage 'em."

We finished the interview. I helped him strip for the physical exam. His dirt-dark head and hands and ankles contrasted with the white skin of the rest of him, like a blackface minstrel offstage. As I went over him, I saw the slippage in tone and tissue of his athlete's body, and felt sad.

"I refuse the rectal," he said. "Find anything? Like liver?"

"Nope," I said, knowing he was wondering if I had palpated a hard liver edge, a sign that the cancer had metastasized already. "Except for some infected sores and dehydration, physical exam normal." Our eyes met again. He shook his head, at the irony of the "normal."

"Cancer, me?" he said, shaking his head. "People always seem to get what they fear most."

"I'll draw bloods and write the order for a Librium detox. We'll get you cleaned up and to bed."

Getting the tubes and needles and putting on the tourniquet and drawing his blood was a relief. "You're not so bad at straight medicine," Malik said sarcastically. "Y'ever think of becoming a *real* doctor?" I smiled. "I know I need to go to groups here, see my sponsor, work the Program, but deep down all I feel is 'fuck it.' I need you, Basch, to help me stay here, get my ass in gear."

"I'll drop by as much as I can."

"Dickheads never learn. You don't 'drop by,' you make appointments with. I'm in hell. I need some order."

I got out my book and made appointments for each day. "Okay, let's go."

"I can't go."

"Why not?"

"Because I'm stark naked, schmucko, and I've got no clean clothes!"

"Sorry. I'll get you something to wear."

"Amazing," he said quietly. "You didn't even ask."

"Ask what?"

"*Why* I got cancer. We've gotten so used to everybody getting cancer, that when somebody gets it, we don't even ask why. We see it as an act of God, which is the one thing it most certainly is not. Uh oh." He rolled his eyes.

Bronia was in the doorway, carrying a suitcase. She marched past me straight to Malik, and from her stride I was afraid she would smack him for insubordination, but she put her hands on him gently and broke into sobs. I left them there together while I went to write his orders.

THE NEXT MORNING Malik announced that he was leaving.

"Nice try, Basch, but no thanks."

He made it out of his room into the foyer before he encountered Frankie, the mental health worker. Frankie, broad and solid, blocked his way. Geneva and Yoman were there. Seeing Malik, the dog whined and waggled expectantly.

"Hello, Leonard," Geneva said. "Going to 'Leisure Skills Group'?"

Malik stood there for a few seconds, swaying. "I didn't come in here of my own free will. I was carried in. It wasn't my choice."

"Since when does a drunk have a choice?" Frankie asked.

" 'Self-centered thought and action,' " Geneva said, "is a killer."

"Screw you," Malik said bitterly, "screw you all. I'm going back to bed."

That was just the beginning. Malik attacked all of us, especially me, his alleged therapist. Anything I said or tried to suggest, or do, or not do—even the quality of my listening—he either trashed directly or mocked perfectly. He took everything I said and batted it back to me, using his uncanny feel for the inner workings of people on me, criticizing me mercilessly. I knew that he was in withdrawal and a little looped on Librium, but still, all his negativism about me and life was hard to take. I felt incompetent and naive, much like I'd felt on my first days on Emerson, faced with a hallful of "borderlines" that Malik said didn't exist. He was infuriating, baffling. Every day when I went to see him, I was called on to use all the skills he had taught me, and all the skills I had learned over the year—how to face someone's rage, how to work the transference, how to keep exploring—trying to just be there with him despite his fatalism, bitterness, and rage.

It wasn't just his negativism that made things hard, it was the sheer force of his presence. For the first time I could see how I, and other psychiatrists, in the presence of someone full of energy, full of the fatal real stuff of living, could take the easy way out, retreat, protect, defend by calling in umpteen Heiler factors, or A.K.'s Freudian bullshit reducing vitality to bad childhoods, or Errol's biology saying it's all bad brain molecules and we can fix it fast because people are basically dogs. Like when the eye doctor clicks in those last few lenses and suddenly you not only see, but see that you have not been seeing, I saw the power of psychiatry to fashion hundreds of ways to deny the truth of human-to-human contact and label the other person as "sick." But if there was one thing I was sure of about Malik, it was that he was not "sick." Mentally, he was one of the healthiest people I'd ever met.

I was not at all sure that I could meet him in his intensity. Often, being with him felt too hot to take. Or too cold, for sometimes he would withdraw under the covers, alone, all ice. I constantly felt like a failure, believing that after eight days he'd walk and start to drink, and it would be my fault. We extended our sessions to an hour and a half. The level of *realness* he demanded was extraordinary. Any wavering, any bullshit, any movement away from this "ruthless encounter" in the present, and he picked it up and threw it back in my face. Sometimes there would come a point where it was like listening to fingernails screeching against a blackboard. Other times the silence was so intense I sensed it was the big one: a beloved person, dying.

I was sitting with an expert who had handed over all expertise to me, while demanding that I not treat him "expertly," but merely as another suffering human being. How was I supposed to use my own experience of suffering to help him, anyhow? I felt lost. On rare occasions I would try to slip in one of the techniques he himself had taught me.

"Don't try that goody-two-shoes Malik bullshit on *me*," he'd say. "Let's just forget it. The only thing that can help me is talking to another drunk."

"I may be a drunk too."

"You? You're not a drunk."

"I've been drinking a lot." I told him about fleeing Misery for a drink or two before facing Zoe in therapy.

"A drink or two?"

"Yeah."

"A drunk would never stop at two. You ain't one."

"So then how can I help you? You need to go to the AA groups, and talk."

"Yeah, but I can't. The staff all know me. I'm too ashamed." I stared at him as if from a distance. "And stop looking at me like I'm already dead. I'm not an object, I'm a person. I'm still here. Jesus fuckin' Christ!"

EPIDEMIC, UNAPOLOGETIC RAIN dimmed the days and pestered the nights. On day three, Malik refused to get out of bed. He was filled with gloom.

"I've never been able to really love anyone, my whole fucking life."

"You?" I said. He didn't respond. "What do you mean?"

"Aw c'mon!" he said, and then, mockingly, " 'What do you meeen?' "

"People think you love them."

"Great, great. It's nice to think that they think that, oh yeah."

"You draw people to you. It's unbelievable how many people have come to visit you in here."

It was true. Malik was like a beloved patriarch on his deathbed in the autumn of his life. Not only was he visited by Bronia and her friends, but by great numbers of Misery workers, from Viv, who came in with a florid dress and a perfume that whacked you hard and a lace hankie, and Primo, who blubbered like a baby, through various Misery social workers and nurses and mental health workers, to just about every member of Buildings and Grounds who chattered awkwardly with him in their particular dialects from Africa or the Caribbean and left a small token of their love, usually a single flower or a bead or, from one ebony-black woman whose neck seemed more constrained than adorned by gold bangles, a doll and pins and in a glassine bag a potion from the Brazilian rain forest containing a piece of skin from the giant anaconda that ate her brother which she said he should smoke to "kill dot Cancer Debil." Then there were those from the AA and NA community, the "Program" people, people from all walks of life, "from Yale to jail," from all over New England, for it turned out that Malik had been active in going on "commitments," where one AA group went to talk to another.

Soon Geneva and I, with his agreement, had to restrict his visitors. Word spread fast, and the torrent of visitors eased to a trickle and then to nothing at all, except one day when an older woman appeared who looked familiar. She turned out to be Mrs. Kondrath-Robb, the nurse on Women's Chronic 9 at Candlewood, the back ward that Malik and I had been the only doctors to venture into. Malik had kept going back weekly. I had not. Another failure.

Now I said to him, "Everybody loves you, Malik."

"Yeah," he said, sinking lower into his pillow, "but I don't love anybody the way I could. I look good, but I'm faking it. I lead a double life, a secret life. I can't love anyone. Can't really get to it with anyone." He paused, shot me a furtive, shy look. "Like I'm not gettin' to it with you."

He turned his head and stared at me, waiting for my answer. I felt a pressure to respond, to try to help, to fix things. But I didn't know what to say or do. Worse, I saw that he knew I didn't. I felt flustered.

"Can't you say *anything*? For Chrissakes I just spill my guts to you, Basch, tell you the worst thing about me, and you just *sit there*? Fuck! Stop thinking about your fuckin' self and start thinkin' about *me*!"

"I am thinking about you—"

"The hell you are."

"You're a lot better at this than me, Malik. I'm trying my best, but—"

"I'm lost, I'm hurting, I need to feel you with me! You're my best friend and I don't know you!"

"Me?"

"What's *your* pain? Your secret, the double life you're leading? What's your suffering, your obsession? What's *yours*?"

"I . . . I don't know."

"Terrific. Basch, you're history. I'm outta here." He got up and walked out into the hallway, heading for the unlocked door.

Frankie the mental health worker stopped him. "Easy does it, Malik."

"I'm dying," he said bitterly, "I might as well die drunk."

"Malik, please," I said, "I'm sorry—"

"Too late, Basch. When it came right down to it—" He coughed, pitiably. "—you couldn't even *ask*."

"Ask?"

"Figure it out."

"Stop." I grabbed his arm. "You will *not* leave. No way."

"Oh that's good," he said mockingly. "Use your authority. Use force. Get violent. That's very good, that's really going to work, on me."

I let go. He walked past us out the door. I walked out after him.

He didn't go far. He was standing on the bridge over the ravine between the Heidelbergs, stamping one foot, then the other, cursing. The wrought-iron imitation gas lamps lit him up like in a film. His breath made small clouds in the mist. I saw the smallness of the clouds as a diminished pulmonary vital capacity, from his cancer.

I stood on the porch, staring at him across the stream of rain. I called to him. He waved me off. Then he took something out of his pocket that glinted in the fake gaslight. A knife? A gun? He bowed his head, struck a match. It went out. He cupped his hands more intently, struck another, and lit a cigar. He puffed, coughed, puffed again. Then he straightened up and stood there, facing me, smoking and coughing. The red tip of the cigar glowed and faded like a geriatric firefly. The shadow Malik cast seemed sharp and solid, as if a source of high wattage was blocked by something deathly opaque. Frankie came out onto the porch.

"Ever been to a meetin', Doc?" Frankie asked as we watched Malik.

"Nope."

"Shit. Biggest disease in medicine, and they don't teach you young docs how to treat it. Only thing that'll save our man Malik is gettin' him to tell his story to another drunk, either his sponsor, or at a meetin'."

"He won't."

"Yeah I know. All us guys, it's like in our nature—when we get into trouble, we think we gotta 'stand tall' and handle it ourself. All that ridiculous John Wayne bullshit. For a man like Malik to ask for help is the hardest thing in the world. But the fellas who make it, well, they go against their nature. Move in the e-zact opposite direction. Ask for help. You identify with this at all?"

"Maybe. How do you get someone like Malik to ask for help?"

"Didja get him to fill out his 'Spiritual Inventory' in the chart?"

"He refused."

"Yeah, well, I guess somebody's gotta get down on his knees."

"Pray? Him?"

"Him too."

"Who else?" Frankie smiled. Horrified, I said, "Me?"

"You're the only one he's talkin' to anymore, Doc. He's choosin' you."

"Yeah, well, suppose I'm all out of God."

"Who said anythin' about God? You don't have to pray to God. You just gotta admit you ain't God, I mean you yourself."

"Who ever said I was?" My long kosher history of the Old Testament God who'd vaporize you if you dared eat a shrimp or soul-kiss a shiksa had scared me off, and I had mostly vaporized Him. "God? The face of Jesus in a plate of linguini?"

"Aw, don't do that, Doc."

"Hundreds saw Him, last week, in the linguini on a billboard in Tampa."

He laughed. From that bulky body came a girlish giggle. "Yeah, well I used to be the worst drunk in the world, Doc. One day I asked for help—not from God, from another drunk. It worked."

"You're saying that it'll help if I pray?"

"Can't hurt, can it? Malik's just about gone now."

"Well how the hell is my praying gonna help him?"

Malik, drenched, was coughing and shivering. "Dunno, Doc, but you got any better ideas?"

I turned to go back inside.

"Hey, dickhead!" Malik called out.

I turned back. "Yeah?"

Malik was holding his cigar in the V of his index and middle finger, and pointing it at me accusingly. He looked like nothing so much as a failed, bitter impresario blaming me for his ruin. "What's yours?" he asked. "What the fuck is *yours*?"

Nineteen

THAT NIGHT I DROVE to the ocean, to moonlight as an emergency room doctor at Collins Community Hospital, which served a once-flourishing fishing port now decaying hopefully to a tourist trap. Solini had been moonlighting there. This was my first time. It was eighty bucks an hour for a twelve-hour shift, from seven at night to seven in the morning, and much of it, according to Henry, would be spent sleeping. I had dug up my battered black bag and instruments that I'd used on our trip around the world, serving as a doctor when needed. The last time had been just about a year before in Changsha, China, after the flooding of the Xiangjiang River.

Now as I drove on through the dark rain—rain that I knew would assure me a busy night—Malik's words echoed in my mind, much as, when a coin spinning on a tabletop falters, the ringing gets more and more insistent as it falls.

"What's *yours*? What's your pain, your secret, your obsession?"

He was saying that the only way I could be with him was to be with my own pain. Yet something was keeping me from it, even from my telling anyone about my own despair, my having prepared to commit suicide. What had he meant when he'd said, "Too late to ask"? Ask what?

Collins Hospital was a classic New England colonial complex overlooking the sea. I walked through the packed waiting room like a gunslinger hired to save the town. Greeting the nurses and orderlies, I eased into the familiar banter of those chosen to work the frayed edge between health and horror. I soon felt at home.

Immediately I was bombed, starting with a kid with an earache and a temp of 105, a man my age dying from a heart attack, two ferocious nosebleeds, a garbageman who'd fallen down a manhole, a kid with a popcorn kernel in her ear which I couldn't get out, a horrifically sick old man from a nursing home who thought I was "Lana Tuna," and several minor car accidents, one after a high-speed police chase that had half the local cops signing in with neck and back pain, going for the gold of workmen's comp. Most I handled with ease, pleased that my body-doctoring skills were still intact.

And there was also something new, for as I worked on these people I realized how much my vision had broadened. Instead of seeing just bodies, I was seeing people, reading people, sensing in people's faces and postures and words and in the intangible stuff, some truth about the person, not only in terms of each life, but in each as part of any life, of life itself. I saw the sorrow behind the smile, the years of pain pulling out the lines from the corners of the mouth and eyes, the rage provoking the scar, the weight of nostalgia tugging down the lip, even the smile behind the sorrow. From my year of focusing on the something else besides what these people were showing me consciously, they had become more translucent yet more substantial, in the way that the translucency of a deep-sea creature reveals the bones, the guts, the feathery beat of the heart, that glassy-ribbed heart.

My way of being with them as a doctor had changed. My instruments—my shiny chrome stethoscope, otoscope, ophthalmoscope, reflex hammer—were not so much instruments to probe the body as tools with which to make contact. Examining a feverish, scared infant making the classic bark of croup, I gave her the bell end of the stethoscope to play with, and let her put it on my own chest before putting it on hers, so that it became for her—and for me, through her laughter—a way of easing her fear. Once I had the feel with a person, he or she caught on, and seemed more interesting. For the first time in my medical career, something bizarre was happening: I, a doctor, was truly curious about them, the patients. How reassuring it was, after so many hands-off months of shrinking, to noodle around in bodies, palpating a belly, percussing a spleen, auscultating a heart, the sounds calling up the anatomy—that squeak a tight aortic valve, that train rumble a leaky mitral. And the beauty of the retina, the only place in the body where blood vessels can be seen directly, a bright red tangle of arterioles against the amber dome, the Sistine of sight.

Not that it was easy. Medicine reflects society, and the society of this dying town was split between the few who owned everything, the Reagan-Bush-Clinton rich, and the anxious rest. The town was full of violence and greed and drugs and people losing jobs and losing hope, all under the mocking eye of the few who, in our tattered democracy because they could pay to control the tax code and the politicians, controlled the many, the few who holed up behind the alarmed granite walls and ironwork gates of their great estates, with private security and private schools and private jets and private clubs and private souls. I was the guy at the end of the ambulance ride, treating the rage and despair.

By eleven I hadn't sat down, eaten, or gone to the bathroom, and that was just the start. A baby came in with a laceration on his forehead, needing two sutures. He was almost blue from screaming. The nurse asked the worried mother to leave, which wrenched me, as it had rarely wrenched me during my internship when I'd viewed mother or father or whoever else was there beside the patient as a mere bother, adding to my time awake, to be gotten rid of. Now, as I strapped the baby down on a papoose board, I saw in his desperate face that of an old man, bald, tormented at being strapped down into a nursing home bed, both faces at once. With a tiny hooked needle clasped in my forceps, I hovered above the baby's face, sweating now, trying to place just two little sutures in that wound. The baby's eyes suddenly became immense, as if the forehead were all eyes, eyes plump as ripe grapes, and his head moved back and forth with remarkable strength despite the nurse's hands, and I thought, What if this needle hits his eye? The point snagged skin. I was amazed again at how tough skin is, even a baby's. I curled it through, snagging the other edge, pulled, tied, cut. Drenched in sweat, I threw in a second suture. Done. I sighed with satisfaction. Undid the damp baby. Handed him back to his mom.

Much of what I saw was psychiatric: belly pain, anxiety, phobias, depression, suicide attempts, hallucinating crazies. Before, these had been "turkeys," unfathomable and untreatable, mocked by us real docs and turfed to the shrink or back out onto the street. Now they were familiar, and easy. In a few minutes I got the feel of where this person stood in the world. I *had* learned something in my year of psychiatry, something about how to listen to intense feeling without flinching, how to make sense of it.

At about midnight there was a lull. I went to see a woman complaining of shortness of breath. She had been to many specialists. No one could find anything wrong except eosinophilia, a high number of allergic cells in her blood. She'd even been to MBH—Man's Best Hospital—with no luck. She was a fine-featured, pleasant woman of fifty, sitting in her emergency room nightie, oxygen mask over her face, gasping for breath. I listened to her story. She was neither crazy nor hypochondriacal. I began asking her not about her breathing, but about her life. One thing led to another. It turned out that she rented out rooms of her house, and that one of her boarders was a magician who kept pigeons in her basement. Curious, I asked about this magician, these pigeons. It turned out that the pigeons were kept in cages near the washer-dryer. Whenever she did the wash, the pigeon shit got blasted up into clouds, which she inhaled.

"That's it," I said, "your lung disease."

"The pigeons?"

"The pigeons' shit. You've got 'pigeon breeder's lung disease.' "

"But what's the treatment?"

"Move the pigeons!"

"I will!"

You listen with curiosity, you hear it all.

I went to bed at two, but was awakened from deep sleep by a nurse, stat. I felt I had slept for ten hours, but it turned out to have been ten minutes. I had that horrible feeling of stumbling up out of a sweet dark dream into a fluorescence and having to face a terrible emergency, trying to remember where I was let alone what to do as a doctor. A two-car collision. Bodies mangled and cut and messed up in unmentionable ways. I was running to and fro and calling surgeons, who came cheerily in, happy to be doing nice civic things like sewing fingers back on hands and hands on wrists and lining up bones straight as five irons. Finally everybody was into operations or casts or cars home. I finished and stood there shivering in the spring cold, for I was wearing only a thin green operating room shirt, about to go back to bed again, but then the nurse said she had a case of child abuse where a father had broken a baby's arm and then another car crash with two great drunken Americans going through the windshield so it was Laceration City and a woman giving birth, which brought back my days at the National Maternity Hospital in Dublin where at eleven-thirty at night we'd get kicked out of The Silent Woman—which so many of the docs and med students hung out at that we nicknamed it "the Office"—and staggered up to Delivery and half-banjaxed on Guinness would pull out a baby or two before staggering back down to bed. And then a kid with a temp of 105 and seizures from it and an old man with a blood pressure of 60 and a temperature of 106—in whose scared tight face I saw that of the baby I'd sewn up earlier—and then, before five, I got a call to do a favor for a local doctor who had been called at home to do it but didn't want to come in, to go up onto the ward of the hospital to pronounce someone dead.

Sleepily, I took the silent elevator up to the top floor and walked the waxy corridor toward the light near the end, stethoscope tapping one side of my belly and then the other like an elephant's trunk. I stopped at the nursing station, got the name, went down to the room.

There lay a man, his body emaciated. His eyes were open and dead and his mouth was open and dead and his color was more blue than white, which meant he was recently dead, the oxygen in his blood vanishing, but not vanished. His age was hard to guess, given his disease. Probably about sixty. A whole life, a whole family, a whole life of learning to creep and crawl and cruise and walk and talk and love and hate and beat out a single down the first base line and make money and woo and wed and have children and sicken and now die. My not knowing anything about him gave his death depth, for it was anyone's death. My death, and Malik's—for here was metastatic cancer.

I laid my stethoscope on his heart and heard nothing.

I went to the nursing station and signed him out as dead and walked down the still smooth corridor to the elevator alone and secure in my mortality. Secure, yes, for I felt comforted that sooner or later someone else would be viewing me this way, as anybody, once alive, now dead. I felt a sense of awe at that, at the brief human day, a blink in the eye of whatever lasts, a part of whatever is whole, the awe at all the faces and bodies I'd seen and treated that night.

Secure in my mortality, I went to bed.

I slept as if dead until seven, then dressed and walked out into the fluorescents. Caroline the night nurse thanked me and I her, for the good job we'd done. I followed the smell of freshly baked muffins to the cafeteria, where I sat watching the manly, insecure construction workers drink coffee and talk sports and "pussy" and eat muffins and get ready to do death-defying ironwork in the name of making more hospital. Then I got into my car, but instead of heading back toward Misery, for some reason I drove down the main street of colonial mansions crowned with widow's walks and through the slums of the seaport with its bars and yuppie shops and then along the sea to the neck of land leading out to the five-mile-long island, half of which was a bird sanctuary, half public beach.

Berry and I had walked here once, a couple of years before, during my internship. She had suggested walking the whole beach in silence. I remembered how, that day, despite the bright sun and deserted beach and optimistic gulls and the hand of the woman I loved clasped in mine, my mind had been busily elsewhere, over and over running a tape of how, compared to others, I was a failure at . . . at . . . I couldn't even recall at what now.

But it had spoiled our day. My obsession with comparing myself to others, and my feeling like a failure, had gotten in the way of my being with her. What insanity.

Now I looked around at the expanse of nipping, sharp sea, the gulls and sandpipers and husks of crabs and sand dollars, and then looked back to the twisted slats of dune fencing and willowy grasses taunting the wind, to the bird sanctuary.

Suddenly I felt cold. Somewhere in this sanctuary Cherokee Putnam had put a gun in his mouth and pulled the trigger.

Realizing then that that was why I had been drawn here, I stood chilled by the wind and warmed by the sun, trying to get my mind around these images. That was what had killed Cherokee: his relentless comparing himself to others and feeling he was not enough, a failure, trapped. A *core ingrati*, he'd called it, an "ungrateful heart."

"The hearts of ambitious people dry up," Malik had said. "The self is insatiable—it can never get enough. Once you get into your self, kid, you can't help but compare yourself to others, and you're doomed."

Now I saw what he meant. Hadn't I done a good job in the emergency room because nothing about *me* was riding on it? No one knew me there, nothing I did would advance or retard my career. I was not into *me*, I was into caring for others. I had relaxed into just doing the job at hand, meeting each challenge without pride, doing things easily, with that relaxation into the truth in the corner of my eye. The meeting of the challenge had created the energy, increased the understanding. Not being focused on myself had opened up my vision, allowed me to read people. I knew all too well the destruction I caused when I went ruthlessly after things with tunnel vision, knocking others aside to get there. My focus on my failures on this beach on that dazzling day had kept me from being with the woman I loved. When I saw the world in terms of myself, I saw narrowly and perversely, I compared myself to others, felt I was never enough, and my obsession with all the others who were enough passed in front of my eyes like the electronic stock quote strip that runs around the front of that tower in Times Square.

But if I saw the world not in terms of me, but as a world of which I am a part, a temporary expression? What might I see?

Suddenly I understood how "self" was at the center of psychiatry, a whole industry sprung up to use the self of the psychiatrist to solidify the self of the patient, using talk, using drugs—it was all the same. The various theories were an invention of complexity in the face of something that was incredibly simple: making connection. As if they had invented the complexity not only to protect themselves from that connection, but also to make their own "selves" seem special, better than or smarter than—any comparative would do—their patients? All these suits of armor and regimented ties, these big black shoes, these laughable words. Make it so complex that you need advanced degrees to do it, and only they could do it, charging enormous prices for their monopoly on the perversion of "selfdom," the suicidal white underbelly of the American Dream, to fight tooth and nail not to be with others, or to be like others, but to be special, separated and individuated from others. What bullshit. And all the while it is connection, not self, that heals.

But how? How to get the self out of the way and just be there?

"Ask."

I stared directly into the sun as it eased aside the coverlets of mist, and saw what Malik had meant. In that moment with him, feeling pressured by him to respond, I thought I should be able to fix it, and not being able to think how to fix it, had said nothing. All I had to do was ask. My self-centeredness had kept me from asking. If I let go of the center, could the right questions be asked? Asked of him? Asked from him, for help? Are they the same?

"What's *yours?*"

Could it be just this, my obsession with comparison?

The way that I, from my earliest memories, had tried to be better than everyone, at grade school, at sports, with girls, in college—organic chemistry!—Oxford, med school, my trying to be better keeping me from connecting, keeping me from helping anyone else—great preparation for the "helping professions!"—the tape of comparing myself to others running in my head, keeping me from having the clarity of heart to take the hand offered by the woman who loved me for myself and in spite of myself too, whom I could mostly hide the tape from, keeping me from being with her at the deepest levels, let alone nurturing others, except for my own success. Always comparing, and at the moments of my greatest success, feeling like I was a great failure. Now I saw how this whole year I'd been comparing myself to my teachers, how, when I was with my patients, I was focusing on trying to be as terrific a shrink as Heiler, or A.K., or Ike, or even Malik, rather than just forgetting myself and being there with them. A.K. was the worst, the real point of her Freudianism being to focus on your own inner machinery, and this focus had first seduced, then isolated, and finally killed Cherokee. With disgust I saw how I had been intent on playing a boy's game of "Follow the Leader," and all the while the people asking me for help were dropping alongside. I was walking along behind the alleged authorities, and all the while chanting under my breath the great American mantra, "not enough, not enough, I am not enough."

And keeping it a secret, even from myself. Hiding it, yes. All the secrets we men keep, the double lives we men live. From the secret pain of Ike White smiling and shaking my hand an hour before he did it, to Cherokee, who never once mentioned his obsession with suicide to me, and all the patients I'd heard it from, like the man who for years seemed to be going out to work each morning but in fact went to shack up with a woman and drink and watch TV till the wife's money ran out, and the cousin's husband whose long affair with the fellow schoolteacher was discovered only when he left the pornographic photos of them on his workbench in the basement in a box filled with forms he'd been given to fill out by students for college recommendations, all of which were still blank. All these double lives, these secrets! All the ways we men stay unseen. My secrets. I'd never really opened up to Malik about my work with Cherokee. I still hadn't told him about my seeing Schlomo fucking Zoe. And I'd yet to tell anyone about my plans to kill myself.

"What the fuck is *yours?*"

"I'm obsessed with comparing myself to others," I said to a nearby gull.

Is it possible? I wondered, staring at the gull and then past it to the sun, seeing it straggle up out of the week of rain and morning's rain like a wet mirage, shaped through the layers of mist to look remarkably like a gilded version of my grandfather's battered homburg hat. Is this "mine"?

"Hey, it's possible," I whispered to the sun, feeling embarrassed at this, such a thin, reedy voice at the billowing intersect of ocean and beach and windy sky, this magnificent edge of dawn's bed. I felt really tired, tired of the old ways of seeing the world, and yet I felt like the sun, my heart rising through the mist, freed.

I wanted desperately to *do* something, to make some sign. I got down on my knees and put my palms to the sand and, that not being enough—there it is again, that "enough" shit!—I lay flat on my belly, putting my face to the sand, it feeling rough, gritty, bathing my eyelids my nose my lips in a mist of grit. Wondering, Is this prayer I hope not, I rubbed my face back and forth in this grit, and then I gathered myself and sprang up into the air like one of the worst psychotics in the world and cried out, "It is possible!" and continued to cry it out as I half ran half floated up the beach, back, feeling for the first time in my life that I was more *like* everyone than not.

The buffoonish gulls and meticulous sandpipers scattered, then re-formed like water in my wake. How could I have helped Cherokee? How can I help Malik?

By riding this sense of "like," by connecting. But how? Something is missing. Whom to ask now, for help?

MALIK REFUSED TO SEE ME.

At three that afternoon I drove to the nursery school. Berry would be out at three-fifteen. I hadn't seen her for a long time, and although we'd talked on the phone maybe once every other week or so, we had stayed away from the pain, and the residual hope.

I stood on the civilian side of the Cyclone-fence swinging gate, looking into the driveway which, given how small the preschoolers were, was big enough, with a slash of grass on either side, to function as their playground. To the left of the driveway were the jungle gym and swings and a tire suspended from three chains, which the kids could swing on and rotate around while other kids pushed. To the right, the sandbox and mud pile and a kids' plastic kitchen set were next to the stairs of the old house that functioned as the school.

As I waited, the "threes" and "fours" were being picked up by their parents, thirty-two splashes of bright kid colors zipping here and there until each got linked up, each little hand finding a big one, attached to a grown-up more drably dressed. Seeing those little hands in those bigger ones, sensing the flutter of big people's love even if clouded by irritation at little people's dirt on pants or failure to wear a hat in the chill of the day, these hands and this flutter had a strangely deep effect on me, as if my heart, so dry as to be brittle, was drinking in some of it, and softening.

A lull. No more kids. I waited. Berry.

She looked older, more substantial, in a way, maybe because of all the small kids. She was dressed in jeans and a T-shirt with the nursery school logo on the front, a kid's drawing of a sun, simple round black circle filled in with yellow, and with black sun rays streaming out. The yellow sun was a face, with a smile. She looked like she had gained weight.

When she saw me, she stopped still. Then without a word she walked to the gate and stared into my eyes.

"Hi," I said.

"What happened to you?" Berry asked.

"You mean where was I?"

"No, no, I mean now. What happened?"

"Why? What do you see?"

"Your eyes are filled with light. What happened?"

"C'mon. I'll tell you." She hesitated. "I know, I know," I said, "it's crazy, to just show up like this. But I've got to talk to you. If you'll just give me an hour, that's all—"

"That's all? You show up out of the blue, your eyes all funny, and you're just going to give me an hour?"

"You want more?"

"Still afraid of that?"

"No, I mean not right now. I need to show you something, at my place. Okay?" She nodded. "C'mon."

As we drove along I told her about my night in the hospital, my morning on the beach, and as I told it I heard it as simple, clear, like when you tell someone your home address. We parked at my house.

"On your face?" she asked. "Really on your face?"

"Very much so."

"In the sand?"

"Still got some grit, in my teeth."

"Roy, that's wonderful!"

"You think?"

"I know." She hesitated. "Shit."

"What?"

"It's just that—I don't know—I was starting to get over your being gone. . . ."

"And?"

"And you're here, you creep. I mean you're really here."

"Like I wasn't, that day on the beach."

"And when I tried to get to you that day, you kept saying, 'But I *am* here, damnit! What's wrong with you? You're too damn sensitive.' " She sighed. "Creep."

"I'm sorry. Really sorry." I took her hand, looked into her eyes, and was filled with a sense of our history together, our care and concern—more—filled with a curiosity of who she was right now, for I saw that despite our years together I didn't really know who this woman was, and I wanted to, desperately. "I love you, you know. I've never stopped."

She said nothing, and looked away, out her window.

"Will you come in?" I asked. "Got something I need to show you." She nodded. I started to get out of the car. She touched my shoulder. I turned back to her.

"It's foolish for me to tell you this, Roy, but me neither."

Now we looked into each other's eyes without shying away—for me as if for the first time, that scary sacred time when I a boy first looked into her a girl's eyes without shying away—and I saw her eyes soften from a woman's to a girl's, and glow a little with tears, as did mine. We were too scared to touch each other.

We got out and I led her upstairs to the turret bedroom and opened the top drawer of the dresser and took out the small IV bottle of normal saline and the polyethylene tubing with the stopcock and butterfly needle and the bottle of phenobarb. She asked, "What's all that for?"

"To kill myself."

She gasped. "No way!" She snatched it all up and held it to her chest. "Do you have any more pills?"

"No."

"I'm getting rid of all this." She flushed the pills down the toilet and wrapped the IV bottle in a towel and smashed it with a hammer and sliced up the tubing into macaroni and bent the butterfly with a pair of pliers. I led her back to the turret and dimmed the chandelier and went around to the five windows and pulled the shades. We faced each other across the bed, our eyes gradually getting used to the darkness, sight coming back in stages, first the outline of her body, then the contour of her face, then her eyes.

For the longest time we said nothing. The bed was a barrier and a link. I sensed the energies flowing back and forth between us as if made of fine filament, say silk, that light that strong, the energies as bright and clear and usual as the ones we as babies possess before they get normalized out of us, and I saw then that this was what she might call "mutual" and I might call "being with" and Malik might call "soul" and we all might call "spirit."

I whispered, "I'm asking you for help."

"I'm here," she whispered back. I heard her crying. She bowed her head, and put her face in her hands. I stood there with my hands at my sides and cried too, not only for her but for my father, who died before I could live with him with any compassion, and before he could see any of my children.

Crying together softened us, lightened us.

I asked, "How can I help you?"

"Just by that, by asking. It works both ways."

"What are you crying about?"

"I'm crying for us."

"Us?"

"And I'm pissed as hell at you."

"I know."

"No you don't. Thanks to you, you creep, I gained eight pounds."

THE NEXT MORNING I stood outside Malik's door, knocking, to no answer. He was still refusing to go to any meetings, refusing to talk to his sponsor or to me. I opened the door and went in. The window shade was drawn against the morning. Light seeped in, in three widening slats.

Malik was lying on his side of the bed, curled up, head bowed, hands tucked into his chest, wearing jeans and a white T-shirt of which the visible portion read "—OREST." I stood, watching. He coughed, once, twice, clutched himself tighter to himself, and settled again.

I walked to the edge of his bed and sat down.

He stirred, sat up, staring at me with puzzlement, and then curiosity.

"How are you?" I asked.

"What's with you?"

"I want to hear about you—"

"No, no," he said, waving me away, "go on."

"I'm not here to talk about me, Malik."

"It's all the same," he said insistently. "Talk."

I stared at him for a moment, reluctant to go along with his deflection of attention from himself to me. He stared back, his eyes steady, suspicious. Deft, he'd always said, you gotta be deft. Don't go at suspicion head-on. I started to tell him about where I was. Things I'd kept secret: my seeing Schlomo screwing Zoe, my preparations for suicide, Zoe coming to my apartment.

"Schlomo!" he said. "The shit!"

"And there's another victim." I told him about Lily Putnam.

"What have you done about it?"

"I can't get either of them to report him, or allow me to. I need help."

"We'll get to that. Go on."

I told him about my emergency room shift. My walk on the beach. "I've been doing a lot of crying," I said, "for my father, for Berry, for all the dead patients this year. I don't know why this is all happening, but it is."

"We don't know shit about 'why' things are, so we make up all kinds of stories—shrinks make up the most bizarre stories—about penises, about brain molecules. Why did Zoe come to your apartment that night?"

"She said she had to. To keep from killing herself."

"Yeah well, what you and she didn't know is, she was the Grace of God, walking into your life."

"And I was that, at first, for you?"

He looked down at his hands. "When I first met you, with Ike just having been destroyed by this place, I felt I had to try to show you what I understood. Over the year, I've watched you being crushed, turning cynical and bitter. Then, out in the woods—you and Solini show up? In here, I saw that if I could save you, I might just save myself."

"Save us?"

"Us. Yeah."

"But how? The deeper I look, the more I see I'm totally obsessed with comparing myself to others! It's hell!"

"Yeah, I know. It's a bitch, isn't it?"

"You too?"

"I'm worse than you—see? There it is."

"But you don't seem trapped by it."

"Oh, I'm great at 'seeming,' oh yeah."

I felt the "click." This was what he had wanted me to "ask" about, and what I'd shied away from, sending him walking out into the rain in disgust.

" 'Seeming' to love?"

Our eyes met. His, dark as dusk, filled with shame and flickered away. In that flickering away from me I had a sense of seeing him from close up and far off, both at once. Seeing him not only right then and there but seeing him as part of his whole life. The brilliant shy kid fleeing his family for the elephants, and from his pain at the plight of "the big fellas" developing a talent for compassion, going on to use his strange brilliance and intensity and sense of other people to focus attention on the experience of others, drawing others to him while deflecting attention from himself, holding back, not really joining in. This whole year, he had been Malik the One Who Understands More than Me, but he had never really connected in the way in which he talked about connecting. Was he too specializing in his defect? I saw now how he'd used alcohol to break through this "seeming," it only seeming to help adding another layer of falsity.

"Buddy?" I said. "You can let me see you, it's okay."

He raised his eyes to mine. I sensed his understanding that I understood. Shame lifted and his eyes pooled with tears. I filled with an appreciation of him, of all that he had come to understand and live. And I saw all that he was about to lose, what we all would lose in losing him. Tears came. I tried to stop them but they wouldn't stop and my body shook with sobs. He and I sat there crying. As naturally as a father might comfort his child after a fall, I brought his head to my shoulder. I hugged him. Felt his bristly growth of beard.

"Fucking cancer fucking toxic shit!" he sobbed into my neck. Through the smell of vomit and night sweat and the poison of alcohol and the boniness of his shoulder and the crab of cancer snapping at the delicate pink air sacs of his lungs, through and for all this, I hugged him and he me.

After a while we sat back. He reached over and handed me a Kleenex, and took one himself. We blew our noses, two sad foghorns in the sickroom.

"Thanks," he said.

"Thank you."

"You know, all that time out in the woods drinking, all the time I've been in here, my mind is going, over and over, 'Malik, you're worse than everybody,' or 'Malik, you're better than everybody.' It's disgusting."

"I know. In my head, I've got a continuous feature playing—'The Roy G. Basch Story.' The more I try to erase it, the more it's there. How can I get rid of it?"

"What worked for me, these two years, is getting down on my knees, morning and night. Ask for help in the morning. Thank for the day's help, at night."

"You prayed?" I felt the little hairs on the back of my neck rise.

"Prayed and meditated. You know how to meditate?"

"No."

"Want me to show you?" I nodded. "This method is the Buddha's own." He sat me next to him on the bed. Told me to close my eyes. "When you look into a mirror," he said, "you see your body. When you look with your eyes closed, you see your mind. And then you've got no excuses—what you see is what you get. You see you. Focus attention on your breath. When your attention wanders, notice what it's wandered to, and bring it gently back to the breath. Don't judge it, just bring it back to the breath. Wanna do five minutes?"

"Sure." I closed my eyes. It was impossible to focus attention on my breathing for more than five seconds at a time. My mind was busy with fragmented images of trivial days. Five minutes seemed an eternity. Malik called time and asked what it had been like. I said, "What a mess."

"No joke. You think 'The Book of Basch' is bad, you should see 'The Legend of Leonard A. Malik.' "

"And this shit is going on in my mind all the time?"

"At least all the time, yop."

"What a waste, what crap! What do I do about it?"

"Do nothing!" he said, his energy rising. "Do as much nothing as possible! Just see it for what it is, just your mind. See that crap—and the anger and shame and sadness for all that crap—and sorrow for all that too—and don't lift a finger. Don't try to fix it. Sit with that sorrow, feel the edge and sharpness of that sorrow. And then—it's unbelievable!—after a while it starts to move. Sorrow can't stay still, kid, it *has to move*! As it moves, it starts to lose its grip on you. You get to know the pettiness and envy so well that when it bites you in your gut—'I'm not enough!'—you recognize it and you say, 'Oh there's that snake biting me in the gut,' and you remember to breathe, and you breathe, you go on. You see it as just a fact. And if we get with the facts, kid, we're free. And if we don't, the snake grows in us and sucks our spirit dry."

"Like it did to Ike White?"

"Like it did to poor fucking Ike White. What killed his spirit was always tryin' to become the Best Shrink in the World, and always feelin' like a failure for not."

We sat quietly together and the weight of this settled, the way the weight of a baby lying on your chest settles as she falls asleep.

"Malik?" It was Frankie at the door. "Patient Speaker Meetin'?"

Malik looked to me. "Will you come with?"

"Sure."

"Frankie, I'm gonna bring my doctor along."

Patient Speaker Meeting was an in-house AA meeting, a kind of dry run for the outside world. The speaker was the same ugly Irish drunk who'd knocked me aside my first day on Heidelberg East. Now he was clean-shaven, in a clean shirt, shaky but speaking clearly. His story was horrific. Alcoholic mother and father, first drink out in the woods with the boys, puking his guts out, vowing never to do it again, and then, the next weekend, doing it again. As a teenager, in order to get money for booze and time off from work to drink it, he had a friend break his arm with a baseball bat. Drunk, he didn't feel it. Afraid that his arm wasn't broken, told him to hit him again. He woke up in the hospital with his arm broken in three places. To escape the law he joined the navy, where he got paid to drink full-time. Discharged, he married, had kids, and his life went to hell. One morning he went out to his car and found a child's bicycle smashed against his front fender. He had no memory of what happened. The police showed up. He'd hit a little girl, broken her leg.

Another morning he awoke to find his wife lying unconscious on the bed, blood all over. Again he remembered nothing. In an alcoholic blackout, he'd beaten her with a Bruins hockey stock. She took the children and left.

I'd heard this story often as a doctor, and knew the ending: jail, or institutions like Misery and Candlewood, or death. My attention wandered to Jill, from whom I'd gotten another postcard: an immense radio telescope strung like a gargantuan spiderweb from peak to peak in Arecibo, Puerto Rico.

Went up! Moved on. Back soon.
Loveya Jill.

Puerto Rico? I thought she was in the Galápagos.

" . . . and so I got my wife and kids back and graduated from college," the Irishman said. "I never saw college in my future—hell, I never saw a *future* in my future. I was workin', goin' to meetin's, doin' good. But a month ago, after I was six years sober, my son got in trouble with the law and I got involved pullin' strings for him. I cut down on meetin's. Stopped callin' my sponsor. One night I found myself in a bar and sat down for a drink or twenty." Everybody laughed. "I was off and runnin'. My sponsor got me in here. One thing I learned: if you're in recovery from alcohol and drugs, it's a good idea to stay sober." More laughter. "Anyway, my insurance runs out today and I call the insurance girl in Tucson and tell her I need to stay. She goes no. I go, 'So what do I do?' She goes, 'Just between you and me, go out and start drinkin', and we'll call it relapse and authorize you to go back in.' " Big laughter. "So for any of you sittin' out there thinkin' it's not possible, I'm here to tell you it is possible. If I can do it, you can do it. This program is the only place that never told me I had to go seek 'outside help.' What helped me is this: don't sit here thinkin', 'I'm better than him' or 'I'm worse than him,' see if you can see how 'I'm like him.' Like they say in the fellowship: 'Identify, don't compare.' "

Malik nudged me in the ribs. I nodded.

". . . and so, if no one today told ya they loved ya, tough shit, don't drink." Big laughter. "Before I leave, I gotta make one more amends." He scanned the room, and his eyes found mine. "When I first got here, I knocked into a young doctor. On purpose. Sorry, Doc." I nodded back. "Thanks."

"Amazing," I said to Malik as we left.

"Yeah. At a meeting, you usually hear something that hits home."

"Malik?" It was Frankie. "Return-to-Work Group," Malik nodded.

"Wait a second," I said. "What do I do about Schlomo?"

"Get Zoe and Lily to meet, and to take action with you."

"I tried. They won't."

"Try again, 'cause now they will."

"Why? Nothing's changed."

"You have. You're different."

"I can't see it."

"That's how you're different. The self can't see its little deaths. You only see changes through the eyes of others—how they act with you, what they see in you." He smiled. I smiled back. "Click." I knew he was thinking, Like you and me now.

"Like you and me now?" I asked.

"See? Congratulations, Basch: you're finally catching up to where you are." We laughed. "Just make sure," he said, "when you meet with Zoe and Lily, that you're not sitting there covering up your spirit with any bullshit concepts in your head."

THE THUNDERHEADS OVER the mountains meant the end of spring. It was the next day, and Zoe again was late for her appointment. As I sat looking out the window at the storm clouds, it was as if I had opened a file cabinet in my mind. I kept seeing the whole year's worth of my meetings with Zoe in vivid detail. Every moment was there, intact. But for that first night when I'd admitted her to Misery with Malik and had felt the "click," my work with her had been a mostly frustrating attempt to locate her and respond to her, and her to me. She didn't know that she had saved me, by showing up at my house that night. At every moment, in each meeting, I had pretty well hidden myself from her.

She arrived with only fifteen minutes left to go, threw herself down in the chair and took off her Yankees cap, fluffing her short light brown hair. We chatted about the change in the weather, about our concern for the well-being of the missing Thorny. I felt a sense of sorrow for her, for what she had been put through this year in the name of psychiatric treatment. And I thought of Cherokee, how he too, lost and looking in good faith for some help, had found me, the wrong person at the wrong time, and it had killed him. If he had wandered into Malik's office, maybe he'd still be alive.

My sorrow deepened. I found myself seeing Zoe in a new way—seeing not just the words but something else, all around and in between, like on a farm on a summer's day you can almost see the breeze, ruffling the wheat. When a technique or a theory would come to mind, I'd hear Malik's voice crying, "Bullshit!" and I'd let go of the idea and keep on listening. Concepts seemed stupid now, given the facts of her suffering—even though she was speaking cheerfully. As I listened, a strange thing happened: I felt her pain so deeply that even though she was not showing it, tears came to my eyes. I was doing more crying in the last three days than in the last thirty years.

"What's wrong?" she asked.

"How do you mean?"

"No, no," she said, shaking her head, moving her hand back and forth between us as if clearing away cobwebs. "What's with you?"

"I'm feeling a lot of sadness for how you've been treated this year."

"By Schlomo?"

"And by me. I . . ." I looked away. But then, remembering how Ike had avoided my eyes, I looked back at her. I saw her quizzical look and held it with my sorrow. Saw it soften to concern. My lip trembled, my throat felt clogged. Wetness was on my cheeks. "I'm sorry, Zoe."

"Here." She handed me the Kleenex box. "What a switch, eh, Doc?"

"Thanks."

"You're like really hurting, aren't you?"

"Uh-huh. It's terrible to see what you've gone through this year. I've tried my best to help you. I hope you know that?"

"Yeah, I do. Oh shit." Tears overflowed her eyes too, and streamed down her cheeks. "Pass me back the Kleenex, will you?"

We cried, tears of sorrow and understanding and, yes, love. For the first time I saw that whatever helps people in psychotherapy has nothing to do with psychology, and everything to do with this, being human with, moving with another person as parts of a whole. Understand, and you love; love, and you understand. Love, understanding, and sorrow are different words for the same thing. "Healing," Malik had said, "is as little a matter of mind as is love."

"Thanks," Zoe said. "I've never felt this before in my life. It's scary, I mean because it's so real."

"Thank you."

"Okay. I'll meet with that other woman. If she like agrees, we'll do whatever we have to together, to get that little sonofabitch."

She left, and I called Lily Putnam. She agreed to see me again. I found her that night in the barn, "mucking out." The smell of horseshit was a kind of comfort, reminding me of lifting hay bales into carts under a full moon on a summer night in Columbia when I was in love with a farmer's daughter.

"Can we talk?" I asked.

"Got to finish this."

"Mind if I help?"

She stared at me, wiping a lock of light brown hair from her eyes. "There are some boots over there. They were his. Do you mind?"

"We'll see." I put on Cherokee's boots, and the rubbery contact they made with the barn floorboards and slippery horseshit felt familiar. We chatted as we mucked, about her children, her parents, about her life and mine, my parents—parent, rather, leading me to telling her of my father's death. "It's strange—I keep wondering where he is. I saw him in his coffin, but it's as if he's still here somehow."

"Lucky you. Cherokee made sure we'd have a closed-coffin affair. But I know what you mean. I still can't believe that Cher's not up in his office above us right now. Have you dreamed about your father?"

"No. You? I mean of Cherokee?"

"Some. He's always young and wonderful." She stopped mucking. "All right. Bring her out here tomorrow at noon. What's her name?" I was astonished. I hadn't mentioned a word about Zoe. Lily repeated, "What's her name?"

"Zoe."

"See you and Zoe tomorrow about noon."

"But why? What happened?"

"You pitched in and helped."

"Mucking?"

"That too. There are moments in life when you either do it or you miss it. Cherokee missed it. You're giving me another chance. Tomorrow at noon. The children will be at school. I'll make a light lunch."

So, I thought, struggling to take off his boots without smearing horseshit all over me, it's not what's said, it's what is. The word is not the thing. The description is not the described.

The next day, seeing the two women together, I was astonished at how alike they looked! Each was tall and slender, with the same shade of light brown hair cut in the same short style. Their eyes were the same light green and their noses were the same shape, that delicate straight line that must have provoked in Schlomo, given his ugly honker, "nose envy." As they took in the fact of their resemblance—not only in physical appearance but in culture and background—I could almost sense their feelings, as the memories of the abuse freshened. It was as if Schlomo's perversion were on view, as if I were seeing his victims through his eyes, as if he were saying, "This is the kind of girl that turns me on. When one of these dolls comes to me to find her a therapist, I keep her for myself."

"The hardest thing for me," Zoe said, "is finding out that there is another victim."

"For me too," Lily said. "And knowing that there must be others."

"Yeah."

"Which, for me," Lily went on, "is the purpose of our meeting?"

"One of the purposes," Zoe said, "yeah."

They began to compare notes. Schlomo's pattern was almost exactly the same with each of them, though it had been going on much longer with Lily. Each had thought that his words to her were unique, and it turned out that his words were almost exactly the same, as if he had practiced and perfected his seduction technique. They started to get into the details, and then stopped. Lily asked me, "Would you mind greatly if we talk alone?"

"Of course not," I said, and left, thinking it might be half an hour.

Three hours later Lily woke me up. Zoe was standing beside her. Their arms were around each other's waist. Like mother and daughter. Their eyes were puffy with crying, their faces flushed with relief.

"We've decided to take action," Lily said.

"Together," Zoe said. "And with your help."

"Great."

"We've composed a letter."

Schlomo Dove:

You have sexually abused both of us in psychotherapy. Our testimony and that of Dr. Roy G. Basch, who witnessed an episode of sexual abuse with one of us (Zoe), will stand as powerful evidence in a court of law. You have done much damage, and we are repairing this, in our own ways.

At this point, for the sake of ourselves and our families, we are not making our abuse public. We demand that you give up your medical license, resign from the Freudian Institute and Mount Misery staff, and stop seeing patients. We also ask that you meet with us, either individually or together, to try to heal the wounds.

Stop voluntarily, or we will take action in the press and courts to stop you.

"Terrific," I said, "except for one thing."

"Yes?" Lily asked.

"If Schlomo's lawyers find out that you two know each other and have talked, they can discredit your testimony. You have to write him separately. Different letters."

"Fine," Lily said.

"And this meeting between the three of us," I went on, "never took place."

"Like what meeting, Doc?" Zoe said. "I don't see any meeting."

SCHLOMO REPLIED IMMEDIATELY. He sent each of the women the same letter:

Professor Schlomo Dove is shocked and deeply hurt at your fantasies of what went on in his consulting chamber. This is an erotic transference—a *psychotic* erotic transference. You are crazy.

Schlomo Dove knows, as do you, that nothing of the kind ever happened. You are out of touch with reality. Schlomo never touched you physically, except for an occasional handshake on Christmas or the 4th of July.

Schlomo Dove will fight tooth and nail in any arena including a court of law to protect his professional honor against this smear campaign. When Schlomo Dove's word is put up against your word—a borderline woman with a history of psychopathology and hospitalization whose detailed record Schlomo has on file, and the word of a first-year psychiatric resident who is known to be unstable and a troublemaker—you don't stand a chance.

Drop this, or Schlomo Dove will sue you to the wall. Nash Michaels, Counsel to Misery, has been retained, and Dr. Lloyal von Nott alerted.

The mature approach would have been to schedule sessions with Dr. Schlomo Dove to work through your psychotic-erotic-borderline-transference. Now it is too late. Schlomo Dove will no longer be available as your therapist, though he will refer you to a skilled psychoanalyst to work through your psychosis.

The doctor will not be humiliated by his patient.

Enclosed is a final bill. Prompt payment is expected. Have a nice life.

More in sadness than anger,
Schlomo Dove, M.D., F.R.A.P.S.

"What do we do now?" Zoe asked the next day in my office, with Lily on the speakerphone from her house.

"We get a lawyer," Lily said. "Do you know any women lawyers, Roy?"

I did. Henry and I had gotten in touch with Hannah in Wyoming, and she too had returned, to finish out the year and to try to help us deal with Schlomo. Hannah had been transformed, her hair and eyebrows back to their natural black, her figure back to full, and her mind back to a healthy remembrance of her first analyst, her eye roll-ups a comfort to her, and, in a funny way, to us. She had started therapy in Jackson Hole, with a showy Jungian rodeo gal who focused on the analysis of shadows and who had recently had a piece in *People* magazine on her "Inner Child of Your Past Lives" approach. The most significant piece of Hannah's transformation was Gilda Plotkin. At Hananh's side when she showed up, Gilda was her former college roommate, who had played great viola to Hannah's prodigal cello in their string quartet. Gilda had gone on to Yale Law School, and after almost a decade in law had bought a ranch out West and continued part-time lawyering, both criminal and civil, in Denver and Jackson Hole. Gilda was a large, robust woman with big hands and a wide-open, wind-burnished face glowing with health, with bright dark eyes and pink cheeks and a nose broken in the past and big strong lips and a prizefighter's chin. She was a cowgirl without a trace of the blues, a brilliant, funny, rough-tough advocate, who seemed unafraid of anything, and was madly in love with Hannah. The two old friends were making beautiful music together as lovers.

Gilda was getting bored, back East. She might welcome the chance to skewer an abuser like Schlomo. So I said to Lily and Zoe, "I sure do. We'll need separate lawyers for each of you."

"Is it all right if I go first, Zoe?" Lily asked. Zoe nodded. "Arrange a meeting as soon as possible, Roy, will you?"

"With pleasure."

MALIK WORKED THE PROGRAM intensely, and worked with his sponsor George and with me and Solini. Henry would hardly let Malik out of his sight.

The night before Malik's discharge, we went with him to the Misery Loves Company meeting in the Farben. They handed out key chains stamped with various lengths of time of sobriety. They called out, "Anybody with one week?" and Malik walked slowly to the front. As people recognized him, he who had up until recently been a pillar of their community, there was a hush. "Go, Malik!" someone shouted. Others took it up. Soon all were clapping. Malik took his key chain and raised it over his head. Then he doubled up coughing. Another hush. He walked back through the pall and sat between George and Henry.

The next day his insurance ran out. He was going back to Bronia.

"I couldn't live with her," he'd said, "but maybe I can die with her."

Solini and I had finally gotten Malik to talk about his cancer. We'd encouraged him to go to the world experts, at the world's best hospitals, down in Boston.

"After what you've seen of the world experts here?" he'd asked.

"Cancer's different," I'd said.

"Right. You have a choice: either get poisoned first and die, or die. You see the paper today? They're finally gonna regulate pesticides a little. Just in time, eh? The time frame of humanity is so stupid! Throw the shit on the lettuce, dump it in the water, and by the time they can prove it kills people, the fat cats who cashed in are retired to Florida. Shit."

Now, Solini and I sat with Malik out on the porch of Heidelberg East, waiting for Bronia to come pick him up. Malik was physically weak, and subdued. Dazed, even foggy. With the year ending, and Solini leaving Misery, we tried to talk with Malik about the horrors we'd seen all year long, and about what more we could do about Schlomo. We wanted advice, but Malik gave none; sitting quietly, he only listened. We lapsed into what felt to me an uncomfortable and uneasy silence. It was a relief when Bronia drove up in the old VW bus, its license plate now one of maximum irony:

BREATHE

We walked out together, a piece of his luggage in each of our hands. Malik walked slowly, on wobbly legs, arms around our shoulders, leaning on us both.

"That sunlight feels terrific!" Malik said, blinking in the glare. It was the first hot day of the year. "You guys should see that forsythia through these amber lenses—I mean it is wild!"

"Cool," Henry said, looking at this wildness and sneezing paroxysmally.

We helped hoist Malik up into the passenger seat.

Through the window I asked, "Do you pray to God, Malik?"

"I don't know about God," he said. "All I know is that I'm not God, and I'm asking for help from something else, outside me. Step Three." He sighed and looked around. "I pray to whatever doesn't exclude others, but includes them. To the flower in the compost, the compost in the flower. I ask for help from this." His eyes swept the landscape, and ours followed. Suddenly I saw the hills like waves and the fields like tides, and the dark green pines hiking up the mountains to crest in white snowcaps like breakers on stone, the light green new maples and indomitable grasses flowing back down into the valleys, the hollows, the glitter of water seeking ocean, then sky, then rain. "From the Divine intelligence behind all this."

"*Omain!*" Bronia said, mashing the gears, letting out the raspy clutch.

"Wait!" Henry cried out. Bronia waited. "Where will you be?"

"Around, awhile," Malik said. Then he smiled, and got that "I'm your coach and I'm callin' the play" look in his eye, and said, "You listenin' up?" Henry and I said we were listening up. "Good. Live your understanding, right now, or it'll destroy you. Got it?"

"Cool," Solini said, "but what if you don't have all that much?"

Malik chuckled. "Live what you have. And remember: never go to a doctor you see on TV. So long."

MY TURMOIL THAT NIGHT was intense. Berry was asleep. Awake, my mind was going over and over my failures as a shrink, a lover, a son, brother, uncle, person, human—even, staring at Berry's cat staring icily at me, as a failed friend to cats.

In the static of all these failures I heard Malik's voice saying, "If you ain't close to God anymore, who moved?"

I got up out of bed and went to a linty corner of my turret. I got down on my knees. The floorboards hurt my kneecaps. The action felt embarrassing. Closing my eyes, in a churlish whisper I said:

"Please help me? Thanks a lot." It was all I could do not to add, "You big dickhead."

Whom was I asking for help?

"The Heroic Saga of Roy G. Basch, Great American" was providing all kinds of images: Charlton Heston in *The Ten Commandments* with God in white beard and bathrobe in the puffy clouds, or the vengeful God of widowed Rabbi Ritvo our tenant on the other side of the wall of our two-family in Columbia who at night screamed in Yiddish at his two spinster daughters.

I was not asking for help from that God. That God was merely my mind. I was not asking for help from myself.

Could I have been asking for help from the eternal disconnections, and the eternal connections that held even them?

Twenty

SOLINI, HANNAH, AND I, as the damp sun of May turned into the flatiron sun of June, began to take action around Misery.

We became extraordinarily curious about the money our patients were spending to stay at Misery. We let them know that it was over twelve hundred dollars a day. Somehow their insurance companies found out that the patients were being labeled with not one but two or three DSM diagnoses solely to keep them in Misery longer, so that the hospital and their doctors could make more nice green money. One day Solini and I were strolling past Emerson. Seeing once again the sign DISSOCIATIVE HOUSE, we felt it our duty to send individual letters to the major insurance companies letting them know that ever since they'd stopped paying for "Borderline Personality Disorder" and started paying for "Dissociative Disorder," Blair Heiler had switched diagnoses. Wasn't it funny how, in the hard science of psychiatry, diagnoses could be so soft?

Insurance started hassling Heiler and others about payment, decapitated right and left, and refused to authorize more nice green money. Patients and their families got caught in the cross fire. We encouraged said patients to walk their concerns directly over to the office of Nash Michaels, Chief Counsel of Misery, or to Dr. Lloyal von Nott, Chief of Misery. Of course patients and their families could not even get past the secretary guarding the outer office to get to the secretary guarding the inner office, let alone to the men themselves. Luckily, somehow the unlisted home numbers of the men themselves—von Nott, Michaels, Heiler, Cabot, Dove, and Lowell—all became readily available to the patients. These unlisted numbers were dialed.

Somehow, Lloyal von Nott's memo to us inviting us to the Misery Capital Campaign Luncheons, where we were asked to reveal the names of our rich patients so that Lloyal and Nash Michaels could hit them up for donations to Misery, turned up on the desk of the *Boston Globe* Spotlight Team. Failing to get through the barricades of secretaries to Lloyal and Nash at Misery, the Spotlight Team dialed their home numbers. The newspaper asked whether this memo, flying in the face of medical ethics, let alone common decency, was perhaps a joke, or a hoax? The media assumed that it, and their signatures on the bottom of it, could not be real.

Nash Michaels and Lloyal von Nott responded with silence.

Silence provoked the *Globe* further. It and TV began trailing them around with videocams, in much the same way they had done with drug dealers, mafiosi, and no-show judges. Lloyal and Nash became no-show shrinks. They flitted to and fro wearing sunglasses and hats and riding in big cars with darkened windows. They unlisted their unlisted numbers. It was amazing how fast this happened. All in a matter of weeks.

We also went after the other side of the ongoing war at Misery, insurance companies. Gilda and Hannah prepared a legal form letter for clients and their families who were having trouble with coverage—either being denied admission to Misery or being kicked out—to send to their insurance companies. Said letter carried documentation of the severity of said client's mental illness, and stated that any injuries to said client or family including suicide were events said insurance would be held strictly liable for. Misery depended on its relationship with insurance, especially with the big mothers like Blue Cross and Liberty Mutual and John Hancock. Since insurance was now calling the shots and could cancel Misery's provider status in a second, in a few days limousines with darkened windows could be seen driving up the hill to the Farben. The limos carried insurance executives, all pink and beer-bellied and encased in the same kind of pin-striped armor as von Nott and his boys. Meetings were held to find out—as one secretary told us:

"What the fuck are you doing, Lloyal, having our subscribers *talk* to us?"

It was astonishing how easily such a solid-seeming system could be shaken to its core. Seemingly as solid as a bank, it was every bit as flimsy.

We went after Schlomo too. We began to name his name. Wherever we went, whatever forum we found ourselves in—staff meetings or AA encounters or on night call on all the various wards of Misery, in talks with friends—we mentioned that we had heard on good evidence that Dr. Schlomo Dove had sexually abused at least two women patients. The women were about to bring charges. Naming his name made us realize how we doctors never did this, never revealed the secrets we knew about another doctor if it might harm his or her reputation. Now, to break the code of silence was scary, but thrilling.

"SCREWING PATIENTS IS LEGAL," Gilda was saying, sitting with me and Hannah and Solini in my office in Toshiba.

"You gotta be joking," I said.

"I don't joke. It's not against the law."

"Of course it's against the law," I said. "Has to be."

"Sexual abuse of a patient by a doctor in this state is not against the law. It's not a crime. Same as in most states, in fact."

"You shittin' us, man?"

"I am not a man."

"You shittin' us?"

"Unless it's done under the influence of drugs. If you fuck them, it's not a crime. If you drug them up and *then* fuck them, then it's a crime. And Schlomo didn't drug them up."

No one said anything for a long time.

"So what do we do now?" Hannah asked.

Gilda went on to explain that Lily and Zoe could file a civil suit, for malpractice. They could also make a complaint to the State Medical Board to take away Schlomo's license to practice, and try to get him thrown out of the Freudian Institute, Misery, and the BMS. And, of course, longer term, the victims could try to influence the state legislature to pass a law to make sex with patients illegal. Minnesota had such a law. We asked Lily and Zoe what they wanted to do.

They wanted to do it all: sue for malpractice, file complaints with the state, the Freudians, Misery, and the BMS. They were excited about the idea of forming a nonprofit organization—which Zoe named TALL: "Therapist Abuse Link Line"—to find other victims. They wanted to talk to the *Globe*, as well.

Gilda informed the state board that she would be filing a complaint with its Ethics Committee against Schlomo Dove. The board informed Gilda that Schlomo Dove was a member of its Ethics Committee.

"Like unreal!" Solini said.

"Hardly," she said. "I've researched it. These pricks are often members of these so-called ethics committees. They get their kicks from it."

Gilda demanded Schlomo recuse himself from the deliberations. Schlomo, in a bravura performance at a semiprivate emergency hearing before the board, a hearing to decide about the issues of the public hearing, convinced a majority of the board members that he was being slurred maliciously and that to remove him from Ethics without due process would set a dangerous precedent for "the hundreds of upstanding physicians threatened by mentally disturbed patients," and might lead to his filing a suit of his own against the board for its proceeding without due process. The board, in secret deliberation, recommended another, strictly private hearing of all parties separately, which would lead to a fairly-strictly-private rehearing of the original semi-private emergency hearing, to see if there were grounds for a public hearing to deal with the matter. Then the board lost the records.

"Even if we get rid of that little *putz*," Gilda said, "his cronies are on the Ethics Committee. The whole thing sucks."

She immediately prepared to file, on behalf of Lily Putnam, a suit for malpractice against Schlomo Dove.

The backlash from Schlomo was swift and vicious. He sent identical letters to Lily and Zoe:

> You two women are not the victims, *I* am the victim. Your complaints are totally false and pretty pathetic. You are severely disturbed women diagnosed as severe borderlines (BPOs, 301.83, with HF—Hysterical Features). Your hospital records will embarrass you and your families in a court of law.
>
> I am assured by my lawyer, Nash Michaels, that your testimonies are further contaminated by the fact that you *obviously* have had extensive talks together to collaborate in fabricating your stories. Dr. Roy G. Basch's record is filled with complaints by nearly every division of Misery, from Chief von Nott all the way down to Buildings and Grounds and Nursing.
>
> If you persist in this "Misery Conspiracy," Dr. Dove will file suit for defamation of character. The monies figure suggested by Schlomo Dove's counsel is $2.75 million. Each.
>
> Grow up, get a life. Any further correspondence should be addressed to N. Michaels, Chief Counsel, Mount Misery.
>
> More in anger than sadness,
> Schlomo Dove, M.D., F.R.A.P.S.

"Let me give it to you straight," Gilda said to Lily. "Juries respond to authority. He has all the authority of Mount Misery, the medical school, and Freud. It's your word against his. In court he will bring up every lurid detail anyone has ever written down about you, and his own lies about you, from his files. He will paint you as crazy, march out expert witnesses to testify that you are crazy and that part of your craziness is your being vindictive, and more experts to testify to his own integrity. This will give the jury the impression that you are at best an ax murderer and that he is at worst a hybrid of Simon Wiesenthal the Nazi hunter and Saint Francis of Assisi. The odds are stacked way against you. The humiliation you will experience, in front of your friends, family—children!—as you are sucked up and spit back out by the press and TV and film industries hungry for your life—the pressure of public degradation, will be unreal. And there is a risk of countersuit."

"So you're saying," Lily said, "that we don't have much of a case."

"Oh, you have a great *case*. You just don't have much of a *chance*."

"But the truth," Lily said, "is that he *did* abuse us both."

"Sweetheart, sweetheart," Gilda said, smiling and shaking her head. "The law is not about truth, but proof. That's what I was taught by the world-expert lawyers at Yale. That's why I bought my spread in Wyoming. Land and livestock are about truth."

A sense of gloom settled over us. We felt the weight of the status quo press up against us, as a mountain might against a climber who is tiring, caught a little too high up in the unexpected cold of a spring afternoon.

"Is there anything that would strengthen our case?" I asked.

"Your *chances*?" I nodded. "Let me think." She reached into a pocket of her cowgirl vest and took out a Swiss army knife, one of the thick ones with blades enough to open a reluctant can or scale and fillet a tough trout. She flicked out a white plastic toothpick and picked away for a while, Malik-like. "Okay. Here's what will give you a chance. Find another victim. With impeccable credentials. Who has contemporaneous evidence—that is, notes which she, the victim, actually wrote down at the time of the abuse. She has to be totally willing to come forward."

"Cool," Solini said. "Anybody know another Schlomo victim?" No one did. "There's got to be like somebody."

"Perhaps if TALL gets the word out," Lily said, "one will come forward."

"If so," Gilda said, "don't talk to her. Send her to another lawyer." She paused. "And if you don't find anyone else, we drop the case?"

"Yes, there would be some relief in that," Lily said. "We could all get on with just trying to heal."

WE TRIED TO FIND another victim, and could not. Days passed, then weeks, and we were stuck. Henry, Hannah, Gilda, and Malik would all be leaving in a few weeks. Momentum would slow, then stop. Time was running out.

Despite my feeling so awake, so alive, so in tune with the onrush of summer, despite seeing so much new life in Berry, my patients, and my friends, there was a hum underneath, as if of heavy machinery, a hum of death. Deaths echo deaths. The hole left by all the deaths of the year was getting bigger, deeper, and wider. I was beginning to feel more and more gloomy about our chances of bringing Schlomo down, about Malik's disease, and about how the hell I was going to survive another two years of my training to become a dear and glorious physician-shrink in Misery.

One night on call I was walking with Solini to pick up my beeper in the Farben when we ran into Win Winthrop and Arnie Bozer, standing in the foyer outside the Conference Room, which now had a shiny brass plaque nailed to its door:

DR. ISAAC WHITE CONFERENCE ROOM
COURTESY OF GLÜCKSSPIEL APOTHEKE LTD.

"Well, hi there, Doctors," Arnie said cheerily. "How's business? Will you be attending today's Resident Support Group with us?"

Henry and I had not gone to A. K. Lowell's group for months.

"Fuck no, Arnie," Solini said.

"Locked out by that bitch," Win cried, enraged, smashing at the door with his fists. He seemed more bulked up than ever. The steroids would explain his rages too. "She meant it."

"Meant what?" I asked.

"Thanks for asking, Roy," Arnie said. "Dr. Lowell said she was tired of us showing up late. She locked the door on the hour. She's in there free-associating."

"Ah, the hell with it," Win said, with one final kick. "Let's go."

"But how would that look?" Arnie asked. "If she should open the door early, and we're not here?"

"Yeah, you're right."

"So how's the family, Win?" Henry asked. He'd always liked Win's older son.

"Who knows? The bitch won't let me see 'em."

"You moved out?" I asked.

"She found out about me and Gloria."

"Gloria?" I said.

"Fire in the belly. And lower."

"But, man, like what about the kids?"

"I'm using the Glücksspiel company lawyer. No way she'll get my money."

"You're not trying to work it out with her?" I asked.

"Cheaper to change. Like Errol. Long as you got a prenup. Warrior cash. 'Victories of the Heart!' "

"And what will you young doctors be doing come July the first?" Arnie asked.

"Quitting," Henry said. "Getting out of this shithole for good."

"I'll be here for year two," I said. "And you?"

"National Institute of Mental Health Prize Fellow," Win said. "And on salary for Glücksspiel. Bly says no more sibling shit, and we all better just *grow up*! But hey listen: Errol referred me a cousin of the Kennedys!"

"Psychopharm is truly fascinating," Arnie said. "I'm rotating on the West myself and it's really interesting. Boy what we can do with drugs now. On July the first Dr. von Nott is sending me to the Harvard Business School, to specialize in the business of psychiatry. My subspecialty training will be in gerontology. The seniors are the fastest-growing segment of the American health-care system and America itself. My expertise is in death and dying."

"Death and dying, you?" I said.

"Working with the dying is the only truly time-limited psychotherapy."

Solini and I were speechless.

Finally Henry said, "Never seen you so happy, Arnie."

"Yes, yes," Arnie said, "I am one happy camper, yes."

"Great drug," Win said, "that Zoloft."

"You're on Zoloft?" Henry said.

"Yes, I am. I like myself on it, but my girlfriend *loves* me on it. We'll be sorry to lose you, Dr. Solini."

"Go fuck yourself, Arnie."

"Thanks, guys," Arnie said, "for sharing."

That on-call night was different. In tune with Viv, I found myself being curious about the people I was doctoring. Whether it was the voice floating on the other end of the line or the people locked up on the wards, even brief contacts were fun. It had nothing to do with how much time I had to spend with the person, and everything to do with how much I was really there with the person. I was finding out that connection can be made in a second or never made in fifty years of marriage, can be present from a thousand miles away and can be absent in the same room. That night, sometimes, I was really there.

"You've been awesome tonight," Viv said as I handed in my beeper at the end of the shift.

"How?"

"You have engaged in no bullshit. It's not something I see very often around here. What the hell happened to you anyways?"

"You tell me. Malik says that whatever happened I'd be the last to know."

"Yeah, well, be careful, Cowboy."

"Why be careful?"

"The good ones get it in the neck."

Leaving, I saw Errol Cabot in his Ferrari growl past, up toward the lead boxes and radioactive isotopes of the West. He had a new bumper sticker:

SO MANY PEDESTRIANS
SO LITTLE TIME

"HAVE YOU GONE UP?" Jill asked a few days later, getting out of her rusty old Buick in front of Heidelberg East. It was raining, a first summer rain, big sprouting drops that hit the hot asphalt like notes from a jazz pianist on a wild riff, raising the scent of boyhood summer in Columbia. We faced each other as the raindrops popped upon our heads.

"You think?" I said. I was stunned by her fullness, her liveness, her beauty, her sensual energy. Her blond hair was again long, as when I'd first met her. She had a sleek dark tan, as if bronzed.

"Lemme see." She put her palms to my temples, and stared into my eyes. I stared back into hers. It was intense. Rain dripped down onto my lips. She said, "You are on the beam! What a treat!"

I went to kiss her. She pulled back. I asked, "What's wrong?"

"You're back with Berry, right?"

"Well . . ."

She kicked me in the shin. "You lying sack of shit!"

"Oww-wow!" I screamed, bending to rub my leg. "Okay, okay, yes I am."

"Good. Someone like you should be back with someone like her."

"And you? You've got someone?" She nodded. My heart fell. "Who?"

"A guy. It's fabulous."

"Fabulous?"

"Mostly. But what can you do? I mean he *is* a guy. Can we walk?"

"In the rain?"

"Sure. I love rain! Everything is so *green*! Like the tropical sea."

We walked through the woods, down the ravine, along the asphalt path through the oaks around the lake, then down into a marshy hollow—where, last New Year's Eve, they'd found the frozen body of Sedders, the Man Who Couldn't Get Admitted to Misery in Time and Had Died Trying—and then onto the mossy carpet up into the high pines, where the scent vaporized up into the dampness of the day.

When we started walking, there were light circles of dry road under the trees that overhung the dark, wet road. We walked for so long that, after the rain had ended, by the time we retraced our steps the road was dry, and what had been light circles of dryness under the trees had now become dark circles of wet. The rain had soaked through the leaves, and the trees had shaded the hot sun, preventing it from drying the damp circles under them. And maybe it was the day itself, or the woman, so bright and alive and fulfilled that I found myself worrying that being with me might jinx her; whatever it was, this cojoint arising of wettening and drying circles was like a metaphor for our lives, no longer lovers but friends. What a challenge to me, a man, to have a woman friend. I who had been taught from my first awareness of boyhood that either you ignored girls completely or you tried to get into their pants.

Jill said she had "gone up." In the Galápagos, a red translucent ball had rolled along the grass at her. "Suddenly I was going faster than light all reddish up to a big silver spaceship." The aliens looked just like the pictures in the tabloids at supermarket checkout counters, less scary than friendly, "like small gooey puppies." Then somehow she'd hitchhiked from the Galápagos to Puerto Rico, where she visited an astronomer who worked at the radio telescope that was trying to receive messages from other life in the universe.

"Sorry if I'm not making sense," she said. "My brain isn't working that well. I'm waiting for my period and I feel like a blimp. So what about you?"

"I've been on an emotional roller coaster."

"Good!"

"Good?"

"For some people that might be a problem, but not for you. So?"

I told her everything. When I finished, she said, "You were gonna kill yourself over *this*? Are you crazy?"

"I guess I was."

"I'm glad you didn't because it would not have been very smart. Funny. I never picked up any 'killing yourself' signal from you. Fifteen minutes with a woman waiting in line to use a ladies' room and you know more about her than fifteen years with a guy. I feel sorry for guys actually." She took my arm, my triceps against her breast. "But I can't get over it—you're so . . ."

"What?"

"I dunno, you're just so *in it* with me, now. Now, we could really get it on!" Her hand brushed my thigh. "But we can't, so keep talking."

I told her about Schlomo.

"Yeah," she said, "I know."

"You *know*?"

"A lot of us who worked here know. He's been doin' it for years. Women go to him to find a therapist. The ones he wants to fuck, he keeps for himself, and the others he sends to somebody else. I went to him. He said he'd be my therapist, and I looked him up and down and said, 'Is this a joke?' "

"Why hasn't anyone tried to stop him?" She laughed. "What's so funny?"

"You. Look, you grew up thinking you had some clout, right? You were the privileged class. Me, and my people, we are the unprivileged class. We *assume* that these guys, the ones running things, are crooked, and perverts. A lot of us mental health workers knew about Schlomo. Patients would tell us, sometimes, and at first we'd tell our bosses—Heiler, Errol, A.K. They'd tell us that the patients were crazy. Where I come from, you go along to get along, or else. Forget it. You can't do nothin' about it."

"You'll see."

"You're actually going to try?"

"You bet. Will you help us, give us names of other victims?"

"No way. I've seen what they can do to you if you mess with them."

We found ourselves in a clearing, staring at a trailer park. The house trailers were parked in neat rows, each with its propane tanks and those aluminum awnings you see on TV wrapped around palm trees when hurricanes hit Florida. A trailer park, in Misery? A fresh sign, in the Misery colors and with the Misery pine tree and moon and duck rampant, read:

MOUNT MISERY AFFILIATED PSYCHIATRISTS

Underneath was a map, with a "You are here" cross and the paths to each of nine house trailers, with a list of names, including:

GENEVA HOOEVENS, M.D. MODULAR UNIT 7

"Mind if I look her up?"

"No. I know her. She's great."

Yoman the seeing-eye dog lay on the steps of Modular 7 beneath a hand-lettered sign:

HERE AT MISERY
THE FLOGGING WILL CONTINUE
UNTIL MORALE IMPROVES.

I knocked. Geneva answered. I introduced Jill, whom she remembered.

"What's with the trailer park?" I asked.

"Misery's in money trouble. There's been a sudden drop in the census. Lloyal and Nash are trying to get rid of me and the other psychiatrists who still believe in talking with patients. It's all drugs now. In a few days they'll close up Heidelberg East for good."

"What? Why?"

"Empty beds. Insurance was only paying for a few days of detox. They'll close the building, add another DSM diagnosis to each patient, and send them all over to a new "Dual Diagnosis Unit," run by Errol Cabot. Errol's going to be putting all the drug addicts and alcoholics on drugs."

"Great. And what's with these house trailers?"

"These house trailers are not 'house trailers.' They are 'temporary Misery-quality modular office structures.' "

We laughed. I told her about Schlomo, and asked if she'd ever heard of him abusing other patients.

"Yes." She thought for a moment. "Could it be twenty years ago already? Yes. I still had my sight. I got a call from an internist who said a young woman patient of his had come to him claiming to have been sexually abused in therapy by Schlomo and would I see her. I met with the woman, and believed her. I was a member of the Freudian Institute. Assured of confidentiality, I filed a complaint. Schlomo was a rising star then. The institute said that unless the woman came forward and made a public complaint, they could do nothing. And she couldn't do that. Too vulnerable."

"Did anything happen?"

"Lots. Schlomo found out, and stopped referring patients to me. I was blacklisted. But it was good, in the end, to give up psychoanalysis. Forced me to learn new things. Like learning new ways to see."

"He's been abusing patients for twenty years?"

"At least twenty."

"Do you know any women who might talk?" I asked.

She thought for a while, but could not come up with anyone. I felt even more discouraged. "But it's such a rich afternoon!" she said happily. "Shall we walk a little, on the path through the woods?"

We started out. Geneva had one of her hands on the dog's harness and the other resting lightly on my arm, as if I were escorting a shy girlfriend to a dance. Having gone blind gradually, she'd been able to cultivate her other senses in synchrony with the decay of her eyes. This time of year, with all the plants and trees in bloom and the moisture of the air acting like a second blossoming, the scent was, as she said, "Heavenly, heavenly." We came to a clearing, a fork in the path where the daylight was made all the more dazzling by the wooded dark and the memory of rain. We stood in that moment's mist and sun. Jill said she had to go.

"See you soon," I said, putting my cheek to hers, my hand reflexively moving to the hillock of her belly, to the free edge of her marvelous breast.

"No you won't," she said, pressing my fingers to her, "I'm leaving tonight for the Amazon."

"The Amazon? Why?"

"Life's easy, if you're on the beam!"

With a hug that took my breath away, her breasts pliant against my chest so that I saw them again naked, half tanned, and swaying, she was gone.

Geneva and I and Yoman walked on slowly, talking.

"This training," I said, "this whole first year of training, has been unreal. I don't know if I can take two more. How can you stay here?"

"I shan't stay much longer. People like me don't stay long in places like this. The Lloyals and Nashes of the world stay, not I."

"It's like everything I've been taught here," I said, "goes against anything I've learned to be true. If I'm sitting there with patients thinking, I can't be with them. It's like 'I think, therefore I am not.' "

"Quite. It's not the method you use, but the person you are. Do you know, the older I get, the more it seems that what we're quote 'taught' is opposite to what really is. We're taught to avoid conflict because it will lead to violence, when in fact it's the very avoidance of conflict that will do so. We're taught that the way to avoid stereotypes is to not look at difference, when in truth it's only by seeing deeply into difference that stereotype is avoided. Even Freud's idea that therapy is a process of making the unconscious conscious? Perhaps we'd all be better off helping people make the conscious unconscious—getting all of our egos out of the way!"

We laughed together. The dog looked up at us, seeming to smile, as dogs do.

"Sounds like something Malik would say," I said.

Stillness. A bird cried, a blue jay. Malik.

Walking on in silence, we heard the *thwap thwap* of tennis balls being hit. Soon we were in view of the tennis court. There, in the cage of chain-link fencing, four people were playing doubles. Even from a distance the intensity of their game was evident. It was being played in hostile silence but for rare curses and complaints from one side of the net.

"Who are they?" Geneva asked.

"Let's see." I led her toward the court. We stopped under the skirts of the big copper beech. I'd fallen asleep here, before that first Ike seminar.

The four were Dr. Blair Heiller, Dr. Errol Cabot, Dr. A. K. Lowell, and Dr. Schlomo Dove. Heiler and Cabot were playing against Lowell and Dove. All wore classic white tennis gear except Schlomo, who was in Converse All-Stars and black socks unrolled below bulging varicose calves. Their rackets were the latest design and alloy, those oversized oval jobs with big sweet spots.

I led Geneva to courtside and stood watching. Each of the players glanced at us in turn, secreting away any reaction, denying we were there.

Heiler was aggressive, hogging the net, slashing away viciously at every shot, and, when he missed, shouting and cursing and throwing his racket in disgust.

Errol was pure macho, his thighs and calves and biceps full of steroids and God knows what other drugs, hogging the court, thundering bulkily between the baseline and the net, thrashing at the ball as if it were a feeling still left alive after ever-higher doses of medications, thrashing with grunts and curses and cries of disbelief at the weird spins and bounces it would take.

In the throat of the curses from Heiler and Cabot, the other side of the net functioned in an eerie silence.

A.K. was, as I knew all too well, a lobber. She lay back, in a defensive and defended position, never leaving the backcourt and baseline, merely trudging to and fro, with plenty of time to gauge the ball coming at her, and, for each ball, even the most hot low drive, somehow with a flick of her wrist sending it up and up and up, lobbed over the heads of the onrushing foes, sending them scrambling back together and calling for it and trying to elbow each other out of the way to hit it, and then, either Errol or Heiler smashing at it as if it were a last hungry mosquito in the bedroom at night, usually failing to hit it at all, or hitting it and his partner or himself, and cursing out the ball or the partner or A.K. for playing "wimp" tennis.

Most bizarre was Schlomo. In all my years as a tennis player, including my stint as captain of the Columbia High Fish Hawk tennis team, I had never come up against a player like Schlomo. He was a slicer. He never hit the ball true. He had perfected a stroke that could put a spin on the ball in many different ways, so that when it bounced, it never bounced the way Errol or Heiler thought it would. It kept you guessing. Sometimes lower than it seemed, sometimes higher, sometimes to the right, sometimes to the left. Just when they thought they had figured out, from Schlomo's stroke motion, which way it would spin, he'd dupe them by somehow with the same motion hitting it dead straight.

And Schlomo cheated. Any close call, any ball hitting the line, he would call "Out!" This would provoke argument from Errol and Heiler, but Schlomo would respond to these accusations with silence, and when A.K. was asked her opinion, she would respond vehemently with as much nothing as I'd ever heard.

Soon the Heiler-Cabots were infuriated. Curses doubled in intensity, rackets crashed to the blacktop. You'd think they all hated each other.

Geneva asked what was happening. I described it blow by blow. My talking during their tense awaiting of service annoyed them. Heiler and Cabot told me to "Be quiet." The other two sent me contemptuous glances.

Suddenly there were other people watching.

Solini and Hannah and the formidable Gilda were across the court from us, their fingers laced into the chain-link fence.

And then who should walk up and lean against the fence behind Heiler and Errol but Mr. K. and the Lady Who Ate Metal Objects. They stood watching, lacing their fingers into the twisted squares of metal, the Metal Lady gnawing at the galvanized alloy with a vengeance.

A few minutes later, Zoe appeared and took up a position directly behind Schlomo Dove. When Schlomo turned and walked back to take his serve, he caught sight of her. He showed no reaction, but his first serve, a vicious slice, sailed long. His second, one of those inept "patty-cake" pops, sailed far over the line, out of bounds. Double fault.

We watched the four shrinks on court flailing away in hatred and contempt. None of us said anything, but the pressure on them was almost palpable. It was only a matter of time before the game would be over. We would stay until it was.

They never even finished the set.

Schlomo walked to the net, gesturing the others to him. They consulted. Heiler and Cabot argued and cursed, to no effect. The four got their gear and walked toward the door of the cage. Suddenly there was a shout:

"Dickheads Incorporate!"

Could it be? The person shouting this, strolling lazily down the path from the Farben, looked a little like Thorny, but rather than the wild-eyed, scraggly-clothed maniac who'd escaped from Misery many weeks ago, here was a clean-shaven, bright-eyed, calm young man in a dark business suit and snappy tie, carrying a briefcase and a laptop.

"Dickheads with Laptops!" he cried out happily.

"Thorny?" I asked, taking his hand as he joined Geneva and me.

"Clean and serene!" he answered. His handshake was as firm as an MBA's.

"Clean and serene?"

"Thorny!" He stared at the shrinks at the net. "Hey hey hey!" he shouted at them. "We got us some Dickheads at Play!"

We laughed, and then we fell silent, watching them watching us.

Then they walked from the net to the gate, opened it, and filed out, one by one.

We stared at them. They couldn't meet the pressure of our outrage. They looked away, saying nothing to each other. They walked the concrete path leading out of the amphitheater formed by the facades of Farben, Toshiba, the Toshiba research foot, and the high ledge of granite and thick woods. The four of them in single file disappeared over a hillock toward the safety of the parking lot and their wonderful cars. Even though we had failed to find another victim, even though it now seemed like the whole thing would just fizzle out and join the other buried violence of the year, I felt great.

The amphitheater was quiet, even still. Then, with a shout, the Metal Lady started running up the path after the shrinks.

"They can't stand it," I said to Geneva.

"Stand what?" she asked.

"Feeling seen. They can't stand feeling seen."

"Yes," she said, taking my arm to leave. "We can't."

FREE THAT WEEKEND, Berry and I did a day hike up the back face of Sunapee to Lake Solitude, picnicked and swam, and drove to Dartmouth for dinner. As we walked up to the Hanover Inn we saw black and white balloons everywhere, tugging up against their tethers in the brisk June breeze. The patio was filled with black people and white people celebrating something. One black and white couple were dancing. The white man wore a black tuxedo; the black woman a white wedding dress.

"There's hope," Berry said.

"Wonderful, yes."

We walked into the lobby. As we approached the counter I saw a short, bald, chubby Jewish-looking man in his fifties, wearing a dark suit, his arm around a much younger woman, who was quite a bit taller than he. She was slender, with an aristocratic face and sharp nose. Her hair was cut short. She wore a light-colored summer dress. Guests at the wedding. As if caught in a black-and-white photo, they stood still, watching the bride and groom cruise the floor.

A chill shot through me. I squeezed Berry's hand.

"What's wrong?" she asked. "Do you know them?"

"No."

"What, then?"

"We've got it. I think I've found another victim."

"Who?"

"A. K. Lowell."

"What?"

"C'mon. We've got to drive back down to my house, before it's too late!"

"But what about dinner?"

"No way. No time. I'll explain as we go. Jesus! C'mon!"

I dragged her, half running, to her Volvo. I drove back up alongside the College Green, beat the yellow light across Main Street and roared down the hill and across the river to the interstate. When we were settled into mindless speed, I told her.

The sudden sight of the two people standing there had made my mind flash on the black-and-white photo that A. K. Lowell had on her desk, which I'd seen the night I'd gone there for dinner, after tennis. A.K., in a summer dress, was standing beside Schlomo Dove. She was taller. His arm was around her. Ike White was standing farther off to one side. Schlomo had been A.K.'s training analyst at the Freudian Institute. Schlomo had been Ike's training analyst too. A.K. had had a six-year-long analysis with Schlomo, five days a week. Ike too. Like Lily and Zoe, in the photo A.K. was young and tall and slender. Her nose was still big and bent, but soon to be straightened. Her light brown hair was short.

"Schlomo must have been screwing *her* too," I said. "During her analysis with him. She's the perfect victim for us—impeccable credentials, and she must have taken notes during her analysis, about everything that went on. And she's tough. No one could rattle her on the witness stand."

"But she'd never admit it."

"I can force her."

"You have proof?"

"I might. That's why we're heading back."

As we drove back down from the mountains, we felt more connected than we'd been in a year. Over and over in my mind I saw that black-and-white photo of the three of them—a smiling Schlomo with his arm around a tentatively smiling young Jewish woman in a summer dress, and there, apart a little, with a pained look on his face, little Isaac White.

OLY JOE'S LEDGER was still in the false ceiling above my chandelier. We took it down, turned the light up, lay back together against the headboard of the bed, and started reading.

There were hundreds of pages divided by that vertical line. The right-hand side was lurid and crude. "I suck your sweet boy's cock till you come," was pretty regular. "When I feel your little boy's cock rip at my asshole my clit gets big as a dick," was not atypical.

"Do you believe this?" I asked Berry.

"It's sickening."

"Uh-ohhh. Here it is. Listen." I read, " 'Sucking your cock isn't like sucking Poppa Schlomo's 'cause his is shorter and thicker and he can be sucked a lot longer before he gets off.' "

I looked up at Berry. Her eyes showed her revulsion.

"But would you actually make that public?" Berry asked.

"Her thinking I would might be enough."

"To make her go public? And ruin her reputation?"

"Ruining Schlomo's might save hers. And she and Ike were best friends. There's a limit, isn't there, even if someone's been psychoanalyzed? Maybe if she smelled blood in the water, if she knew there were two other victims filing suit, she just might take the chance. It might never have to be made public at all, if Schlomo sees the light. It would never come to trial. Gilda says these things never do. If it gets close, they settle out of court. It all comes down to money."

"You're forgetting one thing."

"Which is?"

"She's an analyst. She can claim it was all fantasy, all in her mind. Her countertransference to him."

"Yeah, except for what Oly Joe wrote, in blood."

Reading the entire volume, I found many other passages where A.K., using the powerful tools of psychoanalysis, free-associated from Oly Joe's penis to Schlomo Dove's penis. The descriptions of what went on between A.K. and Schlomo—his "you buy the condoms," the Ziploc bag—matched what Lily and Zoe reported. There was a passage that at first seemed to defy physical possibility, which had Schlomo masturbating her with an unripe banana while she performed fellatio on him. And there were several detailed descriptions of the geography of the Schlomo Dove penis.

First thing the next morning, I drove to my neighborhood L'il Peach convenience store and photocopied several of these pages. Then I drove to the nearest Rank Bank and opened a safe-deposit box and left the ledger there. At ten minutes before the hour I called A.K.'s secretary Nancy. I said I had an urgent matter to take up with A.K. and needed an appointment that day.

"She's just breaking from her nine o'clock. I'll ask her." She put me on hold. She brought me back. "She will not see you."

"When can she see me?"

"I'll put you on hold." She put me on hold, then came back. "Roy?"

"Yeah?"

"She says 'never.' "

"Fine," I said. "Tell her I'll be right over."

I went down the hill from the Farben to Thoreau and sat outside her office. At ten-fifty the door opened. Out came some poor bastard, rail-thin and pale as a pustule, all dressed up in a three-piece suit like A.K.'s, looking as if he'd just spent fifty minutes with a demon. I walked in and stood in front of her desk. She was doing her crossword on the rail-thin pale guy, but she stopped and stared up at me.

"It is in your interest to talk to me." Silence. "Two women who have had Schlomo Dove as their therapist are about to sue him for sexual abuse. He was fucking them during their analyses." Silence. "I know that you too were a victim of his abuse." I thought I caught the slightest hint of movement, a clench of her jaw, but it might have been a play of sun across the skylight, or a bird. "I know from your ledger on Oly Joe. I have the ledger in my possession, locked up tight." I held out one photocopied page. She did not take it. I placed it carefully on her desk.

Seeing her sitting there so alone, so trapped in her mutilated mind, seeing her muscular body and surgically remodeled nose, I felt for her. How sad it all was. But sad as I might have been for her, I was more sad for Cherokee and the gunshot that in a single moment had put a curse on his two young children, and had started a chain of suffering that would echo down through not only their whole lives, but the lives of their children, and their children's children. Outrage swept away my sadness for her.

"I would hate to have to make these notes public," I went on. "If you decide to come forward, as a Schlomo victim, I wouldn't have to, would I?"

A.K. picked up a pencil and held it, eraser down, on the desk. I had never seen this before from her, her holding a pencil vertically, point up, and was encouraged.

"Why, it might never need to be made public at all. Your contacting Schlomo might be enough to scare him off."

The eraser tapped on the desk, once, twice, silently. I could have sworn I saw the sharp point tremble, a breath caught in all this desiccation.

"It's Monday. I'll give you till five o'clock Friday to make up your mind."

Often in the past I had walked out of that vile office feeling like so much deadweight. Now I walked out feeling light.

Twenty-One

A.K. REMAINED SILENT, day after day, all that week. I told Hannah and Henry about the ledger, and swore them to secrecy. As the week went on, I was preoccupied with what was going on with A.K. She faced an impossible choice. I felt some sympathy for her. I recalled Viv and Primo telling me that as a first-year resident in Misery, before she'd gone under analysis with Schlomo, as Aliyah K. Lowenschteiner, she'd been a bright, young, fun-loving, and funny woman. Her nickname, Viv had told me, was "Sunny." Descended from a long line of eminent kosher butchers, not only had she been the first in her family to go to college and med school, but through sheer gutsiness she'd risen to the top of every class, and had gotten admitted into Freudian heaven, the institute. Then one day, she'd gone to the head of the institute, a man analyzed by Freud himself, and, expecting to be matched with a lesser analyst, walked out instead matched with Dr. Schlomo Dove himself. Imagine her joy. She had it made.

I saw how that moment of what she must have seen as her greatest success was in fact the moment of her downfall. She was doomed. Could she have done otherwise? Could she at any moment have stopped? Before the nose job? Before the first touch? Before the first fuck? Before the first banana? I too had felt Schlomo's mesmerizing power. When I'd gone to him to confront him about his abusing Zoe, he'd overpowered me, shamed me, made me doubt my own eyes and ears. To be with that monster five times a week? Who could resist doing what he told you to do, especially when he said it was necessary for the success of the analysis? I saw, then, that Schlomo wasn't even primarily into sex. This was about power. This was rape. Schlomo was a classic rapist.

Friday at five was A.K.'s deadline to come forward. At noon on Friday Solini and Hannah and I sat together in the front row of the newly renamed Mutual of Life Theater, in the Farben. We were attending Misery grand rounds, where the topic was "How to Manage Your Risk as a Psychiatrist." Despite our having heard nothing from A.K., we were flying high: Henry and Hannah were just about done with Misery forever. I, despite the specter of two more years of training, now felt that I had finally come closer to understanding what I'd come to psychiatry from medicine to understand: how to be with people, including patients. The past few weeks working with my patients, I'd felt able to use all that I'd learned during the year.

While our speaking out and taking small actions over the past few weeks may have had some effect, it turned out that Mount Misery was also being rocked by larger explosions in the culture. Things at the hospital were getting more and more chaotic. The algorithms, the decision trees, the boxes adangle from other boxes were banging into each other, coming to rest at weird angles. Just as doctors were no match for businessmen, the hospital was no match for the insurance industry. The industry now more or less owned the hospital, and thus owned the patients too. Talk was no match for drugs. The industry would not be paying for talking any longer. You could almost see the class split in America widening: those who could pay, could talk to a therapist; everybody else would be handed a drug. Most psychiatrists would be pill-pushers. It would be great for the drug industry and the insurance industry. They would be making a lot of money. In some ways, they were becoming indistinguishable, drugs from insurance, insurance from hospitals. Soon, as in publishing and entertainment, it would all be owned by the mammoth multinationals. Risk, once taken by insurance—in fact, risk had been the very reason for insurance, starting with the Medicis—would now be taken only by patients and doctors.

Psychiatry had succumbed to the medical model: diseases, diagnosis, and drugs. Errol was in, Malik out. The shrinks had fallen prey to the very thing they were supposed to heal in their patients: the isolation of one human being from another, and the violence of one human being toward another. What made people sick in the first place was being replicated in the institutions set up to heal them, all these Miserys of the world. In this, allegedly one of the most human specialties in all of medicine, human beings often seemed to matter least. Perhaps it was inevitable, I thought, sitting there in the almost two-hundred-year-old auditorium, given the original concept of the Yankee founders, that diseases of the mind are a kind of flip side of diseases of the body. I now saw how a lot of the world experts in misery acted as if they truly believed there was a medical treatment for the suffering of the soul.

And if, already, some of the millions of schoolkids and adults labeled with ADD—Attention Deficit Disorder—and, put on drugs such as Ritalin, were starting to develop a Tourette-like syndrome, with facial tics and twitches that might be irreversible? Well, it's the price we pay, isn't it, for drugging ourselves to attention, for living better chemically? And if, with the two billion prescriptions for Prozac written during my year in Misery, some of the Prozacians had seen their sex drive wither? Well, wouldn't a bit less sex drive be better for society, as a whole, in the end? And if, as is always the case when you throw something as gross as a drug into something as delicate as a brain, you lessen the human part? Well, maybe we've all had enough of this so-called human part, no?

All year long, whenever my common sense had come up against the received wisdom of Misery, the phrase that had come to mind was: "They must be joking." Today's grand rounds was no exception. Mount Misery had decided to address the hot issue of "Therapist Risk" head-on. At the front of the refurbished old auditorium, on a small toylike stage spread under that beautifully proportioned, long and gradual arc you see on doorways and windows and roofs of Shaker dwellings, sat Dr. Arnold Bozer, Dr. Schlomo Dove, Dr. Blair Heiler, and another man I'd never seen before, all in power suits. Schlomo looked neat and clean, his curly hair full of snappy energy, as if it had been permed.

Dr. Bozer presented the case for discussion, in his words, "a DSM 300.14, Dissociative Disorder, Multiple Personality, a young woman who I had had in therapy on Emerson." With a haughty sarcasm that I knew he had copied from Blair Heiler, Arnie said, "Sometimes she would be Sharon Stone, other times Hillary Clinton, sometimes Bambi's girlfriend Faline, up to a grand total of seventeen multiples. The Sharon Stone multiple claimed that her therapist, me, was abusing her sexually. I have a policy of never touching a patient. I swear I never touched her. Soon thereafter her inpatient insurance ran out and she was discharged to Candlewood, clutching a man's shoe. She still tries to call me sometimes. Gosh, it's embarrassing. She was discharged on Prozac, Ritalin, Placedon and Zephyrill, and nystatin, for her athlete's foot." He sat down.

A tall, handsome, thin man with straight blond hair styled like Bill Clinton's stood up. He was wearing a fine suit and a tie with an insignia with no ducks rampant. This was Dr. Bobby Lee Shpitzer, a Texan who was a world expert on Therapist Risk.

"There's a lot of *schtupping* going on out there," he said. A lot of people laughed. "Lights out, please?"

He proceeded to give a slide show with a commentary that was so witty that soon much of the audience was laughing, as if we were watching *Seinfeld.* At one point he put up a slide of a famous James Thurber cartoon, of a male doctor leering over the headboard of a hospital bed at a female patient. Dr. Shpitzer read the caption out loud: " 'You're not my patient, you're my *meat.*' "

Roars of laughter. Solini grasped my right knee, Hannah my left. I grasped theirs. We all squeezed, hard.

The slide show ended. Dr. Shpitzer then made a heartfelt statement that patient-psychiatrist physical contact was absolutely off limits. Touching the patient, but for a handshake, was off limits. A hug was totally out of bounds. Yet what was the psychiatrist to do when a female patient, maybe a borderline or dissociative or multiple, suddenly got up out of her chair and approached, intent on hugging him? Dr. Shpitzer asked Dr. Dove to demonstrate. Schlomo, ever the showman, popped to his feet.

First Shpitzer said he would show us all what *not* to do, and told Schlomo to go ahead. Playing the woman patient, Schlomo started toward Shpitzer, arms forward. Shpitzer crouched in a martial-arts stance and with a scream—"Hyahh!"—karate-chopped Schlomo's hands down. Roars of laughter from the audience, horror in Henry's and Hannah's faces, squeezes of knees.

Next the world expert showed us the correct response. Again Schlomo danced toward him for a hug. Shpitzer grabbed both wrists, crossed them over each other firmly, pushed them down toward the zone between breasts and genitalia, and said, "No, no. This is not therapy."

Schlomo got up on his tippy-toes and danced coyly. "Please, Doctor, just one little hug?"

Roars of laughter.

"No, no. This is not therapy."

"But you're so cute, Shpitzy! Pretty please? One eentsy-weentsy?"

"No, no. This is not therapy. If you persist, I will terminate."

They stopped. The audience applauded. Schlomo took a grand low bow.

The discussion then centered on variants of this technique. Dr. Shpitzer passed out his brochure, describing his video course—"Six Quick Steps to Avoid the Pitfalls of Risk"—which we could all buy for $399.95. This would allow us to pass our risk-management requirements for state relicensure as shrinks in the comfort and privacy of our very own homes.

Next, Dr. Blair Heiler rose from his chair onstage and went to the podium to offer his comments. "Dr. Bozer did not pay enough attention to the LNT, the Latent Negative Transference. If he had, he would have been able to hate the patient and—"

"*Hate?*" cried a voice from the back. Heads turned.

It was A. K. Lowell, standing up against the back wall, a yellow pencil in her raised hand. "*Hate?*" she said again, triumphantly, having caught her rival red-handed. "What a slip!"

"No, no. *Love!*" Heiler said defiantly, but his face reddened. For many of us this classic Freudian slip was a poignant reminder that he had failed his analysis because of problems with premature termination, anger, and sadism, or Latent Negative Transference, untreated. "Let me decenter myself," Blair said, sitting down, blinking his eyes. Then, with a tremor in his voice, he said, "Dr. Bozer would have been able to *love* his patient."

"You *meant* hate," A.K. said.

"Did not!"

"Did so!"

"*Oy!*" Schlomo said, standing. Up above us on the toy stage, with the other men onstage sitting down, Schlomo seemed tall and solid. He seemed to grow even more solid and powerful as he put a hand on Blair's shoulder and fixed A.K. with his eyes, which, as he tightened his face in anger, became slits, ominous and terrible. It was incredible, just how much power seemed to be beaming out from this chunky little man onstage. "Lowell?" Schlomo said. "Sit!" A.K.'s face went ashen. "*Sit!*" Schlomo hissed. "*Down!*"

Humiliated, A.K. sat down.

I turned to Solini. His forehead was beaded with sweat. I too was sweating. Hannah's eyes were wide with horror. It was the same horror we'd felt that day when, in this same room, we'd seen Lloyal von Nott deny Ike's suicide. Now, our horror had returned. Where had it been?

Schlomo went on as if what had happened had not happened. He gave a classic Freudian explanation of "how this multiple gets men to *schtup* her." As he went on—amusing, intelligent, and sincere—the audience was in the palm of his hand. The three of us looked at each other. In this room almost a year before, Geneva Hooevens had gotten up, spoken out, asked for the truth. I wanted desperately to get up and speak out, but I felt as if a weight were holding me down, making my tongue too heavy to lift. I felt the weight of the others in the room who thought Schlomo was a great man, a brave man for confronting this delicate issue in therapy, and even braver because he could say that while of course the therapist was responsible for abusing the patient sexually and must be held accountable, the patient had a hand in provoking the abuse. I felt the weight not only of those present, but of all those who had sat in this room through its past, the weight of so many years of denying what was being seen in the moment, to preserve what was thought to be known.

"Within the consulting chamber," Schlomo said, "careful Freudian analysis will uncover exactly what leads these women to get themselves sexually abused."

"Right," Hannah whispered, loudly enough to be heard by a few people around us. "They all had light brown hair and looked like boys."

"And like goys," Henry added.

Schlomo glanced at us, but went on, "I applaud Dr. Shpitzer's brilliant program of risk management. Folks, it's just not worth the risk. To hold a patient's hand, to acquiesce to what is, deep down, as much an aggressive act as an erotic one, a hug? Not worth the risk."

"But screwing a patient," I said to Solini, again loud enough for those around us to hear, "now that's *worth* the risk."

As Schlomo went on, his audience sat mesmerized, like snakes by a world-class charmer. Why couldn't I speak? Was I a coward? A defective person? Were Henry and Hannah too? Malik had said that what hurts the victim is not only the cruelty of the abuser but the silence of the bystander. Berry had told me that for women who had been sexually abused as children, the worst was when they'd been put in the position of *knowing* that their younger sister was being abused, and had not been able to speak up. I decided I had to say something. I braced myself. I would stand up and interrupt him. On three. One, two . . .

But I could not. What would I say? How would I say it? It was too big, and the weight of false histories in the room too heavy.

Schlomo went on, gathering momentum, drawing the audience toward him by his being such a high-class mensch. He finished. Applause rolled up toward him. Bowing, smiling, dancing on his toes as the applause splashed over him, he asked, "Any questions?"

Silence.

Now. I tried harder to gather my thoughts. As soon as I got one in line, I felt the pressure of my heart pounding and the eyes that would be upon me as heavy as rocks, and the line broke, and my mind went blank. I looked to Henry and Hannah. Both sat still, as if turned to stone.

Crack!

We jumped at the sound. A gunshot? We turned toward it, behind us in the back.

A. K. Lowell was on her feet again, her snapped yellow pencil in her upraised hands. Her face was flushed with fury. Suddenly I knew what she was about to do.

"You pervert!" she said. "You have sexually abused your patients for years. You sexually abused *me* for years."

Schlomo's hands fumbled at his chest as if he'd been shot or was having a heart attack and then drifted slowly down to his crotch.

A.K. walked out.

All eyes turned back to Schlomo, who stood stock-still.

"Let's go!" I said happily, loudly, to Henry and Hannah.

"Let's make our *move*!" Henry said.

"Cool!" Hannah said.

The three of us stood up and walked. We walked lightly, triumphantly, walked straight on through the deadweight of all these normalized eyes, walked up the aisle and out the door in solidarity with Aliyah K. Lowenschteiner.

OUR TRIUMPH WAS short-lived. An hour later Mr. Beef Telly and Misery Security came to my office to escort me to Dr. Lloyal von Nott's office. As I passed by Viv's bulletproof, our eyes met. In her eyes I saw fear.

A plush carpet gave way to a plusher carpet. I was face-to-face with Lloyal von Nott and Nash Michaels and the chairman of the board of Misery. They were all dressed identically in funereal suits and flat boxy ties, as if by a mother of triplets. Lloyal and Nash looked bad, older, burnt out. Lines like scratches spread across their foreheads, out from the corners of their eyes, and down in defining arcs from their nostrils to their masseters. With the hospital having lost its battle with the insurance industry, they'd been under a lot of pressure. Recently they had responded by releasing a high-gloss and soothing "Annual Misery Report," which made it sound like the hospital was as successful as Disneyworld. As I stared at them I saw them as shiny, buffed to a sheen with secrets, their lies a patina of denial.

"Hello," I said nervously. I felt vulnerable and alone. All my life I'd been in these situations in schools, called in before principals.

"Good-bye," von Nott said, from behind his desk.

"What?"

Mr. Telly's walkie-talkie squawked. He and Security moved to narrow the sightline to von Nott, as if to shield him from me, a Secret Service move.

"You are hereby informed," said Nash Michaels in a voice of Formica, "that this conversation is being recorded. If you would like to have your own counsel present, we will stop right now."

"What's this all about?"

"Counsel refused," Nash said, eyes slithering up to the ceiling. The Toshiba transceiver, which went both ways, was on.

"We shan't keep you," von Nott said.

"I'm in no hurry."

"Ah, but you are. Your contract expires at midnight of thirty June, Wednesday next. We shan't renew your contract. On one July you are history."

"You can't do that."

"We have. You have failed. You are a failure. Your career is over."

The word "failure" bit into me. My dream—my father's dream—of my being a doctor was over. "B-b-but y-you have no grounds."

Von Nott pointed to a thick manila folder on his desk. "Grounds aplenty."

"Y-y-you're getting rid of me b-because I saw Schlomo D-D-Dove have sexual intercourse with Zoe."

"You saw nothing."

"I know what I saw."

"You saw nothing."

"Are you saying I didn't see what I saw?"

"You saw nothing. Unless you saw what wasn't there. This, perhaps you've learned this year, is called an hallucination."

"A. K. Lowell, today in grand rounds—"

"We don't take cases," Nash said, "that we can lose."

Suddenly the breath seemed to go out of me. I felt weak and light-headed. I felt silenced.

The door burst open. Telly crouched, reaching for his stun-gun.

"Solini?" I cried out. The little guy stood there, rolling his wrists.

"When Viv calls *stat*, you move! You pull a Malik—you stick together!"

"Get out," von Nott said.

"Fuck you!"

"Dr. Basch has just been terminated, and you—"

"Fuck you!" Henry shouted, and reached into his jacket. Von Nott ducked down behind his desk; Telly and Security and the chairman dropped to the rug.

What? They thought Henry was reaching for a weapon?

It was a letter. Throwing it down on the glossy desk, he shouted, "Fuck you! I fuckin' quit and fuck you!"

All at once I saw it. Their having their thugs and lawyers and board chairs here, their ducking down behind desks. "Henry! They're afraid of us!"

"Scared shitless of us, man, yeah!"

"You guys," I said, "are afraid of us!"

"Tell it, Roy! Of us!"

The three men in suits exchanged glances. This was outside protocol, beyond the flowcharts and dangling boxes that defined them.

In that moment I saw all the other people that year who'd died and left, died and left. All of them were standing with us, sticking together with us. Even dead and gone their presence right then right there in that pathetic office was vital, powerful. They were here with Henry and me. We all were crowding out these three boys before us, crowding them out, these three boys dressed up so hard to look like real men. Standing there, I saw, in these men, dead souls.

Much as in real medicine I'd learned to see death itself, flitting like a lost moth around people's bodies. I felt a rush of joy, and said, "You fuckers are scared to death of us."

"To like death, man!" Henry sang out, squinching up his face. He was rolling now. "And one more thing: fuck you!"

"Ridiculous," von Nott said, standing back up. I'm sure he thought that his face was stone. But the denial was so thin, splotches of the real bled through. He'd been found out, his secret seen.

"Scared to death!" I said joyfully. "And fuck you all!"

"Diddily diddily death!" Henry sang.

"As we often said in Europe during the war," von Nott said, " 'You haven't a snowball's chance in hell.' "

"The war?" I asked, surprised he'd bring that up now. "And where were you during the war?"

"In Switzerland. I was neutral."

"In that war, you were *neutral?*"

"Get out."

Looking at each in turn, into each set of eyes calcified by cash and deception, I said, "You are dead souls. Dead fucking souls. And you're being killed like you killed Ike White."

"Like Ike, man!" Solini said. "Tell it!"

"Out!"

" 'Check out the real situation—check it out check it out!' " Henry sang.

We danced out, shaking hips, waving index fingers, jiving, singing Bob.

Carried down the hallway on our exhilaration, we found ourselves staring at a nameplate:

SCHLOMO DOVE, M.D., F.R.A.P.S.

"Let's do Schlomo!" Henry shouted.

"Yeah!" I said, and was about to bang on the door when I was stopped by a weird sound coming from inside his office, a raspy sound like when you try to shift gears with a bum clutch. Then I recognized it. It was the defining sound of our times. "A shredder?"

"Turning the truth, man, into confetti. Be cool, Roy. Catch you later."

Solini walked away, to see a patient. I walked over to Viv. She buzzed me in.

"Thanks for sending Solini," I said, feeling safe behind the bulletproof. "How did you know?"

"Cowboy, you looked bad! So how'd it go?"

I told her. As I spoke, the lift left me. I started to feel down, really down. What had I done?

"Congratulations," Viv said.

"For what?"

"Bein' fired from Misery. Wear it like the Congressional Medal of Honor."

"Terrific. I'll have to change the title of my autobiography from 'Notes of an Overachiever' to 'I Was a Failure at Misery.' "

"Failure? In whose eyes, theirs? Thank God they dint call you a success!" I laughed. "Listen, Cowboy-doll," she said, her long fake lashes flying up toward her blond beehive, so that her hazel eyes widened. "I've seen it over and over again: if you're any good, they get rid of you. No one who's any good stays long in Mount Misery."

How right she was. They'd gotten rid of anyone "on the beam": me and Henry and Hannah and Malik and Geneva Hooevens, and many other good therapists, now out in the community. They had succeeded in weeding us out. We were history, soon to be revised. In a few years the word would be that Ike White had not killed himself at all but had died of a fatal disease, say a heart attack, why not? Nobody would be around to tell the truth.

All over America sincere, intelligent, sensitive, and enthusiastic young men and women were heading into these training programs. They hoped to open up even more, and learn how to help those caught in the hell of mental illness. Instead they would learn to close down and shut down and become someone special. They would buy terrific cars and after years of training be able to look into the mirror and—rather than see the truth of the person looking back out of the mirror—see the image.

There would always be a Lloyal, a Nash, always be an Errol, always a Heiler, a Schlomo Dove. The bad news is that you get rid of one, and another takes his place. The good news is that in rising, they are all dying.

And maybe the better news is that with psychiatrists becoming drug pushers instead of listeners, the actual work with human beings will devolve to the ones better at it, the nurses and social workers and mental health workers and alcoholics and addicts in recovery and pastoral counselors way down the flow-chart of Misery, who in many ways had done the most to help patients this year. Those who, with patients day in and day out, through chance encounters and common sense, offering man-on-the-street wisdom gained through facing the suffering in their own lives, helped people heal. Like the basically cheerful often dark-skinned workers in Buildings and Grounds who talked with patients while emptying the trash or mopping the floor or cutting the grass. Years later, if you asked a former patient what had made a difference to make them better, they would point not to a drug or a shrink, but to a connection made with one of these people. These Vivs. And one of the most hopeful signs, now was how patients themselves were organizing, forming support groups with like-minded others, like Zoe's TALL for the abused, or MDA—Manic

Depressive Association—to empower each other to find sensible, common-sense therapists out in the community, and to resist the authority of the world experts in the great institutions, all the Miserys.

"But people think these jackasses are good therapists," I said to Viv, "these world experts. When a relative gets in trouble, people ask their doctor to find them 'the best psychiatrist' and they get thrown to guys like von Nott, or Heiler, or Errol—or Schlomo! There's no way to measure who's any good. Everything takes place behind closed doors. Nobody knows."

"I do."

"How?"

"Simple. With the good ones, their patients get better."

"And what makes them get better?"

"Onny one thing matters, I mean really."

"Yeah?"

"If they like you."

"You think?"

"I know." She smiled. "They like you, Roy. And so do I."

"It's mutual. You are something else!"

"No foolin'."

"But what about Cherokee?"

"That was a very bad tragedy. But you learned from it. Nothin' this whole year taught you as much as him, God bless 'im." She blew her nose, loudly. "So anyways, send me a picher postcard sometimes, willya?"

"I don't know where I'll be."

"You can always call collect."

"How can you stand it here?"

"Somebody's got to, right? What can we do? We can't just walk. Besides," she said, patting her bluish-blond beehive, "women like me are getting in line to inherit the earth. Can I ask you one favor?"

"Anything."

"Can I kiss you?"

I blushed, and my head had barely nodded when I felt her teeth clack against mine—holy moley what an overbite!—and then her lips were on mine, and then to my surprise there was a quick flicker of her tongue on mine.

"Remember, Cowboy. You can always call Misery collect."

MY LADY IN BLACK, Christine, sat with me in my office up in Toshiba late that afternoon. Still Madonna-platinum, she wore a sleeveless black blouse, short black shirt, and black tights with flowers entwining up toward no-man's-land. Her nails and lips were scarlet. I told her I would be leaving Mount Misery.

"What? How can you do this to me?" she said. "After all this, you leave? What the hell's wrong with you? Why are you doing this?"

I wanted to tell her I'd been fired, but I couldn't. "I'm sorry," I said. "I know it makes you angry—"

"You bet! Unbelievable. I take this very seriously. You don't!"

"I do."

"Yeah, sure. Oh boy. Maybe I've been wrong about you. I mean you knew how suicidal Cherokee was," she said, her anger rising, "and about his big insurance policies that were coming due. I know you couldn't tell me, but couldn't you have somehow warned me?"

I felt a hit of dread, a snakebite in my gut.

"Well?" She stared at me, wild-eyed. "C'mon—*respond*!"

Her inflamed anger inflamed my dread. Feeling trapped, I backed away emotionally. Pure dread—old, familiar. Dreadlock.

"Oh God," she said in disgust, tapping a scarlet nail on the arm of the chair.

But then something new happened. All at once I saw this dread so clearly, it began to lessen. For the first time in my life I saw that it was not my psychopathology festering under the enamel of my mind, but merely a fact, called dread. Over and over, through millions of deflections of love, I had learned to become an agent of disconnection, in the name of becoming a man. As women had come toward me in love, I had fled, imagining that I had to do something to win that love. Then I realized: it's not just me, it's all of us men, trying to become champions. We run from the love that is there for the asking, to try to become champions, to win the love we are running from. We men run.

I saw, then, the mean-spiritedness of theories that blamed our mothers or fathers for this. It isn't our mothers or fathers, it's what we learn about preserving the myth of our separate selves by disconnecting from relationships. It's not sick, it's normal. It's all of us normal men caught in the most violent and fragmented time of human history, screwing it up together. When old men call us "soft" for being too connected, and tell us we need to become more quintessentially male, we follow like sheep. And all the while what we need to do is not become more male, but be more connected. Mutually.

All this shot through my mind in an instant. Seeing it so clearly, as not only about me but about my gender, it seemed to ease and lose its grip on me. The muscles of my neck softened. My shoulders eased down. I breathed. The softening and easing and breathing made me realize how hardened and tight

I'd been—I'd actually been holding my breath. Breathing out, I felt a touch of humility. Breathing in, calm. I said:

"Cherokee never told me just how suicidal he was, or about any insurance policies. What did he tell you? Maybe we can understand it, together?"

"You didn't *know*?"

"No, I'm sorry to say I didn't."

"Did you ask?"

"I tried."

"Terrific," she said sarcastically, looking down into her lap.

I understood. The issue wasn't me, or her, but us. The "we" in the room, which seemed so solid right then that you could shape it, yet so ephemeral that it was the unseen historical forces shaping you. It wasn't *my* dread, but merely dread; not *her* anger, but merely anger. The psychopathology wasn't in her or in me, but in the way that we were meeting. Perhaps there was no such thing as "psychopathology" at all.

My job right then was to hold this "we," this connection with her, hold it for both of us. That was my job as a doctor. To use my experience with others who had suffered and my vision born of that experience to bring someone who is out on the edge of the so-called "sick" into the current of the human. To take what seems foreign in a person and see it as native. This is healing. This process is what the healing process is. This is what I signed up for, years ago. This is what old Dr. Starbuck in Columbia did, taking care of the town, inviting me into medicine. This is what I had done moonlighting. This is what good doctors do. We are *with* people at crucial moments in their lives, healing. How hard it had gotten, in these hellish hospitals and institutions encrusted with machines and desiccated hearts and dead souls, to get back to authentic suffering, authentic healing. How much we have lost.

Now I took on the job happily, even with zest. Holding this "us," this connection, right here right now in this suddenly fine moment. Holding this connection as a father learns to hold not so much a crying baby but the connection with a crying baby, a baby overtired and needing to be held and rocked to sleep, a baby who can sense if the arms around her are constricted with anger and trying to control her, or if the arms are open to merely being there with her. If the arms are angry and controlling, the baby will struggle against sleep no matter how tired she is. If the arms are relaxed and open, she will ease down into the feather down of sleep, yes.

"We've had a hard time, Christine. Can we try, together, to understand?"

She looked up at me. I sensed her seeing the depth of my concern. I felt that "click" of opening that I'd felt with Zoe my first night on call.

Click. I saw Christine see it. I sensed her feeling seen. Despite herself, she smiled.

We began to talk about us, and Cherokee. Talk as good friends might, of a mutual friend. Our words were strung together to help hold us. And then all at once we stopped talking and were still. We sat awhile in stillness.

Thwop! Thwop! The sound of tennis balls being hit, coming through the open window, rising from the tennis court below. The sounds were sweet, full of resilience and bounce, reminding me of hearing, through a stethoscope, a healthy heart. The seasons had come round. We both smiled.

She said, "You know what you did that helped me the most?"

"Followed you down to the tennis court."

"Yeah."

"I felt it was such a dumb thing to do at the time," I said. "What helped you, about my doing that?"

"That it was such a dumb thing to do. It showed you were a person. People don't do smart things all the time, they do dumb things. And you hung in with me, through all the dumb things we both did, through Cherokee and everything, you hung in with me."

"We hung in together, yes."

She sat still again, her hands in her lap. "I guess I just don't want to go through life not knowing if I've ever been loved."

She looked up. Our eyes held. "Christine," I said, "you are loved."

In the past she would have cried. Sobbed at the smallest sadness. Now she did not. She smiled, as did I. She asked, "Why are you leaving?"

"I was fired."

"Fired? You? Why?"

"Because I kept doing things like following people down to tennis courts."

"Yeah, well, maybe you don't fit in here. I mean you're basically a sweetie, just trying to understand. I mean the potential, Roy, is there."

We laughed. "We could continue to meet. I'll have an office outside the hospital."

"No. We've done everything we needed to do." She got up. I did too. She looked me squarely in the eyes and took a step toward me. I thought for a second that she was going to throw her arms around me and hug me. She held out her hand. "Thanks," she said, her grip firm. "You did good."

"We did good."

"Yes, we did." With a certain dignity, she walked out.

BERRY AND I TALKED into the small hours of that summery night.

"I don't think I've ever felt so opened up and alive," I said.

"Imagine if you could live every day like that?"

"Who could bear it?"

"How can we bear not to?"

"Makes me think of how we lived all last year, in China, Italy, Istanbul, Morocco—the intensity of it? Why do we settle for less?" We were lying naked in my turret. It was hot; the windows were open to the spongy June night. "Great timing, eh? Just when I finally learn, I get fired."

"Learn to be a psychiatrist?"

"That too. I was thinking finally learn how to be a real doctor."

"Now there's an idea. A real doctor, mmm." She yawned, and snuggled into the crook of my neck. "Hold me, babe, hold me so close we won't ever die."

She dozed off, my arm around her. I too began to doze. But then, in that hypnagogic moment just before sleep, I jerked to attention, that black-and-white photo facing me, as if blown up on a billboard. I went cold and shivered—in that hot June night, I shivered. I was face-to-face with a demon. I shivered with fear, and sickly revulsion. I lay there alone until I couldn't stand it anymore, and woke up Berry.

"Wha-what?" she said.

"I'm sorry, but I've got to tell you something."

" 'Kay." She sat up and faced me, eyes barely opening. "Give me a sec." She yawned, rubbed her eyes, crossed her legs. " 'Kay."

"I know what killed Ike White." She blinked. "Ike was in that photo, standing apart from Schlomo and A.K. Schlomo was Ike's analyst too, at the same time as A.K.'s. Ike and A.K. were best friends. They were in the same class at the Freudian Institute, going to seminars together three times a week. They each saw Schlomo in analysis every day. They were close."

"So?"

"So in that photo, Ike looked like a young boy. He was slender, clean-shaven. His hair was cut short, like A.K.'s, and Lily's, and Zoe's."

"Oh God."

"Yeah. Schlomo was fucking Ike too. Shit." I took a deep breath and tried to breathe out hard, to breathe it all away. "On Ike's face, in that photo, was a look of such sadness. He and A.K. must have suspected Schlomo was screwing each of them." I shook my head. "That first time I met with Cherokee, at six in the morning when he'd told me he thought Schlomo was fucking his wife, I went to Ike for supervision, and told him. I didn't get anywhere with Ike—he said I had to investigate what was probably a delusion. But he didn't totally dismiss it, and when I asked if I should talk directly to Schlomo, he said I definitely should. Almost like he wanted me, or was choosing me, to find out the truth."

"Yes."

"And that same morning I went to see Schlomo, and told him all about it. He said Cherokee was crazy. But later that day, after he'd talked with me,

Schlomo called up Ike. And that night, after saying good-bye to me, Ike killed himself. Was that what had killed him? Hearing, from me, that Schlomo was still at it? Hearing, from Schlomo, that he'd better keep his mouth shut or else?"

"It's sick," Berry said. "It is so so sick."

"That's their word," I said, "and their excuse. Calling it 'sick' is way too easy, it lets 'em off the hook, lets 'em say they're not responsible. Not just sick, no. What it really is, is evil."

IN ACADEMIC MEDICINE the first of July is "change day," when one year ends and we doctors move on to the next. Friends, you enter an academic hospital early in July at no small peril to your life.

I awoke on the morning of June 30 feeling sad. Solini and Hannah had flights booked out that night. Henry was flying to Jamaica, Hannah to Wyoming. Malik, too, was taking a plane that night. Although he wouldn't tell us his destination, I had a sense that he would be going back home to Chicago, to be near his family. We would all meet at the airport that night.

The day dawned crisp and clear. Against the fading forsythia and daffodils, the hell-bent tulips and daredevil lilac blossomed with even more passion. I drove toward the hospital. As Mount Misery rose in the distance it seemed stunningly beautiful. The way college always looked to me the day after the last exam. Misery's high crown of oaked hill seemed a solid underlay to her red-brick buildings set like rubies in green rings of lawn, lawn flowing down the hill and around the lake and then under the massive iron fence and gate, giving way to normal turf, scraggly fields and hills heading toward the mountains. On the Misery campus people strolled to and fro with seeming purpose. Though I now could tell a patient from a doctor on sight, I could no longer tell whose purpose was authentic.

I stayed just long enough to meet Henry in the attic of Toshiba, to help each other empty out our offices.

On the way out, as Henry and I passed Malik's office, we ran into Mr. K. and Solini's reggae man, Carter. They were hoping to catch Malik to say good-bye. Henry asked Carter if there was anything more he could do for him.

"Nope. I'd rather have a bottle in front of me than a frontal lobotomy."

"And you, Mr. K.?" I asked. "How you doing?"

"Lobotomy's not so bad," he said, "if they botch it. A botched lobotomy's almost a match for a perfect birth. Yesterday was my eightieth birthday."

"Eighty?" Solini and I cried out in unison. He looked maybe sixty, tops seventy.

"But you seem so young!" I said. "How have you managed to stay so young?"

"Yes, er, no," he said, as if confused. But then his eyes lit up and he went on, "My secret is this: always stay a little bit out of it."

I drove down off Mount Misery for the last time. Workmen were replacing the sign THOREAU with a sign and logo HEALTHCARE HOUSE. For an instant I felt a stab of regret, recalling the high hope with which I had first ridden up the hill to my first interview with Ike White, where I'd been so dazzled by his compassion and intelligence that I'd enlisted right away to work with him. In the next instant, seeing Misery made small in my rearview mirror, I felt relieved. I would no longer be using the mirrors of sadism and authority to try to catch a glimpse of any truth, in this strange place that those locked up inside had nicknamed "Heaven on the Hill."

WE ALL CONVERGED on the Boston airport that night.

I drove Solini. He was wearing jeans and a bright flowery Hawaiian shirt and his round woolen Rasta cap. He was traveling light, in one hand a new valise, in the other his battered black doctor's bag. The little guy, who had always seemed so cynical, was doing something wildly idealistic—signing up to be the only white doctor in Trenchtown, Jamaica. Bob's hometown.

Hannah and Gilda were already there, traveling heavy, with masses of suitcases, skis and a cello case piled in front of them as they waited in line. Both wore "farmer" jeans, the kind with the bibs and straps and brass buttons, and cow-woman hats. The rancher outfit looked great on the gutsy, broad Gilda, but Hannah, thin down to the hips and dark-haired and looking brittle, reminded me of a city girl having her picture taken on a pony on a day trip to the Catskill Game Farm.

Finally we all sat together on the hard plastic seats that would outlive not only us but civilization. In this polymeric ambience of the airport, we joined those from all walks of life who were taking the leap of faith that heavy metal machines could sail through air. Our own faith had been diminished by having had pilots and mechanics as patients. Often they were alcoholics or addicts or so depressed that they wanted to kill themselves and couldn't care less if they took whole planeloads down with them. I'd seen one pilot in the West with the fixed delusion that metal of course cannot sail through air and that in fact God picked up each plane on takeoff and set each down gently on landing, and that given the sins of the world, God was fed up and about to stop doing it and there would be a rash of crashes. When his insurance ran out he was turfed out on six drugs, and last I heard he was back flying.

Of all the airports I'd seen in my trip around the world, Boston's Logan was the worst. The night before, there had been a screwup. Flights all day had been canceled or delayed. By the time we got there, the place had the feel of a Third World outpost. People were camped out, little families of refugees huddled over candy bars and soft drinks, staring blankly through the foul canned air at nothing, having long ago run out of things to say to each other. Children shrieked and cried.

We waited anxiously for Malik. To our surprise we were joined by Zoe and Thorny. Zoe was beaming. She, and then Lily, had been interviewed by the *Globe*.

"The reporter was great," Zoe said. "She'll protect our identities. And after what A.K. did in public, she's just *got* to come forward. Yesterday another Schlomo victim called TALL! Listen!" She spoke with clarity, and power. The transformation was striking, given where she'd been a year ago, when she came into Misery—a frightened college girl who'd sought power only through men. "So we've got an even better case now. Right, Gilda?"

"Better than better, sweetheart. You may even have a chance. Yeah, if it does go to trial, I reckon you got a chance to nail that predator, for good."

"And what about you, Thorny-babe?" Solini asked.

Before he could answer, Malik appeared. He was dressed in a khaki safari suit and new black Nikes. He too was carrying his black medical bag. Bronia was carrying two of those black mesh knapsack/suitcases made of everything-proof material, a spin-off from the outer space program. Thinking intergalactic, I flashed on Jill. Jill in the jungle now, Jill naked but for a purple velvet choker, Jill gone. Sad.

Malik seemed healthier, not coughing. His eyes behind those tinty lenses were intense and curious, as when I'd first met him. Greetings all around. Zoe took out a camera and asked a woman to take a group photo. At her urging, we smiled. Flash. Done. I realized that Thorny had gotten cut off, and asked, "What about you, Thorny?"

"The South Pacific!" he cried. "An atoll! Thorny and the *Rainbow Warrior* against the dickhead French!"

"Greenpeace?" I asked.

"Thorny!"

"Thorny?"

"Greenpeace! I leave next week!"

"Good for you!" I cried.

"Good for us all! No more 'Family Tree' bullshit—'Tree Family!' " He smiled, all adazzle. "Dickheads Go Green!" We laughed. But then Thorny seemed to crumple a little.

"What's wrong?" Malik asked.

"Lotta shit comin' down, Doc. The last few months, out there on my own sellin' software, well, I got into a relationship with a lady, and, well, it was like puttin' Miracle-Gro on my character defects. Even the South Pacific may not be far away enough!"

Malik took him and Zoe aside. Zoe shook Malik's hand good-bye. Thorny gave him a big hug, shouting out, "Remember, Malik. Before you met me, you was drinkin' Aqua Velva. And no matter where you are, Lenny, I'll be on you in spirit, like white on rice!"

Zoe and Thorny walked away. I felt worried for them, seeing them, still, as too opened up for the world. Yet I also felt envious, seeing them both as having, over the year, found such clear purpose in their lives, while any purpose I'd entered with had, over the year, been lost. I had no idea what I'd be doing, even tomorrow.

"What did you say to them?" I asked Malik.

"I told 'em how, after I got sober, early in my recovery when I was going through hell, I kept saying to my sponsor, George: 'I'm going insane, George! I'm going *insane*!' and he said back to me, 'No, no, Malik, you got it wrong. You're goin' *sane*. You're goin' *sane*.' "

"*Nu*, I'll check us in," said Bronia, her sabra body armor seeming, suddenly, to be falling like wet clothes to the floor, leaving merely a woman in love with a dying man. She marched off into the wilderness of Departures.

"So where are you going, Malik?" Hannah asked.

"Dalhousie, in the Himalayas. There's an orphanage there, run by a woman I studied with, a spiritual teacher. Two hundred children, three attendants, no doctors—until the day after tomor—" A fit of coughing. We waited.

In the wake of this paroxysm it hit home—this was it, the last time we'd all be together. We began to really talk, that rare, intense, back-and-forth you have late at night, say in college, and in love. Malik said how grateful he was to us, for being with him through the year, for hearing the alarm, for waking up. We talked about our love for him, but soon we were talking about our doubt about what we had done all year long—"a year," von Nott had written in a memo recently, "rather typical for Mount Misery"—and doubt about what we could do now.

"And that's it!" Malik said. "That's their power, to get us to doubt. But don't confuse self-doubt with radical questioning. We've each had a hit of vitality this year—each of us—and no institution can stand too much vitality. Not medicine, business, government, not religion, education—none of 'em! And the amazing thing is, is that our doubt is our faith, okay?"

He looked to us, each to each, eye-to-eye, asking, his gaze once again sharp yet kind, the false line between conscious and unconscious revealed and gone, jolting me out of the ordinary, like that feel of grit, that morning, on my cheek. My heart beat harder, my head cleared, my vision sharpened, I was eye-to-eye with him, volt-to-volt. Anything was possible right then.

"And faith itself, in this day and age, is a revolutionary act."

He looked from face to face in our little circle. Then he smiled. "Like sports."

"Last call for USAir flight 1492 to Miami, Boarding Gate Thirty-one."

"Shit," Solini cried. "U.S. Scare and I didn't even hear it." The little guy's good-byes were rushed. "So, man," Henry said, embracing Malik last of all, gulping back sobs, "like what's the last question?"

"Isn't that it?" Malik asked.

"No, no, I mean for real. Gimme one anyway."

"Okay, hotshot, here you go: 'What's *yours*?' "

"Good question," Solini said. He stopped rolling and was still. He knitted up his brow and, starting to roll once again to his internal beat, said, "Mine is this: there's a lot of life out there, man, but you gotta open your eyes to see it? And hey—I got one for you, Malik?"

"I'm all ears."

"Meditate all you want, babe, but tie up your camel?"

"Cool," Malik said.

"So," Solini said, biting his lower lip to keep control, feet and knees and legs and arms starting to rock and roll. "So, Malik, babe. You cool on all a this?"

"I'm cool. You?"

"There it is." The little guy blew his nose in his flowery shirt and hurried off. As he got smaller and smaller he became his shirt and rainbow Rasta cap, and then his shirt and cap became only pops of color, and finally an after-image of green and yellow and scarlet, like an island on a map of an equatorial sea.

"United proudly announces the departure of flight 699 to Denver."

Gilda and Hannah took their leave, sadly, with fading embraces and promises to keep in touch. We watched them, as burdened as pack mules, disappear down the arroyo of Departure toward their flight to Wyoming.

Bronia was still standing in the crowd at Air India. She didn't seem to have moved. As we watched, a large Indian family draped in silk shoved her aside.

Malik and I were alone. I felt our time as precarious as quicksilver. I had a tremendous urge to talk, to ask everything, fast.

Then the strangest thing happened.

We just sat there side by side.

We just sat there.

Eyes open to the madness of the airport, and then beyond, to the lights of the circling planes blinking in the hazy summer night like the fireflies of Tuscany that had lit up Cherokee's heart for a brief moment a year before, we sat there in silence together.

"TIME TO GO, LOVE." Bronia was standing before us with a wheelchair.

A wheelchair? Malik? This friend of mine who, my first day in Misery—it seemed a second ago now—had been chasing down every ball Mr. K. had hit, and with that hoisting-a-turkey-onto-a-truck stroke, was somehow getting it back, now unable to walk? Oh God.

I wheeled him through the frantic crowd to the metal detector. This was it.

"Let me know where you are," I said, "so we can keep in touch."

"You too."

"Wish I knew what I'll be doing."

He nodded. "About 'doing'?"

"Yeah?"

"We'll both be doing the same thing, kid."

"Which is?"

"Learning."

"Learning what?"

"To die well."

A last hug. Bones. He got up out of the wheelchair, walked slowly through the metal detector, and joined Bronia on the other side. She gestured him to get back in, but he started to walk. He walked a few steps. A little out of breath, he stopped, and turned to wave. I waved back. He turned away again and walked a few slow steps, coughing, and walked a few more. I couldn't take my eyes off him. He was the most important organism on the face of the earth right then. The love between us was stretching and stretching to thinner and thinner stuff, until it was as fragile as a filament of breath, and as unbreakable.

As I watched, he bent down, as he had the first day I'd met him and had done so often in the course of this miserable year that I'd stopped noticing it, bent down and picked up a piece of litter. Holding it in his hand, he walked on.

CANYON DE CHELLY

"The planning took place on the top of the Beautiful Goods.
They planned how the strong Earth's Heart should be formed;
How the Mixed Chips should be used, and
How the Sacred Mountain should be made.
How the Sacred Mountain should be made,
Like the Most-High-Power-Whose-Ways-Are-Beautiful."

—NAVAJO MOUNTAIN CHANT

Twenty-Two

TOGETHER WE WATCH the Navajo woman pass by. She seems to come suddenly out of the high desert, a lean black dog following after. White-haired, bronze face weathered, she wears a long purple skirt and brown leather vest. Her blouse is the bright red of arterial blood. Gold lightning flashes across it. Silver and turquoise, like water and sky, are around her neck. A golf umbrella, sectored blue and white, and proclaiming CITIBANK, shades her. She walks past us without eye contact and slips through what seems solid sandstone at the mouth of the trail down into the canyon, her black dog following. As suddenly as they have come, they are gone.

"Did you see that?" Berry asks. "The way she just came out of nowhere and then moved through that rock?"

"Yes," I say, stroking her cheek. "Like a mirage."

I'm leaning back against a boulder. Berry is lying against me, her hair nestled into my chin. Lizzie Qun, naked, is asleep on her chest, her morning bottle, interrupted by sleep, in one hand. The other hand clutches the edge of Berry's bra, white lace in tiny fingers. To feel the sun, Berry has opened her blouse to the waist. Her breasts lift and lower Lizzie's head with each breath.

We are sitting on the ground near the canyon rim. The late-June morning sun is clear and warm and revving up to hot. We sit on Lizzie's green quilt covered with purple birds with triangle yellow beaks and rounded bottoms like toy boats. Our quilt is spread amidst the scrub. As far as the eye can see is rough cracked land, sagebrush, rock and red dune, and clattering sky. On the horizon, a hint of buttes. Above them, dark clouds. We are over a mile high.

"We were right to choose this," I say. "It's so solid. Basic. What a relief."

"Really. Two Jews, a Chinese baby, and a Navajo woman—out in the middle of a desert."

"It's your normal American family, on the way to their new home."

We laugh. Lizzie stirs. She's eight months and four days. She was four months when we met her, and now it's four months and four days that we've had her. The balance of her lifetime has shifted—she's been with us more than she's been with anyone else. Berry and I went back a second time to China, to Changsha, in Hunan Province, to adopt her from Social Welfare Center Number One. We carried her to the ninth floor of the Xiangjiang Hotel while her passport and adoption papers were processed. Having crashed from our infertility, we'd had doubts about adoption. But then, leaning into life, we'd said, "Yes."

Lizzie has a round face with plump cheeks and a mouth made of rose petals. That first time we saw her in the orphanage, we were taken with her eyes. Swaddled so she couldn't much move, she must have lived through her vision. She touches everything with her eyes, as the blind touch everything with their other senses. Her eyes are shaped like teardrops set on their sides. The irises are as dark as the pupils, so that even in the bright desert sunlight you can't see where the matter of the iris ends and the emptiness of the pupil begins. Her eyes give an illusion of wisdom. Four-hundred-year-old eyes. Malik eyes. Her face is so familiar to us already that non-Asian babies seem foreign. We can't stop kissing her.

Yesterday we arrived at Fort Defiance, Arizona, the regional seat of the Indian Health Service, to start our two years of service, I as a doctor, Berry as a teacher and child psychologist. I'll be doctoring a lot of alcoholics and drug addicts. It's been almost a year since I was fired from Misery.

"Shall we open the letter now?" Berry asks.

Awaiting our arrival here yesterday were several letters and postcards. One letter was from India, Dalhousie, in the Himalayas. The handwriting was unfamiliar. I knew it concerned Malik.

"No," I say, "let's wait till we're at the ruins, down in the canyon. They say it's a sacred place."

"Can I make a suggestion, hon?"

"Try me."

"Breathe."

I laugh and do so. "Breathe," Malik had always said. "Find the breath."

This morning in *U.S. News & World Report*, the issue devoted to "The Best Doctors and Hospitals in America," they said that the best psychiatric hospital was McLean but the second best was Mount Misery, and the Best Administrative Psychiatrist in America was Dr. Lloyal von Nott, and that among the "Fifty Best Psychiatrists Under Thirty-Five" was Dr. Winthrop Winthrop.

"What's wrong?" Berry asks. Startled, I wonder how she does it, always seems to know. I tell her what had come into my mind. She says, a little sharply, "Can't you just be here, with us?"

"I want to, but that magazine set my mind spinning like crazy. They call those jokers the best?"

"So what else is new? It's called the 'normal world,' right? We're here to find an alternative. Remember?"

"But it's *outrageous*!"

"Apucha! Kee-ka!"

Lizzie is awake, looking at us, sensing the tension. Berry sits her up. Perfect balance, legs crossed. A little Buddha.

"Play with your daughter. She doesn't know the meaning of that word."

"She doesn't know any words yet."

"Look at her. She wants her dad to be with her. Play with her. I'll clean up."

As I look at her, Lizzie sees me looking, gives a yelp, and smiles. Smiles not only with her mouth but with her whole body, fat shoulders scrunching and arms lifting toward me and fingers grasping not just me but my seeing her—her seeing my seeing. As I join her in this seeing-play, something melts in me, an edge dissolves and all at once I'm with her. The small tight ball of my self breaks apart, letting something else expand. I'm in the world and of the world, feeling the morning sun on my back, the cool breeze on my cheeks, the sense of my wife and baby with me.

"Lizzie Qun!" I say. "Thank God for you!"

"Scree-op!"

"And for you," I say to Berry, appreciating how long we've been together, how hard we've tried to walk the walk together, how together we have finally crossed the divide that separates the sterile from the fertile. Tears come to her eyes, blurred by my own.

"Hey!"

Startled, Berry and I look around. Who said that?

Lizzie? We stare at each other.

"Her first word?" I ask.

"Lizzie?" Berry asks. "Did you say 'Hey'?"

"Scree-op! Amut!"

We laugh.

Berry squeezes my hand. "C'mon, love. Let's hike on down."

Lizzie squeals with delight when she sees me take out the Tough Traveler backpack, her big blue friend. I lift her up, and despite the weight, feel light, as if I too am being lifted. We walk to the edge of the canyon.

It takes my breath away—Berry's too; I hear her "Wow!"—the canyon stretching on and on as far as the eye can see and down so far that the sheep look like toys on a child's blanket.

I'm speechless, jolted out of myself into a perception that's free of any doctrine of a landscape or even of perception itself, a perception of what is. As Malik had shown me, sometimes in therapy you chance upon the real person right there with you, right there right then without bullshit, and I can almost hear Malik's tough, gym rat's voice telling me:

"Live your understanding, kid, right now, or it'll destroy you."

We start on down the trail into the canyon, toward the ruins said to be sacred. The baby on my back, nipple to her lips, starts exchanging formula for air.

THE WHITE HOUSE RUIN faces us, across the riverbed from where we sit. There on the sandy bank of the river is a small grove of cottonwoods and aspens. In this lap of shade, a Navajo man sells jewelry spread out on the hood of his pickup truck. Lifting up above the green tufts of the trees, our eyes are drawn to the cave.

The cave is set in the cliff face like a dark teardrop set on its side. Our eyes search the blackness. The Anasazi, the "Old People," the humans first here tens of thousands of years ago, built these dwellings of wood and fired mud. The lower row of dwellings are faded rose, the color of the cliff. Ladders lead up from their flat roofs to the doorways of another house, set back a little, like a hat set back on a head. This topmost dwelling is white, still white after millennia. It shines through the shadows. The current crop of humans have named it "the White House."

Earlier this morning we read several of the letters and postcards that had been awaiting our arrival.

One postcard showed, front-on, the towering bow of a freighter riding low in rough seas. The bow, fluted from a sharp edge at the bottom to an elegant furl at the top, was crashing down on a rough swell that lifted the foam almost up to its name: *Akatsuki Maru*. There in its path was a tiny rubber life raft with an outboard motor, its name: *Greenpeace*. Standing in the life raft, wearing orange rough-weather slickers upon which was drawn the three-pronged, propeller-shaped symbol for radioactive death, are two men. On the other side of the card, the message:

Dickheads Battle Plutonium Death-Ship!
Wish you were here.
Love, Thorny.

From Jamaica came a postcard of a fat tourist wearing a crappy straw hat, perched on a thin donkey. On the flip side:

There's a lotta life out there, man,
But you gotta open your eyes to see it,
And then it is Ideal. Be cool. Love, Henry.

From Hannah in Wyoming there was a long letter handwritten on "100% tree-free, chlorine-free, acid-free EcoPaper, made of hemp fiber—which requires only one-fourth of the land needed by the same amount of wood—and cereal straw, a by-product of grain production. I thought you'd like it because from the 1st century on, Chinese craftspeople created beautiful papers made from hemp, straw, and common plants." Hannah was seeing patients as a lay analyst, and doing a lot of work with her Jungian rodeo-archetype analyst. Things were going well with Gilda and the livestock, though better with the livestock. "Gilda and I are making fairly beautiful music together, although there are problems. Loveyakid, H."

My mother in Columbia was full of news about her life and golf, and about how nice my father's tombstone looked. Once, when my father was alive, she had pulled me aside and said that what she wanted on her own tombstone was an arrow pointing to his tombstone and the words:

He Pushed Me Into This.

Now she had mellowed. She had chosen a single stone for them both.

I asked Berry, "If you had on your tombstone, 'She Was Wonderful at Relationships,' would that be enough for you?"

"Yes and no."

"How's that?"

"It's good, but I'd want a second line, something like, 'And She Was a Good President Too.' " We laughed. "How 'bout you?"

" 'He Was Enough.' "

"Oh boy."

From Viv, in Esalen, California, came a note on stationery crowded with flowers:

> Cowboy,
>
> Misery downsized and they put Communications under Security. I was fired. They were scared of Primo and the rest of the old Security so they herded them into a room under false pretenses and then surrounded the room with the new Security—an outside group—and fired them and opened the door and they had to walk through the gauntlet. In a "total-quality-control" effort to make Misery "leaner and meaner" they laid off 40% of the workforce. Nash and Lloyal both got big raises, Nash got $234,000 and Lloyal $432,000. I'm using my savings to do the human potential movement thing. Hot tubs 'n' all. Primo sends his best.
>
> Love, Viv.

Poppa Doc, the analyst I'd never gone back to, sent a bill on a note: When you look into a very small looking glass, you see only yourself.

The final letter we read last night was overnight mail from Zoe, telling us about the last days of the trial of Schlomo Dove.

Had there ever been a trial so funny?

Berry and I had been in the courtroom up until the jury went out, when we had to leave for Arizona. Over and over again, like everyone else in the courtroom, we'd found ourselves cracking up with laughter.

A. K. Lowell was first to bring suit for malpractice. Schlomo created many delays. Through his lawyer, a woman named Joanne Green who looked like a sweet young thing but had the soul of a crocodile, Schlomo took both the high road and the low. First he tried to bribe A.K. Then he tried to threaten A.K. Finally he went public with slime on A.K. He responded to the *Globe*'s stories on two other "anonymous victims"—Lily and Zoe—by calling them "a Misery conspiracy" and reiterating his claim that "*Schlomo* is the real victim here." Then he tried to settle with A.K. out of court.

A.K. did not budge. The threat of my going public with her ledger was too great. A date was set for trial.

Schlomo's going public made jury selection difficult. He'd done the talk shows. Everyone had been entertained by him in print and on TV. Schlomo was great on TV. Selection of twelve reasonable, schizoid, reclusive folk who hadn't seen him, or had seen him and had not formed an opinion about him, took time, especially as Schlomo insisted that the only real "jury of Schlomo's peers" would be a dozen top Freudian analysts. Anyone else would be grounds for appeal. It was said that his alleged patient, Dershowitz, was watching.

Twice, just as the trial was about to start, Schlomo pulled the old Mafia trick of crushing chest pain, landing him in intensive care in my old hospital, "the House of God." The second crushing chest pain resulted in the judge convening the trial in the hospital. Schlomo made a terrific recovery. The trial began.

Schlomo's defense was that it was all fantasy. A.K.'s contention was that it was all reality. Both called in world-expert forensic psychiatrists as witnesses, who drew totally opposite conclusions, along the lines that you would expect.

When Schlomo testified he was terrific. Wise, funny, sad, angry. A man of the people. An esteemed professor high above the fray. Mesmerizing.

Even I, knowing the truth, half believed him. It was weird, just how convincing he could be. Not only was he totally entertaining, with his Borscht Belt humor about the accusations, but he came across as a victim himself, filled with—his word, said with a fist clenched over his heart—*tsouris*. This, he explained, was a Yiddish word meaning total grief. He gave the derivation and usage in great and teary detail.

Schlomo conveyed to us all not only his resilient humor, but also his pain, his heartache for everyone involved, especially "my poor *bubbie*, Dr. Lowell." He spoke from his *kishkees*. He laughed through his tears. He dressed so sloppily, looked so ugly, sounded like such a poor schlemiel, it seemed impossible that a woman would fall for him, especially not a woman as strong and sure of herself as A.K. By the end of his testimony I thought he had the jury eating out of his hand. Even the judge, a stern old New Englander named Shipley, tall as a tree and with a face like the Old Man of the Mountain, laughed twice, and once seemed on the edge of tears.

A.K., unfortunately, came across as she was: cold, unknowable and unknown, making no real contact with the jurors. With her soul so hidden, it seemed that she just might be crazy, making all this up. Especially when her stiff, guarded words were seen against the backdrop of Schlomo's spilling his guts in such a seemingly sincere, convincing, and entertaining way.

Schlomo testified under oath that he could not possibly have abused A.K. because he had been impotent for a decade at least. In a spectacular piece of bravado, his wife Dixie Dove took the stand and, with a humility that was truly heart-wrenching, said:

"Yes, Schlomo Dove has been important for at least the last ten years."

Everyone cracked up. Schlomo laughed as hard as anyone. He was enjoying this, his moment of national—hell, international—fame. Half of Hollywood—the psychoanalyzed half—was said to be calling. He was becoming a star.

In cross-examination, A.K.'s lawyer, a fit, handsome fortyish man named

Darney, leaped on this "limp-penis defense." He introduced extensive notes from A.K.'s contemporaneous journal describing Schlomo's erect penis in no small detail.

"And even if you were impotent, Dr. Dove," Darney said, voice rising in accusation, "have you not fingers? A tongue? Toes? Toes, Dr. Dove, have you not toes?"

Attention turned to Schlomo. We all half expected Schlomo to say, "No, they've all been amputated, your honor." But no. Shaking his head in wonderment, Schlomo said, "Toes, ten. *Tsouris*, plenty."

How could you not smile at this?

Finally, after seeing much legal infighting around Exhibit A, the condoms in the Ziploc bag, the jury saw Exhibit B, the bananas. A.K. testified that these were used by Schlomo for masturbating her. Schlomo testified that they were used to make sure his potassium level stayed normal, as he was on diuretics for his heart failure, which, in his words, "is killing me slowly, and deep down is the cause of my impotence."

Ms. Green, Schlomo's sweet young reptile of a lawyer, tried everything to demolish A.K.'s character. She quoted from Schlomo's voluminous notes from his psychoanalysis of her. Nothing suggested the slightest physical involvement. All described just what a depraved sick person A.K. really was. She'd changed her name. She'd changed her nose. Was this not proof of instability?

But A.K. too had taken notes on her psychoanalysis with Schlomo, notes that described in lurid detail their several years of sexual acts. In addition, A.K. was now a respected member of the psychoanalytic community, and marched out witness after witness attesting to her fine character. After all, she had been analyzed, hadn't she, by one of the self-confessed "best analysts in town, if not the world"—Schlomo Dove. Hadn't Dr. Dove, head of the Freudian Institute, put his imprimatur upon her, terminating with her successfully? Hadn't Schlomo, when she'd gone to him for a match with an analyst, told her, "You have all the warmth of the sun, but you keep giving it away to others, leaving you sad and lonely"—and then kept her for himself?

Beside me, Zoe and Lily Putnam squirmed at these words.

The trial kept moving from this sense of human tragedy to farce. Some of it was so surreal that after it happened you couldn't believe that it had happened, except that it had. It was like America in that way, where, ever since Nixon, really, anything you thought of as a flagrant exaggeration of reality turned out, years later, to be a gross underestimate. In just a few decades the surreal in our country had turned real. What did this say about what would count as reality in our future?

The most surreal exchanges were around the Schlomo penis.

Schlomo's lawyer asked A.K. whether the Schlomo penis was circumsized.

"Yes," A.K. said.

"It would please the court," Ms. Green said with a dramatic flourish of her arms and in the voice of a premenstrual diva, "that the correct answer is 'only partially.' The Schlomo Dove penis is only partially circumsized!" Dramatic pause. "Your honor, I rest my case."

Schlomo beamed with pride. As his lawyer sat, he gave her a high five.

"One of the main bones of contention," said Darney, A.K.'s lawyer, in what I thought was a particularly inept turn of phrase, "is the doctor's penis. On the one hand, is it circumsized? On the other hand, is it not? Is it perenially flaccid, or is it capable of erection? Your honor, defense claims it is 'only partially' circumsized—whatever that boils down to, and—to quote Dr. Dove's words in his deposition—'always soft as linguini.' Parenthetically, I would point out that there is linguini, and there is linguini. Uncooked, it is hard. The phrase 'al dente' also comes to mind." The judge rolled his eyes, and gestured counsel to get on with it. "Your honor, counsel sees no other route than to have Dr. Schlomo Dove's penis examined by a medical expert, to see if, number one, it is circumsized or not, and number two, if it can maintain an erection."

"What?" Schlomo screamed, shooting to his feet, "you wanna see if I can get it up?"

"Objection!" Ms. Green screamed, shooting to her feet at the same time. "The penis is a red herring!"

"Oy, what a slip!" Schlomo said.

"OhmyGod," Ms. Green said.

Everyone cracked up, even the judge.

Banging his gavel, shaking his craggy head, the judge then called the attorneys to the side bar. They argued heatedly. The judge recessed, and called them into his chambers. We adjourned for the day.

The next day the judge ruled against A.K. The crafty old judge hinted that—perhaps fearing Dershowitz sinking his teeth into it—the penis would be an awkward exhibit to maintain at the appellate level, "if it could get up that far." The Schlomo penis was put to rest. Advantage, Dove.

The judge charged the jury on "the burden of proof" in such strict terms that it seemed to me our case was lost. Schlomo had been mesmerizing, A.K. unfathomable. Mr. Darney pointed out that in mesmerizing the members of the jury, Schlomo was doing exactly what had been done to seduce A.K. Further, Darney painted a vivid picture of how A.K.'s cool hiddenness and "sour demeanor" were the result of being an abuse survivor. But even to us this seemed a last-ditch effort by a desperate advocate, incidental, doomed to fail.

Berry and I left for our drive to Arizona. The jury stayed out five days. A finding for Schlomo, the defendant, seemed inevitable.

Last night we got the verdict, in Zoe's overnight letter.

The jury found for the plaintiff, A. K. Lowell, on all counts.

A sweet victory for A.K. Only Berry and I and A.K. herself knew just how sweet. I would return her ledger to her. Her own abuse of Oly Joe would remain a secret.

But what did the victory really mean? It was a civil not a criminal victory. Schlomo had been convicted of no crime. His legal expenses, and the monetary awards to A.K., whatever they would turn out to be, would be paid by his malpractice insurance. He would not do a single day in jail, or pay a single penny. In fact, since the award could be as high as a million, all of our malpractice premiums would go up, including mine. *We* would wind up paying, not him. He himself would no longer be required to carry malpractice, since now he would lose his license. Even though he would no longer have a license, there was nothing in the law to keep him from seeing patients as usual, as long as he didn't prescribe them drugs, which he didn't do anyway. His practice might well flourish. Now that he was famous, a household name, he might well make a killing with a book, a film, a miniseries.

In her letter, Zoe said:

> Schlomo's lawyers called me, and Lily, and want to settle out of court. To spare everybody embarrassment, and since he's already been found guilty, we probably will.
>
> TALL is going great. The number of abusers around here is incredible. There's talk of making it a national hot line.
>
> The bill to make sex with a patient a crime is still stalled in the legislature. A state rep named DiMesi keeps shelving it. He's a lawyer with a local practice. When someone asked him why he keeps shelving it, he said, "You think I'm gonna get behind somethin' dat says it's illegal for me to pinch my client's ass?"
>
> But I can't tell you how happy I am, to be working for TALL, doing something I believe in! We're all standing TALL!
>
> Do you know how important you were to me that whole year? How important you still are? You were, you are. Thank you for my life.
>
> In friendship, Zoe
>
> P.S. Any more news of Dr. Malik?

Now we sit across the stream from the White House ruin. Our eyes sometimes rest on the cave mouth and dwellings, sometimes are drawn up the face of the cliff, up the sheer mass along the streaks of purple and red leaking down the rock from the rim and glistening with eons of leachate, metallic ore, dark iron. I take the letter out of my shirt pocket. Fingers trembling, I open it. We read it together.

Our friend Leonard Malik died peacefully today. The body will be cremated and its ashes scattered here in the Himalayas. Donations in his memory may be sent to any endeavor which, in his words, "promotes an enquiry into the meaning of life, or to the orphanage here." He asked us to write to you, his dear friend, and to leave you with this message:

"Find the breath, kid. Don't forget to breathe."

With you in sorrow,
V. Thakar

I find myself smiling. Now I see what he had been showing me all year long. Suffering is forgetfulness, forgetting to breathe, forgetting to be with the life-breath, the spirit. Healing is connection. Isn't that all, isn't that it?

My mind's eye fills with Malik, from the first time I saw him, on the tennis court when I mistook him for a patient and Mr. K. for a doctor, through all the "clicks" I'd felt with him, to my doing the physical on him when he pointed to the acromial knobs of his shoulders and said, "I haven't seen these bones since I was eight years old," and finally to our sitting in silence, saying good-bye. He had asked me for help. I had given it. We had helped each other.

I see him sitting front and center in the photo I carry with me at all times, the color photo of our ragtag group at the airport: his body is sagging, as if against an inner dark weight, and leans to one side. His face is pale and constrained, more pale even than Zoe's face, and more constrained even than Bronia's, but his eyes are alight. He is free.

"It's so simple. That was his gift, to show me how simple it is."

"What's that?" Berry asks sleepily.

"How to be with people, help them grow. What helps is this, just this."

"Mmm. Everything's simple," she murmurs, "if you're really here."

"It's like seeing and loving go together."

"That's excellent, yes."

We sit together in the stillness, in the movement of connection with each other and with nature. The line between living and dead seems fuzzy, as if you could cross back and forth easily. This letter from India might help us cross, if we wish, but urges us to stay on this side for now, watching the flow of the stream and the flow of our grieving, part of all that is human and even all that is not human but merely life, even the life of the stream and the life of the rock.

Suddenly I realize that the night before I had had my first dream about my father since his death. I tell Berry about it.

"He was running upstairs to the second floor of our old house, the two-family we owned. Rabbi Ritvo rented the other half. My father was wearing his raincoat and his rain hat—he looked like a salesman back from a two-week road trip. The hat was one of those brimmed ones, from the thirties. He ran upstairs and seemed eager to talk to me. Eager, but worried. His voice was shaky—either with fear or with love, I don't know which—he'd often get teary when he first saw me again after I'd been away for a while—and he said to me, 'Son, I've just been named Best Dentist on the Jolly Jews basketball team!' And I said, with enthusiasm, 'That's great, Dad!' "

"Wonderful dream," Berry says. "You've made peace with him now."

"With his spirit, yeah." I think of poor Cherokee Putnam, having the colossal bad luck to get me as his therapist during my love affair with Sigmund Freud. If he'd gotten Malik, or me now, he'd still be alive. I say to Berry, "You know, I think I understand how to help people now, I really do."

"Shhh. She's asleep, so we should get some sleep too." Snuggling in, she murmurs, "But that's good, Roy, that's real good. That's why you wanted to be a doctor in the first place, right? Mmmm."

I raise my eyes above the green tufts of the cottonwoods and aspens to the White House ruin, sitting atop the other stone dwellings, and see how the humans who'd lived there a thousand years ago are a part of the rock, by virtue of their endeavor and understanding, and then my sight enlarges to take in the teardrop-shaped cave, and I see how the dwellings are a part of the cave, by virtue of the humans, and then my eyes start up the cliff face, and I see how the cleft is part of the cliff, by virtue of the wind and the rain, and then my eyes slip up the cliff face between two iron oxide streaks to the rim, seeing how the declivity of the canyon is part of the plateau, by virtue of the wind and the water and the fire in the earth, and then my vision lifts lightly up off the trampoline of the rim into the desert sky the color of tropical water, seeing how the sky is part of the earth, by virtue of life itself. That fact is the Divine: the being part of the whole.

And I see how psychiatry had been a mutilation of the Divine, the ripping apart of the fabric, the fragmenting of the whole into parts, the taking of what was in fact the breathing of the soul—the whole rich unknown life of the spirit—and cramming it into a tiny island of the known, named "psychology."

Ike White. Why had he killed himself? Because he lived two seconds ahead of time, or two seconds behind. In expectation, or in memory. He was never present. He never looked you in the eye, never touched you. He had a secret, and that secret was his keeping secrets. He didn't know how to ask. But why had he killed himself that night, after meeting us, the new residents?

Was it because he saw our hope, and he knew all the shit, knew from my telling him about Cherokee that day that I was about to wander into all the

Schlomo shit and God knows what else and how could he tell a bright young idealistic guy who looked up to him a lot that he'd been fucked up the ass for years by Schlomo Dove and knew that A.K. and God knows how many others had been fucked by Schlomo too? Because he was living a lie and it killed him? He was forty-one and a star, but he felt that compared to other stars he was a failure. Buy in to comparison, try to become more and more and better and better, and you can never be enough, because you can never be. I see it as clearly as this sky, as the edge of this baby's quilt upon this sand: Buy in to a self-centered way of living and you make it only up into your late thirties maybe your early forties and then your life drops down around you like pants too big for a cancered body and you're left standing there naked, and even if there's a trophy in your hand and cash in your pocket, your mouth is full of ashes.

If Ike White died of any "fatal disease," that was it: the time bomb of the self. I too had come close, that butterfly needle poised over that bulging vein in my antecubital fossa. And this is normal male life? No. Healthy growth is through and toward connection. We don't have to be heroes, and our alternative is not being wimps. We've just got to live human-sized lives.

Berry and I and Lizzie Qun are here to start living in a place where spirit is not split off and mocked, where, without self-consciousness, we can start to talk about being part of this wholeness, this spiritual life, this faith in life carried on the stream of connections, this sense that if there is a "self" it came as an attempt to organize the onrush of associations from our overriding brain cortex, that any "self" is made up only and wholly of "nonself" parts, and that we can no more use the old way of thinking about "self" and "other" without regard for the mutual connections than we can, at the other end of the spectrum, use the old way of thinking of particles of matter, because the new physics has shown that there are no such things as isolated Newtonian particles like those little plastic balls of organic chemistry, but rather that what we call "particles" of matter are in fact only the mutual relationships among the particles, which means, if you really take that in, that the universe is made up not of fundamental pieces but of a pliant fabric of mutual co-arisings, of relationships and connections, of the very stuff which we, split off as humans, aspire to rejoin.

"This rock," I say to Berry, "is energy, like the sky."

But she's asleep. Lizzie's asleep. I sleep.

After a while our baby awakens us. We put her in the Tough Traveler and head upstream toward the trail mouth, which leads up, and out.

GAINING THE RIM, Lizzie on my back babbling with all the strength of the sun, everything being more real, bulging and blazing, my heart feels ripe.

I sense the baby's energy field, surrounding my head like a halo, reminding me that there's a whole other world out there, beyond words, to which she is attuned, like when she knows that our cat is in the room before she can see or hear it, or when she senses in a person—no matter how attentive to her—a phoniness, and she flinches, turns away and starts to cry. These energies exist, in that world of mere being.

Catching my breath in the rare high air, I turn with Berry and look back, out over the vista, down to where we'd been.

"If there's a heaven," I say, "this is it."

"Khreeeeh op!" says Lizzie Qun, our present moment.

We laugh. Lizzie laughs. We laugh more. Lizzie laughs more.

"I'm so happy!" I say. "No one ever tells you, with a baby, how much fun it is!"

"How could they? It's not something you can tell."

"Isn't it true," I ask, "that before Lizzie Qun, we only seemed to learn things through suffering, and now we're learning through joy?"

"Sweetie!" she says, squeezing my hand. And then suddenly she lets go. "Uh-oh."

"What?"

Berry sniffs our baby's bottom. "She needs changing."

"Who doesn't?"

"Where's the diaper?"

We find the diaper, and lay Lizzie Qun down on the hood of our truck. She smiles, and reaches a hand up toward us, or maybe toward the sky.

LAWS OF MOUNT MISERY

Laws of Mount Misery

I. There are no laws in psychiatry.
II. Psychiatrists specialize in their defects.
III. At a psychiatric emergency, the first procedure is to check your own mental status.
IV. The patient is not the only one with the disease, or without it.
V. In psychiatry, first comes treatment, then comes diagnosis.
VI. The worst psychiatrists charge the most, and world experts are the worst.
VII. Medical school is a liability in becoming a psychotherapist.
VIII. Your colleagues will hurt you more than your patients.
IX. You can learn everything about a person by the way he or she plays a sport.
X. Medical patients don't take their medication fifty percent of the time, and psychiatric patients don't take their medication much at all.
XI. Therapy is part of life, and vice versa.
XII. Healing in psychotherapy has nothing to do with psychology; connection, not self, heals.
XIII. The delivery of psychiatric care is to know as little as possible, and to understand as much as possible, about living through sorrow with others.

ABOUT THE AUTHOR

SAMUEL SHEM (Steve Bergman, M.D.) graduated magna cum laude and Phi Beta Kappa from Harvard College and earned a Ph.D. in physiology from Oxford University, where he was a Rhodes Scholar. He graduated from Harvard Medical School. He is the author of the novels *The House of God* and *Fine* and seven plays, including, with Janet Surrey, *Bill W. and Dr. Bob.* He is on the faculty of Harvard Medical School and The Stone Center, Wellesley College. He lives with his wife and five-year-old daughter near Boston.